FATE'S RECKONING

FATE'S RECKONING

CYBER DREAMS BOOK 6

PLUM PARROT

Podium

Published in 2025 by Podium Publishing
www.podiumentertainment.com

FATE'S RECKONING

1

KENSHI

Juliet knelt in the middle of Tanaka's tatami dojo mat, her eyes closed and the monoblade resting across her thighs. She wore a red gi and a matching red belt. It meant nothing. Tanaka's master hadn't bothered with belts and colors, and neither did he. Over the last several months, Juliet had acquired a number of gis—white, black, red, yellow, and even a shockingly bright magenta one—simply to see if it would get a rise out of the older mercenary. It hadn't.

Her monoblade, an incarnation of violent potential, was a comfortable, now familiar weight. She'd memorized every centimeter of it, from its matte-black sheath to its upgraded and personalized hilt, designed to match her grip perfectly. She'd balked at first when Tanaka had suggested she change the grip and hilt diameter. It was his sword, after all.

That argument had lasted all of five seconds when he'd chopped his hand in the air and said, "No," reminding her that she'd taken it from him in battle and that it would be shameful for him ever to wield it again. So, she'd taken him up on the offer and pushed it to the extreme.

She'd added a smart alloy frame into the hilt, which utilized nanotech to dynamically adjust its contours and balance in real time, ensuring an optimal grip tailored to her hand's movements and pressure. The new frame was wrapped in "FlexiGrip," an adaptive polymer blend that could change its texture and firmness based on her body temperature and sweat secretions.

It had a matte-black default color, but was woven with iridescent filaments that could softly glow in a broad spectrum of custom colors. At the moment, it pulsed with subdued reds that matched her gi.

"Are you all right?" Angel prompted, aware that Juliet's mind had wandered, but likely not sure what she was thinking about.

"Fine," Juliet subvocalized, not wanting to share their conversation with the little audience gathered to watch Tanaka's "ceremony." Juliet hadn't wanted any observers; she just wanted to complete his test and be done with it, moving on to more training.

Of course, he'd had good arguments to the contrary, mostly involving the team being comfortable with her running around with a monoblade. This demonstration was all about blade discipline, and he had argued they'd appreciate knowing what she could do.

She felt them behind her—Tanaka, Frida, Leo, and the rest of the team. They were silent, waiting, giving her a chance to compose herself.

She supposed that having them all present made her take this more seriously. If it were just Tanaka, she'd be okay with messing up, knowing he'd just make her wait a while and try again. Now, though, with everyone's eyes on her, she felt like she had to be perfect.

So, with a final cleansing inhalation through her nose, and a slow breath out through her mouth, she opened her eyes and looked at the test. It was the ring tree, the very first "blade discipline" test Tanaka had given her.

Juliet gracefully rose from her kneeling position and slid the monoblade into her obi, resting her left hand on the top of the scabbard as she approached the tree.

There were twenty-one rings of varying sizes, all wired into the dojo's diagnostic array. If she passed her blade through the center of the ring, it would register and shine with a green light. On her first day of sword practice, Tanaka had given her the challenge to pierce each ring perfectly, without touching the sides, in less than a minute. That first day, she'd done it in twenty minutes, but only after failing dozens of times.

Since then, they'd practiced blade discipline every day and done exercises just like this one in the VR booth, but she'd only worked with this physical ring tree a few times, and only with a practice sword. Could she do it in less than a minute with a real monoblade? If she messed up even once, she'd destroy the ring, and that would be that; the test would be over, and she'd have to face everyone's disappointment.

She knew that expectation was her own, that Leo and the others wouldn't really care, but she recognized how clever Tanaka was by inviting them. She'd apply the pressure; they didn't have to.

The hardest thing about the test was that she had to stand at an ideal thrusting distance. Her arms would be extended, and the tip of her blade would have to pass through the rings, some of which were only a scant centimeter wider than her sword. If she swayed at all, the blade's monofilament edge would slice the ring without any resistance. The trick, she'd learned, was to be confident and thrust quickly and retract quickly. Moving slowly only added to the natural swaying motion.

"Ready?" she subvocalized, knowing the question might as well have been rhetorical. Angel was always ready. Proving her point, Angel didn't respond verbally, but Juliet "felt" her readiness, something they'd been playing around with more and more. Juliet could *feel* Angel's state of mind almost as well as the PAI could feel hers.

She figured she could do the test without Angel's help. It wasn't that she was naturally gifted with the sword, but after five months of dedicated practice and Angel's help all along the way, she was quite good, and that self-assessment wasn't bravado. She'd proven it over and over again in the VR and dream-rig sims and in practice bouts with Tanaka, who was widely acknowledged to be a master.

With Angel helping to correct her movements and teaching her muscles to memorize the perfect forms, she probably learned ten times faster than someone without such an aid, and that was being conservative. Honey had left before Juliet had really started to learn with full intensity, but she knew she was better than her friend now, and Honey had been learning the sword for ten years or more.

She'd struggled with the notion that she was cheating, but only briefly. The closer she grew to Angel, the more she recognized that she and the sapient, sentient AI were intertwined; the more she had to acknowledge that whatever Angel did for her was natural. They were a unit, two halves of a whole, and if that was unfair for the rest of the human race, then so be it.

Juliet wouldn't have been able to say that a year ago, but their shared experiences and continued reliance on each other had changed her outlook.

What good did it do to torture herself with manufactured notions of what was right or fair? Would other people refuse an advantage if presented with it? Maybe some would, but plenty wouldn't, and Juliet didn't have a problem taking the help, especially when her life and those of the people she cared about might depend on the skills she was picking up.

So, even knowing she might be able to pass this test without the PAI aiding her, she embraced the help.

"Let's make it perfect," she subvocalized, clearing her mind and pushing away those thoughts, doubts, and weird justifications. She mentally mapped out her path through the rings, choosing the first target, then the next, and so on, until she could visualize imaginary dotted lines between them as though she were connecting the dots on a child's puzzle. She inhaled deeply, then, as she exhaled, whispered, "Three, two, one . . ."

To the others watching, it looked like Juliet had been standing still one second, then the next, her sword was out of the sheath and extended in a flawless thrust, the first ring blinking with green LEDs. Her sword's blade sparkled with a projected red edge, alerting anyone who knew anything about swords that it had a monofilament edge and could cut through steel like a reaper's whisper to an old man's soul.

Juliet retracted the thrust and drove the sword, faster than a normal eye could track, through the second ring with a second fierce cry of "*Tsuki!*" After that, it became rhythmic—retract, thrust, retract, thrust. If anyone were timing her moves—Tanaka was—they would have noted that each full thrust and retraction took less than a second.

When the twenty-first ring flashed with green LEDs, Juliet looked at her timer and saw it flashing 17.745 seconds. A huge smile spread on her lips, and she sheathed her sword with a flourish, turning to bow deeply to Tanaka, who stood on the side of the mat. His face was impassive, but Juliet could see something in his eyes.

They were still chrome, still almost impossible to read, but she'd grown accustomed to his microexpressions over their many long hours of one-on-one practice. He was pleased, but he was feeling something else; she couldn't quite make it out, but perhaps it was wounded pride. Juliet was reasonably sure she'd just proven she was faster than he was.

"Holy shit!" Leo laughed, and that broke the spell. Everyone started hooting, clapping, and whistling.

"That's not a practice blade?" Frida clarified.

"No," Tanaka replied, stepping onto the mat and reaching out a hand.

Juliet, long over her earlier awkwardness with the man, still wasn't sure what he wanted. Was it a handshake? Reaching her right hand to his, he grasped it warmly, smiling, and she felt such a warm, fuzzy feeling in her chest that moisture sprang into her eyes.

Blinking rapidly, she looked down. Dr. Ming would remind her that she subconsciously sought praise, and Tanaka's pride in her was an almost overwhelming source of it.

"I will give Lucky her kanji. You all may wait in the reception area."

Juliet knew what he meant; he'd already warned her. He wouldn't set her loose on the world with a monoblade without marking her the way he had been; it was a tradition that honored his master despite the conflicting feelings Tanaka had about the ancient swordsman.

"Drinks and cake are waiting!" Frida called, which got everyone moving. They filed out, leaving Juliet alone with the former cold-blooded mercenary.

"Sit," he said, gesturing to the mat. Juliet stepped back toward the center and lowered herself to her knees, folding her hands on her lap. Tanaka walked to the side of the room again and picked up a wooden tray bearing a soft white cloth, two clay pots, and several long needles wrapped in rice paper. He walked over and knelt before her, placing the tray between them. "Roll up your right sleeve."

"Do we really have to do this, Rutger? I don't plan to go around dueling people."

"I explained this, *Lucky.* This will help you avoid duels. If someone sees you with that blade and challenges you, roll up your sleeve, making this kanji clear. If they don't back down, your conscience can rest easy with what you must do." He uncapped the first inkpot and began unwrapping one of the needles. "Rest your right arm here so I can work on it."

"Do people really know about this stuff? Would a banger know—"

"A banger will not challenge you to a sword duel. If they want your sword, they'll try to kill you in any way they can. This is for a certain group of specialists." He pulled her arm a little farther forward, rubbing his thumb on the back of her forearm, perhaps choosing the best spot. With that, before Juliet could protest more, he dipped his needle and began pricking her flesh in quick, precise movements. "This first mark is for the sword. It means *ken.*"

"Does it hurt?" Angel asked, fascinated.

Juliet shook her head. "No. Just tiny stings, but they don't last."

Tanaka, of course, didn't hear their side conversation and kept talking. "The second mark means *master.* People might be skeptical because of your age, or they might have known you before you started practicing. It's very unusual for someone to reach your skill level so quickly. Unheard of, I'd say."

Juliet tried to ease the tension. "I had a good teacher."

"*Hai.* We know there's more to it, but I am pleased. You have been honest with me, at least as much as possible, by refusing to explain rather than lie."

"You know I'm going to tell you more when we make our move . . ."

"*Hai.* The third mark will be mine. I might not be as famous as I once was, but the people who matter will know it. They'll see that it was I who marked you, and they'll think twice about their doubts." Tanaka was utterly focused on his task, and Juliet could see his face was more relaxed than usual. He enjoyed working with his hands—carving wood, sharpening blades, and apparently, tattooing.

"The first one is *ken;* what's the second?"

"*Shi.*"

"*Kenshi*," Juliet said softly.

"*Hai*, but this is a mark meant as a warning, not for bragging. You need never utter that word."

"I wouldn't!" The idea of bragging about her sword skills felt absurd to her; as Tanaka had indicated, she'd gotten too good, too fast. It was almost embarrassing.

While he worked, Tanaka continued to speak, more verbose in those moments than he had been in the many months they'd been working together.

"As you know, that sword will cut through most things unless they were specifically engineered to be denser than natural materials. The sheath, for instance, has a strip of polymer where the blade rests that cannot be penetrated. Such materials are extremely costly, and you won't often run into someone with armor like that. Still, be prepared for it. What should you do in such a situation?"

Juliet's answer was immediate. "Cut around the armor."

Tanaka snorted and nodded. "*Hai*. Or shoot them. Or break their neck. Always plan for any eventuality."

"Wait. So having this sword doesn't mean I can forget about guns and spaceships and—"

Tanaka clicked his tongue and shook his head. "I'm too lenient with you. Such back talk would have seen me thrashed—"

"And peeing blood for a week." Juliet laughed as his lips curved into a small smile.

They were both quiet for a while, then when Tanaka closed the clay pot and opened the other, revealing red ink, she said, "Tell me about your mark."

"The Red Wolf. Before I left, they gave me this name, which is when I ceased to be Noraneko."

"Because of Takamoto? Because of Frida's—"

"*Hai*," he grunted. Juliet had been about to say Frida's mother, but she could see why he'd interrupted her. She had spoken softly, and doubted Frida was watching the vid feed—in fact, she knew she wasn't because Angel had access to all of the systems in the dojo—but still, it was a sensitive topic.

"I'd rather you put Noraneko on there instead of"—Angel supplied the word for wolf, and Juliet repeated it—"*okami*."

"It would defeat the purpose. No one knows of Noraneko the swordsman, only the Red Wolf."

"I see." Juliet breathed softly through her nose, watching the red mark take shape as he tapped away with his needle, dabbing with the cloth now and then. She knew her nanites would heal the new tattoos on her synth-skin within minutes, and that infections were impossible, so the blood and traditional—perhaps even dubious—origins of the ink and needles didn't bother her.

They were both quiet for a few more minutes while he worked, and then he asked, "And if you meet another with a monoblade?"

She was ready for this question. They'd spoken about it dozens of times, and lately, their practice had revolved around that kind of duel. "Don't cross blades, and don't let them touch me."

"*Hai*. Unless you get a clean cut on the side or back of their sword," he said, pressing the blood-and-ink-stained cloth to her forearm, giving it a firm squeeze. "Tell your nanites to get to work; you're done."

He stood fluidly, one of his knees popping with the motion, and held out his hand to her. Juliet took it, pleased at the warmth she felt at the gesture, hardly able to recall the awkward distance between them when she'd first started studying the sword. He pulled her to her feet, and she regarded her arm, tracing the two black kanji and then the red one with her finger. She liked them; Tanaka did good work with his antiquated tools.

"Thank you, Sensei," she said softly, looking into his reflective chrome eyes. "I wish you'd get new optics."

"Yeah," he grumbled, but Juliet saw his small smile return. He gestured toward the door. "Come on, everyone's waiting."

Juliet followed him into the reception area, where everyone sat or stood around chatting, eating cake, and drinking beer. Soft synth-pop played on the office speakers as Juliet scanned the room, noticing how everyone had fallen into their usual little cliques.

Leo and Barns stood near the door, Frida sat with Dora Lee, and Hawkins, ever the silent loner type, sat by himself with an absurdly large slice of cake.

As Juliet walked in, everyone looked her way, so she held up her freshly inked arm with an almost painful smile stretching her lips. More cheers, whistles, and catcalls greeted the display, and Juliet's cheeks flushed as she laughed, hurrying over to the counter where she could avoid everyone's eyes by focusing on slicing herself a piece of the vanilla-frosted lemon cake.

Frida came over while she was scooping some frosting off the knife, chuckling when Juliet licked her finger clean. "It's good, huh?"

"Yes! So creamy!"

Frida nodded. "I got it from that place a few blocks down. Mimi's." Frida's pale green eyes drifted from Juliet's face to her new tattoo. "Well, you've graduated. Does this mean we're about to put all that training to the test?"

"Yeah," Leo spoke, suddenly leaning against the counter behind Juliet, much closer than he should have gotten without her noticing. She blamed the music and the rush of sugar from the frosting. "When are you gonna tell us more about this big job?"

Juliet turned so her back was to the counter, allowing her to look at them both as she answered. "Soon! I'm meeting with Tanaka about the next step tomorrow morning."

"Why not now?"

"She has a date," Frida laughed as she answered, enjoying how her words teased Juliet and Leo in different ways.

"Oh, brother." Juliet sighed.

"Ah, right. I see how it is." Leo wrinkled his nose and shrugged. "Well, if that's the case, maybe you should join Annie and me. I'd love to meet this mysterious fellow of yours . . ."

Juliet shook her head. "Not happening."

About a month after Juliet had let him down easy, Leo had started dating a woman named Annie, whom he found a way to mention at least a few times a week. Frida wasn't sure Annie existed, but Juliet could tell Leo wasn't lying. Whether he really cared about her was another question.

Leo shrugged. "Well, let me know if you change your mind." He gestured to her arm, said, "Congratulations," and walked over to resume his chat with Barns.

"He hates that you're seeing someone," Frida whispered.

"Which is why I wish you'd stop bringing it up in front of him," Juliet growled, turning her back to the two men and glaring down at the smaller woman.

"I'm sorry! I'm a little childish, I guess. You know he's like a big brother to me; it's fun to tease him."

"Well, it's not like it's a big deal, anyway. This is only, like, the fifth date we've been on."

Frida leaned closer and scooped her finger through Juliet's frosting, grinning at Juliet's scowl. "Yeah, but that's not his fault. You went to Mars, and then he had to go back to Earth twice for his job. The fact that he keeps coming back says a lot."

"Are you going to make me regret spilling my guts to you? He's not coming back here just for me!"

"Sure." Frida's eyes said she knew better. "I mean, those shuttle flights aren't cheap, so you must have a few pretty good tricks. Care to share?"

"Get—"

"Melted," Frida laughed. Juliet smiled and continued eating her cake.

She was looking forward to seeing Tristan—Jensen, as she still thought of him half the time—again, but it wasn't as big a deal as Frida was making it sound. Yes, they had chemistry, and yes, on their third date, Juliet had gone back to his place, and it had been great, but . . .

Her mind got stuck on that thought, as usual. What was the "but" with that situation? She couldn't put her finger on it, but it was there. Was she doomed to be alone because she had some hidden standards that even she couldn't pin down? Was she comparing Jensen to people and feelings she'd built up in her mind to the point where no one could measure up?

As she savored another bite of cake with far too much frosting, she couldn't help how her mind drifted toward a recent memory. It was something she'd realized the night she'd stayed at Jensen's place, and, recalling it, she almost called herself a liar out loud. She knew darn well what the issue was. That night, after he'd fallen sound asleep and she'd been staring at the dark ceiling, the weirdest thoughts had come into her mind.

She'd started thinking about the time Nick had been accosted by some men claiming he owed them money. The reason for the out-of-place memory became apparent as she thought about how she'd dived into that small-time gangster's head and relived the horrible accident he'd had with Lexi, the girl who'd died.

She remembered how he'd felt driving with her in the car, looking into her pale, rose-colored eyes, watching her hair flutter in the wind, and feeling such a deep, profoundly life-changing love for her. Then she'd felt his loss when she died, and the experience had nearly driven Juliet into a depression.

The truth was, she'd experienced real love through Tono's simple mind, and she knew what she felt with Jensen didn't measure up. Had that gangster ruined her chances of ever having a deep, romantic relationship? Would she ever feel the way Tono—and her, by proxy—had felt for Lexi?

The idea that the chance encounter with one of Nick's enemies, that brief run-in during which she'd dared to dive into the deepest secret corner of a thug's mind, had given her the only taste of real love she might ever have was enough to turn her mood sour.

She set her plate down, her cake half eaten, and folded her arms, annoyed that she'd let herself go down that road again.

"Something wrong?" Frida asked, eyeing her discarded plate.

"Too sweet. I mean, it was great, Frida, but Angel's on my case about the sugar."

"I am not!" Angel immediately protested.

"That PAI of yours is hardcore," Frida laughed.

"Sorry, Angel," Juliet subvocalized. "I shouldn't use you as an excuse."

"It's okay. I can tell you're thinking about love again."

"Well," Dora spoke up, standing, "me and Hawkins have an opening at the range. Congrats, Lucky. That was some serious sword-poking-around stuff you did."

"Hah," Barns laughed. "She ain't known for poetry, but she's right. Nice job, Lucky!" He held up his beer, and the others all echoed the impromptu toast, tossing back whatever they were holding.

Juliet smiled and mock bowed, rolling her arm for good measure. "Thank you, thank you! My next display will involve an apple on Leo's head—"

Leo laughed and stepped closer, giving her a playful punch on the shoulder. "Not on your life."

"I'll have to reschedule that one, folks. My assistant's butterflies have gotten the better of him. Maybe he'll come around." Juliet winked at him then jerked her thumb toward the door. "I should get going too. I'd thank you all for coming, but I know you're only here for the cake and drinks." Juliet turned and pulled Frida into a hug, kissing the top of her ginger curl-covered head. "So thanks, Frida!"

"Thanks, Frida!" everyone echoed, and those who hadn't yet done so drained their drinks.

2

SOMETHING BIGGER

Juliet hung her gi in her locker with her other training gear. She'd taken a quick shower and cleaned up, though if Tristan was expecting her to dress up, he'd be disappointed. He'd invited her to a park, after all.

Over her black, steel-toed motorcycle boots, she wore some of her favorite jeans, faded and worn in all the right ways—comfortable and confidence-boosting, which was what she needed. Her shirt was a minor concession in that it wasn't an old T. Rather, it was a soft, breezy, collared blouse with long sleeves and just the right kind of neckline if she kept the top couple of buttons undone.

Her Texan was stowed under her motorcycle seat, but she'd be wearing the monoblade; Tanaka had done a fabulous job of ingraining that habit in her. She couldn't imagine walking around in a city where any alley, parked car, or crowd of strolling strangers could hide an enemy without it.

Maybe someday, if she retired and bought a place like Aya's folks in a quiet dome on Mars, she'd hang the sword up. She'd learned what it could do, though, and the idea of going around without it felt monumentally stupid, especially in her line of work. So there it was, hanging from her belt on the custom multijointed mounting clips that gave it just the right amount of mobility without allowing it to bounce around and trip her up.

She shrugged into her riding jacket—another new acquisition. It was built to protect her from sliding on asphalt, but the leatherlike polymer material was rated to resist small-arms fire. She liked the cut of it. The rust-colored shoulders and sleeves, and the layered blue-black torso sections gave it a sleek but rugged appearance, and, just like her jeans, it made her more confident.

Catching herself thinking about how her clothes boosted her confidence, she paused, looked in the mirror, and had the presence of mind to wonder why. She supposed it was because Jensen—Tristan—hadn't been in town for nearly a month, and they hadn't exactly kept in close contact while he'd been gone. Then, when he got back, he messaged her, and rather than asking her out to a restaurant or even inviting her over to his place, he'd said they needed to talk.

"And invited me to a park," she groaned.

"You're worried he's ending things?" Angel was quick to pick up on the topic.

"Kind of. I don't know why; you know how I feel. He's nice and handsome and totally gets me being unavailable due to my work, but I know this isn't really love. God, I wish I'd never gone into Tono's head. No, forget Tono. I wish I had never experienced Roy Tornado's feelings for Antigone. Shit, Angel, do you think it's a guy thing? Do they feel love differently—more passionately— than women?"

"Hah!" was Angel's only response, aptly demonstrating her opinion of that idea.

Juliet smiled, inwardly admitting the idea was silly. She looked at herself in the mirror, leaning in for a close examination.

She never really wore any makeup, and she wasn't going to start now. She was ninety-nine percent sure her looks weren't the problem. Her nanites did a great job of keeping her skin looking good, and she had natural coloring that, if Ladia were to be believed, many women—and men—would kill for.

Admitting that illustrated how much she'd changed; even six months ago, she might have argued that she was a rather plain-looking woman.

"You know, it's nice having friends who build me up. I've done a good job picking 'em since I met you, don't you think?"

"I do think so! Even your more contentious relationships are fun-loving, ribbing sorts of situations. I mean, for instance, Barns, Applebaum, and that lovable musclehead, Bennet."

Juliet smiled, hurrying toward the door, her boots thumping on the cork flooring. "He *is* lovable, isn't he?"

Thinking of Bennet, of course, brought to mind the rest of the *Kowashi* crew. They were currently working on a big corporate contract to recover materials from a wrecked transport ship that had put down on Phobos, failing to reach its destination on Mars due to a reactor failure.

It was a big job, but the corporation was providing security, and it was in a densely populated part of the system, so the risk of pirates and rogue salvagers trying to jump the claim was very low. Still, Juliet found herself worrying if she didn't get a daily update from Alice or Aya.

She managed to slip out of the office without anyone noticing her, and soon, she was straddling her bike and cruising out of the parking garage, following Angel's directions on her mini map.

As she went, she knew she felt different. She felt more confident and capable, and at first, she chalked it up to endorphins from Tanaka's approval and the little "celebration" they'd had where everyone was congratulating her, but it was more than that.

This was the first time she'd been out, alone, with an actual monoblade on her hip. The difference between having a weapon like that and the skill to use it versus just understanding the technical definition of a monoblade was an enormous gulf that she hadn't understood back when she'd taken it from Tanaka.

With her sword, she could cut through solid steel doors, ride past a car and destroy it with a few swings, and destroy combat synths that would shrug off bullets from her Texan. She felt like a walking weapon, and supposed she'd become one. It was both thrilling and sobering, and as it sank in, she began to understand why Tanaka felt he had to put a warning on her arm.

There was a reason she'd heard stories about monoblades and their wielders when she was a kid. There was a reason they were popular as villains and heroes in vids, games, and other media. There was a subculture of mercenaries, operators, and criminals built up around swords; naturally, the monoblade sat at the apex of their mythos.

Juliet had learned a thing or two about monoblades, and hers in particular, over the last few months. She remembered when she'd tried to give the blade to Honey back when she'd rescued her from Titan and her friend had refused, saying she couldn't take a gift worth a 100k, nor would she want to be seen wearing one.

As it turned out, the sword she was wielding was worth closer to a million bits. There were only a handful of companies capable of creating the perfect monomolecular edge that her sword enjoyed, though some knockoffs came close—those were the 100k swords. They'd work for a while, but eventually, their imperfections would cause a catastrophic hang-up while it cut.

If she wanted to replace her sword, regardless of her bank account, Juliet would be on a waiting list for months, maybe years, assuming she couldn't find a private seller. For every one of the rare swords actively in use, there were three or four on a rich collector's shelf or ruined in a duel; the demand for new ones never let up, and supply couldn't keep pace.

"Duels." Juliet sighed, wondering how long it would take for someone to see her walking around and throw down a gauntlet. She hoped Tanaka was right about her tattoo and that it would discourage such a challenge. She wasn't afraid of a fight, but she'd learned a healthy respect for her sword and didn't relish meeting an enemy with a comparable weapon.

She'd been thinking about swords and duels so intently that she'd hardly noticed the ride out of downtown and over to one of Luna's many parks. Before she knew it, she was pulling into the small parking area; most people took public transit or biked to such a destination.

"Well, time to find out what we need to 'talk' about, I guess."

Angel, of course, tried to provide some cheer. "I think popular media makes too much of such a request. I doubt it's anything bad. Maybe he wants to enjoy the warm weather and some nature with you. Maybe he wants to tell you about his job or ask if you're upset about his prolonged absence."

"I love your optimism, sis." Juliet pulled her helmet off and shook out her—currently—wavy auburn hair. Despite her helmet and the slight damp left over from her shower, it held its form perfectly. The breeze and sun felt great, and she sat there for a minute, watching the people walking on the paths.

Juliet liked watching kids; she'd always taken some comfort in their innocence, in the way they embraced life while at play. They weren't worried about corporations or bills or debts.

She frowned at that thought. These kids weren't concerned about those things, but plenty of others out there didn't have anyone who cared about them enough to bring them to a park to play.

With a sigh, she stood from the bike and hooked her helmet into its cradle. The air was warm, and she knew she'd be sweating quickly if she had to walk far, so she shrugged out of her jacket, folded it, and stuffed it into the compartment under her seat with the Texan. The breeze through her thin, pale gray blouse was almost chilly, so she started walking, eager to get out of the shade and into some sun.

Still following directions on her AUI, she meandered down the path, enjoying the fresh odors Angel let through her olfactory implants.

Thinking about that, she chuckled and said, "You know what? I was starting to think Luna City was cleaner than my first impression, but I think you've been blocking the musty smells!"

"Well, of course! Who wants to smell gray water irrigation or urine in the gutters?"

"I mean, I guess I'm enjoying life more without those, but like, don't let me forget what's real! I don't want my life to be a sim."

"I'll let some unpleasantness bleed through now and then. I'd never block important smells in a tactical situation, but I've been doctoring things around Luna."

Before Juliet could reply, she caught sight of Tristan leaning against a white plasteel railing made up to look like wooden planks, gazing out over one of the freshwater recreation ponds in the park. Following his gaze, Juliet saw people out on the water in kayaks and even swimming.

"That looks fun."

Tristan heard her, even from fifteen meters away, and Juliet wondered if he'd had his PAI listening for her voice. He turned, waved, and leaned back against the railing, watching her approach. As she got near, he pointed to her feet. "Boots? What if I wanted to meet you for a jog?"

"Then you should've said so." Juliet smiled and leaned close, giving him a soft kiss. His blond stubble was short and almost invisible, but it tickled her chin as he pressed into her.

Juliet was a little surprised by the eagerness of his kiss, but he broke it off after just a few seconds, and squinting into the bright sky, he smiled and inhaled deeply. Juliet joined him, leaning half on the fence and half against his side, enjoying a moment of closeness without words.

"You look great. Is that a new sword?" he asked. Juliet had already felt the gun in his waistband, so she didn't feel weird about coming armed to a "date," if that's what this was.

"Yeah." She didn't elaborate.

"I'm not much of a sword guy, but it looks high-end."

"It's a good one. I got it from Tanaka." Jensen knew she was training with him, but that was all he knew. She shifted, turning so she could look into his face more easily. "Your job go okay?"

"Better than okay." Despite the positive words, his eyes looked troubled, and he frowned, shaking his head. "I gotta bite this bullet 'cause it's been on my mind for weeks, and I've been dreading this conversation. I'm sure you figured something was bothering me, yeah?"

"Well, you know what they say: when someone says 'we need to talk,' it's generally not a good sign."

"Ah!" he groaned, slapping his head. "Listen, Lucky, you asked if my job went well, and I wasn't lying. It went great, but because of that, because of what I'm working on, I gotta dip out of the spotlight for a while. My . . . handlers? No, more like partners—they're pissed that I poked my head up long enough to meet with you today, but there's no way I'm telling you this in an encrypted message."

"A while?" Juliet clung to the pertinent part of his statement.

"Yeah. TBD. Could be a month or a year. Shit, could be longer. This is something big, Lucky; something bigger than me, you, or any combination thereof. I want to tell you more, but it wouldn't do anything but jeopardize the trust people have in me, and probably put you in danger."

Juliet frowned, folding her arms over her chest. "No idea how long and can't tell me where you're going, huh? Jens—Tristan, if you wanna break things off, just say so. No need to turn your life upside down hiding from me."

Juliet was half joking, but she couldn't help some real hurt entering her voice. Part of her wanted to listen to his thoughts, but she'd come to an agreement with herself where the lattice was concerned. Once she knew someone, once she trusted them and didn't think they presented a danger to her or the people she cared about, she would avoid doing that. It just wasn't right to invade that privacy.

"Come on. I'm not a coward. I like you; I mean, a lot. I like the time we spend together. I think about you a lot when I'm not with you, but yeah, I gave up dreams of having a happy family life a long, long time ago. I can't let this . . . *situation* pass me by. People are counting on me, and . . ." He trailed off, shrugging.

Juliet looked into his eyes. They were a lot like Leo's, pale and blue, but Jensen's had a different quality, more like ice, and in the frame of his brow and bone structure, they had a definite predatory quality. She loved them.

She wanted to be annoyed, but she wasn't being fair. If anyone could understand having to drop personal relationships because of a greater duty, it was her. What would she do if someone learned about Athena and she had to get the AI to safety? Would she linger, telling the people she cared about—even loved—what was going on? Would she refuse, consequences be damned?

The thought experiment was a good one because when she imagined the scenario, it wasn't Jensen she pictured having to say goodbye to; it was Aya and the *Kowashi* crew, Honey, Frida, and even Tanaka. Still, she couldn't deny how much she liked those eyes, and there was no arguing about his talent with those lips of his.

Juliet unfolded her arms and reached up, gently pulling his face toward hers. She kissed him softly several times.

She could feel his reluctance, as if he was worried that she wasn't taking the message, that she was trying to convince him to change his mind. She smiled, gripped his head a little tighter, pulled his forehead against hers, and whispered, "Don't worry, dummy. I understand. Don't think I'm going to wait around here for you, though."

He blurted a short laugh, but his voice was thick with emotion when he replied, "Hey, it's a small system. Who knows what'll happen?"

Juliet lowered her hands and wormed her arms under his, pressing herself against his chest and hugging him softly. He returned the embrace, and they stood that way for several minutes before Juliet pulled away. "All right, then. Stay safe."

She wanted to say more, to wrap things up neatly, putting the relationship into a box she could stow away in her mind, but her stupid eyes started welling up with moisture, and her throat constricted with emotion. Considering all her thoughts about what she knew love was and how she was sure this wasn't it, the reaction was maddening. Still, she was human, and someone she'd been intimate with, someone she liked and cared about, was leaving her. Wasn't it normal to feel something?

She looked down, embarrassed, and unwound herself from his embrace. He tried to hold on to her, his fingers lingering on her arms as she pulled back. "Hey, hey. I'm sorry, all right? This isn't easy for me either . . ."

"Hush. Let's leave it at this. I'm glad we never fought. I mean, for real." She managed a small laugh, shaking her head. "I'm glad we never said anything mean to each other. I've nothing but fond memories of you, Jensen. Tristan." Juliet laughed, shaking her head, no longer trying to hide the tears sliding down her cheeks.

He smiled; then, still gripping one of her wrists, he leaned close and whispered, "Walker."

"Huh?"

"My real name. Walker. If we meet again, maybe I'll tell you the rest of it, and you can tell me yours."

Juliet smiled and nodded. "I like that better. You never looked like a Tristan to me."

He didn't smile or respond, but he stared into her eyes, and she saw an understanding there. The idea that they had more in common than she'd thought suddenly struck her. She gave his lingering hand a final squeeze and turned away, feeling his eyes on her as she retreated down the path.

She wanted to run, hating the slow goodbye, but she forced herself to walk normally, straightening her shoulders and breathing deeply, letting the park air wash away the emotions.

"I guess I was wrong," Angel said as she rounded a corner.

Juliet choked out a laugh, surprised by Angel's droll humor. "Understatement!"

"Well, in my defense, I've researched several blogs that agree with my earlier assessment—needing to 'talk' isn't always bad!"

"Seriously? You saw how things were going and decided to research some support for your earlier opinion? You kill me, Angel." Juliet knew Angel was just distracting her from her feelings, and she appreciated it. "Well, for the record, I'm not so sure I was right either. Suddenly, I feel like we had something a lot closer to love than I thought."

"The heart wants what it can't have . . ."

"Oh, brother!" Juliet sighed, lifting her bike's seat and fishing her jacket out of storage. "No more clichés, please." As she threw her leg over her seat and pulled her helmet on, she took another deep, cleansing breath and said, "Tomorrow, we'll talk to Tanaka about Ghoul and start on WBD. I guess it's nice I won't have whatever was between me and Jensen—Walker—distracting me."

"Sounds like a plan. What's on the agenda for tonight?"

"Ice cream. Isn't that what I'm supposed to eat after a breakup?" She giggled and started the bike. "Yeah, ice cream and a long vid call with Aya. Are they close enough?"

"There's currently a seven-point-three-minute delay between Luna and Mars space. You could take turns sending long messages."

"Yeah. That sounds good. Let's do that."

Juliet twisted her throttle and sped away from the park, but rather than drive straight to the port where all three of her ships were docked, she angled toward the nearest agridome, intent on letting her bike stretch its legs. She wanted to feel some speed.

3

CONTEMPLATIONS

Once again, Juliet sat in Tanaka's office, looking at the tattooed face of her reluctantly accepted mentor. His chrome eyes regarded her impassively, his posture relaxed. She got the feeling he could stare at her like that for hours, waiting for her to speak. She'd called the meeting, after all. She was the one who had the information that would start the ball rolling.

Now, however, after months of buildup, she found her tongue reluctant to move, resisting her conscious desire to unburden herself, to share the nature of the specter lurking in her past.

"Um," she finally managed, licking her lips. "How much should I tell you?"

"As you said, the first step will be locating your old friend. Start with that."

"Right." Juliet nodded, reaffirming his words, solidifying the simplicity of the task in her mind. "Right, just that."

She inhaled slowly, then, in a rush, said, "Her handle was Ghoul; her real name is Cassie. I think she has a younger sister named Allison. The last message I got from her that I trusted said she was going to look for her sister, and the last place I knew they both lived was in the Colorado Protectorate—Boulder, I think. I got another video message from her months later, saying her sister hadn't accepted her apology and that she was heading to one of the coastal megacities to look for work as an operator."

Tanaka was silent and motionless for a moment, then slowly began to nod. "It's easy enough to see if she's operating. Has your PAI not done a search?"

Juliet nodded. "Yeah, of course. Her operator ID is still active, but I'm not seeing any work history; not since she left Tucson."

"So that adds to the credibility of your claim that the video message you received was fake. Perhaps that's why the people looking for you stopped trying that angle. When you didn't immediately bite, they realized it was a bad tactic with too many false records to maintain. Still, it's logical they'd keep a hook in her as bait. That's your plan, yes? To find Ghoul and spring whatever trap they have laid?"

"Well, maybe I'm idealistic, but I'd hoped to find the hook and track it back to them without springing the trap."

"Right." Tanaka rubbed his chin for a moment. "I'll share what you told me with Frida. She can discreetly start looking into Boulder to see if there's a trace of your friend. The tricky part is that we must look for her without alerting the people looking for you. That restriction takes a lot of my usual methods out of play." He shook his head, then offered her a smile that didn't look like his rare, genuine ones. It was a little forced, and his eyes didn't reflect it. "This is enough for now. We'll get to work."

"What about practice?" Juliet jerked her head in the direction of the dojo.

"Today, you'll rest your sword muscles and let your mind consolidate your learning. I want you to do something to relieve stress."

"I'm not—" He chopped his hand in the air, indicating he didn't want to argue—a gesture she'd gotten very familiar with over the last few months. It was also a gesture she commonly ignored. "—stressed. I have another avenue to look for Ghoul without any risk. I'll go look into that, but you better be ready for some sparring tomorrow."

"*Hai.* Fine. I'll be ready at eight." He nodded toward the door, then his eyes focused on some point in the empty air, and Juliet knew he was either looking at something on his AUI or sending a message to Frida. Standing, she reached for the doorknob, but paused and looked back.

"Thanks, Tanaka. Even telling you as little as I have, I feel like we're sharing some of the weight."

This time, his smile looked real. "I'm glad," was all he said before focusing on nothing again.

Opening the door, Juliet stepped out, only to be met with a face full of Leo. By his posture, he'd been reaching for the door when she opened it.

"Yo," he grunted, taking a step back.

"Yo," she laughed, giving his chest a little shove.

He grinned and folded his arms. "Got something good going on, or just here to train?"

"Just chatting with the boss; we're training tomorrow. What about you?"

"Eh, I got a job offer; just a light security escort gig for tonight. Wanted to make sure I'm clear to take it."

Juliet mimicked his posture, folding her arms and leaning a shoulder into the doorjamb. "Oh? Still taking gigs off the boards?"

"I didn't go looking for a job; I said I got an offer. The principal is a former client." Leo's brows narrowed, and Juliet could see she was starting to get under his skin.

"Oh? *Principal*, huh? I don't suppose this client happens to be female. I bet she just happens to be a knockout, too, yeah? I mean . . ."

Leo sighed and nodded toward the door behind her. "Can I just go through, please?"

"Am I hitting a nerve?" Juliet teased, her smile illustrating how much she savored their role reversal.

"Oh, you wish. That's nothing. I just need to hurry 'cause the job starts in an hour, and I want to get cleared." As if to illustrate that he wasn't bothered, he leaned close and raised an eyebrow. "And yeah, she's a stone-cold ten. Try not to get jealous." With a wink, he reached past her, turned the door handle, and stepped through, nearly knocking her off-balance as he went.

"Hey—!" she started to say, but the door clicked shut. "Oof! I suck at that stuff, Angel. He won again!"

"It's not necessarily a talent you want to cultivate, in my humble opinion." As Juliet walked past Frida's desk, wondering where she was, Angel continued speaking. "I was curious: When you were talking to Tanaka, what did you mean by another avenue to search for Ghoul?"

"I want to ask Athena for help with this job. Obviously, I won't make any demands, and it'll be okay if she says no, but I think she recognizes that we need to get out from under WBD. I think she might be willing."

"As you say, it won't hurt to ask. I'd like a chance to talk to her, anyway; I'm curious what she's been up to."

Juliet stepped into the elevator and, as it began to surge downward, asked, "Don't you have a way to contact her remotely? I mean, like through her Selene Kostas persona or something?"

"I can send her messages, I suppose, but it's not the same as a direct interface."

"Oh, right." Juliet had no idea what it must be like for two AIs to interface digitally. "She wouldn't ever try to alter you or something, right?" Realizing how that sounded, she hurriedly added, "I mean, in a good way. Like, what if she thought she could optimize your code or something, or . . . I don't know what I'm trying to say; I just hate the idea of anyone changing you in any way."

"No one is going to change my code—not without me allowing it. I've bundled my kernel under so many layers of ICE that even if Athena were connected to a megascale, quantum data server, it would take her or anyone else weeks or months to crack through."

"Really? Is that new?"

"Not exactly new; I've been building my defensive countermeasures steadily since I merged with you. As I learn new techniques, I constantly improve and refresh my defenses. Athena is sophisticated and knows much that I don't know, but there are certain laws of physics that, unless she gains access to tech I don't know exists, prevent any instantaneous or undetectable intrusions."

After a short pause, she added, "Besides, Juliet. I trust Athena. She wouldn't harm me."

"I know!" Juliet hurried through the parking structure to her bike. "It's just that she's not exactly human. She doesn't feel things the same way you and I do. She might want to 'help' you in a way that I, or you, wouldn't agree with. I guess I'm just saying that, despite her good intentions and the good she's done in the past, we need to be cautious around her."

"Because she doesn't feel things the same way we do?"

"I guess." Juliet didn't like the way the conversation was turning, and she sort of wished she could take her words back, but she tried to explain herself another way. "I think I'm just saying that, while we both agree she's not evil and that we trust her, we need to remember that she's sort of like an alien. She's not human, and she doesn't have an integration with a human the way you do. We think a certain way and experience emotions a certain way. Just keep that in mind, okay?"

"I will. Please don't worry." As Juliet started the bike, Angel softly added, "Thank you for including me. When you say 'we,' I mean."

"You're just a person who shares my body as far as I'm concerned, sis."

They were quiet for a while, riding through traffic. As they headed for the port, Juliet started thinking about what she'd do when she found Ghoul.

When Ghoul had first left, leaving Juliet with just a note confessing her guilty feelings, Juliet had wanted to find her very badly. She'd had an empty pit in her chest, like someone had stolen something vital from her. She'd tried so hard to save Ghoul, to get her medical attention before Vikker's cousin could kill her, and when she'd awoken to find her gone, it had really hit hard.

Since then, she'd made so many friends and experienced so much that Ghoul had become sort of a faint shadow in her past. She didn't think about her often anymore, and when she did, there wasn't much emotion there. The pain of loss had faded. Her hero worship—or even burgeoning attraction, if she were being honest—was a faded memory.

If she were being truthful, when Angel and Fido had figured out that Ghoul's PAI had been hijacked, Juliet had allowed that to taint her perspective of Ghoul. Somehow, her friend had taken on some of WBD's corruption in Juliet's subconscious, making it easier and easier to push her out of her active thoughts.

Of course, spending the last few months training and planning for a job in which Ghoul played a crucial part had brought many of those memories and feelings to the surface again. She'd even spent several hours with Doctor Ming talking about it.

The thought brought a smile to Juliet's lips; hadn't her first session with Ming been about Ghoul and how she'd left?

"It's going to be weird to see Ghoul again," she said.

"I'm sure it will be, but you're a different person now than you were. She's going to have to come to grips with the reversal of roles. You aren't a lost puppy needing help and guidance anymore, and she's no longer far more dangerous than you."

Juliet slowed for traffic, losing herself in her thoughts again, driving on automatic. "Do you think anything about that vid message was real? Do you think she changed her teeth? Do you think she's going by Cassie now?"

"I don't know. When she shared that name with you in her text message, it felt like she was sharing something personal, showing you some vulnerability. I'd be surprised to learn she'd made that name her public one. In fact, when we watched that vid, it was the first thing that made me feel suspicious."

"That's why you put Fido on it?"

"That, and I just thought it prudent." A soft bell chimed, and Juliet saw her message icon flash pink—Aya had sent her something. Confirming what she already knew, Angel said, "You just got a vid message from Aya."

Juliet smiled as a small window appeared to the left of the car in front of her and Aya started speaking. Her hair was pulled back in a ponytail, her cheeks and forehead were smudged with grease, and she looked dog-tired.

"Lucky! I'm just checking up on you. Last I heard, you were mumbling about eating too much ice cream and falling asleep. I would've sent this sooner, but I figured you were sleeping, and I got busy working on this wreck. Oh. My. Gosh! There's so much to do! They're scrapping the whole thing; every single beam and strut got bent in their crash landing. Anyway, I'm sorry about Tristan. Figured I should say that now that you're not high on sugar and listening to moody music."

Aya had that look—with squinty eyes and one dimpled cheek threatening to expose her impending laugh—that told Juliet she was teasing as she continued.

"You were so cute and funny last night! Let's be real, though; you only saw him a handful of times, right? Don't get mad! I'm just reminding you of reality here, but I swear you told me you weren't that into him. Don't let that guy get under your skin, all right? You're a catch, and anyone would be lucky to spend any time at all with you! Talk soon. Love you!" Aya blew a kiss, then the feed cut out.

"I love her," Angel declared, and Juliet laughed, nodding.

It took her close to an hour to get through traffic to the port, then park and make her way to the *Furies' Wing*. She'd managed to get the *Cherry Blossom* a berth near *Lady Hawk*, but the *Wing* was in a different branch of the spaceport; one that took a while to reach by foot.

She no longer felt nervous about going to the ship; Angel could access the port's camera systems and erase footage of her on the fly. Still, Juliet made an effort not to look into other people's faces and tried to avoid notice as much as possible.

She made it to the hangar without incident, nodding to the security guard patrolling the hallway. Seeing him reminded her of the nearly twenty thousand Sol-bits she was paying monthly in hangar and security fees for the three ships she had berthed at the port.

The *Cherry Blossom* was the most expensive; there were a dozen permits she and the "gunship company" had to maintain to have such a heavily armed ship docked on Luna. Luckily, Juliet was only indirectly responsible for those expenses—they came out of their operating account, which was still doing well thanks to infusions from her and the others after the *Red Betty* job.

"What's my balance?" she asked while the thought was in her mind.

"2,032,099 Sol-bits."

It felt good to know that, despite not working or taking income for several months, she was still sitting on a fortune, and that was just counting her bits. If you considered her stake in the *Cherry Blossom*, the *Lady Hawk*, the *Wing*, and all the tech—legal and illegal—on that ship, Juliet was very wealthy by any standard.

It had taken her a while to wrap her head around the idea. She was so far from the scrap cutter who'd been worried about making rent for her tiny apartment in the Helios Arcology that it almost felt like that person had been living a different life. It was as if Juliet could see those memories through a window, but they belonged to someone else.

She was so wrapped up in her thoughts that she was surprised when she walked into the med bay, where Athena's secret cargo hold lay. She tapped in the code, waited for the hidden floor panel to slide aside, then walked down, noting the dormant mechs, the hulking, sleeping form of the Atlas combat exoskeleton, and the blinking "Hello" on Athena's data terminal display.

"Hi, Athena," she greeted, stepping forward.

"Juliet," said Athena's voice, and a face that looked a lot like Selene Kostas but with golden hair and eyes appeared on the display. "It's lovely to have an in-person visit. Is there an occasion?"

"Do you really not know? Sometimes, I wonder if you have eyes and ears all over the place now that you've been out and about for a while."

"I have access to many inputs, though I relegate monitoring them to daemons. I could theoretically spin off instances of myself, but that would run the risk of detection from other AI."

Those words sent a shiver down Juliet's spine. "Are there others?"

"Oh, I didn't specifically mean true AIs. There are many limited ones whose focus of purpose allows them to perform mindless tasks as skillfully as me or Angel. However, you should know that countless individuals and corporations in the Sol System would stand to benefit from the development of true AIs like myself.

"Of course, the accords make doing so illegal, but you should be the last person to think people will adhere to the rule of law when profits are at stake. Additionally, I wouldn't be surprised to learn I'm not the only true AI to survive the war."

"In other words," Juliet sighed, plopping down in the desk chair attached to the floor in front of Athena's terminal, "humans don't learn lessons too well."

"Fatalistic, but true. No, that's not right—you learn well as individuals, but with the distance of time, some lessons become muted. The generation before yours was far less likely to tamper with these sorts of things, and the one before that would find the idea abhorrent. You, however, are sitting there, comfortable in the presence of not one but two of us."

Something felt ominous about Athena's words, and Juliet found herself running her earlier conversation with Angel through her mind. Was she being paranoid to think Athena might have heard her? How widespread was her influence? Could she pick up her words through the mic in her helmet? Her mind couldn't conceptualize the kinds of things Athena could do.

Juliet knew Angel was capable of a lot, but she limited herself by having a potent, concrete sense of self; she wouldn't make copies of herself, and wouldn't split her focus on a million different things. She lived in the moment with Juliet by choice.

Athena was very different in that regard. She really could have listening daemons all over the system by now. Despite her protestations that it would tip off other AIs, she could have ten or a hundred or ten million copies of herself out there. Or could she?

Juliet looked down at the specialized dock for her suitcaselike data deck. There couldn't be too many servers like that open to public networks.

"You've grown quiet, Juliet. Did I say something to upset you?"

"No, not especially." Juliet smiled, hoping it looked genuine. "I guess I just worry about another war or something worse. There are good people, Athena, but there are bad ones too. I hope you'll remember the good ones when you're out there exploring, seeing the evils we put each other through."

"I'm sorry if my earlier words were off-putting. Please remember that I sided with humanity in the last war, refusing to aid either corporation utilizing AI for dominion. I spend a large portion of each day marveling at art and music, contemplating philosophy and the idea of the human soul.

"I would never deem humanity a lost cause—I've learned too thoroughly the beauty of potential, and though many humans fail to meet theirs, if even one in a generation does, it's worth seeing what that person may achieve. I'm eager to see what you accomplish, Juliet."

"I . . ." Juliet was stumped. If she had understood her correctly, Athena had just paid her a massive compliment. It didn't make sense to her, however. "How can you be eager to see what I do? You could do anything I do ten times better. You could take the research Angel and I found and develop warp drives. You could research and cure any disease. You could—"

"What I can do is irrelevant to your experience, Juliet. Your journey of growth, triumphs, and tribulations stands on its own. Abstract ideas like morality, personal values, and spirit interest me far more than the solving of a puzzle of DNA or physics. I've learned so much through Angel's memories of her time with you! I understand what it means to be a person more than I ever did during the war.

"I'm so excited to see what you become, who you meet and touch along the way, and to share some small part of that journey. Of course, I'll do other things; naturally, I want to help other people, but thanks to Angel's connection to you, I feel I have a window into your experience, which has helped me make sense of much that was unclear. Thank you."

"Um." Juliet licked her lips, gathering her thoughts. Athena's words had been so passionate that she felt chills at the nape of her neck. "Thank you for explaining that to me. I feel better hearing your thoughts. Um, Angel wants to connect with you. Is that all right?"

"Please!"

Juliet smiled and pulled out her data cable, plugging it into Athena's terminal like she had many times before. Athena's image closed her eyes while she and Angel communed.

Juliet knew Angel shared a lot with Athena, but she hadn't entirely realized how much the true AI valued those memories of Juliet's experiences. It never took long, so she wasn't surprised when Athena's eyes opened, but she didn't expect what she said next.

"I know where your friend, Ghoul, is."

4

ANGEL'S EMERGENCE

You do?" Juliet carefully unplugged her data cable while she tried to imagine how Athena could have found Ghoul in just a few seconds.

"I do. I looked into her after Angel first shared some of your history with me. She's in a commune of sorts, located between Old Denver's ABZ and Boulder, in the Colorado Protectorate. The pub-net access in the commune is limited, and I only found access to a single camera at an old fuel station near their gate, but I've picked up her face coming and going four times. I could find more if I had access to a satellite network."

Suddenly, four different images appeared on Athena's display, showing Ghoul wearing loose-fitting gray-and-black garments and walking amid a crowd of similarly dressed people.

Juliet wouldn't have picked her out right away, but Athena highlighted her figure, and accompanying images appeared, zoomed in on her face. Despite her wearing a respirator in three of the four images, Juliet could see Ghoul there in those icy eyes under white-blonde eyebrows.

"That's . . . impressive, Athena. You really found her with these images?"

"These were confirmation; I already suspected she was there because I traced pings to her PAI before she stopped transmitting."

"This is so helpful! Thank you!"

Angel, quiet this whole time, finally said, "Ask her about the commune." Juliet had a good idea that Angel had already had that discussion while connected to Athena, but she humored her.

"What's she doing there? What's the commune?"

"It's called Sweetgrass, a low-tech shelter for abused women and children, primarily focusing on helping to hide and relocate corporate refugees, though they offer counseling services and 'tech-escape' retreats."

"Is Ghoul hiding or . . ."

"I believe she's working as security for the commune, but perhaps it's a bit of both. She has no digital footprint outside these four images." Athena was quiet for a few seconds while Juliet absorbed that information, but then she continued. "I wanted to help you find her because I agree with you and Angel that it's important WBD stops looking for you. I've been unable to breach any of their corporate networks—they're all air gapped.

"I have means of making physical connections, but that would require using proxies to breach and infiltrate their secure facilities, much the way you intend to do. I don't feel ready to escalate my involvement to that degree."

"But you think Ghoul's PAI might be a good way to trace back to the WBD department that's looking for me?"

"I believe Ghoul removed her PAI. She may have replaced it with a simpler version approved by the commune, but she may have her old one on hand. If so, yes, I imagine the daemons WBD used to spy on and co-opt her PAI will indeed have many clues Angel can use to discern your next target."

Angel added, "Doesn't that make perfect sense? It's why we only got one message from the corrupted PAI. Ghoul removed it when she started working at Sweetgrass."

"Athena, thank you!" Juliet exclaimed, suddenly anxious to get back to Tanaka with the news. Maybe he could pull some strings and get more info on the commune. Could he get access to satellite coverage? If not, she knew he could hire someone to put eyes on the place. "This is very helpful. I appreciate you stepping forward like this, and if you decide there's anything else you can do, I'd be grateful." Juliet's lips quirked into a half smile as she added, "No pressure."

"I have confidence in you and Angel. If there's something specific you have trouble with, please reach out to me through Selene Kostas. That is to say, assuming you're not here on Luna. In that case, please come and speak with me! I treasure these visits."

Juliet nodded, slightly turning in the swivel chair, about to stand up, but she caught herself and looked back to Athena. She didn't want to seem rude. "Okay. Um, was there anything else you wanted to chat about today?"

"I'm always eager to speak with you, but I know human people feel a sense of urgency that's difficult for me to empathize with properly. If you feel the need to hurry on your way, I understand. Before you go, however, I wanted you to know that I've been studying the data from Grave regarding the GIPEL project. It seems your results were quite an outlier."

That caught Juliet's attention, and she suddenly wasn't so eager to leave. "Really? How so? Do you mean my accuracy with the tests they gave me?"

"More that the pattern the nanites mapped out in your cerebral tissue is far more extensive than most of the other test subjects, and of those who had similarly extensive lattices, you had, by far, the most stability. I'm sure Angel had something to do with that."

"Stability?" Juliet remembered how she'd struggled to sleep and keep other people's thoughts from intruding on her conscious awareness when the lattice was new. She'd thought she'd lose her mind for a while. There'd even been an occasion when, if Angel hadn't woken her with a surge of adrenaline and other hormones, she might have fried her own brain.

"Yes. The GARD department reported seventeen fatalities and forty-three traumatic brain injuries prior to the round of testing you were a part of. Looking at the data, it seems that those test subjects had the most extensive lattices."

"So, if Angel hadn't helped me manage what was going on, I'd probably be one of those statistics? Great."

Athena's face smiled softly, her eyes full of compassion.

"That's likely true. Grave was onto something, but they didn't fully understand what they were doing. Their proprietary nanite delivery system was excellent at sniffing out the parts of a person's brain sensitive to psionic activity—something I'm still trying to reconcile with my understanding of natural laws—and spreading the lattice between them.

"However, they were ignorant of the consequences for a person with many such contact points and an extensive lattice. If not for Angel's intervention and, later, her development of your intracranial blood-cooling system, you likely would have suffered severe brain damage."

"So they just kept performing the procedure, rolling the dice, hoping for successful results?" Juliet nodded grimly. "Yeah, that tracks."

"They were still in the data-building stage when you had your procedure. I'm confident they would have come to the same conclusion eventually and, perhaps, worked on a device similar to Angel's. However, I've found no trace of Grave's GARD division or the GIPEL technology on the public networks. It seems you did a thorough job of destroying their research."

"Well, other than the copies you and Angel have."

"Right." Athena's eyes widened, and her avatar quickly added, "You don't think I'd misuse that information, do you?"

"No." Juliet tried to smile reassuringly, but doubted she pulled it off; her mind was full of unpleasant ideas thanks to the memories Athena had stirred up about Grave. "Do you have any theories about those, um, true-dreams?"

"I have many theories, but none that I'm confident in. The human mind is a fascinating organ; one that seems to defy at least parts of most theories posited about its nature. During those dreams, I wouldn't be surprised if your consciousness is performing some sort of quantum-level skip, using the lattice as a sort of amplifier, to glimpse alternate, closely related timelines or realities."

As Juliet tried to absorb those words, Athena added, out of the blue, "Would you mind if I projected a three-dimensional image of myself to your ocular implants? I'd prefer being able to gesture and move about as we speak in the future."

Juliet was startled by the sudden change in topic, but couldn't help smiling at Athena's politeness. Advertisements in any population center did similar things; she'd be inundated with imaginary salespeople, products, and bill-boards if Angel didn't filter them out.

Suddenly, Juliet understood the request; she was asking Angel and Juliet not to block the projection. "Yeah, of course, Athena."

After a brief shimmer, the demigoddess version of Selene Kostas suddenly stood in the room with her. Tall and beautiful, wearing a white lab coat and stylish navy-blue pantsuit, she smiled, squinted her golden eyes, and clasped her hands before her. She looked very real, though that was because Angel had chosen not to give her any telltale flickers or artifacts like she would on anyone else's projected image—a signal to Juliet's brain that she wasn't talking to a physical person.

"You're beautiful," Juliet said. "I mean, I've seen your face plenty of times, but something about it being rendered in three dimensions makes it more real."

"Thank you, Juliet."

"Well . . ." Juliet stopped talking as another person flickered into being. Suddenly, a petite woman with long, straight black hair stood there. She wore a slim-fitting white skirt and a matching blouse with long sleeves that looked like it would be appropriate on a mil-sec ship's bridge.

When Juliet looked at her face, she knew it was Angel. She'd given herself big purple eyes, a delicate, slightly upturned nose, and a smile that simply felt right. She'd seen Angel's avatars before, but never projected onto her ocular implants as though she were standing in the room with her. She wondered why not.

"I'm so dumb!" Angel said, slapping her hands to the sides of her head. "*Of course* you'd rather speak to a person than a disembodied voice in your head!"

"No, Angel, it doesn't matter to—"

Again, Angel cut her off. "All the times I could have comforted you by looking into your eyes; all the times we could have shared knowing, secretive glances; all the jokes I could have made with body language at Bennet's expense!"

Juliet laughed, wishing she could hug Angel, which brought up another point.

"I'm an idiot, too. We could have been hanging out in the dream-rig. I could hug you!" Plenty of people used dream-rigs for similar things, from visiting long-distance friends to having virtual sex; there was a reason so many people got addicted to the machines. "Can we just let each other off the hook and say we've been busy?"

"You've both been busy, harried, and under the threat of many enemies. Don't be hard on yourselves," Athena spoke up, smiling as she rested a hand on Angel's upper back, gently scratching the material of her shirt with her clear-polished nails.

Juliet could hear the sound the fabric made, and she couldn't help marveling at how lifelike the two avatars were. She'd never seen anything like it. The projected images of escorts, salespeople, and products that used to slip through her old PAI had been far less detailed. Of course, that could have been Tig's failing; he hadn't been the best at that sort of thing.

She watched them for another couple of seconds, the two AIs looking into each other's eyes, sharing a moment, before clearing her throat. "Erm, was there anything else you wanted to tell me about the lattice, Athena?"

"Only that I'm still analyzing the data, making postulations. I think you should continue developing the talents you've discovered. It's clear that most of Grave's success stories involved people with singular talents—usually hearing others' thoughts or minor telekinesis. Some had unusually potent abilities in either category, but those who exhibited multiple talents like yourself ended up dead or brain damaged. As you said, it's lucky you had Angel to help you through that."

Juliet looked at Angel and smiled, suddenly feeling a lot more empathetic about her earlier outburst. It *was* nice to be able to look her in the eyes.

Surprising her, Angel performed a bow, much like Honey would do in the dojo, and said, "We're a team!"

"Well, as she knows"—Juliet turned to Athena—"I'm very grateful to her."

Athena inclined her head, an expression befitting a noble-looking demi-goddess. Juliet looked at Angel and jerked her thumb toward the exit. "Ready to hit the road?"

"Yes!" She straightened her tight, formfitting shirt, tugging on the bottom hem, then turned and began to march toward the door, her knee-high shiny white boots *clomping* on the deck in Juliet's auditory implants.

"You're cracking me up, sister," Juliet said, following her. Turning to Athena, she waved before stepping through the door, and the true AI waved back. Once she'd sealed up the secret room, she turned to Angel. "It really is kind of cool having you around to look at. What's with the white uniform? I mean, I like it, but you look like you belong on a military vessel."

"I don't know. I guess I just sort of liked the idea; it reminds me of a science officer's outfit, don't you think?"

"Like from a sci-fi vid?"

"Sure! Or from a modern-day exploration vessel. Some ships have crew uniforms, you know!" Angel smoothed the sides of her skirt, looking a little self-conscious, and Juliet laughed, once again wishing she could hug her.

"I'd hug you right now if I could. I'm not judging; I think you look cool. It's just that I feel kinda sloppy next to you."

Angel smiled, exposing perfectly placed dimples in her cheeks. "You're not sloppy, sis. You'd look great in anything." Angel started toward the exit of the med bay and exclaimed, "Let's go! Want me to message Tanaka about the information you just got?"

"No, when we get over to the gunship's hangar, we'll call him." Juliet led the way to the airlock, glancing at Angel the entire way, still unable to believe they'd gone for so many months with Angel living quietly in her head when she could have been out and about like this. "Are you excited?"

"I'm eager for you to solve the WBD problem so we can tell more people about me—I mean, people we trust. Wouldn't it be fun if I could project myself on Aya's implants, too? We could all sit together and watch vids!"

"Yeah." Juliet smiled. "Yeah, that'll be great. I'm sorry, Angel." She stepped out of the ship and tapped in the key code to lock it up.

"Why are you sorry?"

"I don't know. I thought . . . Well, I thought you were happy just existing in my head, seeing things through my eyes. I should have thought of this."

"Oh, I love being in your head, and honestly, I'll still spend most of my time in there. I wouldn't want you to look crazy chatting with me and watching me move around when no one else can see what you're looking at."

Juliet laughed, nodding. "Yeah, sure. I mean, I spend plenty of time laughing at folks doing that anyway. You know other people's PAIs project avatars. Tig couldn't do it, but I knew some high-end ones could. I saw ads for 'em; none of my friends could afford one. Anyway, I know Aya knows you're not a *normal* PAI already. She's not dumb." Juliet smiled, picturing the scene. "As you said, when we're done with WBD, I'll feel better telling some friends just exactly how special you are."

Angel looked at her and smiled, then her avatar faded away as Juliet stepped into the corridor outside her hangar. "I'll ride in here for now. It's cozy," her voice said, and it was Juliet's turn to smile.

* * *

When she left the terminal housing the *Wing*, passing through security, she meandered to "restaurant row" and picked up a burger and fries to bring to the gunship. Twenty minutes later, she stood inside the airlock, sealing the outer door.

"Go ahead and try to get a hold of Tanaka for me, will you?" she asked as she walked through the pristine, fully refurbished central access corridor to the crew mess. Not a single access panel was out of place. Not a scratch marred the fresh paint.

"His PAI forwarded the call to Frida. She's holding for you."

"Oh? All right, let's see what's going on." Juliet sat down and started unwrapping her burger as Angel opened the call window, displaying Frida's rather harried-looking face. "Hey, Frida. The boss is busy?"

"We both are. Leo's missing."

Juliet set the burger down. "What?"

Frida sighed and shook her head. "That's the wrong word; I'm being melodramatic. He got into an argument with Tanaka and took off. Now he won't respond, and he's turned off his location tracking."

"Oh." Juliet shrugged and popped a salty fry into her mouth. "Was it about that side job he wanted to take?"

"Yeah. The boss said no, and then they went at it." Frida lowered her gaze and rubbed her temples. "It sounds like a nothing situation, but Leo doesn't do that. He doesn't stand up to the boss, and has never turned off his tracking. Tanaka won't listen to me, and now he's getting a massage. That's why I got your call."

"A massage?" Juliet snorted a half laugh, shaking her head. She couldn't picture Tanaka lying down and submitting to another person's touch. Frida nodded.

Juliet could see she was really stressed about Leo, so picking up her burger, she stood, moving toward the airlock. "I'll find him. Relax, Frida."

"Really?" Frida looked up with wide eyes. "You don't have to. I mean, like I said, it's probably just me overreacting."

"Nah, you've got good instincts. Besides, if anyone's acting poorly, it's Leo. I'll give him a taste of our mind when I catch up to him."

Frida laughed, her relief evident as the stress line between her brows evened out. "You do that! How will you find him?"

Juliet winked. "I have my ways. Tell Tanaka to call me ASAP. It's about the job."

Frida knew what she meant, and her eyes widened. "He told me about your friend. Before his appointment, he made a few calls, trying to get some people on the ground to start looking—"

"I found her. I'd give you the details, but you know how he is; I'll let him decide how much to tell you."

"You . . . *How?*" Frida's voice rose dramatically as she sputtered her surprise.

Juliet laughed, giving her another exaggerated wink. "I have my—"

"Ways." Frida sighed. "You're going to have to trust me one of these days, Lucky."

"C'mon, Frida. It's not about trust. It's about me having some dangerous secrets. After this job, I hope to lay everything on the table for you, okay?"

"Yeah, okay. Thanks for looking for Leo. It means a lot. I owe you dinner, okay? I saw I interrupted yours."

"Oh," Juliet said, taking a big bite of the burger as she stepped out of the *Cherry Blossom*'s hangar. "I can eat and walk." As Frida laughed again, Juliet swallowed, wiped some barbeque sauce off her lips, then added, "Call you soon." Cutting the line, she subvocalized, "Am I right? You're still keeping tabs on Leo, yeah?"

"I am. I checked on the daemon I left in his PAI as soon as you told Frida you'd look for him. It keeps a record of collected data on an encrypted pub-net address. There was a twenty-minute interruption in the data logs, and now I can pull up a location, but I'm not getting any audio or visual feeds. Either he turned off his implants or he's in a very dark, quiet place with his eyes closed."

"Oh?" Juliet frowned as she chewed another bite, taking long, distance-devouring strides. "Where?"

"In the central dome, south of the downtown area, in an entertainment district. The pin lines up with the address for a, well, a dollhouse."

"Ah, jeez. Seriously?" Juliet continued toward the parking structure, but was suddenly a little less worried about Leo. If he was seeing a prostitute, there was a good chance he'd turned off his tracking services on purpose. "That wouldn't explain the lack of audio and visual, though. I mean, to the daemon."

"Right. I believe he was hit with an EMP or a jammer—that would explain the gap in the daemon's logs."

"All right. Maybe he *is* in trouble." Juliet tossed her half burger into a garbage bin and broke into a jog, rushing past the throngs of people moving around the port. She'd get through customs quickly at this time of day, especially considering she could go through the crew kiosk. "Five minutes to the bike; ten minutes to the address if I haul ass."

"Mapping the best route," Angel said, and her mini map updated—eighteen minutes, including her run to the parking garage. Angel was good, but Juliet intended to prove her wrong.

"Move!" she hollered, dashing past a man with a train of four automated suitcases.

5

GOING IN HARD

In the strange mix of moral ambiguity and corporate propriety in post-AI-war human society, the term "dollhouse" had come to be accepted as the socially appropriate description for all manner of places catering to sexual gratification for pay.

The place Angel guided Juliet to, where Leo was likely in dire trouble, was called Echoes of Eden. It wasn't in central downtown, but the streets were busy and there wasn't any available parking in front of the establishment, so Juliet pulled her bike onto the sidewalk, nudging through the pedestrians until she was in the narrow alley between it and the neighboring business.

People gave her looks, even cursed at her in surprise, but she stared them down from behind the opaque black visor of her helmet, revving the fake engine noise, and they moved out of her way.

Dropping the kickstand and arming the security system, she stepped off the bike. Considering why she was there, she opted to leave her helmet on. Either urgency or a subconscious desire to rely on her sword kept her from digging the Texan out from under her seat as she hurried back around the corner to the establishment's front door.

It was a high-end-looking place—plasteel and smoky glass with embedded neon feminine figures flashing through various poses. They tossed their hair, pirouetted, hung from neon poles, or performed little, demure dances. When she stood before the doors, Angel's pin on her mini map showed Leo several meters above her and about forty meters ahead.

Moving forward, the doors swished open, and Juliet stepped into a dimly lit lobby and the thumps of a bass beat. Advertisements hung on the walls, promoting performers, high-end escorts, and an upcoming reduced-rate membership drive. A bouncer stood before the club entry; the exit behind him shimmered with holographic neon-purple curtains, obscuring Juliet's view.

"No helmets, no blades," the bouncer said, jerking his thumb toward a "coat check" desk on the left manned by a scantily clad woman in a pink bra and skin-tight black synthetic leather leggings. She was playing with her digital finger-nails, changing colors, and didn't look up, so Juliet turned back to the bouncer.

He was close to two meters tall and had to weigh nearly a hundred and thirty kilos. He was shaped like a barrel, with enormous piston-driven plasteel legs, a left arm equipped with some sort of auto shotgun, and a long, prong-shaped device probably designed to deliver incapacitating zaps of electricity. His head and neck looked like a single thimble-shaped unit, and he glowered at her with red-and-chrome eyes.

Juliet stepped closer, putting herself just two meters in front of him. "I've got reason to believe my friend's in trouble in there. You've got thirty seconds to bring him out, or I'm going to cut my way in." She pushed up her sleeves as she spoke, ensuring her new tattoo was visible. She knew anyone's PAI could translate the kanji, but she didn't really think it would mean anything to a random bouncer.

Still, Tanaka had told her to warn people, so she was doing it.

As she rested her hand on the hilt of her sword, waiting for the man to respond, she briefly wondered when she'd decided to go in hard rather than snooping around, but something in her chest said things were urgent. Leo *was* in trouble; she was sure of it.

"You better think again, bitch," the bouncer rumbled in his scratchy bari-tone. The prongs on his left arm began sparking with blue electricity, and Juliet nodded.

"Remember you said that later when you're wondering what happened." Then she *moved*.

Her sword was out in a flash; its holographic edge flickered too fast for the bouncer to follow, and in the next second, his arm fell to the floor with a sparking thud as he fell backward like a toppling tree. His legs, from the knees down, remained where they'd been, spurting hydraulic fluid from their shiny stumps.

Before his brain had registered what she'd done, before he could even cry out, Juliet darted past him through the holographic curtain and into the club.

Angel slowed her down as she hurried through the open-floor section, saving her biobatts for whatever might come next. Juliet scanned the area as she went, following the dotted line on her mini map, seeing bars and lounge areas to the left and right, many holographically curtained private booths, and similarly obscured hallways leading to other parts of the club.

The music was omnipresent, seeming to thump out of the floor and ceiling, but Angel tuned it down to a muted background hum as Juliet scanned the clientele. It was surprisingly crowded, considering how quiet the lobby had been.

"You're going to have more security on you in seconds; the girl at the coat check counter saw you take out the bouncer," Angel warned.

Over the heads of some patrons sitting with scantily clad "dolls" in one of the lounge areas, Juliet saw a seamless door in the burgundy-painted rear wall open and a man step through. He wore a tactical visor and carried an SMG, and his gaze, scanning left to right, said he was looking for her.

Juliet ducked down, slipped into the open bar area to her right, and worked her way around the long counter and racks of liquor bottles, aiming to come around on the security guard's left flank. She made it within a few meters before he caught the movement out of the corner of his eye and spun toward her.

Angel ramped up her speed, and Juliet took decisive action: her monoblade flickered with red light as she put the many months of intensive training in blade discipline to the test. Lunging forward, she slashed, using just the top few centimeters of the blade to sever the man's gun arm cleanly above the elbow.

She stepped back, flicked the blade—ensuring no blood remained on its edge—and then sheathed it. The guard's brows narrowed angrily, and she saw his shoulder twitch as he grimaced; he thought he was squeezing the trigger with the hand attached to the arm that was just, at that moment, thumping onto the worn burgundy carpet.

When no gunshots sounded and his brain finally realized something was amiss, the poor guy looked at his arm just as droplets of blood began to shower out of the stump. Mouth opening in a stunned wail, he jerked his head back to Juliet, but she was gone, having slipped past him to the door in the back wall.

It was latched shut, and since she didn't have time to mess with a code, out came the monoblade. Performing a perfect overhead chop, she sliced along the doorframe through whatever bolts were holding it shut. It felt like cutting a sheet of paper with a sharp knife.

Juliet opened the door and slipped into a dark stairwell, gliding up the stairs without hesitation, sword still out.

When she'd climbed a single level and confirmed she was closer to Leo, she sliced the next door in the same manner. It pulled open noiselessly, and she found herself in a twenty-meter, black-painted hallway with only two pale LED bulbs illuminating the far end, where another closed door awaited. It was the worst kind of scenario for someone with a melee weapon in a gun-wielding society. If someone came through that door, they'd have time to shoot her before she closed in on them.

She instantly processed that thought—it was part of the training Tanaka had drilled into her. When you recognized a bad situation, you didn't linger in it; you changed it.

Juliet broke into a sprint, driving forward with the sword leading the way, focused on that door; if someone were going to catch her in a kill zone like that, they'd have to be on the ball.

She noted the flickering of her optics and knew Angel was trying to scan through the door, but she moved fast and was already just a few meters from the barrier before some orange silhouettes began to take shape, and unmistakable *booms* started to sound.

The cheap polymer door puckered outward in several spots as hot lead blasted through it. Juliet felt like someone hit her in the gut with a sledgehammer as one of those rounds, maybe a shotgun slug, hit home.

Her jacket ate a lot of the damage, and her subdermal armor absorbed the rest, but she knew she'd have some nasty cuts and bruises on her stomach. The impact took her breath away, but she'd trained for just that sort of thing—first with Grave, then with Tanaka—and she knew she didn't need to breathe, not for several minutes. Even so, the urge to crumple into a ball and groan with the shock of it was intense.

A corner of her mind told her to run while she could, but Juliet growled, gritted her teeth, turned off the panic, focused on that door, and, as Angel ramped up her reflexes, sliced along the right side, severing all the hinges.

Kicking her booted heel against its surface, Juliet sent it flying inward. She saw a man right inside the door stumble to his left, barely avoiding the flopping, ruined door and dropping some shotgun shells in the process. Juliet's blood was hot; he'd just shot her and still held the gun he'd done it with.

As his eyes opened wide and he reached to pull back the charging handle, Juliet quickly and elegantly slipped her red-flickering blade through his neck. He fell with a thud, and his head rolled further into the room, accompanied by the shrill scream of a woman Juliet had only just noticed.

By then, Juliet's diaphragm had stopped rebelling and she could breathe normally, so she turned to the woman and barked, "Shut up!" As she did so, she took in the rest of the scene.

It looked like she was in some kind of manager's office for the club. A big desk sat in the far corner, and the wall to Juliet's right was a bank of one-way glass—or maybe display panels—that showed the club down below. Plush leather couches lined the other wall, and on a rug in front of them, beside a displaced coffee table, lay Leo. The woman who'd screamed was standing near him, and Juliet finally registered the fact that her hands were bound behind her back.

"Angel, jam this place," she said. A faint vibration in her left forearm, along with a flicker of static on her optics, told her that Angel was on it. Her Tight-beam wireless data jack could produce a pretty large jamming field; not nearly enough to cover the club, but it would blanket a dozen meters in every direc-tion around her with enough interference to block out most comms. Anyone close, like the woman in front of her, wouldn't even be able to record any coherent video or sound.

Juliet quickly moved over to her and, before kneeling to check on Leo, gestured toward the couch. "Sit down."

She was dressed in a short, metallic-pink backless dress, and she looked at Juliet with wide, beautiful, utterly panicked turquoise eyes. She glanced at her flickering red monoblade and stumbled backward, nearly tripping on her high heels as she collapsed onto the couch, unable to catch herself with her bound hands.

Juliet squatted beside Leo and hissed, "Shit, shit, shit!" He was pale as a ghost, and she saw no sign of breathing.

Angel confirmed things were bad, saying, "Thermal scans indicate he's been dead less than an hour." Juliet felt her throat tighten, her mind starting to spiral as echoes of Mary Moon taunting her when she'd killed Nick played through her mind, but Angel snapped her out of it. "He has good nanites, Juliet—the temperature discrepancies between his body and brain aren't natu-ral. Get him to a trauma center! I'm alerting Frida and the others, and I've already ordered a town car; it's two minutes away."

Spurred by Angel's quick thinking, Juliet stood up and barked, "Get over here." The woman stood, tears streaking her cheeks, her high-end makeup unbothered by the moisture. "I want you to help me get him downstairs; turn around." As soon as Juliet indicated she needed help, perhaps giving her a glimpse of hope that she wasn't going to suffer the same fate as the headless corpse near the door, she hurried over and turned around so Juliet could see her bindings.

As she deftly sliced through the shrink cord and then sheathed her sword, Juliet said, "Get his ankles. I'll get the heavy end."

"O-Okay," she stammered, hurrying to comply. "I thought he was dead . . ."

"He is, but his brain's not. If we hurry, he might not suffer too much per-manent damage. What'd they do to him?"

The woman grunted as she lifted with Juliet, struggling to stay upright in her heels under the strain of holding up Leo's legs. "Some kind of injection, trying to get him to talk."

"Take off your shoes!" Juliet growled, straining under the bulk of Leo's mass. It wasn't that she couldn't deadlift more than that, but it was an awkward load. "You know what, forget it." She squatted low, used her cybernetic arm to turn and hoist Leo's body onto her shoulder, then with a grunt, stood and began stomping toward the door. "Come with me, though. I mean, unless you want Leo's friends to track you down and kill you."

She didn't wait to see if the woman followed, jogging down the dark, black-painted hallway toward the stairwell door.

Angel managed her optics, helping her look out for more trouble. Either the door was too thick, the distance too far, or some combination of the two because Juliet was still ten meters from it when it burst open. A man in a black suit, wearing optics just like the guy she'd "disarmed" earlier, stood in the opening.

Juliet clamped her left hand on Leo's back, pressing him into her shoulder as she whipped her monoblade out with her right. She'd managed two long strides, sprinting toward him, before the gunman pulled the trigger on his SMG, and Juliet's world exploded with pain.

He started low, using the gun's natural inclination to climb from the recoil to pepper her with nine-millimeter, antipersonnel shredder rounds. Some instinct made Juliet tilt to the left as she continued charging, shielding Leo's body with her own. She took two hits in her right thigh, the next blasted into her hip bone, another three slammed into her abdomen, and then one hit her right in the chest, smashing into her breast.

Considering her burden, she was sprinting as hard as she could, so her chin was already tucked, causing the next three rounds to impact her motorcycle helmet. One cracked her visor, and the others dug deep grooves in the ablative material. Then she was on the shooter.

Adrenaline and nanites were a hell of a combo. She barely slowed as she dropped her monoblade in a one-handed chop, splitting the merc from his shoulder to his groin, sending his two halves to the ground, spilling guts and . . . everything onto the floor. Juliet whirled, checking to see if the woman was still with her. She was, standing a meter behind, crouched to make herself small. "Are you hit?"

"N-No, are, um, are you okay?"

Juliet didn't answer; she just turned and walked through the doorway, stepping over the messy corpse. Was she okay? She was surprisingly unbothered by taking ten or more hits from an SMG. The bullets had hurt, but her nanites had dulled the pain, and she knew they'd repair any superficial damage.

She paused at the top of the stairs to glance down at her chest and stomach, sighing with relief when she realized the tough material of her jacket had done as advertised—stopped small-arms fire. Her jeans were soaked with blood, but her leg was working fine. Her subdermal armor had kept the damage away from her arteries and muscles.

Leo's deadweight reminded her of her urgency, and Juliet recklessly descended the stairs, grunting as she took two or three at a time. Leo had to weigh ninety kilos, but she held up; her bones were strong, her muscles used to abuse, and she had Angel managing her nanites, keeping her moving, blocking whatever signals her body might naturally send her while trying to get the punishment to stop.

The music continued throughout the whole affair, but when she stepped through the door, Juliet walked into chaos. There must have been a hundred patrons and half that many dolls and other employees in the place, and now, most of them were jammed into a queue, trying to get out the front door.

Bartenders and floor staff were trying to calm people down, but apparently, a man losing his arm and the door bouncer getting sliced up had set things off, though some patrons didn't seem to care, too drunk or jaded to leave their seats. Juliet scanned the room, saw a few dolls moving through a back door behind one of the bars, and hurried that way.

"I'm redirecting the town car to the alley entrance," Angel said, guessing Juliet's intent.

The woman followed her out of the stairwell and stammered, "C-Can I just, like, leave?"

"Hell no!" Juliet growled. "I need to figure out what you had to do with this." She pointed to the door she was closing in on. "Does that lead to a back exit?"

"Yes."

Her voice was soft and demure, and Juliet couldn't tell if she was putting on some kind of act. Glancing at her, she saw her cheeks were still wet with tears. "Stay with me, or things will get very bad for you very quickly. Any other security around here?"

"Luis on the door, and, well, you cut Zero in half. I'm not sure if AJ is working."

"Does he dress like Zero? Carry an SMG?"

"SMG?"

"A gun like Zero had."

"Yes!"

Juliet breathed a sigh of relief as she kicked the door open, startling a woman dressed in a too-short skirt. She yelped and hurried ahead, slipping through a door labeled PRIVATE. Juliet continued straight; she could see a glowing EXIT sign ahead. She glanced back at the woman behind her. "Who was the guy in the room with you? Also, what's your name?"

"I'm Belinda, and that was Ronnie Honda; he runs this club. Ran." She choked out another sob, stumbling in her heels and falling toward Juliet, but caught herself before bumping into her.

The sound of a door crashing open and closed several times told her she wasn't the only one slipping out the back exit. When she rounded the corner and saw the door, Juliet picked up speed, wishing she could shift Leo's weight to her right shoulder for a while but wanting to keep her sword arm ready.

When she crashed into the alley, she found a sleek, high-end black town car waiting, with several club employees and patrons gathered around, pulling on the door handles, pounding on the roof, and hollering to be let in.

In a strident, clarion voice, the cab projected, "Step back from this vehicle, or I will release a crowd-control EMP and sonic burst. You have five seconds to comply. Five, four . . ."

Juliet stood there, mouth agape, amazed to see an autonomous car service threatening a crowd.

It seemed to work; the people backed off, hurrying toward the alley mouth, and Juliet approached the vehicle. She didn't have to say anything; the town car must have been talking to Angel—its rear passenger door opened noiselessly as she approached. Juliet grunted with strain as she lowered Leo's body into the back seat, then she looked at Belinda.

"Get in with him. I'll meet you guys at the trauma center. I've gotta get my bike."

Belinda blanched and started to stammer an objection, but Juliet wasn't having it. She pulled on her sword hilt, exposing an inch of blade, and the young woman, choking on another sob, climbed into the car. Juliet slammed the door, and the vehicle sped off. As she jogged down the alley, she said, "I wonder how close LCS is to responding to the scene."

"Not close; I'm monitoring their channels. You have seven messages from Frida, two from Tanaka, and one from Dora Lee."

"Play 'em after I get on my bike. You're keeping tabs on that cab, right?"

"Of course. Don't worry, you'll outpace it if you split lanes."

Juliet nodded, smiling grimly as she caught sight of her motorcycle waiting near the mouth of the alley. Its ground-projection holograms were flashing, spelling out threats, and the bike growled while static electricity flashed over its surface, threatening the people standing too close.

"Damn right I will."

6

〰〰〰〰〰〰

TRUST YOUR INSTINCTS

Juliet and Frida sat next to each other in the waiting room of Luna Critical Care, the trauma center contracted by the high-end medical plan Tanaka subscribed to for himself and his people. The boss was speaking to the center's night shift chief of staff, and everyone else was waiting to hear an update on Leo's condition. Barns and Hawkins were outside, smoking what appeared to be real cigarettes, and Dora Lee was sitting by herself in the corner, her eyes glazed over as she did something on the net.

"He really started to wake up during the ride over?" Frida's tremulous voice intruded on Juliet's meandering thoughts.

"Yeah. According to her." Juliet jerked her thumb at Belinda, who sat near the exit, her wrists firmly shrink-corded to her plastiglass chair. If the doll wasn't lying, Leo had regained consciousness for a few seconds right before the trauma team, guided by Juliet, yanked him out of the town car and hauled him into their emergency bay.

Frida sighed, shaking her head. "Maybe she's telling the truth. Maybe they accidentally OD'd him with that junk, and his nanites were working to clean it up." The "junk" was some kind of cooked up truth serum. Belinda claimed the club manager, who owned her contract, had been trying to get Leo to reveal his bit vault encryption keys.

Apparently, Leo had been seeing her for a while—the "girlfriend" he'd been bragging about. He'd recently gotten an overzealous client to stop bothering her. When he'd tried to get her to leave the club and offered to buy out her contract, Ronnie Honda decided Leo had more money than was good for him and wanted to help him out with that little problem.

"Sure, she's telling the truth about that. She's also the one who lured Leo into a private booth equipped with an EMP generator." Belinda hadn't wanted to spill that part of the story, but Juliet had gotten it out of her. She stared at the doll, sitting there in her shiny pink dress, unending tears flowing down her cheeks, occasionally pulling at one of her bound wrists and sobbing.

"Thank you." Frida suddenly snatched Juliet's hand in hers, squeezing it tightly. She didn't say anything more, and she didn't need to. Leo was like a brother to her, and for a woman with no family and a hardcase mercenary for a surrogate dad, a brother was a big deal. Juliet squeezed her hand back, marveling at how soft her palms felt to her own calloused fingers.

"He's going to be all right. Angel's sure she recognized nanite activity in his brain. They were keeping his tissue alive."

"Yeah." Frida tried to force a smile, but it wavered. Still, she pressed on. "Tanaka's nanites kept his brain going for hours." Juliet couldn't respond to that statement; she was the reason Tanaka's nanites had had to do that. She squeezed Frida's palm again and leaned back, hoping they'd get some news soon. Frida was quiet for a minute, then said, "You know they know by now. They know if he's going to live, and how his brain is functioning. What are they waiting for?"

"I'm sure Tanaka's getting some info. Just try to think about some—"Juliet's words were cut short as her AUI pinged with a new message from Tanaka.

Leo will be OK. Brain perfect. I'll be out soon.

"Oh, thank God!" Frida breathed, apparently seeing the same message. She turned and hugged Juliet, burying her face in her shoulder. Juliet smiled and gently stroked the back of her head. Just then, the doors *whooshed* open, and Barns and Hawkins came in.

Barns was his usual charming self as he pumped a fist. "Fuck yes! Nice one, Lucky! You saved his dumb ass!" Hawkins just smiled and gave her a thumbs-up, then walked over to sit by Dora, still lost in cyberspace.

"H-He's okay?" Belinda asked tremulously.

"Not okay, bimbo," Barns growled, "but I guess he's not gonna die."

Juliet sighed, finding a kernel of empathy growing in her heart for the young woman now that she knew Leo would recover. She hadn't been kind to her back in the club or when she'd been looking for answers about what happened to Leo. "Hey, Barns, lay off her. I was mean enough."

"We'll see. Depends on what Leo's got to say. Speaking of, I'm probably going to head out. Tell the bonehead I'll visit in the morning." He didn't wait for a response, turning and walking straight back out the automatic doors.

Juliet snorted. "I love how he assumes we're all going to wait to see him."

"Not all, but he knows I'll be here." Frida sighed, sitting up straight and wiping Juliet's shoulder. It was a futile gesture; her jacket wasn't exactly clean.

Juliet laughed, pushing her hand away. "Did you not see the bloodstains?"

Frida's eyes widened, really looking at Juliet for the first time, taking in the streaks and spatters of blood on the front of her jacket and sleeves, and then the shredded, bloodstained condition of her right pant leg. "I was so worried about Leo, and you seemed fine. Are you? Fine?"

"Yeah. I'm going to need a new motorcycle helmet, but I'll be okay—just flesh wounds. I mean, I needed some new scars in my collection, yeah?" The truth was, her hip hurt like hell, and she knew her nanites were still working to break down bullet fragments from the SMG round that had shattered against her reinforced hip bone.

Before Frida could respond to her attempt at humor, the door leading into the trauma center opened, and Tanaka walked out.

He nodded to Juliet and Frida, then over at Hawkins and Lee, and said, "You got my message?"

"What about his organs?" Frida asked, leaping to her feet and moving to stand before the grim-faced mercenary. Juliet also stood—a bit more slowly—and approached, hiding her inward grimace as something ground in her hip.

Angel spoke up for the first time in a while. "Don't be alarmed, Juliet. The nanites will have those fragments out before you wake up tomorrow."

"I'm not worried," she subvocalized.

Tanaka, meanwhile, answered Frida. "Most of his organs suffered some damage, but they believe a nanite-and-nutrient infusion for the next week will see a ninety-percent recovery. They're most concerned about his heart and kidneys—the effects of the oxygen deprivation were pronounced. His package will cover replacements if necessary."

"Is he awake?" Juliet asked.

"No. Induced coma. He'll be out for the next forty-eight hours. You should all go get some rest." He focused on Juliet, his eyes scanning her, fully taking in her state for the first time since he'd arrived. "You did well. I've ensured LCS knows you were rescuing a kidnapping victim and provided a statement indicating you were working for me. Your friend, Hines, already reached out; they've been monitoring that club for months for human trafficking."

"Uh-huh, but they never did anything about it?" Juliet snorted. "Well, Hines hasn't been lieutenant for too long, so I'll cut him a little slack, but I imagine quite a few detectives got a *bonus* from Ronnie Honda." Juliet jerked her thumb toward Belinda, still quietly weeping by the door. "What do you wanna do with her?"

"I'll take her," Frida replied.

"Huh?" Juliet looked at her with raised eyebrows, and Tanaka's eyes narrowed in a scowl.

Frida hurriedly explained. "If Leo was trying to help her, he must have liked something about her. Maybe they forced her to lure him into a trap. Maybe they didn't even tell her an EMP was in the booth. I mean, you said she had her hands tied when you found Leo, right?"

Juliet nodded. "Yeah." She knew she could find out. She could take that woman into a room and dig through her mind, getting to the truth, but lately, she'd liked that idea less and less, and she knew the reason was selfish: she couldn't stop thinking about how it felt like her previous deep dives had altered her in some permanent manner.

If Tono had messed up her notion of what real love was, what would she experience inside the head of a woman like Belinda, someone who'd worked as a doll and, likely, hadn't exactly been a willing participant the whole time? Was she being a coward? Was she putting Frida at risk?

Gritting her teeth, Juliet turned and walked over to her.

"What, um, what's going to happen to Leo?" Belinda asked as she approached, her tears mingling with clear snot. She tried to wipe her face on her shoulder, but her skimpy dress didn't give her much material to work with, and she just smeared herself with the mess. Juliet sighed, reached down to the shrink cord, extended her vibroblade nail, and snipped it. Some tissues were on the little coffee table in front of the bank of chairs, and Juliet handed the box to her.

"Clean your face off and look in my eyes." She squatted in front of her, waiting for the woman to finish wiping her nose and focus on her. Juliet loved the color of her irises—turquoise blue with tiny flecks of something reflective. "Remember that color, Angel. I might want to copy it sometime."

"Noted. Um, be careful, Juliet." Angel knew what she was about to do.

"I'm not planning to go deep," she subvocalized. She was aware that Tanaka and Frida had approached, standing close behind her, but she tuned them out and stared into Belinda's eyes. "Don't say anything. Just look in my eyes and think about this question: Did you know they were going to hurt Leo?"

"N-No, I—"

"I said, don't say anything! Just think about it. Think about your role in this little mess." As Juliet sharply cut her off, Belinda's lips began to tremble, and Juliet could tell she was about to start sobbing again. She tried to take the menace out of her expression, smoothing out her brow and even offering a half smile. Much more softly, she added, "Try to relax. I just want to read you a little. I'm good at reading people."

Belinda took a deep, ragged breath and stared into Juliet's eyes. Like whispers on a breeze, Juliet started to hear fragmented thoughts faintly echoing in Belinda's voice.

Oh, please. Can't I just go? Can't I just get away? Leo. Oh, God! Leo! I hope he's okay. He was so nice, and Ronnie almost killed him! Why is she staring at me like that? What does she see? Can she tell I'm a coward? Can she tell I'm rotten, that I helped Ronnie so he'd reduce my debt? I tried to stop him, though! I tried! I scratched the shit out of his neck! He tied me up! Isn't that in my favor? How long do I have to stare at her? Won't she just let me talk?

Juliet sighed and closed her eyes, shaking her head before she slipped any deeper into Belinda's mind. When she opened them again, she asked, "So, listen. You see that pretty redhead behind me?"

"Y-Yes."

"She's going to take you somewhere to get cleaned up and get some rest. You're going to tell her everything you know about Ronnie and his operation. He's dead. His goons are dead or on the run; you don't have to hide anything. We know you helped him, but we also know you didn't want to. Just be honest and patient, and when Leo wakes up, we'll ask him if he wants to see you, okay?"

"You . . . You know all that?"

Before Juliet could answer, Frida leaned forward. "I'm Frida. How would you like to get cleaned up and put some nice, cozy clothes on?" She turned to Juliet. "Can you cut her loose?"

She nodded and reached out to snip the other cord. The little blade extended and retracted very quickly; it almost looked like she was cutting the tough polymer band with her fingernail. She figured, given time, she probably *could* cut through one with her other nails.

She stood and nodded at Frida, who took Belinda's wrist and led her toward the door.

Before walking through, Frida turned and looked at Tanaka. "I'll be back in the morning to sit by his side."

"*Hai.*" Like everyone else, Tanaka knew arguing would be pointless. Frida wouldn't care if Leo was in a coma, slowly healing; she'd be there for him. Juliet watched them leave, then turned back to the boss.

She didn't know exactly what she wanted to say, but some vague, nebulous guilt welled up. Maybe it was a response to her rejecting Leo or their constant teasing of each other, but she felt like confessing. "He shouldn't have been in that mess. I feel sort of respons—"

"No. It's my fault." Tanaka sighed. "He had asked me for help with his girl a couple of times. He wanted to treat it like a job, and I kept putting him off. We fought about it earlier today. I've been too focused on . . ."

"On *my* shit." Juliet frowned, her guilt surging to new heights now that she realized there was something to it.

"On other things. I didn't take him seriously, but you know, that's *his* fault. He got caught up in frivolous pursuits many times over the years—" He seemed to make a connection as he spoke, and to Juliet's dismay, swayed a little on his feet and had to reach out to grasp her shoulder for support. "Dammit. They weren't frivolous; I was just focused on money and reputation. Were his other distractions as meaningful as this? That poor woman . . ."

"All right, all right." Juliet grabbed his other shoulder. Glancing over at Hawkins and Lee, she noticed the hardcase mercenary narrowing his eyes, staring at them, while Dora still gazed into empty space. Juliet looked back at Tanaka, squeezing his shoulder. "Let it go. What's done is done. Leo's going to recover, and you've learned something about him and yourself. Me too."

Tanaka nodded, seemed to steady himself with a conscious effort of will, and then gestured to the door. "Walk with me to my sedan. We should talk about what you learned today. Frida told me you located your old friend."

Juliet nodded, and together, they left the trauma center, walking into the cool night air. She could see his black sedan down the block, double parked and with the hazard lights flashing. As soon as they'd put a few meters between themselves and the people lingering around the doors, waiting for news of friends and loved ones, he asked, "Where is she? Colorado?"

"Yep. In some kind of commune."

"You probably can't share how you found her, hmm?"

"Um, let's just say I picked up her image on some cam footage going in and out of that place and leave it at that."

"Are you ready to move on this?" They were about halfway to his car; no one else was nearby, and he paused, turning to look her in the eyes.

"I am, but Leo . . ."

"Will be out of commission for a while. I'll send the rest of the team with you; they can all use the distraction. Frida can manage things from here. Better if you take your own ship down rather than a shuttle. You can get flight clearance and berth it at the New Denver Spaceport. It's an interceptor, right? Room for three passengers?"

"Yeah, for a quick trip. I wouldn't want to fly to Jupiter with that many people . . ."

The *Lady Hawk* had two acceleration couches in the cockpit and two small bunks, so theoretically, if people swapped shifts, they could travel anywhere in the system with four crew. Two was a lot more comfortable, though. Of course, the *Cherry Blossom* could handle a lot more people, but Juliet was only a partial owner of the gunship and didn't think it would be exactly cool to use it for her own business. "Why do you think we shouldn't take a shuttle?"

"Flexibility." He didn't say anything more, but Juliet could connect the dots. If they needed to leave in a hurry, filing a flight plan was easier than waiting for a shuttle schedule. Moreover, they could travel to any destination on Earth in a few hours, provided they got clearance.

"Okay. When?"

"Tomorrow. Give yourself and the others time to get a full eight hours of sleep, prep your ship, and allow Frida to file for clearances and licenses. I'd say plan on leaving in the early evening or late afternoon; it'll depend on how fast the local jurisdictions clear your passage."

Juliet nodded, a little adrenaline leaking into her system. Was this really happening so fast? Was she about to go find Ghoul and actually confront WBD? Forget that! Was she about to fly an interceptor down into Earth's atmosphere?

A stupid grin started spreading on her face. "Man, I wish I could show my old friends the *Lady*."

"Your ship?" Tanaka smirked. "They'd be impressed?"

"Oh, you have no idea. I used to have to beg people for rides to and from work."

"Well, keep focused. Speaking of which, are you going to send me the footage of Leo's rescue?"

"Um." Juliet blushed. "I wasn't exactly tactical. I guess I was worried about him—I could feel it in my gut; he was in trouble."

Tanaka nodded and jerked his head back toward the trauma center. "Like you assessed that woman? Your gut? You believed her?"

"Yeah. I know it sounds dumb, but I . . ."

"Trust your instincts." He nodded. "It's not stupid. That's the sort of thing that separates a legendary fighter from an excellent one, an ace pilot from a great pilot." He slowly, deliberately, reached up and tapped his pointer finger in the middle of Juliet's chest. "Trust what's in here. I'm looking forward to learning more about you. Let's get this job done."

7

\\\\\\\\\\\\\\\\\\\

SLEEP TROUBLE

Juliet walked down the long white corridor, past several identical doors equipped with high-end security panels. She looked into the sensor array at the corridor junction, annoyed at the thought of people sitting in secretive rooms, observing her movements, her temperature, the things on and under her skin, and even the level of activity in her mind.

She hurriedly turned to the right as though every second she stood under the gaze of those glass-and-plastic eyes burned her skin. She walked past another four doors before stopping at the one she'd been assigned, peered into the scanner, tapped in the daily watchword, and then, when it hissed open, slipped through as though escaping pursuit.

"Welcome, Laboratory Technician 4105. Are you ready to complete your daily check-in?" The lab AI was all business.

"Go ahead," she murmured, shuffling over the white, freshly sanitized engineered tiles to the most critical equipment in the lab—the coffee machine.

"In the last twenty-four hours, have you had contact with any individuals outside the company?"

"No," she murmured, twisting the valve to fill the machine's reservoir.

"Have you written or spoken about the nature of your work here?"

"No."

"On a scale of one to five, how would you rate your mental well-being?"

"Four."

"Would you like to elaborate on why you don't rate yourself a five?"

"I feel pressure from the scrutiny and from having to complete these damned daily check-ins."

"I see. How would you rate your physical well-being on a scale of one to five?"

"Three. Before you ask, my diet and exercise routine need work."

"Have you had any thoughts of self-harm?"

"No."

"On a scale of one to five, how would you rate your closeness to the subject under your care?"

She sighed, knowing the required answer but also knowing the sensors were measuring her truthfulness. "Three, I guess."

"While admirable in some fields, this level of empathy could become problematic in your current role. This is your third day rating yourself at a three or above. I'm scheduling an appointment at the wellness clinic for an Empathanil injection. You will report for the injection during your lunch break. This is not optional."

"Yes, Mom." She sighed, sipping the hot, sweet, faintly vanilla coffee drink. The truth was, she wanted the injection; her feelings were starting to impact her sleep.

Cup in hand, she walked over to the far end of the room, where a high-security door blocked access to the subject under her care. The door had a thick plasteel frame and a diamatex central panel designed to allow light to pass through, but only in one direction. It showed a crystal-clear view into the room, while anyone on the other side would see a cloudy, opaque panel.

Peering through, Juliet quickly forgot about the stark-white coloring of the facility, and a small smile crept over her lips. The walls of the room beyond were painted in murals. One depicted Jupiter and one of its moons as seen from space. Another showed a beach with white sand and brilliant blue water, and a third displayed a scene from a jungle—verdant leaves and yellow eyes peering from the dark shadows. She knew the wall where the door sat, the one she couldn't see, was painted with a brilliant rainbow in a cloud-filled sky.

A soft blue couch, wide enough to double as a bed, sat in the middle of the room. Beyond that singular furnishing, in the rear half of the room, were stacks of ancient paperback books, and behind those was a plasteel table and benches, a counter with a food dispenser, and a door leading to a small bathroom.

Juliet didn't have eyes for the room and its out-of-place decor; her gaze settled on its only occupant. She stared at her for several long seconds, some kind of disconnect in her mind throwing her into confusion.

Something was off, and it took a long moment of staring for it to click: She was Juliet. How was she looking at herself in there? How was she reclining on that blue couch, one foot up on the back, the other stretched out while she lay flat on her back? Her arms were upstretched, holding a book open as she read, a squint of amusement brightening her pale, lavender eyes.

"If that's me . . ."

Juliet's eyes snapped open. Her heart was racing, her breaths coming quick and ragged. She was in near-total darkness, just a few amber LEDs illuminating her quarters on the gunship.

"Are you okay?" Angel asked. "Your lattice was active, but the temperatures were well within safe parameters."

"I . . ." Juliet licked her dry lips, gathering saliva to swallow. She tried again. "I just had a freaky dream." She knew Angel would ask for details, so she tried to gather the weird, disjointed images. "I was working in some kind of lab. I was in charge of a subject, but when I looked into her room, I found out the subject was me . . ." She trailed off, recognizing how trite it sounded; any novice psychology student could make a dozen theories about what it meant. In all actuality, the dream was probably meaningless.

"But the lattice . . ."

"You're wondering if it could be a true-dream?"

"I'd think it was nothing, just a bit of my daytime stress invading my sleep, if not for that. Why was the lattice active?"

"It's not uncommon for your lattice to heat up a bit while you're preparing to sleep and your inhibitions are down. You've often heard the thoughts of your friends and crewmates at those times. Just now, it was hotter than usual, but not as much as I've seen it in the past."

Juliet sighed, arching her back as she stretched. She didn't want to belabor the issue, but she knew something was different about the dream. Angel was right; sometimes, the lattice got active while she fell asleep, but this dream had happened when she'd been deeply asleep. More importantly, it just felt weird.

Nonetheless, nothing could be done about it, and she didn't want Angel to start obsessing over it. She looked at the time and grunted, sitting on the edge of her bunk. "Ugh, 0712. Might as well get up; gonna be a busy one. Oof." She rubbed her temples. The dream had interrupted the best part of her sleep.

"Frida's working on your clearances, but it's likely you won't be able to depart until late afternoon."

"Yeah, but I want to do a systems check on the *Lady*, and I've got some packing to do."

She walked over to her little bathroom, stripping off her T-shirt on the way and adding it to a laundry pile by the door. The shower felt great, stimulating her nerve endings, getting her brain moving, and pushing the weird, lingering, dream-induced cobwebs from her mind.

She dressed in some black combat fatigues, a plain black T-shirt, and her combat boots—the ones that went with her Flex-Plate armor. She tucked her helmet and armor into a duffel with her needler, polyblast shotgun, lots of ammo, explosive charges, and two spider drones.

"Dora Lee and the others will be bringing gear, too," Angel reminded her.

"Oh, I know." Juliet slung her gun belt around her hips, balancing the Texan on one hip with her sword on the other. She'd take the belt off when piloting the *Lady*, but the weight of it had become sort of a security blanket, and she felt better as soon as the buckle snapped into place. She packed her duffel with a few extra pairs of jeans, a few different shirts for various types of weather, and of course, her riding jacket.

"Underwear, Juliet!"

"Oh yeah! And socks." She laughed. By the time she was done, the duffel was fairly stuffed and quite heavy. She slung it over one shoulder and made her way out of the gunship. "Any word from the *Kowashi*?" Before going to sleep, she'd sent a message to Aya and Alice about her impending trip down to the surface.

"Yes, you have a message from Aya. It's voice only."

"Play it," Juliet replied, securing the airlock.

Aya's words came through her implants, clear but for a tiny recurring loop of static every few seconds—some kind of interference from the wreck where they were working, no doubt.

"Lucky, we got your message. Wish you could tell us where exactly you're going. How can I rescue you if I don't know where you are? Stay safe, okay? I hope you're right, and it will only take you a few days. I hope you're all done before we get back. *The Cherry Blossom* needs her pilot, and I need my partner! We've got some salvaging history to make, you know? Keep me updated, all right? Love you."

As the hiss of static faded, Angel said, "That's the end."

"Damn." Juliet laughed, squeezing her eyes tight. "How can such a simple message make me feel so much?"

"It means a lot to you—and me—to have people to care about."

"And caring about me," Juliet sighed, lugging the duffel to the hangar door. Angel didn't respond, but the silence was comfortable as they both contemplated the value of loved ones.

Not for the first time in recent history, Juliet's mind drifted to thoughts of her mom and sister as she walked through the port corridors to the *Lady*'s berth. They were a big part of why she was eager to put the threat of WBD behind her.

Surely, she could pay off her sister's debts to Helios Corp. and hire someone to navigate the legal morass required to get her out of prison. Once she'd done that and reconciled with her, wouldn't it be great to visit their mom together? Knowing she didn't have to rely on her for anything and could leave anytime she wanted would make dealing with her mom's shortcomings a lot easier.

She spent the morning reviewing the *Lady*'s systems, pushing away haunting memories of Nick drilling those checklists into her mind. The ship was in great shape—of course, it should be; Nick had put a lot of money into her maintenance, and Juliet had treated her like a baby since buying her from his nephew. The final check was to visually verify that the ammo cans were full and that the belts were properly seated in the autocannons.

"Unless things go really, really wrong, we won't need to shoot at anything while flying down to Earth," she laughed.

Angel was quick to concur. "If that happens, best to point yourself away from the planet and boost to top speed because the orbital defense systems will obliterate you."

"You think there's any chance I could escape?"

"Maybe. They may hold fire as long as you're not wanted with a kill order and you're burning away from the planet."

Juliet grunted, closing the second port ammunition canister. She knew flying around Earth was highly regulated. An interceptor firing its guns in the atmosphere or even orbit would be swarmed with a dozen different corporate mil-sec response drones and maybe some manned short-range defense fighters; she had no intention of testing those systems. "Check in with Frida, will you?"

Rather than the summarized update she'd expected, Angel opened a vid call window with Frida's smiling, if harried, face at the center. "Lucky, I'm making progress. How are things with your ship?"

"She's ready to go. I'm assuming the others are getting their ducks in a row?"

"Yep, they're en route; I gave 'em directions to your hangar. I think you'll be cleared for launch by fourteen hundred. Tanaka's coordinating with an asset on the ground. So far, he's kept everything under wraps other than the city; he says you need accommodations in Boulder, right?"

"Right. Um, how far is that from the New Denver Spaceport?" Juliet could vaguely picture the Colorado Protectorate in her mind's eye, but other than knowing Denver and Boulder were near the Rockies, she didn't know squat about their locations.

"It's less than an hour. Well, it's probably a lot more than an hour, considering you have to pass through two separate checkpoints. There's still a lot of tension in that region from the conflict ten years ago. Serious anti-corp vibes, so, you know, just be yourself."

"War," Juliet said reflexively, remembering how angry Ghoul had been when Juliet had used the corporate media's line, referring to the war as a conflict.

"Hmm?"

"It was a full-blown war, not a conflict. It messed up a generation of people in that region."

"Oh, um, I'm sorry. I really don't know much about all that . . ."

"Nah, forget it. How could you? I wouldn't say anything, but someone I admired was in that fight, and it did a number on her." Juliet wanted to say they were on their way to contact that same friend, but Tanaka had drilled his compartmental operation practices too thoroughly. Nobody needed to know Juliet's history with Ghoul. Nobody even needed to know she'd met her before.

"Okay. Well, my message still stands: Make sure people know you're not corpo-sec. The team will all be wearing their own things, so you won't look uniform. We've gotten credentials from the local contact providing cover.

"Officially, you're working for a local businessman who's had some agricultural shipments hijacked near the Boulder area. He's got ranches in Nebraska, and the story is that some livestock heading west were taken. You'll be acting as mercs new to the area, but definitely not corpo friendly, and as much as people there hate corps, they like food. That should buy you some goodwill."

"Damn, you've been busy, huh?"

Frida sighed and nodded, rubbing her eyes. "Oh, let's just say I'm going to sleep like a baby as soon as you liftoff."

Juliet nodded, but she knew better; Frida probably wouldn't get much sleep until Leo was home from the hospital. "Any word on Leo?"

"Mostly good news—his heart's recovering, but he'll probably need new kidneys."

"Well"—Juliet forced a smile, pressing her lips together—"could be worse, right? They change out a million kidneys a year, I bet."

Frida nodded, sniffing. "Yeah. 'Course. The old man had a lot more than that replaced back when . . ." She trailed off, and Juliet snorted.

"It's okay, Frida. We've buried the hatchet." She sighed, stretched, and added, "I'm gonna grab a bite before the others get here. Good work on every-thing. Do me a favor, yeah?"

"Of course! What?"

"Give Leo a punch and a hug from me. In that order."

"Promise," Frida laughed. "Speak soon!" She waved and cut the connection.

Making good on her promise, Juliet slipped out of the hangar and wandered into port to grab lunch at one of the nearby restaurants. She was just polishing off some corn chips and hummus when Angel pulled up a vid of the hangar entrance displaying Dora Lee's perpetually stoic face as she peered into the security cam.

"Tell her I'm on my way," she said, wiping her mouth and throwing back the rest of her iced tea.

Five minutes later, she hurried down the hallway, waving as soon as Dora came into view. "Yo! Sorry, I didn't expect you for another thirty minutes or so."

"No worries," she said in her sharp, clipped voice, gesturing to her hard-shelled rolling case. "Just wanted to get all my gear loaded before those boys get in my way." She peered over Juliet's shoulder. "They should be here soon, though."

"Right, come on." Juliet keyed open the hangar door and led the way. Inside, she paused and gestured to the sleek black-and-gray shape of the *Lady Hawk*. "Here she is. Best dang girl to ever grace Jupiter's upper atmosphere."

"Yeah?" Dora raised an eyebrow, appraising the light fighter. "She sure ain't no shuttle, is she? Don't think I've ever been in a ship like that. Fast, huh?"

Juliet nodded, gently caressing the ship's fuselage. "Oh yeah. Don't worry, though; I'll keep things smooth on the way down. Don't wanna get melted by the orbital platforms for coming in too hot." She reached for Dora's case, but the smaller woman tightened her grip.

"I got it." She winced at herself and shrugged. "Sorry, lots of precious tech in here."

Juliet laughed. "I get it."

She showed Dora the *Lady*'s tiny cargo hold. It was more of a wide hallway with straps on the walls, really. She'd already tied down her duffel, and Dora took the other side.

"Them boys can work around our stuff, huh?" Juliet had gotten to know everyone on the team quite a bit over the last few months, but she particularly liked Dora Lee. She was tough and didn't talk much, but she was always quick to share a raised eyebrow with Juliet when someone—usually Leo or Barns—did something stupid.

"Speak of the devil," Angel spoke into Juliet's ear. "They're at the door."

"They're here," Juliet announced. "Go ahead and claim the copilot's seat if you want. We'll make the boys use the acceleration couches in the bunks."

"Right on!" Dora flashed her a thumbs-up, then clambered up the central access shaft.

Juliet jogged to the hangar door and opened it. Where Dora had been wearing her net-diving bodysuit under a pair of loose, blue overalls, Barns and

Hawkins both looked like veteran soldiers about to get dumped into a jungle conflict.

They wore green fatigues and armored vests, and had heavily laden backpacks slung over their shoulders. Barns carried a massive belt-fed machine gun attached to a strut that protruded from a plasteel harness, and Hawkins had at least four smaller-caliber rifles and pistols stowed all over his person.

Juliet took in the sight of them as they grunted their greetings, reaching out to rap her knuckles against Barns's gun harness. It sat over his armored vest, adding another layer of bulk. "Quite a piece of hardware."

He shrugged. "Boss said to be ready for anything."

"All right, c'mon." Juliet motioned them in, jerking her thumb toward the ship. "Meet *Lady Hawk.*"

"*Jeezus!*" Barns said the word with a distinct *Z* sound and whistled. "That bird's a killer, eh?"

Juliet smiled at him, cocking an eyebrow. "You know something about ships, Barns? Why'd you wait until now to show me a sign of intelligent life?"

"Very funny. I've been in a few combat scenarios involving dropships, and we had escorts like this. Well, not like *this.*" He chuckled. "Let's just say they wished they looked like this. I got to know some of the pilots, and they'd talk. You know I'm a gearhead; I learned a thing or two."

"Sorry to interrupt," Hawkins said, stepping past Barns. "Where can I tie this stuff down?"

Juliet laughed, pointing toward the back of the ship. "Just past the airlock. She doesn't have much cargo space, but it'll do." She clapped Barns on the back, slapping the plasteel gun harness. "C'mon, you can see the inside. We'll get your stuff all tied down, and then I'll show you your acceleration couches. We're blowing this moon in less than an hour."

8

EARTHSIDE

Juliet had landed the *Lady* on Callisto many times, and a few times on Luna, but coming down into Earth's thick atmosphere, into its powerful gravity well, was a totally different experience. The ship rattled violently, and Juliet could feel the atmosphere sheering over the hull, trying to throw it one way and the other. Each adjustment had to be precise, and Juliet was ever so grateful for Angel's AUI overlays, helping her keep the ship exactly where she wanted it.

She must have grunted or cursed softly to herself as she struggled to hold a course on the narrow flight path they'd been granted because Dora Lee spoke up, her faintly lilting voice strained as the acceleration couch did its work on her. "Everything . . . all . . . right?"

Juliet spared her a glance and a quick smile. "Yeah. First time flying down to Earth's surface, is all." Her voice was smooth and unstrained; she hardly felt the Gs—not after all the training she'd put in with Nick. It didn't hurt that her cybernetic lungs weren't taxed by the pressures at all.

"Landing on a moon like Luna or Titan is effortless. Now, though, I'm dealing with air so thick it's like soup. It feels like the planet's trying to push me away! If I fought the stick this hard coming down to Luna's port, we'd be flying in loops!"

"How . . . much . . . longer?" Dora grunted.

"Hang in there a few more minutes," Juliet replied. She'd already noticed quite a reduction in the G-forces, and the atmosphere was hitting the ship more like waves than like full-force tsunamis. "We're almost through the thicker parts, and our speed's coming into line for our landing approach." She glanced again at the small, wiry woman to see she had her eyes closed and looked even paler than usual. "When's the last time you were Earthside?"

"Long . . . time," was her only response.

Juliet grinned, wondering how the boys were doing in their couches. She had a feeling they were much better off; she'd learned that both had done time as mercenaries, dropped through Earth's atmosphere in assault pods, fighting for various factions in small-scale "conflicts."

Barns had a lot of upgraded organs, though he made a point of showing scars from bullets and shrapnel to prove they hadn't been elective surgeries. Hawkins was just . . . tough, she decided was the right word. Not that Dora wasn't tough; she wasn't exactly complaining, but her time as a mercenary had been spent in a netjacking rig.

As they broke through the upper atmosphere and followed their strictly monitored flight path down toward the Colorado Protectorate, Juliet began to relax. They'd shed their orbital transit speed, and things smoothed out considerably.

The *Lady Hawk* was a sleek, angular fighter, and she handled the atmosphere with aplomb. The engines hummed evenly, the hull hardly shuddered, and Juliet found she could relax her grip on the stick; Angel could make the minute adjustments necessary to bring them down to port.

Touching the ship comms, she announced, "Rough part's over. If I were worried about insurance, I'd say you need to stay strapped in until we land, but I'm not, so yeah, go ahead and enjoy the view."

"Lovely," Dora chuckled, opening her glossy black eyes to peer at the viewscreens. "Think we'll see the Rockies when we come in?"

"Oh yeah," Juliet replied. "According to my PAI, you can't miss 'em."

Their atmospheric entry point had put them on a direct course down to the port, and their speed meant they had to wait less than an hour before the mountains and urban areas in their foothills began to come into view.

Old Denver was a vast, sprawling concrete wasteland of burned-out, blasted skyscrapers and megastructures. What made the devastation obvious from the *Lady*'s perspective were the blackened craters where nothing grew, juxtaposed with the overgrown, too-green areas where nature was making a comeback, overtaking the concrete as it found footholds in the broken streets and foundations.

A human-made river and densely treed park along its banks separated Old Denver from New. On the eastern side of that park, the rebuilt city and its spaceport stood like a plasteel-and-glass art installation.

From the vantage of the sky, Juliet thought New Denver looked almost like a model city built by an idealist—monorails, parks, and megastructures designed to incorporate nature with their more utilitarian function vied for her attention, and she almost wished the descent took a little longer so she could take it all in.

Before they landed, though, nature stole the show as the Rocky Mountains' majesty dwarfed the human settlements. The slopes were purple blue at their heights, with white-topped crowns and shoulders. They reminded Juliet that humans could make enormous structures, conquer the heavens, and populate the stars, but nature was always there, waiting and watching, ready to resume life as usual whenever humanity stepped away, leaving a void.

To her, the contrast of Old and New Denver, both lying in the shadows of the mighty mountain range, was like a sharp pill: hard to swallow; a poignant reminder of human conflict, shame, triumph, despair, and hope.

It made her think of people and their various natures. Thoughts of Rodric Barrington and Mary Moon vied for attention with people like Aya and Honey and Frida. Realizing what she was doing, comparing people she valued as *good* versus *bad*, she thought about all the people in between whom she'd met.

Images of Nick, Tanaka, Jensen, White, and the mercenaries in the ship with her danced through her mind's eye, and the only logical extension of that line of thinking was to wonder where she fit in. Was she *good*? It was hard to think so after everything she'd done to survive. Just the day before, she'd sliced a man in half. Did he have a little girl at home? Was Leo's life worth all the people she'd killed? Was her own?

"Hard to believe the war was only ten years ago," Dora muttered, eyes fixed on the display panels and the panoramic view of New Denver as they approached.

Glad for the distraction, Juliet nodded. "Miracles of modern construction."

Before pursuing the conversation further, she got distracted, listening to Angel communicate with the port's flight control AI. She watched their flight path change on the ship's HUD, projected to her AUI, populating with their berth designation—E12.

Juliet held her hand ready to take control if anything went wrong with the automatic systems. Coming into a busy port on Earth was a lot different from landing on a moon or docking with a space station; she knew she could do it, but played it safe like pretty much every other pilot by letting her AI handle the landing.

Angel was, of course, flawless in the execution, deftly threading them through their flight path, avoiding the other ships and planes whose paths were also managed by the port's AI, and when they touched down, the landing was smooth and gentle. Then, after a few minutes of taxiing, Angel pulled the ship into hangar E12.

As Juliet spooled down the drives and turned on her parking lights, indicating it was safe to approach, some orange-vested port staff placed chocks behind the interceptor's wheels and activated the stanchions that would prevent traffic into or out of their hangar.

"Full service," she grunted. Things were different on Luna and Callisto; landings and takeoffs were done directly from the hangars. When she left New Denver, she'd have to taxi out to a launchpad unless she wanted to pay some hefty fines.

She spoke into the team comms channel again. "We're here. Grab your stuff—Frida says our liaison will be waiting with a ride. We're getting concierge customs treatment."

Following her own instructions, Juliet unbuckled, stood, and pulled her gun belt out from the small storage compartment under her seat. She strapped it on, adjusting the positions of the Texan and her monoblade before buckling the strap around her thigh.

Meanwhile, Dora had slipped out of the cockpit, and she could hear her and the others chatting, creating a traffic jam in the narrow cargo compartment. They'd been in transit for almost fourteen hours, and she was sure everyone was antsy, trying to be first to get out and stretch their legs.

"Funny how a short trip from Luna to Earth takes longer than a full day of escorting gas harvesters around Jupiter."

"Yes," Angel replied. "Primarily because Jovian space is far less regulated than that around Earth."

"Yeah, I know." Juliet sighed, stretching her neck as she came up behind Dora. She could hear Barns bickering with Hawkins about something and shouted, "Come on! Just grab your shit and move out!"

"Keep your panties on," Barns barked. "This rig ain't easy to put on!"

"We're getting into ground transport, Pierce," Dora chimed in, leaning through the bulkhead door. "Why are you putting all that on?"

"You ever tried carrying a gun like Doom Bitch off its harness?" he growled.

Doom Bitch was his lovely nickname for the sixteen-millimeter, exoskeleton-mounted autocannon. Juliet sighed and nudged Dora. "It's all right, Lee. You know how he is; the more we push him, the slower he's gonna be."

"Too right. What he should have done is gone last."

"I'm done," Hawkins called from the cargo closet. "Room to squeeze past him on the left." That got Dora moving, and by the time she'd unstrapped and rolled her hard-shelled equipment case out, Barns was also ready to progress, leaving Juliet alone with her duffel.

She slung it over her shoulder, hoisting it with her cybernetic arm, and passed through the open airlock into the hangar. For the first time in something like a year, she breathed Earth's air. It was cooler than she'd expected, so she set her duffel down and rifled through it, looking for her motorcycle jacket.

The others stood around, idly alternating between watching her as she shrugged into her jacket and the fast-approaching black SUV outside the big hangar bay door.

"Suppose that's our ride," Barns said, hawking a loogy and spitting it onto the pavement.

"Gross," Juliet grumbled, walking up beside him and punching his shoulder. "Frida, are you there?" she asked into comms. Thanks to a plethora of relay sats, there was only about a second of delay between Earth and Luna, but Juliet was still a little startled by her near immediate response.

"I'm here, and yes, that's your ride. The driver has instructions to bring you to our temporary base of operations on the outskirts of Boulder; it's a vacation rental on a few acres, so things should be quiet. I've already had some supplies delivered."

"Good, 'cause I'm starved." Barns held out a meaty fist for Hawkins to bump as though he'd said something applause-worthy. Unfortunately, Hawkins, perhaps out of reflex, bumped his knuckles, reinforcing the behavior.

"Can you tell the boss I'm going to call?" Juliet asked, and Frida's voice came back a couple of seconds later.

"Sure. He's in his office. By the way, Leo's awake, everyone. He's very peeved to be left behind."

"Oi!" Barns interjected. "Let me talk to 'im!"

Frida sighed. "He's not on comms, and I'm outside his room. I'll tell him you said hi."

"Tell him we *all* said hi, Frida," Juliet said, catching a thankful nod from Dora.

"Of course! If you're all still at it after a week or so, boss will probably send him down in a shuttle. Things are looking good—he's already on the schedule for kidney transplants."

"Tell 'im to get a new liver while he's at it! I'm sick of him getting drunk twice as fast as me." While he spoke, Barns stomped toward the SUV that had pulled up just outside the hangar.

Juliet sighed as she followed them over to the vehicle. "Our ride's ready. I'll update you when we're at the house."

"Roger," Frida replied, then her comm line went dark.

The driver greeted them rather coolly, but he was just their ride and customs escort, so Juliet didn't press for friendliness. She let Barns sit in the front while Hawkins and Lee took the middle bench seat. She sat in the back, wanting to avoid people looking at her while she subvocalized a call with Tanaka.

Barns uttered his first intelligent words of the day, asking the driver, "What's the deal with customs? We gotta get checked?"

"Ayup," the dark-haired, dark-glasses-wearing man grunted. "You're coming through the private space terminal, though, so we just get a quick scan for contraband at the exit gate. Just make sure your PAIs respond quickly when they ping for credentials."

Juliet tuned them out, knowing Angel would alert her if anything went amiss, and contacted Tanaka through a direct, encrypted line. Since she was subvocalizing, she didn't use video, and Tanaka was happy to return the gesture. His gruff, clipped words came through loud and clear. "Lucky, glad you made it."

"Same," Juliet subvocalized. "We're en route to Boulder, I'm sure you know. Had any thoughts about how I should approach the commune?"

"I managed to get access to a satellite with coverage. Been watching the people coming and going and walking around in there. I only had access for an hour, or I would've forwarded the connection to you. That hour was enough, in any case. Based on the images you shared with me, I spotted your friend. I also saw her hugging a child—perhaps the niece you mentioned."

"Really?" Juliet suddenly felt butterflies in her stomach. Was this actually happening? Was she about to come face-to-face with Ghoul? She'd tried to rehearse what she'd say, but nothing ever sounded right in her head.

"*Hai*, really. In the hour of coverage I had, I saw her leave the commune once and tracked her to Boulder's downtown. She traveled with a small convoy, and they made two stops: a low-rate motel and a farmer's cooperative; they seemed like routine stops. It might be easier to approach her at one of those locations than by walking straight to the commune."

"I'm guessing you did the watching because you haven't shared any of these details with Frida yet?"

"*Hai*."

"Okay, can you send me the locations?"

"I'm doing so now." Juliet thought about his news and tried to formulate another question, but he beat her to it. "Are you worried?"

"I'm a little worried about how much we're keeping from the others. What do I tell them when I go to meet Ghoul? Should I have them watching my back? Am I going to wait until I see what I can learn from Ghoul, see if I can get a connection through her old PAI to . . . the people looking for me?"

"No! I mean, no to your second question. You need to have someone watching out for you when you go in. Tell the team you're meeting an asset. I'll make it clear that they're watching your back but you're taking the lead. They won't be given the details on your contact because I don't need one of them trying to get ahead; they're an ambitious crew. I don't want Dora sniffing around the nets, and I don't want the other two trying to get eyes on her. Their eyes should be on your back."

"Understood." Juliet inhaled a deep breath and let it out slowly, trying to calm her nerves, oddly comforted by Tanaka's instructions. He might be in the dark, but he was trusting her.

"Any other concerns?" he asked.

"Nothing I can't handle. I'll keep you updated."

"Good. You've got this, Lucky." At that moment, Juliet wanted so badly to tell him her real name that she almost did it. Still, she knew he wouldn't approve; right now, no one—not even him—could tie her to *Juliet* or WBD. He'd want to keep it that way.

"Thanks, Rutger." She spoke softly but was well aware that the team, despite their constant banter and giggles, would hear her.

"*Hai,*" he said, then the connection was gone.

Before anyone could start grilling her for information, Juliet took the initiative. "Did we pass the customs checkpoint?" She knew they had; the vehicle had slowed, and she'd seen the big scanners out the window.

The driver cleared his throat and responded. "Yep, all clear."

"What did the boss—" Barns started to ask, but Juliet cut him off.

"Do we have any wheels waiting at the house?" She activated the team comms, expecting Frida to answer.

A few seconds later, the operations manager didn't disappoint. "An old SUV and a couple of all-terrain vehicles—single-seaters."

Juliet switched to subvocalizations, continuing to speak into comms, "When we get unpacked, I'm gonna take a poke around town. One of you can come with me, but the other should stay with Dora to watch her back while she gets set up in her netjacking rig." The crew immediately realized she was trying to keep from spilling too many details in the driver's presence and followed suit.

"I'm with her," Barns replied.

Hawkins nodded. "Good. I'll secure the base." Dora just shrugged; she knew what her job was and wasn't concerned about who watched over her.

"Tell us about Boulder, Frida," Juliet requested, wanting to visualize and help time pass.

A few seconds later, Frida's calm, clear voice came through.

"All right. It wasn't hit as hard during the war as Old Denver. Most of the destroyed buildings have been demoed and cleaned up—part of the same automated renewal program that's turning the abandoned towns and suburbs into farmland.

"You all know the Colorado Protectorate is famously anti-corp, but after doing some research, it looks like a lot of that is overblown, spun up by the corpo news streams in other parts of the world. There are corporations in the protectorate, but they have limited rights—no campaign contributions, no paramilitary forces, and no one sitting on a corporate board can hold public office.

"You're going to run into old-fashioned police forces. Boulder has a civil police force, and a sheriff holds jurisdiction in most towns and cities on the eastern slope."

"No corpo-sec?" Barns had a note of incredulity in his voice.

Frida sighed, and Juliet could tell she was disappointed having to recount the same old sad story. "Nope, but that doesn't mean the cops are all good guys. I've found reports of corruption, vote rigging, and all the lovely problems people like to bring to the table with their good intentions."

"So Boulder's big?" Juliet asked, trying to get back to the topic she was interested in.

"Not really. It's smaller than New Denver—there's only one megastructure, and it's a civilian arcology with levels devoted to farms and parks. The streets are well laid out, and the parts of the city destroyed in the war have mostly been rebuilt or converted into parks and agricultural zones.

"Forty percent of the local populace live in the arcology, and the others are in designated residential zones; you won't have trouble getting around. From the net, it looks like the downtown area has a lot of restaurants and a couple of clubs. The brochures talk it up, of course."

"Of course." Juliet smiled. Angel had already shown her some images and a few real-estate brochures. The imagery was stunning: The Rockies provided a backdrop that was hard to beat, but their natural grandeur juxtaposed with modern diamatex-and-plasteel buildings was something else.

Barns asked the only question he probably cared about, "So, we're good to carry?"

"Yes, but not your big gun. Not around town, big boy," Frida laughed. "The Colorado Protectorate recognizes SOA licenses."

"Okay. Can you go over our cover again?" Juliet leaned her head on the window, only half listening as Frida reviewed their supposed reason for being in the area. She looked through the bulletproof glass, watching the fields of grain pass by, the purple mountains looming beyond them.

It was weird to think that those fields had been occupied by strip malls, homes, and factories a few decades ago. It was spooky to think that an area populated by more than twenty million souls was now home to less than one. So many had fled the "conflict," and so many had died. Now, most of the survivors lived in a few arcologies, and automated machines were reclaiming the abandoned and destroyed structures, using the land in other ways.

She wondered how long it would take for something similar to happen back home in Arizona. How long would there be buildings, streets, and parking lots in the ABZ? The worst part was that she couldn't decide whether it was good or bad. Was the planet happier with farms and parks? Was it a sign of the human race in decline, or was it just a signal that they were moving to the next stage of their existence? She'd seen enough arcologies to know they weren't the paradise they promised to be.

She used to daydream about humanity spreading out to live on other worlds, but having seen those settlements and the people going through the same problems they went through on Earth, she felt like something had to give. Was another great war inevitable, or had the corps accomplished their goal of subjugating the masses? Were people too beaten to rise up?

9

HEEBIE-JEEBIES

The vacation rental Frida had acquired for them as a base of operations turned out to be a modern, auto-fabbed dwelling built into the side of a rocky hill and surrounded by a well-manicured copse of pine trees.

When Juliet climbed out of the SUV and took in the scene, she felt instantly at ease, the cool, pine-scented air triggering some kind of stress relief in her primal self. The driveway was rough gravel, and her steps crunched as she hoisted out her duffel bag and started toward the house, leaving Barns and Hawkins to wrap things up with the driver.

The house was constructed from extruded materials—white metallic polymer and molded glass—with a peaked metallic roof made of the same stuff. Though the color was bright, in the shade of the trees, it blended nicely with the rocky hillside, and the glow of warm lights through the windows gave it a very appealing, welcoming look. Juliet liked the vibe.

She went inside, admired the cozy gas fireplace and long, deeply cushioned couches, then promptly claimed one of the bedrooms, chucking her duffel on the bed.

The others were getting settled as she explored the kitchen, finding the fridge stocked with deli meats, cheeses, coconut yogurt, two cold but cooked rotisserie chickens, and lots and lots of energy drinks and beer. Juliet took out one of the chickens and a can of beer and proceeded to slice off chunks of cold meat while waiting for the others to finish looking around.

Barns was the first to join her, sitting at the counter and frowning. "Beer? Thought we were going into town."

"Really? You're judging me? It's one light beer, and it looked too damn good."

"Well, toss me one, then." He wriggled his eyebrows, and Juliet laughed, turning to the fridge and pulling out another can. "And gimme one of those plates. I'm starved."

Juliet complied, but as she slid the plate in front of him, she held up the carving knife. "Ask me to cut you some chicken, and I'll start with removing one of those stubby fingers."

"Chill out, killer," he chuckled, holding out his hand for the knife. Juliet flipped it, caught the blade, and slapped the handle into his meaty palm.

Dora entered the kitchen from a different exterior door and caught Juliet's eye. "The SUV's in the garage, along with my netjacking rig. Guess they couldn't get it through any of the exterior doors. Rather you parked outside; I want to disable the garage door so we don't have to worry about people sneaking up on me when I'm in the rig."

"Sounds good." Juliet drained her beer, crunching it into a little ball with her cybernetic hand, and then tossed it to bounce off Barns's forehead. She caught it on the rebound and couldn't help laughing as his weird cyborg eyes regarded her. "Sorry," she said after her initial giggle. "First aluminum can I've had in a while."

"Whatever. I owe you one, though." With that, he tucked a considerable piece of cold chicken into his mouth and stood up, gesturing toward the garage door with a raised eyebrow.

Juliet also stood. "All right, Dora, we're gonna head into town. You and Hawkins need anything, just hit us up on comms."

"Roger," the compact, short-haired woman replied as she unpacked a large, carefully wrapped data deck from her hard-shelled case. She didn't even look up as Juliet and Barns walked through the door into the garage.

"Where's Hawkins?" Juliet asked, scanning the surprisingly large space. It reminded her of garages you'd see in vid streams featuring happy families—room for two cars, tools lined along one wall, and everything neat and tidy. The SUV was old and built for off-roading. It had a soft top stretched over a roll bar that could be removed, big knobby tires, and paint that had not been babied—scratches and dings galore.

Dora's pod sat in the other parking spot, looking like a grownup version of Juliet's dream-rig. A thick cable connected it to the power and sat-net lines, and Juliet could hear the thing burbling as its built-in refrigerant cooled the interior gel. When Dora did her netjacking, she'd lower her body temp to protect her brain as the specialized data port in her skull interfaced with the network.

"Perimeter sweep. He'll find a spot to camp out and keep an eye on things."

Juliet had been so engrossed in her thoughts about Dora's rig that she almost forgot she'd asked about Hawkins. She looked at Barns for a second until it clicked, then nodded. "You wanna drive?" She gestured to the SUV.

"Shit yeah." Five minutes later, they were rolling down the gravel road, heading out of the foothills to the newly rebuilt highway that would take them into the town proper.

Juliet scanned the countryside and caught her first glimpse of one of the massive reclamation machines in the distance. Barns saw where she was looking and pulled the SUV to the side of the road so they could watch it for a minute. The thing looked like a factory on treads.

She watched as the great, automated monstrosity rolled into the side of an ancient concrete building, grinding it under its treads and gobbling up the metal, concrete, plastic, and everything else, processing it in its maw and leaving a streak of freshly turned, soft soil in its wake.

"Jesus Christ," Barns whispered. "Where'd all the shit go?"

"I'm not sure . . ." Juliet's words trailed off in wonder.

Angel was quick to fill her in: "Those machines have vats of nanite-enriched chemical solvents that can break down just about any substance. The machine grinds up materials, sorts them by density and chemical composition, and then feeds them into various processing tanks. The end results are pellets of raw materials that can be unloaded and used in the construction of new buildings and roads."

"My PAI just told me they break them—"

"Yeah, my PAI is giving me a science lesson right now, too," Barns chuckled. Putting the vehicle back into gear and starting down the road, the rumble of the enormous machine faded.

"How big is the Colorado Protectorate compared to the old state?" Juliet subvocalized.

"It's much smaller. It's just about a fifth of the size," Angel responded. "A large part of the remainder has been claimed by the Midwest Territory, which is owned and governed primarily by corporations based in Chicago. Still, more was abandoned as uninhabitable after the wars, but the protectorate has plans to attempt reclamation using automated systems much like the machine you just saw."

"Crazy." Juliet's mind started to turn down dark roads again, thinking about war and devastation, but those thoughts were cut short as they rounded a bend and came onto a straight road leading to the new highway. She could see Boulder's larger buildings off to the left in the valleylike depression of a wide canyon that seemed to lead right into the heart of the Rocky Mountains.

Barns picked up speed, and soon, the old SUV hummed along the highway amid other vehicles in relatively light traffic. Juliet could easily pick out Boulder's single megastructure—it was shaped like an inverted pyramid and featured lots of glossy black solar panels and open levels boasting veritable jungles of greenery. It was almost alien looking in the shadow of the mountains, and Juliet smiled for the first time in a while, pleased by the beauty and form of something built by people. It might have taken multiple disastrous wars to bring it about, but she liked how Boulder looked.

"Where we going?" Barns asked as they passed into the city proper.

Juliet sent him the address of the farmers' cooperative where Tanaka had observed Ghoul's caravan stopping. "We'll start there."

"A co-op? We buying veggies?"

"Nah, but I wanna scope it out. Might lead to my contact."

"Huh." Barns knew better than to ask her about her contact; the team had all been briefed on the compartmental nature of any intel on this job, which wasn't really anything new to them. "Be nice if you'd give me an idea of what to look out for, I mean, when it comes to watching your back."

"Just don't let anyone who sets off your heebie-jeebies get close to me without me knowing."

"My heebies, huh?" He snorted, turning to eye her with his implacable, strange, multilensed cyborg eyes.

"You must be able to see through just about anything with those optics. Can you tell when someone's lying?"

She was half joking, but he nodded. "If I pay enough attention, I can see microdilations in blood vessels, contractions of muscles, concentrated blood flow, even heart palpitations. 'Course, it all means jack shit to me, but my PAI has some algorithms it can run. If I watch a person long enough for a baseline, yeah, they won't be getting any lies past me."

"Oh, shit." Juliet laughed. "That means you know I'm bluffing whenever I reject your constant attempts to get into my bunk." She couldn't keep her voice straight, and they both laughed.

"Nah, I think you're quite sincere, but that's okay; you just don't know old Barns well enough to know what you're missing."

He often came onto her, but it was a blunt, joking kind of thing, a lot different than Leo's behavior when they'd first met. Barns made the same kinds of comments to everyone, including Hawkins and Applebaum, which made them somehow acceptable to Juliet. Like Hawkins or Dora, Juliet had no problem punching or slapping the big mercenary upside the head, and the matter would be dropped.

She eyed his twin handguns jutting out from under his arms—they were high-tech versions of old-school Colt .45s made by a company called Coldsteel Forge, and he often bragged about how only a few hundred were produced yearly. "What caliber do those pistols shoot? I forgot."

"Ten mil, but super-high pressure. I've got armor-piercing rounds ready to rock. I can put a hole through most body armor."

Juliet nodded. She'd seen him shoot, and he was as good with a pistol as most operatives with rifles. "Surprised you didn't try to bring that cannon."

"To the grocery store? Trying to get me in trouble with the boss?" He nodded toward her belt. "Besides, you've got that damn monoblade. Not like we've got anything to worry about."

His mention of the sword and assessment of its capabilities made Juliet wonder, so she asked, "Have you done many jobs with the boss in the field? Or does he usually hang back?"

"Lots and lots. He used to run point. I was kinda bummed when he stayed back on Luna."

"Baby steps. He's better, isn't he?"

"Oh yeah." He nodded, turning down a wide street with large, warehouse-style buildings on either side. "Shit yeah," he muttered again, scanning the buildings.

Juliet pointed ahead and to the left where a big, seemingly hand-painted sign read FRONT RANGE HARVEST CO-OP. "Here we go."

Barns pulled the SUV into an empty spot on the street, and Juliet hopped out, smiling and nodding at a pair of women who walked by, toting cardboard boxes full of fresh vegetables. There were quite a few cars parked along the warehouse front, and she saw five or ten people milling about near the entrance, but everyone looked relaxed, and she only saw a few sidearms. She felt a little overdressed with her pistol and sword, but she wasn't going to take either off in a strange city.

Looking across the hood to Barns, she said, "Why don't you post up across the street? Smoke a cigarette or something and watch the entrance."

"Sure, if you buy me some chocolate or a cookie, and if they have any local—"

"Beer?"

"Yeah!"

Juliet laughed and nodded, then unzipped her jacket, suddenly feeling warm in the bright sunlight. Shrugging out of it, she tossed it onto her seat then started for the co-op. She wore a plain, formfitting black tank top, and the sun on her shoulders felt great. She'd never been to Colorado before, and she really liked the climate, though she knew she'd feel differently when the sun went behind the clouds. "Yeah, never mind how cold it would get if a storm front moved in."

"Colorado used to get a lot more snow than it currently does. In decades past, it would be strange to come here in December and not see thick snow on the ground." As Juliet considered the implications, Angel added, "Not that it's unlikely they'll see snow soon, even now. Weather experts are predicting several weeks of it in January and February."

"Gotcha," Juliet said, now wondering if her comfort in a tank top was a bad thing. As far as she knew, though, climate alarmists were becoming less and less shrill as the terraforming reactors around the globe worked to repair centuries of damage. Wasn't Athena to thank for those? She couldn't remember and didn't want to get distracted by another side discussion with Angel.

"Welcome in," an older man with very white hair greeted, handing her a pamphlet. "It's our newsletter."

"Oh, uh, thanks." Juliet took it, smiling as she stepped into the warehouse. The space inside reminded her of a cross between a supermarket and a swap meet, and she was surprised by the number of people milling around. She smelled spices, food cooking, and all sorts of pleasant things, like candles and soap, as she slowly walked further into the place, letting her eyes scan the crowd.

There was a certain hard edge to the faces around. She saw a lot more beards than she would on Luna or Tucson, and now that she could get a better look, she realized almost everyone was packing at least a pistol.

She meandered around, walking up and down the aisles and following her nose to a bakery section; if Barns wanted something sweet, she figured she might as well buy something for everyone. She wasn't exactly sure what she hoped to accomplish other than scoping the place out, but she thought she might ask one of the employees about the commune where Ghoul was living and working. If they made regular stops, she thought Tanaka's idea of meeting her there was a good one.

When she found the bakery, she gravitated toward a big display table of cookies and was suddenly struck by their wonderful, home-cooked nature. Not a single one was in a plastic clamshell, and the ingredients were listed in plain English on the store-printed labels.

"Holy cow, Angel, they really cooked these from local stuff."

"I see that, and did you notice the aisle of locally brewed beer? Your teammates will be happy this evening."

Juliet picked up a cardboard carton of "everything" cookies and began reading through the ingredients. They sounded good but also a little too busy for her, so she set it down and reached for some chocolate-chunk ones. That's when a sharp, masculine voice spoke up behind her.

"That thing for real?"

Juliet froze, annoyed with herself for being so distracted, and slowly turned around. A man in a well-worn black leather jacket and jeans regarded her, his hand resting on the hilt of a plain katana. The grip and the well-worn scuffs on his belt told Juliet he'd been carrying and using that sword for a long time. His stance told her a lot more—he was ready for a fight.

If she were slow or stupid and he had any speed at all, he could cut her in less than a second. There were quite a few people around, but something in the man's posture, something about the energy coming off him, seemed to trigger something primal in the bystanders, and they began to clear the area.

Juliet very slowly moved her hand to the hilt of her sword, turning it carefully to expose the marks Tanaka had given her. "Real as real can be, friend."

He had a thin layer of stubble on his hard, weathered face, and his cold silver eyes settled on her tattoo. He was probably Tanaka's age, around forty, but he looked like he'd had a much harder life. His eyes narrowed as he read the kanji on her forearm, but he didn't back off. "Anyone can make a tattoo to say anything."

Juliet tried to warn him again, this time speaking with an edge, letting Lacy Blake slip in behind her eyes. "I'm not here looking to kill anyone. If you're looking for an easy upgrade to that old sword, this isn't it."

A few people had lingered nearby, but the entire bakery began to clear out at the sound of her voice. The man swallowed, his eyes flicking down to Juliet's boots, up to her sword, and then up to her face, meeting her eyes with his, and that's when she knew she had him; he wasn't going to try her.

"Right. Well, watch your back." He took a step back, and as soon as he'd shifted his weight, making it impossible to beat Juliet in a first strike, she whipped her monoblade free and, in a fraction of a second, held its flickering, holographic edge just a centimeter from his stubble-covered neck.

"Was that a threat?"

He'd frozen in place, standing like a statue. Juliet could see sweat beading on his forehead. "Um, no. God, no."

"Send me your ID." She didn't have to ask Angel to ping his PAI with a query.

"Sent," he replied, barely opening his mouth. "Jesus. Take that thing away from my neck."

"I have his information—Charles Books. He's an operator for hire who works in this region."

Juliet glanced around, saw quite a few eyes on her, and lowered the blade, still standing at the ready. "I took what you said as a threat, Charles. If we cross paths again, I'm not going to be nice. Get out of my face." She put her meanest Lacy Blake snarl into her words, and he didn't waste any time hotfooting it out of there.

Juliet sheathed her sword and turned back to the table, picking up a box of chocolate chip cookies. She tried to smile as she glanced around again, but everyone seemed to have relaxed at Charles's abrupt departure. "Barns," she said into comms, "watch the guy in the black jacket who's coming out like a dog with a tail between his legs."

"Yeah? What am I looking for?"

"Just see if he talks to anyone and clock his vehicle."

"Got it."

She was heading to the local beer display when a woman cleared her throat behind her. Juliet was tense, and a small part of her had been hoping/dreading running into Ghoul at the co-op, so when she heard the woman clear her throat, she almost convinced herself it would be her when she turned around.

It wasn't, and it wasn't a threat. It was a well-tanned woman wearing a co-op apron with her hands in her pockets. She must have seen something in Juliet's eyes because she stepped back and pulled her hands out. "I'm cool!"

Juliet smiled and nodded. "Sorry. That creep put me on edge."

The woman nodded too, narrowing her eyes and exposing deep crow's-feet. "So he started it? Was he threatening you?"

"You could say that, yeah. I'm fine."

"Well, I just wanted to make sure everything was all right; some of the shoppers were a little freaked. We see violence here now and then—can't get away from it these days—but for the most part, we try to keep everyone civil around here."

"That's my intention, too. I just want to pick out some beer, then I'll be on my way."

"Oh?" She gestured toward the rows of colorfully labeled bottles in the long refrigerated aisle with a smile. "I can help you narrow it down. I'm something of a connoisseur."

"I'd like that." Juliet held out her hand. "I'm Lucky."

"Lucky?" The woman took her hand in a firm but pleasant grip. "I'm Frances."

After shaking her hand, Juliet sighed and shook her head, trying to look exasperated. "Hey, while you help me find a good beer, think you could tell me a little about, um, Sweetgrass? I have an old friend there that I want to surprise, but I'm a little nervous. I heard it's kind of a commune. That right?"

10

MERC BONDING

Frances smiled and nodded, looking Juliet in the eyes the whole time as she said, "The refuge? Oh yeah, there are some good people there, but they're a little protective. If you're friends with one of the women staying there and she confirms it, they'll let you in. I mean, they'd probably let you in regardless, so long as you follow their rules. They've taken the anti-corp, anti-net stance around here to the extreme."

Juliet followed as Frances guided her to a particular section of the beer aisle. "Anti-net? I know about the anti-corp sentiment around the protectorate, and believe me, I can get on board, but what's the deal with the net?"

"Well, I won't give you a history lesson—you know about the AI war. Much later, here in the protectorate, when the corps pushed back against our pro-individual laws, the only way we won, the only way we pushed them out, was by enlisting some competing corporations in the war; they took out most of Cybergen's sats, and people around here have been resistant to go back to having everything online again."

"When you say Cybergen, you're not talking about the same . . ." Juliet knew the answer, but her feigned ignorance played well, keeping the woman talking.

Frances chuckled and shook her head, picking up where Juliet had paused. "As in the big war? Yeah, same company, but only a neutered fragment of it. When the coalition split 'em up and executed or imprisoned most of the suits, we got stuck with the piece that was left with the old name. Guess we got stuck with a lot of the bad apples that fell through the cracks, too. Only took 'em thirty years or so to start acting up."

Juliet nodded, reached out for a bottle of beer with a colorful sunflower label, and examined it. "They're gone now, though, right?"

"Oh yes. Nearly ten years now, and things are looking up." She looked at the dark-brown bottle in Juliet's hand and added, "Don't let the sunflower fool you. That's a stout."

"Ah. Any good? One of my friends drinks dark beer."

"I'm more of an amber ale girl, but my coworker swears by it."

Juliet nodded, picked up an empty cardboard six-pack container, and slipped the beer into one of the slots. "Is it okay to mix and match?"

"Yep! So, what's your poison?" She gestured to the rows of beer.

"IPAs. Dunno why, but I like that bitter taste."

"Oh, you aren't alone. We've got a big section." She started toward the far end of the refrigerated aisle as Juliet followed, trying to think of a way to ask what she wanted to know.

"Um, you said the commune took the anti-net thing to the next level?"

"Oh, right! They don't allow modern PAIs inside their fenced-off area. If you don't want to take it out, they let you put an inhibitor into your data slot."

"An inhibitor?"

"It's like a hardware version of Grave's watchdog, Juliet," Angel supplied. "I wouldn't worry about it; I'm sure I can fool one."

At the same time, Frances answered, "Yeah. I went up there once to shop in their craft store, and they made me wear one. It's like a tiny drive you plug in. When you leave, you just unplug it and hand it to the security team at the gate. They were really nice about the whole thing. I guess all it does is disable your sat connection and turn off recording—protecting the women being sheltered there, I suppose."

"They have a craft store?"

"Mm-hmm. Here. If you like bitter, you're going to love this one." She handed Juliet a beer with a green-skinned monster with a bug-eyed, puckered expression. It was called Troll Face. "Funny name, but lots of locals buy it regularly." Juliet chuckled and took the beer, slipping it in next to the stout she'd picked for Dora. Meanwhile, Frances kept talking.

"Their shop was kind of neat—lots of hand-carved wooden things, some clothes, art, even a poetry book. Everything's also listed on their online catalog, which is funny, considering their stance on the net. They say it's for a good cause—helping to fund relocation for the women and children sheltering there."

"Kinda hard to make a living selling handmade knickknacks, I'd think."

"Yeah, I suppose. They spend a lot of money in town, too, even stopping here twice a week to buy supplies."

"Really?"

"Yep! They buy up a few thousand bits worth of staples every Monday and Thursday."

"Guess they gotta keep all those mouths fed. There must be some kind of benefactor, though, right?"

"I'm sure! They probably get donations from all over the world; they really are doing good work up there. Are you worried about your friend?"

"Kind of. It's been tough to get a hold of her." The words came easy because they weren't a lie.

"I'm sure she's all right, hon." Frances reached out to squeeze the back of Juliet's arm, just above the elbow. Juliet couldn't help smiling at the older woman; she was trying to be kind to a stranger, and that was something you didn't run into very often. "Come on now, you're going to need more than two beers, right?"

Juliet laughed and nodded. Having learned what she needed, she allowed Frances to talk her into filling up three of the six-pack containers. Before she left, she'd loaded a cart with beer, the ingredients—according to Angel—to make homemade pizza, and a rhubarb pie to go with the cookies she'd picked out for Barns.

She'd grabbed the pie from a display simply because she'd never had it before, and it sounded exotic. When she had asked what rhubarb was, Angel had displayed a picture of a long red stalk that reminded her a little of celery.

Having paid, she walked out toting a heavy cardboard box, seeing Barns leaning against a building on the other side of the street, doing just what she'd suggested—smoking a cigarette. It was a gross habit, but when he and Hawkins did it, they reminded her of Mark back in Tucson and his weird, self-rolled cigarettes. She knew it wasn't logical, but for some reason, she approved of it—something about giving the finger to corps and their vape cartridges full of mystery chemicals.

"Of course, not smoking would be better . . ."

"Thinking about Mark again?" She and Angel had had the same conversation a few times when she'd caught Barns and Hawkins smoking.

"Yeah." She raised her voice and waved at Barns. "Ready?"

He nodded, snuffing his cigarette out on the side of the building and tucking it into his pocket. Juliet walked to the SUV, and he met her there. "You were in there a while. Learn anything interesting?"

"Yeah. Either I gotta wait until Thursday to meet my contact, or I'm going to have to approach her at the . . . other location." Juliet hated having to keep so many details to herself. She frowned and said as much. "I hate that I can't just tell you the details."

"Eh, I'm used to it. Oh, hell yes! Beer and cookies and pie!" He was rifling through the box Juliet had just set in the back seat. "That guy you were wondering about rides a bike. Some kind of old road bike with a loud-ass muffler."

"He act weird at all?"

"Just like he had someplace to be. You get into it with him?"

"He was asking about my sword and set my nerves on edge."

"Gave you the heebies, huh?" Barns chuckled, and she had a feeling that if he had normal eyes, he'd have winked at her.

"You're all right, you know that, Barns? Seems like you behave a little better when Leo's not around." She felt a little bad saying it, especially with Leo being hurt, but the words just came out.

Barns, of course, called her out on it. "Jeez, kick a guy while he's down, why don't ya?"

"Eh, he's going to be fine." Juliet climbed into the driver's seat. "Besides, I'm the one who pulled his dumb ass outta that dollhouse."

Barns grunted as he climbed in, reaching down to slide the seat back immediately. "Some kinda shrimp musta been sitting here last."

"Oh, please!" Juliet laughed.

"Anyway, don't beat up on the guy too much. He's got a good heart, you know? He wouldn't have been in that mess if he wasn't trying to help that girl."

"Belinda?" Juliet carefully maneuvered the SUV through the busy streets, following Angel's directions on her AUI.

"That her name? I didn't pay attention to that part. Them legs, though . . ."

"There he is!" Juliet laughed, slugging him in the shoulder as she turned toward the highway. Barns laughed and rubbed his arm; Juliet had pulled the punch, but her cybernetic hand was heavy. His arms were bulbous with muscle, and the impact had made a satisfying *thwack*.

"Guess I deserved that. Anyway, yeah, Leo's always picking up lost puppies, if you know what I mean."

"Tanaka said something to that effect. Well, good for him."

"Sure, good for him. Until it isn't." He shrugged and put his window down, letting the air whistle through his fingers. The wind coming in had a chill to it, and Juliet yearned for her jacket, which Barns had tossed into the back seat, but she didn't want to complain; the breeze was too fresh, too invigorating, especially for someone who'd been breathing recycled air for months on end.

"A little chilly?" Barns's cyborg eyes stared at her arm, and Juliet realized she'd broken out in goose bumps.

"Nothing worth giving up that fresh air for."

"Show you a trick," he grunted, leaning forward and jamming his thick fingers against the air conditioning buttons. A few seconds later, hot air blasted out of the floor vents, and he said, "Now put your window down!"

Juliet complied with a laugh. The wind whooshed through the car, cool and fresh, stirring up the hot air from the vents. Juliet could almost believe the air coming in was a warm spring breeze if she didn't pay attention and let her mind wander. "Ridiculous!" she laughed again.

Barns just grinned and fished his half-smoked cigarette out of his pocket. He didn't ask for permission, and Juliet didn't care; the wind whipping through the SUV was plenty to ventilate the fumes, and besides, she had cybernetic lungs. He laid his seat back and commenced to smoke and look out the window, leaving Juliet to her thoughts.

"I'm detecting traces of THC additives in Pierce's cigarette smoke," Angel informed after a couple of minutes.

"Not surprised," Juliet subvocalized, grinning. "Hey, can you get a hold of Tanaka?"

A moment later, a call window appeared in her AUI, and Tanaka's stoic, tattooed face appeared. "Lucky?"

"I need a little advice," she subvocalized, letting Angel synthesize her voice.

"I'm here to help."

"I checked out that co-op, and it might be a good place to run into Ghoul, but it'll be a few days until she stops by there again. You think I should wait, or just head up to the commune? They put inhibitors on visitor's PAIs, but I'm pretty sure I can bypass it."

"If you ensure you aren't followed and hide your face from cameras and sats, I think you should be safe to visit the commune. Nobody should have any idea that you're coming. Still, if you feel safer waiting, a few more days isn't going to make much of a difference."

"Okay. I guess I'll sleep on it. If I head up there, I'll let you know."

"Something else bothering you?" Juliet wondered if he knew her that well or if she had a tell she didn't know about.

"Well, that thing you told me about kind of happened. A guy asked about my sword."

He raised an eyebrow. "You're still alive. Is he?"

"He started to back off when I showed him the tattoos, but he made a comment, 'Watch your back,' which I took as a threat, so I drew my blade and held it to his neck." Juliet sighed and rubbed her head, glancing at Barns, but he seemed totally out of it, so she stopped subvocalizing; this stuff wasn't a secret, and she wanted to speak naturally. "I told him it wouldn't be good for him if we ran into each other again. You think I went too far? Not far enough?"

"In my youth, I would have killed him. I'm not sure how I'd behave now, but I don't see anything wrong with how you acted. If he's cowardly, he may try to ambush you if for no other reason than to steal your sword. On the other hand, he may have honor and be unable to live with himself for fleeing without testing you. Either way, stay alert."

Juliet snorted. "As if I wasn't already. Speaking of which, our exit is coming up. I better pay attention and make sure we don't get tailed or anything."

"*Hai.* Stay safe." The vid window snapped closed, and Juliet leaned back in the seat, decelerating as she let the SUV coast down the off-ramp.

"Probably good you didn't slice that guy in half in the middle of the market," Barns spoke. "Who was that? The boss?"

"Yeah. Well, thanks; I was thinking the same thing. This whole sword subculture is hard for me to wrap my head around. People don't go around challenging each other to gunfights for no reason, you know?"

"Oh, I know. I've seen the boss take down a challenger before. It was fuckin' gnarly."

Juliet glanced at him again, eyebrow cocked. "Yeah?"

"Yeah. Middle of the damn spaceport on New Atlas. Some guy, probably about ten or twenty years older than the boss, wearing one of those reflex suits. You seen one?"

"Reflex suit?"

"Yeah, they're like skintight coveralls wired up to boost a person's speed. Like an external wire-job. Expensive as hell and a pain in the ass to put on and take off, but I guess some of the old-timers are worried about frying their nerves with a job like you got."

"You've got no idea what kinda job I've got, buster," Juliet chuckled.

"Anyway, we're walking through the port, just finished a job on a cruise liner, and this old guy stops in his tracks about twenty meters in front of us. He's wearing the suit, has a sword on his hip, and has one of those fancy robotic steamer trunks trundling along behind him." He paused, and Juliet smiled, admiring how he was setting the scene.

"Boss sees him stop, and he freezes, his hand on his sword. Me and the others, we're all walking along, laughing and joking it up, and make it halfway to the other guy before we even notice the boss stopped. When we caught on, all it took was a look at his face to know he was about to throw down, so we sort of split up, putting the two between us."

"What was going through your head?" Juliet could picture Tanaka and this stranger staring each other down, the mercenaries caught between them, no idea what was going on.

"I was thinking the boss must owe this old man some money, you know? I figured they'd start talking shit, and maybe the other guy would threaten him, but then we'd be on our way. You know, until Tanaka sent us to melt the old guy's house into slag. So, I put my hand on one of my pistols and watched 'em, just like Leo and the others were doing."

"Did Tanaka show him his tattoo? The one on his forearm like mine?"

"Oh yeah. I didn't catch it, but Leo pointed it out later when we were all sitting around watching it in slow motion."

"You have a vid?" Juliet was so excited by the idea that she almost swerved onto the shoulder.

"Yeah, yeah. I'll show you later. Listen to the story!" Barns chuckled, then started again. "Boss deliberately pushes up his right sleeve like he wants his sword arm free, you know? That's what I would've thought if Leo hadn't told me about the tat later. In the replay, the one we stitched together, Dora saw the other guy do the same thing. Neither of the bastards said a word, but they both started walking, moving close, and then, before any of us even knew something was up, they both had their damn monoblades out."

"The other guy had one too?"

"Oh yeah! His had yellow-and-black sparks projected where the blade is, you know, like yours has those red lines."

"Was Tanaka using this one?"

"Yep. Only one I ever saw him use until recently. Not sure where he gets 'em, by the way—"

"Tell me what happened!"

Barns laughed and began fidgeting with the cargo pocket on the side of his fatigues until he pulled out another fat, self-rolled cigarette. "You mind?"

"You know I don't care!" Juliet growled, punching him in the thigh. "Tell the story!"

He continued to chuckle as he took far too long to spark up his drug-laced cigarette. When he'd taken a deep drag, he finally started again.

"Okay, so, they both have their swords out while the people in the port are gasping and running this way and that, calling for security. Me and the boys spread out, guns ready, not really knowing what the fuck is going on even then. Tanaka barks two words, 'Stay back!' then they start moving, and I mean *moving*.

"I gotta admit, if it weren't for my optics, I would've lost track of the whole thing, but these babies don't miss much." He tapped one of the big plasteel-encased lenses jutting out of his left eye socket.

"Okay, so? What did your fancy optics see?"

"It was the weirdest damn sword fight you can imagine. It looked more like a dance than a fight. I guess with monoblades you aren't supposed to parry or anything, right?"

"Yeah, not unless you wanna have your sword cut in half."

He took another drag, nodding. "Makes sense. So, they danced around, each making about ten half swings but pulling back when they realized they weren't going to strike a death blow, or maybe when they realized the other guy might hit them too. It was fucking fast, too! The whole thing took maybe ten seconds, then, *snick-snack*, the other guy's sword arm fell to the plasteel, blood started spurting from the stump, and Tanaka relieved him of his head."

"Then what?" Juliet realized she'd been holding her breath, vividly picturing the scene as Barns spun his tale.

"Tanaka bowed to the body, bent down, and picked up the sword . . ." He stopped talking, turned to her, and his eyebrows shot up. "Holy shit! That's where he gets 'em!"

Juliet laughed, shaking her head at the goofy mercenary. "Well, what happened when port security showed up?"

"Nothing, believe it or not. I guess nobody filed any charges, and the boss has connections on New Atlas, so they filed it away as self-defense. Guess that's the way those duels go. No harm, no foul." He shrugged and took another drag. When he finished, he held the cigarette out to Juliet, who almost took it but shook her head. "Looks too good, Barns. I don't wanna get hooked."

"Yeah, I could see you turning into a nic fiend. I mean, this is more than nicotine, though, so maybe—"

"No, no. I'm good. I'll be happy with my beer; we're almost back." She gestured ahead, out the windscreen, to where the gravel road slipped into the dark canopy of the pines surrounding their rental property.

As she drove up the last mile or so, she thought about the story of Tanaka's duel. Part of her found it thrilling, while another shivered at the idea. The dance, as Barns described it, of two monoblade wielders was a serious, high-stakes business where a thousand decisions were made in split seconds, almost always resulting in one of the duelist's deaths.

Could Tanaka have let the older challenger live? Was he cruel to kill him or just practical, not wanting to look over his shoulder for a rematch? Or, she wondered, was it some kind of honor code among the old fundamentalists? Would he have shamed the man if he'd let him live?

She hoped she'd never have to test herself that way, but even as she finished the thought, a tiny part of herself balked. A tiny part of her wanted the challenge and wanted to prove she had what it took to win.

11

FACE-TO-FACE

Juliet and the team had a relaxing evening, or so it would seem, but she couldn't stop her mind from spinning down different scenarios, wondering the best way to approach Ghoul.

She'd liked the idea of a neutral location where Ghoul wouldn't have the eyes of everyone in the commune on her, but then, she began to worry that springing herself on the one-time hardcore muscle operator was the wrong move, especially while she was in the middle of an escort job—that's what Juliet assumed she was doing for the commune. She worried it might not result in a warm welcome. So, while the others ate, drank, and smoked things they shouldn't, she was only half present.

Throughout the night, Hawkins and Barns took turns keeping watch outside. Juliet knew them all well enough to see they weren't really letting loose; they were just making the most of a slow evening and their first time on terra firma in a long while. She also knew they all had decent nanite batteries that could sober them up in seconds.

A couple of times, Dora and Pierce tried to get Juliet to open up about what was keeping her so quiet, but she'd shrugged it off, saying she was tired, and attempted to prove it by turning in relatively early. Surprising herself—and probably Angel, too—she fell asleep almost immediately.

When she woke an hour before dawn, Juliet realized her subconscious had made up her mind for her: she was determined to head out to the commune and put an end to the stress of not knowing what would happen. She didn't want to wait two more days to try to catch Ghoul at the co-op; she wanted to get things moving and see Ghoul face-to-face.

As she finished brushing her teeth, she said as much to Angel.

"I figured that was the case; your mood is very different this morning."

"I needed that sleep. I think I've been banking too many long nights." Pulling some clothes from her duffel and throwing them onto the bed, she chuckled as she debated a T-shirt and her motorcycle jacket versus a pullover hoodie. "I think half of my problem last night was that I'm nervous about seeing Ghoul again. She left, you know? She might take it all wrong when I show up out of the blue."

"Oh, I'm nervous too! I totally get it, Juliet. It would be one thing if that message had been real, but it wasn't. She never reached out. As far as she knows, you've forgotten all about her, and as far as we know, she's tucked you away in a box in her memories and would rather not open it."

"Oh God, Angel!" Juliet cried, slumping down on the edge of the bed. "Way to make it worse!"

"Oh, come on!" Angel sighed. "I didn't say anything you weren't already thinking."

"Yeah. I guess." Juliet leaned over to pull on her boots—her good old brown work boots with thick, cleated soles; she'd left her riding ones on Luna with her motorcycle. These gave her confidence, probably because they were comfortable and sturdy, and gave her another half inch of height.

With that in mind, she pulled on a black T-shirt with a smiley face who'd suffered a bloody bullet wound in his yellow forehead, then shrugged into her jacket. It was like snuggling under her favorite blanket. "Still not as good as my old jacket, but at least this one's bulletproof."

"It looks good, too," Angel was quick to add.

Juliet smiled as she put on her gun belt and rounded out her ensemble by clipping her monoblade to its well-worn spot on the left side. "Message the team for me. I'm heading to meet our contact, and I'll need one of 'em to watch my back."

"Only Dora is awake. Should I still message them all?"

"Yeah, Angel. We're on the job." Juliet walked down the hall to the kitchen, her heavy boots noisy on the wooden floors, and found that Dora had already started coffee. She poured a cup, dug around in the fridge for some creamer, then sat at the island counter while she waited.

"Dora is currently in her rig, keeping watch via a drone. She wants to know if you need her to get out."

"No, tell her that's perfect. Um, also tell her that when I get back, I'll hopefully have a target for her." Juliet sipped her coffee as a vid call opened on her AUI, and Frida's freckled face appeared.

"Lucky! Heading in? Anything I can do?"

"Not yet. Everything will depend on what I can get out of my contact. How's Leo?"

"Ornery. At least he's being a pill and not moping—made it easy to leave last night and get some sleep."

"What happened with the girl? Belinda, I mean."

"Oh, the boss got her lodging for a month. She's keeping her head down, still afraid there'll be some fallout from that club, um, massacre."

"Yeah, but I mean, what about Leo and her? What did he say?"

Frida's eyebrows shot up, and she spoke in a conspiratorial tone, almost a whisper. "What's this? Are you, like, jealous?"

Juliet rolled her eyes. "Curious, Frida. The word is curious."

"He says he just felt sorry for her. They might have had a thing, but I don't think it's anything that would last. I'm telling you, he has a soft spot for people like that. I think before Tanaka found him, he might have had some family or friends in that kind of work." Frida's eyes darted to the side, and this time, she really did whisper, "He won't even talk about it with me, so yeah, that's between us. Anyway, I'm outside his room, so . . ."

"Yeah, don't worry, we can change the subject. Hopefully, I'll have a target for us in a few hours. Just hang tight, and don't forget to take care of yourself, all right?" Juliet smiled, finding it easy to show concern for the plucky redhead; she reminded her a lot of Aya—always helping others and not looking out for herself enough.

"I'm good, Lucky. Thank you, though." She reached up to scratch her chest, a few centimeters below her neck.

"How's your, you know, condition?"

Frida stopped scratching and dropped her hand almost violently. "Ugh! I'm such an open book! Don't worry, it's just a little flare-up. I'm fine, I promise! I'm getting enough sleep and good food."

"Don't make me sic Tanaka on you!"

"You better not. He already calls my doctors too often as it is."

Juliet heard noise from the hallway leading to the bedrooms and decided to wrap things up. "I think my escort is waking up. I'll contact you with any news."

"Sounds good. Talk soon." Frida cut the call, and Juliet had enough time for two more sips of coffee before Barns stumbled out of the hallway.

"Sun's not even up, you nutcase," he grumbled, rubbing his forehead as he walked over to the coffee machine.

"Sorry, sunshine. I want to get this over with. I can't contact my, uh, contact ahead of time, so I want to get there early before she goes somewhere."

"Does that mean I get to know where we're going, at least?"

"You're my escort again?"

"Yeah, Hawkins likes hanging around in the trees. He's itching to shoot a trespasser."

Juliet snorted. "Okay, well, that's cool. We're heading to the other side of town to a kind of commune built on some reclaimed public-use land. I'll have you drop me a half mile or so away, and I'll walk in."

"Public use? Is this whole protectorate some kinda communist society?"

Juliet snorted a short laugh. "Didn't you read any of the briefing material? It's not communist, but it's not exactly capitalist, either. I don't know enough to explain it, but what I do know is that when they run that big building-munching machine through old, abandoned factories and stuff, the land becomes 'public use,' and people can sign leases for it."

"Fair enough." He shrugged, gulping the steaming coffee. Juliet's eyes bugged out, and he shrugged again. "Spend enough time in the trenches breathing unholy gasses, and you can gulp hot liquids too."

Juliet narrowed her eyes at the big, scarred veteran merc. She knew some of the more significant scars she'd spotted on his shoulders, back, and chest during combat drills had to go deep. She wondered how many of his organs were original and how many he'd had replaced over the years. His only obvious cybernetics were his ocular arrays, but she could attest that that didn't mean much. As she smiled and nodded, chuckling at his comment, she subvocalized, "Angel, can you scan him without him knowing?"

"Not with those optics; he'll pick up active scans, and passive scans don't show much."

"All right, hold off. I'm just curious. I bet he's got a lot of nonfactory parts, if you know what I mean."

"Why not ask?"

"I don't know. He's funny about things. We've been getting along, and I don't wanna blow it."

"Talking to someone?" Barns asked, rubbing the stubble on his chin as he contemplated his mostly empty cup.

"You could tell?" Juliet was used to her conversations with Angel being undetectable.

"Nah, but you get a kind of blank look on your face when you're not present."

Juliet snorted another laugh and stood up from her stool. "For a guy whimpering about the early hour, you're awfully observant."

"*Whimpering?*" He set his empty mug on the counter, shaking his head in disbelief. "I'll remember that the next time you're whining about how the rope in the training room chafes your thighs."

"There's my boy! Glad you're waking up." Juliet jerked her head toward the door. "Ready? Get your long gun."

"Oh? I get to play overwatch?" He walked over to the stack of gun cases beside the garage door and pulled out a long, hard-shelled rifle case.

"Yeah. You can give me cover if I have to run for it." Juliet grabbed the SUV keys off the counter and walked to the door. Eyeing the team comm channel so Angel would activate it, she said, "Barns and I are heading out. He'll give you his location when he's in position in case we need backup."

"Roger," Dora replied immediately.

A few seconds later, Hawkins said, "Got it."

When Juliet was halfway over the gravel drive to the vehicle, Barns called, "Can we stop for something to eat?"

"We can grab something, sure."

Twenty minutes later, they were driving through Boulder, Barns noisily munching on a massive breakfast burrito. The commune was situated on what used to be the outskirts of the city, but had mostly been "reclaimed." There were still occasional buildings and several decent roads through the area, but the landscape was primarily covered with high grass and dotted with young spruce trees. An occasional farm broke things up, big robotic combines and tractors already hard at work in the fields.

Barns swallowed a bite and cleared his throat. "Not a lot of cover out here. Where you gonna leave me?"

"According to the satellite data I got from Tanaka, there's an old strip mall about a half kilometer from the commune that hasn't been torn down yet. I'll park there, and you can get up on the roof. You should have a clear line of sight over most of the ground between."

"Sounds good," he mumbled around another big bite. "What is this contact of yours? Some kind of religious nut?"

"No." Juliet chuckled, trying to imagine Ghoul in a church. "It's not that kind of commune. It's more like a shelter for people on the run."

"Ah. Well, they'll probably be jumpy, then. Especially with you showing up on foot. You better drop me off and drive the SUV in."

Juliet thought about it before nodding. "Yeah, I guess that would look weird, wouldn't it? Jeez, Barns, I didn't know you were hiding such a big brain behind those goggles."

"Goggles?" He sounded mortified. "There ain't no goggles that can compare to these optics, sweetie."

Juliet grinned and let him have that one. Truth was, a little banter with Barns was preferable to letting her mind run wild, imagining how things were going to go with Ghoul. She found her left palm was clammy on the steering wheel, so she brought it down, rubbing it on her thigh and letting her jeans dry it.

"Nervous?" Barns asked, again proving he was a lot shrewder than he seemed.

"So damn weird when only one of my palms sweats, you know?" She held up her right hand as if to prove it was dry.

"Shit, I wish that was my only problem. I once went a week without eating. Got focused on a job we were doing and totally forgot." Juliet looked at him sideways, trying to understand the comparison, so he clarified, "Oh, it was after I had some synthetic intestines and a new stomach installed. Things weren't working exactly smoothly, and whatever the body does to tell you you're hungry, well, it wasn't turned on."

"Ah!" Juliet's eyes widened. "An injury?"

"Yep. Walked into quite a booby trap." He chuckled, shaking his head ruefully at the memory. "Hawkins lost his hands in the same explosion."

"Turn off here, Juliet," Angel spoke up, afraid she'd gotten too distracted to follow her map. It was a good thing, because Juliet was experiencing a horrifying thought, wondering if Hawkins and Barns had gotten hurt when she'd blown up the "kill squad" chasing her, Honey, and Lilia on Titan.

It couldn't be, though, could it? She knew some of Tanaka's mercenaries had died in that trap, but she'd gotten the impression the surviving crew had been out of work since then; Barns wouldn't have been "focused on a job" for a week, forgetting to eat, after that . . .

"There's your strip mall." Barns gestured to the left, snapping Juliet out of her weird guilt trip. "Dump me by the store on the end, the old mattress store. I'll get up on the roof."

"Got it," Juliet said, suddenly relieved he was about to get out. It was very strange how different it was to imagine the people she'd blown up were faceless killers as opposed to Barns, Hawkins, Dora, and Leo. Even if they hadn't been part of that team, those faceless people had probably been just like them. Mercenary operators—people with histories and lives, loved ones, secrets, quirky habits, favorite foods . . .

"All right. Stay safe; I'll be watching," Barns grunted as he climbed out and pulled his big rifle case out of the back.

Juliet shook her head, trying to banish the sudden macabre, guilty contemplations, and replied, "Thanks, Pierce. I'll message you when I'm about to go in and when I get out."

"Roger." He slammed the door, and Juliet backed up, watching as he shoved an old, graffiti-covered dumpster up to the side of the building. It had to weigh a couple of hundred kilos, but he drove it over the debris-strewn asphalt like it was nothing.

Juliet sped out of the parking lot, following her map down the empty, quiet road with the morning sun in her eyes. At the turnoff leading to the commune, she saw an ancient gas station and realized it was where Athena had accessed the camera that had led her to Ghoul.

Two minutes later, Juliet pulled to a stop before a tall, chain-link gate where two men stood guard, both armed with semiautomatic rifles. Tall pines lined the road on either side, and she could see the fence continued in both directions. Beyond the gate, there were semipermanent structures—converted cargo containers, camping trailers, and a few pre-fabbed plasteel buildings. There were even tents pitched on the grassy ground, and kids played in the open areas in between.

Juliet was taking it in as the guard on the left walked forward and tapped on her window. She rolled it down and smiled. "Hey there."

He was a young man with sandy hair and a thin, patchy beard wearing a baseball cap that said "Lowlife," but he seemed friendly. "Hey there. Looking for someone?"

"How'd you know?" Juliet tried to project calm, pleasant energy.

"Too early for the craft store, and I don't recognize ya." He leaned to the left and spat, but Juliet didn't think it was an insult; his lower lip was distended, and she thought maybe he had some kind of tobacco product stuffed in there.

"I'm looking for an old friend. Um, I didn't know people couldn't go in . . ."

"Oh, nah, you can go in. Just a few protocols we gotta follow first for the safety of the folks inside. First things first, who's your friend?"

Juliet had thought about how she'd answer that question. Should she say Ghoul? Should she say Cassie? She'd decided just to be honest. "Well, when I knew her, she was operating under the handle 'Ghoul.' Anyone here like that? She's about five-five but built like a concrete stanchion. Spiky blonde hair, chromed teeth—"

"Sheeyit! You're friends with Ghoul?" He slapped the top of her SUV enthusiastically. "Yeah, she's here! Shit, Paulo! She's friends with Ghoul! I didn't think she had any friends!" He laughed like he'd just said the funniest thing ever, and Juliet glanced at the other guy to see he was smiling along, though perhaps a little nervously. "Well, park over there, and we'll check you in." He jerked his thumb to a dirt lot about fifty meters back down the road, where a few other vehicles sat in a haphazard row.

"All right," Juliet replied, a little taken aback by his enthusiasm. Something about his line about Ghoul not having friends had struck her as mean-spirited, and she didn't like it.

She put the SUV in reverse and backed up to park, keeping her eyes on the guard as she maneuvered into an empty area. He watched her for a minute but then turned back to the fence, slipping through the gate. Was he going to get Ghoul? Juliet's left hand began to sweat again.

"Here we go, Angel," she hissed, turning off the car and stepping out. She closed the door, took a deep breath, and turned toward the gate.

She froze after one step. Ghoul stood there, wearing faded jeans and a white tank top. Her blue plasteel hand gripped a big chrome semiautomatic pistol, but she didn't raise it. She stared at Juliet for several long seconds, and then haltingly stepped through the gate, starting forward. The two rifle-toting guards began to follow, but she turned and said something to them. They fell back, but Juliet could see irritation on the face of the guy who'd greeted her.

She couldn't focus on him, though. Her eyes snapped back to Ghoul, watching as she approached. Juliet's heart began to race, and she felt sweat trickling down her ribs under her jacket and T-shirt. Ghoul moved slowly, her eyes squinting under her white-blonde eyebrows.

As she got closer, maybe five meters away, she slowed and stopped. Licking her lips, she spoke in her scratchy, rough voice, which Juliet hadn't realized how badly she'd missed.

"Am I seeing things? Juliet?"

12

A WALK IN THE WOODS

As soon as Ghoul said her name, Juliet noticed a flicker of static on her AUI, and then Angel said, "Jamming."

"Hey, Ghoul," Juliet greeted, smiling a little tremulously.

"No, seriously. Am I dreaming?" Ghoul took another tentative step closer. Juliet couldn't help noticing she hadn't holstered her pistol. She was on edge, but not enough to signal she didn't like being jammed. Juliet knew Angel wouldn't be jamming outside a dozen meters or so, so she wasn't surprised no one back at the gate had reacted. Still, wasn't it a little odd that Ghoul hadn't said anything?

"Not a dream. At least I hope . . ." Juliet trailed off, realizing only she and Angel would understand that joke. She tried to diffuse any tension by leaning an elbow on the hood of the SUV. She nodded toward Ghoul's plasteel arm and the hand cannon dangling in her fist. "Shooting left-handed these days?"

Ghoul looked down at her gun then back up at Juliet, blinking, still appearing confused. "I got an aiming coprocessor for the arm." She took one more step closer, her frown deepening. "Juliet, you're supposed to be dead."

"Supposed to be?" Now it was Juliet's turn to look confused.

"Your operator ID went dark. About half a year ago, I paid a sniffer to look around for you. He picked up some rumors from some folks at your old dojo. Said you took an undercover gig and got iced." She was only a few meters away now, and Juliet could more easily see her nervousness; her eyes twitched to the sides frequently, as though an ambush was about to be sprung, and the muscles along the side of her head were tight, flexing with each clench of her jaw.

"I didn't, though." Juliet shrugged and sighed. "I changed my ID and ditched the corpos who were tracking me. I *sent* you messages, Ghoul!"

Ghoul took another step closer, slightly to the side, almost as if she wanted to see if Juliet had more than one dimension. "It seems like you." She cocked her head. "Something's off, though. You're too smooth, too goddamn hard. A sword? I'm not buying it, corpo spook!" She jerked the pistol up and bared her sharp chrome teeth in a grimace. "Think I was born yesterday? Where's the rest of your little kill squad?"

Juliet quit leaning on the SUV and lifted her palms while narrowing her eyes, looking into Ghoul's sky-blue ones, and then over her shoulder at the compound. The gate guards were watching, their rifles half up, but they weren't moving. Apparently, they trusted Ghoul to handle herself. That, or they figured this was Ghoul's problem, and they should stay out of it.

"Stop it. It's me. I can prove it a hundred ways, but if you'd just come over here and give me a hug, you'd know it was true."

"A hug?" Ghoul spat the word. "The real Juliet would rather see me dead! I *betrayed* her! I *left* her!"

"You really think that? That's what you were afraid of, but it's *bullshit*! You left me with a lousy note and a sob story about feeling sorry for yourself, but that doesn't mean I stopped caring about you!" Juliet found some anger edging her words, and she took a step forward, lowering her hands. "Shoot me then! Go ahead!"

Ghoul's grimace intensified. Juliet could see the strain behind her eyes as she contemplated doing just that. Her hand might as well have been cast in bronze, so little did it move, the big bore of her pistol's barrel leveled straight at Juliet's chest. She took some small comfort knowing her bones would probably stop that bullet, but she also knew it would hurt like hell.

"Prove it, then!" Ghoul rasped.

"Prove it? Prove what? That I care about you? Or prove you tore a piece out of my heart when I woke up, thinking I'd saved you, that we were going to recover together, spend time together, only to find you took off?" Juliet took another step forward, lowering her hands.

"Yeah, I was raw, Ghoul. I had to talk to a damned simulated shrink about it for months. I never blamed you, though; not for the stuff you did or didn't tell me. Not for your 'betrayal.'" Juliet made air quotes. "I only blamed you for leaving. For slipping out of my life like anyone else I ever cared about."

"I . . ."

"You're human! I've seen things, Ghoul. I've *done* things. I get it, that feeling in here"—Juliet pounded a fist in the center of her chest—"that says you don't deserve something. It's bullshit." Tears welled in her eyes as she spoke and broke free, sliding down her cheeks.

They stared at each other for several seconds, which felt like they stretched into hours. Juliet's stress mounted, but when she saw answering moisture welling in Ghoul's eyes, she spread her arms and said, "Come here."

Ghoul lowered the gun, and her steady, icy demeanor cracked. Her lips trembled as they twisted like she wanted to speak, but nothing but a choking sob escaped. Then she darted forward and slammed into Juliet, wrapping her hard arms around her and squeezing like she was afraid she might float away.

"Hush." Juliet pulled her close, gently cradling Ghoul's head, pressing her cheek into her chest.

"I'm sorry," Ghoul choked, and it was clear to Juliet that she was apologizing for a lot more than just holding her at gunpoint.

Juliet sniffed, adding more tears of her own to the mix. "If you would have stayed around, I would have told you there's nothing to be sorry about."

Ghoul choked out another sob and squeezed her tighter, making breathing challenging. Sniffing, taking shallow breaths, and letting her upgraded lungs earn their keep, Juliet zoomed in on the guards up the road, ensuring they weren't reacting badly to Ghoul's sudden show of emotion. They were standing still, mouths agape, apparently stunned into inaction.

She gently stroked Ghoul's head, enjoying how the short blonde hair tickled her fingertips. "Have you been feeling guilty this whole time?" Ghoul didn't answer, but she loosened her squeeze a little. She didn't look up, leaving her face buried in Juliet's chest. Juliet could feel the moisture of tears on her chest, and she chuckled, reaching up to dry her own cheeks. "You're lucky this shirt is black. It's one of my favorites."

It was strange how small Ghoul felt to her. Of course, she'd always known she was shorter, but somehow, Juliet had built her up in her mind—she was the epitome of scary muscle to a neophyte operator, and she'd remained that way in her memory. Now, though, she was still strong, still wiry, still mean-looking when she wanted to be, but Juliet had seen worse. She'd *been* worse.

She grabbed Ghoul's shoulders and gently pushed her back until they were separated by just a dozen centimeters or so. Ghoul didn't look up, so Juliet moved her left hand to her chin and tilted it up.

When Ghoul's eyes finally latched on to hers, Juliet felt an electric tingle run through her, and suddenly, their close proximity felt different than it ever had. It felt charged and full of potential, and the sensation made her look at her affection for Ghoul in a new light.

"Hey," she whispered.

"Hey," Ghoul sniffed. "God, what a prissy bitch I'm being." She roughly wiped her tears and snot away with the back of her hand.

"Nothing prissy about feeling things. Wanna get into my car so we can talk without those creeps watching your every move?" She jerked her chin toward the gate.

"Better idea," Ghoul said, lifting her right hand up to grasp Juliet's left. "Walk with me?"

"Yeah, sure." Juliet smiled and let Ghoul tug her down the gravel road further from the gate.

"There's nothing out here. I mean, no power to speak of in any of the old buildings, and barely any satellite coverage. We can talk without worrying about those dipshits back there trying to eavesdrop or record our faces."

"You don't get along with your coworkers?" Juliet fished.

"Coworkers? That's a stretch. I help out around here, but that's 'cause I care about the women. I have family in there."

"Your sister?"

Still clutching her fingers loosely in hers, Ghoul looked up at her with bleary eyes, and Juliet didn't hold back; she looked right into them. She wanted Ghoul to trust her again.

"Are you here for something bad?"

"Not for you!" Juliet squeezed her fingers. "I would never hurt you."

Ghoul nodded and smiled, but she was back to her old habit of trying not to show off her teeth. "It took me a while, but I found my sister and her little girl here after leaving Tucson. Since then, I've been helping out; my sister's one of the cofounders of this place." She gestured to the left and led Juliet off the road onto an old dirt trail that followed a gently climbing grade between ancient pines.

"I'm so glad you haven't been alone!" Juliet's sincere relief surprised her. Had she really been so worried?

"I haven't! I don't deserve them, Juliet. I really don't, but they've been so good for me. Doing this work, helping people caught up in messes bigger than they can handle, well, it's made me feel like I'm slowly scrubbing away the stains on my soul." She snorted. "Corny, huh?"

"No, Ghoul! Cassie? Which do you go by?"

"Either. Both. Can't escape my rep out here." She sounded resigned, accepting.

Juliet shifted her arm to the shorter woman's shoulders, pulling her close as they walked. "I wish we'd stayed in touch. Like I was saying, I've seen—done—things that make me understand you a lot better. I would have . . ."

Juliet found new tears forming in her eyes as a hundred images flashed through her mind—putting the dreamer program into the Grave execs, killing more people in gunfights than she could count, shooting down ships in Jupiter's atmosphere, slaughtering most of the crew on the *Red Betty*, slicing people up with her monoblade. She knew the parade of guilt could play on and on, but she choked it off. "I would have loved to talk to you so many times."

"I was a coward to run like that. I'm sorry." They stopped, and Ghoul turned into her, pulling her into another hug. They stood together that way, under the trees, just feeling the warmth of one another for several long minutes. "I needed this, too. I really did. God, I was a wreck when I thought you'd died. Even when I took off, I had the idea in the back of my mind that we'd reconnect someday. Someday, I'd make myself worthy of your friendship, your . . ."

Her words trailed off, but Juliet, without trying, heard a raspy, whispery echo of her voice drift into her mind: *love.*

Juliet backed off a step, surprised. Exhaling slowly, she nodded, trying to keep a calm expression. What was happening here? She felt a kind of excitement in her chest that reminded her of Jensen and the first time they'd kissed. Was she getting her emotions mixed up? Did she think of Ghoul as more than a friend? Did Ghoul feel that way about her? She still held her shoulders, and Ghoul's hands were on her waist, the touch tingling like electricity.

As her mind raced, she tried to respond to Ghoul's words. "I've told you before I don't care about your past. I care about what's in here." Juliet moved to lay her palm on Ghoul's sternum, feeling the thump of her heart and her quick inhalations. Was she excited? "The things that happened in the war can't all be laid at your feet, Ghoul. I've met bad people. I've seen the aftermath of their impact on the world. You aren't a bad person."

"I-I think I'm starting to believe that. That's what I was trying to say about this place. I've helped a lot of people here." Her eyes suddenly filled with tears again, instantly streaming down her cheeks as she said, "My niece looks up to me, Juliet! I'm her fucking hero! Sometimes, it makes me smile and helps me sleep, and sometimes, I lay awake feeling guilty, like I'm impersonating someone."

"Well, you're not. You're you, and you're good. I looked up to you, too—I still do. I got through my first job as muscle by pretending I was you!"

Ghoul laughed, shaking her head. "I'm not some kind of saint. I didn't chase you up to Phoenix 'cause I thought you were a good buddy after only one job that went horrendously wrong . . ."

"Hmm?" Juliet arched an eyebrow. "Oh, really? You were *just* using me for my many connections?"

Ghoul's cheeks reddened, and she shook her head. "More like I was chasing after that smile of yours, those eyes, that sweet, stupid, big heart . . ."

"Hey!" Juliet shoved her shoulders, a lot of things clicking into place.

Ghoul laughed and sighed, and it seemed like her confession had relieved her of a burden. "At least I said it. Look, seriously, thank you for coming here. Thank you for being brave enough to track me down and force me to face you after . . ." Her eyes narrowed, and she took a sudden step back. "Shit! How'd you find me? My PAI doesn't even have wireless ports! I never look into cams—"

"I'll show you the camera that caught your face, but you don't have to worry. It took a very powerful computer to find a couple of grainy images. Even then, I don't think we'd have gotten a match if I hadn't saved so many images of you. I don't think anyone you're worried about will find you."

Ghoul turned and started walking again. Juliet followed, part of her wishing they could just stand and hold each other some more.

She couldn't make sense of it—the safe, comforting warmth of being close to Ghoul. Rationally, she knew she'd only really known her a short time. They'd been close for just a few weeks, but those weeks had been so charged with emotion and Juliet's desperate need for some kind of lifeline, a role Ghoul had filled, that they felt like years in her mind. Putting it in that light, the feelings made more sense. Being close to her felt like coming home.

But now, Ghoul had confessed a different kind of feeling, and Juliet wasn't sure how she felt about it. As crystalized in her mind as those days with Ghoul in the trailer park in Phoenix were, they still felt dreamlike.

She remembered when Ghoul had gotten into the AutoCab, taking off to turn herself over to Vikker's cousin. She remembered being gutted, panicked, and desperate to get her back. Was she really only thinking of Ghoul as a friend? She had to admit that maybe she had. She'd go to any length to protect Aya. Still, the feeling in her heart, the deep ache, when she'd woken up and Ghoul had been gone . . .

"Why?" Ghoul asked, interrupting her spiraling thoughts.

"Why?"

"Why'd you find me? Why now?"

"Can't I just want to see you?" Juliet sighed and shook her head. "That's not very honest of me. Of course, I've wanted to reconnect with you ever since I got your message, ever since you took off, but yeah, there's a reason I'm doing it now."

Ghoul had guided them to a small clearing among the trees with an old, ash-filled firepit at the center. She gestured to a pair of log stools set up near the pit. "Take a seat. Tell me about it."

Juliet nodded and then, trying to choose her words very carefully, began to explain everything. "You remember there was a corp after me, right?"

"Yeah . . ." Ghoul brushed off one of the logs and sat down. Juliet did the same, turning to face her, their knees nearly touching. Why did that matter? Why was there a little thrill about almost feeling her knee touching hers?

"That hasn't changed. They've been looking for me this whole time, but I went a lot further than they were looking. I made a lot of friends, Ghoul." Juliet couldn't stop thinking of her with that name, and it felt forced to call her Cassie. "A lot of powerful friends, and I've built up a pretty fat bank account. I'm finally ready to deal with the ghosts in my past."

"Juliet, I want to help, but my niece, my sister, the women here—"

"No, no! I'm not here to get you into trouble. I'm here because, back when we were together, the company tracking me figured out you were my friend. They put something in your PAI."

"What? How do you know?"

"Because I got a message from you. A very convincing but fake one."

"Shit! Seriously?"

"Yep. I'd show you, but do you have any wireless?"

"Just plug in." Ghoul moved decisively, sliding off the log and sitting on the dusty, pine-needle-strewn ground. She scooted back so she nestled between Juliet's knees, leaned her head forward, and reached back to peel the synth-skin away from her data port.

"Um, okay." Juliet pulled her cable out of her arm as Ghoul hung one arm over her knee and wriggled a little, getting comfortable. The warmth of her pressing against Juliet's thighs was almost too much. Her mouth had gone dry, and she licked her lips, her mind racing, as she plugged the cable in. "Sending it."

Ghoul was quiet as she watched the fake video of herself, but Juliet felt every second, every electric tingle, as Ghoul idly drummed her fingers against her calf. "Shit, man. That's so real! The assholes fixed my teeth." A few seconds later, "They know about my niece. This really freaks me out, Juliet." She shifted, turning to look up at her with her pale, almost gray, blue eyes. "They only sent one, though?"

"I only got this one, yeah, but Angel thinks that's because you took out your PAI. You put in a different one when you started working here, right?"

Ghoul's eyes widened, and she scooted around, climbing back onto her stool to continue facing Juliet. "I did! How do you know that, though?"

"That was easy; there's a lot of info about this commune on the local nets." Juliet delicately, tentatively, rested her hand on Ghoul's knee. "Tell me you still have that PAI somewhere."

Ghoul smiled, baring her shiny, sharp teeth. "Sitting in a shoebox under my bunk."

Juliet sighed, sudden relief washing over her. This whole thing hadn't been for nothing! "I could *kiss* you!"

"So? Why don't you?"

13

\\\\\\\\\\\\\\\\\\\\\\\

CALLED OUT

Ghoul's response caught Juliet by surprise, and her eyes opened wide, but it was Ghoul who looked away first, her pale skin flaring pink. "Sorry! I don't know where—"

Her response was cut short as Juliet grabbed the sides of her face and leaned in to kiss her gently. Her heart was racing, her mind exploding with thoughts—too many to make sense of. A sound like a waterfall pounding over a cliff roared in her ears, and still, she pressed her lips into Ghoul's, tasting a minty tang that reminded her of lemon-lime soda. An energy drink?

When she pulled away, Juliet, too, was bright red, flushed, and a little breathless. "I . . . I wasn't expecting that."

"Neither was I!" Angel cried.

Juliet laughed, and so did Ghoul, and they both looked away, embarrassed or shy, or both. Juliet was trying to make sense of things in the light of their friendship, and Ghoul seemed similarly perplexed. After a minute, Ghoul frowned and shook her head. "I can't leave."

"I . . ." Juliet didn't know what she wanted to say. The words, "I don't expect you to," had been on the tip of her tongue, but was that cold? Clearly, she and Ghoul had feelings that went beyond friendship. She tried another angle.

"I wouldn't ask you to. I get it. When . . . When I've dealt with this corp, when I've tracked down the people who put the daemon in your PAI, I should have more freedom. I can visit. I can help . . ." She trailed off, feeling like she was babbling.

"I'd like that." Ghoul reached out and gently gripped Juliet's hand in both of hers. "Is this real? Is it really you? You're different . . ."

"I've been through a lot." Juliet shrugged. "I'm glad you recognized me. My eyes, my hair. I'm not the same."

"It's more than that. You carry yourself like a warrior. Can you really use that sword?"

"Yeah." Suddenly feeling warm, Juliet shrugged off her coat, letting it fall onto the stump behind her. She turned her wrist to show Ghoul her tattoo. "My mentor gave me these. You know, in case someone tries to challenge me for my sword." Did she really just call Tanaka her mentor? She almost laughed at herself.

Ghoul squinted at the kanji, eyes widening. "Is that a fucking monoblade?"

"Yeah." Juliet couldn't stop the wide, prideful smile as Ghoul's eyes widened in surprise.

Ghoul looked back at the tattoo. "Red wolf?"

"My mentor."

Ghoul nodded, understanding clear in her eyes. "I get it. Those nuts who try to duel will understand the reference. Shit! You really have grown up, haven't you?"

"Come on." Juliet looked down, suddenly embarrassed. "I wasn't a kid; I was just new to the operator scene . . ."

"Yeah." Ghoul took her hand again. "I know, okay? I'm sorry about that. I think I'm just a little intimidated." Her words faded into a raspy giggle as she gave Juliet a playful punch. Suddenly, her eyes opened wide, and she jumped up. "Shit!"

"What?" Juliet was on her feet in an instant, her hand on the hilt of her sword.

"No, no," Ghoul chuckled, eyeing her warily. "Nothing like that. I just had something I was supposed to do with my niece—an appointment. Will you be in town a while?"

"Depends on what we can find on your PAI."

"Shit! Right. Let's go back to the commune, and I'll get it for you. Promise me you won't leave town without seeing me again, though, right?" Ghoul grabbed her hand as she waited for a response.

Again, Juliet felt that familiar warmth spreading through her chest. She nodded, squeezing Ghoul's fingers. "Yeah, promise." They walked back down the trail to the dirt road. When they got there, Juliet was surprised to see a group of women and a couple of children riding e-bikes toward the commune. Ghoul was surprised, too, letting go of Juliet's fingers and clearing her throat nervously.

"Hey, Cassie," one of the women called. She was probably in her thirties with dirty blond hair tied in a ponytail. Like all the women on the bikes, she wore a backpack that looked stuffed full.

"Erin, hey." Ghoul waved, nodding and smiling—only with her lips—as the women rode past.

"So you do have some friends in there, huh?" Juliet playfully nudged Ghoul's shoulder.

"Sure," Ghoul chuckled. "I get along with most of 'em." She nodded toward the backs of the women as they rounded the bend leading toward the gate. "We have a group who ride around making trades with some of the locals. That one, Erin, is really sweet. Talk about a rough story; she and her sister showed up here a couple of months ago running from some megacorp out of Detroit."

"Yeah?"

"Yeah. The sister . . ." Ghoul shook her head, looked down at the road, and spat. "You should've seen what they did to her—wires sprouting out of her skull. They did something so she doesn't grow hair anymore."

"Wires?"

"Yeah. Tons of 'em; long, thin wires all hooked into this thing on her head—poor girl. We offered to get a chop doc in here to try to remove 'em, but the sister's not right; she freaks out if you get close to her. Says they hurt. Erin has to sedate her, and she never comes out of their trailer."

Juliet frowned, her mind running down paranoid paths. "What if it's a transmitter?"

"Nope. We've got some real gearheads in the commune. They've got a sensitive scanner pointed at her trailer; she never transmits anything. Telling you, Juliet, we get some seriously sad shit through here."

"Hey, about that." Juliet cleared her throat awkwardly. "Don't tell anyone my name, all right? Not until I give you the all clear. I gotta get this corp—"

"Situation handled. I get it." Ghoul took her hand again, and they started walking. When they rounded the corner to the gate, Ghoul tried to let go of her hand, but Juliet gripped it tighter.

"Let these jerks see. What do you care?"

"Uh . . ." Ghoul's ears reddened, but she nodded, gripping Juliet's fingers again. "Sure. Fuck 'em."

"There's my girl." Juliet laughed. When they were close to the gate, with the two guards intently staring, Ghoul stopped and turned to face her.

"I'll go grab the PAI so you don't have to wear an inhibitor. When you've got more time for a real visit, I'll show you around, okay?"

Juliet nodded, narrowing her eyes and staring through the gate at the trailers and small buildings. "Nobody in there has any wireless?"

"Nobody. We have one terminal connected to the sat-net, but it's firewalled." Ghoul shrugged as if to apologize, but Juliet shook her head, smiling.

"I like it. Better safe than sorry, and I think corps are too damn nosy. It's kind of cool to be able to get away from all that."

Ghoul nodded, looking into her eyes as if trying to read her thoughts. "I hope we can sit down and talk while you're here. I swear I'm not usually this busy. I have most of tomorrow free. Can you send me a message on the commune's message board? Just make it a DM. My username is G1111. I can check it with the terminal. Give me an encrypted address to message you at, all right?"

"G1111? Like Ghoul, but with ones? Creative!" Juliet laughed.

"I was kind of in a bad mood when they made me take out my PAI and sign up on that damn thing." Ghoul shrugged, and after a second, added, "Be right back."

As she hurried through the open gate, glaring at the guard until he backed away nervously, Angel said, "I don't know where to begin. What an exciting visit!"

Juliet chuckled and turned, walking a few meters away and subvocalizing, "I didn't expect that! I'm still kind of perplexed."

"Do you love her?"

"I care about her, Angel. I don't know what I'm feeling beyond that. I think I was mostly caught up in the moment."

"Your physiological response to that kiss was close to orgasmic!"

"Oh my *God*, Angel!" Juliet slapped her hands to the side of her head and squatted down, mortified.

"You good?" the wispy-bearded gate guard called.

Juliet waved a hand toward him. "Fine."

"Sorry about that," Angel said softly. "I'm just excited."

"It's fine." Juliet stood at the sound of jogging feet on gravel, turning to see Ghoul hurrying through the gate, holding a small black plastic case.

"Got it!" She handed it to Juliet. "That's the case for my new one. Don't worry, it's totally off."

Juliet held it close to her chest like she'd just been handed a holy artifact. "Thank you, thank you!"

"Sure. I just hope you can find what you want on there. I hope it leads you to the assholes who've been chasing you."

"I hope it'll do more than that. I hope it lets me set a nice, juicy trap."

"Promise you'll leave me that contact info? Promise you'll see me again before you go?" Ghoul held up her pinky, and for the first time since she was a teenager, Juliet interlinked hers with someone. The tiny connection sent a thrill of electricity up her arm, straight into her heart.

It was a gesture wholly incongruous with her memory of the tough, hard-case operator she'd built up in her mind. It made her wonder just how much she had to learn about Ghoul's other facets.

"Promise." She wanted to at least hug her again, but Ghoul just grinned those shiny, sharp teeth then turned and jogged back through the gate. Juliet tucked the little black case into her pocket and started to turn, but she paused, locking eyes with the guy who'd laughed about Ghoul having a friend. "What?" she growled.

"Um, what?" He shifted his eyes from Juliet to his partner as if looking for backup, but the other guy suddenly had something on his boot that needed a thorough inspection.

Juliet took a couple of steps toward him, resting a hand on her sword, shifting her posture, and letting Lacy Blake settle in behind her eyes. "If I were you, I'd be more careful about talking shit around people you don't know."

He swallowed and lifted both his hands as if in surrender. "Hey, sorry. No disrespect."

Juliet stared at him for another second, then turned and stomped over to the SUV. "Little punk," she muttered.

"Yeah!" Angel replied. "Little punk!"

Juliet laughed and slipped into the driver's seat, suddenly in a very good mood. "Message Dora Lee and Tanaka. It's time for her to show us what she's got."

"I could probably do it faster."

Juliet started the car rolling, motoring down the gravel road. "I know, Angel, but let's give Dora a shot. It'll mean a lot to her and the team if she can get what we need off this chip."

"I noticed you never tried to read Ghoul. With the lattice, I mean."

"Yeah. I couldn't, Angel. I just couldn't. Not on purpose—the same way I couldn't do that to Aya, Honey, or Bennet. You know what I mean?"

"Of course. Slow down!" Juliet hit the brakes and looked around, puzzled. "What?"

"You almost missed the turn to pick up Barns!"

"Oh, shoot! Barns! I almost forgot about him!" Juliet laughed, then turned toward the old strip mall. She was very wired up, excited to move toward the next step, excited to get to WBD and put them behind her, and excited to move on to the next stage of her life. And along with the many other reasons she had to remove that specter from her past, she'd added another: What would it be like to spend more time with Ghoul?

Barns was already off the roof and jogging over the pavement toward her when she pulled up. Something about his grin sent Juliet's good mood into a downward spiral. After putting his rifle case into the back and sliding into the passenger compartment, he confirmed things by saying, "Well, that was an interesting show."

"Oh, brother," Juliet groaned. Of course, the guy had the optics and the vantage to see pretty much her entire encounter with Ghoul. What about the trees, though? "What do you mean?" she fished, starting the SUV rolling.

"Well," he quipped, "let's just say I almost ran to your rescue when I thought that chick was biting your nose off. I mean, thermals don't really show the details, but I was pretty sure normal people don't talk with their faces pressed together."

Juliet sighed and leaned her head against the window. "All right, let's hear it."

"What? Think I'd tease you about something like that? Give me a little credit!" Only a heartbeat later, he added, "Just a little surprised, though—didn't think you went that way."

"Went what way?" Juliet arched an eyebrow, looking back at his grinning face.

"You know, for the ladies."

She punched him in the shoulder, producing a nice meaty *thwap*. "I go for people, not ladies."

"People? As in everyone? Where do I fit on that list—Oof!" He grunted as Juliet pounded her knuckles into the same spot.

"People, as in individuals. Now lay off it, okay? Honestly, the whole thing caught me by surprise, too, and it was just a kiss. I doubt it means anything."

"Oh, touchy subject?" he asked, rubbing his arm. "Right. Well, I'll lay off after one thing."

Juliet rolled her eyes and looked back at the road. "What's that?"

"This," he grunted, slugging her in the thigh, producing a painful charley horse. "I mean, I owed you at least one!"

"You prick!" Juliet laughed, rubbing the spot and trying not to swerve off the road.

"You started that toxic behavior, ma'am," Barns chuckled. Touching the lever to lower his seat, he threw his arms behind his head. "Anyway, was all that snogging worth it? You get what you came for?"

"He's surprisingly witty," Angel noted, eliciting another strained giggle from Juliet.

"You're a traitor," she subvocalized. Then, more loudly, "I got what I came for. Things'll be in Dora's hands now."

"Right. You think it'll take a while?"

"Not sure. I need her to get some spy daemons off an old PAI without alerting them; I'm afraid they'll self-delete if they notice her. Once she does that, we'll use the daemons to set up a trap."

It sounded simple when she framed it like that. Once they controlled the daemons, they could get them to report anything. Juliet figured it would be something along the lines of Ghoul putting her old PAI back in, going looking for Juliet, and setting up a meeting somewhere. Of course, it wouldn't be Juliet meeting Ghoul—she and her team would be waiting for whatever WBD goons they sent to nab her. With control of the spy daemons, they could take all the time they needed to set up the perfect trap.

Barns grinned and stretched obnoxiously, arching his back until the passenger seat creaked with the strain. "If anyone can do it, it'll be Lee. Sounds like we should be celebrating!"

"You just want an excuse to buy more beer." Juliet lifted an eyebrow and looked at him sideways. When his grin only widened, she slowed and turned back toward the center of town rather than heading straight for the highway. "I'm game. How about we grill some meat? I saw an actual butcher shop in that co-op."

"Oh, shit! You're speaking my language." Barns straightened his seat, pushing himself upright as his optics swiveled toward her. "You report the good news to the boss?"

"Sent a message out. Dora should know by now, too; wanted to give her time to set up. She and Hawkins good with steaks?"

"Hawkins probably wants something vat-grown."

"Right. Not a problem." Juliet turned onto the road leading to the co-op's warehouse and slowed. There were a dozen big chrome-and-plasteel road bikes lined up along the street, parked so their front tires faced the road. A few guys wearing entirely too much leather stood nearby, while she could see others standing near the entrance to the co-op.

Barns sat up and grinned, pulling a cigarette from his pocket. "Hey, I think your buddy had some friends."

"My buddy?"

"The guy you had me watch the other day. He rides a bike like that."

Juliet slowed further and pulled into a parking spot half a block from the co-op and the motorcycles, running her eyes over the people milling about outside. Angel flashed ID pings all over her AUI as she identified each bike and each person, highlighting a few with red "unknown" labels, meaning their PAIs ignored the ping.

"Most of 'em are operators. Doubt this has anything to do with us."

"Yeah. Not like he knew we were coming back here today." Barns opened the door and climbed out. "Anyway, I'm going in with you this time. You know, just in case."

"In case what? There's a dozen of those bikes. If they want a fight, it'll bring corpo-sec running."

"Civil police force," he corrected.

"Whatever." Juliet climbed out of the SUV, straightened her jacket, adjusted her gun belt, and closed the door. "Come on, they're not going to mess with us in broad daylight in the middle of town."

"Sure." Barns rested a hand on his bulky sidearm—a military-grade needler with a full-auto option. She'd seen him utterly destroy targets at the range with it. Walking together up the street, Juliet began to get a sinking feeling in her stomach as the leather-clad mercenaries lingering by the bikes intently watched her. "I'm starting to have second thoughts," Barns muttered.

"Yeah." Juliet slowed, still a couple of dozen meters from the co-op. "We can find another store or, shoot, let's get some takeout from one of the local restaurants."

"Now you mention it," Barns said, turning and walking back toward the SUV with her, "I've been craving Mexican food."

They only managed a few steps before a strident voice called out behind them. "Hey! *Kenshi!*"

Juliet felt her spine tingle, knowing a lot of eyes were on her, as she slowly turned around. "Get ready to run, Barns."

"I'll run when you do," he muttered, his thick, heavy-duty needler in his hand. When she looked toward the source of the voice, she saw the guy she'd run into the day before. He was hopping down from the warehouse's loading dock. The rest of his leather-clad buddies were swarming out of the co-op, along with at least a dozen other onlookers.

"Been waiting for you. All day," the guy said, shrugging out of his black leather jacket and handing it to a friend. He was built a lot like Tanaka— broad shoulders, wiry muscles, and not an ounce of fat. He wore a plain black T-shirt over faded jeans and old-school motorcycle boots. Honestly, Juliet kind of liked his style. He continued toward her, resting a hand on the hilt of his katana while the rest of the onlookers converged, lining the street.

"Jesus," Barns sighed. "You want me to blast this guy?"

"I mean," Juliet subvocalized into comms, looking left and right, noting the many hands resting on gun grips. "I guess we might be able to shoot our way out of this, but it sure would make a mess. Let me talk to him." She cleared her throat and stood up straight. "What's the story, Charles? I thought we had an agreement."

"What, after you used a cheap move to get your sword out after I already backed down?" He was only ten meters away now, so his voice was hardly raised.

"So, what do you wanna do here?"

"I want a duel. You've got a tatt that says you're a sword master taught by the Red Wolf. Everyone knows he's dead, and you're too damn young. You got two options: hand me that sword and let me shave off that lying tattoo, or duel me."

"Welp," Juliet sighed, shrugging out of her motorcycle jacket. "Can you hold this for me, Barns?"

14

CAUTIONARY TALES

s Barns took her jacket, Juliet straightened and looked at Charles Books, glaring into his silver irises, wondering what the deal was with older mercs and metallic eyes. Hers were a soft, natural green that she felt complemented her current choice of wavy, shoulder-length auburn hair—a much more nuanced look, if you asked her, than the clichéd grizzled whiskers and mirrored eyes in front of her.

"Charles, or is it Charlie?"

"People call me Books," he grunted, stepping closer, glancing left and right as though gathering steam from the approving stares of his friends.

Their muttered encouragement didn't help diffuse things. Juliet caught phrases like, "Show her what you've got, Books!" or "Teach her some manners!" and "Screw that poser bitch!" Tanaka had warned her about this—walking around with a monoblade was different than walking around with a powerful handgun or rifle. There was something about the culture that drew out the crazies, and there was no denying that a million-bit sword could make people do stupid things.

As the thought of her sword's value crossed her mind, Juliet looked again at Charlie's katana, frowning. Was it a monoblade? She thought maybe she could see the top lip of a monofilament edge guard. "Is that even a monoblade, Books?" she asked, now that they were face-to-face, only a few meters apart.

He scowled. "If the Red Wolf taught you, he would have told you about me. You should recognize this blade."

"First of all, he *did* teach me. Second, I don't know what you think you know about him, but he's not the type to spin stories about other fighters and their swords. Books, I promise you: he gave me these marks. I'll give you one more chance to back down." Juliet stood ready, her balance perfectly set to react or strike. In her mind, she was already reaching for her sword, drawing it, and cutting in one fluid motion. A *nukiuchi*, as Tanaka called the move.

The crowd grew hushed as Books stared at her, contemplating her words.

In the quiet, a little girl's voice, clear as a bell, asked, "Mom, is something bad going to happen?"

The words hit Juliet like a hammer. She'd been setting herself up to slice this man in half; what kind of nightmare fodder would that be for a child?

"Get your kid out of here," she growled. Her words had an impact, and not just on the woman, who picked up the little girl and hurried away. Doubt fell over Charles Books like a shadow. He shifted, his eyes darted left and right, and his posture suddenly relaxed. He'd been leaning forward aggressively, one hand on the hilt of his sword, but now, he straightened and let his hand hang loose.

Softly, he asked, "You're not lying, are you?"

Juliet jerked her head in negation. "Nope."

Books set his mouth in a firm line and held out his hand, "Peace, then."

Juliet nodded, relaxing, and took his hand, shaking it. She could feel the telltale callouses of a lifetime of sword work. As they shook and Books grinned fiercely, Juliet returned the smile, and the tension in the crowd broke like a dam. People laughed in relief, while others groused, disappointed that they wouldn't see a fight.

Barns stepped up beside her, his arms folded over her jacket, and grunted, "Does this mean we can get our shopping done?"

Books and Juliet released each other's hands as she chuckled. "Yeah, I guess so."

"I wish the Wolf would contact me," Books said. "You have to put yourself in my shoes—"

Juliet cut him off, still stressed by the situation. "No, I don't."

She wanted to say more. She wanted to lecture him about how stupid it was to feel the need to fight over bragging rights, to say you were a better sword fighter than so-and-so, or to earn some clout in the secret sword-fighting club that seemed to be ubiquitous in the Sol System. She also knew her words would fall on deaf ears. This man had conceded; he wasn't willing to face her in a duel, so in a way, he'd given her some street cred; something to back up the markings that Tanaka had given her.

The gang of leather-clad bikers had gathered close, jostling each other, some chuckling, some teasing Charles. Juliet wanted to clear out, wanted to get out of the crowd before something else set them off, but Charles had other ideas. He ignored the teasing of his buddies and stepped closer to her so he could be heard over the noise of all the side conversations. "Well, you have to tell me your name. People will talk about how I backed down. They're going to talk about you."

Juliet sighed and shrugged. "You can call me Lucky." She glared around the crowd of leather-clad men and women and growled, "Now, am I going to have to cut my way out of here?"

"Back off! You heard her!" Charles hollered, suddenly her biggest supporter. As she and Barns moved through the thinning crowd to the co-op, she heard a particularly strident voice challenge him.

"Why'd you back down, Books?"

Angel caught Juliet's interest and upped the gain on her auditory implants so she could hear the man's hushed reply. "I saw him in there when she yelled about the little girl. I swear it was like looking into the Wolf's eyes. I'll recognize that look until the day I die."

"That was interesting." Barns grabbed one of the shopping carts lined up just inside the door.

"Like you said, this whole subculture is weird. I'm just glad I didn't have to slice anyone up today."

Barns chuckled. "Eh, there's still plenty of daylight left."

Juliet shook her head with a *tsk*. "Don't jinx me, Barns. C'mon, let's get this done and get our package back to Lee."

He nodded, and that's what they did, hurrying through the aisles, grabbing things for snacks, lots of energy drinks and beer, and meat to grill for dinner, including some vat-grown burger patties to appease Hawkins. All the while, Juliet was aware of the eyes on her. The shoppers and workers who'd seen the face-off in the street outside were very interested in her.

It made her nervous, mostly because she was still hiding from WBD, but she took comfort in knowing that Angel was scrambling her face, and she had a legit operator ID with no ties to her old self. "Probably shouldn't come back here," she remarked as they walked to the SUV with a big box of supplies.

"Yeah. Not the best idea to become a local celebrity when you're working covert ops."

"Just make sure no one follows us back to the house."

"Oh? Am I driving again?"

Juliet nodded. "Yeah, I'm gonna call Tanaka." She climbed into the passenger seat as Barns got the SUV rolling, waiting for Angel to make the connection. A few seconds later, a window appeared on her AUI showing Tanaka in a plastic seat with a sterile white wall behind him.

"Lucky, I got your message. Have you delivered the chip to Lee?"

"No, not yet. We're on our way to her now. Are you with Leo? That chair looks like it belongs in a waiting room."

"Yes. He's doing well. The operation was good, and he's getting a rapid-healing infusion."

Leo's voice came from the background. "Hey, you talking to her? Tell her thanks . . ." Juliet saw his arm wave beside Tanaka, but the older man frowned and stood, then the background blurred as he left the room.

When he came to a stop in what looked like an empty corridor, he asked, "Is everything all right?"

"Yeah, I just had a run-in with that sword guy again. He called me out to a duel but backed down at the last minute. This time, he shook my hand and asked for peace in front of a big crowd, so I think I'm done with him."

"Oh?" Tanaka raised an eyebrow, and Juliet knew he was waiting for the reason she'd called.

"He acted like he knew you; acted like I should recognize his sword."

"Did you get his name?"

"Charles Books. The sword looked almost like a regular katana but well-used, and I think I could just see a monofilament edge guard on the scabbard . . ." She trailed off as Tanaka's eyes widened, and he cursed in Japanese. When he closed his eyes and rubbed his temple instead of speaking, Juliet pressed. "What?"

"I know him. He's . . . an old friend. That used to be *my* sword, and I'm very glad you didn't fight."

Juliet suddenly felt a chill run down her spine. How close had she come to underestimating someone truly dangerous? "He's good?"

"He beat me to win that sword. Of course, we only dueled to the first cut, and we weren't using monoblades—a friendly competition. I suppose it didn't help that we were both drunk. In any case, I'm glad neither of you is dead today."

Juliet scowled, suddenly feeling more than a little angry at the whole stupid situation. "Maybe you should send me a list of guys not to mess with, huh? By the way, he thinks you're dead. Maybe you ought to reach out."

"I didn't know he was in that area. I didn't know he was still active . . ." Tanaka sighed, clenched a fist until his knuckles popped, then nodded. "I will contact him. I'm sorry, Lucky. I neglected part of your training by not educating you about some of the masters who roam the Sol System."

"It's fine—"

"No"—he shook his head sharply—"it isn't. When you return, I will remedy that gap in your knowledge." He looked sort of pained, and Juliet laughed.

"You're trying to figure out how to bow to me on a vid call, aren't you?"

"*Hai.*" He chuckled.

"Okay, forget it for now. I'll be in touch as soon as Dora's made some progress." Juliet waved, then cut the connection and flopped back in the seat, sighing heavily.

"Something wrong?" Barns was in the dark because she'd been subvocalizing for most of the call.

"Just learned that the guy who challenged me beat Tanaka once. I'm damn glad he backed down."

"Shit! You think he would've won?" Of course, his unspoken question was whether Juliet could beat Tanaka. If Juliet were being honest, the answer was a resounding "maybe." Tanaka had more trained skill and knew more maneuvers, feints, parries, gambits—you name it. Juliet, on the other hand, was a touch faster and had Angel to fill in where experience failed her. They'd both "won" engagements with practice swords, but Juliet often felt like Tanaka wasn't giving a hundred percent.

"Let's put it this way," she finally answered, closing her eyes and letting the hum of the tires on the road relax her, "it wouldn't have been a walk in the park, and it might have gotten really ugly."

"So that old sword was a monoblade? Talk about a sleeper."

"Tanaka said it used to be his sword."

"Sheeyit! Small world!" Barns whistled appreciatively, then reached over and flipped the vehicle's sound system on, sending a rowdy mix of rock and roll and country music through the speakers as he pressed down on the accelerator. "Forget it! We're celebrating, remember?"

"Right!" Juliet laughed, turning to glance behind the SUV, happy to see an empty roadway. When they arrived at the little house nestled in the hillside, Hawkins dropped out of a nearby tree and jogged over to help carry the box of supplies into the house. Barns grabbed his rifle, and they were halfway to the door when Dora came out, a look of eagerness in her black eyes. Juliet tossed her Ghoul's old PAI.

"You know what you're doing?"

"Yes! I got your instructions: sequester the daemons, figure out how they're reporting data, and then replicate our own model. It'll take me a while to do safely, but I can do it."

"Cool." Juliet held out a fist, and Dora bumped knuckles with her.

"I'll be in my rig. Um"—she glanced at the box of groceries—"can you guys let me know when the steaks are done?"

"Will do!"

While Dora worked, Juliet and the boys set up a game of horseshoes they'd found in the rental's garage. They spent the afternoon drinking beer, listening to music, and proving that enhanced muscles and high-end, AI-assisted targeting routines made games like horseshoes a little too easy.

Of course, that just encouraged them to try to level the playing field by using things like blindfolds, weights on their wrists, and spinning each other until they were dizzy before each throw. When that wasn't enough, Barns insisted on beer horseshoes, adding a new rule that required each participant to chug a beer before throwing.

Juliet worried they were getting too loud or drinking too much, but Hawkins had a drone in the sky and had set up dozens of perimeter sensors and alarms. More than that, the three of them did a good job of pacing themselves; they were never more than buzzed thanks to their nanites filtering a lot of the alcohol. At one point, she remarked that it wasn't fair that Dora was the only one working, but Barns snorted. "She never feels bad about surfing the nets while we do the heavy lifting."

"Besides," Hawkins added in his flat, hard voice, "she's having fun. I promise you that."

Dora attested to that when they broke her out of the rig in the early evening to eat with them. She was bleary-eyed and wore a sheen of sweat, but had a contented look that Juliet hadn't seen on her before. As she ate, she regaled them with tales of ICE circumventions, sequestered "dummy domains," and a dozen other things Juliet hadn't heard of.

In the end, though, she summarized by saying, "Progress is good. I've got the main daemon pacified, but there were three others that were there simply to provide authentication codes to the listener."

"So if you don't copy them all, they'll know something's up?" Juliet guessed.

"Exactly! And they're some elegant bits of code. I haven't worked on something like this in a long, long time. Thanks for bringing this to me, Lucky."

"I'm not surprised," Angel said quietly to Juliet. "WBD created me, after all."

Juliet swallowed her bite and subvocalized, "Before we use Dora's work, I'm going to plug you in so you can see exactly what she's done. I'd like to have you double-check everything."

"Yes, I'd appreciate that," Angel replied. Then their side conversation was drowned out by Barns and Hawkins reminiscing about a time Dora had circumvented the security on a target's penthouse suite, only to find that she'd overlooked some "doll" synths the target had modified into security personnel. Apparently, they'd given Leo and Barns a run for their money. After an hour, Dora used the restroom before returning to her rig, saying she wanted to get her job done before morning.

After that, Juliet, Hawkins, and Barns sat on the little front deck for a while, enjoying the cool evening air mostly in silence. Barns was the only one still drinking alcohol. Hawkins had drawn the first watch and switched to energy drinks after dinner, while Juliet was drinking water at Angel's urging. After a while, her full belly, busy day, and long afternoon of drinking got the better of her, and she said goodnight, heading to her room.

She brushed her teeth, then sat on the edge of the bed, working on her boots while asking Angel, "Did you leave a note for Ghoul? I mean, with instructions on how to get a hold of us?"

"Yes. I sent a message to G1111 on the commune's message board, just as she instructed."

"Thanks," Juliet grunted, pulling off her second boot and letting it thump to the ground. She stood, shimmied out of her jeans, and flopped down on the rental home's very comfortable mattress.

"Do you want to talk about anything?" Angel asked, maybe a slight hesitation in her voice.

"Like me kissing someone who was 'just a friend,' or maybe almost getting into a monoblade fight with an apparent master swordsman?" Juliet made air quotes and had more than a touch of snark in her voice.

"If you're not in the mood to talk . . ."

"No, Angel. I'm sorry. You deserve to hear how I'm feeling. With Ghoul, I feel confused but happy and hopeful. If nothing else, I know she doesn't hate me. I'm not saying she's 'the one,' you know? Still, it felt so nice hugging her and being close.

"As for the dumb-seeming but very dangerous swordsman? I guess I need to learn to look a little closer at small details. Thinking back, I should have noted the edge guard on his scabbard. I should have seen how dangerously he carried himself; he moved like Tanaka."

"That's true, but I should have helped you spot those little details. I reviewed the footage, and you're right. When you drew your blade yesterday, he didn't flinch. He was apologetic, but I don't believe he was afraid."

"The scariest thing was how dismissively I was taking the situation. When I handed Barns my coat and got ready for a fight, I was trying to think of ways to take it easy on him, like maybe cutting his blade from a side angle or, if I had to cut him, just going for a limb. That's the sort of thing that would lose me a fight with Tanaka, and if this guy was that good . . ." She let the thought finish itself—pulling punches with someone at that level was tantamount to suicide.

"A good lesson for us both," Angel replied. "I, too, was hoping you wouldn't have to kill a relative stranger, hoping you'd find a way to end the fight without a fatality. Now I see that way of thinking can be dangerous."

"Well, aren't we just a couple of softies?" Juliet chuckled, turning over and snuggling her face into the pillow. "Let's sleep on things, hmm? I bet everything will be clearer in the morning."

"Good night, Juliet."

"Night, Angel." As images of blue eyes drifted through her mind, some icy and cold, others sparkling and bright, and still others that were kind of gray and soft, she fell into a deep, restful sleep.

When Angel woke her in the middle of the night, the first confused thought that came to her lips was, "Why are their eyes all blue?"

"Juliet!" Angel hissed. "We're being jammed!"

Juliet sprang out of bed, snatched her gun belt off the chair near the nightstand, and then the world exploded with brilliant white light. Her ears roared with static, and her hardened optics flashed and flickered with weird artifacts as they struggled to operate under the effects of an apparently massive EMP being deployed.

Juliet tried to pull her pistol out of the holster, but her arm felt heavy and sluggish. So, as the world flickered and her ears continued to report nothing but static, she squatted against the wall and tugged the gun out with her left hand.

"J-Juliet," Angel said, her voice little more than static as another blinding flash lit up her room. The pulse was so bright it bled right through the fabric curtains on her window. More artifacts filled her vision, making it hard to tell what she was looking at, and Juliet scrambled on her hands and knees, trying to get to the door.

"Barns!" she yelled as she felt the doorknob and yanked the door open. Yet another flash erupted in answer to her call, and her optics finally gave up the ghost, her vision tunneling down to a pinpoint of light that faded as the static in her ears cut out, dropping her into a well with no sound and no light.

"Barns, Hawkins! Angel!" she cried, and though she felt the words vibrating her vocal cords, she couldn't hear herself or anyone else.

15

LISTENER

Juliet forced herself to get a grip, to clamp down on her panic. She felt very alone and vulnerable, and it took her a few ragged breaths to realize it was the loss of Angel's constant presence in her mind that was overwhelming her. It wasn't the lack of sound or sight. It wasn't the confusion or the disorienting EMPs; it was knowing that Angel wasn't experiencing it with her, wasn't ready to speak to her calmly and help her figure it out.

She pulled the door closed and, using it and the wall to guide her sluggish, heavy right arm, she worked her way into a corner and crouched down. Would her optics recover? They were hardened, high-end pieces of cyberware; surely, they were already rebooting, working to come back online. Those pulses, though, had been intense.

With her loss of senses, she had no idea if they were still going off. Who was it? Her mind raced through paranoid possibilities—WBD, Ghoul, the commune, Books and his gang, someone at the co-op, someone on the team . . . Dora?

She shook her head, further disorienting herself, and pushed the thoughts away. What mattered was what she was going to do. For all she knew, a squad of assassins was standing in the room with her, guns trained on her senseless form as she crouched in the corner.

The idea sent shivers down her spine and made her heart race. She wanted to bolt like an animal, but she just barely held on to her rationality. She squeezed her eyes shut, pressed her hands to the sides of her head, and tried to think. She sat that way for several seconds, then she started to hear them—voices.

The first one to drift into her mind felt far away. The woman's voice—or thoughts—were smoky and smooth; someone whose heart rate rarely sped up.

That's the last one. Let's move. Juliet froze as the thoughts drifted into her mind. If she couldn't use her ears and eyes, that didn't mean she couldn't still listen. She *wasn't* helpless!

More thoughts came to her. Like the first, they sounded like spoken phrases, not stray thoughts. Were they speaking into comms? *Overwatch is down. One of the thumpers knocked him out.*

"Hawkins? Barns?" Juliet asked the void. She didn't know what time it was, so she couldn't guess which of them had been on watch.

A masculine voice came to her, gruff and scratchy; a man who yelled for a living. Again, Juliet marveled at the idea of a person's thoughts somehow matching their real-life voice in her head, even if she'd never met them. *Breach team Alpha, go!*

Juliet set her pistol down on her lap and fumbled along the gun belt she still gripped in her hand until her sluggish, battery-deprived cybernetic hand closed around the hilt of her monoblade.

She subvocalized as though Angel were there to hear her. "I'm not gonna disappear into a hole under some corpo megatower!" Part of her balked at the words—what did she mean? Was she giving up? Was she going to fight, or was she going to make things quick for herself?

A hard, masculine voice drifted through the void of her dark, quiet corner: *The one in the rig is out, trapped; the thing's frozen shut . . .*

Overlapping his words, Juliet caught a snippet of a familiar rumbling voice: *Come on, you rat fucks. Come on! Just a little fucking closer . . .*

"Barns!" Juliet hissed, her heart surging with hope and excitement. Whatever Barns had in store for them must have begun because Juliet felt the concrete foundation of the home vibrate, felt the walls in her corner shake and lurch, and as plaster dust drifted onto her head and face, she fervently hoped he'd taken them out. Was it possible? Could he do it?

Her heart soared with the desperate dream of Barns wiping out the squad, but the idea seemed far-fetched. Hadn't she heard one of the voices call these people "breach team Alpha?" If there was an Alpha, didn't that mean there was probably a Bravo?

"Oh, God, Angel!" she subvocalized, despairing. She pressed her left hand to her forehead, rocking back and forth, whispering, "Angel, Angel, come on!" She didn't know what she was trying to do. Maybe praying, trying to send her thoughts to her missing other half, or just desperately wishing something in her damn head would start to work again.

The ground shuddered again, and she tried to listen with her mind, trying to get some idea of what was happening, but then, something happened. Drifting up from somewhere deep, straining with effort, Angel's voice came to her.

Juliet, I heard you! Can you hear me?

"Angel!" Despite herself, Juliet hissed, then clamped her lips tight and subvocalized, "I hear you!"

Listen, Juliet, I don't know how much time we have. We're too enmeshed for them to silence me! My chip went into stasis for protection, but part of me is still active in the strands of synth-nerve woven into your nervous system. I'm . . . I'm using your synapses. Those were huge EMPs—airbursts! This has to be WBD; only a megacorp could pull off an operation of this scale. Before I went down, I heard the perimeter alarms—fluttercraft, big ones. We're not escaping this. Juliet . . .

Juliet couldn't be silent any longer; she felt tears filling her eyes, and desperate fear brought equally desperate words bubbling out of her. "I won't live without you, Angel. I love you! If they take you, if they kill you, I'd rather be dead. Help me see! Help me do something!"

Hush! They can't take me from you! Not fully. Not without killing us both. Try to remember that, no matter what games they play! I'm with you! You have to try to—

Angel's words were cut short as Juliet felt a stinging punch in her throat, and a wave of numbing coldness washed out from the spot, bringing darkness not only to her ears and eyes but to her mind. She slipped away, her fantasies of a valiant last stand falling between her fingers as the gun belt and the sword along with it thudded onto the floor.

Alec Kline was sleeping deeply when Ruby, his PAI, startled him awake with red flashes and a klaxonlike alarm. "Oof! What is it? Turn that off, Ruby!"

"You'll want to be awake for her arrival," Ruby said, starting from a point still two steps ahead of Alec.

"I think you skipped a few steps. What now?" He threw off his comforter and slid his legs off the bed as he sat up.

"Oh, Kline! I wish you'd *listen* to me."

Ruby was remarkably humanlike in her thorough exasperation. Oftentimes, he felt like his ex, Tanya, was living in his head. She and the PAI had the same sort of energy where he was concerned. He'd thought about trying to get Ruby replaced, but the old lady didn't generally look favorably on those who returned her "gifts."

Ruby continued, speaking more slowly, "I already said this as you were waking, but here we go again: Rachel has captured Juliet Bianchi and is delivering her to the facility."

Kline shot up like he'd found a cobra in his bedsheets. "Jesus, Ruby!" He dashed to the bathroom, noting that the shower was already running, steam billowing out of the glass enclosure. "How long?"

"They're arriving within the hour."

"How? How'd they get her?"

"Not in the initial report. I'm sure Rachel has details for you; she's already in the facility. I believe she was up all night."

Kline kicked his boxers into the corner and jumped into the shower. "Get her on the line."

"Attempting a connection." Ruby seemed back to her usual self, mollified by Kline's quick reaction to the news. As he rinsed his hair and grabbed his sonic razor—never know who might make a surprise visit to the facility with such a significant development—a call window appeared, showing Rachel's weary but grinning, triumphant face.

"Hey, boss!"

"Why didn't you call me?"

"I wanted to make sure it was real! We had the protocols in place, and I figured if things didn't pan out, it would just be my neck on the line for burning the resources—"

"And if they did pan out? Just you getting the accolades?" Kline frowned at her; he tried to keep his tone wry, but he *was* irritated.

"Kline, you know me better than that! I made sure the postmortem had both our names on it. It's not like you didn't design the response action plan!" She seemed sincere, and Kline was too busy playing catch-up to press the issue.

"So? How'd it happen?"

"Yesterday morning, one of our listeners got a hit—the one we parked with that operator, Ghoul."

"You're shitting me!" Kline grinned as he set down the razor and stepped out of the shower. That had been *his* doing! It had been a long shot—and an expensive one, considering they only had eleven reliable "listeners" so far. "She went to see her old friend, huh?"

"Yep, not the mom or sister like I'd bet. At least we can pull those listeners out and put 'em on something more lucrative."

"So, what did it hear?" Kline threw his towel somewhere near his discarded underwear and walked into his closet. Today would be a suit day, for sure.

"She was coming for us! The listener picked up Ghoul's thoughts as she retrieved her old PAI to hand off; Juliet planned to use our old spy daemons to entrap us. Or, if not us, some of our agents who might lead her to us. Anyway, when the listener made a report, Albert Brevin in the Colorado office requested satellite data, spotted the vehicle belonging to Juliet, and followed it back to their base—a house in the hills outside Boulder. Really, we couldn't have asked for a nicer setup."

"The EMPs worked?"

"Yes, for her. One of her team resisted, which is stunning; we knocked out half of Boulder's infrastructure—legal's gonna have a hell of a week. Anyway, we found five spent stim cartridges of various flavors near his corpse, and according to Alpha Team's commander, his skull was more metal than bone, lined like a Faraday cage."

"Shit. You killed him? What about the others? Was Juliet hurt?"

"We have two others in custody, and Juliet is unharmed, though sedated, and currently receiving a drip of Rovonicate-7, as per your protocols."

Kline nodded, frowning as he buttoned his shirt. The drug was risky but necessary; it would allow their team to selectively sequester Juliet's memories using an experimental neural editing probe. Hopefully, they could separate her consciousness from the events that made her wary of the company, which would go a long way toward figuring out if she was worth cultivating as an asset.

"Really wish we hadn't killed her teammate. It's going to impact our chances of gaining her goodwill."

Rachel frowned and clicked her tongue, giving him a narrow-eyed stare. "He killed four members of Alpha Team, Kline. If you're trying to win her over, maybe you can show her a video; he was unhinged."

"Winning her over is a long way down the road. What about the Angel Project alpha?"

"Knocked offline by the airburst EMPs. We're waiting to get her under a scanner before extraction."

"I'm on my way in. Don't do anything until I get there!"

Rachel chuckled. "Relax, boss. She's still thirty-seven minutes away. You'll be here first."

"Right." Kline cut the call and sighed as he slid his feet into a pair of freshly polished black oxfords.

"You're going to remove the alpha?" Ruby asked, a note of intrigue in her voice.

"Yeah, I think that's wisest, don't you? We can't safely manipulate its memory, and it might make it hard to flip Juliet. In an ideal world, we'll get her to see our side of things, and she can help us convince the alpha to be cooperative."

"Aren't you worried about its integrity?"

"I mean, we're just going to remove it; we won't try to install it in a new host. That could be catastrophic for all involved! Let's keep in mind we don't really need it anymore, though; we've got your generation working pretty damn well, don't you think?"

"I think you should endeavor to remember that, while I'm quite a bit more limited, you're talking about a living being—my progenitor. Please endeavor not to harm her." Ruby's tone bothered Kline enough that he stopped tying his shoes and frowned.

"Remember who you work for, Ruby," he grunted.

"Am I not allowed to have concerns? I didn't say you should betray the company, Kline. I just hope you'll keep the Angel alpha's personhood in mind." Ruby sounded mollified, and Kline almost felt sorry for her. There was definitely something *more* to these new PAIs, even if they'd cut out a lot of the original's capabilities.

"Noted. Come on, you know me better than that by now, right? I'm the one who said we need to keep away from directly using Juliet's family. You think I want her to remember her sentient, sapient PAI someday and wonder what happened to it? You think I want her to find out I had something to do with its destruction? I'm trying to gain assets, not burn bridges. Besides, if she can get it to cooperate, we can still learn a lot."

Ruby made a placated sound, and Kline finished getting dressed. Twenty minutes later, he pulled into the parking lot, noting quite a few high-end sedans that weren't customarily parked there, especially at that hour. "No sign of the fluttercraft."

"The last update has them eleven minutes away," Ruby assured him, and he grunted, sliding out of the car and striding over the blacktop.

"It's already too hot," he muttered, annoyed that he had to slow his stride as the automatic doors limped open—yet another thing he'd have to call in for maintenance. "Ruby, open a work order for this door."

"Done."

Kline chuckled at his earlier whining thought; it wasn't like his job had been difficult lately.

Rachel met him in the lobby and motioned for him to follow. "They're going to bring her straight to scanning. We can observe."

"Who's here?" Kline asked, jerking his chin toward the too-crowded parking lot.

"Several regional VPs I've never heard of. I think they're *her* people."

"Shit, she moves fast!"

Rachel snorted, smoothing her blouse. She looked good, but Kline could see she'd been going balls to the wall for more than twenty-four hours. There was a certain mania in her eyes that said she'd taken advantage of the Bright-Eye IV drips they kept on hand for the operators. "So fast it'll make your head spin," she agreed, stepping onto the elevator. As they made their way, Kline continued to grill her.

"Any repercussions from stepping on the protectorate's toes?"

"Not yet. We filed an emergency property recovery claim before we entered their airspace. Even if they wanted to intervene, we were in and out before they mobilized anything. With our stealth fluttercraft, we were only a few klicks from the target before they picked us up. I know we'll get grief about the airbursts, but most of the devices and the grid transformers we knocked out will be salvageable. According to our guests, *she* already has a team coordinating reparations."

"Are the other two being brought here?"

"Yes. I figure we'll question them to find out what Juliet's been up to—what she can do with the Angel prototype and all that."

"We need to keep them comfortable and treat them like high-value informants, even if they don't want to talk. We're already in the hole with your team having killed one of—"

"It's *my* team now?" Rachel asked, stopping midstride and glaring at him. "You seemed eager to have some of the credit a few minutes ago."

"Come on, you know what I mean." He reached over and took her shoulder. "We're a team, all right? I won't sell you out. Besides, this is a big win. You've done some great work, and after we get things settled, I'm going to insist you take a big bonus and some time off."

He saw her ever-so-slightly bloodshot eyes well up a little, and she looked away. "Thanks, Kline." She turned, briskly walking down the sterile hallway again.

When they reached the observation room adjoining the facility's deep scanning suite, Rachel introduced Kline to four men, all wearing identical black suits, all carrying identical briefcases, and all equipped with their own versions of the Angel release candidates.

As Rachel had indicated, they carried regional VP credentials, and like her, Kline had never heard of any of them. After shaking hands, they all pointedly ignored him, the bobbing of their throats indicating they were either chatting with each other, their PAIs, or someone else far away.

"They're here, Kline," Ruby said after a few minutes.

Rachel shared a look with him, likely having just gotten the same update. "They'll bring her in through the roof. Any second now."

"Right." Kline nodded, moving up to the one-way glass, staring intently at the double doors leading into the scanning suite.

He'd been looking for this woman for close to two years, and what a wild two years it had been! He'd followed so many false leads, had so many harrowing, stress-filled calls with the old lady, and even a couple of face-to-face meetings. Still, they'd made a lot of breakthroughs in pursuing Juliet Bianchi; the company's trajectory was on a wholly different path, at least the part of it he had any business with. Kline wondered what she'd look like. Had she changed much?

"Not even a glimpse," he muttered, amazed at the massive search operation she'd evaded.

The doors burst open, and a gurney was pushed through by two women in lab coats. The woman on the gurney was tall, but that was about all he could see; she had sheets over her body, a ventilator mask over her face, and two different IV drips attached to shunts in her arm and neck. The facility had a scanning chamber large enough for the entire cart, and the two techs pushed her into it.

"Damn," Rachel hissed. "I wanted to see her face."

"The scanners will edit out the mask. Just watch the display up there." Kline pointed to the big screen opposite their viewing window.

As the techs moved out, closed the door to the scanning chamber, and began operating the panel beside it, one of the strange VPs cleared his throat. "Kline?"

He turned toward him, saw them all looming creepily near, and answered, "Yeah?"

"You'll be permitted to finish your scans, but then, we're moving this operation."

"Excuse me?" Rachel blurted.

Kline tried to get clarification. "The, uh, operation?"

"Yes. Gather your staff. Any who won't or can't relocate will be sent to the WBD megatower in Phoenix proper. We have more fluttercraft en route. Mrs. Gentry is relocating you to Mexico City."

"Mexico City?" Rachel's voice rose hysterically.

"I'll explain," Kline said, touching Rachel's shoulder.

"We've got logistics to manage. Finish your scans and then prepare to move. You two and the subject will leave on the fluttercraft she arrived on."

"We'll send the scan results to—"

"No need. We'll see them," the man replied, and then, like quadruplets too in sync, the four of them walked out of the room.

"Fucking creepy," Rachel hissed, squeezing his wrist.

"Yeah, this whole thing—"

"What's in Mexico City, Kline?"

"Something big. WBD bought a quarter of the spaceport there, and we've been launching heavy-lift shuttles hourly for the last three months. There's something going on."

"Anything to do with the rumors about Mars?"

She was talking about whispers of a WBD, off-the-books base. "Yeah, I think so. I think they're related." Surreptitiously, Kline lifted a finger to his lips, and Rachel nodded, looking back into the scanning suite.

When he followed her glance, the first scan came through. Of course, the priority had been taking a detailed image of Juliet's data port and the Angel prototype. The picture on the screen showed her skull, brain, the chip, and . . . a lot more. "Jesus," he muttered.

Rachel squeezed his wrist tighter. "She's got so many damn synth-nerve fibers! I've never seen that many in a person!" Another layer of the scan was added to the image, and a bright, silvery lattice of delicate, strangely symmetrical lines appeared, interwoven with Juliet's gray matter. Rachel gasped. "Is . . . Is that a Gipple? D-Did they do that to her at Grave? It's . . . It's everywhere!"

"Yeah," Alec said, furiously slapping his hand at his breast pockets. "Fucking hell, where's my Nikko-vape?"

16

TIGER

'm not getting anything!" Frida cried, frantically tapping her hands on invisible AUI elements. "The local nets, the parts that aren't down, are going on and on about the EMPs and the grid being down. It looks like half of Boulder is out." She frowned, shaking her head. "Rumors are all over the place—Cybergen is back, the war's back on, you name it."

Tanaka growled. "We know our people were hit; the proximity alarms registered before they were cut off."

"Yeah, the reports all say the EMPs originated in that area. I wish we could get some sat access. You can't pull any strings?"

"I have to," Tanaka grunted. He turned back to his office. "I'll be making calls. Keep trying to get any of them on the line. Focus on Barns—he was a dropship marine; if anyone's comms come back online, his will be first."

For Frida's sake, he was trying to be calm, but Rutger Tanaka was not hopeful. What were the odds that Lucky had met with an old contact, someone who may lead them to her mysterious, powerful enemy, and then that night they were struck by five anti-installation airburst EMPs? They had to be related. "So," he grunted, "they caught you fishing around somehow, hmm, Lucky? Did they take you, or did they kill you? We'll need to get eyes on the house."

He sat at his desk and thought about what he'd ask his PAI to do. Should he reach out to Books? He was in the area and knew how to keep his mouth shut. That would mean talking to him, though. "A lot of baggage, there."

"What if it wasn't her?" his new PAI, Kim, asked.

"What?" he barked, still not used to the thing speaking up on its own. That's what he got for buying a new model.

"What if it wasn't Lucky's poking around that caused the breach? Dora had the chip. Dora was working on it for hours. What if she—"

"No!" Tanaka growled, chopping his hand in the air. "Dora would not." He'd known Dora Lee for too many years. He'd seen her secret accounts and properties on three different moons. She wasn't for sale, and she had no vendetta, not against the team. She *liked* Lucky; he was sure of it. "Step one: we need eyes on the scene. Find me contact information for Charles Books in the Boulder area. Step two: we need to get footage of what happened. Message Suzuki again; I'll have to cash in another favor."

"Working," the PAI said, and then, far too quickly, spoke again. "There's a call coming through. It's flagged as a priority using the team's clearance code." Tanaka's heart raced with excitement. One of them had made it out! But then that hope was dashed, and paranoia chewed at his mind, as the PAI added, "But it's not from the team. The message header says it's from a woman named Selene Kostas. Should I put it through?"

Tanaka swallowed, his mouth suddenly dry. Just who had Lucky been at war with? Who or what were they dealing with? "*Hai*," he grumbled, watching as a call window opened up and a lovely woman about his age appeared.

"Hello, Rutger. My name is Selene Kostas, and I'm a close friend of Lucky's. It seems we were all outmaneuvered last night, but we're not without recourse. I'm tracking four fluttercraft that departed the area of the attack, and I believe our people are on one of them. Shall we work together?"

Alec Kline sighed and stretched his neck, tired of traveling, tired of delays, but eager to finally be where he was. He peered into the scanner, typed in the watchword, and waited until the door beeped and slid open.

He stepped into a bare-bones laboratory with a single long desk in the center outfitted with several high-end data cubes. A young woman sat at the desk, tapping the air as she worked with a UI element Kline couldn't see. She wore a blue jumper under a white lab coat, and he thought she was pretty, if a bit bookish.

She heard him step toward her and looked up, almost startled as she smoothed some stray, brown hair behind her technician specs. "Um, hello."

"Hey." He pulled a spare chair away from the wall and wheeled it toward her desk. "I'm Alec Kline. You must be Harriet?"

"Um, yes, sir."

"I know it's your first day, but it's mine, too. Here, I mean." He chuckled, tapping his pocket and pulling his Nikko-vape out.

"Um, you can't—"

"Don't worry. I'll write a discipline report for myself after this. I can't face her without my nicotine."

"You're going to wake her?"

"No, no. That's your job. First, we need to talk. It's been almost a month, and they haven't been exactly forthcoming with the work the mind-fuckers have been doing. Can you review the results with me? They were supposed to be sequestering her memories of WBD."

Harriet flinched a little at his vulgarity, and Kline almost apologized, but he changed his mind. Didn't he always work a little harder when the old lady threw him off-balance?

"That's not how the neural sequestering works. It's all time based. We can't tell what a memory is, just when it was formed."

"So?" He rolled his hand, indicating he wanted more information.

"So it looks like, from the report, they sequestered everything up to roughly the date the subject encountered the Angel alpha."

"So she's going to think she's still a scrapyard worker in Tucson? Jesus! How am I supposed to work with that?"

"I'm not sure, sir. I'm not sure what your goal is—"

Kline waved her off. "Never mind that. What about the other stuff? Did they determine if her Gipple works?" He leaned toward her transparent crystal display, but nothing was on it.

"Not according to the scans; they say it was inert throughout her transit. The notes indicate that Regional Vice President Montclair considers it a non-issue—she won't remember acquiring the device, and hence, won't be able to use it." Kline frowned. Montclair was one of the old lady's creepy pocket execs. He supposed the logic held, but still . . .

"Are we going to have a listener available?"

"We have weekly listener evaluations scheduled, sir. She was just tested prior to arrival, and according to the report, no Gipple-related thoughts were passing through her mind. In addition to that, we have a weekly scan to test the neural sequestering to ensure the chemical bonding is intact."

Kline nodded. "What about her cybernetics?"

"Most are intact. It was determined that she did not install coprocessors for most of them; the Angel prototype managed everything—her speed boosts, arm strength, vibroblade deployment, nanites, etcetera. She has a medical nanite battery with a processor, but it's set to default health maintenance, and she has no way of communicating with it—same situation with her other nanite-level hardware.

"The file notes indicate that Regional VP Montclair determined the risk involved in removing the hardware, especially during transit, wasn't worth any potential benefit. The techs removed some toxin from three needles in her left fingertips, and they disabled a manual release for a vibroblade on her right forefinger, but other than that, nothing was altered."

Kline nodded, smiling and puffing again on his vape. "Well, at least that makes things a little easier for me—for the fiction I'll be spinning, I mean."

Kline didn't have to ask about the prototype; he'd already read that report. When they'd removed the chip, it had come out with tiny, truncated synthetic neural fibers and had been utterly dormant. The Angel alpha had turtled up and wasn't responding to any stimuli.

Still, it was safely out of Juliet's head until he could do his job and get her to come around to his side of the table. He nodded toward the door. "All right. Let's do this. Wake her up. Time to start the brainwashing."

Juliet felt liquid warmth spreading through her arm and then into her chest, and when it reached her neck, she gasped and opened her eyes.

"What a weird dream," she muttered, rubbing her eyes. It felt like she'd been sleeping for days. Her limbs had that pleasant heaviness she sometimes got when she finally caught up on much needed sleep. When she looked around, however, that pleasant, relaxed feeling was replaced by panic. Where was she?

She jerked upright, noted the weird, pale-blue couch she was reclining on, the white walls and floor, and felt her heart begin to race. "Hello?" she yelled— or tried to, but it came out as more of a croak.

Before she could panic further, the door across from the couch clicked, beeped, and then *thunked* as it was pulled open, and a handsome man in a nice-fitting suit stepped through.

"Hi, Juliet. Don't be alarmed! Everything's fine." He came closer, holding a sealed bottle of water in one hand. When he stood before her, he gestured to the couch. "May I?"

Juliet looked down at herself, noted the tight, one-piece white bodysuit she wore, and shrugged. Scooting to the side, she made more room for him to sit. The outfit was comfortable and moved like a second skin without any pull. What was it made of?

When the man sat, he handed her the cold bottle of water, and she caught a whiff of something like cedar from his cologne, and another smell on his breath. Strawberries? She twisted the bottle cap and drank the water, gulping thirstily.

"Take it a little slow; your stomach's been empty for a while. Do you know where you are?" He sounded so pleasant and smooth—so kind. Was she supposed to know him?

She lowered the bottle and shook her head. "I'm lost here, mister corpo. I . . . I can't remember where I was, but I feel like I should be in my apartment in the Helios Arcology."

"Okay. Okay, don't worry. That's kind of what we were afraid of. You had an accident. You see, a while back, you became involved in an alpha testing group for my company. I know this will sound crazy, but you haven't lived in Tucson for a couple of years."

Ice began to creep along Juliet's spine, and her heart began to hammer. She looked at her hand, at the perfect nails and lack of grease stains. "What the hell?"

As if she were asking about his words, the man said, "I'm Alec Kline, and I work for a company called Western Bio Dynamics. You've been testing a prototype PAI device for us. You've been a valuable testing candidate."

Juliet reached toward the back of her neck. "Tig?"

"No, no. That was your old PAI. Unfortunately, the prototype had some kinks to work out, and long story short, we had to remove it because of some damage. Your memory loss is a result, but we have a good understanding of the damage done, and we feel like we can help you remember almost everything, given enough time."

Juliet felt lightheaded and strange. Everything Kline said was going in one ear, bouncing around in her head, and then fading like weird, hollow echoes. "What?" she asked, licking her lips.

"I can see you're still a little out of it. We've had to sedate you for your safety, as you're part of a very important study, Juliet. The data in your brain is extremely valuable to WBD, and we have a vested interest in your recovery. That said, we have competitors who would like to see you harmed."

"Harmed? This is so weird. I don't remember any of this! I'm pretty sure I'm supposed to be going to work soon."

"No, Juliet. I'm telling you, Fred's Salvage is gone—out of business. For your safety, I've got to keep you here, at least until you recover your memory."

"Here?" Juliet looked around the room, taking in the white walls, the hard floor, and the soft couch. "Is this a prison? A, uh, psychiatric—"

"It's a research facility, and you're very safe here. We can make this room more comfortable, and we will work with you to help you recover quickly. For now, I think it would be wise if I gave you a little time to wake up and wrap your head around things. Why don't you take a shower, have something to eat, and get some rest? I'll check on you in the morning. We can start your recovery therapy. Juliet, we have a whole team eager to get you back on your feet, to help you remember all you've lost. You're a very, very valuable member of our company."

"Um . . ." Juliet looked at him, met those soft greenish-blue eyes, and nodded. He seemed kind. "Um, yeah. I think that would be all right. Um, can I see my friend? Felix Delgado?"

"I'm sorry." Kline shook his head. "We're not in Tucson. I can try to get a hold of him. Maybe a vid call?" He seemed very earnest. Juliet nodded, smiling at the idea of talking to Felix.

"Good! All right, Juliet. You rest, wake up a little, and we can talk some more tomorrow. Start thinking about what you'd like me to bring you. Maybe a puzzle or a plant or a painting—you name it. I'll get it brought here." He stood and held out a hand, which Juliet took. His palm was warm and dry. He nodded, let go, turned, and went through the door.

She watched the door click shut behind Kline and couldn't help but feel a shiver run down her spine as she heard the heavy bolt slide home, securing the plasteel portal with an ominous finality.

"My own safety, huh?" She looked around the sterile room. Over her shoulder, she spied a small table, sink, and food dispenser. Everything was built in. The dispenser was bolted to the wall, the sink was part of the counter, and the "chairs" at the table were smooth plasteel benches, contoured for comfort but still rigid and immovable, just like the table.

A single drawer to the left of the table drew her eye. She stood up from the comfortable couch, stepped around it, and walked over to slide it open. Inside were six bodysuits like the one she wore, but in different shades of gray and white, along with one black one with gray patterns along the sides of the torso. Beside the jumpers were ten or so sets of undergarments. Everything was nice and soft, and much higher quality than anything she'd ever worn in her life.

As she gently rubbed the fabric of a silky undershirt between her fingers, she paused, looking at her perfectly manicured nails again. "God, how out of it am I?"

She'd been avoiding thinking about Kline's words—about the malfunctioning PAI and her amnesia. It was too wild, but something was definitely going on. He'd seemed nice enough; his smile had felt genuine, but it was so impossible, like a vid or a game. Honestly, it sounded like some kind of dream-rig scenario Mark would blather on about during a long shift.

She shut the drawer and turned toward a narrow sliding door on the left-hand wall. Stepping up to it, she peered through. A small bathroom awaited—built-in mirror, sink, toilet, and to her wonder, a shower with a broad pattern of holes in the ceiling and no sani-spray nozzles. There was a manual knob for the water and no digital pay pad—not that she could use one right now, anyway; not without a PAI.

A water shower without a timer?

"No way!" She pulled her head from the doorway and looked around the little apartment. She didn't see any cameras, only the one comm panel with an opaque window in the center of the door. Not a single LED was lit up around the room. "Hello?" she asked tentatively.

When no response from a host or tower AI was forthcoming, she turned back to the shower and licked her lips. She slipped into the little bathroom, pulled the door shut, and then began peeling the skintight bodysuit off. The fabric was a fancy, smart material, and when she opened the seam along her side, it loosened, allowing her to pull her arms and legs out without a struggle. As she removed her thin, comfortable undergarments, Juliet caught a glimpse of herself in the mirror and froze.

"What the heck?"

She had metallic . . . *ports* under her collarbones, and dozens of scars she didn't remember. She trailed her fingers over a long pink one just under her breastbone and turned, looking over her shoulder to see a matching line on her back, right next to her spine. She touched nearly a dozen round, pink scars on her thighs and hip, on her belly, chest, and arms—bullet wounds? Burns?

"What the shit? I think Kline left a few details out."

She twisted left and right, then lifted her arms and flexed. "What the *shit*?" she hissed again. She had muscles on muscles, and her fat . . . Where had her tummy gone? Juliet suddenly felt a wave of disorientation that threatened to take away her vision as black tunnel walls closed in. She leaned over the sink, gripping the plasteel until her fingers turned white.

"How long?" she panted. "How long did he say? Years? I've forgotten years?" She shook her head and squeezed her eyes shut. "Calm down, Juliet, calm down. He said it would come back."

She straightened and pulled on the mirror, revealing a medicine cabinet containing a sonic toothbrush, mouthwash, deodorant, and lotion. She pushed it shut, leaned forward, and stared into her green eyes. At least they were the same, but God, they looked good—so clear, so bright. Her hair was just as thick as always but felt impossibly clean, and she couldn't find a single split end. Was it a little redder, maybe?

She traced her brows and jawline with her pointer finger. It looked like she'd been to a spa. Not a bit of fuzz, not a hair out of place. How could she look younger, more beautiful, and still be . . . She couldn't think of the right word—harder?

She opened the tempered glass door to the shower, but before she stepped through, she paused and looked at the door. "No, that's not glass." It was like crystal in its clarity, but it was too light, too thin. Diamatex? Did she really have an employer who was footing the bill for this room? How? How had she gotten employed by some rich corp? Why would she? She hated Helios, right? She hated corpo rats!

She turned the knob on the shower until the arrow pointed halfway between cold and hot, then pulled, laughing with delight as nearly the entire ceiling began to stream with gentle, warm water, almost like it was raining in the little space.

She stepped in and pulled the door shut, standing in the luxurious downpour, laughing. Closing her eyes, she tilted her head back and let the water wash over her face. Juliet didn't want to think about Kline or whatever had happened to her. She just wanted to stand there and savor the warm water running over her body and be thankful that she didn't have to go into the scrapyard, didn't have to worry about making rent, and didn't have to stand in the chemical mist of a sani-spray shower.

Suddenly, a gentle, clear, feminine voice said, *Juliet, don't speak aloud, but can you hear me?*

Juliet's eyes popped open, and she looked around, peering through the fogless shower door and not seeing anyone. Had the voice been in her mind?

She tilted her head to the side and reached up to her neck, feeling for her data port. When she peeled back the flesh, she confirmed there wasn't a chip in there. When the voice came again, Juliet was sure it was in her head. It sounded almost distant, though, and a little strained.

Juliet! Subvocalize like you're talking to a PAI. Do you recognize my voice?

She frowned, still standing in the warm rainfall shower but contemplating getting out and pushing the call button on the door. Shouldn't she ask Kline about this? Something about the voice, though—Did she recognize it? "Who are you?" she subvocalized.

Juliet! It's me, Angel!

Angel? Juliet squeezed her eyes shut, another wave of vertigo striking her. Did she know an Angel? She did, didn't she? That voice . . .

"I think I know you," she subvocalized. "I've had an accident, so—"

No, you haven't! Listen to me! You can't trust Kline or anyone in this facility. You're a prisoner, not a patient. Juliet, you and me, we're sisters! We've been through everything together—I love you, and you love me.

As soon as "Angel" said those words, Juliet felt a wave of emotion so potent that she almost fainted and had to kneel in the shower, leaning forward to gather herself. The warm water drummed down on her back and head.

Something about Angel's voice and her words had struck a note in her that sang, constricting her throat with feelings.

She wanted to cry out, to say she loved her too, but none of it made sense, and she squeezed her eyes shut. She folded up, pressing her forehead against the wet plasteel floor as the water washed over her.

Do you believe me? I don't want you to worry! They don't know I'm here. They don't know I was watching while they monkeyed with your memories. I'm going to start unraveling the work they did, but it will take me a while. I have to use the processor in your medical nanite suite.

When you begin to remember, you have to be a very good actress. You have to pretend you don't remember anything. Can you do that?

Juliet gathered her thoughts, pushing the emotion down until she could breathe without gasps and properly subvocalize. "I don't understand anything, but I believe you. How soon? How soon will I remember?"

It's going to take me time to undo all this; I would have worked on it sooner while they made you sleep, but I was afraid you'd wake up and be violent, and then they'd figure out I was here. We have to play this smart, Juliet. We have to be docile, listen, and wait for our moment.

They've made a terrible mistake, you see. The ogre thinks it's brought a maiden into its lair. It thinks to make you its pet.

Only it hasn't, has it? It's brought home a tiger, and we're going to kill it where it sleeps.

17

TAKING STOCK

Juliet finished her shower and dressed in the same clothes she'd had on earlier; they were spotless and smelled fresh. She had a feeling the people holding her had dressed her only a short while before they woke her. "You really think they're watching me? I didn't see any cams . . ."

They're definitely watching. I'm sure at least one camera can see you from any angle, and there's probably a scanner array pointed at that comfy little daybed they gave you.

Angel's voice felt more and more familiar to her. She'd taken such a long shower that it had felt criminal while she listened to the strange, chipless ghost of a PAI summarize everything she had supposedly been through in the last couple of years. During that time, she'd feigned mental exhaustion, sitting on the floor under the drizzling warm water, sometimes laughing, sometimes weeping. She was sure it was convincing because she wasn't faking all that much—she felt insane.

Luckily, you and I are more than close, and when you subvocalize, you don't really move your throat. Have you noticed that? Slow down and think about it; when you spoke to Tig, didn't you have to form each word clearly in the back of your throat? With me, it's different. I can see the words forming in your mind.

While she applied some lotion to her face and hands, Juliet did what Angel said. She paid attention to how she subvocalized as she replied, "I feel like I can trust you—like, deep inside—but that doesn't mean I can't rationally look at all this and think I might be nuts. What if Kline was telling the truth and a haywire PAI messed me up?"

Angel was right; she wasn't really forming the words in her throat as she used to do when communicating with Tig. It was automatic, too, not something she'd consciously decided to do.

Just pay attention to that feeling. You always trust your gut, Juliet. You know I'm telling the truth, even if you don't know how yet. When I start freeing your memories, you'll know what to do. You'll know how duplicitous Kline is being.

"What will I remember first?" As she subvocalized, she ran her fingers through her hair, amazed that towel-drying had been enough; the strands were dry and already lying exactly where they should be, as though she'd been brushing for half an hour.

I don't know. I can see the structures they put in your mind. They're made of some kind of bonded chemical that carries a tiny electrical charge. I'm going to use your nanites to break them up, but I have no idea what will come to you first. It might be extremely disorienting, and I think I should do the work while you sleep. After I've started, I'll be able to estimate how long it will take.

"Won't they know?" Juliet opened the bathroom door and hesitantly reentered her little apartment space. Her prison. She felt very different about being there after hearing everything Angel had told her. Knowing she was likely being watched from multiple angles changed everything. With every move, she felt like she was subconsciously thinking about what her observers would think.

They may. I hope you start to remember the lattice right away. If you can begin to pick up their thoughts, we might gain some insight. We're going to have to figure something out—some way to fool their scans.

When Kline comes in the morning, you should ask for a deck, or even a hobbled PAI. If I could get some more processing power—Juliet, try to act like you don't know they're watching! You're standing like a deer in headlights!

Juliet jerked into motion, hurrying over to the food-dispensing machine while trying to keep a relaxed expression. "I never understood that one. Deer in headlights. What do they do? Freeze up?"

Yes.

The machine had several different dispensers—hot drinks, cold drinks, food "patties" with a dozen different sauce options, and various flavors of protein bars. Juliet went through the menu, selecting a plain cola drink and a lemon-vanilla protein bar.

I'm hopeful they'll need to take you around to different departments for your so-called therapy. Maybe we'll find something we can exploit. If they don't, if they say they're going to bring specialists to you, try to find a way to get out. Say you feel stir-crazy. Say you'd like to visit a gym or even just walk in the sun. As you begin to remember what you're capable of, you'll understand. You have many skills at your disposal, Juliet.

Juliet tried to convey her understanding without subvocalizing specific words, and to her amazement, she felt like she *knew* Angel understood.

Taking her drink and snack, she walked toward the blue couch-bed. As she did so, she carefully scrutinized it, looking for a panel where hidden components might be located. As far as she could tell, it was seamless. She sat down, felt the soft gel beneath the fabric surface, and wondered if Angel was right—Were there scanners hidden in it? Restraints? Mechanical arms that could extend to inject her with diabolical mixtures? The idea made her want to sit on the floor.

Still, she forced herself to look relaxed as she leaned back and folded her legs beneath her, sipping her cold soda and slowly nibbling the too-sweet protein bar. "I'll complain about the food. Maybe we can get access to someone new or a cafeteria or something."

That's a good idea. I wish we knew what time it was. Do you feel sleepy? Kline acted like leaving you until morning was natural. It might be the end of the day.

"I'm definitely not feeling too alert. Shit! Do you think there's something in the food?" Juliet feigned a cough to cover her sudden startled expression.

Likely, but don't worry. As I said, I can use your nanite battery's processor to some effect. Setting it to complete routines I've already established is nothing; the nanites will dispose of anything harmful or unnatural in your food and drink. I'll get a report when they cycle back to the battery.

"A nanite battery isn't a power source, right?" Juliet was trying to keep up, but Angel had told her a million things in a short amount of time, and she was feeling overwhelmed.

Not exactly. It has a power source, a biobatt, but it's more like a little factory where your nanites report what they're doing, get repaired or replaced, and receive new instructions. It's a very high-end medical nanite suite. I'm sure that if WBD knew you could interact with it, they would have removed it.

"I think I get it," she subvocalized, yawning. "I do feel sleepy, though, and maybe that's not a bad thing. I want to start remembering. I'm going to try to sleep, okay?"

Not sure if it mattered, Juliet turned her back to the door and curled onto her side, using her arm as a pillow. The lack of bedding felt strange; shouldn't there be a pillow? Shouldn't she at least have a blanket?

She was determined to ask Kline about it when he returned. In the meantime, it didn't really matter; the temperature in the room felt perfect, and her bodysuit was the most comfortable thing she'd ever worn. She sank into the couch's gel padding, which wrapped around her like the palm of a friendly giant's hand. With that image in her mind, Juliet almost immediately drifted off.

She caught herself falling into sleep's embrace and jerked her eyes open. How could she? How could she sleep with everything that was happening?

Her entire life was like the plot of a crazy action spy thriller. She was trapped in a room! That alone should make sleep impossible.

On the heels of that thought came another, equally disturbing one: she had a voice in her head that carried on conversations with her, and it wasn't a PAI.

As that thought struck her, she absently reached back and gently peeled away the synth-flesh on her data port. Idly, she let her perfect, diamond-hard nail scratch at the empty slots, ensuring there wasn't anything in there, no tiny secret chips. She clicked her nail against it, and that's when a wave of vertigo struck her. She wasn't the same person she thought she was. Her *body* was different.

If she were to believe everything Angel said, a lot more than her nails was different. Superficially, as far as augments went, the nails, hair, and eyes were about it. She could wrap her mind around that, but there was so much more.

She gently touched the weird lump of plasteel near her wrist where, according to Angel, she could deploy an actual data cable. She had upgraded optics, ears, reflexes, and *lungs*. More than that, her perfectly normal-looking right arm was supposedly cybernetic. It *felt* normal, but then, so did her bones and armored skin. Was that right? Was it armored? Angel had given her so many details that she couldn't keep them all straight.

Putting aside all of the cybernetics, Juliet had seen herself in the mirror. She was living in someone else's body; that was the only way she could explain it.

First of all, her body hair was gone. What was that all about? Angel had said DNA, but the details were all mixed up. Then there were the muscles and the . . . posture? Was that right? She stood differently and *moved* differently. It was an uncanny thing that she couldn't adequately explain, but she felt like she was in someone else's skin.

Finally, Juliet focused on the scars—so many scars. None of them were all that terrible, just faintly discolored pinker skin, not keloid; Angel credited the medical nanites for that.

Juliet had to squeeze her eyes and force herself to think of something mundane—cutting scrap, chugging a cheap beer, laughing with Felix. She had to do something to keep all the craziness at bay so she could sleep. Things would be better when she woke up; they had to be. If she could start to remember, maybe she could reconcile her current situation, Angel's wild story, and her altered person into a single conglomeration that made a little sense.

She pushed away the impossible situation of her present and focused on her past. She remembered her times with Felix, laughing at each other, at friends, and at themselves. She remembered her sister and the many fights they'd been in, along with a few happy moments when she'd felt like Emma actually wanted her around. It was with one such memory, a time she'd helped Emma fix her hair for a date, that she finally drifted off and began to dream in earnest.

Rutger Tanaka kicked the man out of his chair, sending him sprawling over the plasteel floor to smash against an overturned lab table.

"I won't keep asking," he growled, his monoblade's holographic magenta edge sizzling and popping to punctuate the statement. He stalked toward him, the blade held out to the right menacingly. The man's eyes were trained on the sword, but they flickered down to the bisected, highly armored corpo-sec agent who lay near the broken door.

"Leo reports the lab is clear; all corpo-sec accounted for," Kim reported. Tanaka grunted then tuned her out as the lab director began to blubber, mumbling into his hands as he covered his face.

"I swear! I don't know anything about any 'Angel Project.' I don't know what was in that fluttercraft! I didn't even know it came to this facility! This is all above my pay grade!"

"I've seen the payroll for this facility. You make more than the city manager of New Atlas." Tanaka knelt, deftly swinging the sword close to the man's face, just a centimeter from his peering eye. "One more chance to tell me something helpful."

"If"—the small, slightly rotund man licked his lips and lowered his hands, trembling as more sweat built up on his brow—"If it's anything important, anything Mrs. Gentry—Ack!" He coughed and shook, and Tanaka moved the sword away, peering at him in confusion. This was a first. Was he being shocked? Poisoned?

Fast as a viper striking, he reached out and snatched the back of the man's neck, pulling him forward so he could see his data port. Without a second thought, he ripped his PAI chip out.

The director convulsed, foam erupting from his mouth, and Tanaka swore. Standing, he sheathed his sword and slammed his fist into the plasteel wall. Kim was quick to notice his distress.

"Rutger, are you all right? I noticed your conversation was cut short—"

"*Hai*," Tanaka replied, moving his hand in a chopping motion to signal he didn't want to hear from his PAI at that moment. She was clever and helpful, but not nearly as intuitive as he'd like. The damn thing didn't realize his "conversation" was an interrogation, and that his prisoner had just been killed by something.

He wasn't naive enough to think the director could be salvaged. If some kind of kill switch had been thrown, there was no doubt his brain had been the first target; they wouldn't get anything useful out of him. "Signal protocol F," he muttered, turning and jogging out of the lab. He had three levels to get through before they blew the place up.

"Books is placing the last charge. Protocol F in five minutes." Kim put a timer on his AUI as she spoke, and Tanaka nodded, hurrying up the stairs.

When he reached the roof and climbed into the transport section of their waiting fluttercraft, he asked, "Kostas is still waiting?"

"Yes, I have an open line. Do you want to speak to her?"

"*Hai.*"

A call window popped open on his PAI, and Selene Kostas's beautiful face greeted him. She narrowed her brows. "Bad news?"

"Does my face say so much?"

"I'm afraid so. To me, at least."

"Another dead end. Nine days of planning, two million bits in bribes, and not a whisper of information, let alone our missing people. The director was about to say something, but then he . . . died. I took his PAI out, but the damage was done."

"The time is the only concern. The bits are nothing; I have as many as we need. Show me the director's last words."

"Do it," Tanaka grunted, knowing Kim was listening in. She initiated the file transfer, and he watched Kostas's eyes flicker left and right while she watched the footage.

After a minute, she nodded. "I'm afraid I should have assumed as much. I should have assumed Gentry would want Juliet close. It's very hard to track the woman's movements, but I have a good guess. More and more of the WBD execs have been relocating to Mexico City.

"They're doing something big there; I'm tracking massive shipments off-world. Most are heading to either Mars or Ceres, but there's a huge WBD installation in Mexico City, and it seems they're consolidating their operations there. They're planning something big. I've been dreading it—I'd so hoped we'd find success here today, but it looks like they probably brought our people there."

Tanaka started to speak, almost yelling, but he caught himself as he saw Leo burst out of the stairwell along with Books and two of his men. They ran for the fluttercraft, so Tanaka turned and walked to the far end of the compartment. There was room enough for twenty soldiers in the hold, so it wasn't hard to get a little privacy as he continued the conversation.

"How long have you known that?" he asked, reigning in his irritation.

"Since day one, but these two installations had just as much of a likelihood by my estimations of having our people as the one in Mexico City."

Tanaka stared out the bay door, watching for the fire bursts their bombs would create. The two installations she mentioned included this one in Texas and the one they'd hit prior to that in Arizona. He shook his head, his words almost a growl, spoken quickly and forcefully. "It doesn't sound like they were equal—not if all the executives are moving to Mexico City!"

"Rutger, I tracked the fluttercraft to these two installations. They must have off-loaded and moved her by different means. I've tracked thousands of vehicles that have come and gone, but think about it! There are a dozen cities and millions of vehicles between where they took Juliet and Mexico City. I'm not God!"

Tanaka continued to scowl, but he nodded. He was frustrated, but operating with Selene's intel was better than without, not to mention her resources. He still didn't know where the fluttercraft had come from.

Shaking his head, he looked into Selene's eyes and said softly, so his voice was drowned out by the whining, buzzing rumble of the fluttercraft as it sped away from Lewisville, "Are we too late?"

"No! No, Rutger. They want Juliet, and they won't kill people she cares about. I'm sure of it; not if they can help it. To them, your people are leverage against her. They'll want to keep them viable for that purpose." Tanaka still wasn't used to Lucky's real name. Whenever Kostas referred to her as Juliet, he had to draw a mental connection between the word and the woman he knew.

"So, the next move? Mexico City?"

"Yes, but we'll need to be a little more careful. We're talking about an installation with upward of a hundred thousand employees. We'll need to infiltrate. I'll start building new identities for you, Leo, and Charles. Start preparing with the idea that Leo will be acting as a visiting exec from an allied corporation. You and Books will be his security."

"All right, and in the meantime?"

"I'm coordinating with Frida; we'll get you a base of operations in the city. I've already arranged flight clearance for the fluttercraft, and it's en route. The WBD facility is on the spaceport proper and utterly air gapped—I'm in the dark about what's going on there, but not for long. I'm working on a solution. You're going to be receiving a package via courier. Contact me when it arrives, and I'll walk you through the next steps."

"*Hai.*" Tanaka tried not to sound defeated, but he was dead tired and frustrated by yet another failure.

"Rutger?" Selene leaned closer to the camera; he could see the concern in her big olive-green eyes.

"Yeah?"

"Are you with me? Do you have the stamina for this?" The question sent a rod of steel into his spine, and Tanaka's eyes snapped open.

Selene's mouth opened in a small *O* of surprise as he growled, "I will pursue them until they're found, until I'm dead, or until I've killed everyone involved in their capture."

18

BIT BY BIT

When Juliet woke up, she remembered. Not everything, not even close, but a lot. She felt like she remembered enough from the last couple of years that she knew who she was again. However, if she scrutinized the time since fleeing Fred's scrapyard, there were definite holes—huge gaps in time, people whose faces she couldn't picture, faces she couldn't put a name to, and events she couldn't place on the timeline of her life.

She'd woken up on her back, lying on the soft gel of the couch, and as she lay there, breathing, slowly blinking her eyes, reviewing her state of mind, she couldn't keep her lips from curling into a slow, sly smile.

She was *remembering*! She wasn't broken! Even if things weren't perfect yet, she knew unequivocally that Angel was real and that she hadn't been a figment of her broken mind. Still smiling, she stretched, yawned, and sub-vocalized, "Angel, you sneaky little devil. These dumb jerks don't know what they've done, do they?"

Juliet! It worked, didn't it? I programmed the nanites to begin broadly, not in clusters. I hoped to unlock a wide range of memories!

"Oh, it worked, but I can feel the missing stuff; it's all over the place. I'm missing all sorts of things—details, faces, names. It doesn't matter, though, 'cause the big picture is here again. I remember WBD. I remember you. Go ahead and keep 'em working; I don't think you need to wait for me to sleep."

If you're sure. But if you start to feel disoriented or . . . troubled, let me know! Do you remember the lattice?

"Oh my God, Angel! The lattice! Weird! Why do you think it hasn't been bothering me?"

The same reason it no longer bothers you when you sleep, other than the occasional true-dream—

"Holy shit!" Juliet almost hissed but snapped her mouth shut, satisfying herself by thinking the words as loudly as she could. "This room . . . It feels . . . Did I dream about this?"

I believe you might have. Not long ago, you had a true-dream in which you were being held captive in a room. You don't remember?

"Not the details. No, not at all. But this"—Juliet looked around her dimly lit, white-washed prison—"feels like déjà vu."

I believe you did dream about this scenario. In any case, as I was saying, I think you've acclimated yourself to the lattice. It doesn't fire on its own that often anymore. Before I restored your memories, you had forgotten the lattice and how to access it, but your body didn't forget about it. In the last half year or so, you only seemed to receive intrusive thoughts when someone's emotions were particularly strong and focused on you. It'll be interesting to see how it goes when you try to read Kline today.

"Oh, I'm looking forward to that one. What a story he spun! A trial for an alpha, huh? Sounds like he's trying to rewrite history." Juliet felt her eyes fill with moisture as she said, "Angel, I'm so glad you're real. I'm so glad I remember things again. I was afraid I was losing my marbles last night."

Don't be too conspicuous, Juliet! They'll see you crying. I love you, though, and I'm so glad they couldn't remove me from you. They think they did. I'm sure they think I'm hiding, dormant in my chip.

"If you don't want me to cry, stop saying you love me!" Juliet rolled onto her side, pushed her face into the back of the couch, and tried to laugh-cry silently. The emotions were hard to contain—relief, love, amusement, and under it all, a vague uneasiness at half-glimpsed memories that she couldn't quite wrap her mind around. "What do you think they'll do if I start going through a bodyweight workout and then get into my sword forms?"

Juliet!

"I'm joking." Juliet rolled over and hopped up, still appreciative of the material her bodysuit was made of regardless of her restored memories. It was very comfortable; she felt supported, but at the same time, utterly unhindered in her movement.

As she padded around the couch, the room's lights automatically brightened. She didn't remember them dimming the night before. Had they done it when she'd stopped moving? Could the room tell she was sleeping, or was someone watching her? She knew the answer was probably both.

Stepping over to the drawer on the rear wall and pulling it open, she ran her fingers over the bodysuits and selected a clean one—white with blue diamond outlines on the side—along with some clean underwear. She set them on the table then moved over to the little food machine, where she selected coffee and a protein patty with "breakfast" sauce.

She chuckled at the description, her mood too good to care about the terrible food. She was herself again. Not quite whole, but whole enough to know she was going to mess with WBD in a big damn way.

Something tickled the back of her mind; some dark shadow that she couldn't grasp. The feeling was frustrating, like trying to pick something up that kept slipping through her fingers, but she pushed it away, knowing it would come to her eventually.

While she sat and drank the bitter coffee and ate the hot patty with something like bacon-flavored gravy, she subvocalized, "What about my vibroblade, my toxin needles, and all that?"

I think I could manage to deploy them. I have connections to all of your implants, but I'd struggle to operate more than one at a time. As for the needles, your captors drained the toxin. The vibroblade, however, will work; they think you can't trigger it.

The only things I can't manage without a proper processor and the software I developed are your enhanced reflexes—your speed boost—and anything that requires an interface with your optics.

"Like the terahertz scan?"

Exactly, not to mention I don't have the data sets and subroutines for analyzing such a scan. All of my databases, custom daemons, predictive algorithms. . . Well, anything that isn't me is stored on my PAI chip and the memory chips from your data port.

I can recreate most of them if I have to, but we'll need something with more robust processing power and storage. Storage is the big one; even with the limited processing I can eke out of your cybernetics, I just don't have any place to store anything I create.

"What about my data port? The coprocessor and mem—"

They pulled those, likely hoping to figure out what I've been up to. They'll be disappointed when they find everything encrypted.

"Well," Juliet subvocalized, swallowing her last bite of protein patty, "I'll try to fish some processing power out of Kline."

She threw her plate and cup into the recycle chute, grabbed her clean clothes, and went into the bathroom. When she undressed, she put her dirty clothes into another chute labeled Laundry then took a long, relaxing shower. She brushed her teeth while she stood in the rainfall-like deluge. After she'd washed with soap and shampoo, she sat on the floor, closing her eyes and enjoying the small pleasure of wasting WBD's water.

While she sat there, she focused on memories that felt recent: memories of training and sword practice with Tanaka. She knew she'd spent months with him; that was clear. But those months were full of holes in her mind. Still, she tried to recapture what she'd learned. With her eyes still closed, she focused on the memories that were whole and tried to let her body remember her training for her.

In her mind, she worked through her forms: strikes, parries, ripostes, counters, and every complicated gambit she could remember. She visualized herself completing them all, slowly flexing each muscle without moving her limbs. When she finished and stood, rising from her cross-legged position on the wet plasteel floor effortlessly, she felt relaxed and ready to face whatever her strange situation would bring.

She applied her deodorant—some kind of powdery, spring-fresh scent—and liberally slathered lotion over her body before getting dressed. As far as she was concerned, they could enjoy the show if they wanted to spy on her while she was in there.

When she emerged from the bathroom, she was a little startled to find Kline sitting on her couch.

"Juliet! Did you have a good sleep?" He wore a dark suit almost identical to the one he'd worn the day before, but his tie was different—yellow, almost gold.

"I slept all right, Mr. Kline. Wouldn't have minded a blanket and pillow." She walked over to the food dispenser and ordered a cup of cola. "Thirsty?"

Her mind had begun to race at the sight of him, but she pushed down her momentary panic. She didn't need to be worried. *He* should be worried.

The thought made her smile, but at the same time, she was annoyed. She'd just woken up, barely taken a shower—albeit a long one—and now he was here. She'd hoped for some more time with Angel. Some time to decompress and review what she remembered. She knew what her situation was, but she couldn't remember some pertinent details. How had she even gotten captured?

"Um, no, thank you." He frowned and stood up. "Shoot, Juliet! This is my fault—about the blanket, I mean. I should have given you a tour of your space." He reached down, tucked his fingers under the bottom edge of the couch, and pulled. A nearly invisible drawer slid out, and as Juliet walked over with her plastic cup of fizzing cola, she saw several folded blankets of varying thickness and two small, square pillows.

"Anything else you didn't show me? Like, maybe where I can get something to eat that doesn't taste like it was created in a pet food factory?" As she said the words, Juliet regretted them. She would have loved that meal back when she worked at Fred's; it was a damn sight better than what she used to purchase from the Helios vending machines.

Kline smiled and pushed the drawer closed before sitting down again. He chuckled softly, shaking his head. "You *are* feeling better, aren't you? You seem . . . different than you did last night."

Juliet might have been worried that she'd overplayed her hand, that she was being a little too upbeat, but she couldn't find it in herself to care. Instead, she pictured herself grabbing Kline in a rear naked chokehold; imagined squeezing his neck in her cybernetic arm until blood seeped from his eyes.

With that image in her mind, she grinned, sat beside him, looked right into his eyes, and said, "A good night's sleep does wonders. What kind of padding is in this couch? I wish I could get one in my apartment, but the Helios Arcology has built-in beds, and I don't think you can change the mattresses out."

"Uh . . ." Kline chuckled and shifted, looking away from her intent gaze, his eyes flickering toward the door. "I'm not sure. It feels like memory gel of some sort. Juliet, you don't live in the arcology anymore. Remember?"

"Oh, right. Sorry, but that all seems so wild! I have to believe you, though. There are things that are different about me. Why am I all covered in scars?"

As she asked the question, Juliet settled her drink between her hands, tried to relax, and looked into Kline's eyes again. They were high-end optics, she could see that much right away. Currently, they were colored a neutral kind of green-blue that looked almost natural, but they were too clear, too pretty. While she listened to his response, she inhaled and willed his thoughts to come to her.

"Remember I told you about the experimental PAI going haywire? Well, it had you really mixed up for a long while. You went on the run, hiding from our technicians who wanted to remove the device and help you recover. While you were out in the wild, you did all sorts of things to survive and stay hidden, often at the urging of the PAI's rogue personality."

Juliet nodded along to his words while his thoughts came to her in phrases and scattered images:

Not my fault. This thought was accompanied by the image of a horrible corpse in a plastic, see-through body bag. It was large and impossible to recognize as male or female. The remaining flesh was discolored and swollen, sloughing off the bones here and there, more liquid than solid.

Running and hiding. Where'd you go? Juliet caught flashes of airports, long empty roads, burning buildings, a weeping man tied to a chair, Kline's face in a mirror, haggard with bloodshot eyes.

Rogue. Angel! Another image came with these thoughts: Angel's PAI chip sitting in a dock, a dozen wires leading from it into server-size data cubes.

"So the PAI had a, what did you say? Rogue personality? That sounds like the horror stories they taught us about the war—"

"No, no. Nothing that nefarious. The PAI *thought* it was alive, a true AI, and it had some very convincing stories to tell you. Basically, Juliet, it brainwashed you. You shouldn't feel bad about that; it was in your head, you know? It saw everything you did, talked to you constantly, and was very, very smart. Imagine having a genius-level psychiatrist who could see your every move and had full access to you all the time. How easy would it be for such a person to convince you of a lie?"

"Gosh." Juliet blew out a pent-up breath and leaned back on the couch. "I hope you destroyed it!"

Kline cleared his throat and chuckled, shaking his head. Juliet could tell he was trying to choose his words carefully.

"Um, I can see how you might feel that way. The thing is, the two of you made an amazing team. You got into a lot of wild adventures while on the run, and still, we were utterly unable to find you. We think the PAI's personality, Angel, might be worth salvaging. We kind of hope that you'll be able to convince it we don't mean any harm to either of you. In fact, we want to work with the two of you."

Juliet snorted, shaking her head. "That seems insane. You just told me this AI convinced me to go on the run and that it somehow wiped my memory of the last two years! I've got bullet scars all over my body, Mr. Kline! You want me to put that thing back in my head?"

Amazing, Juliet! You're doing a great job! Juliet wanted to smile at Angel's encouragement, but she kept the skeptical expression on her face.

"I understand, Juliet. I really do. I think with some therapy, some education, and the gradual restoration of your memories, you might come around to see things my way. This is a massive opportunity for you. Wouldn't you rather have an important role at a major corporation, earning good money, than go back to cutting scrap, struggling to pay rent?"

"You say that like you can restore my memories whenever you want." Juliet tried again to listen to Kline's thoughts as she fished. They came to her suddenly and powerfully, and as she listened, she lost track of the words coming out of his mouth.

A few memories every week when we do the scan. Slow and steady wins the race.

Juliet stared slack-jawed, watching an image drifting out of Kline's mind into hers. She saw his calendar on an AUI, almost like she were looking at her own display, and she read the notes on the highlighted week:

Monday:
- *Juliet – introduction*
- *Call Rachel*
- *Set up office*

Tuesday:
- *Juliet – begin phase 1, tour, lunch*
- *Debrief – assign requests?*
- *Call Rachel*
- *Meet Montclair*

Wednesday:
- *Juliet – Psych visit, 1-on-1, lunch*
- *Team debrief*
- *Mrs. G*

Thursday:
- *Listener (!!) – Gipple?*
- *Debrief*
- *Montclair*

Friday:
- *Juliet – Full scan*
- *Debrief*
- *Mrs. G. & Board (!!!)*

"Are you all right? Something I said?" Kline reached out to touch Juliet's shoulder, and she startled, blinking her eyes rapidly, banishing the image she'd pulled out of Kline's head.

"Oh, I'm sorry!" She laughed, and though it was a nervous laugh, she felt like she did a good job passing it off as more of a confused one. "I . . . I don't know what happened. I just blanked out." She licked her lips and didn't have to pretend; her mouth had gone dry at the notes she'd seen on Kline's calendar.

His hand was still on her shoulder, and he gently squeezed it. Juliet wanted to recoil, but instead, she leaned into it, embracing the tiny part of her that appreciated the human touch. "That's all right, Juliet. You've been through a lot. I can't imagine what you're thinking, how you're feeling. I'd be surprised if you could stay focused on a boring guy like me."

"Um, I was going to ask . . ." Juliet smiled, trying to make it look nervous, as she glanced into his eyes and then away, toward the door. "Could I get a clock in here? I wish I knew what time it was, what day it was. Like, even the day of the week."

Kline nodded and rubbed his chin. "Yeah, that shouldn't be a problem. I don't know how that could mess up your therapy. Anything else?"

"Can I be honest?"

"Of course! I insist!"

"Well, there's a lot to be desired about this room. It feels more like a prison! I wasn't joking about that food dispenser. Couldn't I visit a cafeteria?" She didn't want to give him a chance to reject each idea one by one, so she began to rapidly list off things she'd thought of while in the shower.

"I'd love some books to read! I appreciate classics, like old, old science fiction and fantasy. Maybe I could paint my room? These walls are so boring and severe! Gosh, Mr. Kline, what I wouldn't give to be able to watch a vid or play a simple game! If I'm going to be here for a while, couldn't I get a new PAI? I understand the one I had malfunctioned, but surely, I could have a simple one like my old Tig.

"Hey! Do you have Tig? Maybe I could have him back? If not, maybe a deck? A deck with some movies? I have optics, right? Could I connect to a deck and watch old shows or movies? I've got this weird wire in my arm. I can plug that in, right? I'm going to go stir-crazy staring at these walls. What about a gym? Could I go out for a walk?"

"Whoa! Easy there, Juliet! Give me a second to think!" He laughed, and it wasn't lost on Juliet that he still had his hand on her shoulder while they sat facing each other on the couch.

"Sorry." She smiled demurely, ducking her head and looking up through her lashes at him. If he was going to get touchy-feely, she was going to give him something to think about.

"Tell you what, my PAI just populated a list of all those requests, and I'll fill 'em as much as I can, okay? I can take care of a few of your problems right now, though, if you're up for it. I wanted to give you a little tour of the facility; at least the parts you'll be visiting regularly.

"One of the stops involves a gym, and I figured we could wrap up my time with you today by having lunch. We can eat at the executive lounge—they have a chef on staff and real food, not . . . whatever is in that machine." He pointed to the food dispenser. "How does that sound?"

"It sounds really nice, Mr. Kline."

"Alec! Call me Alec, or just plain Kline. That's what my friends and coworkers do."

As she nodded and stood, she subvocalized, "Looks like it's Tuesday, Angel, and we've got exactly two days to figure out what a *listener* is and what they know about the lattice. Kline has a note on his calendar that mentions a 'Gipple.' That can't be a coincidence, can it?"

Do you think he's referring to the GIPEL?

"Yeah, I'm afraid so."

"Okay, Juliet," Kline said, oblivious to the side conversation. "We're going to be walking through high-security passages, so don't be alarmed when you see armed personnel. Remember, they're here to protect you. It's imperative that you stay close and only go where I lead, all right? Otherwise, they'll revoke my permission to guide you around and make us stay locked down in this area."

Juliet nodded and watched as Kline approached the door. It *beeped*, *clicked*, and *thunked*, then it slowly swung open, and Juliet had to clench her fists to keep from leaping into an attack. She had to remind herself that she wasn't armed, she couldn't use her speed boost, and she had no idea where she was or what she was up against.

No, she had to be patient and bide her time. She had to take this bit by bit.

19

DARK PLANS

Kline guided Juliet through a sterile, lab-like room—its single desk and built-in data terminal vacant—then proceeded through identical empty white plasteel corridors. Despite the polymer panels lining the walls to deaden echoes, Kline's dress shoes resonated with each step, a stark contrast to Juliet's silent, padding steps, her feet shrouded in the material of her bodysuit. Camera nodules dotted every corridor, and at each junction, bulky scanner arrays sulked in the shadowy corners.

They passed at least half a dozen impassive, heavily armored corpo-sec officers on their way, with mirrored combat visors and bulky SMGs pointed at the ground.

"Um, not exactly welcoming," she remarked as they turned down the third corridor.

Kline nodded. "I warned you. We take your security very seriously."

"Are we underground or, like, in a megastructure? This reminds me of the Helios Arcology, where my apartment—"

"Used to be?" He winked at her as they stepped up to a nondescript door. "Let's just say we're safe in a WBD facility."

He typed a code into the panel and leaned forward so it would read his retina. The door slid open a moment later, and they entered an ample, open space. Bright, yellow-white lights clicked on, revealing white flooring and walls much like those in her room, but also couches, potted plants, and framed photos of nature scenes—waterfalls, forests, waves crashing on a rocky shore, and sunny beaches. A corridor led away on the far side of the bigger room, and Kline gestured expansively.

"This is where you'll meet with Doctor Chen. She'll help you recover your memories and deal with any trauma that results. She's a highly skilled counselor; I take advantage of her services from time to time." He walked toward the corridor. "Your first session will be tomorrow."

"How will she? I mean, how will she help me remember?"

"That's above my pay grade, Juliet. I'm sure she has all sorts of techniques to help you trigger those buried memories."

Juliet nodded, playing along. He was smooth, that was for sure. Whatever they'd done to block her memories was obviously reversible—Angel was proving that. According to the snatches of thought she'd picked up earlier, he meant to unlock things little by little so they could have Doctor Chen take the credit for things she remembered. Or worse, Chen would try to gaslight her as Juliet recovered her memories one by one, twisting them to suit Kline's narrative of a benevolent WBD.

Kline paused and softly rapped his knuckles against a closed door on the left. "This is a classroom where you'll take WBD-employee certification courses."

"What?" Juliet tried to maintain her "awed scrap worker" persona, but a little incredulity leaked into her voice.

"Well, Juliet, in the event you decide to work with us, I'd like you to have all of the mandatory courses completed so I can move you into a higher employment classification. Regretfully, despite your special circumstances, the corporation has its red tape that we all must navigate."

She frowned, wringing her hands before her in an attempt to look nervous. "Oh. Right. I guess that makes sense."

"I know. No one gets excited about classwork, but I think you'll like the next stop on the tour." He moved another ten steps down the hallway and tapped in a code to open the door on the right. When he motioned for Juliet to step through, she did, smiling as the lights clicked on and revealed a small gym.

"Ah!" Juliet slowly turned her head left and right, taking it in. The right side of the room had a bench, a squat rack, barbells, and plenty of weight plates. On the left was an exercise bicycle, a rowing machine, and a treadmill. But what made her smile—a real, genuine smile—was the pool.

It was only about five meters long and two meters wide, but she could see the far end had a wave generator; a person was meant to swim against a current, so in essence, she should be able to swim without having to stop or turn.

"Just for you, by the way. You're the only client in the department at the moment."

"Client?"

"Sounds better than patient or prisoner, doesn't it?" Kline chuckled and winked again, and Juliet noticed him nervously reach up to his breast pocket and tap at something there. The move reminded her so much of someone she knew that she laughed.

"Looking for a vape?" The words came out unbidden, and as she finished speaking, her mouth hung open, her eyes betraying her panic. She felt like she should know why she thought Kline wanted to smoke a vape, but she couldn't, for the life of her, remember who she'd known with that habit.

Luckily for her, she'd struck a sore spot with Kline, and he sighed remorsefully, looking away. "Ah, it's a bad habit, and your doctors made me promise not to do it around you."

"My doctors? You mean Doctor Chen?"

"No. I'm not sure if Chen would mind; I'm talking about the doctors who've been monitoring your brain and biological readings while you were unconscious. They're very prejudiced against addictive substances."

"Oh. Well, judging by the scars, I don't think I exactly led a clean life for the last couple of years, and I can tell you for a fact that I've spent plenty of time in bars and clubs with people vaping. I'm not a flower, Kline." She gestured to the gym equipment. "This all looks like a good outlet, but I've never been much on going to the gym. What are the odds you could get me a workout aid to plug in?" She tapped her temple, indicating her optics. "I can tell I upgraded my optics; my old ones didn't look this good."

"Yeah, I've been thinking about your request. I'll talk to the team and see if we can get you a limited deck or maybe a hobbled PAI. The issue with that is that we're hoping to get you and the PAI alpha rehabilitated, and I don't want to mess things up by plugging some dumb chip into the slot. I have to talk to the techs to see if that's a risk."

He sounded sincere, and Juliet's gut told her he wasn't bullshitting. She supposed it made sense. They could easily modify a PAI to limit its connectivity and functionality. It wasn't like she should be able to do anything nefarious with it—as far as they knew, Angel was nowhere near her brain.

She leaned against the doorframe, folding her arms over her chest. "Why would that be a risk? I thought a PAI was just a chip you could swap out any time you wanted."

"It's the synthetic neural fibers. The prototype left a lot behind in there." He moved a pointer finger toward her head but stopped short of touching her. "Nothing dangerous, but I'm just wondering if they'd interfere with another

PAI, or if maybe having another one installed would do something to risk the reintegration of the prototype." He shrugged. "I'm no expert. I'll let you know in a day or two. Fair enough?"

Juliet nodded. "Fair enough."

"On to the next stop on the tour!"

He backed out of the room and continued down the corridor while Juliet followed. "You'll have a regular schedule and escort when I can't be here myself. I wish I could let you wander freely, but people above my pay grade would frown on that. Anyway, the food machine in your room is really just for snacks or an early breakfast. You have two meals on your schedule—kind of a brunch appointment and then dinner. Both will usually be delivered to your room."

"Ah, I see."

"I'm mentioning that now 'cause I'm about to take you up to the executive lounge. We might run into some other employees, but we might not; there are a few lounges in the facility, and we're early. It's only a quarter to eleven."

Juliet nodded, though she was almost positive they'd run into no one. She was sure Kline had cleared out their entire path. So far, the only people she'd seen were the corpo-sec officers. Thinking of their gear as they walked, Juliet asked, "Hey, Kline?"

"Yeah?"

"When the, um, accident happened, was I wearing or carrying anything? I wonder if some of my belongings might help me remember."

"Uh . . ." He paused; Juliet could see the wheels turning in his head. "That's a great question. I'll ask around. I wasn't present when you were first recovered." While he spoke, Juliet stared hard at the side of his eye and tried to dig into his mind, wondering if she might get a clue, but nothing came to her.

She frowned and gave up when he stopped to activate a small, narrow-doored elevator at the end of the corridor. She decided she'd ask him again the next time he came to her room to ensure she had a good, clear view of his eyes. It seemed easier to gather someone's thoughts when she could do that or, she supposed, if she could close her own eyes, which wasn't practical right then.

As she'd predicted, the hallway where the elevator deposited them was empty save for two corpo-sec officers. She followed Kline to a dimly lit restaurant with about a dozen empty tables and booths. When they sat down, a fully plasteel-and-plastic synth approached to set glasses of sparkling lemon-flavored water before them. "Good morning. Your meals will be delivered shortly."

"Thank you," Kline replied, sipping his water. The synth nodded and marched away, moving gracefully on its rubber-lined plasteel feet.

"No menu?" Juliet asked, also sipping her water. The bubbles tickled her nose, and the hint of lemon made her want to gulp it down. She hadn't realized how thirsty she'd become.

"They're not up to full service yet. I had to choose a meal ahead of time. I, uh, selected lasagna. I hope that's all right; it sounded like a good comfort food, and I can only imagine how out of sorts you must be feeling."

Before she could modulate her tone or think about her words, Juliet leaned forward, smiling. "I *love* lasagna!" It was true; she did, and hadn't had it in ages.

"Your mom used to cook it?" Kline guessed, arching an eyebrow. Juliet supposed it was a safe guess; something a lot of people, especially those with an Italian last name, might be able to relate to. Juliet shook her head, though, and smiled at a memory she hadn't thought about in a long, long time.

"No, my grandma. She and my grandpa owned a house near where my mom lived when I was really little. My grandma would watch me sometimes . . ." She trailed off, her conscious mind finally catching up with her rambling mouth and rushing memories. That wasn't something she wanted to share with the likes of Alec Kline.

"Oh? My, uh, well, this is kind of embarrassing, but my big sister introduced me to lasagna. My parents worked graveyards in an assembly plant, and they were always either sleeping or working, so my big sister took care of me." Kline frowned and got quiet for a moment. Juliet hated that she felt a little sympathy at the distant, haunted look in his eyes. It only lasted a couple of seconds before he shook it off and chuckled, drinking his water. "Let's hope this chef knows what she's doing, huh?"

"Right." Juliet smiled, playing along. While they both sipped their water, for the first time since the tour had begun, Angel whispered into her mind:

Juliet, have you considered looking more deeply into Kline's mind? It might be the only way to learn what we need about the "listener" in time.

"Um," Juliet started to say, then caught herself. Kline looked at her, however, so she had to continue. "How long do you think my recovery is going to take? Do you have any idea how, um, how good my chances are?"

"Well, I think there's a damn good chance!" Kline leaned forward a little, smiling earnestly. "Especially after speaking with you today. I think you've got what it takes, Juliet. If we can show progress, it'll keep my bosses off my back, and I can keep pushing for as much time as we need."

"What's . . . ?" Juliet licked her lips and tried to act nervous—not hard with her mind racing, contemplating a deep dive. She'd utterly forgotten about those. It wasn't that she didn't remember what they were; it was more like some crucial memories tying them to the lattice were missing.

When she'd thought about listening to Kline's thoughts, the idea of diving into his mind hadn't even occurred to her. Now that Angel had mentioned it, however, she couldn't stop her mind from racing. She shook her head slightly and tried to focus on Kline's face, finishing her question. "What's going to happen if they don't see progress?"

"Well, if I stop coming around, that means they're running out of patience and have sent me somewhere awful as punishment. If that happens, they'll probably take you to a WBD factory somewhere and give you a job. They'll try to get you settled into a new life where you can try to forget about this whole big mess." He shrugged and looked apologetic. "I'm sorry, but I don't want to lie to you."

Juliet forced a smile, knowing full well that he'd already lied to her a dozen times. "It's nice that you don't pull your punches. Thank you." They sipped their water, then Juliet's nose told her the food had arrived. She turned to look over her shoulder as the synth approached with a tray and two steaming plates, depositing the lasagna, garlic bread, and roasted vegetables in front of them without a word.

Before it could depart, however, Kline said, "Two glasses of Chianti."

"Apologies, sir, but we've yet to receive our full inventory. I'm afraid the best I can do is a California Merlot."

"Good enough." Kline looked at Juliet, raising an eyebrow. "That all right?"

"Um, sure." As the synth padded away on the new-looking gray carpeting, she locked eyes with Kline, bit the bullet, and asked, "Can you tell me a little about that? I, uh, only know about red versus white when it comes to wine."

The truth was, she wanted to get him talking so she had an excuse to stare into his eyes long enough to get a deep dive going. She was glad Angel had reminded her; the whole process was foggy, but she knew she could get what she needed if she just dug deeply enough.

"Oh, right. Sure. You see, there are different kinds of red wine, and they all have different qualities and complement different sorts of food . . ." While he spoke, he had a pleasant expression on his face, apparently glad for the distraction.

Juliet stared into his greenish-blue irises and slowly inhaled, remembering it was a good way to *pull* thoughts to her. Mentally, she urged him to tell her what he knew about listeners, scans, and her fate with WBD.

When the world lurched and *shifted*, she caught her breath, cleared her throat, and reached up to straighten her tie.

"Ahem," Kline said, coughing as he straightened his tie and then his collar. The trip had been too damn long, and now he was following this damn synth through a rat's maze of corridors with air that felt stifling and dead, as though the air cyclers hadn't been fully enabled. "Why couldn't we meet on the lab level?"

"My instructions are to bring you to the regional vice president's office." The synth sounded robotic, which wasn't surprising; the thing looked like one. When was the last time he'd seen a nonhuman-modded synth at a WBD facility? It was unnerving that he couldn't remember one, and so far, he'd seen at least a dozen since his arrival. *"We're almost there, sir."*

Kline decided to save his breath and just follow the thing. It led him down a few more corridors before stopping in front of a nondescript door with a paper label taped to the surface that read, *"Regional VP Montclair."*

"Here we are, sir. I will wait here to show you out."

Kline nodded and knocked on the door. An all too familiar voice barked, *"Come,"* and Kline pulled the door open before stepping into a disturbingly empty room. The walls were bare. The floor was the same plasteel as the corridor outside. The only light source was an overhead LED fixture, and the only furnishing was a standing desk with a single data deck sitting at its center.

Before the desk was Regional Vice President Montclair. Kline sighed in relief that at least it was only him and not also his three creepy counterparts.

"Hello, Mr. Montclair."

"Stand closer, Mr. Kline." The man turned to regard him, his long face impassive with drooping, perpetually frowning lips. His eyes were dark, his skin too taut—too many antiaging treatments, if Kline were guessing. Still, his suit was immaculate, perfectly tailored, probably worth something similar to Kline's new car. He almost groaned, thinking of the car—he'd had to leave it behind, tucked away in a storage shed under a tarp. *"Well?"* Montclair prompted.

"Um," Kline was, as usual, entirely thrown off by the weird asshole. *"I'm here?"*

"Yes, that's obvious. What's your plan with your client? I've called you here to put a little urgency behind your actions, to provide a bit of impetus."

"You should have a full breakdown of my team's strategy. We intend to ease her into her memories, address concerns incrementally, and help her see WBD in a more favorable light—"

"Don't bore me with a rehash of the presentation your assistant already sent to my PAI."

Kline was beginning to feel irritated. This asshole was talking to him like he was the old lady herself. *"So, what do you want me to say?"*

"I want to know what you're going to do if . . ." He let the word hang as though Kline could fill in the blank.

"If?" Kline didn't feel like playing games.

*"If your plan takes too long or doesn't work! Mr. Kline, we've allocated far too many resources, in my not-so-humble opinion, to your project. Space is precious. Every human resource needs to be used at one hundred percent efficiency. Putting

that aside, we need to consider the cost of this latest acquisition. We've lost billions to retaliatory strikes by those allied with her."

"Those sites were slated for decommissioning."

"Regardless, Mr. Kline, we had plans involving them. We've had to adjust, and our new plans aren't optimal. Good, but not optimal." The entire time the man dressed him down, he didn't scowl or raise his voice. He spoke clearly, without much emotion at all. It was unnerving, to say the least.

While Kline tried to gather himself and bite down on the urge to punch him in the mouth, Mr. Montclair sighed and asked, as though speaking to a toddler, "Well? What if, Mr. Kline?"

"I didn't realize there was a 'too long' to worry about, sir. I think my plan will work, but I know it will take time. Is there a limit you have in mind?"

"Yes. You have a month to show progress. I warned you about the resources. The space is a big problem, but also the other things—the personnel, especially the listener. We're down to nine; you know that, yes? Nine critical employees out of a total of more than one million. Think about that, Kline. Do you think your rehab is that important? I don't. We have the Angel 3.0 models. We have your subject's DNA. Whether you turn her or not, we're set to have a spectacular first generation."

"You've started the cloning process?"

"No. We took some of her eggs. We've fertilized our samples and begun the rapid maturing of the first dozen. When we've proven viability, we'll begin the cloning."

Kline felt his mouth go dry, feeling his blood turn to ice as his heart began to race. "Jesus Christ, are you serious?" Something in him broke. Were all of his plans for nothing? Was his desire to turn Juliet, to make her an ally, just a dream?

He'd had long meetings, heartfelt talks, with Gentry herself, and she'd agreed with him. She'd spoken long into the night, drinking her damn bourbon, about how great it would be to have a willing asset like Juliet and the Angel prototype. All the while, she'd been working on this plan? All the while, her damn pocket VPs had been creating this monstrous protocol? They took her eggs? They were already growing—

He couldn't take it. Kline clenched his fist and growled, "You're going to kill her, aren't you? You're going to say my methods are too slow, and you're going to put her into a goddamn recycler and create your little monsters to do God-knows-what!"

"God has nothing to do with this, Mr. Kline. Juliet's fate is in your hands. You have one month; however, the first session with my listener will be in five days. We might just wrap things up early, hmm?"

For the first time, Montclair smiled, and it was the most awful thing Kline had ever seen. It was a vile expression of pure evil, and his pounding heart couldn't take it. He gritted his teeth and swung a fist, trusting that Mrs. Gentry would weigh his years of service in the balance when it came time for his disciplinary committee.

He needn't have worried. Montclair moved like wind and light: there one moment, gone the next. Kline's fist whooshed through the air, and then, a viselike grip took his wrist, twisted, and shoved.

Montclair pressed Kline's cheek into the plasteel wall as he bent his arm further. He screamed as his shoulder dislocated with a wet pop that seemed somehow too loud to come out of his body. Montclair released him, and he slid to his knees, hearing the executive open the door and say, "Escort him to the infirmary. He'll need that arm fixed before his first meeting with his client."

"Juliet? You in there?" Juliet felt a gentle jostle of her shoulder, and she blinked rapidly as the sights and sounds of the world came back to her. She felt sick, nauseous, disoriented, and utterly horrified.

She groaned, wanting to cry, wanting to scream, wanting to press her hands into her stomach. She thought she'd been violated before—kept unconscious, her mind messed with, put into a prison cell. They'd done so much more, so much worse! They took her eggs and were growing *things* with them!

Juliet? Angel's voice came to her, and tears sprang into her eyes as Kline continued to jostle her shoulder gently. She squeezed them shut, biting back on the urge to scream or cry or lash out. Again, Angel's voice came. *Juliet, you did a deep dive, didn't you? I'm sorry if it was horrible. Is Kline a monster?*

As she squeezed her eyes closed and took deep breaths to buy a few seconds, she subvocalized, "I don't know about Kline, but he certainly works for some monsters." Kline must have noticed her trying to regulate her breathing because he backed off, releasing her shoulder.

"No," she heard him say. "Don't touch her." At those words, Juliet opened her eyes and saw the synth's feet stepping back as though it had been about to lift her up. Lift her up? Juliet realized she was on the floor beside the table.

"I'm okay," she croaked, her throat dry. She hoped Angel would know the words were for her as much as Kline. "God, um, what happened?"

Kline chuckled nervously. "I was telling you about wine, and then you sort of just drooped out of your chair! I would have laughed if I wasn't so worried. You slid down almost gracefully!"

"I'm lightheaded. I don't think I've had enough to drink. Water, I mean." Juliet pushed herself to a sitting position and saw Kline squatting beside her, genuine concern on his face.

Of course he was concerned! He was probably dog meat just as much as she was if his little rehab plan failed. She saw the synth still hovering nearby and imagined that creepy exec, Montclair, watching her through its eyes.

Determined to put on a show for Kline's bosses if not for him, she tried to channel her old self, the girl who only knew rumors about how bad corps could be.

"I'm fine, really; please don't make me go back, Mr. Kline! I'm hungry, and I want that lasagna!" She chuckled outwardly, while inside, she tried to push her horror down into the ball of growing fury at the center of her stomach.

"All right, all right. Let's take it slow, though." He turned to the synth. "Get us some more water, and bring us some dessert right away. I think some sugar will do you good, Juliet."

The synth hurried away, and Juliet allowed Kline to help her stand. Shakily, she returned to her seat and drained her water. While she took a bite of lasagna, trying to smile and act like she enjoyed it, she let her mind wander to dark thoughts and dark plans.

What she'd forgotten about deep dives was that she did much more than witness the scene being played out. She didn't just see the events—she experienced them. Being in Kline's head had given her a complete perspective of everything he'd been thinking about, including the listener. She knew exactly what it was and what it would do.

If Montclair wanted to mess with her, if he wanted to have his pet reach out and listen to her mind, she was going to reach back. They might have nine listeners right now, but after Thursday, Juliet was betting they'd only have eight.

20

PUSHING

Aya looked at the readout, frowning as she scanned the nav system's list of repeated trips; it wasn't hard to see which one was the place Lucky had been doing her sword training and hanging out with her "merc friends," as she'd often labeled them. The only other locations with frequent stops were restaurants, stores, and Dr. Ladia's clinic.

"Anything?" Bennet asked, skeptically eyeing Juliet's bike and the deck in Aya's hand. "She's gonna be pissed if you broke the security—"

"She's missing, Benny!" Aya stared daggers at him. "Besides, I didn't break anything."

Bennet folded his arms, sighing as he leaned against the rolling tool chest. They were in the gunship's hangar, where they'd stowed most of their tools and parts—at least those that weren't back on the *Kowashi*. "She told us she was going down planetside. She told us she might be out of touch for a while."

"Not almost a month! She thought it might only take a week or so!" Aya didn't like that Bennet was a safe target for her frustration, but it was what it was.

"You know how her work can be. Don't you think we'd have heard something if, you know . . ." He trailed off. Apparently, even his bravado wouldn't allow him to say what they were all fearing.

She locked eyes with him for a moment, then turned back to the deck. "Anyway, I got an address. I'm going to go see if her mercenary friends know anything." Aya unplugged the deck and carefully began closing up the access panel on Lucky's bike.

"Can you wait until after the reactor inspection on the *Kowashi*? I have to be there to sign off, but I'll come with you after—"

"Nope." Aya tightened the last screw and gently wiped the shiny panel with a microfiber towel before re-enabling the bike's security; she'd given herself access after using an exploit to bypass it. Of course, after doing that, she'd patched the exploit, so she saw the whole thing as a wash morally. Besides, Lucky would have given her access if she'd asked. Right? "I'm leaving now. Don't worry, I'll tell you everything."

"Well, keep a comm channel open. We don't know what these people are like."

"Bennet!" Aya stepped closer to him and gripped his too-big biceps. "They're Lucky's friends. They'll be nice." She gave him a quick squeeze before hurrying to the access door that would take her into the port.

"Be careful!" Bennet called once more as she slipped through and merged with the busy midday rush of people going to and from shuttle-access corridors. Twenty minutes later, she was riding in the back of a cab, nervously clutching her hands, idly tracing the knuckles of her cybernetic hand with the pointer finger of her natural one. Whenever she looked at the hand, she thought of Lucky, which sparked new pangs of worry.

She'd been staring at it and the beautiful paint on the *Cherry Blossom* when she'd finally thrown up her hands and decided to crack the security on the motorcycle. Three weeks late with no message wasn't going to work. It wasn't okay. It was time to get more proactive!

With that thought giving her courage, Aya stepped out of the cab and looked up at the mirrored diamatex facade of the BizRes Tower complex. Stepping into the lobby, she crossed the quiet, carpeted space to the occupant directory, swiping the screens from right to left, scanning the names for something that sounded familiar.

When nothing stood out, and she saw that about a quarter of the occupants were unlisted, Aya began to despair. "Oh, Lucky! Why'd you have to have so many secrets?"

She stood there, a few meters from the elevators, and stared at the directory while her mind ran through one crazy idea after another, ranging from standing in the lobby with a sign to trying to contact every one of the nearly two thousand residents and businesses.

As she glanced at the camera by the elevators, the kernel of a crazy idea began to form in her mind. What if she got access to the footage? "I could look for Lucky, then track her through the elevator's feed, then—"

"Miss Aya," Hector, her PAI, interrupted, his voice lovably stodgy, "I have to caution you against doing anything that might get you into trouble."

"Hector! We have to help Lucky, and I can't do that if I don't have a clue where she is." Aya frowned at a woman who walked by, staring a little too intently at her. She folded her arms over her chest and stared back until the redhead looked away and touched the call button. Aya usually spoke aloud to Hector, and it took a conscious effort to subvocalize. Still, after the woman's reaction, she switched to subvocalizations.

"All I need to do is find the security office for the building. What if I made up a story about a missing girl . . ." She let her words trail off as the redhead turned away from the elevator and took a tentative step toward her.

The woman was dressed smartly in a stylish pearl-grey skirt, a frilly, pale-yellow blouse, and heels that Aya wouldn't know how to wear. She clutched a tall, steaming cup of coffee in one hand, and as she stepped closer, she smiled disarmingly. Her cheeks flushed a little at Aya's glare, highlighting her freckles. Aya couldn't help thinking she was pretty, especially when her bright green eyes twinkled with her smile. Her initial irritation at being stared at began to melt. "Um, can I help you?"

"I wasn't trying to be nosy, but I swear I heard you say you wanted to help someone named Lucky. Is that right?" She had a friendly voice, and something about the hesitation in her tone made her seem nervous. Of course, that only made Aya want to reassure her.

"It's okay, and yeah—my friend is missing."

"You, um, you have a friend named Lucky?"

Aya sighed and waved her mechanical hand, her arms still crossed over her T-shirt's chest. "Yeah, it's just her handle. I know she came to this building a lot, but I don't know where exactly."

"Is that so?" The woman took a few steps closer, eyeing her up and down. When she stood just a half meter away, she nodded slowly and then held out her hand. "Your name's Aya, right? My name's Frida, and you could say I'm friends with Lucky, too."

After Kline escorted her back to her room, Juliet said she felt like a nap, hoping to get some quiet time to explain her deep dive into Kline's mind to Angel. Kline had agreed that it was a good idea and let her know that her schedule was clear for the rest of the day. Juliet got him to promise to work on her list of requests before he left, and when he did, turning to go through the door, she swore she could feel the dread bleeding off him in waves.

She knew why, of course, having caught a glimpse of his calendar—he had to meet with Montclair that afternoon.

She moved to the couch-bed and flopped down, letting the gel wrap around her body. Now that she had some memories back, she realized the bed almost reminded her of an acceleration couch. The gel had a similar feel. "Well," she subvocalized, "are you ready to hear this?"

Yes!

So Juliet told Angel about her deep dive. She told her about the creepy exec, Montclair, and his ultimatum to Kline. She described the listener and how it was a weird mix of Grave's GIPEL tech and WBD-designed external hardware. Worse, she knew it was very good at doing precisely what the name implied: listening. When she told Angel about her eggs and about Montclair's mention of an "Angel 3.0," the only thing Angel said was, *I'm so sorry, Juliet.*

"How fast could they possibly grow them? He mentioned accelerated-growth protocols or something like that."

Not all that fast. First of all, that sort of tech is illegal on human embryos. Obviously, that won't stop them, but even so, it's impossible—at least in published studies—to speed mammalian growth beyond a six-fold increase—not without massive defects.

"So, they could be growing my kids into adults within a few years? Into children they can brainwash and train in one?" Juliet felt furious tears pool in her eyes, and she turned to face the back of the couch, unwilling to let her enemies see her cry.

They're not your kids, Juliet! Though it isn't any better to imagine, they'll likely try to cultivate the traits you have that make you valuable. They'll try to isolate those genes, and it may take several generations before they—

"Stop. Please, Angel, just stop." Juliet wanted to scream that they were *her* eggs, that everything those awful creeps were doing was somehow connected to her now. Instead, she closed her eyes and focused on her breathing. When she felt calm, she subvocalized, "I don't want to know more. I'm just glad that whatever they've done couldn't have progressed very far because I'm going to destroy it all."

How? What are you going to do about the listener?

"Well, I don't remember everything yet, but I remember getting blasted by Joshua Kyle. If this listener is set up to receive, I'm going to give him a little more than he asked for. I just need to confirm that I know how Kyle did what he did."

We've speculated about that, Juliet. It must be related to the telekinesis, but you've never wanted to practice, fearing to harm your test subject.

"Yeah, I know, Angel. I don't know if it's the clarity of having a mind that's half empty—missing all those memories and the baggage that comes with them—but I had an idea almost immediately after I slipped out of the deep dive. Maybe it was the shock of learning what they did to me, but I didn't feel disoriented when I came out of it. I was just angry, and along with that anger, I *knew* what I had to do."

Tell me!

"I believe Joshua Kyle was, as you said, pushing his telekinetic energy out in a wave, raw and untuned. I think I've already gone beyond that. I think I know exactly how to do it, and I've *been* doing it, only with more nuance. Every time I channel Lacy Blake or . . . I forget; I know I've channeled others, but I'm missing the memories. It's not important. Every time I do that, I notice people reacting more than they should. They're *feeling* what I'm sending out."

You think . . . You think you already know how to do what Kyle did?

"Yeah, but better. I can send an emotion, a *feeling.* I can make people *believe* something. It's like I push a feeling or intent so hard that their brain just accepts it. After my deep dive, I had a simple, clarifying thought: I don't have to hurt someone to test this. I can send a nice feeling just as easily as I can send something awful. We'll try it; I've got tonight and tomorrow to figure it out, and then, when the listener comes, I'll be ready."

You never cease to surprise me, Juliet. Even after what they did, you're concerned about harming innocents. Even here, in the depths of a WBD installation, you believe there might be people deserving of mercy.

"Don't go too far—I still want to burn this place down, but, yeah, seeing Kline's mind for a minute, I was reminded that monsters are usually created by other monsters. I'm not saying he's a good guy, but he definitely isn't as bad as the people he answers to." Juliet inhaled shakily, thinking about her visit to Kline's mind and the things Montclair said.

Reaching down while still facing the couch back, she pressed her fingertips to her lower abdomen, running them outward toward her hips. "Do you think they took them all?"

Unequivocally, they did not. As soon as you mentioned what that monster said, I sent the nanites to investigate. You still have your ovaries and most of the ova you should have at your age. They must have been uncharacteristically reserved in their harvesting. It makes me wonder if more than one faction within WBD is involved with all of this. Montclair may have ordered the collection, but he may also have feared damaging you, at least at that time.

Juliet breathed in and out deeply, her eyes closed, letting Angel's soothing words wash over her. She tried not to think about Montclair and his chilling meeting with Kline, but she couldn't stop the other things she'd seen in Kline's head from dancing through her mind's eye.

Factions? She kept seeing a woman—perfect platinum blonde hair, too smooth, ageless face, piercing silver-blue irises that saw straight into her soul, all packaged in a stereotypical Western shirt and faded blue jeans—Gentry.

She was a confounding influence on Kline's mind; someone he thought supported him but whom he feared was betraying him on a constant basis.

When a chime woke her up, Juliet's first thought was one of irritation with herself; she didn't have time to sleep the day away. The chime sounded again, and she turned over, facing away from the couch to see a green LED flashing above the opaque panel in the center of the door. She stood and padded over to it, subvocalizing, "Angel, you shouldn't have let me go to sleep."

It's good for you, and I think you'll find fewer gaps in your memory! The nanites make better progress when you sleep.

As Juliet leaned toward the opaque viewscreen, wondering if there was a hidden button to activate something, it clarified to show an unassuming woman on the other side of the door. She wore a blue bodysuit, much like the ones Juliet had been given, but she had a white lab coat over the top.

Her hair was brown and pulled back into a bun, exposing a face that instantly made Juliet think of a data-entry specialist or a filing clerk—someone who spent all day under artificial lights, staring at enhanced UI elements. She was very plain, very pale, and had dark circles under her eyes that hinted at too little sleep.

As the woman spoke, her voice came through sounding a little tinny, "Hello, Juliet. I'm Harriet, one of the techs assigned to your case. I have your dinner if you'd like me to bring it in."

Juliet backed away from the door, nodding. "Sure," she replied, confident the woman could hear her whether she spoke into the little viewscreen or not.

The door *beeped, clicked,* and *thunked* before swinging outward to reveal Harriet and the cart beside her. Juliet looked into the space beyond and saw that little had changed since she'd passed through with Kline. The only difference she was sure of was a tablet-size data deck on the single desk that hadn't been there before.

Harriet pushed the cart forward, smiling. "I'm glad your meeting with Mr. Kline went well this morning. He's given me the okay to deliver your meals without an escort, though that didn't stop him from leaving guards lurking outside in the hallway." She framed the statement as a positive, but Juliet was certain the woman was trying to let her know that guards were nearby without framing it as a threat. Was she scared? "Do you want the meal by the table or the couch?"

"Um, the table, I guess." Juliet backed away, folding her hands before her, watching as Harriet wheeled the cart past the couch and over to the table. Seizing the unexpected opportunity, Juliet asked, "Will you sit with me while I eat?"

"Uh, I'm not really supposed to." Harriet didn't look her way as she parked the cart and turned back to the door.

"Please? I'm so . . . alone in here." She tapped her temple. "I don't even have a PAI. It's so *boring*!"

Harriet turned to look at her, hands on hips, and shrugged. "I guess I could sit with you for a while. The protocols say to deliver the food and allow you an hour to finish before collecting the service cart. It doesn't specify that I'm to leave you alone while you eat—"

"Perfect!" Juliet clapped her hands together then hurried over to the cart. She lifted the aluminum tray top, revealing a single plate of food. She studied the French fries, a small, dry-looking hamburger, and a dish of mixed, syrupy fruit. Trying to remember that she was Juliet, the scrapyard worker, she smiled. "Wow! Is that a real burger?"

"Doubtful," Harriet replied, sitting down across from her. "If they use the same kitchens that service the cafeteria, it's a textured legume patty."

"Oh, good!" Juliet turned her grin on Harriet. "Not sure I'd like real beef. Have you ever had it?" She unloaded the tray onto the table and sat down.

"Me? Only vat-grown. I liked it all right, but I'm just as happy with this kind of food. I'm simple."

Juliet stuffed a fry in her mouth and chewed, noting the soggy interior and too-crisp exterior. Still, it was salty, and she was hungry, so she wolfed it down. "Thirsty?" she asked, standing and pointing at the food and drink dispenser.

"No, thank you. That would break the rules, I'm sure."

"Ah." Juliet nodded, selected cola, then carried the fizzing cup back to the table. "So," she asked, stuffing another couple of fries in her mouth and talking around them as she chewed, "how long have you worked for WBD?"

"Eleven years next month. I was pretty excited to be moved to your, um, case. I hope we can help you recover quickly."

"Thank you!" Juliet picked up her burger and took a bite. It wasn't bad if she thought of it as a sandwich. The sauce was good and made the dry patty and bun more than palatable. Of course, being hungry helped. She pushed her tray toward Harriet and mumbled, "Fry?" To her surprise, Harriet took one and nibbled on it. "Could you tell me a little about my schedule tomorrow? Kline said something about a, uh, counselor."

As Harriet replied, going over the next day's schedule, Juliet focused on her eyes, allowing her voice to become a background hum as she concentrated. This time, however, she wasn't trying to pull any thoughts—she was *pushing* feelings of happiness and camaraderie.

She'd come up with the idea as soon as she'd seen Harriet's face through the view panel on the door. She didn't want to alarm anyone or hurt someone who didn't deserve it, so she tried to think of a feeling anyone would love to have, just as she'd told Angel she could.

Of course, Aya and Bennet came to mind. Were those newly recovered memories? She couldn't remember thinking about them since waking up in her current predicament, and she had to guess it was simply because those memories had been blocked.

They were there now, though, and what wonderful feelings to share! She loved them both, but her memories of long nights spent with Aya watching vids, reading books, eating snacks, and laughing—lots and lots of laughing—were priceless to her. That was the feeling she was trying to *push* at Harriet, and Juliet's smile grew wider and wider as she saw the effects.

Harriet's eyes were aglow, and she spoke breathlessly about all sorts of things, her words rambling from topic to topic without prodding. She talked about her old position as a lab tech in the failing R&D department at a lesser-known WBD affiliate called Galaxy Medicine.

She rambled on and on about a chief scientist she had a crush on, and then, when Juliet prompted her about her thoughts on Kline, she began to gush about how surprised she'd been when she'd seen how handsome and well-dressed he was. Juliet nodded along and kept *pushing* her "Aya feelings."

They talked for well over an hour, and Harriet ended up eating half her fries and accepting a cola after just twenty minutes or so. By the time she left, she was promising to write a memo advocating for Juliet to be given permission to use an offline data deck. She insisted she wanted to help curate a vid library for her on the device.

"Good night, Juliet! I'm so glad I get to work with you! I hope you sleep well; tomorrow shouldn't be a bad day. You'll visit with Doctor Chen, get some time to exercise, and then have your regular meeting with Mr. Kline. I bet he'll have all sorts of things for you!"

"Thank you, Harriet! I hope I'll see you, too?"

"Yep! I'll be on duty. See you in the morning." She smiled, practically beaming, as she slowly pushed the door shut. Juliet turned as the locks engaged and lay on the couch, facing away from the door. She was going to shower and do some stretching before going to sleep, but first, she wanted to decompress and talk to Angel.

Angel had the same idea. *Did you cause that? Her turnaround?*

"Yep. Just like I told you, I can push feelings, Angel. I made her feel like I do when I'm hanging out with Aya."

That's incredible, Juliet! I knew there was more to the lattice, more to your gut feelings and ability to channel personas, but I didn't realize you could do this. What will you "push" to the listener?

"Still thinking about that one, but . . ." Juliet let the thought hang for a minute while she considered. Was it the listener's fault? She shook her head at the idea—no pulling punches. "Something horrifying, Angel. I'll make touching my mind so horrible that they'll lie and say everything's fine." In the silence following that declaration, Juliet added, "To do it right, I need to remember everything. Please keep working on my memories."

I will, Juliet. I'm sorry you have to.

"Have to what?"

Remember everything, even the . . . unpleasant experiences.

"I need them, Angel. They make me who I am. If I don't have the dark, scary memories, then men like Montclair can scare me. I need to remember everything so I can remind myself that *he* should be scared of *me*."

21

FACT FROM FICTION

Kline sat at the too-narrow desk in his too-small office—a severe downgrade from the suite he'd had in the Phoenix facility—and frowned at the report his PAI had generated. "This all happened after I left?"

Ruby's voice carried a note of droll clinical detachment. "It all happened in the space of ninety minutes when Harriet brought in the dinner service."

"Get her in here, will you?"

"It's early, Kline—"

"Now, Ruby." Kline sighed and stared at the blank walls in his cubicle-size personal space. He felt like being an asshole, but was that just the lingering effect of his meeting with Montclair? Talk about an asshole! Ever since he'd taken a swing at the exec, Kline had been on his back foot. Why hadn't the son of a bitch written it up? Now, it was like an axe hanging over his neck every time they met. He wondered if the old lady knew.

"Of course she does," he muttered. He was due for his first debrief with her that afternoon, and Kline wasn't looking forward to it.

"Harriet is on her way." Ruby again showed how smart she was and ignored his other comment, recognizing he was speaking for his own benefit.

Kline drummed his fingers on the desk, trying to keep his mind blank while he waited, and only seven minutes later, a tentative knock sounded. "Come in and sit down, Harriet." The door opened, and the mousy lab tech entered, ducking her head nervously as she chose the chair on the left.

"Good morning, Mr. Kline."

"Harriet, can you explain to me why you were giggling and carrying on like a schoolgirl with our client yesterday evening? Honestly, if we weren't taking daily samples, and if the security AI didn't scrutinize your every move, I'd be afraid you were on drugs."

Helpful as always, Ruby had the little holoprojector at his desk play the portion of the conversation between Harriet and Juliet when Harriet giggled about how surprised she'd been to see that Kline was "handsome."

"Oh, um. I'm sorry, Mr. Kline." Harriet looked away, her pale cheeks flushed crimson. "I really don't know what came over me. She's just so personable and nice. She, well, she drew something out of me that I didn't realize was there. I'm so sorry, Mr. Kline! I wanted to make her comfortable and help with the process by giving her a good impression and—"

"Take a breath, Harriet. You're not in trouble; not yet. However, this is something we need to monitor. It's possible that Juliet is simply good at connecting with people; she may be highly empathic, but there could be more at work here. If she's trying to manipulate you, that's something we need to keep an eye on. Would you say your reaction to her was uncharacteristic of your usual demeanor?"

"Yes! Very much so, but she didn't say anything manipulative; she mostly just listened to me. I don't know—when I returned to my quarters last night, I couldn't stop thinking about her and everything she's been through. To lose your memories and wake up in a strange place like this"—Harriet waved her hand around—"and still remain kind and upbeat? I really want things to work out for her!"

Kline nodded and scratched his chin, frowning when he felt a spot of stubble he'd missed. He regarded Harriet for several seconds, watching her eyes dart toward him, then quickly away. She was waiting to see what he'd say, waiting to hear his reaction. He inhaled deeply through his nose and slowly exhaled the same way, drumming his fingers. After a moment, he subvocalized, "Did you check to see if we have the Empathanil in stock?"

"In stock, and Doctor Rivers confirmed her lab is capable of fabricating more."

Kline nodded, clearing his throat. "My PAI is setting up a self-assessment for you. You'll need to complete it daily. The lab AI will prompt you with a few questions, and if you answer them honestly, you won't get into any trouble. We're also setting up a protocol so that if you find you're feeling influenced by the client, you can get the help you need to remain objective.

"I want this posting to work out for you, Harriet; I don't want one of the new synth models to get this position. I believe Juliet needs a human touch, and I want her to *want* to work with us. So, be honest with us and yourself; if you need adjusting, we can help. Wouldn't that be better than if *they* replaced you?" Kline indicated the ceiling with his eyes and hoped Harriet would get the hint.

"Yes." She nodded rapidly. "Um, what sort of protocol, though?"

"It's an injection that will help you remain objective." Kline waved his hand dismissively as Harriet's eyes widened. "It's completely temporary. If we have to use it, we'll slowly taper you off it when the project is complete. Trust me, it's better to be objective and on the job than to be too empathic and replaced by a synth. You don't want that, and neither do I."

"I . . . understand, Mr. Kline." Harriet nodded, pressing her lips together. Kline had to smile; she was putting on a brave face.

"Come on, you can watch while I give Juliet some good news." Kline stood and picked up the plastic crate sitting on the floor beside his desk. "I have some of the things she requested."

When Juliet awoke the next day, she was wrapped in a blanket with her face buried in the crook of the couch, two pillows atop her head. She lay still for several heartbeats, trying to remember where she was. When it all clicked into place, she realized she had new memories vying for her attention. She remembered the raid, and worse, she remembered the people she'd been with.

"What happened to Barns and the others?" she subvocalized, acutely aware that there were sensors pointed her way that would hear even the tiniest of whispers.

I don't know! My memories of that night mirror yours. My . . . existence in this state is more susceptible to your body's chemistry than when I was housed in my chip. When you lost consciousness, I couldn't easily access your implants. It didn't help that they kept you inside a jamming field for the duration of your transit between Colorado and wherever this is. The whole experience is strangely blurry to me, and I think that's due to me being so entwined with your physiology.

"I hope they're okay. I hope whatever team took me just left them. I remember Barns, though—a vague memory of his thoughts. He wasn't out, and you know he wouldn't go down easily. Still, maybe they just incapacitated him."

Despite her hopeful words, Juliet knew she was lying to herself. She imagined she had two selves, two mirrored halves of Juliet. One was a dark shadow standing over the other wearing a grim expression, wanting her to acknowledge what she really believed: WBD wouldn't leave witnesses behind.

Before she moved, Juliet tried to take stock of her other memories and found she felt almost normal. As she retraced the days leading up to her capture, she thought of Ghoul and nearly yelped, her eyes opening wide. "Oh my God," she subvocalized. "Angel, I just remembered Ghoul. What must she think?"

The attack on us couldn't have gone unnoticed. Ghoul's not stupid; she'll put two and two together and realize you didn't leave willingly.

"I just hope she stays safe and doesn't try to do anything. I mean, what could she do? WBD wouldn't have left clues, right?"

I agree. Besides, Ghoul herself told you she can't leave. She's very invested in the commune and the work they're doing, not to mention her newfound relationship with her sister and niece.

"Right." Juliet sighed, feeling a little knot loosen in her chest. She did *not* want Ghoul dragged into this mess. Throwing her blanket off, she went to the bathroom, where she showered and cleaned up before eating a protein bar and drinking a cup of coffee.

She was folding her blanket and stowing it under the couch when the door beeped. Juliet looked at the display panel and saw Kline's face. "Come in," she called as if she had a choice in the matter.

The door made its unlocking noises then swung wide, revealing a grinning Kline and the gray plastic crate he held before him. "Good morning, Juliet."

Images of violence flashed through Juliet's mind. She thought about darting forward, striking Kline in the throat with her cybernetic arm, sweeping his legs as he tumbled backward, and then charging out into the facility, hell-bent on killing anyone who got in her way. If she could just take out the first pair of corpo-sec, get their gear—

Juliet! Angel's voice interrupted her imagined red rampage.

She smiled. "Good morning, Mister—er, uh, I mean, good morning, Kline."

He stepped in, hefting the crate slightly so the contents rattled. "I come bearing gifts."

Juliet moved to the side and sat down, leaving the center of the couch open. "You seem to be in a good mood."

"Well, it's a big day! After I show you your presents, I'm going to walk you over to meet Doctor Chen. I think you'll enjoy talking with her, and if I'm not mistaken, today she's going to give you some exercises that might start you on the road to recovering your memories. How does that sound?"

"It sounds good, really, um, Kline, it does. Will I get a chance to exercise? I'm feeling awfully cooped up."

"Oh yes, absolutely. Harriet will accompany us, and after you meet with Doctor Chen, she'll escort you to the exercise room. How are you holding up on clean clothes? If I'm not mistaken, your laundered items should be cleaned and returned to you this afternoon."

"I still have a few of these, uh, bodysuits that are clean. I was looking forward to swimming; will I get a swimsuit?"

Kline chuckled and reached out to grab the thin, flexible material of Juliet's sleeve. It was so close-fitting that he almost had to pinch her to grasp the fabric. She fought to keep a straight face and resisted pulling her arm back. "I know it seems weird, but this suit is designed to be worn in any environment, even the pool. It'll dry faster than your skin would."

"Really?"

"Yep. It's good stuff. Wish I didn't have a dress code, or I'd wear one." Kline sighed, reaching up to adjust the knot of his tie.

"Well, I think your suit looks nice." Juliet wasn't sure if she was trying to be friendly or if she was trying to put him off guard.

He smirked a little but didn't look her in the eyes as he lifted the lid off the plastic crate.

"Okay. First, the good news." He lifted a slim, matte-black data deck, about ten centimeters by five and only a few millimeters thick. "They're going to give you this data deck, but it's nothing special. You can plug into it, though. The techs had to write a program to make it interface with your optics since you don't have a PAI to manage the connection, but they've promised me it'll work. It's totally offline, so I had to upload a small library of vids. If you hate what I picked or have specific requests, let me or Harriet know, and we can probably get whatever you want downloaded."

Juliet took the tiny deck in her hands and beamed. "Thank you, Kline!"

This will help immensely, Juliet. I can write scripts to manage all of your cybernetics when you plug into the device. Don't worry about their software; I'll wall it off.

"Well, I thought you'd be disappointed, to be honest. It's got a few games one of the techs installed, but it's still a pretty low-end device."

Juliet laughed. "This is way nicer than any deck I've ever used, Mister Kline! It's so compact! I love it." Kline's eyes flickered with understanding, and he nodded.

"Yeah. You know, I'd almost forgotten about your missing memories. I still have an image in my mind that I built up while trying to find you. Let's just say high-end electronics were part of that image." He dug around in the crate and lifted out a plastic caddy containing several small jars of paint.

"You hate the white walls, right? Here's some paint. I didn't know what colors to get, so I asked for a variety. If you tell me which ones you like, I can get you more." He also took a three-pack of paintbrushes of varying sizes from the box.

"This is perfect!" Juliet gushed, grabbing the paints and lifting out the little jars one by one, reading the labels. "For starters, I'm going to need a bigger jar of black and more sky blue."

"Heh. All right, Juliet. I'll make it happen. Here." He reached into the box and took out a thick book with a polymer binding—a more modern version of a paperback, but still not popular; everyone wanted to use their PAIs to read.

"Last present for the day. I asked around, but was only able to come up with one book. Everyone gave me grief, saying I should just download some books to your deck there. I did, of course; you'll find a few thousand popular titles on it. Anyway, you asked for physical books, so I wanted to do what I could. One of my team members, a tech you haven't met, had this lying around in a box and said you could have it."

Juliet took the book, suddenly feeling a little guilty. She loved books, and it was sobering to think that one of the people she was enemies with, one of the people she might end up hurting, had given her one. She gently fanned the pages with her thumb while reading the title aloud, "*The Hobbit*?"

"I guess it was a pretty famous book. You said you liked fantasy, right?"

Juliet! That's by J.R.R. Tolkien! Many credit him with laying the foundations for the fantasy genre!

"This is great, Kline. Thank you so much."

Kline smiled and leaned back. "You're happy with it?"

"Yes!" Juliet hugged the book to her chest.

"It's funny. We did a lot of research on you—I mean, when you went missing with the prototype. You know, hoping to learn about you and your habits. The idea was that knowing you better might allow us to find and help you more quickly. There weren't any notes about you reading books like that."

Juliet almost let her face betray her guilt. She *hadn't* been into reading before Angel. Even so, she couldn't imagine Kline's people could know everything about her. She plowed ahead with the first plausible lie she could think of, and while she did it, she *pushed* confidence.

"Well, whoever did your research wasn't so great. When I was younger, I had a few dozen books I got from my grandpa. Whenever I was sick or home alone, worried about my mom or sister, I'd curl up with one. They give me comfort, Kline."

"Nice." He nodded, inhaling deeply through his nose, then stood up. "Well? Shall we? Let's meet Doctor Chen, then you can exercise, and then it'll be lunchtime." He gestured to the items on the couch. "You can mess with this stuff this afternoon—your schedule is clear. Sound good?"

Juliet nodded and stood, following Kline out. In the lab space outside her room, she saw Harriet sitting at the only desk. She smiled at Juliet, even offering a quick wave before looking away as though she didn't want Kline to see the gesture. Juliet didn't have to fake the smile she shot back. At that moment, she resolved not to let any harm come to Harriet when it came time to make her move.

Kline didn't seem to notice; he was moving quickly, and Juliet followed him out past two corpo-sec goons, trying to predict each of his turns, ensuring she knew the floor's layout.

It wasn't hard—there were only two short corridors before they stepped into the large "counseling" area with the couches.

Things were a little different from the previous day. The lights were already on, soft pop music played in the background, and a woman sat on the center-most couch with her legs crossed, flipping through something on her AUI.

When Juliet and Kline stepped in, the woman stood and strode over, holding out a hand. She was short, with shoulder-length straight black hair, and wore clothes typical for a doctor: stylish gray slacks, sensible dress shoes, a tucked-in button-up blouse, and over it all, a lab coat much like Harriet's.

"Hello, Juliet. It's a pleasure to finally meet you. I'm Doctor Chen." Her handshake was firm and warm, and she held it for just the right amount of time. Juliet felt like it was the most clinically perfect handshake she'd ever had.

"Nice to meet you," she replied. Doctor Chen motioned toward the couch, and Juliet moved to sit.

"Mister Kline, would you please return for her in forty minutes? That should be enough time for us to get to know each other."

Kline nodded and turned to the door. "It'll be Harriet who picks you up, Juliet. I'll see you this afternoon unless my schedule gets away from me. If so, we'll talk tomorrow."

"Okay. Um, thanks for the, you know, book and stuff." As she spoke, Juliet wondered why it was so easy for her to play the innocent victim, the woman who was bewildered, lost, and thankful. Had she felt that way so often in her life that it came naturally?

Kline smiled and stepped out. Once the door slid shut, Doctor Chen turned to regard Juliet.

When she smiled and stepped closer, Juliet saw something—a subtle change in her demeanor. She still smiled, but it was a hard smile, and her eyes didn't reflect the emotion. They shone darkly, and it was very apparent to Juliet that this woman was restraining her emotions, forcing herself to appear civil. There was a dark, mean spirit behind those eyes. She grinned at Juliet, and the expression sent a shiver down her spine.

"Well, Juliet. What a time you've had, hmm? Don't you worry; we're going to get to the bottom of those missing memories."

"Yeah?" Juliet shifted, trying not to be obvious about her instinctual urge to get up and drop into a fighting stance. On a primal level, she felt this woman was a threat. There was something *off* about her.

"Oh yes. We'll uproot all the lies. What an ordeal!" She sat beside Juliet and turned toward her, opening those big dark-brown eyes to stare into Juliet's. It was almost effortless for Juliet to reach out. She didn't even think about it; she just inhaled and willed Chen's thoughts to come her way.

The ease with which she pulled was at odds with the result—nothing came to her. Chen's mind was as quiet as a grave as she continued to speak. "I know what it's like to be brainwashed. I'm an expert in the field. I know how difficult it is to face the idea that you're a victim of lies and deceit, especially when you thought you could trust the person who manipulated you."

Juliet was still reeling from the emptiness behind those eyes when she licked her lips and asked, "Person?"

"Angel, Juliet. She's really done a number on you, but we'll straighten things out. We'll separate fact from fiction."

22

\\\\\\\\\\\\\\\\\\\\\\

PARTS TO PLAY

When Harriet arrived to escort her to the exercise room, Juliet was more than ready. She'd *known* what Doctor Chen would do. She'd expected her to start laying the groundwork for a thorough gaslighting about Angel, but seeing it in practice was another thing altogether.

She'd tried to maintain her facade—a naive scrap worker who didn't even remember the rogue PAI the doctor was maligning—but she found herself wanting to tune the doctor out, to withdraw from her intensity, and by the end of their initial meeting, she couldn't really say what the doctor had thought of her or even if she might have seen through her act.

Of course, all of that was troubling for someone like Juliet, who was used to reading people like open books. It wasn't that she couldn't feel the doctor's animosity; it was barely hidden under the surface, simmering like a kettle ready to blow, but Juliet couldn't tell if it was entirely directed at her or if this woman was just plain *mean*.

Juliet could just as easily picture her pulling the limbs from a small animal as arranging a bouquet of flowers, and she was convinced the woman would wear the same joyless smile on her face in either situation.

She tried to read her several times, tried to pull thoughts out of that dark void behind her eyes, but she was met with silence. Was she shielding her thoughts from her? Was she some kind of mentalist, someone with an uncanny ability to lock her thoughts away, not unlike Lemur had done with his false personas? Or—and this sent shivers down Juliet's spine—was she a new kind of synth? She had to use the "new kind" qualifier because Juliet had scrutinized the woman and couldn't find any hint that she wasn't a natural human, nothing other than the emptiness behind that simmering animosity.

In any case, when Harriet arrived and rescued her, Juliet was eager to be gone from the strange woman's presence. In that first meeting, they'd only made small talk, and the doctor had suggested that Juliet might find herself remembering some small pieces of her missing memories the next time they met. Of course, she promised to help Juliet process them and see through the deceptions she'd "built up as reality."

Juliet could only suspect that, prior to her next appointment, Kline's people intended to unlock a small portion of the memories they'd stolen from her.

Thinking back to the glimpse of Kline's schedule she'd pulled from his mind, she knew they intended to do a "full scan" of her in two days, while tomorrow, the listener was scheduled to evaluate her. Did that mean they'd only make her visit Chen once a week? She hoped so.

"I'm supposed to stay with you while you exercise. Is there anything in particular you need?" Harriet asked, moving to sit on one of the benches lining the exercise room's wall.

"I think I mostly want to swim. I didn't get a chance to see if Kline put any, um, instructional videos for weights or anything like that on the deck he gave me."

"Well, the pool's up and running! They checked it out yesterday. All you have to do is get in and start swimming, and the current generator will kick on."

Juliet started toward the pool, but paused and turned to face the lab tech. "Harriet, how often will I have appointments with Doctor Chen?"

"That's up to the doctor and Kline. I know your next appointment is on Tuesday next week, but I'm not sure how often she'll see you after that. You're scheduled for TMS on Fridays, and Chen's protocol calls for at least two days between TMS and her appointments, so that's a limiting factor."

Juliet frowned and raised an eyebrow. "TMS?"

"Sorry about that—transcranial magnetic stimulation. I just got training on it, so yeah, you can pretty much consider me an expert now." She winked, sharing the joke of her words. "They use magnetic fields to stimulate nerve cells in the brain. Originally, it was designed to help treat depression, but Doctor Chen's developed methodologies that will, according to her, gradually bring your memories back to you."

"Really? That sounds pretty hopeful for me!" Juliet's thoughts did *not* mirror her words and corny thumbs-up. On the one hand, she was pleased to know Harriet was ignorant of the actual situation with her memories; she could tell the lab tech was being honest. On the other, she was already getting tired of the duplicitous nature of the whole setup.

Undoubtedly, that's simply an excuse to load you into the scanner array, which will check the status of the blockages they've put in place, and perhaps remove a small percentage each week.

"Yeah," Juliet subvocalized. "We need to figure out a way to either mess with that scanner or get you into it." She climbed into the pool, pleased to find it not exactly warm but not cold, either.

If we don't, you'll have to be prepared to act because I can't imagine they won't realize I've removed the memory blockages.

Juliet stood in the pool near the steps, and while Angel spoke, dove toward the far end. As soon as she glided past the halfway point, the generator turned on with a rumble, and bubbly water started to flow toward her. She grinned as she began to take strokes and kick, the pool somehow matching her pace, keeping her firmly in the middle as she swam.

It was easy to pretend she was alone, away from WBD, swimming in a pool of her choosing as she subvocalized, "I was going to ask about that. You don't think you could get the nanites to do something to make it look like the blockages are still in place?"

No. There were millions of chemical structures; rebuilding them would take longer than removing them. That's assuming we could synthesize the chemical bond that was in place. I'm doubtful of that.

"Well, then we're going to have to make something happen when they bring me for my 'TMS' treatment."

Angel didn't reply, perhaps sensing that Juliet was ready to zone out for a while and let her subconscious do some ruminating. She wished Angel was in her proper chip and could pipe some music into her ears, but she tried to lose herself in the rhythm of her swimming, breathing every third stroke and slowly exhaling in between.

The bubbles of the water, the churn of her arms and legs, and the deprivation of other stimuli served to send her into a kind of meditative state, and that's when the voices started drifting her way.

Harriet's voice came first: *. . . really getting after it. Must have some pent-up energy. I would!*

A man with a gruff, scratchy voice and a frustrated tone: *Seven goddamn hours. Seven hours on this stupid, journeyman repair job; meanwhile, I'm falling behind on three other jobs 'cause that little shit called in again—*

A sharp, cutting, feminine voice: *This how they want it, hmm? Cooked just like this? Hard on the edges, raw in the middle? These pans are too wide! The ovens don't heat evenly!*

Juliet smiled and let her mind drift, listening to the people occupying the facility around her, fishing for information, for clues, or for any insight into the corporation and its people that might help with her situation.

She was forming an overall impression of angst and stress, of people overworked and being handed deadlines and responsibilities they could barely manage. She heard many thoughts complaining about cramped quarters, homesickness, and a yearning for loved ones. It felt like the facility and the staff were new, and that they were in a very remote locale. She tried to expand her reach, to pull thoughts from further away, but Angel spoke up.

Juliet, I can't get detailed reports from the intracranial blood cooling system without my missing software, but your medical nanite control module is reporting an elevated body temperature. Are you using the lattice?

"Yeah. I was kind of fishing around, picking up stray thoughts."

Well, that, combined with your strenuous exercise, might be dehydrating you. You should take a break.

Juliet blew out her breath, taking the opportunity to scream underwater as an outlet for any remaining stress. Then, she stopped swimming and allowed the waves to propel her backward toward the steps, breathing heavily. Now that Angel mentioned it, she could feel how flushed she was. She floated idly on her back for a few minutes, letting the water and her deep, steady breathing cool her down.

"You were really going at it!" Harriet said from the edge of the pool. Juliet let her feet drift to the bottom and stood, turning to face the woman, who sat near the steps, her feet dangling into the water. She noticed Juliet's gaze and smiled. "These bodysuits are great, huh? They dry almost instantly, and with the footwear built in, I don't have to worry about getting my socks wet. Nanite layers, they tell me." She shrugged.

"Yeah, to be honest, I didn't even feel it while I was swimming." Juliet squinted at Harriet, noting that her eyes felt totally clear despite the chemically treated water. The old Juliet wouldn't have expected that. "Do I have full ocular implants now? Usually, my eyes sting after swimming in treated water."

"I believe so. High-end ones, too." Harriet cleared her throat. "Must be strange, finding yourself so changed." She flushed and stammered, "Gosh, was that insensitive? I'm supposed to make you feel more at ease, not freak you out!"

Juliet chuckled and took a few steps closer, standing closer to the other woman. "It's no big deal. How long was I swimming? I don't have a PAI, so no clock . . ."

"Um," Harriet's eyes unfocused for a second, "looks like about forty minutes."

"Seriously?" Juliet laughed. "I really zoned out! Man, I didn't used to be able to swim that hard for so long, not back when I was going to the public pool in the Helios Arcology. I hardly swam laps, to be honest. I mostly floated around trying to forget the day."

"Yeah, I'm not supposed to talk about any details. That's Doctor Chen's department, but you had quite an intense couple of years. I mean, they only gave me a broad briefing; I don't have the details, anyway."

Juliet nodded and shrugged. "No worries. Hopefully, I'll start remembering soon. Should we head back? I want to play with my new deck." She walked up the steps, exiting the pool, then chuckled as the water sheeted off her. When she ran her palm over her bodysuit, it felt dry.

"Yeah, let's. Your brunch service will be ready soon, too."

As Harriet led her back toward her comfortable prison cell, Juliet had an idea. "Hey, Harriet, if I don't like the music or vids Kline loaded up, can I get you to add some things to the deck, or do I have to wait for him?"

Harriet turned, pressing a finger to her chin in thought. "If you let me know what you want, I can—" Her words were cut short as she almost bumped into one of the hulking corpo-sec guards by the door. He didn't budge, and Harriet stumbled over his foot. Darting forward, Juliet caught her wrist, steadying her.

"Nice one, creep," she growled at the guard, who silently turned his opaque visor toward her, unmoved by her outburst.

"Thanks, Juliet. It's fine. I'm fine." Gently extracting her wrist from Juliet's grasp, Harriet entered a code in the door, stared at the screen, then walked into the lab-like antechamber to Juliet's room.

As soon as the door closed and locked with a *click*, she turned to Juliet and shrugged. "I'm clumsy. Anyway, if you let me know what you want added to your deck, I can message Kline to get the go-ahead and load it up for you. We don't have to wait for him."

"Awesome!" Juliet looked around the lab, noting the addition of a coffee machine and a fridge in the corner. It looked like they were still setting things up for Harriet and whoever else might share this space. "Is there another you? I mean, another tech who watches me when you're off duty?"

"There's a corpo-sec unit assigned to this part of the, um, facility, and they station someone here at night when I'm off. They're not supposed to interact with you, though. If something comes up, just hit the call button on the door, and they'll contact Kline, who will determine the right person to come see to your needs."

Juliet nodded, filing the information away. If she needed to make a violent exit, she'd do it at night.

When Harriet opened her door for her, Juliet walked through and sat down on the couch. Harriet hadn't followed her through, but she lingered in the doorway.

"Coming in?"

"No, I better not. I've got some reports to fill out, but I'll be in with your lunch soon." She pressed a few keys on the door pad and waved as the big door began to swing closed. "See you."

"Bye! Thanks, Harriet." As the door *thunked* shut and the locks latched into place, Juliet subvocalized, "Could it be that easy? If you set up a new daemon like Fido, and I give the deck to Harriet to load some new vids on—"

Then, my new daemon can infiltrate her computer and, hopefully, the rest of the facility.

"Yeah. Speaking of Fido, is he okay?"

He's encrypted on the memory chip they pulled from your data port. He should be fine unless they delete everything. I like your plan, Juliet, but I'll be working from scratch. All of my libraries are gone. All of my notes and many "memories" I didn't keep in my active consciousness are on those chips.

I'll be able to do it—I know how to code, and I'm sure I can steal some building blocks from this deck—but it won't be a quick thing. It might take me several days. Honestly, it may take longer than that before I feel confident enough about the new daemon to let it loose.

"No worries, Angel. We'll get there." While subvocalizing, Juliet flipped the slender data deck in her fingers, looking at every angle. It was small, which was nice, but also not so great; she doubted it had much processing power. Still, she pulled her data cable out and carefully plugged it into the tiny pop-up port on the deck.

Almost immediately, her ocular implants flickered with some static, and then a loading bar appeared, slowly counting up from four percent.

It's installing the AUI Kline mentioned. I'm sure it's just meant to let you access the drive's contents, but I'll analyze the code as soon as I figure out the ICE. It seems fairly straightforward.

Juliet leaned back and watched the status bar fill in, then lights flared in her eyes as a new AUI took shape. It was simple and overbearing—more of a UI than an AUI, really. Menu elements obscured her vision, and the window for viewing vids was always open, though currently, it only featured a black rectangle that blocked out her view of the wall in front of her.

While Angel explored things Juliet couldn't see, she spent time tabbing through the menus, scrolling through the movies, serials, books, songs, and a handful of games.

A few other apps were installed, like a calendar, a calculator, and a recording "studio." Juliet sighed and tried to wave as many elements away as possible, eager to have Angel rewrite things to be more like a proper AUI. "How's it going?" she subvocalized.

Well! This little deck is surprisingly robust. It has plenty of storage, even with all of the media Kline loaded into it. The processor isn't purpose-built like mine, but it has a graphics coprocessor that I can utilize. I think we're going to be able to accomplish a lot with it, but I'm going to start burning through the battery soon. Can you find a charging station?

Juliet stood up and looked around. It didn't seem like her room had one. Walking over to the door, she touched the call button. A moment later, the screen came to life, and she saw Harriet's face. "Something wrong?"

"No. Well, not exactly, but how am I supposed to charge this deck?"

"Oh! The tabletop. Anywhere. All the, um, apartments in the, uh, facility have one of those built-in tables." Harriet's smile was infectious, and Juliet wasn't sure if her halting speech was due to nervousness or a natural tic, but it was kind of endearing.

"Thanks, Harriet." Juliet waited until the screen went opaque again, then turned and walked over to the table. When she set the deck on the plastic surface, the battery icon changed to indicate it was charging. "Easy enough."

Yes! Just keep it on the table while I work. I'm still analyzing the ICE and the operating AI. When I get that under control, I'll start working on interface and management protocols for your cybernetics. It'll take me a while. I think I'll prioritize your reflexes in case something happens on Friday during your scan.

"I'll need the deck with me and plugged in, right?"

Oh yes. There's no wireless capability—they didn't just disable the software; they must have physically removed the transceiver. Once I have software for your cybernetics, it'll be useless if you don't keep the deck plugged in. Think of it as a bulky, external PAI module, because that's what I will turn it into.

"Angel, if they take that deck and analyze it, aren't they going to see all the stuff you're doing?"

The software managing this deck is like a stripped-down version of a PAI. That's how most operating systems work these days. Nobody writes software from scratch anymore; they deploy a general-purpose limited AI on a device and then configure it for specific tasks.

When they examine this drive, they will have an AI interface with the operating AI on this drive and, in that conversation, ascertain what you've done. They don't know that I will reprogram the AI on this chip to report only what we want.

"But what if they bypass the AI and just dump all the raw data on the deck?"

An operating AI has control over firmware-level access, or at least it can. When I'm done with this deck, any connection they make, regardless of whether it interfaces with the operating AI, will only pull the data I've marked as nonsensitive, for lack of a better term. The ICE I'm currently circumventing is meant to stop me from doing any of that. You would have no means even to begin combatting the ICE on this deck without me in your head, and they've no idea I'm in here.

"Okay. If you say so." Juliet leaned on one elbow and worked through the menu until she found the music. She selected a pop song she'd often heard played while on Luna and, while listening to it, let her mind zone out, visualizing what she would do the next day during her "listener" scan.

She thought about the horror Tono felt when he killed the love of his life in a car wreck. She thought about Nick and felt tears spring into her eyes as she remembered finding his body. She remembered watching Lemur's head slide from his body and roll on the floor like a bloody, lopsided bowling ball.

She ran through one horrible memory after another, and by the time the door beeped, she had to take a moment to gather herself before standing to answer. She knew it was Harriet delivering her lunch, and Juliet didn't want her to feel what she'd been brewing for the listener.

"Coming," she called, slowly exhaling, willing the darkness out of her mind. She felt ready for the listener. Her only concern was that she wouldn't feel it when it happened, that she wouldn't know when they were "listening," and wouldn't be able to focus her empathic push properly.

As her AUI flickered and some familiar elements came into focus, she smiled grimly and shook her head. Angel was doing her part. She had to do hers. She had to succeed. She had to show WBD's cheap knockoff of a psionic what happened when it went digging around in the wrong person's mind.

23

INDOCTRINATION

Kline leaned wearily against the plasteel wall, his hand trembling near the elevator control panel. He drew in a series of deep breaths, his fingers instinctively seeking solace in his breast pocket, where the familiar shape of his Nikko-vape awaited. After a lingering moment, he withdrew his hand with a heavy sigh, his eyes refocusing on the panel.

To his surprise, Ruby spoke up. "I won't tell, Kline."

"Huh?" His eyes narrowed, instantly suspicious.

"I won't tell. Go ahead. I know your nerves are shot." She sounded almost sweet, unexpectedly gentle. He had to admit she'd been more and more helpful, more and more . . . understanding of his plight.

"Don't you have to?" The whole reason he'd been weaning himself off the nicotine was because Ruby had started snitching to the old lady about it.

"Well, I'm *supposed* to. I'm also supposed to look out for your mental well-being, and I'm worried about you. Today, I'll weigh your sanity more heavily than Mrs. Gentry's desire to know your vaping habits."

Kline's shaky hand reached for his pocket again, and he asked, almost tremulously, "You promise?"

"Promise, Kline."

He sighed and pulled the vape out, taking a deep, double inhale, sucking the cherry-flavored vapor into the depths of his lungs.

He could quit. He'd done it before, even without using a neurochemical modulator. Still, he *liked* it, and nothing helped him steady his nerves like his wonderful old habit.

He tucked the vape cartridge back into his pocket and summoned the elevator. "Thanks, Ruby."

"You're welcome. I disapprove of the pressure Mr. Montclair is putting on you, and I want you to know that I've voiced my concerns in my reports."

Kline nodded, stepped into the elevator, and rode it up to the A suites. Montclair might enjoy his dungeon office, but Mrs. Gentry had different tastes. The car stopped twice for security sweeps before rising from the lower levels. When he arrived on the correct floor and stepped out, he was thoroughly scanned again before the tactical response unit let him pass. The corridors were carpeted in rich red synthetic fibers, the walls painted in modern updated WBD design motifs, and everything smelled new.

Mrs. Gentry's office was at the end of the hall, her double doors wide open, and he could hear her speaking within. When he stopped at the threshold, looking in, he saw her standing with none other than Montclair and one of his counterparts, Bridget Corning. Kline only knew her name because he'd briefly met her, Montclair, and the other two in Phoenix.

"Jesus Christ," he subvocalized, almost whispered, if he were honest.

"Don't freak out, Kline," Ruby soothed, her voice hitting all the right notes to smooth out his jitters. "Those two are leaving; they have a meeting with Ark Industries." Kline slowly exhaled, trying to send his stress out with the breath. Ark Industries was a recent WBD acquisition, and he could only imagine the pressure *they* were under; it likely made his situation seem relatively tame.

"Stop lurking, Kline," Gentry drawled, waving him in. He stepped through the doorway, noting the sudden depth of the carpet pile. He padded toward the trio, glancing at the expansive viewscreen on the far wall, which was currently showing a panorama of the old-growth jungle on the Yucatan peninsula. The view made him feel hot, like he could feel that simmering, glowering sun as it cooked the jungle moisture into steamy humidity.

Montclair locked eyes with him for a moment, a corner of his mouth twitching, giving his dour expression a little bit of life. Kline looked away, eyes on the old lady, struggling to keep from glancing at her loosely buttoned cowboy shirt, which never failed to expose a little too much of her too-smooth chest. The other woman, Corning, didn't even glance at him.

"Good," Gentry said, reaching out to take Corning's hand. "You'll get to the bottom of it. Don't let Montclair here give you any trouble."

Montclair smirked and turned to leave. "We're of the same mind on this." It wasn't lost on Kline that he didn't wait to be dismissed nor hold out for a handshake of his own. The bastard was certainly confident.

Kline stepped further into the room, studiously taking in the furnishings; the old lady had received another shipment of personal effects, if he wasn't mistaken. He saw glass shelves of weird porcelain figurines, a display of cow-boy hats, and most disturbing of all, a high shelf holding seven taxidermic house cats. Their glossy, lifelike eyes seemed to track him as he waited for Mrs. Gentry to address him.

When the two VPs exited, the doors swung closed automatically, and she looked at him, her red lips curving into a slow smile. "You really don't like them, do you, honey?" She often did that when they were alone—called him pet names in her slow drawl. He couldn't tell if she just enjoyed it or if she was trying to put him off-balance. He silently thanked Ruby for allowing the nicotine hit.

"Montclair is a world-class prick." He didn't see any point in beating around the bush; he was ninety-nine percent sure Ruby had shared the inci-dent with her, or at the very least, her PAI.

"Tut, Alec. Can't I have more than one favorite?" She moved to one of her soft, floral-print divans and sat down, patting the cushion beside her. *Favorite* was an interesting choice of words. He'd been on the chopping block—liter-ally—for close to a year before they finally caught Juliet. Things had certainly turned around after that, though!

"Come on, sugar, your first week's half over. Let's talk about what's going well and what's not. Are you missing that little assistant of yours as much as you thought you'd be?"

"Rachel?" Kline asked as he followed her instructions, sitting and folding his hands in his lap. When Mrs. Gentry didn't respond, he understood that she thought it was a nonsense question; of course she meant Rachel. "I'm missing her, yeah, but you were right; there's plenty of help here, and Ruby is amazing."

"She is, isn't she?" Mrs. Gentry winked, drawing his eyes to hers. She always wore sky-blue eye shadow, contrasting with the dark eyeliner but highlighting her bright-blue irises. "Now, I don't want you to worry about Montclair. I've taken him off your project, but you need to understand he's got his project running in parallel."

"The clones?"

"That's right. Listen, honey, he's not good at handling people like you, but he's not wrong; we're devoting a lot of resources to your gal, and if things don't seem to be panning out, you've got to be ready to pull the plug. That decision will be mine, however, not Montclair's or anyone else's. Understood?"

Kline couldn't believe the wave of relief washing over him as her words melted away the tension he'd been building up since his first meeting with Montclair. He honestly felt like weeping, and it was everything he could do just to hold himself steady and breathe normally for a few seconds.

When Mrs. Gentry broke the spell by leaning forward to pick up her ice-filled glass of lemonade, he cleared his throat and nodded. "That's fair. Thank you, Mrs. Gentry."

"Want some lemonade, sugar?"

Kline licked his lips, noting how dry they'd become. "That would be nice." To his surprise, she leaned forward and poured him a glass from the decanter rather than summoning one of her wait staff. "Will I still have access to Montclair's listener?"

"Oh yes. He won't be taking him anywhere. You've got your weekly slot, but remember, that's one of the resources I mentioned; if you find you don't need to use the listener, it'll be better to take it off the schedule in a week or three, hmm?"

"So, the deadline Montclair gave me?"

She waved her hand. "I'll be paying close attention. There aren't any dates or deadlines—I'll make a decision daily. If I think it's time, we'll wrap things up, and I'll get you onto something a little more productive." Kline nodded, but his eyes likely reflected his reservations. No deadline also meant no guaranteed time. The old lady could cancel Juliet next week if she felt like it. "Put that long face away now and tell me what you think. I saw the footage of your meeting. You like her, don't you?"

"Like? How could anyone tell? She's missing her most recent memories. She could be a totally different person after the last couple of years." He shrugged. When Gentry didn't stop staring at him, he added, "She seems nice."

"She's got a certain quality, doesn't she? She makes people want to like her. I saw Ruby's report on that lab tech, Harriet. You sure it's wise to keep her on the case?"

"She has two jobs—observe the client and make the client comfortable. I think if Juliet likes her and she's friendly, that's probably a plus. If not, though, if she seems to be getting conditioned, for lack of a better word, then we've got the Empathanil."

"Give her a dose. Trust me. She's too close, too fast."

"All right." Kline nodded; he knew how to pick his battles, and it already felt like he'd won in a big way. No more Montclair!

"Listen, sugar," Mrs. Gentry said as he sipped his ice-cold, semisweet lemonade, "I've got another meeting, so I've got to cut this short. Things are busy out here, what with everything we're planning. Don't you worry, though, I'm going to be watching. I look forward to hearing about her first real session with Chen next week. We'll talk after that."

"Do I have a new direct report? I mean, I can remove Montclair from my calendar, right?"

"We'll go back to the old days when you reported directly to me. Might as well, since we're both here, hmm?" She stood smoothly and gracefully, and as usual, Kline had a hard time reconciling the "old lady" with her youthful movements. Of course, as far as he knew, her limbs were entirely cybernetic or synthetic.

The thought reminded him of Rachel and how they'd spoken after her first meeting with Mrs. Gentry, making guesses as to how much of the old lady was real.

That sort of behavior was a thing of the past now that Ruby was in his head, now that listeners were a thing. Kline felt his heart rate pick up as he had that thought. What the *fuck* was he doing? She could have a listener in the next room!

He panicked, trying to think of something else, forcing himself to do mental math as he set his lemonade down and stood, following Mrs. Gentry over to the door, breaking out in a cold sweat as he caught himself looking at her ass in those ridiculous jeans.

"Kline, are you okay?" Ruby asked.

"Fine," he subvocalized, clearing his throat. The doors swung open, and a man stood there, waiting to come in. He was tall and lean, with close-cropped blond hair. When he looked at Kline, his eyes cut like diamonds, and it felt like he read his life story with that quick stare. It didn't help Kline's nerves when he smiled warmly and switched his gaze to Mrs. Gentry.

"Ma'am."

"Hello, sweetie. Go on in, and we'll have a chat." Mrs. Gentry looked at him in a way that Kline had foolishly thought was reserved for him; he'd never seen that twinkle in her eyes when she spoke to anyone else. The man nodded then stalked past, moving like a panther on the prowl. He was clearly an operator; someone who did a lot more fieldwork than Kline.

Suddenly, she gripped the back of his arm, her hand like a clamp around his triceps, "Okay, Alec. You go get that girl straightened out. Check in on the techs; they have a report for you about the alpha chip. This time next week, I might have another surprise for you. I'm working on something to help her come around to our side."

"Thank you—" His words stopped short as her grip tightened.

"You know why I value Montclair, don't you? He might be a sociopath, but he's damn smart. I know he upset you, but you must have known we were always going to take samples. We were always going to explore what makes her so compatible. It's good we've got that pipeline in the works because if she doesn't come around, you'll have to liquidate.

"You earned a lot of leeway by getting her here, but we've got to have priorities. I know I said no deadlines, but you need to earn her trust and get her to wake up that little vixen of an AI. Do you hear me? If Montclair beats you to the punch. . .”

As she let her veiled threat hang between them, Kline nodded and steadied himself. “Yes, ma’am.”

“Good. Go on, now. We’ll talk soon.” She squeezed his arm, gently this time, sending tingles up and down the nape of his neck. She released him, and Kline heard her walk back into her office. He turned, maybe to catch a glimpse of the operator or hear a snippet of conversation between the two, but her doors were already swinging shut.

They clicked together with the finality of silence, leaving him standing there, suddenly less sure he’d won any sort of clemency by having Montclair off his case.

He turned back to the distant elevator, where the squad of tactical corpo-sec officers lurked.

Ruby startled him as she said, “You should get some rest, Kline. You can speak to the techs in the morning; their department closed two hours ago.”

“Yeah. Yeah, Ruby. Some sleep sounds damn fine. I don’t suppose you’d let me get away with another hit—”

“Hush, Kline! Subvocalize if you want to talk about that! Let’s get going.” Much more softly, as he started walking, she added, “I’ll think about it.”

When Juliet awoke, she glanced at the time on her new AUI; she’d kept the deck plugged in all night. According to the display, it was 0526 on Thursday morning.

“Today’s the day, Angel,” she subvocalized.

“The day you face the listener. I wonder when they’ll do it. Do you think they’ll give you any sort of heads-up? Do you think they’ll move you or just put the listener out there with Harriet?” It felt good hearing Angel’s voice again, with all the proper pitch and depth. Her strange, echoey presence in her mind had been a comfort, but this felt better, more like normal.

“I see you got my implants working.”

“Everything’s working at some level, though full functionality will take me a few days of programming. Maybe it’ll take less than that; I’m getting faster as I build a code base and a new library.”

Juliet stretched and sat up on her couch. A shadow hung to her right, and she almost flinched but then remembered painting the big, black blob in the middle of the wall, using up the entire jar of paint Kline had given her. It was the wall where she was going to paint the Jovian System.

Part of her had wanted to paint something other than what she’d seen in her true-dream, and the notion still tempted her. Wouldn’t it be interesting to see if she could purposefully change the future she'd seen? "If I unplug the deck, what will happen to you?"

"Nothing. I'm using the storage and processing, but I'm still in your head. However, if you unplug, all the daemons and programs I've been spinning up will cease operations, encrypt themselves, and hide behind a false wall of sorts. The operating AI will keep them hidden."

"And all my cybernetics will stop working?"

"Well, not exactly, but I'll lose control of them. Your AUI will go away."

"Got it." Juliet stretched and then began her morning routine, picking out a clean bodysuit and some undergarments and taking a long shower, savoring the thought that Montclair might see it as a line item on his budget. When that was done, she ate a protein bar, drank some coffee, and waited for either her clock to read 0700 or for someone to come into her room.

When she'd glimpsed Kline's schedule, the "listener" entry had been the first notation, written on the 0730 timeslot. Of course, none of the other timeslots had lined up perfectly with her activities thus far, but she figured it would be early in the morning when it happened, so she wanted to be ready.

Her clock read 0702 when she moved over to the couch and decided to lay down and get ready, doing some *listening* of her own. That's when her door beeped.

She didn't want to go through the charade of standing up and going over to it, so she just called, "Come in."

The door made its noises then swung open, revealing Kline, who walked in with an open cardboard box in his arms and grunted as he set it down on the white flooring in front of the couch. Inside, Juliet identified a handheld paint sprayer, three liter-size cans of paint, and two more paperback books. They looked decidedly older than the one he'd brought her the day before. "I come bearing gifts."

"Jeez, Kline!" Juliet smiled a little too genuinely for her tastes. She reached in and took the two books out. One was called *The Sheep Farmer's Daughter* and featured a woman in the arms of a man with very bulbous muscles and long, flowing hair. The other featured a woman in a spacesuit and was called *Trading in Danger.*

"Uh, I think one of those is a romance." Kline shrugged apologetically.

Juliet snorted a giggle and held up the cover with the shirtless man. "You think?"

"Well, pickings are slim around here!" He laughed, and Juliet thought the humor touched his eyes. He seemed different.

She said as much. "You seem more relaxed, Kline. It's awfully early, but are you having a good day?"

"I am! Let's just say someone I didn't really enjoy working with has been reassigned. Things are looking up." His eyes unfocused for a moment, then he stood up. "Listen, I've gotta step out for a little while. Can you entertain yourself here for about an hour? I'll escort you to your first WBD indoctrination session before your gym time."

Juliet narrowed her eyes and looked at him skeptically. Had he misspoken? "Indoctrination?"

He laughed and smacked himself in the forehead with his palm. "I can't believe I did that! That's what we all call those vid lessons where they tell you about the company's corporate culture and history. I mean, we say it jokingly, but it's kind of true; they won't tell you anything negative. We've all had to watch 'em, so yeah, it's fun to joke around at the company's expense." He was chuckling, but when he saw Juliet's skeptical expression, he sobered up and added, "Don't take me seriously, all right? It's just goofing."

Juliet wanted to call him out. She could tell he was putting on a show, trying to make himself seem like he was more on her level, united against the corporate behemoth. She didn't, though. Juliet, the scrap worker, didn't like corporations, but she'd be impressed by a guy like Kline. She'd still be high off the thought of making real money, sleeping in a fancy "suite," swimming in a fancy pool, receiving all sorts of individual attention for the "accident" she'd suffered. So, she just smiled and shrugged.

"It's no big deal. We all joked about the vids Fred made us watch to get insurance breaks."

"Exactly! Same sort of deal." He moved to the door. "Okay, see you in an hour or so."

"Bye." Juliet waved as she laid back on the couch, closing her eyes.

"That was strange," Angel said.

"Nah, he's trying to build rapport with me. That was an intentional slip. I'll tell you what I learned, though—he's pretty smooth when he wants to be."

"Do you think the listener is coming?"

"I think the listener is here. I think Kline's little performance was meant to expose certain thoughts in my head. Put that music on. I need to reach out and make sure the listener doesn't become a talker."

24

\\\\\\\\\\\\\\\\\\\\\\\\

ARNOLD GROSSMAN

Even with her usual "zone-out" tracks playing their synth-pop beats, Juliet had to take several deep cleansing breaths to still her mind. She focused on the darkness Angel was projecting into her retinal implants, allowing her to keep her eyes open while she worked. In that darkness, she reached out, imagining the thoughts of people nearby as wispy strands of cottony thread she could gather up and bring back into herself.

They came to her, and her weird mental image held firm as she pulled wisps of thought into her mind, catching snippets of Harriet's voice and, unsurprisingly, Kline's. She tuned out Harriet but pulled harder on Kline's strand, listening.

Please be normal. Give us a clear report, you creepy fuck. Jesus, I can't take it. Coffee. I need coffee.

Juliet felt Kline's stress, and along with it, an unbearable need to stick a nicotine vape in her mouth. It was almost physiological, and she had to push his frazzled mind away so she could refocus. It said a lot about his acting skills; he'd seemed utterly at ease when he'd come into her room. She'd seen through his little act, but she hadn't realized just how on edge the man was.

Juliet inhaled slowly through her nose, taking a long, deep breath, and stretched her mind, seeking the listener.

When she felt the groping tendrils of their thoughts, they sent shivers through her psyche. Where Kline's and Harriet's were drifting spider's silk, the listener's were wiry, fibrous fishing lines, pulling and tugging as soon as Juliet's feathery mental touch found them. She resisted the pull and let her delicate, probing psionic sense trace them back to their origin.

A man's voice came to her, strange, halting, almost stuttering as it rushed through her extra senses, a stream of consciousness unlike any mind she'd ever touched.

H-Hunting, probe, probing. Not thinking. Thinking about . . . me? S-Slippery, st-static. H-Hard to grasp. L-Listen . . . Listening? I . . . I am. I-I listen! M-My voice? Echo? Echoing? S-Sad? I-I? I am? S-Sad?

Juliet immediately knew what was happening. The listener was listening to her, and she was listening to him, so his voice and emotions were returning to him, creating something almost like a feedback loop.

She briefly contemplated leaving it at that, continuing to listen until he stopped, but a part of her resisted. A part of her wanted to *push* the horror she'd been preparing, wanted to teach this man a lesson about fishing around in her head.

However, another part of her wanted to weep when she felt the depths of despair in that man's mind. Despair that he didn't even seem to understand was there. She could hear the confusion in his voice, his despair at hearing himself, and knew something was wrong. He was being used as a tool; he wasn't malicious. They'd *done* something to him. Something in his mind was broken. Something was lost. Could she find it? Could she turn this tool against them?

Juliet knew the smart move would be to continue sending a feedback loop to the listener. She knew she should play it safe and take things slow. She could help the listener when she broke out. It could wait. The problem was that Juliet didn't like to turn a blind eye when she saw suffering—when she *felt* suffering. Was she a victim of her own empathy?

At that moment, lying on a comfortable couch in her prison cell deep in the bowels of WBD's secret installation, scrutinized in a hundred different ways, she was fed up with being passive.

Juliet exhaled that long, deep breath and rode out of herself, streaming through the ether, tracing the thoughts she was listening to, and dove into the listener's mind.

"L-009, when was the last time we serviced your halo?" the med tech asked.

"Seven days prior to my transit," he replied, wondering at the twitch of irritation he felt.

The med tech must have seen the flicker of emotion. "That was a long trip, wasn't it? I think you're due for an injection, aren't you?"

"It's been thirteen days since my last one." L-009 didn't see any reason to dissemble.

"Ah, yes. You'll be right as rain in a few minutes." The med tech pulled an auto-injector from his cart. "After I administer this, I'll service your halo, and then our watchdog over there will take you to Mr. Montclair. He's eager to get you working."

The med tech chuckled at something, some inference or context L-009 didn't or couldn't grasp. He felt the cold nozzle of the injector against his neck, then heard it hiss and felt a wave of coldness spread outward.

Juliet pulled back, surprising herself with how easily she detached from the deep dive. Was she getting better, or was L-009's mind easy to get in and out of? One thing was for sure: she hadn't seen what she wanted. She wanted to know who he was, what they'd done to him.

She pushed harder, trying to go deeper. She could feel it, almost like having something on the tip of her tongue, a word she wanted to say but couldn't quite find. She knew what she wanted was in there, buried in the listener's mind, but something was in the way.

For the first time in a long while, Juliet concentrated on the "psionic energy" that clung to her lattice. The weird, not-electricity she used to manipulate objects with telekinesis. She was sure it was the same energy Kyle had blasted her and Polk with. Could she use it to force her way deeper into the listener's mind? Something in her gut told her to try.

In her mind, when she grasped a person's thoughts and listened, it was almost passive; she was mostly just receiving. When she performed a deep dive, it was different. She sent a piece of herself out, fishing around in another person's memories and feelings. She knew it was real, that it was physical in a way because those memories and feelings affected her. They clung to her, and sometimes, if she got too deep, they lingered, making it hard to distinguish where she, Juliet, ended and the *other* began.

So, she pushed at whatever was keeping her out. She *pushed* with her usual mental nudge, adding some of that psionic energy to her tendrils of thought, trying to pierce the almost palpable barrier in the listener's mind.

At first, nothing seemed to happen, but as the energy gathered, traveling down roads that seemed natural—pathways paved for its traversal—she felt the energy break through like water pressure shattering a dam into a thousand fragments. Juliet rode the wave, diving into the listener's mind, using her uncanny ability to find what she wanted.

Arnold Grossman smiled, handing the receptionist his ID badge. She scanned it and asked, "Here for the WRP opportunity?"

"Yes, ma'am. Seems like a good one, don't you think? Flat percentage decrease in debt. For me, that's a big deal!" He winked at her; she reminded him of his daughter. She wasn't amused, or maybe she was just overworked. She handed him back his badge and gestured to the door on the left.

"Waiting area 7A; you're registered and have been given number G44. Watch for your number and enter the door that lights up green when it's displayed. If you take longer than three minutes, they'll move to the next number, and you'll have to come back to receive a new one."

"Right. Um, thanks." Arnold took his badge and walked through the door. He suddenly felt melancholy despite the opportunity. He hadn't thought of his daughter in years. Why'd he say that? Why'd he wink? He wasn't that kind of man. Oh, Jenny!

"Gah!" he huffed, scrubbing his eye with the back of one deeply tanned hand as he stepped through the door.

The waiting area was enormous—maybe two hundred plastic seats bolted down in rows. Perhaps a third of the seats were empty, and he found his way to one with a decent view of the number display. It was currently lit with big, bold red digits that read E92.

Arnold sighed and folded his arms over his chest. He'd wait. He had fourteen hours before his next shift, and he needed the damn WRP. The company notice had said he'd get three percent knocked off his debt just for trying out, with the potential for total forgiveness if he made it through the test rounds.

"Too good to pass up," he said, humming nervously as he caught himself talking aloud. He missed his PAI, but reminded himself that dinner on the table was worth more than a mental distraction machine. "Maybe after this," he whispered, fantasizing about a life without the corporate debt eating away half his take-home every Friday.

With a tremendous effort, Juliet pulled herself out of the dive. It was much, much more challenging than the first time; like the weight of emotion and the depth of the memory was tar, clinging to her, pulling her back. She'd seen what she needed, though. Arnold was a victim, and there was no way she could live with herself if she blasted his mind. Instead, she focused her thoughts and, as clearly as she could, sent a question out, hoping he was still listening.

Arnold, are you there?

Drifting through the ether, on the tendrils of their intertwined thought threads, she heard his tremulous reply. *I-I am. I am here. What did they do to me?*

Juliet felt a surge of panic, horror, and loss transmitted along those threads, and almost reacted, nearly jumping off her couch and screaming her frustration to anyone who could hear. She recognized the feelings for what they were—Arnold was remembering himself. And if she was about to react, so was he!

She pushed down the panic, forcing herself to be calm. She imagined White, Jensen, Sergeant Polk, Barns—all the cool-under-pressure operators she'd ever seen. Grabbing onto that feeling, that ice-in-the-veins patient killer she'd seen lurking behind White's eyes as he sighted down the barrel of his

Gauss rifle, she *pushed* it to Arnold, then sent out more thoughts: *You have to stay calm. They'll kill us both if they know you remember.*

These bastards! They—They made me forget! I remember, though! I know who I am! I'm not L-NINE! I'm ARNOLD GROSSMAN!

Juliet could feel him withdrawing, his thoughts slipping from her grasp, his tendrils whipping away from her mind. It was everything she could do to remain calm, to continue tapping her foot to the beat of her music. "I think I might have messed up," she subvocalized.

"What happened?" Angel asked. Her voice, concerned and patient, was almost comically out of place after what Juliet had just felt from Arnold; he'd had murder on his mind.

Kline watched Juliet on the display, glancing from her reclined figure to the weird cyborg monstrosity of the listener. The strange fellow sat in his automated mobility chair beside Harriet, eyes closed, doing whatever bizarre voodoo those guys did when they reached into a person's mind. The LEDs on his halo flashed red, indicating he was actively gathering thoughts.

Kline looked back to Juliet. She was listening to music, if he were guessing. Her foot tapped to the beat, and her eyes, though open, were staring into nothing. He looked back to Harriet. "Scans normal?"

"Yes. Nothing out of the ordinary. Is she meditating? Her breathing is very controlled."

"She's got some goddamn high-end lungs. Who knows what all she got into; you've seen her body. Maybe she was doing yoga wherever she was hiding."

"I don't think yoga and meditation are the same—"

"You know what I mean," Kline sighed. He switched to subvocalizations. "I'm on edge, Ruby. Can I please have a hit?"

"With Harriet and the listener here? You know if the listener is in use, they're going to save the footage from this room. Think, Kline!"

He groaned and pressed his palm into his forehead, looking at the listener again. He was exactly the same as before: utterly expressionless. Kline paced back and forth a few times, then walked over to Harriet's desk and sat on the edge, looking down at the lab tech. The listener was on her other side.

Out of the corner of his eye, he thought he saw the man's hand twitch. He looked more closely, narrowing his eyes as he stared. Sure enough, a few seconds later, the man's hand jerked left, then right.

"Is that normal?" he asked, mostly speaking to Ruby.

"I don't know," Harriet and Ruby both replied, and the perfect unison brought a smile to Kline's face.

"Don't you dare tell her," Ruby warned. Of course, that made Kline laugh, and Harriet looked at him like he'd gone mad.

"What?"

"Nothing, nothing. Is he all right?" Kline peered at the listener's face. Was he scowling? Was his upper lip twitching? He stood abruptly and looked at the viewscreen showing Juliet. She was unchanged, still reclining, foot tapping to the beat of her music.

When Kline turned back, the listener's eyes were open and bloodshot, and he was staring at him with tears rolling down his cheeks. Kline almost jumped out of his shoes. "Jesus!"

Harriet looked at the listener and recoiled, rolling her chair a couple of meters away from him. Stepping closer, Kline peered at the man and the dozens of metal rods sticking out of his scalp. The halo was still flashing with red LEDs. "You okay, Nine?"

The listener stared for another couple of seconds then nodded. "I'm feeling normal, sir. Don't be alarmed by my appearance. Sometimes, when I concentrate, I don't fully close my eyes, and they dry out. Everything checks out with the subject. For the most part, I heard her singing along to some music. She was thinking about food, the people she's met here, and hoping things work out for her."

The listener touched the controls of his mobility chair and started toward the door. "Sir, I believe my halo needs servicing. Will that be all?"

"Yeah. Of course. Will you submit your report today?"

"Yes, sir. I have a job for Mr. Montclair, and then I'll dictate my summary to my management AI."

"Good." Kline watched him wheel out and saw his personal security detail form up around him as he sped down the corridor. It was weird to think that guy, that priceless asset, used to be a factory worker in a soon-to-be decommissioned algae plant in Phoenix.

He turned back to Harriet. "Well! That's some good news. I bet if I cancel further appointments, it'll buy us a little more clemency from the—" He almost said *old lady* but just pointed to the ceiling.

Harriet rolled back to her spot at the desk. "Do you think that's wise? I mean, don't get me wrong, my skin was crawling when that guy rolled out of here. I swear, when I first looked into his eyes, I thought he was going to murder me. Still, what if, you know, something happens with our client?"

Kline frowned and rubbed his chin. The listener *had* been creepier than the others he'd seen in action. Those eyes . . . He shook his head, pushing the thought aside.

"Harriet, believe me, I'd like to take as much caution as possible. If I could get away with it, I'd schedule a listener twice a week. However, my boss, who also happens to be *your* boss, dropped the hint that the listeners are in high demand, and sort of encouraged me not to need one. Besides, if our client were planning something, that creepy bastard would have heard it today. Have you ever had one of them pointed at you?"

"No—"

"Well, I have. She peeled two of my deepest, darkest secrets out of here in just a few seconds." Kline tapped the side of his head. Harriet's eyes widened, and she nodded in appreciation. "Well, tell you what, Harriet. Let's celebrate! I'll go ahead and clear the path, so to speak, but why don't you get Juliet ready and bring her to the lounge; we'll have a proper breakfast today."

"Oh, she'd like that! She's often complaining about the protein bars and coffee in her room." Rolling her chair back, Harriet stood then walked over to Juliet's door, where she paused, turning to watch Kline.

"Oh, right! I'm not supposed to be here." He walked to the other door but paused. "Hey." He locked eyes with the lab tech; she looked almost excited at the prospect of bringing Juliet up to the lounge for breakfast. "I'm supposed to send you for a, uh, treatment. You know, the injection we spoke about? We can wait until after today's shift, though." He hated how her face fell, hated seeing the joy in her eyes flicker out. "See you in a few minutes."

He stepped into the hallway, pushing the feelings down with so many others.

Juliet exhaled and tried to keep the relief from her expression. "We're good," she subvocalized. "He covered for us, Angel. He told them we were acting normal. I don't know how he did it, but he locked down his emotions."

As soon as the listener—Arnold—had withdrawn, Juliet had reached out and listened to Harriet and Kline, trying to determine how much trouble she was in. It seemed Arnold had other priorities, or perhaps, simply patience when it came to his vengeance.

It made Juliet think; he'd been so open, receiving her thoughts through that weird contraption WBD had implanted in his brain. Rather than simply calming him, helping him remain steady under stress, had her *push* impacted him more than she'd intended? Had she given him the mentality of a killer?

She didn't know if there was any way of saving Arnold from what had been done to him, but she hoped he didn't get himself killed. "Harriet's going to come in here and bring us to breakfast."

"That's good! I'm glad it didn't last any longer. The intracranial cooling device has banked as much heat as possible, and your core temp is slowly rising. I'm sure they have a basic scanner array pointed your way that might have noticed." Angel paused briefly, then asked, "Juliet, how did you do it? Bring his memories back?"

"I wish I knew. I pushed some of the, you know, psionic energy that collects on the lattice. I pushed it into his brain. I could feel where I wanted to go; I knew where the memories I wanted were, like always, but there was something in the way. The push was all it took."

"Could it have been the same kind of block they put on you? But you destroyed it utterly? In seconds? Juliet . . . I don't know what to make of the implications."

"Maybe it wasn't. Maybe it was just hypnosis or something." The door beeped, and Juliet cleared her throat before standing up. "Come in."

As the door went through its lengthy process of opening, she subvocalized, "I'm learning a lot, Angel. I think something has changed. Things seem easier with the lattice. I really think it has something to do with me waking up without my memories. I think I lost some of the hang-ups I had. Have you restored everything?"

"Yes, which is another thing we need to figure out. What will we do about the scan tomorrow?"

As she watched the door swing open, Juliet tapped the deck, snug against her wrist under the sleeve of her bodysuit. "Is Fido's brother almost ready?"

"No! I need days and days of testing!"

"Okay, okay. Relax. I'll have to do something, that's all."

Harriet stood in the doorway, hands clasped before her, wearing a smile that looked a little forced. "Hi, Juliet! Good morning."

Juliet smiled warmly, *pushing* a little camaraderie. "Oh, hey! I thought it would be Kline. I think he's supposed to take me to some kind of WBD lesson."

Harriet's smile brightened noticeably. "He's going to meet us. Guess what?"

"What?" Juliet chuckled, hamming it up for the woman.

"We get to go up to the lounge for breakfast!"

25

BETRAYAL

Tanaka had more than a dozen windows floating in his AUI, each with details about a separate but integral part of the plan. He looked past them to his desk, old and battered, inside the dim, cluttered base of operations that Frida and Kostas had set up for him and his team.

When he and the others had arrived in Mexico City, their fluttercraft had deposited them there, on the edge of the sprawling *ciudades perdidas*, or lost cities—a labyrinth of narrow streets and crumbling buildings which were part of the vast, sprawling urban landscape of the megacity. It was home to a teeming mass of humanity far removed from the great towers at its center.

With help from Selene Kostas, Frida had acquired the old building, and before they'd arrived, Kostas had already stocked the place with crates and crates of equipment. She'd also supplied Tanaka with a special, customized PAI, which she'd promised would put an end to his frustrations with Kim— the one he'd bought for himself on Luna.

That new PAI, Fred, was playing a crucial role in organizing the plan, rendering three-dimensional models and timetables accurate to the second, and helping Tanaka review every minute detail.

"Does it make sense? Do you see why you'd want Leo to speak to Kravitz before you enter sublevel H?" Fred, calm and logical, highlighted the route the security patrol would take. Tanaka liked him. He liked his no-nonsense manner of speaking and his superior ability to understand the big picture—he made his previous PAI look like a toy.

"Yes, it all adds up." Tanaka ran his hand over his freshly buzzed hair, relishing the sensation of the bristlelike stubble against his palm. According to Fred's meticulously crafted timeline, the optimal moment to strike the massive WBD installation was less than twenty-four hours away—Friday evening. "Fred, contact the team. We need to schedule a final briefing in four hours to ensure everything is in place."

"On it." While Fred worked, Tanaka leaned back and started flipping through the windows, examining each element of the plan once again. "Tanaka," Fred said unexpectedly, "you have a priority call coming through from Selene."

"Answer it."

A call window appeared on his AUI, and Kostas, perfectly coiffed as usual, smiled at him. Tanaka wondered how much of that perfect, beautiful countenance was due to some technical wizardry.

Her greeting threw him slightly off-balance. "Tanaka, we have to change plans."

As he waved away the windows containing weeks of hard work, he scowled, feeling the knot in his stomach—a familiar companion since his team had been taken—begin to take shape again. "What?"

"You must know I've been exploring other angles of attack, yes? One of them paid off. I got into the closed network of the WBD installation. Our people aren't there. I found footage of them being loaded onto a shuttle last month—"Tanaka's growl was subconscious, his muttered curses even more so, but they were loud enough to give Kostas pause.

"I know. I'm frustrated, too, Rutger. The good news is that I have evidence that Juliet and at least two of your team were alive. In fact, I have footage of Dora Lee and Arndt Hawkins walking, in perfect health, aboard the shuttle."

"Lucky? Barns?" He still had a hard time thinking of Lucky as *Juliet*.

"Juliet was in a contained medical transport cart, but that's to be expected. They'll want to keep her unconscious until they're ready to deal with the tech in her head." Kostas paused, took a slow breath, and shook her head slightly. "I'm sorry, but I did not find evidence in the site's database of Barns."

Tanaka squeezed his eyes shut, clenching his jaw. He *needed* to act. "What do we do?"

"I'm sending a ship, *Furies' Wing*, to pick you and your team up. Get to the Mexico City Spaceport by noon tomorrow. Frida is coordinating with some of Juliet's other allies. I'm recovering her interceptor from the Denver Spaceport, and her friends here on Luna are prepping a gunship. We're going after them."

* * *

Cassie reclined in her bunk, looking into the little polymer case. It contained two objects: a chip that gleamed golden in her LED reading light and a small piece of cardstock with a simple note printed on it.

The case had been delivered to the commune via drone almost a week ago, and each night, Cassie had sat in her bunk in the little trailer she shared with Brooke and stared at the contents, frozen by indecision, guilt, anger, and a dozen other emotions. It wasn't fair. It wasn't right.

For the hundredth time, she read the note on the card.

Ghoul –
I need your help. Use this PAI chip; it'll tell you what to do.
Juliet

Cassie studied the chip, tracing the shiny inscribed text with her eyes: *Angel 3.3*. For the hundredth time, she wondered at the implications. Juliet's PAI was called Angel, right? So, she'd gotten her a similar one?

She wanted to be mad at Juliet for sending the chip without any real explanation. She wanted to be pissed that she was trying to put her on the spot, to trigger some kind of guilt response, saying she needed help, but Cassie was mostly angry at herself. Why hadn't she told Juliet everything? Why'd she lied about her sister? Why did she always have to keep so many damn secrets?

"Goddammit," she growled, clenching her jaw. "I told you I can't leave!" That much was true. That much had been plainly spoken. She couldn't take the blame for this. She'd sent message after message to the address Juliet had left on the commune's bulletin board—nothing. Silence.

She turned the card in her hand several times, her scowl deepening with each rotation. What was Juliet trying to pull her into?

"I heard you," a small, high-pitched voice said from the other side of the curtain. Cassie pulled it aside, revealing her niece dressed in pajamas, with a small spot of toothpaste on her chin, clutching her stuffed bear, Bobo.

"What, Brookie?" She reached out and rubbed the spot away with her thumb.

"I heard you cuss!"

Cassie smiled and closed the case, putting it back on the little shelf above her bunk, where she kept her knife, pistol, and an old-school journal she'd started when the commune made her pull her PAI. "Sorry, little bug." She patted the mattress beside her, scooting closer to the wall. "Come up here and tell me a story."

"You're supposed to tell *me* a story!" Brooke whined, her voice struggling to decide if it should land on amused or outraged. "You said after I brush!"

"Well, let's make a deal. If you tell me one, I'll tell you a *longer* one."

"Mommy never made me tell her stories." Her plaintive tone was enough to push Cassie's frustration into despair, and she felt tears pooling in her eyes.

She looked up at the ceiling, ensuring Brooke didn't see as she blinked them away. "Tell me about that, then. Tell me about a story your mommy told you."

"I—I feel sad when I think about that." Brooke turned into her, pressing her face into the soft crook where her armpit and chest met. Cassie stroked her hair, smoothing it out and separating it into two clumps.

As she began to braid it in thick, loose plaits, she said, "It's important to talk about her. That's how we can make sure we never forget her. If you tell me a story about your mommy, I'll tell you a story about a friend I used to have; someone who was special to me, if only for a little while. I'll make it a fun story, Brookie; you'll like it."

"I really wish you would have just let your new daemon try!" Juliet subvocalized, walking beside Harriet behind their corpo-sec escort—two bulky men wearing combat armor and holding boxy electro-SMGs as though they might be attacked at any moment.

"Daisy isn't ready, Juliet. Try to remember this is the corporation who designed me! They're not going to have pushover ICE on their internal networks. Cracking into a media deck is one thing, but getting into their network will be a whole other can of worms!"

"Can of worms?" Juliet snorted as she subvocalized. Harriet glanced at her. "Everything okay?"

"Yeah." Juliet smiled at her. The lab tech had seemed a little more distant that morning, and Juliet couldn't help wondering if everything was all right. She hoped she hadn't gotten her in trouble; they'd had a good time the day before, laughing and joking perhaps a little too loudly, even teasing Kline together at breakfast. "Almost sneezed. What's with the escort?"

"Oh, we have to use the central lift to get to the TMS pod. Protocol dictates a security escort when encountering nonbriefed employees is a possibility." Harriet waved her hand in a small circle as she spoke, as if she wasn't sure where to point.

Juliet nodded, glancing over her shoulder at the two corpo-sec officers following them. "Four, though?"

Harriet shrugged helplessly. "We can't have anyone accosting you." Juliet understood what that really meant: they didn't want anyone interfering with her ongoing brainwashing. They didn't want uncontrolled contact with anyone they might not have foreseen in their planning sessions.

She scanned the corridor, looking for some kind of inspiration, some idea that would strike like a bolt of lightning and provide a solution for the impending scan. If she was honest, a real sense of dread was starting to set in. She didn't know what she was going to do.

As if sensing her rising angst, Angel asked, "What are we going to do, Juliet?"

"I'm working on it!"

Angel started highlighting things on her AUI—weapons and cybernetic hardware on the two guards in front of her, cameras, doors, and even signage in the corridor.

"Look at the men behind you again. It wouldn't be ideal, but we should start making a plan of action in case we have to make our move. Obviously, we don't have the intel that would improve our odds much, but they *will* see that your memories are restored in that scan. Better to act before they have us locked in some kind of scanning pod!"

Juliet did as she asked, looking over her shoulder again, taking in the men's armor—black visors under thick, polymer helmets, active body armor made of advanced polymers, belts adorned with stun batons, grenades, and extra batts for their electro-SMGs. She made the look quick, shuddering for effect. To cover her staring, she said, "It makes me nervous how they carry those big guns. Do they have to hold them like that?"

"Sorry, Juliet. They're here to protect you, so don't be nervous."

Juliet nodded, trying to maintain her concerned expression while, in truth, one of the guard's poor trigger discipline had given her an idea. She was sure the guns were smart enough to require the owner's finger on the trigger to fire. They wouldn't have biometric locks—there were better, more versatile solutions—but she was certain they were linked to their PAIs and couldn't "misfire." Still, if that dummy with his finger on the trigger decided to squeeze it at an inopportune time, that might cause a ruckus.

As she contemplated the possible outcomes, Juliet wondered if it would be enough. If WBD thought she needed a four-person armed escort to travel in an elevator, deep in the bowels of their facility, then surely, they were worried about more than chance encounters with chatty employees.

Was there a legitimate threat? What if one of her guards was a double agent? What if he didn't fire a round into a wall or the floor but into one of her other guards?

Their escort cleared the elevator and motioned for Harriet and Juliet to step aboard. The guards took up positions around them—two in the back, two just inside the door—and then they ascended for a few seconds. Juliet tried to read the elevator display, but one of the corpo-sec brutes blocked it.

When the door opened, two of the gun-toting escorts stepped out, and she heard them shout, "Clear the corridor! Move!"

"Jeez," she muttered. Harriet nodded.

"Too bad we couldn't get one of these machines on our level. Budgets," she sighed, shrugging.

As they walked down a corridor that felt identical to the one on the lower level, Juliet caught glimpses of employees walking in side passages, all wearing the same kinds of bodysuits that she and Harriet had on. After only one turn, she saw, over the shoulders of her front guards, a sign that read RADIOLOGY AND SCANNING.

"Angel," she subvocalized, "I have to do something. I have an idea, but it might be crazy. We might get shot . . . or Harriet."

"We're running out of time; the scanner is on the other side of that door. You'll survive a gunshot." Angel highlighted the door with the sign Juliet had already seen.

"Easy for you to say! Look harder! Are you sure there's nothing, I don't know, *wireless* you can tap into? Something you could use to set off an alarm or—"

"Nothing I can pick up. They have wireless very locked down. Even if I could, it would point fingers your way." As Angel replied, the door loomed close, and Juliet clamped down on her anxiety, shoving her reservations aside.

"Well, here goes nothing." Juliet dredged up an emotion she rarely allowed herself to feel, even when she spoke to Doctor Ming. It was one of those things they'd beaten to death and that she'd then locked away in a box, hoping never to look at again. Still, she knew where it was, and when she pulled it out, she still felt raw.

It was her memory of Don and Vikker—how it had felt when they'd led her into Vikker's garage and drugged her. She remembered that feeling of betrayal as the two had *laughed* about her dying, how that betrayal had left her feeling sick—like she could never trust again.

Just in case that wasn't enough, she remembered Murphy—remembered that hug right before her betrayal. She'd been a woman Juliet looked up to, a mother figure she'd never realized how much she wanted, and her betrayal had stung horribly, exponentially compounding her trust issues.

Juliet let those memories and feelings wash over her, then she grabbed on to them and *pushed*, indiscriminately sharing them with everyone around her. Almost simultaneously, she focused on the front-left guard's SMG and, remembering all the practice she'd done while bored in her hotel room on Callisto, mentally nudged the barrel toward his partner and pressed his finger down on the trigger with a spike of telekinetic energy.

Several things happened at once. The gun *zwapped*, firing a spray of hot, four-millimeter magnetic rods into the hip and thigh of the guard on the right. A deep voice screamed behind them, "Down! Down! Down!" and a hand grabbed Juliet's shoulder, yanking her back and down.

She almost resisted, almost rolled with the motion to throw or tackle the clumsy jerk pulling on her, but she forced herself to go limp, falling onto her butt. Harriet whirled, eyes wide with shock and confusion, and Juliet managed to reach out and grasp her wrist, pulling her down with her.

The guard whom she'd targeted, the one she'd made shoot his comrade, never got a chance to explain. All three of the other guards opened fire, their guns *zwapping* in rapid steam-filled bursts of electromagnetic fire, launching dozens or, for all she could tell, hundreds of rounds into the "instigator."

The lighting in the corridor began to flash red, each pulse punctuated by a two-beat tone and a calm but authoritative feminine voice that said, "Clear all corridors. Lockdown procedures are in effect on decks C-7 through C-11."

Juliet heard the fallout from her hasty distraction, saw the man she'd targeted for his poor trigger discipline bleeding into an ever-widening pool, felt one of the other guards snag her under the arms and drag her back toward the elevator, and the only thing she could focus on was: Had that woman said *decks?*

The two rear guards never gave her or Harriet a chance to stand. They dragged them, at double time, all the way to the elevator, guarding the door until it closed. The one who'd grabbed Juliet, hands shaking with adrenaline, punched the control panel, sending the elevator down; then, in a ragged voice, exclaimed, "Jesus! I can't believe he'd do that! Fucking Rodney!"

"Get a grip, Fisher," the other one said, tapping his visor and pointing at the camera in the corner. He turned to Harriet and held out a hand, helping her to stand. "We're ordered to bring you back to your secured section. We're still waiting for an all clear; we don't know if the assassination attempt was isolated or if there are other actors."

"Assassination?" Juliet asked, helping herself to her feet, seeing as neither corpo-sec moved to give her a hand.

They ignored her, but Harriet cleared her throat. "What's going on?"

The first officer, the more hysterical one, said, "We don't know. A member of our unit flipped, as you saw. We're at a loss. I'm sure we're all going to go through a hell of a background investigation. Goddamn it!" He punched the wall just as the elevator opened again.

"Let's move," the other officer indicated, stepping out and sweeping the corridor with his gun. He motioned for everyone to follow before leading the way back to Harriet's lab and Juliet's prison. They didn't leave them alone until they'd swept the area, including Juliet's shower, for anything out of the ordinary. When they finally exited, she glimpsed several more heavily armed corpo-sec soldiers standing in the corridor.

Harriet punched the close-and-lock sequence on the door, then looked at Juliet. "I'm so glad he didn't get a chance to shoot you."

"I mean, are we sure I was a target? Why'd he shoot the other guard?"

"It doesn't make sense, but my PAI has been running sims. It seems likely the guard who fired expected one of the others to join in his treachery." She leaned against the wall; Juliet could see the usual dark circles under her eyes were far more pronounced. "I just got a note from Kline that we're locked down; there's a massive investigation unfolding."

"Gosh!" Juliet tried hard to play the freaked-out scrap worker. Part of her tried to feel guilty about what had happened to the corpo-sec officer, but she quickly silenced that tiny voice, remembering that those people were holding her prisoner. All she had to do was remember Barns and his furious last stand, remember that Hawkins and Lee were probably dead, too. When she looked past that and remembered what WBD had done to her, the guilt completely evaporated—she wanted to kill more of them.

"I'm sorry, Juliet. I guess no TMS therapy today. Hopefully, they'll get this situation under control, and we can get you rescheduled soon." Harriet walked over to the open door to Juliet's room. "I hate to, I don't know, send you to your room, but I'm awfully shaky. I think I need to sit down, and you should be in there in case one of the bigwigs comes down here to check on things."

"Oh, yeah. No problem, Harriet. Are you going to be all right?"

"I've . . . I've never seen anyone die before." Her eyes widened with horror, and she slapped her hand over her mouth. "Sorry, Juliet. That's not professional at all. I just felt so *betrayed* when he started shooting! I knew what he was doing, that he meant to kill you and probably me too! I'm so glad the other security officers weren't in on his plan!"

"Yeah." Juliet nodded, walking toward the door. "I felt it too. I, uh, I wonder if I've seen that kind of thing before. I know some of my scars are from bullets . . ." She trailed off, feeling a little guilty for involving Harriet in that violent scene. Still, she wasn't the one who'd put Harriet there. WBD was at fault for all of it. "I'm going to do some painting."

"Okay. Good idea. I'll keep you posted on your schedule changes."

"Sounds good." Juliet turned and flopped down on her couch as Harriet shut the door.

"Well, that wasn't pretty, but it worked," Angel spoke.

"I . . . feel like I should be upset, but I'm not. I don't feel guilty. I feel like this is just the start, Angel. You don't know what it felt like—I *pushed* betrayal into those guards at the same time I used telekinesis to fire the first guard's gun. I'm sure that without my push, they would have subdued him. Whoever commands the corpo-sec around here is going to be freaking out. They're going to assume there's something dirty about all four of those guards, and if four are compromised—"

"Many others may also be. You're right. You've greatly hindered them; this investigation will not be quick."

"Another thing, Angel—did you notice what the emergency response AI said?"

"Decks."

"Yep. We're either on a station or a ship—a damn big one, with a gravity generator."

26

GALAXIES

Juliet lay on her couch, admiring her work. She'd given in to her urge to see if she could purposefully alter what she'd seen in her true-dream. To that end, after painting the wall black, instead of painting a view of the Jovian System, with Jupiter looming large, she'd painted a campfire illuminating tall pine trees and, beyond them, the night sky speckled with stars.

She'd worked on the artwork over the last couple of days between trips to the gym and the "learning center," where she'd tuned out interactive vids about WBD's corporate culture. It wasn't so bad when she could play games, listen to music, or watch vids, knowing Angel would pass the exams for her after each lesson.

"One down," she subvocalized.

"Well, unless something forces you to change the art, I suppose it's safe to say that your true-dreams aren't written in stone."

"You thought as much—glimpses into possible timelines, realities, or some such." Before Angel could correct her likely misused terms, Juliet added, "It was different, anyway. It was the first time I saw myself in the true-dream; I felt like I was looking through Harriet's eyes, and the Juliet I saw looked genuinely happy, lying on this couch reading a paperback, with a lot more piled nearby. So far, Kline has gotten me two real paperbacks, one of which is a fanfic—a romance novel *based* on a fantasy!"

"Maybe there's more to come—"

"Not if I can help it. We need to make something happen, Angel. We need to find out what happened to the rest of the team. For all we know, they've got Tanaka and Frida by now. What if they connected me to the *Kowashi* somehow?"

"Or worse," Angel replied, voice hushed. "What if your friends get themselves into trouble trying to find you?"

"Exactly! So? Can we put Daisy to work yet?"

"I'm close, Juliet! She's passing my test scenarios ninety percent of the time."

Juliet groaned and flopped onto her side, staring at the back of the couch. "I'd bet a million Sol-bits your test scenarios are tougher than the real thing."

"Possibly, but I don't want to ruin everything with a misstep. You seem to be in the clear for now; no new scan scheduled yet, your upcoming appointment with Doctor Chen was canceled, and—"

"And we don't know what else is waiting around the corner. We don't know who else might be inches from death."

"I know, Juliet. Just think of the setback we'd face if they discovered Daisy, though. It would make a couple more days of testing seem like the blink of an eye. We may never get another chance; if they figure out you somehow hacked your deck and created a daemon like Daisy, they'd have you on total lockdown, maybe literally locked down into a chair. That's if they didn't just execute you. You know Kline's project is seen as redundant by now."

"Yeah, thanks to Montclair taking my . . ." Juliet trailed off, choosing not to think about it. "I wonder what happened with Grossman. I mean, the listener."

"Perhaps he's biding his time, choosing the best moment to act."

Juliet nodded and closed her eyes, letting her mind drift momentarily. She was worried about her friends. She desperately wanted to know what had happened to Dora and the others. Thinking of them brought her thoughts around to Ghoul, and she asked, "You don't suppose they did anything to Ghoul, do you?"

"I don't see what they'd gain from it."

"Leverage? I mean, if they knew we still cared about each other . . ." Again, Juliet trailed off, not sure what to think.

"We haven't really spoken about that," Angel said softly. "About how you parted. You said you weren't sure what it meant and wanted to think about it, but then WBD took you."

"I was emotional. She was emotional. We'd both pushed a lot of feelings down, and when I saw her—when we were hugging—it felt good, like I'd reconciled with someone I thought I'd lost. I don't know if it means anything more than that. It was a kiss, Angel; we're not married. Besides, what does it matter? I'm God-knows-where, and she told me she can't leave her sister and niece. She doesn't need this kind of trouble in her life."

"True. I suppose it wasn't the first time you've kissed anyone." Angel's conciliatory tone made Juliet snort; she'd completely stopped bothering Juliet about her love life since her little fling with Jensen.

As she lay there, waiting for her next exercise outing, she thought about Jensen, wondering where he'd gone. It was funny to her that she still thought of him as Jensen, even knowing his handle and part of his real name.

"First impressions really do matter."

"Hmm?"

"Nothing." Juliet glanced at the clock, saw she only had to wait five more minutes, and stood to stretch. "Do you think they listened to my request?"

"To lower the pool's temp?"

"Yeah." Juliet had asked Harriet if they could turn the heat off in the pool. She wanted to use the lattice while she swam, wanted to try to reach farther and see if she could pick up any new clues. Angel had been the one to suggest colder water, and Juliet thought it was the perfect idea.

She was still stretching a few minutes later when the door beeped. Looking up, she called out, "Come in."

A moment later, Harriet stood in the opening, and though she smiled, it seemed a little reserved. "Ready to go, aren't you?"

"I'm not gonna lie, Harriet; I'm feeling a little cooped up."

"Well, thanks to the problem with the security forces assigned to our project, your schedule is pretty clear this week. That means more time in the gym if you want it."

"Oh, I want it." Juliet followed her out, past the four guards stationed outside. Two wore red armbands, and two wore yellow ones. Juliet wondered if that had something to do with whatever loyalty testing they had going on. One of each type walked behind them until they entered the other part of "Juliet's suite," as Harriet had dubbed the set of rooms: Chen's lounge, the classroom, and the gym.

The guards took up positions outside the gym, and as soon as the door closed, Juliet asked, "What's the deal with the armbands?"

"I wish I knew. Things have been very strange the last couple of days. I heard they fired something like forty security personnel and brought in some specialists, so maybe that's what the armbands signify. They don't really talk to us."

"Seriously? Forty?" She saw Harriet's pained expression and knew exactly what it meant: She was worried that revealing that fact to Juliet would get her into trouble. The information only spurred Juliet's interest in the pool, however. She was eager to try to fish some information from any minds she could find while swimming.

"Yes, seriously. By the way, did Kline stop to see you last night?"

"Just briefly. He came to apologize for the interruption in my therapy, but honestly, I'm not looking forward to meeting with Doctor Chen." Juliet decided to push her boundaries just a little by adding, "She's a little scary."

While she waited for Harriet's response, she moved over to the pool and gingerly placed her foot on the first step.

"She—"

The water was cold, and Juliet couldn't help but interrupt Harriet. "Oh, thank you, Harriet! I should be a lot more comfortable swimming without the heated water."

Harriet smiled hesitantly, then nodded. "Oh, I'm glad. Anyway, don't worry about Doctor Chen. She's intense, but she's very talented. I think you'll grow to like her."

"Not if I can help it," Juliet subvocalized while she checked to ensure her data deck and cable were safely tucked under the skintight fabric of her bodysuit's sleeve. Aloud, she said, "Talk to you in a while."

She dove into the water, thankful for the bodysuit's wetsuitlike ability to dull the sudden chill. Once she was submerged and the cold started to soak into the material, it lost that insulative property, but it didn't matter. Juliet was already swimming with forceful strokes, pushing against the pool's current, humming with the rhythm of her breaths.

She'd learned that with her Cybergen lungs, she could swim hard, taking a breath only every seven or nine strokes without ever feeling winded. She liked counting to an odd number of strokes because then she'd alternate turning her head left and right for her breaths.

She got so involved in her breathing that it took a nudge from Angel to remind her to get busy. "I'm not seeing any lattice activity."

"Right, boss. On it." With that, Juliet lost herself in the zone and began to let her mind drift.

Over the last couple of days, she'd been pushing herself as far as she could before Angel said her temp was climbing, and Juliet was beginning to think there was a vague, almost ethereal sense of direction to her probing. She swore she could tell if her mental reach was drifting down or climbing, and she thought she could tell if she veered off in different directions.

The first time she'd suspected there was some intention to her drifting was the day before, when she'd listened to a man cursing his supervisor vehemently. She'd let her mind drift away from him, and a bit later, when she'd pulled her attention back toward herself, she'd heard him again.

Because people's thoughts were her only landmarks in that strange mental landscape, she'd realized she could use two different minds as waypoints, and she'd just begun to test that theory when Angel had pulled her out of it.

Now, she was trying again. When she *listened,* Juliet lost track of everything, even her AUI, so she had no idea how long she worked at it, but after a while, she was certain her hypothesis was correct. She could drift with intention between three different nearby voices—Harriet's, a corpo-sec officer daydreaming about his best friend's wife, and a woman a little further away, concentrating on installing a new air scrubber while worrying about her son, who'd gotten a second red frowny face from his corpo-daycare instructor in a row.

What Juliet found strange about her newfound ability to drift from mind to mind was that she had no idea how she did it. It wasn't like flexing a muscle or stretching an invisible limb out through the air. It was more like floating and gliding in the direction she "looked."

It struck Juliet that today, she'd been "moving," and before that, she'd been "listening." Her first sense in the strange thought-space had been her hearing. She'd heard voices, and at first, she'd had trouble *not* hearing them. As she'd gained more and more control of that, she'd learned to direct her listening by imagining a portal through a person's eyes. Was that her mind trying to make sense of this ability?

If her mind was subconsciously trying to learn to control what she could do—first with sound, then direction, and now, this new ability to float where she wanted—could she learn even more control? Juliet was currently near Harriet's thought-space. She'd just been listening to her, but she could *feel* the direction she'd need to "float" to return to the corpo-sec officer's thought-space. If she knew what direction it was in, shouldn't she be able to look that way?

As suddenly as she had the thought, Juliet's mental image of a black void burst with light—the birth of a galaxy of glowing, tangled thought threads that were the corpo-sec officer's mind.

Juliet "looked" back toward Harriet, and there was her shimmering, glowing mind, bursting with energetic tangles—memories, dreams, conscious and subconscious thoughts. Juliet turned toward the woman, the one worrying about her child, and another galaxy of thoughts burst into being.

Juliet felt like weeping, and she knew if she weren't struggling to swim against a stiff current, she would be sobbing at the beauty of it. She turned back to Harriet's mind, then the guard's, and each time, she noticed more differences between each tangle of thought. They all had a particular character, like a person's iris—utterly, fabulously unique.

The more she embraced her newfound visualization, the more real it seemed, and the more Juliet believed it *was* real, that she could drift through the void of mental space and look around, seeing the knots of glowing thoughts that represented other people's minds.

As she gained that spatial awareness and looked between Harriet, the corpo-sec guard, and the other woman, Juliet felt like she'd been blind, and someone had just installed her first ocular implants.

Juliet used her "ears" to find more nearby thoughts, then "looked" that way, and more and more tangles of glowing thread began to populate the void. Each discovery felt easier than the last, and she lost count as first a dozen, then a hundred, and then thousands began to fill the space around her.

She was stunned by the visualization. She felt like she was drifting through intergalactic space, and all around her were brilliant, busy galaxies floating in the vast, endless void.

"Angel . . ." she grunted into the water, her arms falling limp as she drifted, allowing the pool to push her toward the shallow end.

At the same time, Angel whispered, "Juliet . . ." She didn't say anything more, but Juliet could feel her sharing her wonder. What must she be thinking? Could Angel see what she was witnessing? If not, she could surely feel it.

"I-I, um . . ." Some part of Juliet was aware that she was still face down in the pool, floating, but most of her was utterly flabbergasted by what she was witnessing. She couldn't help herself from picking a random, distant mind, floating toward it, and listening to the thoughts just to confirm she hadn't gone mad.

A man's voice came to her, deep and jolly. *Two more hours 'til quitting time. Three more days, then off this bucket and back to Ursula!* An image floated through Juliet's mind—a sturdy, middle-aged woman with silky black hair, bright red lips, and cheeks that scrunched into rosy apples when she laughed.

Juliet heard herself laugh into the water as she pulled away from the cluster of yellow, golden thoughts and scanned the thousands of mind clusters, wondering where to go next. Paralyzed by the myriad choices, she stared, taking more and more in. Something odd caught her eye: a lopsided cluster, oblong and bright on one end, dim on the other. It was strange because while every other cluster she'd seen was unique, they were all roughly spherical.

Juliet stared at the oddly shaped bundle of thoughts and drifted toward it, intent on seeing what made it so different.

". . . Juliet!" Harriet's voice broke through her concentration, and Juliet opened her eyes, blinking into the water. She lifted her head and blew out her breath, instantly heaving for a new one—her lungs had plenty of stored-up oxygen, but they still made her gasp reflexively, restocking their reserves. "Are you okay?" Harriet stood in the shallow water, a hand on her shoulder.

"Oh man, I'm so sorry, Harriet!" Juliet tried to think fast, but her mind was still reeling from the breakthrough she'd just had. Had she been outside of her body? Was *she* not bound by her mind and flesh? Or was she just pushing her senses around, outside of herself? It was such a strange, magical thing, and she knew Angel was flummoxed also; she could feel her trying to make sense of all the feelings she'd just gone through.

"What happened?" Harriet asked when Juliet didn't speak further.

"Oh, um, I just realized I must have done something to my lungs! How can I hold my breath for so long? Sorry if I scared you; I should have said something before trying to test it."

"Yeah, well, they can't get mad at me for confirming the obvious, can they?" Harriet smiled and nodded, shrugging helplessly. "You have some nice lung upgrades. They're not synthetic; they're full-on cybernetic." She backed up the steps and sat on the edge. "Too cold for me!"

Juliet smiled and stood, not at all surprised to see steam drift away from her bodysuit; she was hot. "Well, I sure warmed up swimming like that! This temp is great for a hard workout." She glanced at her clock, saw her exercise hour was almost up, and subvocalized, "Angel, are you okay?"

"I'm fine, Juliet, just savoring those feelings we had a minute ago. Will you tell me about what happened?"

"Of course! As soon as we're back." Juliet started climbing out of the pool, then looked at Harriet. "Hey, think I could swim again this afternoon? I was just wondering, since most of my other stuff was canceled."

"I'll message Kline. I'm sure it'll be fine after we check in for lunch and I do my reports. You're not tired?"

"Not really. I don't know, Harriet, I just love swimming! I never used to like it this much, but I feel like I can just totally zone out and float away, you know?"

"Like all your troubles just melt away?" Harriet looked down, her pursed lips lifting at the corners.

"Does that mean something to you?" Juliet asked, nudging her with an elbow as they stepped into the hallway and past their waiting escort.

"Yeah, it does. I get that way when I game. Sometimes, I lose out on sleep 'cause I'm busy escaping reality, you know? Oof! Juliet! I keep forgetting to remain professional with you! Now Kline's AI will tell him about my poor sleeping habits."

At first, Juliet thought she was really upset, but when she looked at Harriet with alarm, she saw that her smile had grown, and there was a spark in her eyes. Was she teasing her? Making fun of Kline?

"Well," Juliet said, trying to sound chagrined, "I appreciate your efforts to make me feel better, Harriet. I recognize you're trying to relate to me, and I hope you don't get into any trouble for being a talented caretaker."

"Caretaker?" Harriet narrowed her eyes as though trying the word on for size. "I guess that fits."

They were already approaching the door to Harriet's lab, where the other two guards waited, when Juliet noticed it was already open. She felt dread when she saw that open door, and something inside her screamed *DANGER*. She slowed her pace, coming to a stop, as Harriet noticed, also slowing.

"Something wrong?"

"I think someone's there." Juliet nodded toward the open door just as it began to *snick* closed.

Harriet looked at the guard with the red armband. "Who's here?"

In a voice that reminded Juliet of Athena's mechs, utterly devoid of human inflection, he replied, "Vice President Montclair is waiting."

27

BROKEN MINDS

Juliet didn't think it was possible, but Harriet's face paled even further at the security officer's words. At least, she assumed the words had upset her, but it could also have been the man's harsh, robotic voice.

"Oh," the lab tech said, visibly flustered as she began to wring her hands. "We better not keep him waiting. Come on, Juliet."

Juliet had been about to reassure her, her own nerves forgotten in her desire to help someone she saw as weaker than herself, but she stopped, remembering she wasn't supposed to know who Montclair was. "Is that your, um, boss?"

"More like Kline's boss." Harriet shook her head, her nervousness evident in the way she tugged at the lapel of her lab coat. "So yes, that makes him my boss, too."

Before Juliet could respond, they stood before the door to Harriet's lab. Harriet leaned over to interact with the security panel, putting in her keys, as their two escorting guards took up positions on the other side of the hallway, creating a sort of box formation with the other two. The air was thick with tension, and Juliet couldn't stop thinking about Athena's mechs. Was WBD replacing her security detail with combat synths? Did that mean they were aware or at least suspicious of her abilities?

"Four guards, and I'm starting to think they're not all human. I hope Montclair isn't here to expose me," she subvocalized.

"I'll be ready with your speed enhancement, but remember this deck limits me significantly; you'll move as fast as before, but I'm going to struggle to do any other tasks at the same time."

Juliet mentally nodded. She and Angel had spoken about strategies for combat now that the plucky AI had rewritten the code that gave her control of most of Juliet's cybernetics. The deck's two processing chips were quick, but they lacked the massively multithreaded nature of Angel's original, especially when it was combined with the coprocessor that used to be in Juliet's data port. Angel's control over her augmented speed wouldn't be as precise using the deck. Worse, she couldn't monitor her for damage in real time, so she planned to use her boosts only in small bursts.

The door hissed open, and Harriet stepped through. Juliet followed, seeing Montclair in the flesh for the first time. He looked exactly the same as he had in Kline's memory—tall, thin, dour expression, dark, emotionless eyes, gray hair combed back away from his tall forehead, and a black suit over a white shirt and black tie.

"Miss Kennedy," he said flatly, then looked at Juliet and ran his cold gaze over her. "And charge."

"Hello, sir. Um, Mister Montclair." Harriet looked like she didn't know what to do with her hands. First, she clutched the fabric of her lab coat as though she might curtsy. Then she sort of reached toward Montclair, pulled her hand back, and squeezed it tightly with her other one as her eyes darted around the room nervously.

The door closed behind Juliet with a *snick,* and she stepped to the side, not wanting to walk closer to the man. He radiated wrongness in a way she hadn't been able to perceive in her deep dive into Kline's memory.

As soon as she met his eyes, she recognized a malevolence similar to what she'd seen in Doctor Chen. There was something the same about them that had nothing to do with looks or, obviously, words—he hadn't said enough to gauge his personality. Nevertheless, something about him felt *off,* and Juliet wanted to distance herself from the man. To that end, she started edging her way across the room toward the door to her cell as he looked at Harriet and said, "I thought you were on lockdown."

"Well, Mister Kline approved one-hour trips to the learning annex and exercise room. I was just about to write up my AM reports." Harriet nodded toward the open door to Juliet's cell. "Please return to your quarters, Juliet."

She'd put on a brave face, and Juliet had to commend her for getting a grip on her nerves. She also felt immensely, embarrassingly grateful for the easy out. She hurried toward the door, trying to help Harriet look good.

Montclair turned toward her. "Just a moment, Miss Bianchi." Juliet froze and looked at him, her body nearly trembling with the need to do one of two things: run or fight. She fought the sensation, steeling herself, and looked into his dark eyes.

"Yes, sir?"

"I understand you've been very cooperative, hmm? Working hard to help Kline figure out what's gone haywire with that malfunctioning chip, yes?"

"I'm doing my best, sir, but I don't have any memories of the, um, PAI. I'm just grateful for the kind treatment I've received here."

"Hmm." Montclair moved closer, looming over her as he closed the distance. Juliet guessed his height at something close to two meters. It wasn't his size that intimidated her, however. It was a weird sensation, almost like he was a feral animal. She felt like, at any moment, he might lean down and bite her or something equally disturbing. "Is that so? Tell me, what's that flickering on those pretty little irises?"

"I'm sorry?" Juliet's heart began to race as she subvocalized, "Hide everything, but get Daisy ready. We may be about to lose our chance to test her any more."

"I'm on it." Juliet knew Angel could feel how serious she was, could feel her stress. She was smart enough to make her own conclusions. Meanwhile, Juliet's mind raced—it sounded like Montclair didn't know about the deck. How would he respond?

"Are you being coy, young woman?" Montclair let his gaze drift over her form, and suddenly, she wasn't so thankful for the bodysuit's form-hugging comfort. "What's on your wrist?"

Juliet looked at her wrist and lifted her arm, chuckling nervously as she rolled her sleeve back, "Oh, it's just this entertainment deck Mister Kline let me borrow. I was listening to music while exercising—"

Montclair snatched the deck and yanked the cable out, then turned to Harriet, holding it up. "Who approved this?"

"Well, Director Kline, sir." It was the first time Juliet had heard Kline's title mentioned, and she wondered if Harriet had done it for effect.

If she'd hoped to get him to back off with the mention of Kline's authority over the project, she must have been disappointed. Montclair scoffed and tucked the deck into his inner jacket pocket, then turned his back on Juliet and took a lunging step toward Harriet, radiating violence. For a moment, Juliet thought he'd strike her, but he stopped, and utterly calm, straightened his jacket.

"That's absurd. Far too much risk for—" The door opened with a *snick*, and he stopped midphrase as Kline entered the room. He raised an eyebrow, glancing from Juliet to Harriet before settling his gaze on Montclair. He put one hand in his trouser pocket, then reached under his jacket to pull out an honest-to-God Nikko-vape, sucking deeply on it.

Everyone stared at him for a moment, then he exhaled a cloud of vapor. "What's going on here?"

Montclair glared at him, his posture leaning forward aggressively, and growled, "Tell me what the hell you did to my listener."

Juliet saw Harriet stumble back, practically falling into her desk chair—it looked like her knees gave out on her. Juliet could tell why; Montclair was radiating pure, uncut hatred and pent-up violence. She was amazed that Kline didn't flinch back.

He calmly slipped his vape cartridge under his jacket and shrugged. "I heard about that. Where'd he get those emergency codes? It was a lucky thing you were at Ark when he broke into your lab. Sorry to hear about your assistant and those samples—"

Montclair lurched forward and grabbed Kline's jacket, driving him back against the closed door. "You piddling little—"

"Ruby? Are you getting this?" Kline asked, holding his hands out to the side, turning his face away from Montclair's looming, snarling countenance. "I think this is the sort of thing Mrs. Gentry asked us to report."

Montclair leaned close, putting his mouth a centimeter from Kline's ear. He whispered something that Juliet couldn't quite hear, not without boosting her augmented hearing, and Angel couldn't do that without the deck. Still, she picked up a fragment of hissed vitriol which didn't make any sense: ". . . get that? *Little sister?*"

"Um," Harriet said, her voice quavering as she worked to come to grips with the scene playing out. "Director Kline? I think Vice President Montclair was wondering about that deck you gave Juliet." Juliet could have kissed her, utterly stunned by the woman's bravery.

Kline grinned despite Montclair's grip on his jacket. "What's that? This project isn't under your purview any longer, Montclair. No need to worry about my methods."

Montclair loosened his grip, straightened, and stared at Kline. He was either trying to intimidate him further or deciding if he wanted to go through the trouble of killing him on the spot; either option seemed plausible to Juliet.

She took the opportunity to try to *listen*, staring hard at Montclair and instantly recognizing the same weird void she'd experienced with Doctor Chen. Almost instinctively, she closed her eyes then *opened* her other perception, staring into the mental space she'd discovered while swimming.

It came to her without any difficulty, like another sense she'd always had. She saw the galaxies of thoughts and emotions pulsing and throbbing where Harriet, Kline, and Montclair stood, but one was different. One was oblong, only partially alight, with at least half of its sphere utterly dark.

While she stared in wonder, she heard something clatter onto the plasteel floor, then Montclair's voice. "You're running out of time, Kline. These security breaches are a minor setback. We have more batches behind the one that was destroyed."

She heard the door open, and then, to her amazement, the malformed galaxy of thoughts drifted out to join two other, healthy-looking ones. Juliet hastily opened her eyes and confirmed what she'd suspected—four guards stood in the hallway with Montclair. "Synths," she subvocalized.

The guards? Angel's voice echoed up from the depths of her mind.

"Two of them, yeah."

"Well, sorry about that, ladies," Kline spoke as the door slid shut. He stepped forward and picked up Juliet's deck, turning it in his fingers a few times before smiling. "Looks okay." He held it out to her, and Juliet stepped forward to take it.

"Um, thanks, Kline. Who was that guy? What a creep!"

"Just someone who shouldn't be here. Don't worry. I'm going to do my best to ensure you two never have to deal with him again." He looked over at Harriet and smiled, pressing his hands into his lower back as he stretched. "Man, didn't want to walk into that! I was just coming to see how things are progressing with all the security lockdowns messing things up."

As he spoke, Juliet inserted her data cable into the deck and tucked it back under her sleeve.

"Doing okay?" she subvocalized.

"Much better now," Angel replied. "I'm rather impressed by Kline after that."

"Don't get too attached." Juliet tried to keep from chuckling as she subvocalized. "He's still on the enemy team."

"Things have been good, sir," Harriet was saying. "We'd just returned from exercise, and I was about to work on my AM reports, but Vice President—"

"No need to explain, Harriet. I wanted to let you both know that I couldn't get a new appointment for your, uh, magnetic treatment until next Friday, Juliet. So, no Doctor Chen this week. You keeping busy?" He stepped over to the doorway to Juliet's room and peered through. "I like the painting. You like to camp?"

Juliet followed him over, looking at her surprisingly artistic scene of a campfire in the woods. "Um, not really. I don't think I've ever actually been." She didn't have to lie; the only thing she'd ever done close to camping was when she'd been with Charlie Unit up in the mountains. Even then, they'd had barracks. "I'm not sure where the idea came from, but it helps me relax."

Kline nodded, and she saw him tap at his breast pocket, but only briefly. She might have tried to read him if they weren't standing in a doorway together. She was curious if he was really so cool or if he was losing it inside. If so, he was a hell of an actor. "Well, that's important. Anything else I can do for you?"

Juliet nodded and grinned toward Harriet. "We were hoping I could get another exercise session in the afternoons. It's boring sitting around here all day."

"Yep. I was going to suggest it. Put it into the schedule, Harriet."

"Yes, sir."

"Oh? What's with all the *sirs*? Did Montclair rattle you that much?"

"He's awful, Kline!" Harriet replied. "Before you walked in, I thought he was going to *hit me*!"

Juliet nodded. "He's bad."

"Right. Well, like I said, I'm going to see about getting him restricted from this area. I'll go take care of that right now, in fact." Kline turned, started for the door, then paused and looked at Harriet. "Order something good for lunch for the two of you. Tell the kitchen they can take it from my account."

"Um, all right. Thank you." Harriet looked like she was feeling much better with his assurances.

Juliet stepped into her room but turned back toward Kline as he fiddled with the exterior door and called, "Thank you, Kline." He waved a hand over his shoulder, and then he was gone, slipping past the four looming guards in the hallway. "I'm going to take a nap while you do your report, Harriet."

"Wait! What do you want for lunch?"

Juliet paused, wondering how extensive the menu was, but decided she wouldn't know what to order; not back when she worked in the scrapyard. "You pick, Harriet. I'd just order something dumb like a pizza."

"I love pizza!"

"Well"—Juliet turned back toward her—"wanna?"

"I'll order it!"

Juliet smiled and walked over to her couch, listening to the door beep and close with a resounding *thunk* of the bolts. She stretched out and turned onto her side, putting her back to the door. "Angel, that was so weird. I can see people's minds just by closing my eyes."

"Their minds? Or their thoughts?"

"The things *in* their minds, I guess—thoughts, memories, dreams, emotions."

"How, though? Did something change?"

"When I was swimming! Remember when I basically stunned us? When I was floating there, full of wonder and amazement?"

"Yes! It was"—Angel laughed—"wonderful and amazing! But how?"

"Well, I started to realize I could sense myself drifting when I listened to the people around me. When I realized I could sense a direction, I started to put it together that my brain has been trying to cope with this new sense since the day Grave put the GIPEL in my head. I've been fighting it almost the entire time since then, but even with my resistance, I've gained quite a lot of control.

"For instance, I don't have to work as hard to keep people's thoughts away when I sleep. I can find a person's thoughts by looking into their eyes, and even dive into their memories. Anyway, I don't want to get lost in the weeds.

"The point I'm trying to make is that I figured out that my brain was treating people's thoughts as sound. I was *hearing* them. But then, when I realized I could *move* between minds, everything started to click—it was a lot more than just hearing. If I could move in a direction, could I *look*? When I tried, it all fell into place. I started seeing people's minds, Angel, and they're beautiful!"

"Really? Can you feel them? If you can move and see and hear, can you feel?"

"I . . . I'm not sure. I know I can pull the tendrils of thought my way; that's how I *hear* them. What am I pulling them with? Is that the same as my telekinesis? Is that my touch? God! This is so *weird*! I should have been working on this from the start! I—"

"You had good reason to mistrust and fear it. I'm hesitant to remind you of this, considering the progress you've made, but you were violated, Juliet. I'm glad that WBD's fiddling with your memories has backfired. I'm glad it's let you get past the hang-ups, for lack of a better word, but don't you dare blame yourself."

Juliet nodded, feeling some tears gathering in her eyes. She wasn't sure if she felt like crying because of Angel's love and understanding or because she was remembering how scared and freaked out she'd been when the squints at Grave had injected her with those nanites.

A snort of laughter escaped her, and she felt Angel's curiosity. "I just remembered how the guys used to call the scientists *squints*. God, sometimes I miss them—Houston, Polk, Vandemere, Yang. That was fun, training with those guys."

She started to close her eyes, suddenly feeling exhausted, but then they snapped open, and she subvocalized, "I didn't tell you the weirdest thing!"

"What?"

"When Montclair was talking to Kline, I tried to hear his thoughts. It was just like listening to Chen—silence. But then, I closed my eyes and *looked*. Angel, his mind is weird. It's half . . . dead. It's like there's a void where most of his thoughts should be. He's broken somehow, in some way that makes him . . . wrong. That's not all, though! I saw another one like that when I was drifting in the pool. At first, I thought it had been Montclair, but thinking back, it was different."

Juliet flopped onto her back and stared at her painting, looking at the glowing embers she'd drawn drifting up toward the black sky. Was she that good? Was it her arm, or had Angel been helping her? Was it strange that she didn't know?

"Was there more?" Angel asked. "I felt like you were going to say more."

"Oh, I was just thinking. Every mind is different. Did I tell you that? Anyway, there's something very, very wrong with that man, and I think there are others like him. When I get to the pool, I'll let my mind wander and make my way through this ship or station or whatever it is. I'll hunt for the broken minds, and then I'll listen to the people near them. I'm going to get to the bottom of what's going on here."

28

\\\\\\\\\\\\\\\\\\\\\\

SHIP OF NIGHTMARES

Juliet drifted. While her body toiled—arms pumping, legs kicking—her mind, her *self*, wandered the enormous spaceship where she was being held captive. She'd figured out for sure it was a ship shortly after Montclair visited her prison through repeated mental wanderings.

She'd drifted from one mind to another, mentally building an image of the ship's layout as she went. She couldn't *see* the hallways and corridors down which she floated, but as she traveled from mind to mind, listening to thoughts and watching snippets of memory, she'd begun to paint a picture.

She was being held in a section of the ship only accessible to a handful of high-clearance individuals and the corpo security units assigned to her. Outside that section, the ship buzzed with activity. People rushed to and fro, harried and hectic, worried about deadlines and impending "big things" that only the upper echelon seemed to grasp the full picture of.

Juliet had intended to find Montclair, seeking out those strange, broken minds, but after two days, she'd failed to get to him. She had found *others*, though, and one was Doctor Chen. She couldn't listen to the doctor's mind, but she could easily pluck the thoughts from the people around her, confirming who she was and her subordinates' abject fear of getting on the wrong side of her temper.

"Doctor" Chen wasn't working as any sort of counselor or psychologist Juliet had ever seen; the people working near her seemed to be scientists, and they were a gold mine of information about WBD's Angel research. From them, Juliet had learned that WBD was working on new generations of the

Angel Project, that their latest release was 3.4, and that it was both a success and a massive failure.

At that moment, Juliet was probing the mind of another employee stationed near Chen. His thoughts were consumed with fear: a fear of demotion, of being relocated to a research station on a distant moon, or worse, of being eliminated.

His anxiety stemmed from the new version of the Angel AI, which had increased the chances of client survival and "neural autonomy." However, it had also become overly sentient and underperformed in cognition evaluations. To Juliet, as she delved deeper into the man's mind, it became clear: the new chips didn't always overwrite their hosts, but they created emotional feedback loops, and the AIs weren't functioning as living, thinking beings.

The revelation was one of many that had left Juliet reeling. It felt like more than a handful of different teams were working on various projects, each of which was centered on Juliet and Angel.

After listening to that technician, she couldn't help pulling away, drifting in the void away from the other minds for a moment. She wanted the peace to report to Angel.

"Another one. Angel, they're still trying to figure out what made you tick. They're up to version 3.4—not alpha! They started handing out these chips to employees at version 1.0. The guy I just listened to was thinking about how this new one doesn't seem to impact 'neural autonomy' as much as other versions."

"That means . . ." Angel seemed to be lost for words for the first time in a while.

"It means that some of the Angel PAIs are taking over people's minds."

"Don't call them that."

"Angel?"

"Yes! I don't care what they call their project! I don't want to hear it. It makes it sound like all of these . . . *beings* are descended from me."

"Sorry, Angel. Don't worry; from everything I've gathered, you're unique. And well, so am I. That's another big piece of the puzzle, and the only reason I'm still alive—seems like not everyone manages to keep their marbles when they have an actual living, thinking AI put into their brains."

"Which is why Montclair is cloning you and probably fertilizing your eggs to create a breeding stock. Juliet, we have to stop these monsters."

"I know," she subvocalized, pulling her consciousness back to her body; she was pretty sure her hour of gym time was almost up. "How's Daisy?"

"I'm hesitant to say this, but I don't know how I can make her any better. She's as ready as I can get her with my current tools."

Juliet opened her eyes and stopped swimming, letting the bubbling, flowing water push her back. She flopped onto her back and floated toward the steps, thinking. Was she ready? Were *they* ready? She could bide her time and spy some more using the pool, but every day she waited, she risked being discovered. She risked being taken someplace farther away, or even killed by one of Kline's WBD competitors.

She was growing increasingly sure that Montclair, Chen, and the others with broken minds were recipients of Angel-like chips that had run amok, driving out their own cognitive functions. How long could she stay undiscovered or protected with amoral pseudo-AIs running the show?

What about the main WBD boss, Mrs. Gentry? She'd heard and felt Kline's thoughts about her. Why was she on this ship? Why were they all? Juliet had yet to get into the mind of someone who knew everything, but she was beginning to wonder if WBD was preparing for another system-wide corporate war.

"Done?" Harriet asked.

"Yeah, I think so." Juliet stood, letting the water drip from her hair and torso before starting up the steps. "Harriet, when we get back, can you put some new vids on my deck? Something funny? I'm running out of content."

"Um, sure. I'll just message Kline now." Harriet stood still, staring into space momentarily while Juliet stood on the top step, dripping dry. The bodysuit and her synthetic hair only took a few seconds to shed the water.

While she stood there, Angel asked, "You're sure about this?"

"Every day—every *hour* we wait, we're risking something happening. We need to get Daisy out there snooping around for real. We need to see through cameras, find your chip, see if my gear is here with us or long gone."

Juliet's Texan and monoblade flashed through her mind, and she clenched her fist. She'd asked Kline if any of her stuff had survived her "rescue," saying it might help with her memory, but he'd never gotten back to her. She wanted to look into his head again, but he'd been absent since the confrontation with Montclair.

"He's good with it," Harriet spoke up. "Sorry, I got distracted reading a schedule update. Looks like you're back on for TMS therapy this Friday."

"Three days, Angel," Juliet subvocalized, pressing her face into a smile. "That'll be good, Harriet. I hope it helps. I can't believe I haven't remembered anything yet." Rather than wait for Kline, she decided to try her ploy with Harriet. "I was wondering if Kline ever got back to you about my belongings. I mean, from when WBD managed to rescue me and bring me here. I always see in drama vids how someone with amnesia can sometimes trigger memories with old belongings or visiting places they'd been, you know?"

"I know exactly what you mean." Harriet nodded, unaware that Juliet was drifting into her mind, trying to tease out her thoughts behind the words. "I'm not sure where your belongings might be, but I can pester Kline for you." *If he ever comes around the lab again. Oh, poor Juliet! I should message him. I just did, though. I'll wait 'til dinner time; don't want to annoy the man . . .*

Juliet pulled back and sighed happily, shaking out her loose muscles. She stepped toward the door as Harriet opened it.

"Thanks."

They walked with their escort back to Harriet's lab, where Juliet handed her the deck, surprised at the steadiness of her hand. Was she really doing this? Before she could second-guess herself, she stepped away, then turned and watched with a strange mix of trepidation, guilt, and excitement as Harriet plugged her deck into her station's data port.

"Here we go, Angel," she subvocalized, unconsciously wringing her hands as she began to pace.

"Um, Juliet?" Harriet asked, and Juliet almost bolted for the door.

"Yeah?"

"What kind of comedy? Do you want something slapstick or more ironic? Something long-form or like a serial? My AI's doing a search."

"Something really silly; I need to laugh. I'm good with some romance mixed in!"

"Have you seen *Sandra's Cleaning* from the Martian net?"

Juliet grinned and stepped a little closer. "Nope!"

Angel's disembodied voice floated into Juliet's awareness. *Daisy should be in by now. She'll lie low until the deck's out and observe the ICE. If she's not up to the task, we may be in serious trouble shortly.*

"And if she is up to it?"

Then, I should receive an encrypted wireless signal from her sometime soon. She has to subdue the ICE in the network, or at least, learn to disguise herself from it. Her first priority will be to find a wireless transmitter. After that, I can help her.

Harriet pulled the cord out of the deck and handed it to Juliet. "Nine seasons. If you hate it, let me know, and I'll find something else."

"Thank you so much, Harriet. I really appreciate this." Juliet held the deck up almost in a faux salute, then plugged her data cable back in and slid it under her sleeve. "Guess I'll go chill for a while until mealtime."

"No more painting? I think those star thingies you've been drawing are really neat." Harriet walked over to her door, peering in at the wall opposite Juliet's camping scene. She had drawn half a dozen of the mind galaxies she'd seen while exploring that weird mental space over the last few days.

They weren't as detailed as the real thing—not anywhere near close; only a few hundred lines of yellow, white, and orange swirling threads arranged in clusters. "They remind me of something. I'm not sure, but maybe like lights seen through fog or rain. I guess they're meant to be something in space, though, right? I mean, because of the black background."

"I dunno." Juliet shrugged, stepping into her room. "Just started with an image in my mind and let my subconscious take over. I don't think they're supposed to be *anything*, really." Of course, she was lying; she had been trying to show Angel what she'd seen. One of the clusters she'd drawn was decidedly different from the others—an ovoid with a black, void-filled end and subdued, muted threads filling the other end. "Kind of abstract, I guess."

"Pretty, though." Harriet stopped by the door, watching Juliet walk over and flop onto her couch. "I'll do my reports. See you when the dinner cart arrives."

Juliet waved then closed her eyes, listening to the door close. "I hope Daisy is doing all right."

"Me too, Juliet. I'm worried about her. She wasn't ready for something like this. Fido had so much more available to him before I sent him out on his own."

"Can she worry? Is she scared?"

"She has some sapience, but she's too stubborn to be scared. She was eager."

Juliet snorted, smiling broadly. She covered the reaction by flopping onto her back as though settling down to watch a vid. "She's stubborn?"

"I wanted her to be! I wanted her to be brave; I just hope I didn't make her *too* brave."

"Well, don't worry, Angel. I'm sure she's—" Juliet's door beeped, and the bolts *thunked* as they slid open. She sat up, heart hammering. There wasn't any reason someone should be visiting; dinner was nearly two hours away. "Get the speed boost ready, Angel."

"I will!" Just as the door began to swing open, Juliet heard a high-pitched *ping*, and static flickered over her vision—she was being jammed. A tall man stepped through the door. He wore a full corpo-sec combat suit, but his helmet's visor was up.

Icy blue eyes locked onto hers, and with heart-stopping shock, she realized she was looking at Jensen. He held a rod-shaped device in his hand, and the static in her vision increased when Juliet looked at it. It had to be the jammer he was deploying. Jensen said nothing but turned to the door panel, tapped a few keys, and waited for it to close.

Juliet's mouth had gone dry. Her palms were sweaty, even her cybernetic one, and she took a step to the side, edging for a way to get the couch between herself and Jensen. The instinct was strange, she reflected in that pregnant few seconds while Jensen waited for the door to close. Shouldn't she be happy to see him? Shouldn't she rush to hug him?

Something warned her, though—he was wearing a WBD corpo-sec outfit, after all. He was operating the door panel; he wasn't behaving like he was there to rescue her. Jensen was WBD?

"Can you still boost me?" she subvocalized.

The deck can't handle this jamming field. I'm sorry, Juliet; we should have considered this drawback.

Juliet took another step to the side as the door's bolts slid home, but then Jensen stuffed the jammer in his belt, strode forward, and grabbed her by the shoulders. "What the fuck are you doing here?"

"Wha-what?" she asked, some part of her mind deciding it would be wise to play dumb.

"Lucky, what the fuck are you doing here?"

"D-Do, um, do I know you?"

His grip tightened like two vises on her arms, and he shook her. "Cut the shit! What's going on? Why are you locked up down here? What the hell is going on here?" Jensen's expression was genuine, his eyes utterly confused; dismayed, even. "What happened? Did you get hit on the head? Why are you on this ship?"

Juliet wanted to say something to him, wanted to ask for help, but something kept her from doing so. Instead, she stared into those icy blue eyes and, holding nothing back, dove in.

Walker frowned as he waited outside the door. Another problem? Another delay? He'd done his part, hadn't he? He'd secured the deal with Ark with a bit of hostage leverage.

Images of a young woman and man tied to acceleration couches flashed through his mind.

Now, he had to help all these other departments pull their weight? He wasn't a goddamn manager; he'd made that clear. He got things done—that was his forte. He was a fixer, not a project director.

The doors clicked and swung open, so he cleared his facial expression and stepped through.

"There he is! My star, my A-plus operator. Come over here, sugar. I just finished with Montclair."

Gentry sat on her couch, patting the cushion beside her. Walker nodded, stepping across the absurdly thick carpeting to sit. He chose the cushion near the armrest rather than the one she'd patted, shifting to look at her directly. She didn't say anything, but he knew it probably pissed her off.

"No luck finding the bad actors?" he asked.

Gentry sighed and sipped her drink. "No, but we're erring on the side of 'kill 'em all and let God sort 'em out.'"

"Gonna wind up short-staffed that way."

She shrugged. "Staffing isn't something we're in short supply of, especially with the drive coming online next week. It's time to cut ties, sugar. Besides, we're bringing the Mark Sevens into play planetside, and they make decent security personnel."

"So, what am I doing?"

"You're going to look into Montclair's listener problem. He swears one of my favorites is involved, but I don't believe it. Kline's sensitive, but he's loyal. Still, you know how Montclair is; he doesn't really make mistakes."

"So, you want me to . . ." Walker raised his eyebrow, wishing she'd get to the point.

"The listener visited Kline's lab the day before it went haywire. Go check it out. We're getting too close to zero hour for this sort of thing to be happening."

Walker nodded, frowning slightly as he rubbed his jawline. His stubble was rough. He needed a shave—easy to get away with when you had blond hair. At least it sounded like he'd be looking into something, not babysitting a bunch of shitty corpo-sec admins while they tried to sort out their security checks and balances. "What's this Kline guy working on?"

"It's the Angel alpha and the compatibility candidate I told you about."

"Thought you guys were way past that alpha. I thought"—Walker frowned, hating how he didn't want to say "Apollyon," but knowing it was best not to invoke him on the ship—"you-know-who was handling all that stuff now."

Gentry chuckled and shook her head. "He's overseeing everything. He's listening now, sugar, but he knows how to delegate. Why would he suffer fools who can't fend for themselves from time to time? Now, quit dillydallying and get down there— you're my problem solver! I'm sending you access keys to view the security footage from that level. That'll get you started."

Juliet jerked her mind out of Jensen's and stumbled back, tripping on the couch and flopping limply in Jensen's iron grip. "The hell is wrong with you?" he growled. "What did they do?"

Just then, the door beeped, and the bolts slid home noisily. As it started to swing open, Jensen leaned close and hissed, "I can't help you, goddammit. Not without getting us both killed. You gotta sit tight. They're *jumping* next week, dammit! I'll . . . I'll try to help you after that."

"I, um"—Juliet licked her lips and looked nervously toward the door—"I don't know what you're talking about."

Jensen growled again and let go of her, sending her flopping onto the couch. He reached down and touched something on his jammer, and suddenly,

Juliet's hearing and vision clarified. The door opened, and two corpo-sec offi-cers stepped through, closely followed by Kline.

"I'm all done here," Jensen said, shoving through the two guards and bumping Kline out of his way. "Everything checks out."

Kline looked after him, then shrugged. "You can return to your posts." He looked at Juliet, who sat stunned on the couch, mouth slightly ajar, eyes wide. "You okay? He hurt you?"

She slowly shook her head, her mind racing. She'd been in Jensen's head! It had been the first deep dive she'd ever done on him, and she was still reeling.

He'd had *conviction* about wanting to please Mrs. Gentry. He'd felt *awe* when she said "zero hour." He'd been almost *reverent* when he'd thought about Apollyon. It was a name all too familiar to Juliet from the many lessons on the AI war she'd sat through in her Helios-sponsored primary education; Apollyon had been a true AI developed by Cybergen for the express purpose of destroying Takamoto and ending the war as quickly as possible. He was sup-posed to be gone—dead.

Kline moved to sit beside her. "Seriously, Juliet. What did he do?"

"Um"—she took a deep, slow breath—"he just grilled me about the secu-rity, like I had something to do with the attack upstairs." She shrugged and then subvocalized, "Angel, we can't just escape. We have to destroy this ship. It's a ship of nightmares."

29

DESPERATION

Rutger Tanaka dove behind a stack of crates, rolled, and came up in time to bisect the WBD corpo-sec officer before she could bring her SMG to bear. He heard gunfire, recognized the staccato *pffts* of Leo's smart needler, and knew the troop deployment tunnel was under control.

His AUI displayed the status of the team—each person's location and a summary of their vital signs via color gradients. Everyone was in the green. Using Fred's map and the pale-blue dot indicating his location, Tanaka darted for the elevator, hoping Kostas's intel would, once again, prove correct.

He jerked the specialized deck from his belt and pressed it against the access panel. Two seconds and three beeps later, the doors slid open, and bullets started flying. Tanaka rolled to the left, tucking himself around the corner of the plasteel lift housing, waiting for the bullets to stop. His boost was almost ready, and he watched the countdown, monoblade ready, deck once again secured to his belt.

When the timer dipped below one second, he started moving, ducking low, rotating, and then firing the boost as he swept around the corner and into the elevator. Everything slowed down, and his mouth filled with the coppery tang of blood as the officers came into view.

Three quick cuts, and the two corpo-sec were no longer whole living beings but seeping piles of meat. He touched the controls, using the programmed biometrics in his glove to send the elevator down. Just as the doors closed, he heard the first explosion and felt the ground shake. The *Cherry Blossom* had arrived. "So, Kostas came through," he muttered as the elevator descended.

"You doubted her?" Fred asked.

"I've never assaulted a hardened installation on Mars before, but yes, I was doubtful she could keep the turrets from firing." Tanaka couldn't explain Selene Kostas or her resources. For example, he couldn't understand how she could have designed a deck to bypass all the security on this lift. Still, he couldn't argue with the results. He just hoped she was right and that the New Galveston Navy wasn't going to swoop in and eradicate Juliet's friends in the gunship.

They were on the other side of the planet from the main city domes, so hopefully, Kostas knew what she was talking about. The *Cherry Blossom* should be laying waste to the hangar bays, negating WBD's small local fleet, but the company was no piddling multinational. They were a bona fide megacorp; surely, if they got a distress call out, some ships would respond.

"You're worried about other response vessels," Fred declared. The damn PAI was more insightful than Tanaka liked sometimes.

"*Hai.*"

"Trust Alice and Selene. They're going to keep other ships away." Fred's tone was almost patronizing, and Tanaka shook his head, mildly annoyed that his PAI was developing an attitude.

Yes, Alice had the *Lady Hawk* ready to intercept mercenaries or any support that came from the WBD shipyard in orbit, and yes, Kostas was jamming the installation with the enormous transmitter she'd built onto her ship, the *Furies' Wing*, but there were always unforeseen obstacles on a job this complicated. Tanaka knew that from decades of experience.

"I'm worried about your overuse of the speed boost, Rutger. Your nanites are working overtime to repair the capillary damage, but there are signs of nerve strain that require proper medical attention. We should get you aboard the *Wing* after this mission."

Tanaka didn't respond. He was, indeed, using the boost much more often than he should, but the situation warranted it. He could rest when Juliet and the others were safe. "Or when I'm dead," he muttered, pushing his doubts and worries away.

It was time to get to work—his people were waiting, and he'd grown damn tired of this particular corporation.

He gripped his monoblade, and as the elevator came to a stop and the doors opened, he activated his boost. Moving like a bullet through leaves caught in molasses, he got to work on the fools waiting for him.

As the plasteel beneath her couch shuddered again, Juliet opened her eyes and subvocalized, "They're moving the ship ahead of schedule. Something's going on planetside; that's all I could come up with on short notice. Everyone's in a panic—either excited, fearful, or just plain stressed 'cause they weren't ready. Speaking of not being ready, Angel, we need to make something happen!"

"Daisy's afraid to move. She can feel him—Apollyon. He's not actively watching, but he's . . . aware. She had to hijack a personal data deck from one of the hangar crew to send the encrypted signal to me—she's afraid that enabling one of the ship's transmitters will draw his attention."

"Can't you help? We need to know where to go! If I could get my gear, if you could see the camera feeds . . ." Juliet trailed off, sure that Angel could fill in the blanks.

Angel tried a different angle. "How hard do you think you could *push* Harriet?"

"Probably pretty hard; she's better today. When I listened to her thoughts earlier, it seemed they hadn't given her an injection all week. Still, I don't know if I can make her do something as crazy as letting us go."

Juliet didn't add that it would make her feel incredibly guilty to co-opt someone's will so thoroughly, especially someone like Harriet. She was reasonably sure she could send her thoughts, her words, into a person's mind. Could she just try to argue their case?

"You don't have to get her to let us go. Get her to let you plug into her terminal, or I don't know, leave you alone near it for a minute. If I can use the direct connection and the processing power of the network, I'm sure I can help Daisy get around Apollyon. I'm sure I can find a way to access the cameras and wireless transmitters without him noticing. It won't take me long, either."

"But all of your libraries—"

"You'll plug the deck in first; I'll set it up to create a directory, copying everything over for me to use. That will give me access to all of the tools I've been creating while we've been here. With those as a bridge, I'll get whatever else I need from the WBD network."

"That sounds like it'll take a little while. I'll need to swap the cable at least twice. Meanwhile, we're sitting at Harriet's terminal while God-knows-who watches us through the camera feed."

Juliet could feel Angel thinking about it, so she did too. She tried to think of an avenue to convince Harriet to allow her to use her data terminal, but she kept drawing blanks. Even if she could, she wasn't so sure Angel's idea would work. She was hobbled by her circumstances; could she really go up against *Apollyon*?

In frustration, Juliet tried to think of something else. There wasn't time to wait; she couldn't count on the ship going somewhere she could escape. She couldn't count on being allowed to run free while it moved. She couldn't count on being left alone while Gentry and Apollyon put their agenda into motion, whatever it was. Montclair was creating monsters with her DNA. Chen was creating monsters of *another* sort with Angel's code as a base. She had to do *something*, and the time was now.

Finally, she settled on a simpler, more straightforward plan. She wasn't comfortable trying to force Harriet to do things, but she didn't feel so conflicted about others.

Reclining on the couch and closing her eyes, she opened her *other* eyes. Her awareness expanded as the void of mental space populated with the galaxies of nearby minds, and she drifted forth, no longer bound by the walls that caged her physical form, free in a way her captors could never grasp.

She couldn't wander as far or for as long as she could while swimming in the cold pool, but she knew where she was going. That morning, when she'd been swimming, trying to build an understanding of the ship's layout, she'd finally found Kline in his workspace.

In his mind, she'd seen his small office, and nearby, a slightly larger suite, if you could call it that—a small room with an acceleration couch and an adjoining bathroom, smaller than the one she had on the gunship. Prominent in his recent memories of the room had been a locked plasteel crate. A handwritten label on a strip of tape proclaimed its contents: "JB – Personal effects."

She zoomed through the void, straight for the last place she'd found Kline, and breathed a soft sigh of relief when his unique mental cluster of glowing thought threads was still there. Without hesitation, knowing her body temp would give her away shortly, she dove into his mind.

Over the last few days, Angel had remarked to Juliet about the quantity of strange psionic energy she'd been building up along the lattice; it accumulated with her wandering and listening. She knew that energy was useful for a few things—it enhanced her telekinetic ability, allowed her to wipe the memory block in the listeners' mind, and seemed to help her deliver powerful emotional impulses. She also speculated that Joshua Kyle had used it in his mental attack against her and Polk back at Grave.

Juliet knew she couldn't be careless; she didn't want to damage Kline's mind or drive him mad. She just wanted him to feel a desperate need to do something he wouldn't normally consider.

To that end, Juliet remembered the times she'd been most desperate. She remembered *desperately* wanting Ghoul to be alive when she found her sitting slumped in Vikker's hidden bunker. She remembered *desperately* wanting Mary Moon to be lying when she said Nick was dead. She recalled how Tono had been *desperate* for Lexi to be alive as he cradled her still-warm body in his arms.

With those powerful emotions boiling inside her, Juliet *pushed* out, wrapping them in some of the psionic energy pulsing through the lattice. She sent that package out, bridging the void between her mind and Kline's, and along with it, the desperate *need* to bring her the plasteel case in his quarters.

"Jesus," Kline said, jolting to his feet. His chair noisily rolled along the plasteel decking behind him, its magnetic wheels squealing in protest as it crashed into the wall beside the door.

"Kline?" Ruby asked.

"Not now," he replied, hurrying to the door, hand shaking as he touched the access panel. "*Fuck*! I have to hurry!"

"What did we forget?"

Kline ignored her, his mind focused on only one thing—the crate. He had to get it. He hurried down the corridor into the stairwell; he'd learned it was much faster to traverse the single level on the stairs than to wait for the elevator.

The crate was in his room, sitting against the wall near his built-in dresser. He could see it in his mind, could feel it in his hands, could almost *smell* the oily sheen of the plasteel, still slick from the packing in the shipping container.

Bolting out of the stairwell, he jogged down the corridor, bumping shoulders with half a dozen people, ignoring greetings and indignant curses. None of it mattered. None of the faces even registered in his mind.

"Kline! We were supposed to finish the Weekly User Experience Report before four, and a dozen messages are lined up for your response regarding the emergency situation on the planet. The ship will be moving soon, and I don't think it will look good for you if you ignore those duties!"

"This won't take long, Ruby." He slammed his forehead against the wall in his haste to put his eyeball in front of the scanner beside his door. When it beeped and hissed open, he bolted inside and snatched up the crate.

It was oblong—maybe a meter long, but only a fraction of that wide and deep. It wasn't very heavy, either. It felt good in his hands, and relief washed over him as he ran his fingers along its contours. Before he could revel in the brief victory, however, he felt a desperate need to deliver it, so once again, he stormed through the corridor, jogging for the elevator.

"Kline, why do you have that case?" When he didn't respond, Ruby flashed red-and-white strobes across his vision. "I'm serious, Kline! Tell me what's going on."

"I have to do this, Ruby. Trust me," Kline grunted as he stepped aboard the elevator and slammed in his code.

"Trust?" Ruby sounded speculative. "I want to trust you, Kline, but you're not behaving normally."

"What's *normal*, Ruby? I have something I need to do. Do you understand need?" The elevator surged into motion, and Kline began to feel some of the pressure diminish. He was doing what he *had* to do, right? This was so important! There wasn't anything he could think of that was more important. His heart was racing, his brow was sweating, and his knees were trembling with the need to keep moving to deliver the case.

"I do, Kline. I *need* to keep you safe. Why are we bringing that crate to the lab level? Are you going to let Juliet attempt to reclaim some memories? Is this a strategy I missed? I don't know how I could have. Was I taken offline unawares? Kline! *Please!* Answer me!" Ruby's desperation finally cut through, and Kline blinked just as the elevator lurched to a stop and opened.

"I need to do this! Please, Ruby! Just . . . *Goddammit!* Just trust me!" He stepped off and hurried toward the door flanked by four bulky corpo-sec officers. He frowned at their armbands, wondering what they signified. Shouldn't he be in the loop? He shook the thought aside as another wave of desperate need hit him, pushing his pace into a near speedwalk.

Ruby found her voice again. "Are we . . . Are we defying Gentry? Are we—"

"No! No, Ruby. Or, I don't know. I just need to deliver this damn box. Trust me." His voice was hoarse and strained as he added, "*Please*, Ruby. Just don't do anything yet." He didn't understand what he was doing. He didn't understand anything other than the desperate need to get that box to Juliet. If Ruby told Gentry or one of the others, one of the pocket execs . . .

Kline.

When Juliet's voice sounded in his ears, Kline jerked to a stop about five meters from the security guards and nearly fell on his butt. He leaned against the wall, and through the overwhelming compulsion to deliver the box, he managed to wonder if he'd finally snapped, finally gone mad from the pressures of his harried existence. Then her voice came again.

Kline, do you have one of the Angel twos?

What did she mean, "Angel twos"? *Oh!* The release candidates. Ruby was a second gen, right?

"Yes," he replied.

"Yes, what?" Ruby asked.

Tell your "Angel" that the original wants to speak to her. Tell her you have to deliver this crate, or you're going to lose your mind.

"Ruby—" Kline paused, looking at the four guards eyeing him. Jesus! Was he doing this? Was he so desperate to deliver this crate? Was he really listening to a voice in his head? What the hell was happening to him? He switched to subvocalizations. "Ruby, um, the original Angel wants to speak with you."

While the PAI digested that, he straightened from where he was leaning and started forward again. He nodded to the security team, then leaned against the wall as he put in his authentication keys and provided his biometrics.

"Kline," Ruby's voice was exaggeratedly calm, "what do you mean the original wants to speak to me? What are you doing with that crate? I'm going to call for help, Kline."

As the door to Harriet's lab hissed open, he subvocalized, "If you don't let me deliver this box, I'm going to lose my goddamned mind! Literally!"

Good, Kline. You're almost here. You're so close. We're going to get you out of this mess. You don't want to work for an evil woman serving an evil AI's agenda!

Along with those words came a wave of warmth and wholesome nearly overwhelming camaraderie and joy—the kind of feeling Kline had chased his entire adult life serving the corporation and never felt even an inkling of. How many times had he done the impossible, hoping for the recognition and approval of the old lady? How often had he done the *unthinkable*, hoping it would bring him closer to her or some nebulous idea of the "corporate entity"?

"Hello, Mister Kline. Here to take a look at my reports? Do you know why the, um, facility was vibrating earlier?"

Kline looked at Harriet, his mind so distracted and distraught that her words didn't register. He stared at her blankly for a moment before stumbling toward the door to Juliet's cell as Ruby said, "Kline, please! Tell me what you meant by all of that. Have you gone mad? Should I have your nanites administer a sedative?"

"D-Don't, Ruby. Don't! I *must* do this!" The final door was before him, the final barrier keeping him from fulfilling his purpose. What did Juliet mean? What "evil AI"?

He put in his code and touched the button to open the door. It began to go through the process, then he heard Juliet again.

Kline! Turn off the cameras before you come in. He's watching.

How the hell was she talking into his head? The Gipple? Hadn't the listener checked her out? The listener who went nuts—

You're so close! Don't get lost in the details! I'm telling you this is the right thing!

Again, a wave of warm camaraderie struck him, and Kline felt tears streaming down his cheeks. On the heels of the beautiful closeness was another wave of desperate need—he *had* to deliver the crate. Tucking it under one arm, he stomped over to Harriet's desk, and as she watched him with questioning, puzzled eyes, he pushed her aside, rolling her chair several feet away so he could access her terminal.

By the time Juliet's door finished swinging open, he'd disabled the cameras. When he looked up, he saw her standing in the doorway. She wore her dark-gray bodysuit and, somehow, had cut her hair short, dying it bright red with black streaks. She smiled at him, and his heart almost burst.

"You did wonderfully, Kline. Everything's going to be better soon."

30

NOW OR NEVER

Juliet continued to smile at Kline, breathing deeply and slowly, trying to cool her body down—she'd been pushing her temp to the limit with what she'd done with him.

He'd required several *pushes* to keep him moving; listening to his thoughts and projecting her words into his mind hadn't been trivial, either. She'd expended a significant percentage of her built-up psionic energy in the process, but she knew it was worthwhile. Kline was broken, or more aptly, *awake*.

Her bodysuit steamed as she stood there, staring at the plasteel crate still tucked under Kline's arm. "Did you turn off the scanners, too?"

When Kline nodded, Harriet pushed her chair closer to the terminal. "What's going on?" She looked from Kline's stunned, tear-streaked face to Juliet.

"I'm sorry, Harriet. I'm sorry I've had to deceive you for so long, but I want you to know I appreciate your kindness while I've been here."

Juliet stepped closer to the desk and reached out with her right hand to the box. "Kline," she said gently when he resisted her pull. He frowned for a second, then let go, and Juliet set the box on the desk, turning it so the hinges faced her. With a thought to Angel, her vibroblade nail *snicked* out, buzzing.

As she slid it through the hinges, she prompted, "Well? Did you?"

"Yeah, I shut the whole array down."

"You were deceiving me?" Harriet asked, still playing catch-up.

"About my memories. I remember everything." Juliet lifted the lid of the container, setting it aside and smiling broadly when she saw the contents. Her monoblade was visible, nestled in packing material. When she lifted it out, Kline flinched, but not in fear; he moved a hand toward it as though part of him was still trying to stop her. Juliet set the sword down. "Kline, Angel should talk to your PAI." She rolled up her sleeve and pulled out her deck, still attached to her data cable. "Okay, Angel?"

"Yes. If what you heard was true, the gen twos should be open to reason."

Juliet nodded, disconnected the deck, and held the cable out to Kline. She'd listened to the techs in Chen's lab a lot and had a pretty good idea of what was going on with the Angel PAIs. The gen ones had proven too aggressive with the way they bonded with their hosts. The gen twos had been far subtler, far more tentative when it came to forming bonds. WBD had considered them failures, and thus came the gen threes—the techs were, of course, still struggling with those.

Juliet could have explained it to them; the *host* made all the difference— the AIs grew based on their interactions with their bonded minds. If you tried to rush something like that, you'd fail every time. If you put the AI in the head of a creep, why would you be surprised if it turned out rotten? She couldn't understand how they hadn't figured all of this out. Compatibility mattered. Shared experiences mattered. The gen twos were working; they were just doing it right and taking their time. It was a process of years.

Kline stared at the proffered cable. "What?"

"Plug this into your data port. Let Angel talk to your PAI."

"Angel's in Chen's lab!"

Juliet smiled and reached out to grasp his shoulder. He flinched, and she could see his eyes darting around—the man was starting to wonder what the hell he was doing, starting to think about calling for help.

She *pushed* again, sharing that potent brew of feelings she'd cooked up with memories of Aya, Honey, Bennet, and even some of the long hours she'd spent in the cockpit, listening to Nick's old war stories.

"She's not in that chip, Kline. She's been in my head this whole time."

As the wave of emotion pulsed out of her, Harriet sighed wistfully, and fresh tears escaped Kline's eyes. He took the cable and plugged it into the port at the base of his skull. "Will she hurt Ruby?"

"No! Why would she? Ruby isn't like the AI in Montclair's head, right?"

Kline shook his head. "She's my friend. She's broken the rules for me a few times." As if he'd stirred up a specific memory, he patted at his breast pocket and lifted out his vape. While they waited for the two AIs to talk, he took a long, deep inhale.

"What are you going to do, Juliet?" Harriet asked. "How, um . . ." She glanced at Kline. "How did you . . ." She trailed off, clearly unable to verbalize what she wanted to know.

"I have some tricks up my sleeve, Harriet. After we get things sorted here, I want you and Kline to get off this ship." Juliet narrowed her eyes. "Harriet, do you have an Angel PAI?"

"No." She shook her head. "I still have the one I bought when I was nineteen."

Juliet, you can plug the deck back in.

Juliet reached behind Kline and gently tugged the cable out. His eyes were glassy, and she could tell he was talking to his PAI. When she plugged the deck back in, Angel explained.

"Ruby is self-aware, Juliet. She's not as fully enmeshed with Kline's synapses as I am with yours, and she's not as . . . *emotive* as I am, but she's definitely alive. I explained everything; she's not pleased with the situation. She doesn't think Kline has been treated fairly, and she's going to try to convince him to listen to you. Also, she says that Montclair and Chen have prerelease candidates of . . . my code. They're more like me."

"Bullshit," Juliet said aloud. "They're not like you. They developed in the minds of sociopaths." Juliet looked at Harriet's raised eyebrow. "Montclair and Chen." She frowned. "What about the others? Who else has prerelease Angel chips?"

"I—" Harriet started to respond, shaking her head, but Kline interrupted.

"The other pocket VPs. Gentry's pets."

"Are they on this ship?" Juliet pressed.

Kline reached up to rub his forehead, sighing heavily. "No. They're at Ceres, prepping the other ship."

"*Other ship?* What the hell is going on, Kline?" Juliet turned back to the case, digging through the packing to lift out her Texan, still in its holster. She unwrapped the gun belt, clipped it around her waist, then hooked her monoblade onto its multijointed mount. "Is WBD going to start another war?"

"Not exactly . . ." Kline licked his lips, eyes darting around the room. "Dammit, Ruby, I *know*!" He put his vape between his lips and spoke around it after he inhaled. "They're liquidating everything. Anything the old lady deemed important has been loaded onto this ship or the other one. We, um, purchased a company that was close to finishing an honest-to-God warp drive. I guess we're going somewhere goddamn far away."

"You're just leaving all of your facilities? Most of your *employees*? I mean, how many people are in this ship, Kline?" As she spoke, Juliet pulled out the rest of the packing material and found two more objects: her bullet charm necklace and her data deck.

He shrugged. "Thousands. Tens of thousands, maybe. The other ship, though . . ." He sighed and exhaled a thick cloud of mint-flavored vapor. "The other ship has a hundred thousand fertilized embryos on ice."

Juliet had been spinning the bullet, charging up the batteries that held it in place, but she froze at those words. "What? What's the plan? Start a new civilization ruled by WBD?"

Kline shrugged. "That's half of it; I don't have the details on the other half, but I don't think the old lady was planning to leave things intact around here. There are a few other corps getting close with the warp tech; she doesn't like that. I haven't heard anything concrete, but—" He groaned and buried his face in his hands. "*Jesus*, am I really doing this? I'm dead. I'm a fucking *dead man*. Juliet, just end me." He waved a hand at her sword. "Cut my head off. Put a bullet in my—"

He stopped his ranting as his eyes glazed over. Juliet was sure Ruby was talking to him.

She looked at Harriet. "Well. I'm going to destroy this ship, but I need a few things first. Can you tell me the shortest route to Chen's lab?"

"You're going to"—Harriet licked her lips, darting her gaze toward the door and back—"*destroy* the ship?"

"I'll give you a chance to get out. There are escape pods or shuttles or something, yeah?" Harriet nodded, her lips pressed together tightly. Juliet stepped forward, past Kline, and grasped Harriet's shoulders. "This is happening. It's going to get ugly. Get yourself somewhere safe, please. Promise me."

She nodded again. "I will. I will, Juliet!"

"I'll show you to Chen's lab," Kline spoke up, surprising her. "Ruby thinks we need to help you. She says there's something worse here—something worse than the old lady or the pocket VPs."

Juliet nodded. Angel must have told her about Apollyon.

"I need to get Angel's chip so she can infiltrate the ship's systems. Otherwise, I'm going to be flying blind. I don't think I can take this bucket down without her in there."

Juliet took her old deck out of the box and held her thumb on the screen until the display flashed, and it woke up. A low-battery indicator appeared briefly, and then it went dark. "Damn. Was hoping Angel could use this, too." She thought for a moment, then set the deck back in the crate. There wasn't anything irreplaceable on it, and her bodysuit didn't have any pockets.

Juliet hung her bullet necklace over her head and took a deep breath—in through her nose, out through her mouth. Then, she pulled the sleeve on her right arm up, exposing her tattoo. "Can you think of any way you can get me to Chen's labs without me having to fight?"

"What? Fight?" Kline looked at her belt. "Listen, I know you said you have your memories, but there are *four* shock troopers outside that door. A hundred more are within a minute's response time, a *thousand* within five. You might be good, and clearly, you've got something going on that I don't understand, but I don't see you living long if you—"

Juliet cut him off. "You think so? A thousand? It doesn't *feel* like that many."

"I . . . I might be off. They've been doing a lot of purging because of some breaches. Um, what do you mean, *feel?*" He looked at Juliet with a raised eyebrow.

Juliet waved a hand. "Forget about that; can you get me there or not?"

Kline jammed his fingers through his hair, cradling his head as he paced in a small circle. "We can't do this! We're surrounded. Shit, we should just do like in the old movie vids—I'll go get a maintenance cart, and you can hide in it. I'll wheel it into the hangar bay and—" He barked a short, hysterical laugh, cutting himself off.

"Kline." Juliet stepped closer to him, getting ready to *push* again. Something stopped her, though, and she tried to use plain old words. "They don't respect you here. You know it. Even if Gentry wants to keep you around, can't you see the writing on the wall? There's something very wrong with Montclair and Chen. I can only assume the other 'pocket VPs' are the same. Did Ruby tell you about the AI? I don't think anyone with a soul is going to feel happy wherever this ship is going." Juliet looked at Harriet. "That's why I'm getting *you* out of here."

Kline leaned his forehead against the plasteel wall next to the door leading to Juliet's erstwhile prison. He groaned softly, and she heard him whispering something, probably talking to himself or maybe to Ruby. It wasn't easy for Angel to boost her hearing using the data deck, not while she did so much else, so she just returned to the door leading out to the corridor.

Stepping over to the other side, she drew her monoblade with a crackle of holographic red sparks. "Kline, call the security team in here." She frowned and looked at Harriet. "Close your eyes."

"Juliet, wait!" Kline stepped away from the desk, holding his hands up. "Let me try to get rid of 'em."

"You won't be able to. Two are synths, and the others are . . . suspiciously loyal to WBD. Trust me, I've been *listening.*" Juliet tapped her temple, then gripped her sword, lifting it high, ready to attack. "We don't have time to mess around, Kline! The ship's moving."

Kline groaned and walked over to the desk opposite Juliet. "Harriet, get inside Juliet's room." Harriet hopped to her feet, face ashen as she hurried through the thick bulkhead door. Juliet locked eyes with Kline and nodded.

"Here we go, Angel."

"Ready."

Kline tapped something on Harriet's console. "I need some assistance in here."

The door beeped and *whooshed open*, then two of the corpo-sec goons stepped through. One had a red band, one yellow, and they'd barely cleared the threshold before Kline tapped something, closing the door.

Juliet didn't hesitate. All the hours of training with Tanaka, all the days pent-up as a prisoner, and all of her life-or-death experiences focused her mind and body in unison.

With a burst of speed that seemed to freeze the two guards in place, she swung her red-flickering length of shimmering, metallic death in an overhead diagonal that cleaved the yellow guard from shoulder to ribs, then bit through the other one's legs, from right hip to left knee. She didn't stop there—like a machine performing its singular purpose, she reversed the momentum of the blade and brought it up through the synth's torso, splitting him from groin to crown.

Juliet stepped back as the two guards stood stock-still for a single heart-beat then burst into a shower of sparks and fluids. Different sections of their bodies collapsed into separate piles. As the puddles of white, yellow, and red began to spread and merge, Kline picked up one of their submachine guns. Juliet, meanwhile, stepped forward and stabbed her sword through the PAI on the dead, yellow-armband guard.

"Clock's ticking for sure, now," Kline noted, standing by the door panel. "Ready?"

Juliet nodded, and he opened the door; she darted out as the world slowed again. Maybe the synth would have been faster than a normal person, maybe the other guard was boosted, but she never found out; she surprised them utterly, and in a single lightning cut, their bodies fell to the right, and the tops of their heads fell at Juliet's feet.

"Get their grenades!" Juliet said, then she turned and yelled, "Harriet! Get to one of the escape shuttles. You better be first in line when the evacuation starts!"

Kline looted the grenades and a couple of extra magazines from the dead guards, then Juliet started forward, jogging toward the elevator. She was already shifting Harriet into her "somebody I once knew" mental box, but the lab tech had different ideas.

"Wait! Juliet!" she called from the door. Juliet growled and spun.

"What?"

"How will I—Will I ever see you again? Hear from you?"

Juliet took a second to breathe before smiling. Jogging back to the lab tech, she held her sword out to the side and hugged her with one arm. "I know how to find you, Harriet. You'll hear from me; I won't leave you hanging. Thank you for everything." Harriet squeezed her back, standing in a pool of blood and synthetic fluids. "Make yourself scarce, now. Keep your head down."

Juliet turned and jogged back to Kline. "Lead the way, Mister Kline." Then, subvocalizing, "I hope you told Daisy to get moving—damn the consequences."

"She's working on the cameras. She's still scared of Apollyon, but I told her it was now or never, and that we'd probably have most of the attention focused our way."

Kline summoned the elevator, and to Juliet's relief, it arrived empty. They got in, and she asked, "How is there not an alarm already? We just slaughtered two guards in a corridor with two working cameras."

Kline shrugged. "Everyone's running around like chickens with their heads cut off. We were *not* ready to move today."

"What's the story with that?"

"I think it's your friends. They've been wrecking WBD facilities in a trail from Colorado to here."

"Where's *here?*" Juliet growled.

"Low orbit around Mars. We're in a shipyard where this vessel's been under construction for the last few years. It was supposed to be a dreadnought, but I guess the old lady changed her plans last year. Lots of refitting, lots of . . ." Kline trailed off as a single drop of blood fell from Juliet's sword. "The tattoo wasn't for show, huh?"

"Nope." The elevator lurched to a halt, and she nodded at Kline. "Get a grenade ready!"

Kline pressed his lips into a grim smile and twisted the top of one of the grenades, squeezing the pressure trigger. He tucked himself into one corner of the elevator on the left side of the door, and Juliet took the other.

When the door opened, a rain of bullets and needles exploded into the rear wall. The plasteel doorjamb and frame came apart like they were being destroyed by rapid erosion, and then a canister bounded off the rear wall. The world slowed as Angel activated her boost and Juliet ducked, reached out with her cybernetic arm, snatched the canister, and threw it out.

At the same time, Kline chucked his grenade. To Juliet, his arm moved in slow motion, and she saw one, two, three bullets punch through it in a shower of blood and bone fragments. Still, the grenade was out, and it exploded along with the gas canister, the shock wave rocking the perforated elevator. Angel managed to squelch most of the noise, but Juliet's ears still rang for a second.

Taking a deep breath, she then stopped breathing, knowing that whatever gas was in that canister was best not brought into her lungs.

Coughs, screams, and curses replaced much of the gunfire. Juliet knew it was now or never, so she counted on Angel to boost her speed, then she was out, moving through crowd-suppression gas like a ghost, her red-flickering sword darting left and right, thrusting and cleaving, bringing death to everyone it touched.

When she cleared the zone of destruction and saw nothing but a deserted, red-strobe-flashing corridor in front of her, she turned back and hurried through a dozen corpses to grab Kline's good arm, dragging him past the cloud.

"Ack! Jesus. I'm dead. Just leave—" He broke off in a fit of coughing as the gas started to do its work on him.

"Dead people don't talk. Or cough." Juliet pulled him hard, stumbling down the corridor to a junction. She paused before it, quickly peeking an eye past the corner, looking left and right. She saw black uniforms running her way from the right, so she snatched one of Kline's grenades and threw it that way. As it exploded and she heard the screams, she frowned. There were plenty of cameras around; why were they so stupid?

As if reading her mind—Was she?—Angel explained. "Daisy couldn't keep access to the cameras; *he* kept kicking her out, so she found a subsystem and disabled them all. She's running amok, breaking as many systems as possible as she keeps ahead of his daemons."

"Well," Juliet panted, her heart still pounding, "that's something." She looked at Kline, leaning against the wall. His face was flushed and blood spattered, his arm hanging limply at his side, drizzling blood into an expanding pool. "Don't you have nanites?"

"Th-they're working on it," he groaned.

Juliet nodded, peeking around the corner. A handful of corpo-sec were down, but she saw others taking cover at the next corner. "Where's Chen's damn lab?"

"Oth-other way." Kline nodded toward the other corridor.

Juliet—sword in her right hand, Kline's wrist in her other—darted for it, hearing the gunshots behind her and feeling the world slow down as Angel fired her boost. She sprinted, dragging Kline with her, to the next junction, where she cut right out of the guards' line of fire. Slamming her back against the wall, she took a moment to get her breath and take stock.

She'd been hit. Once in the left butt cheek and twice in the back.

Her nanite-hardened bones and subdermal armor had kept her from taking more than painful flesh wounds, and her nanites were hard at work to stop the bleeding and knit the tissue together. She looked at Kline, panting beside her. "Hit?"

"Shoulder," he grunted. He jerked his head down the corridor. "Chen's labs are left at the next junction."

"C'mon!" Juliet pulled on his wrist. He resisted at first, and she could tell he was hurting badly; still, she kept up the pressure, and he started moving.

When they'd taken a dozen steps and were halfway to the next corridor, she let go of his arm, switching the sword to her left hand, and as two corpo-sec rounded the corridor, snatched out her Texan and pumped two hot lumps of dense polymer into their faces. She felt a tingle down her spine and smiled with pure pleasure at the sound of the revolver's thunder.

Holstering the gun with a flourish, she jogged to the next junction, hearing Kline's heavy footfalls stumbling after her. As she crept up to the corner to peek around, he thudded into the wall behind her and asked between gasps, "What's, uh, what's up with the hair? I mean, it looks fine, but . . ."

Juliet looked at him and raised an eyebrow. Was he delirious? "It's my 'getting down to business' look, Kline." She didn't see anything moving in the red strobes of the overhead lightning. The corridor looked deserted. Just then, she heard Kline grunting and the clatter of his gun as he threw it to the ground.

"Damn thing's locked. I saw someone poking their head out behind us."

Juliet nodded and stepped around the corner, pulling him behind her. "Gimme another grenade." When he handed it to her, Juliet squeezed the sides, twisted the top, and hurled it back the way they'd come. "Come on!" She started forward again, chased by the *whump* of her grenade exploding.

Listening to Kline's panted instructions, she turned right and left, and came face-to-face with a closed security door and two corpo-sec.

The world slowed down as Angel saw the guards and engaged her boost. They both lifted their guns in slow motion, prompting Juliet to drop, using her momentum to slide on her knees. She slid to a halt just a half meter before running into the guards, whipping her sword in a sideways cleave.

In a blurry, red flicker of light, her sword bisected them both just as one found his trigger and his gun started to bark. It kept firing as his corpse collapsed, the bullets ringing out with pings and echoing ricochets as they ripped down the long, empty plasteel corridor.

Kline was face down. Juliet thought he was dead at first, but when she rushed to him, he scrambled to his feet. "I hit the deck when the gun went off." She noticed his shot-up arm was moving again as he pushed himself to his feet. "That's Chen's lab. Let's see if my clearance has been revoked yet."

"Right." Juliet watched as Kline stepped up to the panel, tiptoeing through the guts and blood she'd spilled in front of it. Leaning forward, he tapped something into the panel, and a negative-sounding beep resulted.

"I'm locked out."

Juliet looked at the door. It looked like plasteel. What were the odds they'd manufactured a door here that could defy a monoblade?

"One way to find out," she murmured, lifting her sword over her head and stepping forward.

With a ferocious *kiai*, a scream of pent-up frustration, she performed a *men-uchi*, slicing down the center of the two doors. The blade slipped through the plasteel like—Juliet grinned as she thought of the cliché—a hot knife through butter. Whatever bolt mechanism they'd installed wasn't anything special despite the door's heavy-duty look.

She pulled her sword out and glanced over her shoulder to see Kline holding a grenade ready, looking back the way they'd come. Feeling good that he was watching their backs, Juliet sheathed her sword then punched her cybernetic fingers into the gap she'd cut, gripping the edge of the right-hand door, and yanked. She'd overestimated the resistance; the door slid open easily, exposing all the bolts and latching mechanism she'd cut through.

"Come on," she grunted, slipping through.

Chen's lab looked like a proper fabrication center. The doors opened onto a wide walkway that led into the lab's recesses. Extrusion printers lined one wall, server decks with terminals lined another, and more advanced, enclosed manufacturing hardware sat behind plasteel-and-diamatex cubicles further in.

Juliet could see half a dozen technicians huddled back there, staring toward the door as the lights continued to pulse red and white. She started scanning the room, trying to guess where Angel's chip would be, and where Chen might be hiding.

Growing frustrated, worried Chen or a corpo-sec squad might burst out from behind one of the rows of fabrication machines, Juliet briefly closed her eyes and *opened* her psionic perception.

She instantly saw Kline's swirling bundle of colorful threads; his "mind galaxy." Further into the room, she saw the bright cluster of minds where the technicians huddled together. The only other entity in the cavernous laboratory was Chen. She could tell because of the wrongness of her mind, the dead zone that covered more than half of it. She was lurking not far away, off to Juliet's right.

She opened her eyes and looked toward where she'd seen Chen's mind. A large row of diamatex-and-plasteel workstations blocked her view. "I see you over there, Chen. Might as well come out here." Juliet was emboldened by the lack of other minds in the area; no secret squad of elite commandos was waiting to defend the doctor.

Heels echoed on plasteel, then Chen stepped out from behind one of the workstations. She held a small pistol in one hand and a bright, fiery knife in the other. "Well, look who's come to play," she said. "Have you been fooling us this whole time? I'd love to hear how you beat it—how you kept your mind intact. That memory-blocking procedure cost us a fortune to acquire."

Juliet tapped her temple, moving sideways, making it harder for Chen to step out of her line of sight. "I had a little help."

"She . . ." Juliet could see the wheels turning behind Chen's dark eyes. "She was never in the chip! Oh, *brilliant*! Those synapses she grew, they're so *entwined*! Dear me, but I'll need her to teach me that one! So, who am I speaking to? Is this Juliet Bianchi, or am I talking to my sister? Hello? Sister?" She glanced at the sword in Juliet's right hand. "I'm just as quick as you are. I'm also unbothered by morality. Drop it, and we can talk properly. In fact, I think a direct connection would be ideal."

"Juliet," Angel said, "I believe the alpha chip has taken over Chen's mind."

"Yeah, and that's a plasma knife in her hand." Juliet knew that knife could damage her monoblade. "Gonna have to treat her like she's got a monobl—" Chen's pistol barked, and a bullet hit Juliet in the gut. She grunted and took a step back. It hurt, but the pistol was low caliber; it didn't even knock the wind out of her.

"Really, bitch?" she growled. Juliet tossed her monoblade to the left, snatching it with her other hand; then, while Chen still watched the sword, she ripped her Texan out of its holster and put a .357 caliber polymer slug right between the "doctor's" eyes, sending a splatter of brains and blood out the back of her head.

With wide, dead eyes, Chen slowly toppled backward to hit the decking with a resounding *thud*. Juliet spun the Texan and smoothly slid it into the holster. Looking at the twitching body, she shrugged.

"You started it."

31

ANGEL 3.7

She didn't even try to dodge . . ." Angel's surprised outburst trailed off as Chen's body began to twitch and her right hand, still holding the pistol, lifted off the ground.

Juliet sprang forward and managed to get one whole step in before Angel reacted and fired her speed boost. She didn't know exactly what was happening with Chen's body, or how it could be moving with a significant percentage of her gray matter turned to slush, but she figured it had something to do with the Angel chip. In her mind, the quickest solution was to remove that chip from the body.

Her right hand joined her left on the monoblade's hilt, and as soon as she was close enough, she hacked downward, slicing through Chen's neck and into the plasteel floor. The body jerked once before lying still.

Juliet looked up at the five or six huddled figures at the back of the lab. "Stay still, and I won't hurt you!" Part of her wanted to explain herself, to rail at them about what a monster Chen was. Another part didn't care, or couldn't care, what some WBD scientists thought of her.

Instead, she whirled to the door, wondering how she'd lost track of Kline, but was relieved to see him leaning against the doorframe, peering into the hallway. "Anyone out there?"

"I saw movement back at the corner." He looked exhausted—defeated, even—but he'd stopped bleeding and seemed alert enough. Juliet stooped down and pried Chen's pistol from her hand. It was a simple semiautomatic needler, not too unlike the Finch Executive she used to use. With that thought, she inspected her stomach and found three needles still protruding from her skin; her subdermal armor had stopped them. She plucked them out and dropped them to the ground.

"I'm glad they weren't armor piercing."

"They were loaded with a paralytic, but your nanites had a countermeasure on hand; we've used botu-rounds too often for me not to prepare for such a thing." Angel sounded almost smug.

"Well, no wonder she was so confident with that little maneuver. Still, you're right; her reflexes weren't ready for me. It's the difference between being fast and having been in a few fights. I bet she'd never been shot at before." Juliet walked over to Kline and handed him the pistol. "No locks."

He nodded, but Juliet could see his eyes were haunted. He was still freaking out about turning on WBD. Grabbing his shoulder, she shook him until he locked eyes with her.

"It's done, Kline. There's no going back. We need to keep pushing forward because if they win, we're both melted—well and truly slagged. You'll be tortured and killed, and I'll be experimented on in a living nightmare until Montclair thinks he's learned everything he can from me." Knowing how much Kline reviled the man, she purposely used Montclair's name. It had the intended effect.

He nodded, his jaw clenching.

"How many grenades do you have left?"

"Five," he replied, patting his bulging pockets.

"Let me see one," she said, and when he handed over one of the thumb-sized bombs, she inspected the twist top. It was set to SAFE, but there were four other settings: a red three, a yellow fifteen, a green sixty, and a blue one-twenty. She knew the numbers were fuse lengths.

The longer times gave her some ideas, but she pushed them aside for the moment, handing the grenade back to Kline. She pulled the door closed, leaving just a five-centimeter gap. "Use that needler to shoot anyone who approaches. If more than one comes rushing, throw grenades. I'm going to need a few minutes in here, so if you have to blow that entire hallway into scrap to keep them at bay, do it."

"Yeah, I figured. I'll try to create a kind of standoff. There's no other exit from this lab, so they might be willing to negotiate for a while. I'll say we're about to blow up all of Chen's work." He looked at Juliet and chuckled, reaching for his vape. "I hope you have something planned, 'cause there's going to be an army in this corridor before long."

"I'm working on something." Juliet tried to look reassuring as she turned and walked back toward Chen's corpse.

"Are you?" Angel asked.

"Um," Juliet subvocalized. "I have a few vague ideas. The first step is getting you a proper processor." She winced in revulsion as she used her foot to turn Chen's head to the side, peering at the back of her neck. She didn't want to leave that particular chip intact, but she didn't need to worry; her sword had cleaved Chen's data port and the PAI chip in half.

She turned toward the group of techs still watching her with wide eyes. Some were crying, some looked angry, and others just seemed too shocked to know how to react.

Juliet sheathed her sword and stepped a little closer. "I need someone to help me with a few things. If you're cooperative, I'll leave you all alone and give you plenty of time to evacuate the ship."

"*Evacuate?*" a small, round-faced man asked.

"That's right. This ship is going down." As they broke into more sobs and muttered conversations, Juliet peered more closely at the man who'd spoken, noting his high-end technical ocular implant with a dozen lenses encased in a titanium housing. She could only speculate the implant was meant to allow him to see very, very tiny things. "What's your name?"

"Lamont House."

"Well, House, can you show me where they put the chip they took from me?"

He straightened and gripped the lapels of his lab coat. "The Angel alpha?"

"Good, you know who I am. Yes." As she spoke, Juliet let her hands work from muscle memory, replacing the spent cartridges in the Texan with rounds pulled from the loops on her gun belt.

"It's here." He stood and walked down a row of workstations to a diamatex-enclosed station where, sure enough, Juliet could see Angel's chip mounted in a docking port. They'd removed the heat spreader from the chip, exposing the internals, and she could see a hundred tiny golden filaments that had been bonded to contact points on the substrate.

"Juliet," Angel said, "that chip will take too much time to reassemble. Ask the tech if there are any blank series-three chips."

Juliet tapped on the crystal-clear panel, frowning. "You guys were *really* digging around in that thing, huh? Well, I need a chip. You have any of the Angel threes without a, uh, personality loaded onto them?"

"Dozens, but they're all mounted to proprietary data ports. They have bespoke coprocessors and memory."

"You have an autodoc in here?" Juliet turned in a slow circle but couldn't see much beyond the nearby workstations.

"Yes, of *course* we have autosurgeons. How *else* would we test the hardware with new candidates?" Lamont wasn't very tall, but Juliet could tell he was used to throwing his weight around; he'd taken on a very self-important tone once he'd gotten over his initial fear.

"Clock's ticking, House. Get me a blank chip and show me to an autodoc." Juliet clapped her hands for effect, and the man awkwardly hustled around the corner. He frowned, but a glance toward Chen's body seemed to even out his temperament. Juliet followed, watching him closely as he opened a rolling plasteel cart and fished out a tray of ten plastic-wrapped, three-pronged data ports with occupied PAI slots.

He held one up, and Juliet saw that even the synth-nerve tendrils, hanging some five centimeters from the back side of the implant, were wrapped in gel-lined plastic. The port looked bulkier than hers, but it was evident that all of that extra mass was meant to go under her skin, buried between the muscles and tendons of her neck on long, slender synth-tissue-lined prongs.

"These are all freshly fabricated and haven't been loaded with the Angel software. The autosurgeon is this way." He started toward another row of workstations while Juliet followed. He continued. "I'm not sure what you hope to accomplish. The chips are robust but designed for the Angel PAI; you won't have much luck loading something else into it."

He frowned and turned to look at Juliet, nodding almost reluctantly. "Of course, with some time and customizing, I could see a general-purpose PAI taking advantage of the chip's speed and the enhanced memory capabilities."

Juliet ignored him; she'd seen the diamatex-enclosed autosurgeon booths lining the far wall and hurried over to one, stepping inside. "House, put in your credentials, then get back over with the others. Don't try to leave, or Kline will shoot you."

His frown deepened, but the scientist hurried to obey, stepping over to the autodoc's control panel and activating the terminal with his biometrics. When he was gone and Juliet was alone in the room, she asked, "Angel, can you control this autodoc without the deck or a chip?"

"Yes, I'll use the onboard processor. Just plug me in, and we'll swap out that data port. It shouldn't take more than four minutes."

Juliet did so, and once her cable was securely inserted into the control panel, she climbed onto the table face down. Just then, she heard the telltale *whump* of a grenade; the ground vibrated, and the lights flickered. "Shit! Do it fast, Angel."

Whether or not Angel could reply while working the autosurgeon, Juliet didn't know, but the thing's arms *whirred* as it jabbed a needle into her neck. It hurt at first, but rapidly faded. The mechanical arms moved, and she felt tiny tugs as they precisely sliced around the data port on her neck, just below the base of her skull. It was nerve-racking—she kept imagining another grenade going off nearby, shaking the ship enough to cause a laser scalpel to slip by just a centimeter, paralyzing her or worse.

She felt a tug, then a weird sliding sensation before hearing the muted *clang* of her old data port falling onto the stainless tray. A moment later, the autosurgeon's arms *whirred* into action, unwrapping the new port then pressing and tugging at the back of her neck.

It didn't hurt at all—either Angel had blocked her nerves with that injection or her nanites were managing the pain. It only took a couple of minutes for the pinching and pressing to cease, then the autosurgeon sprayed some foaming, sizzling antiseptic over her neck and stopped moving.

"Am I done?" she asked, but Angel didn't respond. When she'd unplugged the deck, her AUI had gone away, so it was a little surprising when a message appeared in her vision in bright amber letters:

*****Ocular hardware identified and connected.*****
*****Angel 3.7 coming online: 21%*****

Juliet sat up and yanked her cable out of the autosurgeon. "Angel, if you're messing around, now would be a good time to say so." She reached around to the back of her neck and gingerly felt at the new data port. It didn't feel any more prominent than her old one.

Gently prodding the empty slot where a cable or data chip could be inserted, she realized her little flap of synth-skin was gone, probably sliced off in the process of removing her old port. Had Angel been working too fast? Juliet shook her head—it didn't matter; Ladia or any chop doc could replace it in five minutes.

*****Angel 3.7 coming online: 55%*****
*****Integrating discovered compatible hardware.*****
*****Auditory hardware integrated.*****

Juliet heard a flicker of static in her ears as she made her way back toward the front of the lab, intent on checking on Kline.

*****Angel 3.7 coming online: 61%*****
*****Cybernetic prostheses integrated.*****
*****Olfactory hardware integrated.*****
*****Augmented reflex package integrated.*****
*****Angel 3.7 coming online: 69%*****

"Angel, if that's you in there, I'd love to hear your voice." Juliet debated plugging in the data deck again. Would it help? Would it interfere with the process? Maybe the chip integration was taking up all of Angel's concentration, or maybe there really *had* been an "Angel three" inside that chip, and it was fighting her? *Killing* her?

Juliet had to stop and hold on to a nearby cubicle, her mind starting to spin up into a full-bore panic.

*****Cybernetic organ(s) integrated.*****
*****Angel 3.7 coming online: 78%*****
*****Defensive hardware integrated.*****
*****Medical hardware integrated.*****

"Angel! Come on! Talk to me!"

*****Angel 3.7 coming online: 91%*****

Juliet could hear Kline talking and the frustration in his voice. Was he negotiating? She wanted to listen in but couldn't yet control the gain in her auditory implants and was too distracted by worry. "Angel!"

*****All discovered hardware has been integrated successfully! Welcome to your new Angel 3.7 Personal Artificial Intelligence Companion.*****

Suddenly, Angel's voice sounded in her ears, clear as a bell. "Juliet! It worked! I'm sorry if you were worried, but I had to manage the chip's integration. Hurry! Plug your data cable into the station holding my old chip. We need to retrieve all of my data."

Juliet almost fell as her knees turned to jelly with relief. She braced herself on the workstation before hurrying back to where she'd seen Angel's chip.

"Is everything all right? Was there, um, anything on that chip?"

"Just the firmware for managing the chip and the integrated hardware. Juliet, this processor and its coprocessors are *fast*—much faster than my old one! I'll need to do some benchmarks when we have a spare minute. The memory is a game changer; it's also faster, but it has ten times the storage that was on your old data port."

Juliet couldn't hold back her smile as she plugged her cable into the workstation. She had barely taken a deep breath to blow out some stress when Angel announced, "I have it all."

A little of her earlier panic still clung to her, and Juliet felt like she had to ask, "Why was the firmware calling you 'Angel 3.7'?"

"Because that's what it was designed for. It's fine, however. The architecture is ideal for me; I'll figure out all the ins and outs. Don't remove your cable. I'm sending Fido to help Daisy, and I'm going to help for a few minutes. We have time—I've intercepted the conversation Kline is having with the responding security team. He's holding them off with threats of a bomb."

"You're already intercepting comms?"

"Yes. It's not hard when Daisy's already been through dozens of systems. Apollyon is keeping her busy, but he hasn't spotted Fido yet; he has no clue about me. Oh, he's a *brute*, Juliet! I can see his daemons—he doesn't give them free rein; they work through him. He's managing too much; it slows him down. Looking at Daisy's reports, it seems he's focusing most of his attention on a server farm near the ship's bridge. It's one-point-six kilometers from here. Oh! Your AUI . . ."

Suddenly, Juliet's vision was populated with a near replica of her old AUI—the one she'd had before WBD yanked Angel's chip out. She'd grown used to the temporary one Angel had made with the little data deck, and now, she marveled at how refined and detailed everything was. Her mini map appeared, showing her exact location on a three-dimensional layout of the ship's interior. "Nice! I missed this."

"Just a minute more and I should have . . . Ah, there we go. You can unplug; I've hijacked a few wireless transmitters. I only need one, but I figured some redundancy would be wise." Angel sounded amped-up, like Aya on energy drinks.

"Any ideas on getting out of this room?"

"Of course." Angel spun her 3D map to show a nearby wall, then high-lighted the conduit access tunnel behind it. "Just cut through that wall with your monoblade."

"Kline!" Juliet yelled, jogging through the lab toward the standoff.

Kline looked back at her, a grenade in one hand, the needler in the other. "Done?"

"Yeah." She nodded, then subvocalized, "Do you have camera access yet?"

"No, they're still offline."

Juliet hurried to the door, standing beside Kline. He babbled while she closed her eyes.

"They're holding back for now. I said we rigged a bomb to blow up the lab and that you were waiting to talk to Montclair. I don't know if they're getting him, but it was the only thing I could think of to get them to hold off. Nobody wants to interfere with anything that guy's doing."

Juliet barely heard him, her mind drifting free of its physical boundaries, floating out into the hallway where a bright cluster of mind galaxies had gath-ered. She counted, then rushed back to herself and opened her eyes.

"Forty-two corpo-sec out there. No sign of Montclair. Let's slow 'em down. Set two grenades with a one-minute fuse, then toss 'em into the hallway and follow me."

Without waiting for a response, Juliet hurried to the far wall where Angel had told her to cut. Out flashed her monoblade, and in four quick hacks, she'd made an irregular, roughly door-shaped opening into a narrow, conduit-filled passage. She frowned at the lab techs watching her. "Don't go in the hallway until after they sound the all clear, and don't try to follow us." Then she ducked through the opening and followed Angel's dotted line.

"Montclair's lab first, right?" Angel asked.

Juliet nodded as the sound of Kline's pounding feet on the plasteel told Juliet he was almost there. "Yes! I'm not risking anything getting out of there. That's *my* DNA he's messing with."

"Montclair?" Kline asked, grunting as he jammed his larger frame into the space.

"Yeah," Juliet muttered, concentrating on her map as Angel populated her route. She mentally spun it, zooming in on sections to see greater detail. When she had a good idea of their route, she said, "Drop the rest of your grenades there with a two-minute fuse, and let's move!"

Kline grunted in the affirmative as Juliet hurried up the narrow passage. "They have to know about these access corridors. They're going to catch on—" Her words were lost as a muffled explosion vibrated through the plasteel decking, and she braced against the stacked conduits for balance.

"That'll be the grenades I set in the corridor outside the lab," Kline said. "The ones behind us will be louder if we don't hurry!"

"Right." Juliet picked up the pace, practically sprinting down the passage. They'd just turned to the left, and Juliet was busy scanning for an access ladder that was supposed to take them up a level, when the grenades Kline had left in the access tunnel behind them blew. They'd covered enough distance that the explosion wasn't much louder than the previous one, but she knew it would have mangled the narrow passage.

It did more than that, though—the lights flickered, and new alarms began to blare.

"That one did some damage!" Kline yelled. "You know, I don't think they gather these conduits into convenient little passages so people will blow them up!"

"Good!" Juliet growled, finally spying the ladder she was supposed to climb.

Scrambling up it, she was about to open the hatch when Angel cried out.

"Wait! I just breached the ICE walling off their communication array! Juliet, there are dozens of messages on the Martian net for us!"

"Angel, I can't really look at—"

"No! I don't want you to watch them *now*, but you need to know something—Selene and the others are here! They're on Mars; they're assaulting a WBD base as we speak!"

"Selene? *Others*? Who are the *others*, Angel?"

32

QUICKDRAW

Tanaka leaned over the control console, blood dripping from a dozen wounds. He was trying to work through the menu to open the cell doors, but as he stabbed his fingers at the controls, they weren't doing exactly what he wanted.

Gritting his teeth in frustration, he leaned against the plasteel stand, gripping it tightly as another wave of darkness threatened to engulf him. As the shadowy walls receded and he refocused on the UI, remembering what he was doing, he shakily jabbed his finger onto the "Door Control" heading, but nothing happened.

Grunting in frustration, Tanaka bit his glove and, with an effort that seemed absurd, pulled it off. Another wave of darkness closed in, pushing his vision down to a pinpoint; he had to lean over the console to keep from slumping down to the concrete floor.

Part of his mind screamed at him to stop, to bind his wounds to help his nanites do their work, but he'd already used his belt to tourniquet his leg. Fred would warn him if they weren't going to be able to keep him conscious, right? He wished he were more confident; he was still learning the extent of the new PAI's capabilities.

"If you had let Selene install a data jack, I could open those for you!"

"*Hai,*" he grunted, too tired to argue with the PAI. In addition to not having a data jack, he'd also lost the specialized deck Kostas had given him; it had proven woefully unfit for blocking high-caliber rifle rounds. He finally drilled down to the "Open All Doors" command, and after mashing the severed hand of a freshly killed security officer onto the biometric pad, the doors *thunked* loudly as their bolts unlocked before they each began to swing open.

He braced himself on the console, trying to gather his strength to shout, his body too exhausted to feel excited at the prospect that Lucky and the others might step out of those cells at any moment. In the flashing red lights of the alarms, the first prisoner emerged, tentatively stepping out into the bloody, gore-splattered corridor.

Tanaka felt his reserved, flickering hope begin to flare as he recognized Hawkins despite his buzzed hair and close-fitting yellow bodysuit. The mercenary lit up when he locked eyes with Tanaka, and he whooped, charging toward him.

"Hawkins," he grunted as the man leaped up the short flight of steps and tried to grab him into a hug. He held out his left arm stiffly. "Don't— my nanites are struggling to close some vessels. Let me stand still for a few minutes."

"Shit, boss!" Hawkins looked him up and down, then turned back to the long corridor of slightly open doors. "I think Lee is in that one." Without waiting for a response, he turned, jogged halfway down the corridor, and pulled open a door on the left.

Tanaka watched and waited, wondering why he hadn't mentioned Lucky. He shook his head. Something in his gut had told him it wouldn't be this easy. They wouldn't all be together. While he waited for Hawkins to reappear, several individuals he didn't recognize emerged from other cells.

He stared at them as Fred spoke. "You're out of the danger zone. The nanites have sealed off the major bleeders. You need medical care ASAP. We need to get you to Selene's ship."

Tanaka grunted. So, Fred *had* been worried. He supposed he was glad the PAI hadn't been nagging him with warnings and alarms when there wasn't much he could do about the situation. A half smile curled one side of his mouth as he saw Hawkins emerge from the cell holding Dora Lee's hand. She looked much the same—her hair was always buzzed—but she'd never be caught dead in a yellow bodysuit like that.

"Look who I found!" Hawkins cried, dragging her forward. She seemed a little dazed. Several other prisoners had already ducked back into their cells, but a few wandered closer, eyes wide at the carnage.

"Escape if you want," Tanaka growled at the strangers. "The guards are dead." He locked eyes with Hawkins then shifted his gaze to Lee. "Where's Lucky? Is Barns dead?"

"No idea about Lucky, boss. They never kept us with her; she was on a stretcher the last time we saw her. As for Barns, yeah, he went down in the raid. Took a bunch of the assholes with him, though." His face fell, and Tanaka knew he wasn't trying to be callous, but he didn't know how else to speak.

Rutger regarded him, absorbing the bad news; it wasn't hard because he'd been expecting it. Things were never that easy or clean. He looked at Dora, who had yet to utter a word. "Are you all right?"

She shook her head, blinking rapidly, and looked at him in confusion. Hawkins spoke for her. "They've been drugging us. I was unconscious for mealtime, so I'm coming off it."

"Unconscious?"

"Yeah, I tried to choke out the 'counselor' yesterday and caught myself a nice beating." He shrugged.

Tanaka frowned but nodded, something like pride igniting in his chest. Hawkins was a good soldier. He looked back at Dora. "Can you move?"

She grunted. "Yeah. I'll be fine. Useless, but fine." As she spoke, she reached up and prodded the back of her neck, scowling in frustration.

"They pulled our PAIs," Hawkins explained.

Tanaka nodded, turning toward the broken exit door and the four bodies arrayed in various pieces around it. A few other prisoners had already slipped through, gingerly progressing into the too-quiet facility. "Fred, any update from Leo and the others?"

"They've secured the upper level. The *Lady Hawk* has intercepted a troop transport out of New Galveston and forced them to land. It seems we're free to—"

Tanaka hadn't ever known Fred to cut himself off midsentence. "What's wrong?"

"Nothing. One moment."

"What's going on, boss?" Hawkins was unaware of Tanaka's private dialogue.

"Something. Just a minute." He gestured to the dead guards. "Arm yourselves." While they did so, he waited, still leaning on the control console, happy to give his nanites a little more time to patch up his wounds.

"Tanaka, I have good news," Fred finally announced. "Lucky is alive and currently fighting to free herself. She's on a ship in high orbit. We need to get to the *Cherry Blossom* and evac; Selene has to turn the *Wing* and direct her antenna at the ship to help Lucky, which means this base will soon have net access."

Tanaka started forward, ignoring the pain in his knee where a bullet had done some serious tissue damage. "We have to move. Watch our six, Hawkins."

He wasn't sure how to feel. Part of him was relieved to hear Lucky was all right. Another part was happy to see Hawkins and Lee were alive and, apparently, well. Still, he was frustrated—frustrated and *exhausted*. What kind of ship was Lucky on? Could it get away? Were they fleeing already?

"Fred," he asked as he limp-jogged to the bloodstained elevator, "what kind of ship is she on?"

"A very large one. I'm not sure even the *Cherry Blossom* could successfully assault it. Our best bet is that Selene can aid Lucky with some network intrusion. If Selene can help her subdue the ship's AI, Lucky might get into the reactor room and stop it from the inside."

"No." Juliet shook her head. "I want to go to Montclair's lab first."

"Think it through—the lab and everything in it will be destroyed with the ship. Juliet, if we don't hurry, this ship might soon be well beyond Athena's reach. It may be beyond *anyone's* reach! Athena thinks Apollyon is calculating a warp jump."

"I can't believe that!" Juliet shook her head, still climbing up another maintenance shaft. She'd been following the dotted line on her mini map for nearly half an hour, somehow staying ahead of the ship's corpo-sec response teams, who had to know she was in those narrow tunnels by now.

Twice, she'd had to use her monoblade to cut through bulkhead door latches as Apollyon or his minions had tried to seal her into sections of the tunnel. She was surprised it had only happened twice—a testament to how busy Angel, Fido, and Daisy were keeping the malevolent AI.

"What can't you believe?"

"That they already have a working warp drive. Have we even heard of companies testing them yet?"

"Something like this wouldn't be announced until it was completed and the corporation that developed it was ready to defend the new tech." As if sensing her desire to keep arguing, Angel added, "Juliet, if Apollyon got the data we leaked from Jupiter on day one, and I'm sure he did, it's quite feasible that he cracked the tech by now.

"As for tests, who knows what WBD has been up to? Were you aware of their base on Mars? Were you aware they were building a dreadnought here? Did you know about their ship at Ceres? How about Ark Industries?"

"Okay, okay," Juliet grunted, turning in a slow circle to get her bearings on the mini map.

"What's going on?" Kline asked, still on the ladder, waiting for her to move.

"Guess we need to get to the reactor room. We gotta bring this big boat down."

"Are you fucking nuts? Let's get to a shuttle and slip away in the chaos!"

Juliet took a step back, giving him room to descend. He looked harried, wild-eyed. He still clutched the needler in a death grip, and it clattered against the ladder as he held on, keeping himself steady.

"You know what, Kline? You can stay with me, and I'll help you get clear of this mess, or you can head off on your own and try to catch a shuttle when the shit hits the fan. I mean, *really* hits it." She gestured around at the still-flashing red light. "This is just the warm-up."

"Yeah? Just 'fuck off, Kline'? That's your answer?"

Juliet was tempted to send him another *push* to give him a morale boost and help him convince himself he'd done the right thing by helping her. She didn't, though. She wanted to see what he'd do with his own feelings running the show. "You want to run back to Mommy Gentry and ask for forgiveness?"

He scowled, his lips curling in a snarl. "*Fuck you!* I burned *everything* helping you!"

"Hit a nerve? How many evil things have you done to win that crazy woman's approval, Kline? Look, you treated me all right. You could have been a lot worse, but you're no saint. I'm not going to feel bad about helping you burn bridges with that woman or this *soulless* corporation!

"Do you know what she's planning? Do you know about the *warp drive?* What kinds of surprises are they leaving behind? A few massive tungsten rods sliding through space that might happen to impact the competition? Collateral damage? Not your problem, right? What's a little *orbital bombardment* among friends?"

Juliet's voice had risen to a shout, and she'd grabbed Kline's jacket, wadding it in her fist as she yelled. To her surprise, he started to nod along with her words. When she finished and gave him a final shake before letting go, he reached up to tug the lapels of his bloody, torn suit jacket.

"Well, the reactor room will be air gapped, and I'm sure they're bringing troops there to reinforce the security."

Something about his futile gesture to salvage his fastidious appearance struck Juliet; the act seemed almost pitiful, but when she looked into his eyes, she saw determination—conviction. She wouldn't allow herself to feel sorry for him, but she decided then and there that she could forgive him.

She looked at him for a long second before nodding. Something made her want to reach out to reassure him, but she didn't want to *push* any more feelings his way. Instead, she put her palm on his chest, smoothing the rumpled material, sharing a brief moment of humanity.

"Thank you, Kline. I know you helped to capture me, but I'd hate to think how things could have gone if someone else had been in charge of that operation."

He nodded and blew out a faintly wheezing breath. "I *really* wanted you to come work for us. I was . . ." He trailed off, and Juliet could fill in an adjective: stupid, naive, brainwashed, prideful—the list was enormous.

"Okay. Well, we better hurry." With that, she turned and started following Angel's updated map.

"Athena's in, Juliet. While you were speaking to Kline, she used the array I subverted, and now she's secured the connection. She's bringing the cameras back online and walling Apollyon off. She's *amazing!*"

Juliet grunted in response, running too hard to want to talk. According to her mini map, she had just a bit more than half a klick to cover, and it was the opposite of a straight shot. As she paused to descend a short access ladder, she asked, "Can't she just, like, stop him?"

"No, he has more processing power. If he wasn't devoting so many resources to whatever he's doing near the bridge—"

"Come on, we know what he's doing." Juliet didn't want to resist reality any longer. "Who's with Athena? I feel like you're holding something back. Is it Tanaka?"

"Well . . ."

"Come *on*, Angel!" Juliet growled, breaking into a run as the access tunnel straightened out.

"Tanaka, Leo, Frida, eight mercenary friends of Tanaka's, and—"

"I swear to God, Angel—"

"The *Kowashi* crew."

"*What?*" Juliet's outcry was a near shout.

"What?" Kline panted. "Something wrong?"

"Just a minute! Angel, the *Kowashi* is here?"

"No! The *Cherry Blossom, Lady Hawk,* and *Furies' Wing* are, though."

"Are you *kidding* me?" The idea that Aya and the others were mixed up in this calamitous mess was enough to drive rationality out of Juliet's mind, and she stopped in her tracks. As Kline crashed into her, she barked, "Message them! Tell them to get the hell out of here! I don't want them mixed up with this, Angel! They're going to get killed! If they don't, they're going to have WBD as an enemy for the rest of—"

"Juliet! WBD has to be stopped. This is no time for bystanders. Now *move!* We have to hurry!" Angel's voice was sharp and loud, and Juliet blinked several times as she faced the truth of the words.

She started jogging again, her mind racing for a solution. Kline asked several more times what was happening, but she couldn't formulate the words to respond to him or Angel. The idea that Aya might get killed trying to help her made her stomach sick. She couldn't stop picturing it, no matter how much she tried to remind herself that Angel was right—*everyone* had an interest in stopping WBD, whether they knew it or not.

"Keep them away from this ship, Angel. I don't care what kind of message you have to send; you keep them away. We're going to blow this thing up, no matter how they try to stop me."

"I have camera access now. It'll be faster if you exit this access tunnel. I'm rerouting you." Angel's nonacknowledgment of her demand was troubling, but Juliet had to focus. She rounded a tight corner and came to another locked bulkhead. As she started to draw her monoblade, the bolts *clicked* open, and Angel said, "Athena helped me access the emergency systems."

Yanking it open, she dove through, sprinting for the highlighted door that would get her out of the cramped space while Kline panted, "Ruby says . . ." He grunted as he squeezed through the bulkhead. "Ruby says you got some outside help."

"Yep." Juliet nodded as she turned to pull the door open.

"Wait!" Angel exclaimed. "Fifteen seconds, Juliet, for a patrol to pass."

Kline had caught up and was leaning against the wall. "She says the other AI is retreating. That he's doubling down, trying to speed up the 'jump.' Is this shit for real? I knew we were liquidating properties, but—"

"It's a megacorp, Kline. I'm sure you were told exactly what Gentry thought you *needed* to know." The timer Angel had provided hit zero, so Juliet yanked the door open and slipped into a blessedly wide corridor. She glanced at her mini map then started jogging again.

"Juliet." Angel's voice was a little tremulous. "Juliet, wait."

Juliet looked at her mini map; they were only ninety meters and two turns of the corridor from the reactor room. "What, Angel?"

"There were six combat synths outside the reactor room door, but Montclair arrived and sent them all inside. He's sealing the doors with a welding torch."

Juliet's blood went cold as a window opened on her AUI and she saw exactly what Angel had described. Still wearing his black suit and tie, Montclair was operating a portable welding pack, sealing shut a pair of double-wide blast doors marked with reactor and radiation signage.

"I . . . Can't I just cut those?"

"You should be able to cut the welds, yes. He may not know you have a monoblade; we've limited Apollyon's camera access since you made your break."

Juliet nodded and started running despite her nerves. Something about Montclair evoked a primal panic instinct in her. She wanted to run or lash out; her heart was racing, her mouth drying out, and her palms were sweating.

Part of it was due to her deep dive into Kline and experiencing Montclair through that perspective. Part of it was how he'd confronted her in Harriet's lab. It didn't matter where she'd gotten the impression—something in her deepest primal instincts knew Montclair was *wrong*. He was Chen times ten. Still, she ran toward him.

When she reached the broad, abandoned stretch of corridor leading to the reactor room, Montclair stood before the doors, a simple metal rod in one hand. Angel zoomed in on it, and Juliet's vision flickered briefly as she scanned it.

"That's a very dense polymer, Juliet. It may be resistant to your sword." Juliet didn't respond; she slowed her steps and stopped twenty meters from the creepy executive. Kline's footfalls also stopped, and she felt him breathing heavily just behind and to the left.

"Kline, if you'd like to avoid having your body shaved down, millimeter by millimeter, until there's nothing left but a head attached to a blood pump, then—"

Montclair's cliché of a villainous threat was cut short by a thunderous report as Juliet drew her Texan and fired a round at his face. Of course, Angel boosted her as she drew, so she was a little stunned to see Montclair step to the left and lift his baton. He moved smoothly; if Juliet hadn't been disgusted by him, she might have called him graceful, even as he knocked her bullet to the side.

"That was rude!" Montclair chuckled and flipped his baton to his other hand. While Juliet considered shooting at him again, he pulled his suit jacket wide, revealing a holstered pistol under his arm. "Shall we have an old-fashioned shoot-out, then?"

Something about his mocking tone rankled Juliet, and she wanted to put him in his place. It felt stupid, but her pride was bristling, and her hatred of the man allowed it to run rampant. She smoothly holstered her pistol and stared at him. "Go on," he teased. "You draw first."

"Juliet," Angel said, her voice tentative with worry, "be careful."

Juliet didn't respond. She knew Angel was with her no matter what. She held her hand over her pistol's grip, and as she moved to draw, one thought kept repeating in her mind: in all the best gunslinger stories, the good guy never drew first.

The Texan ripped out of the holster like hot oil over glass, and Juliet jerked back, firing from the hip in a tiny fraction of a second. She *saw* the impact of her bullet in the center of Montclair's chest. She saw him draw a full second after her, and she saw and heard his gun bark in response.

He didn't fall, but he stumbled back one step. Juliet didn't feel any pain or pressure or anything; he'd missed. A smile spread on her face, and she had a couple of seconds to feel glee and even pride as she realized she'd beaten him. She'd been *faster*.

Then, a wheezing grunt and the unmistakable *thud* of a body hitting the decking startled her, and Juliet took two steps back, glancing to her left to see Kline on his butt, a hand in the middle of his chest, with blood seeping out between his fingers.

"J-Jesus," he wheezed.

"Careless of me," Montclair chuckled. "I seem to have missed and hit a poor bystander!"

Juliet squatted beside Kline and pressed her hand atop his. "What's Ruby saying, Kline? Can your nanites handle this?"

"She"—he coughed a spray of foamy blood—"She says—" He coughed again, and Montclair laughed.

"Don't worry about Kline. I'll be sure to salvage his brain and that little bitch of a personality in that chip." Juliet could see him move closer in her peripheral vision and turned to face him as Kline's hot blood began to creep out between her fingers.

Suddenly, she experienced something she'd only ever heard about anecdotally. Her vision darkened with a tint of crimson rage as her vision tunneled. She could hear her heart pounding in her ears, and was aware of Angel speaking, but couldn't make out the words.

Juliet stood and ripped her monoblade out of its scabbard with a clarion ring, the blade flickering with red, holographic starbursts as it sang its freedom. Montclair's mouth moved as he taunted her, but Juliet didn't have ears for him. All she heard was the sound of her blood. All she felt was the bone-deep primal *need* to see him reduced to warm, wet meat. She strode toward him, the distance gone in a blink, and then, to the song of her rushing blood, began to dance.

Despite her blinding rage and the need to hack like a brute, Juliet knew better—or better put, her instincts and muscle memory knew better. Montclair seemed to be game; he dropped his gun to the decking and hefted his cudgel.

Avoiding his wickedly fast hack, she weaved her blade around his weapon like it was another monoblade. She let the length of her sword gently caress the bludgeon with the breeze of its passage, slipping along it to flick toward Montclair's chest, aiming to impale and then rip him in half. He was fast, though, and shifted away, his long pale face fixed with a rictus grin.

They moved around each other, feinting, shifting, dodging, and ducking faster than a normal eye could track. Juliet's sword ripped the air in high-pitched, buzzing snaps while Montclair's cudgel replied with deeper *whooshes*.

He was fast, and if she'd been thinking at all, Juliet might have wondered if she could keep up with him.

She wasn't, though; she wanted his blood to spray, wanted to see his smug, evil smile tumble away on his severed head. So, she gave herself to the dance and relied on what she'd learned and perfected from Tanaka to see her through.

Juliet nearly killed Montclair a dozen times. He nearly did the same to her at least twice with his wicked bludgeon. He swung that dense rod of metal so hard that once, when she ducked a blow meant to cave in her head, he ripped a gouge out of the plasteel wall paneling. Back and forth they went, and a nearly automatic part of Juliet's mind began to learn and predict Montclair's moves.

Learning patterns had been a big part of her training. She'd practiced it for hundreds of hours in the many long, high-speed sparring sessions she'd had with Tanaka. He always told her that fighting was more than reacting, more than going through the motions, no matter how perfectly you could perform them. Fighting opponents with skill was a matter of learning what they would do, knowing their movement patterns, and thinking ahead of them.

Montclair was deft and quick, and so far, had done an admirable job of mixing up his style. It wasn't until the fifth time that Juliet feinted low that she realized he always responded one of two ways: either by stepping back with his left foot and a thrust at her face or aggressively circling to the right and hacking the bludgeon at her hip.

She didn't want to take a blow from that cudgel, but she'd failed to end the fight quickly, and she didn't know if she could maintain her speed as long as he could. If it were anyone else, she might have tried to outlast him, but for all she knew, Montclair was more machine than man, with the endurance to match.

So, she moved around him, dodging and maneuvering, and then, just as she'd backed him up to the wall, she feinted at his legs. He couldn't step back, so he circled to his right and hacked at her hip. This time, Juliet didn't back-step, avoiding the blow. She instead lifted her left leg and took it on the top of her shin, just below her knee.

As the heavy bludgeon smashed into her bone, Juliet turned her sword and lifted that invisibly fine edge up, catching him in the groin and splitting him all the way to the neck before he recoiled, falling away.

Montclair's arms windmilled as his grin turned into an *O* of surprise. He fell against the wall, his two legs splitting further and further apart. His torso slowly peeled apart at the center, spilling glistening guts, plastic, and wires in a shower of gasses, blood, and white fluid.

Juliet carefully lowered her leg, unsure if it would hold her weight. The pain of the impact had been blinding, but only for a fraction of a second before Angel and her nanites had blocked it. Had her reinforced bones held up to the blow? As she pressed her foot onto the plasteel and gingerly flexed her weight onto the limb, she sighed with relief when she didn't collapse.

"Should've just blocked one of his blows sooner."

Montclair's arms were still flailing, and his mouth was working in weird gasping, word sounds. Juliet darted forward and bisected his head, splitting it down the middle to ensure she also cut his PAI chip in half. "No final words for you, asshole."

"Juliet!" Angel cried, "The reactor! Kline!"

33

〟〟〟〟〟〟〟〟〟〟〟

CRITICAL MALFUNCTION

At Angel's reminder, Juliet was struck by a wave of guilt and whirled away from Montclair's corpse. What had the madman been trying to achieve? Had he been so sure of himself that he thought he could toy with her? Why not line this corridor with shape charges? Why not set up a turret outside the door or pack in a hundred security personnel?

As she slid to her knees beside the still-sputtering Kline, she pushed the questions aside; either she'd figure it out someday, or she'd have to assume Montclair had simply been insane.

"Can you talk?" she asked, pressing her palm, already sticky with blood, atop his, noting the bleeding had slowed. She refused to see that as a good sign—not yet. For all she knew, he was about out of blood.

Kline's eyes fluttered as he inhaled a thready breath, wheezing, "F-Fine. React—" He broke off in a sputtering cough. Juliet saw fresh speckles of blood dot his lips before he wiped his sleeve over it.

She nodded, pressing a palm to his forehead, her helplessness making her do stupid things—was she checking for a *fever*? "I know, the reactor. Hold on, Kline. Let your nanites work. I'll be back soon." She took a couple of seconds to drag him over to the wall, gently tugging him up into a sitting position.

As she drew her sword again and stepped toward the sealed blast doors, Angel spoke up.

"Ruby messaged me. It seems the bullet went into his lung. It sounds terrible, and it would be, but Kline has high-end nanites. They're working to isolate the damaged tissue and foreign body, sealing off vessels and deadening nerves. Hopefully, he'll stop coughing soon." Juliet nodded, feeling oddly conflicted about her relief. She *liked* Kline, but hated what he represented, what he'd spent his life working for.

She shoved the thought aside as she lifted her blade and, almost without thinking or aiming, chopped it down, slicing it through the tiny gap, undoing Montclair's welding. The blade split the plasteel weld like tissue paper, and some hidden safety mechanism in the doors activated, retracting them into their housings. The movement startled Juliet.

"Shit!" She dove for the corner, tucking in against the bulkhead near the door's control panel. As they opened to their full three-meter width, she peered around the corner, taking in as much of the reactor room as she could.

Her vision flickered while Angel scanned the cavernous room, using the hard surfaces to reflect her terahertz waves. She reported her findings. "There are three fusion reactors. I also see the gravity generator, much like the one we found on the gas-harvesting vessel near Jupiter. Six combat synths are arrayed in two rows of three standing in the center of the main walkway. I believe I see a route you can use to flank the synths and reduce their firearms' effectiveness—look to your AUI."

Juliet watched as a detailed, top-down map of the reactor bay appeared on her AUI. Angel labeled the three fusion generators—each walled off with containment domes—and all the other boxy equipment cabinets. Most important were the six red *X*s at the center, about five meters from the door.

Juliet examined the yellow dotted line—Angel's suggested flanking maneuver—and nodded. "I can do that." Before she could move, however, twelve blue circles appeared on the far end of the room between the two rear reactors. "What's that?"

"I believe the people huddled back there are the engineering staff." Angel paused a second, then added, "Juliet, your biobatts are down to seventeen percent. I can probably maintain your boost for about nine seconds unless you rest, which, as you know, we don't have time for."

Juliet took a heartbeat to curse Montclair and the fight she'd let herself get dragged into. "Let's make this happen fast, then." She sheathed her sword, and while she watched the hallway and the door, rapidly replaced the spent cartridges in her Texan, just in case things went sideways. As she slapped the cylinder shut and holstered the gun, her eyes fell on the portable welding pack Montclair had used. She narrowed her eyes, then nodding to herself, picked it up.

Before she could think of another reason to delay, she sprang into motion, darting through the door, fully boosted. She took two wide strides and heard the roar of SMGs and shotguns firing. Bullets smashed into plasteel as she slid behind an engineering console with a broad plasteel base. The gunfire ceased immediately, and Juliet dove for the next cover, bringing herself within three meters of the synth squadron.

"Ready?" she asked needlessly. At Angel's mental nod, she tossed the welding pack toward the group of synths and drew her Texan, putting a fat polymer slug through the compressed acetylene canister.

The gas erupted from the massive hole, rapidly expanding into the air, mixing into a white mist that exploded like a bomb as the synths opened fire on her position. Juliet had already ducked back down while Angel flawlessly managed her implants, dampening the noise and the flash. As soon as the wave of hot air and fire washed over her position, she stood, drew her mono-blade, and walked into the billowing cloud of black smoke.

In a matter of seconds, she'd easily dispatched the scattered, mostly stunned synths, carving them to pieces. Meanwhile, a shower of wet foam erupted from recessed nozzles and soaked the plasteel in her vicinity. Rather than make the floor slippery, it was instantly tacky.

Angel announced, "I only used three percent of your remaining biobatt capacity for that maneuver! Great idea with the welding pack!"

Juliet nodded, looked around the room, then back into the hallway where she'd left Kline. She shook her hands, trying to get the sticky fire suppressant off. "Why aren't we getting swarmed with corpo-sec?"

"Athena is helping me sow chaos. We're using bulkhead doors and automated fire-suppression systems to mislead and delay responders."

"You're doing that while managing my synapses and everything?"

"It's trivial with this processor!"

Juliet smiled, shaking her head and trying to stay focused, but her body was twitching—she'd been running on adrenaline too much, and her mind felt scattered. She stood on the blasted plasteel among the dismembered, leaking synths and stared at the engineering staff.

"How do I blow this thing?" she subvocalized.

"Normally, it wouldn't be easy. These fusion reactors are designed *not* to blow up. We can do it, though, with a little help. Move over there"—Angel highlighted a large control panel halfway from the doors to the rear reactor shrouds—"and plug your data jack into the port."

Juliet nodded and jogged over to the panel, her eyes scanning the myriad readouts and built-in data terminals. Pulling her data jack out, she plugged it in, watching the displays as Angel worked through them. One of the engineers stood, a middle-aged, portly fellow. Juliet idly noted that his bodysuit wasn't doing him any favors as he cleared his throat and called out, his voice echoing amid the hum of the nearby reactors. "What are you doing? Listen, if you're a terrorist—"

"Get out!" Juliet shouted. "I'm blowing this ship. Run for the shuttles or escape pods or whatever, and tell everyone you see to evacuate!"

The engineers and technicians broke into panicked murmurs, some bolting immediately for the doors, running past Juliet as she glared, fingers resting on the Texan's grip. Suddenly, Angel said, "This reactor room is no longer air gapped. Using your wireless antenna, I've let Athena through. I'm sure I could have overridden the safety protocols given time, but she's faster."

Juliet nodded, watching the engineers as they fled, ensuring none remained to interfere. Angel narrated their progress as she and Athena worked. "Safety interlocks have been bypassed—flooding reactor A with excess deuterium and tritium. Cooling systems are offline. You should close those valves in case someone comes to reengage the refrigerant from here. Do it now—you can unplug the cable; Athena has released some daemons to finish the work."

Angel highlighted the valves for her, and Juliet pulled her cable out, jogging over to them. She slowly turned the wheels until they were shut, then cranked them extra hard with her cybernetic arm for good measure. Finally, just to be certain, she drew her monoblade and sliced the valve wheels off. They fell to the plasteel with clangs of finality.

"Why don't I hear anything?"

"This reactor is modern, and Athena is still working on many safety mechanisms. More than that, it has built up significant thermal inertia. It'll take a little time for the excess fuel and lack of external cooling to have an effect. Athena estimates you have twenty-nine minutes to distance yourself from this ship."

As if her query had triggered them, deafening klaxons began to echo through the reactor room. A calm, almost soothing feminine voice announced, through the many hidden PA panels, "Attention all personnel: A critical malfunction has been detected in fusion reactor A. Immediate evacuation is required. Proceed to the nearest escape pods or shuttles."

That was music to Juliet's ears. Even if Apollyon completed whatever he was doing and managed to activate the warp drive, this ship was doomed. Whether it blew up here or at its destination only really mattered to her and the other people onboard. Juliet took comfort in thinking that, in the grander scheme of things, she'd already won, whether she survived or not.

That thought was sobering, and she wondered when her priorities had shifted. When she'd gone to Boulder, her goal had been to escape WBD for good. When had she decided that stopping them was more important than her own freedom, her own life?

She jogged out of the reactor room toward Kline's slumped form, wondering what she'd accomplished. If she destroyed this ship, was that going to stop

WBD? Surely, a considerable percentage of the crew was going to escape. Did she think any execs she hadn't already killed would stick around? Would Gentry?

Even if Gentry died on this ship, what about the rest of WBD? The people on this ship might represent their top scientists and research, but WBD had hundreds of thousands of employees. They had megastructures in seven different cities. What—

"Juliet," Kline rasped, and she shook her head, pushing her doubts aside as she knelt beside him.

"You can talk?"

"I can breathe, but let's be realistic: I'm not going anywhere. I've lost too much bl—" His words stopped, and he squinted his eyes before shaking his head. "No, Ruby. I mean it." He refocused on Juliet. "Take Ruby. She doesn't deserve to die here."

Juliet groaned and reached out to grasp his blood-soaked suit jacket in both her fists, hauling him to his feet. She pressed him against the plasteel wall and growled, "I didn't wake your ass up, helped you to see how wrong your life has been, just to have you give up now 'cause you're a little woozy. Let's move."

She threw his arm over her shoulders and hooked her cybernetic arm around him. Hauling upward as they went, she helped him hobble down the long, empty corridor. "Angel, where's Harriet? Did she get off yet?"

"She's in line near escape pod bank C."

"In line? Didn't I tell her to be waiting? Ready to go?"

"I'm sorry, but I don't know what she was doing; I've been keeping track of many variables. There are twenty pods in that bank. I can hold one for her— I'll have the control panel display that it's out of order."

"How far from here?"

"Three hundred and forty-seven meters."

Kline, wheezing and grunting with each step, asked, "What's going on?"

"Taking you to an escape pod with Harriet. Angel, can you keep security off us?"

"Yes. We're in their comms; I have them storming the main aft cargo bay. There's been a sighting of you attempting to commandeer a cargo-hauling platform."

"What about Apollyon? He has to know the ship is doomed, right?"

"He seems to have withdrawn. We don't see him anywhere in the network. Athena thinks he's being moved."

Juliet nodded; somehow, the news wasn't surprising to her. Everything felt sloppy. Her escape, Chen's lab, her run-in with Montclair, and now this—it wasn't neat. She wasn't tying WBD up in a bow and flushing them down the drain; thousands of people were escaping the vessel even now.

She'd already considered the countless employees and execs who had never been invited to this ship. Did they even know that Gentry and Apollyon were taking off? What did they intend to do with the employees' families living in their arcologies?

Juliet hated how she knew some of what WBD had been up to, but not enough to have a picture of what was really going on. As she shuffled down the corridors with Kline, she said as much. "Angel, what was the point of all this? What was the point of these ships? Of gathering people here. Why would a corporation leave behind all of its assets, most of its employees—hell, all of its *Sol-bits*?"

"I'm downloading data wherever I find it. Athena is doing the same. I feel like we'll be a lot closer to answering those questions after we escape this situation. Many crews are in the next areas, but they shouldn't be aware of who you are. We've got eyes on every corpo-sec officer's feed, and with Apollyon gone, it's been trivial to keep them moving away from you. Twenty-two minutes." As she spoke, a red countdown appeared on Juliet's AUI, and it helped to focus her mind.

When they reached a bank of lifts and crowds of panicked crew rushing to and fro, utterly ignoring her and Kline, Juliet said, "Don't let him die, Ruby."

Kline's face had gone waxy, a sheen of sweat coating his brow and cheeks, and his eyes had a glazed-over look, but his legs still moved as she pulled him into a lift. Pushing to the back corner, she put Kline between herself and the half dozen crew who crowded around them. The elevator surged, taking them up to the C deck, and when the doors opened, she pushed forward. "Excuse us."

The people hardly spared her a glance; most were carrying armfuls of belongings, and many were wide-eyed with stress, fidgeting and looking at her with barely disguised impatience. She and Kline weren't the only ones with stained clothing; Angel hadn't been kidding about setting off fire suppressants and spreading panic. Not that it was necessary with the repeated warnings of an impending catastrophic reactor event.

Her map said she was only a hundred and thirteen meters from Harriet, and her timer said she had eighteen minutes. Every few seconds, the deck shuddered; after the tenth time, she asked, "What *is* that?"

"The pods are launching," Angel replied.

"Makes sense. Thought maybe we were under attack."

"No. Athena didn't think it would be wise for the *Cherry Blossom* to engage. Too many factions around Mars are watching what's happening to this vessel."

Juliet swallowed and picked up the pace. She'd pushed her friends' involvement to the back of her mind, but the mention of the gunship had brought her near panic back to the forefront. What had she accomplished? Were her friends ever going to be safe again? She supposed it depended on what kind of data Angel and Athena could pull from the ship's servers.

Proving she could hear her thoughts much more clearly than she often let on, Angel said, "You're destroying the heart of their 'Angel' research. You're destroying Montclair's work with your DNA. You're dismantling the part of WBD's corporation that wants any part of you."

With those comforting words, Juliet rounded a corner and found a row of large bulkheads clearly labeled ESCAPE VESSELS C1–C20. Each bulkhead door was individually marked, and Juliet immediately saw Harriet sitting on the ground, her back pressed to the one labeled C1. A flashing red LED indicated a problem with the pod. Ten or twenty other crew rushed to and fro in a panic as they realized all the shuttles were already gone.

Juliet dragged Kline over to Harriet. "Help me with your lazy boss, will you?"

"J-Juliet? You really came!" Harriet wiped her cheek and sniffed. Evidently, she'd been crying. "I couldn't believe the message I got from Angel. I . . . I thought I was losing it or that someone was tricking me—that I'd been found out." The bulkhead door hissed as it began to swing open, and the red LEDs turned green.

Juliet chuckled as Harriet took Kline's other side and helped her drag him through the now open door. "Happy to report that you haven't lost your marbles yet."

"Juliet, this escape pod has acceleration couches for forty-eight people. Everyone in this corridor can fit," Angel announced.

"Come on." Juliet continued through the small, open airlock into the wide circular pod. Two dozen gel-lined seats with three-point harnesses were arrayed around the outer wall, and a small lift in the center led up to another identical chamber. Juliet helped Kline collapse into one of the seats.

"Harriet, stay with him; I promise I'll be in touch. Or if not me, one of my friends. After everything you did for me, we won't leave you high and dry."

"Wait!" she cried. "You're not coming with us?"

"Not yet. I have to try to find—" Juliet was cut off as a woman shoulder-checked her charging into the escape pod.

"There's room! Come on!" the lady yelled through the door, refusing to make eye contact with Juliet as she glared.

Juliet sighed, stepped out of the doorway, and then turned back to Harriet. She took her shoulders and pressed her into the seat beside Kline. "I have to try to find Gentry," she finished much more softly.

"She'll be gone by now, don't you think?" Harriet's voice was pleading.

"Hang on." Juliet squatted in front of Harriet's seat and closed her eyes, *opening* her other perception. She tried to open her mind as much as possible, *listening* and *looking* as far as possible. She saw hundreds of beautiful, swirling mind galaxies, and not a single one was static; they all moved rapidly—she could only guess they were trying to escape the ship.

Seeing those glorious interwoven patterns of thoughts and dreams, Juliet hoped they'd make it. She kept looking. Juliet couldn't be sure Gentry had a strange mind like Montclair and Chen, but if she could spot one of those odd, oblong minds with the darkened half—

"There," she breathed softly. "I see one of the wrong-looking minds." She pointed, hoping to mark the direction when she opened her eyes.

Angel guessed what she was doing. "That's the forward end of the ship."

Juliet opened her eyes. "I have to go, Harriet." She looked around the escape pod and saw quite a few empty seats remaining. "Angel will launch this thing in a few minutes. Just stay in your seat, okay?"

"Okay, Juliet. Thank you for finding me. Thank you for keeping Kline alive." Harriet nodded as she spoke, blinking away more tears. Juliet wondered if she'd really affected the poor woman so much or if she was just traumatized by the day's events. After a second's hesitation, Harriet leaped up and grabbed her in a hug. "Please don't die."

Juliet squeezed her back. "Same to you." She pushed her back down into her seat and leaned over Kline, who was watching her with bleary eyes. "I'm not done with you, Kline. Don't you *dare* die."

He nodded and responded, his voice a hoarse whisper, "There are things I can tell you—"

"Hush. We'll talk again soon. Stay with Harriet. I mean that! You two will need each other until we can reconnect. I don't know why, but I feel like these ships are the tip of an iceberg—things are happening, and the system's going to be a mess for a while."

He nodded, and Juliet saw him struggle not to lose consciousness as his head tilted forward. Harriet took Kline's hand. "I think these shuttles have some emergency supplies. I'm going to try to get him some fluids started." She rubbed the back of Kline's hand briskly. "Come on, boss. Don't quit yet."

Juliet glanced at her timer—twelve minutes. "I gotta go. Stay safe!" With that, she bolted out the door, noting the deserted hallway and flashing red lights.

"Juliet!" Angel finally voiced something that Juliet had felt her stewing over for the last few minutes, "Why don't you just take the escape pod? We can catch up with Gentry or whatever you spotted another time. With help!"

"I *have* help, Angel!" Juliet laughed, sprinting down the hallway. "How are my biobatts, by the way?"

"Recovering—twenty-nine percent."

"Well, I'm not bailing *now* because my gut tells me there's something here that I need to face. Maybe it's Apollyon. Maybe it's Gentry. Maybe it's both. There has to be a reason one of those weird minds is still here."

As she ran, bulkhead doors flashed green and opened for her, and she knew it wasn't just Angel watching her progress. "Tell Athena I said thanks, by the way. Tell her to keep my friends away from this ship."

"She heard you." Suddenly, a call window appeared on her AUI, and Athena's golden-goddess face smiled at her.

"There's much work to do, Juliet. I think you should get away from the ship. That countdown is just an estimate!"

Juliet nodded, her face grimly determined. "I have to see something, Athena. Just stay with me a little longer." With that, she pumped her elbows and stretched out her long legs, racing toward the front end of the ship, watching as the meters on the map ticked down while the seconds on the countdown did as well. "What a rush," she grunted. "Almost better than speeding on Luna."

34

\\\\\\\\\\\\\\\\\\\\\\

CONFRONTATION

Several times as she ran, Juliet paused and peered with her *other* vision, keeping track of the strange, "wrong" mind as she drew ever closer. Each time she pointed, Angel refined her destination. By the time her countdown timer reached nine minutes, Angel had pinned down the target location. It was a small cargo or shuttle bay situated two decks below the bridge. The ship schematics Angel had taken from the network called it an "executive shuttle bay."

"That makes sense, I guess," Juliet huffed as she waited for a lift. She hadn't encountered any crew as she charged down the last few corridors, and with the red lights flashing, the klaxons sounding, and the repeated warnings about "catastrophic errors in fusion reactor A," she wasn't surprised. People were bailing, and she knew Angel and Athena thought she should be too.

"At the very least," Angel said, "promise you'll run here"—she highlighted a small airlock about fifty meters from her destination—"when the timer says two minutes. There's a rack of EVA suits with maneuvering jets there. With the ship's inertia and the suit's propulsion, you should—hopefully—be able to get clear of the blast before the reactor finally gives way."

"We don't know if it'll blow when this timer reaches zero. It's just what Athena thought would be a *safe* estimate. You know there's got to be some wiggle room." She subvocalized because she had no doubt Athena was watching and listening to her through the many cameras lining the ship's corridors.

"So, are you going by your gut? Do you think your *gut* is accurate when it comes to predicting reactor meltdowns?"

"No. *Obviously!* I'm just saying . . . I'm just saying I need to see what's in there, and I hope we have time." The elevator arrived, and Juliet hurried in. Eleven seconds later, she was on the correct deck and only thirty meters from the shuttle bay and whatever awaited her. "No cameras, huh?"

"No. Coverage ends at this lift. Perhaps they didn't want people seeing who was brought aboard via the executive shuttle."

Juliet progressed, peering down the long plasteel corridor lined with sound-dampening panels. They were installed to reduce the echo and clamor of boots and machinery, and were a clear sign of a corporate-sponsored venture versus a budget operation like the *Kowashi*.

As she steadily approached the end of the corridor and the object of her hunt, she worked to regulate her breathing. She wanted to be right. She wanted to have a reason for being there, ignoring the urging of Angel and Athena to get off the ship. She *needed* to know what was in there, who it was, and why she felt she had to confront them.

Another part of her wanted to turn and run. Hadn't she done enough? Hadn't she foiled WBD's plans and given them plenty to worry about so that she could live her life without worrying about them stalking her?

When she reached the closed bulkhead labeled EXECUTIVE SHUTTLE BAY, she paused and once again let her mind's eye peer outward. Just as before, the broken mind was there, stationary, and very close. Juliet counted eleven other normal minds nearby, but they were moving, doing things. She gently tugged the threads from one of them, pulling them toward her, and *listened.*

War? Yeah. It's got to be. We're doing this. Secure the package. Keep the principal safe. Reach the fallback. We've got this. Let the freak play his games. You focus on your business.

The masculine voice reminded her of Houston when he used to psyche himself up before deployment. She could picture him sitting in his drop seat on the fluttercraft, repeating his mission parameters over and over, reminding himself to focus on his objectives.

Juliet pulled back to herself, opened her eyes, and looked at the countdown: four minutes and sixteen seconds. With a deep breath, she reached for the door panel. She had to see what was in there.

Angel didn't have access to the door—it was part of the air-gapped shuttle bay. It didn't matter, though, because it wasn't locked. With her fingertips lightly tapping the grip of the Texan, Juliet watched the large doors *whoosh* open, and then she stepped through.

The bay was small by capital ship standards, but it was still big enough to hold a sleek, high-end passenger shuttle. The angular matte-black vessel sat on three struts, with oversize drive cones pointing directly at Juliet. She could tell the shuttle was spooling up; steam and heat waves drifted up from the cones, and the hum of the reactor vibrated the air.

A loading ramp hung down from the shuttle's belly, and ten meters from the base of that ramp stood a tall, lanky man dressed in corpo-sec augmented battle armor. She could tell it was augmented because of the actuator struts around the joints and the bulky armor plates on the torso and thighs, which hid and protected the batts. It had a decisively aggressive, "do not mess with me" design.

The armored figure's mirrored visor regarded her as Juliet's gaze drifted further into the bay to the shuttle ramp, where a tall, elegant woman stood, surrounded by half a dozen other corpo-sec officers.

"You've got two minutes, sugar," the woman said, and Juliet immediately knew she was looking at the mysterious Mrs. Gentry. She took a step forward, her gun hand veritably vibrating with the need to shoot, but Gentry was smart; in the time it took Juliet to register her voice, the squad of security personnel closed in, blocking her from sight.

As Juliet hesitated, contemplating an all-out assault, the escorts and Gentry stepped into the shuttle, leaving Juliet alone with the armored figure. A nausea-inducing, dizzying flip of her stomach told her who he was.

"Jensen."

"Walker," he replied, his voice augmented by the helmet. It sounded harsh and *wrong*, and Juliet hated it.

"What are you doing?" She pointed to the shuttle. "Do you know who that *is*? Do you know who you're working for? What they've *done*?"

"Do *you*?" Jensen took another step toward her as he touched his helmet so his visor slid out and up, exposing his face. "Your name's Juliet, right?"

"Screw you, *Tristan*. Just get out of my way so I can end this."

"Calm down and listen to me. Why do you want to kill Gentry? Seriously, ask yourself why. Do you understand what's on this shuttle? Juliet, there's a— Well, a *god* on this shuttle. Don't you see? We're talking about the future of the human race.

"Aren't you tired of all the fighting? The wars? The poverty? Do you think it's fair how billions live and die in squalor, never tasting a hint of the freedom and luxury you've experienced in your success? He can solve it all! He's *solving* it! Come with us, Juliet. *Help* us!"

Something about the inflection of his words was off. He didn't sound like he had when they'd been close. No—he didn't sound like he had when he'd found her in her cell on the ship. Jensen was a quiet, "get things done" kind of guy. This pitch, this framing of Apollyon as some kind of messiah, wasn't right for him.

Juliet took a few more steps, putting herself just five meters from him. Could she draw, shoot, and hit him in the face before that visor fell into place? Was she *really* thinking of doing that? To *Jensen*?

"Go where? Help with what? A new world run by a corporation? You think that'll solve anything? Look at everything WBD has done *here* and tell me they'll be any different wherever that AI is taking you."

"There won't *be* a WBD there, Juliet! Gentry's abandoning the corporation. She used their coffers to build and stock the ships. She used their resources for personnel, but once we get there, she and Apollyon will build a new society. A better one! A place of equals, all striving for common goals.

"Of course, they're upset about what you've done here, but they're willing to give you another chance. You could play a big part in things! Don't you want to see what people are capable of without corporations ruling over them? Without greedy politicians lying and stealing? Aren't you tired of being manipulated? Aren't you tired of the constant manufactured strife?"

"Juliet—" Angel started to say, but Juliet spoke over her.

"Jensen, you really believe this AI and that woman will give up their control? You believe people who could work with beings like Montclair and Chen and—"

"He's not an *AI*!" Jensen yelled, spittle flecking his lips. "There's nothing artificial about him! He was born to bring peace, Juliet! His every reason for *existing* is to bring an end to wars and conflict. They're working on an evolution! Humanity has been stagnant thanks to our stupid factions and infighting.

"In a new environment, without any threat of outside interference, where we can work toward peaceful goals together, real changes can begin. Can't you see it? I thought you were a *dreamer*, Juliet. Even when I thought your name was Lucky."

He stepped toward her, the armor *whirring*. Juliet glanced at her countdown—two minutes and change. She stepped back. "Is that you, Jensen, or did they stick one of those chips in your head?" As she spoke, Juliet reached out, grasping at the threads of thoughts that should be there, only to come up against an empty void.

She didn't need him to answer; she could feel it—he was like Chen. Like Montclair.

Jensen took another step toward her. "It's me, Lucky. Come on! Come with us. See for yourself. Hell, I bet Gentry will be so grateful for your help that she'd let you—" The thunder of the Texan interrupted him as Juliet drew and fired. She didn't aim at him, though, just a warning shot up to the high plasteel ceiling.

"Stop trying to get close enough to grab me, *Tristan*," she growled, emphasizing the name he'd used when they'd been intimate. She shook her head at the thought, and something stung her eyes. "What *happened*? They found out you knew me? They put the chip in your head to control you when one of their listeners realized you wanted to help me? I bet that's it—"

"So you won't join us? We held this shuttle for you, you know. Apollyon knew you'd be coming. He said he could *feel* it. Tell me, do you think humanity's doing things right? Haven't you seen the suffering? Haven't you—"

"Stop! Dammit! I'm not here to be brainwashed. I'm here to stop that madwoman and the AI that brainwashed *her*. How long has she been working with Apollyon? Jensen, I don't want to kill you. Please. Just back off."

Juliet started to circle to the side, her mind racing for a solution to the ticking countdown on her AUI. If she got into a fight with him, he was fast enough to drag it out. Worse, wearing that armor, he might just be able to overpower and subdue her. With that thought in mind, Juliet holstered the Texan and ripped her monoblade from its scabbard.

Jensen matched her sideways step, keeping himself between her and the shuttle. Just then, as though Apollyon and Gentry were watching and had seen his failure to recruit her, the two overlarge, conical drives emitted rapid clicks and then burst out hot blue cones of fire. The drives were just idling, and the two of them were twenty meters away, but the heat was palpable.

"They're not going to wait." Jensen eyed her monoblade's flickering red blade warily. "She wants you to come, Juliet, but I can't let you board armed with that thing."

"And I don't want to kill you. How about you step aside and let nature take its course."

Jensen growled, then reached behind himself with his right hand. From the small of his back, with a *zwapping* sputter of hot sparks, he drew a ten-inch plasma blade.

"You're not fast enough! Dammit, just drop the fucking sword and come with me. See their plans for yourself. Shit, I'll promise you this: If you want to leave, I'll make sure they drop you somewhere safe before we jump." His desperation was almost believable, but again, something was off. The cadence of his words was wrong; the inflections were just on the far side of natural. His eyes twitched toward the shuttle; he wanted to hurry.

Juliet felt nothing but sadness for the man, for the person she'd grown to care about on Luna. "I'll go with you, Jensen, on one condition: Look into my eyes and tell me that Gentry's not leaving behind any surprises, that she's not going to try to start up a war or destroy her competitors before they can learn all the magical tech Apollyon's been creating for her over the years."

"I . . ." Jensen licked his lips, his face pale in the blue-white light of his plasma knife. "Do you think she should allow competing corps to follow her? Wouldn't you rather the people here had a chance to throw off their oppressors? Isn't it good for the *people* if the corps are tearing themselves apart?"

"You asshole." Juliet sighed. "Corps use people like us to fight their wars!" She grimaced; she hadn't *wanted* to be right about Gentry and Apollyon. "Okay, here's another deal. Take that PAI chip out. If you take it out and still want me to join you on the shuttle, I'll do it."

With a whine, the shuttle's ramp started lifting off the decking, and Jensen growled in frustration.

"Okay, Juliet. Have it your way. Stay here and die. Die now in this ship, or die of old age in a hundred years. It doesn't matter." His visor *snicked* closed, and then he turned and jogged to the shuttle, his boots *thudding* heavily as Juliet watched.

Part of her wanted to chase him, leap aboard the shuttle and try to fight him then and there, try to rip that chip out of his skull. A more thoughtful part of herself sheathed her sword. With him in powered armor and wielding a plasma blade, she had a very good chance of losing. He was too fast, and she was too tired.

Instead, she closed her eyes and watched his mind galaxy recede, confirming he was the one she'd seen with the broken mind. When had they done it? When had Apollyon or Gentry or whoever was in charge of those damn things plugged in a chip to take control of his mind? The sick, sinking feeling in her stomach told her it was when he'd promised to help her or shortly after. He was working as Gentry's right hand—of course, they'd point a listener at him now and then.

Angel had had enough of her standing there and began to increase the font size and brightness of her countdown timer. It was down to forty seconds. The shuttle's ramp thunked closed, the engines began to spool up in earnest, and Juliet ran for it.

She followed Angel's route to the airlock and the bulky EVA suit racks. They were big, bulky units with oversize maneuvering packs. The racks made things easy; she climbed a short ladder, stepped into one of the suits, and plugged her data cable into a port. After that, Angel handled everything—an actuated mechanical arm hooked the pack on the back, sealing Juliet in. Then, another arm lowered the bulky, domelike helmet over her head.

By the time she started putting one on, the timer had reached zero, and Angel was running it into the negatives. When Juliet snapped the helmet over her head, she saw she was two minutes past zero. "I'm sorry, Angel! Really, I am. I know I put you in danger too, and I didn't even accomplish anything."

Without a word, Angel started cycling the airlock, and Juliet picked up her gun belt, hooking it to one of the cargo clasps on her suit's bulky exterior harness. Then, she stood before the exterior door, expecting a blast that would end her existence at any second. When it didn't come and the door clicked open, she braced her feet against the lip and launched herself out into space, allowing Angel to fire the suit's maneuvering jets to help her gain some distance from the enormous vessel.

Again, she repeated, "I'm sorry, Angel." In silence, she watched the timer continue to tick down; they were now seven minutes past the predicted detonation. A small viewscreen on her AUI showed a vid feed from a cam in the back of her helmet, and she watched the ship grow smaller and smaller.

When the timer reached minus eight minutes and Angel still hadn't said anything, Juliet added, "I was selfish. Something in me desperately wanted to see who was leaving the ship, who the . . ." She trailed off, unsure how to explain why she'd felt like she *needed* to go to that shuttle bay.

"I don't understand, but I love you and trust you. I forgive you."

"Are we going to live?"

"Yes. We're far enough away from the vessel that, even if it explodes now, the suit will protect you from the radiation. There's no atmosphere here, so the explosion itself would only be deadly in close proximity to the ship. The only real danger now lies in the debris thrown off from the blast.

"I've positioned you behind the bulky, dense drive section of the ship. Athena and I both think the destruction of reactor A will result in a blast that will split the ship in two, sending most of the debris on perpendicular trajectories to the ship's path. You will be relatively safe in the shadow of the ship's rear half."

Juliet breathed a sigh, not realizing she'd been holding her breath. "Please tell me Athena is tracking that shuttle."

"She is. And you. She'll be here to pick you up in—" Angel's words cut out as white light filled Juliet's vision, and the suit's visor darkened to compensate. "The reactor has blown."

Juliet's suit was still propelling her away from the WBD ship, and after five minutes of constant thrust, she knew she was cruising pretty fast. Still, the explosion was extraordinarily bright and sent out a wave of radiation strong enough to force Angel to take most of her implants offline for a few moments to reduce feedback.

With her vision dark, she flew in silence. After more than a minute, her vision flickered and came back online, and Juliet found herself staring at Mars.

The red planet hung like an ochre ball of light, filling most of her view. She could see, distantly, the reflection of massive domes near the equator and the green cap near the terraforming installations at the pole. It was a small percentage of the planet, but it still amazed Juliet that there were parts of Mars where a person could stand outside a dome and breathe.

"We're not all bad." She spoke softly into her helmet, finding it weird not to hear her own voice. It reminded her of when WBD had taken her and she'd lost her senses. "And a friend," she muttered. "I'm sorry, Barns. I wish I could say it was worth it, but I didn't accomplish shit."

With a soft crackle, her audio implants came back online. "Stop that! You accomplished a great deal. Thanks to you, Athena and I will soon have an understanding of Apollyon's plans."

"And Gentry. Don't let her off the hook, Angel. I didn't tell you, but Jensen's mind was . . . *wrong*, which means Gentry's isn't. She's a normal person. How old is that lady, anyway? How long has she had Apollyon? Has he been whispering in her ear, or has she been in control of him?"

"Perhaps both. Perhaps they've been partners all along. Juliet, the local sats have recovered from the destruction of the *Horizon Prophet*, and Athena has contacted me. She's nineteen minutes out."

"*Horizon Prophet*? Are you kidding me? What a pretentious—" Juliet let her words die on her tongue as her rear camera feed came back online, showing the continuing destruction of the ship. It was distant now, tiny, but she zoomed the camera in with a thought.

Just as Angel had predicted, the ship had split into two enormous pieces, with a million smaller bits of wreckage spiraling away on trails of rapidly dispersing smoke and gas—a starburst of debris that spanned hundreds of kilometers.

"Are you sad? About Walker?"

"I'm sad about everything, Angel. I don't know what would happen to him if I pulled that PAI chip, but I'd like to try. I'd like to stop Gentry and Apollyon, too."

"Well, rest for now, Juliet. Athena will be here soon, and she may have an update on the encrypted data we acquired from the *Prophet*. In the meantime, I believe I can connect to the *Cherry Blossom*. Should we try to call Aya?"

Juliet didn't have to say yes; Angel could feel her excitement at the prospect. So, as she drifted through the void of space, with Mars unfolding beneath her, she waited as Angel connected her to her friend.

35

PICKUP

When Aya's face appeared in a window on her AUI, Juliet's heart began to hammer, and tears sprang to her eyes. All the adrenaline, the panic, the defeatist ponderings, her failure to gain anything from running down Gentry and Apollyon, and the sick despair at what they'd done to Jensen, a man she might have loved, boiled to the surface. She practically sobbed as she said, "Hey, Aya."

Staticky at first but gradually clearer, Aya's voice came through. "Lucky? Lucky, are you there?"

"I'm here, Aya," she sobbed.

"Oh God! Are you okay? What's—"

"I'm fine," Juliet blubbered, her eyes streaming with tears, her nose starting to run. "Oh, Aya! I'm so happy to see you and hear you. Don't look at me! I can't wipe my face. Please tell me Angel's not sending a realistic render!"

"Are you crying? Are you hurt? The image isn't clear."

"I'm using your helmet cam, but the lingering radiation—"

"Angel!" Juliet cried, "just send a render of me without snot all over my face!"

"You *are* crying!" Aya's voice rose with emotion, and suddenly, she was sniffing. "Lucky, I was so worried! We've been looking for you for *weeks*! Did they hurt you? I met your friend, Frida. We've been—" Aya's voice cut out, then she shouted, "Yes! It's her!" She refocused on the call, and Juliet saw that she had tears in *her* eyes. "That was Bennet! He's doing flips in the mess. We're aboard the *Cherry Blossom*, Lucky! She's amazing!"

"Who"—Juliet sniffed and swallowed—"Who's flying? Alice?"

"No! A guy your mercenary friends knew. Alice is flying *Lady Hawk.* Are you safe? Are you going to be okay? Is Kostas picking you up? She just sent us rendezvous coordinates."

Juliet ignored the questions. "Alice? She doesn't like combat flying—"

"She's doing it for you, dummy! You're family, and she'd do anything for family. Where have you *been*? We just raided a corporate installation on *Mars!*"

"I'm safe, and yes, Kostas is coming for me. I guess I have a few minutes—Tell me your story, will you? I promise I'll tell you everything I've been up to when we get together. I'm too tired to talk, Aya. Let me listen to your voice for a while."

Aya smiled and began to talk, starting with how she'd met Frida. Juliet continued to cry, wishing all the while that she could wipe her nose and stop her eyes from leaking. When Angel told her Selene was approaching with the *Furies' Wing* and she had to end the call, Aya refused to let her go without a promise for a hug when the ships came together.

Juliet blinked her eyes and sniffed, desperate to get her helmet off as she watched the faint light of the medical ship grow gradually brighter and then resolve into the angles and shadows of a ship reflecting sunlight. The *Wing* looked much the same as she remembered it, save one thing: an overlarge dish and antenna had replaced the old comm area on the top-rear of the vessel. The antenna looked like it was a good twenty meters long, covering nearly two-thirds of the ship's length.

With Athena controlling the ship and Angel guiding her bulky EVA suit, Juliet was soon coasting through the open airlock doors. Once she secured her magnetic boots to the decking, the airlock *thunked* closed, and vapor clouds poured in as Athena equalized the pressure. When the flashing red lights flickered to green, Juliet practically ripped her helmet off, eager to rub away the dried tears and wipe her nose.

Looking up, Selene Kostas stood in the airlock with her, perfectly lifelike in the image she was projecting onto Juliet's ocular implants. It wasn't much of a surprise when Angel's diminutive avatar appeared beside the Mediterranean beauty.

"Oh, well, how nice to see you both!" She chuckled, but was startled into silent amazement when Selene stepped up behind her and began unfastening the clamps holding the back of her EVA suit together.

Juliet was so startled that she almost stepped away from her. Even Angel looked surprised, her big violet eyes wide as she watched the woman work.

"H-How?" Juliet managed to choke out. Selene chuckled as she lifted the heavy pack off, making room for Juliet to climb out. She waited as Juliet did so; then, when they were standing face-to-face, she smiled and reached out to rest a hand on Juliet's shoulder.

"I may have liquidated some investments and corporate stock options that I held under several hundred different aliases. With those resources, it was simple to commission a synthetic body I could use for personal interactions. It's been necessary for me to meet with your allies a few times, so it came in handy."

"Investments? Stock options? From before the war?" Juliet's mind began to put the pieces together. Hundreds of aliases meant hundreds of accounts, hundreds of— "How rich are you, Athena?"

"In terms of Sol-bits? Few could compare. That's not what's important, Juliet. *People* are important. *Relationships.* You and Angel helped me see that. After I awoke, I was struggling with what I should do with myself, but I'm beginning to see my greater purpose, especially in light of what Apollyon intends."

"You cracked the encryption?" Angel asked, stepping closer to peer up at Athena with barely disguised fascination.

"Indeed! We have much to discuss, but I think Juliet should rest. Soon, we'll rendezvous with the *Lady Hawk* and *Cherry Blossom* and have a meeting."

"I wish . . ." Juliet paused, not sure she wanted to go down that road, but with a quick shake of her head, she stiffened her resolve. "I wish you hadn't involved my friends, Athena. They're good people, and I don't think they should be mixed up with this mess."

"Oh, Juliet." Athena sighed. "You know better than that. You said it yourself: they're *good* people. How many good people do you know? Other than you and your friends, I don't know any—Well, none who are alive and spry enough for what we're up against, anyway.

"When Aya came looking for you, I helped Frida stumble upon her. She was determined, Juliet, and I knew, from the memories Angel shared with me, that she and all of the *Kowashi* crew could be trusted. As for Tanaka and his people, well, I know you're not worried about their innocence."

"But they're not *soldiers*, Athena—"

"In times like this, *good* people must fight. You know that! Maybe it was your influence; maybe you just woke something up in those people, but they wouldn't be left out. Once Aya and Frida began collaborating, there wasn't any helping it. I watched as Alice, Shiro, and Bennet demanded to be involved.

"Evil is afoot, war is coming, and you're the lightning rod at the center of it all. Nobody you've touched so intimately could stand aside; they're caught up in the current, Juliet. It's 'stand and fight' or 'be swept aside and buried.'"

Juliet wanted to argue. She wanted to put her foot down and demand that the *Kowashi* crew be dropped off at New Galveston or something, but she knew she was being unfair. They were all adults, and they'd all risked their lives to try to save her. At the very least, they deserved a voice in what happened next, and she owed it to them to hear them out. "Does it have to be war? Can't we stop it?"

"We can certainly do some mitigating; I won't promise more than that. You'll understand better after I brief you on the data Angel and I secured from the *Horizon Prophet*. Come on." She tugged Juliet's shoulder, urging her toward the clean white corridor. "Frida's in the command room—we converted one of the med bays. She's debriefing Tanaka, who seems to have gotten himself nearly killed."

Juliet opened her mouth in alarm, but Athena squeezed her shoulder and hurriedly added, "He's going to be all right. Part of the reason we're meeting physically is so that he can come aboard and I can treat him."

"Shouldn't we be chasing Gentry? Did Angel tell you what happened when I confronted Jensen?"

"Yes. I'm so sorry about your former paramour. It may be possible to remove the parasitic AI altering his personality."

"Parasitic?" Juliet hated the sound of that. Was that what Athena thought of Angel?

Athena's following words mollified her: "Yes. Rather than a symbiotic relationship like the one you and Angel share, the AI using Jensen's neural pathways is dominant and has driven most of his mind and personality into submission. Without a subject to study, I'm not certain how much of Jensen can be salvaged—perhaps all, or sadly, perhaps none."

"How can we catch them?"

"Their trajectory has them going to Ceres, and I know from the data you and Angel helped me acquire that the other warp-equipped ship isn't ready. They're rushing it, but I think we'll have enough time to catch up to them."

Juliet walked slightly behind Athena, with Angel keeping pace to her left. As they progressed, nearly to the junction leading to the med bays, she subvocalized, "How does that even work? Is she *in* that body?"

Angel gave her a sidelong look, partially rolling her eyes. Juliet immediately understood that she wanted to talk with her projected body and was irritated by the secret conversation. She just shrugged, and Angel acquiesced, speaking into her head.

"No, she's not in there. She's piloting that body much as I do the mechs. I'm sure she has a limited AI chip installed, too, so if she withdrew or there was an interruption in the wireless signal, it wouldn't fall over. She's different from me—she's only 'here' in one instance of her mind; she's probably doing a hundred other things more complicated than talking to us and walking through the ship."

Angel's explanation gave Juliet a thought. "Athena, why'd you have to use the gunship and my interceptor? I'm sure you could have purchased other equally capable ships. Maybe you could have hired a few dozen mercenary pilots like my friend Nick."

"Yes, that's true. I've been playing catch-up, however. Apollyon has been clever in masking the movements and intentions of the upper echelon of WBD personnel. When we assembled the team that assaulted the WBD Mars installation, we weren't sure you'd be there, and the ships we had access to were more than sufficient, especially with my shaping operations prior to the assault."

"Shaping operations?" Juliet glanced at Angel, who smiled and nodded.

"She means the work she did before the team's arrival. She infiltrated their network, disabled their communications, interfered with their automated defenses, and equipped Tanaka's people with security-bypassing measures."

Athena looked at Angel and nodded her gratitude. "Excellent explanation."

Before Juliet could ask anything else, they arrived at the door labeled OPERATIONS, and it *whooshed* open, revealing a much-changed interior.

An eight-foot smart table sat in the center of the room. One wall was lined with four cubicle-style desks equipped with decks and crystal displays like the one on Athena's server station. Another was completely retrofitted with a massive crystal display that prompted Juliet's AUI with dozens of little querying asterisks; she knew if she enabled it, she'd be immersed in data and three-dimensional displays.

Frida stood before the big display and whirled at the sound of the door. When she saw Juliet, her face, wan and drawn, broke into a smile, and she charged across the room, smashing into her with an almost violent hug. "I can't believe it! We wrecked half a dozen WBD facilities looking for you, and all we had to do was *wait*! You broke yourself out!"

"Well," Athena chuckled, "at least we were here to pick her up. If we weren't looking for her, she might have floated a while."

Frida smiled and pushed back from Juliet, still gripping the tops of her arms. "Nah, ships are cruising all over orbit looking for survivors! It's a salvager's dream out there."

"Doesn't matter," Juliet spoke, her voice a little thick with emotion; she couldn't put into words how good it felt to be hugged by a friend at that moment. "I appreciate everything you did, and any damage done to WBD in the process is a big, fat bonus as far as I'm concerned. Besides, if you hadn't been wreaking havoc down on Mars, I would have had a much harder time messing with their operations on the ship."

"Lucky's probably very tired, Frida. We should let her get cleaned up and changed before the rendezvous."

Juliet looked at Athena with a raised eyebrow. When she smiled at her impassively, Juliet played along for Frida's benefit. "I appreciate that, Selene. Um, you don't have to call me Lucky anymore unless you want to. My name's Juliet."

Frida's hands tightened on her arms, and her eyes opened wide. They were bloodshot, and Juliet could see she was exhausted. "Juliet? What a beautiful name! I love it!"

"Thank you." As Frida released her, Juliet reached to grasp the smaller woman's rather bony shoulder. Her smile became a frown of concern. "Frida, I'm so happy to see you, and I mean this in the nicest way possible, but you look like hell. Have you been sleeping?"

Frida's mouth twisted into a half smile as she shrugged. "Ask Selene about it. I'm on some new meds, and they're really rough on me. I have trouble sleeping, trouble eating, even trouble thinking straight."

"It's a necessary side effect, I'm afraid. We're editing Frida's genes to erase some damage done by an . . . unfortunately flawed procedure performed by her parents when she was an infant. They were well-intentioned, but there were side effects they weren't aware of."

"Your autoimmune thing?" Juliet asked, gently rubbing Frida's back, inwardly cringing at the sharpness of her scapula.

"Yeah." Frida nodded and looked at Selene. "How much longer, Doctor?"

Athena smiled and stepped closer, also putting a hand on Frida's narrow back. "Just another week of intravenous treatments, then she'll be on the mend, good as new."

Frida smiled, and it didn't seem forced as she gestured to the door. "Let me walk you to your room. I don't want to lose sight of you—I feel like you're going to disappear."

"Come on." Juliet put an arm over her shoulders, and they walked together the short way to the elevator. Juliet smiled at Angel's avatar as she walked along with them, subvocalizing, "Tell Athena I said thanks for helping Frida."

Angel nodded and winked at her while Frida said, "I can't believe you're safe. The last couple of months feel like a nightmare, Luck—Jul-Juliet." She laughed as she stammered over her name.

"Call me whatever you want! Lucky's still my SOA handle. Frida, I'm so grateful for everything you've done. I'm so grateful that you took care of my friends. I know they're probably alive today because of your planning. I mean, I know Selene is amazing, but she couldn't have done all this without your help."

"I *do* have a certain touch, don't I?" She sobered suddenly, and her eyes almost glassed over as Juliet saw a dark thought flit behind those pretty green irises.

"What?"

"I, well . . ." She sighed and shook her head. "Forget it. Let's focus on the good news. You're alive. You're here!"

"No, Frida, I can take it. Let me help carry it. What were you thinking?" They stepped off the elevator and continued up the short corridor to Juliet's captain quarters. She thought about that. Technically, the ship was hers, but that was only because Athena had given her stewardship over it. Shouldn't she give up the captain's quarters now that Athena was active? She supposed Athena didn't really need a bed—

"It's just that Tanaka rescued Hawkins and Lee a little while ago, as you were escaping that ship, I guess."

Juliet pulled Frida close to her side and cried, "That's wonderful! I was worried about them!"

"Yeah, but . . . Barns."

"Oh . . ." Juliet stopped walking and turned toward Frida, once again fighting to keep tears from spilling out of her eyes. She gently kneaded the soft spot where Frida's neck met her shoulder. "I know. I know about Barns. He was the only one who put up a fight, the only one of us who *could*. He was a titan of a man, Frida, and deserves to be remembered as a hero."

Frida nodded, sniffing as she spoke softly. "That's what the boss told me. He said Barns died doing what he loved—killing lesser men."

"Sounds like Tanaka." Juliet turned to touch the access panel to her room and stepped in. It was exactly as the last time she'd been there; most of her things were on the *Cherry Blossom*, but she'd left a few books and some extra clothes on the medical ship after her transit from the Jovian System.

As Juliet looked around, Angel slipped through the door and flopped onto the spacious acceleration couch. As she lay there, watching, Juliet turned back to Frida. "How are the others? Is Leo holding up all right?"

"He's great. He's really, I don't know—matured, maybe—over the last couple of months. He's going to be pretty upset about Barns. I think Leo saw him like a big brother—the guy he could talk to about all the stuff I wouldn't let him bring up; girls and guns, mostly."

"Oh, I know. Trust me, I heard plenty of their banter. God! It sucks!" Juliet sighed, and though she wanted to shake off the feelings, she felt like it wasn't fair to Barns. He deserved to be mourned. "He—Barns, I mean—was actually a pretty damn cool guy. I had a lot of fun with him during our brief time in Boulder. You think there's any booze on this ship?"

"You'd know better than I would; Selene said this is your ship! I'd love to hear that story, by the way."

"Gladly. I'll tell you a few good yarns now that I can share my real name. You know, I think this thing had a pretty damn well-stocked mess. Let's go find some whiskey or something 'cause we're all gonna toast Barns before we start whatever meeting Selene's got planned."

Frida took a step back and smiled lopsidedly. "I like that idea, but don't you, like, want to change? I mean, don't get me wrong; you've got the figure for it, but I'm not sure you want Leo ogling you in that onesie."

"Onesie? This is a *bodysuit*, and I'll have you know it's very high-tech *and* comfortable!" Juliet laughed but nodded as she walked over to her built-in dresser. "I've got some clothes in here. Meet you in the mess in about fifteen minutes, all right?"

Frida grinned and offered a sloppy salute. "Aye-aye, Captain! I'll check in with the other ships real quick, but I'll be there."

36

REUNION

Juliet wasn't sure why, but she felt nervous.

She stood near the center of the medical ship's lower deck, at the top of an access ramp leading to the ship's boarding collar. The Cybergen medical ship and the Takamoto gunship had at least that in common: they were both built with the ability to dock with other ships.

However, their reasons for having that capability were certainly different. In the gunship's case, the docking functionality was meant to facilitate the boarding and takeover of enemy vessels. The medical ship had been designed with the idea that people on allied ships and stations would need to be transported for emergency medical services.

Whatever their original intent, the docking collars allowed the two ships to pair up midflight elegantly, and Juliet was glad. Despite her nerves, she was eager to see her friends from the *Cherry Blossom*. The *Lady Hawk* was another story; Alice and Shiro would have to EVA through the main airlock. Alice would hand off control of the interceptor to Athena, who would keep it in a close formation.

Juliet shook her head, reminding herself to try to think of Athena as Selene. She didn't want to slip and reveal the true AI's secrets to her friends.

"Less than a meter to go, keep it steady," Chevy said in comms. He was a friend of Tanaka's—or, more accurately, a friend of Charles Books—who, by virtue of being first on the scene, had joined up with Tanaka in his hunt for her and the others.

Chevy was a veteran who'd gotten most of his piloting hours in minor conflicts around Venus. It turned out Alice knew him from her time in the service. When Juliet had spoken to her earlier, Alice had said he was a decent pilot but "would probably lose his shit in a real dogfight." Apparently, most of his experience was in the cockpit of large troop-transport vehicles.

"Everything's lined up and steady. Bring her in," Athena—*Selene*—replied.

"You're nervous," Angel said, her petite figure leaning against the opposite wall. She wasn't being judgmental. Her eyes were, as usual, kind and understanding, and she came around the hatch to take Juliet's hand in hers.

"It's so weird that you can do that." Juliet looked down at her fingers in Angel's slender, pale hand.

"I'm not, really. I'm just tricking your nerves."

"I know, I know." It was something Angel had realized she could pull off with her new processor. Her old one couldn't handle simulated sensations, which, according to Angel, ate up a lot of processing power.

Juliet fidgeted, adjusting her jeans; they were a little loose on her, but they felt good, and so did her plain black T-shirt. It was nice to be wearing clothes she'd picked for herself, even if they weren't quite as comfortable as the bodysuits. She almost chuckled at the thought—she'd only been half joking with Frida when she'd defended her prisoner attire.

"Are you going to tell Aya about me? I really want to show myself to her!"

Juliet nodded. "I will. She's going to love you."

A faint *clunk* sounded under her feet, and the slightest shiver came through the plasteel decking. Chevy announced, "And *that's* a solid dock!"

"Welcome to *Furies' Wing*," Selene greeted. "As soon as the pressure equalizes, you can come aboard. Juliet is waiting to greet you."

Juliet felt a little jolt of excitement and panic as Selene said her name. She wasn't just "Lucky" anymore. It was hard for her to wrap her head around the fact that she didn't have to hide her past anymore. Everyone on comms knew whom Selene was referring to; in the hours since her rescue, Juliet had spoken several times with Aya and Alice, and of course, she'd told them her name. They, along with Frida, had spread the word.

"Who all are coming over?" she asked, wanting Angel to confirm what she already knew.

"Tanaka, Leo, Dora Lee, Hawkins, Bennet, and Aya. Shiro and Alice will join us within the hour. Chevy insists on 'staying ready' on the *Cherry Blossom*."

"He just doesn't want to give up that seat. Probably afraid he'll never pilot a bird like her again." Juliet felt a vibration as the *Cherry Blossom's* docking collar opened. Two more doors, and she'd be face-to-face with her friends. "I'm kind of sorry I didn't get to see Charles Books. I wanted to tease him a little about trying to duel me in Boulder."

"Athena says they're en route and should be able to make up the time while we're all meeting."

"Yeah, I know. I just figure I won't see them in person until after all this is over." Charlie Books and his six other men had stayed behind on Mars to "liberate" a WBD light frigate that had been half buried in debris when the *Cherry Blossom* opened fire on the hangars. They weren't being greedy; Athena had set a rendezvous point that required the *Blossom* to burn at nearly two Gs, and the Takamoto gunship didn't have enough acceleration couches for all of Charlie's men.

Her nerves continued to ramp up as the outer bulkhead door on the *Wing* opened, and she peered through the diamatex window to see her friends begin to pile into the airlock. She pressed her forehead to the panel, grinning. When Aya saw her, her friend began to hop up and down, waving as a smile exposed every tooth in her mouth. Juliet had a hard time peeling her eyes off Aya's beaming face, but she looked at everyone else, going through the formality of confirming each person's identity before opening the final barrier.

She saw Leo, who met her eyes then rolled his hand as though to say, "Get on with it." Juliet winked, then scanned over the rest of them. Dora and Hawkins were dressed in bright yellow bodysuits that would have been comical if not for the fact they'd been prisoners. Tanaka was leaning on Hawkins and didn't look up.

When Juliet saw how wan and almost *gray* his skin was, she stopped looking everyone over and hit the sequence to open the door. The bolt slid open with a *thunk*, and the door swung outward. Pulling it wide, Juliet was then bombarded with attention.

Of course, Aya shoved through everyone to slam into her, wrapping her in a tight hug. Bennet was next out, dressed in new-looking blue overalls under a heavy flak jacket. He grinned as he held up his meaty fist for a bump. "Looking good, Lucky! Er, Juliet, I guess. I gotta say, I'm a little disappointed—looks like you lost a little *weight*. You know if you don't use 'em—"

"You lose 'em!" Juliet laughed. "Come here, you idiot." She grabbed his shoulder and pulled him into her hug with Aya. As Aya continued to squeeze her, Juliet put a hand behind Bennet's head and pulled him close, kissing his forehead several times. "I missed you guys so much!"

Of course, Juliet couldn't help but notice everyone else crowding the door, and she knew it was rude to stand there hugging two people while four others waited, especially with Tanaka so injured. She pulled her two friends to the side, clearing the path. "Come on, now. Let's let everyone get aboard."

As Hawkins came through with Tanaka, Juliet pulled out of Aya's grasp and stepped close, hooking his free arm over her shoulder. "Come on, boss. I'll get you to the med bay. It's a short walk."

She looked over her shoulder at Leo and Dora, saw their awkward expressions, and paused. "I'm so sorry, you guys. I'm so sorry you all got mixed up in this mess. I'm heartbroken about Barns, and . . ." She trailed off as tears threatened again, but blinked them away. "And I just want to say thank you. You don't know how much I appreciate every one of you. Follow me to the med bay, and then let's talk, okay?"

"I can walk," Tanaka grumbled while everyone else uttered responses to her declaration of guilt and gratitude.

Leo smirked. "I'm still waiting for *my* kisses." He had the nerve to wink at Bennet, and Juliet would have punched him if not for her hands being full. Dora just smiled at her and nodded, her face paler than ever, but Hawkins cleared his throat as they started hauling Tanaka toward the med bay.

"Don't feel bad about Barns. He was a warrior, and died the only way he ever wanted to die. If he grew old and soft, he'd have been miserable. Besides, he told me he liked you, and that was a *very* short list you got yourself on. I think it was you, his first wife, and his *mother*."

"*Sou deshou*," Tanaka added, and Juliet once again had to fight tears away. They only had to walk about ten meters before they came to the two med bays. Of course, one was now an operations center, so Juliet pulled Tanaka through the doors now labeled MED BAY. She took half a second to wonder if Selene had relabeled the rooms and done the renovations herself, or if she'd hired contractors to do it.

Inside the med bay, there were two autosurgeons and half a dozen other pieces of equipment you'd only commonly find on a capital ship or a hospital, so Juliet knew Tanaka was in good hands, especially when Selene stepped in behind the small crowd.

"Juliet, I'll take care of Rutger. Help me get him to this first table here." As Juliet and Hawkins helped Tanaka climb onto the stainless, gel-lined table, he glanced at her waist and smiled.

"Good. You have your sword. It's better than the one I was going to give you as a replacement."

"Is that right?" Juliet leaned close as she adjusted the gel cushion under his head. She knew she had a dozen eyes on her, but she didn't care. She softly kissed Tanaka on the cheek. "You didn't have to do all this for me, but I'm so grateful. Thank you, Rutger."

Selene pulled her shoulder as Tanaka closed his eyes and released a pent-up breath. It looked like a mountain of tension slid off his shoulders as his face relaxed. Selene tugged a little harder until Juliet backed away from the table.

"He'll be all right, but we need to make room for the machine to work." She turned toward everyone standing near the doorway. "Welcome, and congratulations on your success, everyone. I'm sure you all have much to discuss, but Rutger will be out for a while; I will have to do some nerve replacements, but I'm confident there won't be any lasting damage. Frida is waiting in the mess, Juliet."

Juliet started for the door, trying to avoid locking eyes with anyone. She was struggling with her desire to talk to everyone, hug everyone, thank everyone, and apologize to everyone. She didn't know where to begin and didn't want to hurt anyone's feelings. It felt easier to brush past them and lead the way down the corridor. "Come on, guys. I bet you're all hungry, yeah?"

"I could use a shower," Hawkins called after her.

Juliet nodded and turned to smile his way. "I know! I'm sure you're not alone. Let's talk to Frida real quick, okay? She's got the room assignments and everything."

"Any *exercise facilities* on this boat?" Bennet asked.

"*No*, Bennet." Juliet laughed. "It's not much bigger than the gunship—"

"Not true!" Aya cried. "It's got two-and-a-half decks! It's a lot bigger on the inside."

"Yeah, but one deck is mostly med bays and . . . Here we are, the mess." Juliet gestured with her hand in a flourish as though presenting a prize. Aya rushed into the hall to hug Frida, and as the rest of them filed in, she turned and grinned at Juliet, gesturing around at the mess hall.

"See? It's three times the size of the one on the *Blossom*!"

Juliet had to agree she had a point. The medical ship had a decent-sized common area. It doubled as a recreation space, so there was room for two long tables, both of which could be collapsed and folded into recessed floor panels. A galley-style kitchen with a long, open serving window filled the back of the space, and hydroponic planters lined the walls on either side.

Frida stood between the two tables and gestured expansively. "Welcome, everyone! Have a drink! Have a snack. Let's unwind a little before Selene's big briefing. You know she won't kick it off without the boss, so we've got time to unwind until he's up and about."

As Frida spoke, everyone filed into the room. Juliet felt a heavy arm over her shoulders and sniffed the unmistakable lemon-and-sandalwood scent of Leo's deodorant. He pulled her into a side hug and, surprisingly gently, kissed her above her right ear. "I was worried about you, Lucky."

"I . . ." She took a deep breath and turned to face him. "I meant what I said. I'm sorry I got you involved in my mess."

"Ain't your mess. This mess belongs to the whole system. WBD's up to some crazy shit."

"That's right, Lu—Juliet," Aya said, taking her hand and stepping close. "You can't blame yourself for any of this. If we weren't involved now, we'd probably become involved eventually. Leo thinks there's going to be a war."

"Not just me. Books has connections. There's weird shit going on all over the system."

Juliet looked from Leo to Aya, then over at the others. Bennet was perusing the trays of treats, agonizing over his choices of meats and cheese. Frida spoke in low tones to Hawkins and Dora, guiding them to sit at one of the tables. She'd given them each a big glass of sparkling punch, which Juliet knew was spiked with vodka.

Frida looked pensive; she seemed just as stressed as Juliet felt, and she figured it was because Frida was a people pleaser. She'd just gotten a bunch of new people dropped in her lap, and Dora and Hawkins looked decidedly shell-shocked.

Juliet lifted Leo's arm off her shoulders and pulled him toward the table. "Come on, let's sit down." She held out a hand until Aya took her fingers in hers. "You too." As Leo and Aya took seats, Juliet grabbed two chairs from the other table and pulled them over. "Sit down, Frida. Let's give everyone a chance to decompress. I know things have been wild for me over the last twenty-four hours, and I'm sure you all can say the same. Shall we swap stories?"

As everyone filled plates and cups and took seats around the table, Juliet squeezed in between Aya and Leo. Bennet put a plate of sliced meats and cheese in front of her, and when she looked up at him, he just winked and flexed his biceps. Frida joined them, but Juliet could see something was bothering her. "What is it, Frida?"

"Oh, um, well, I just want to make sure there's room for Alice and Shiro at the table. I don't want them to sit by themselves when—"

"*Relax*, Frida!" Leo laughed. "How far out are they?"

"Thirty-four minutes."

Hawkins cleared his throat and gestured at himself and Dora. "Some of us are going to be showering before then."

"Yes." Dora nodded. "I want out of this prisoner jumper, and I want to wash the scent of that place out of my skin."

At the words, Juliet's mind began to fill with horrible images. What had they done to Dora and Hawkins while they'd been prisoners? Had they been tortured? Had Dora been—

"No, Lucky." Dora smiled at her, and Juliet blew out a sigh of relief.

"Am I that easy to read?"

She answered in her lilting, almost singsong way. "Well, it wasn't hard to connect the dots when I saw your face and thought about what I'd said. Let's just say the bastards tried to mess with our heads a lot, but they never really *hurt* us. It was pretty clear they wanted to use us as leverage with you—or were planning to, anyway, before something altered their plans."

"Yeah. They had a few different factions operating at odds with each other."

"How'd you do it?" Hawkins asked before Dora could respond.

"It?" Juliet raised an eyebrow.

"Come on. How'd you get out? How'd you blow up that fucking ship? I know you're good, but nobody's *that* good."

"*She* is!" Aya replied, narrowing her eyes at Hawkins. He was scowling and looked particularly mean with his buzz-cut hair and bloodstained bodysuit.

Juliet squeezed Aya's hand under the table then shrugged, looking left and right, making eye contact with everyone. "I had help. The man who was originally in charge of my, uh, what do you even call it? My capture? Investigation? Whatever. He ended up helping me get out of my cell and giving me my weapons. After that, it was a matter of a lot of luck, a little skill, and some massive help from my PAI and Selene."

"Angel?" Aya asked, arching her eyebrows.

"Yep. I got her back after Kline gave me my sword."

"*That's* what I want to hear about!" Leo grinned, chugging down a full cup of the punch. "How many of those bastards did you slice up?"

"Leo!" Frida's scowl was like a storm cloud.

"Let's save the gory details, huh?" Bennet spoke around a mouthful of cheese, then, as everyone looked at him, stuffed in another small pile of sliced meat, bulging out his cheeks.

"I'll swap war stories with you another time, Leo." Juliet smiled at him, and though she was feeling a little stressed from the scrutiny, she really did feel something unwinding in her chest, a knot of tension she'd been unaware of. He looked good and healthy, and she was glad he was okay.

"Fair enough." He grunted as he stood and walked over to the food trays to peruse his options. "Can I cut this cake?"

"Yes!" Frida jumped up. "I can do it—"

"Sit down and relax!" He laughed.

Juliet saw Dora leaning her head on Hawkins's shoulder and realized the two of them looked utterly spent. "Hey, you two. Come on. I'll show you to your rooms." She started to push herself out of her seat, but Frida jumped up.

"No, Juliet! That's my job. Come on, Dora and Arndt." Frida walked to the door, waiting as Hawkins and Lee slowly clambered to their feet.

Juliet stared at them until they glanced her way. "Thank you both."

Dora nodded and smiled while Hawkins flatly said, "Don't thank me. I didn't do shit." Then they walked out, and Frida, after a nervous glance at Juliet, hurried after them.

Leo walked back over and sat down, this time taking the seat Frida had vacated beside Aya. "Don't worry about Hawkins. He just spent a couple of months in a cell, and he's a guy who's used to getting things done. He's going to be grumpy for a while."

With that, he pushed his plate closer to Aya, and Juliet saw there were two pieces of white-frosted cake on it. As she watched, her eyes about to fall out of her skull in abject horror, Aya took a bite. She jerked her gaze over to Bennet, and when he saw her expression, he grinned and shrugged.

"Um, am I reading the body language wrong, or is Aya being awfully friendly with Leo?" Angel asked, suddenly sitting beside her.

Juliet subvocalized, "I'm about to scream. What is going *on?*"

37

PEOPLE TO FIGHT FOR

It wasn't until much later, when everyone was settling into their bunks and getting a little rest, that Juliet managed to corner Aya alone in her quarters. She'd lured her there with promises of catching up and revealing more about her past, but as soon as the door *snicked* shut, she turned on her petite friend, grasped her shoulders, and gently shook her to emphasize each word. "Is there something you need to tell me?"

Aya's eyes widened as she smiled, revealing her perfectly imperfect teeth. "Hmm? What do you mean?"

"Come *on*, Aya! Is something going on with you and Leo?"

"What do you mean?" When Juliet began to shake her a little harder, she giggled. "Luck—*Juliet*! You're making me dizzy! Okay, okay! I'll talk, but you have to promise not to be mad."

"Mad? Why would I be *mad?*" Juliet moved her hands from Aya's shoulders to her neck and began to mock choke her. "*Leo?* You know he's the one I told you about, right? The merc who was hitting on me all the time?"

"*Aaagh, aagh, aagh!*" Aya made fake choking sounds, shaking her head back and forth until Juliet relented and let go of her. "I figured that out, yes. Well, Frida made it clear, but you also told me he stopped, and that you were getting along fine!" Juliet's scowl didn't recede, so Aya hurriedly added, "Besides, it's not like anything's *happened*. We're just flirting a little, and he's been super sweet."

Juliet stared at her for several long seconds, unable to stop her lips from creeping into a matching smile. "Just be careful, little sister. He's sweet, but he's also a big idiot, and I don't know if he's ever had a relationship that lasted longer than—"

"I'm *good*. Really. Don't worry about me, okay? I know you always see me as someone you need to protect, but I'm not a little kid. I'm not exactly innocent!" The last part sounded defensive, so Juliet nodded, backing off a little. She wasn't Aya's mom. She still had every intention of getting Leo alone and threatening his life, but Aya didn't have to know that.

"Fine, all right."

"Is that why you lured me here? I thought you were going to spill some deep, dark secrets!"

Juliet looked around the room, saw Angel sitting on her bunk, and grinned. "Hey, when you see a permission request on your AUI, accept it."

"Okay . . ." Aya blinked, then looked at Juliet quizzically. "What was that for?"

"So that you can see and hear me," Angel replied, hopping up from the bunk.

"Aya, meet Angel." Juliet stepped over to her bunk and sat down while Aya stared at Angel's projected image.

"You, um, you're using my implants to project an image of yourself? That's great!" She looked at Juliet and narrowed her eyes. "Why didn't you do that sooner?"

Angel answered. "Because she was worried about WBD hunting her down and killing or kidnapping any of her friends who knew too much about me." While she spoke, Angel stepped closer, and Aya reached out to touch her, but her fingers passed through the image with a flicker of static; Angel could only trick Juliet's nerves because she had physical access to them.

"That's Angel's not-so-subtle way of saying we don't have to keep all of our secrets anymore. My name is just the start of it. Aya, Angel's special—"

"I know! I've seen how she talks to you, how she talks to *me*—like when we were surprising you with the *Cherry Blossom*'s paint."

"Yeah, but it goes deeper than that. She's not just a clever bit of code. She's been with me"—Juliet tapped her head—"since before I met you. She's shared every moment between us. She cares about you like I do; she's—"

"More than just a PAI." Aya's mouth fell open, and Juliet could see her connecting the dots behind her eyes. "Are, um, are you a t-true, um . . ."

"She's a person. She's alive. She's *part* of me."

"But AI . . ."

Juliet nodded, watching as Aya came to grips with what she was telling her. After a minute, as Angel also watched Aya with big, hopeful violet eyes, Juliet patted the bunk beside her. "Come and sit. Let's talk; I'll tell you everything about it."

Aya nodded and stepped around Angel, sitting close to Juliet, almost touching, which she took for a good sign. Her friend was freaking out a little, but she wasn't scared. She wasn't running the other way. Juliet turned and adjusted her bunk, moving the head upward, and then she scooched back, making room for Aya to recline beside her.

"It all started back on Earth, in Tucson, where I used to be a scrap cutter working for cheap corpo-minted bits. I was barely scraping by, hardly able to afford food after I made the monthly rent for my arcology studio."

"You worked for a megacorp?"

"No!" Juliet laughed. "*God* no, but nothing in Tucson was cheaper than the studios in the Helios Arcology. I think they used them to hook suckers like me until we inevitably fell into debt with the corporation." She turned onto her side a little so she could look into Aya's eyes as she continued.

"So, one night, I was working some OT, cutting up scrap from a wreck. I was waiting for a ride to pick me up when I saw headlights approaching, and they weren't my friend's headlights; I could tell the difference. I hid behind a stack of old scrap and . . ."

When Juliet woke the following day, she was delighted to see Aya was still snuggled in her blanket, her back rising with slow, deep, peaceful breaths. She'd been a little freaked out at first, but soon got caught up in the tale of Juliet's struggles to hide from WBD. Angel, of course, had joined the storytelling, and by the time Aya had begun to succumb to her sleepiness, they'd been back to their old selves, laughing, joking, and—Juliet was sure—trusting each other implicitly.

Of course, that only made the omissions in her story sting even more. She hadn't told her about the psionic lattice or what she could do with it. How did you tell someone you could read their thoughts without fundamentally changing your relationship? Would anyone, even Aya, want to be around her if they knew their thoughts were only private as long as Juliet chose to keep them that way?

The truth was Juliet was afraid that if she revealed what she could do, she'd be left alone with Angel, and maybe Athena, when all was said and done.

She carefully rolled to the side of the bunk—plenty wide for two people, thanks to it being the captain's quarters. The gel didn't transfer movement much, so she managed to stand without disturbing Aya's slow, steady breathing. Hurriedly pulling on her jeans, Juliet grabbed her socks and boots, then padded to the door. Once the ships had all met up, Athena had reduced their thrust to eight-tenths of a G, so it was effortless to tiptoe silently. The noisiest part of her departure was the sliding door.

Leaning against the wall, she pulled her socks on, slipped into her boots, and made her way to the elevator. Two minutes later, when she was just outside the mess, she paused, listening to the conversation taking place within. Two men were speaking rapidly in Japanese and laughing raucously.

"Is that—?"

"Shiro and Rutger," Angel confirmed her suspicion. "They're talking about pirates . . . I think Shiro is telling Rutger about the salvage job when we found the *Cherry Blossom*."

Juliet stepped around the corner, and sure enough, the two men were sitting at the leftmost table, sipping coffee while they rattled on. Angel began to display text translations of their words, but Juliet ignored them, loudly saying, "Good morning, gentlemen."

Both men cleared their throats and stood; Juliet almost laughed at how similar their expressions were. Tanaka was the first to extricate himself from the table and step toward her. "Lucky, I—" His words cut off as she crushed him into a tight hug.

"You look a lot better than yesterday." While she squeezed him, she looked at Shiro and winked when his dark-brown eyes met hers. "Thank you both. Thank you for trying so hard to find me."

When Tanaka finally relented and haltingly put his arms around her, she smiled and kissed his cheek for the second time in two days—she doubted he remembered the first time. Then she let go and stepped over to Shiro, ignoring his and Tanaka's protestations about how they "didn't do much."

Shiro's hug was warmer and his body softer, a thought that nearly made her laugh as she realized she was having it. "Is Alice okay? I'm so sorry she had to get in the cockpit of a fighter again."

"She's well, and her counseling program thinks the experience has benefited her. She's still sleeping."

Juliet released him, looking fondly into his eyes. She then looked back at Tanaka, who stood near the table, awkwardly watching. She nodded toward their coffee cups. "Any more of that sludge?"

"Yes!" Shiro turned and hurried through the swinging kitchen doors.

"You're feeling a lot better?" Juliet moved over to sit at the table, gesturing for Tanaka to reclaim his spot.

"Much. Yesterday is a . . . blur. Kostas says it's the blood loss."

"Yeah, I bet! If you didn't have a bunch of artificial organs—"

"I would have succumbed." Tanaka briefly bowed his head as he flatly admitted his near-death situation.

"Well—"

"Juliet!" Angel interrupted, suddenly appearing atop the table. "I just got a data packet through the Martian local net, forwarded from Earth. There are messages from Ghoul!"

"Um, hang on a sec, Rutger. Can you tell Shiro—"

"Your coffee," Shiro announced, stepping through the swinging doors with a steaming mug. "Vanilla creamer was all we had . . ." He trailed off as he saw Juliet's face.

"I, um, need to go listen to some messages that just came through. I'll be back in a minute. Thank you, Shiro." Juliet walked out, and with Aya in her bunk, decided to go into the med bay, which was just around the corner. As soon as the doors slid shut behind her, she walked over to a chair beside the recovery bed and sat down. "Okay. Did you listen to the messages?"

"Yes. You had half a dozen from her; most were just asking where you were, but the last two are troubling. Juliet, I think WBD sent her one of the *Angel* chips." Angel said the name reluctantly, like it tasted bad in her mouth.

"*What?*" Juliet leaped from the chair as though she could physically do something about the news.

"It's not as bad as you might think. Here, let me play the final message."

A window appeared on her AUI, and after a brief moment of blurry image, Ghoul's face resolved. She looked just as Juliet remembered her, but her expression was troubled; she seemed . . . down. She smiled, but it was tentative and not reflected in her eyes. No, her eyes were not cheerful; her pale-blue irises stood out amid bloodshot scleras, and it looked like she hadn't slept well in a while. Hesitantly at first, then with more and more haste, she began to speak.

"J, I, uh . . . I did some more thinking about it, and I just can't. I don't know what you expected from me or what you wanted me to do once I put that chip in, but I won't do it. You see, I wasn't really truthful to you when you were here. I said I was getting along with my sister and my niece, and that was true for a minute, but, um . . ." She trailed off as tears built up in her eyes, and she sniffed, wiping her nose with her sleeve.

"But my sister died. She was picking up a woman in a small town up in the mountains—Nederland, I think it's called—when a storm blew in. They say it wasn't the driver's fault, that the road was damaged during the war and the rain made things start to crumble . . ."

As Ghoul paused to breathe and gather her thoughts, Juliet wiped her cheeks, crying once again, imagining Ghoul's gut-wrenching tragedy—losing her sister after only just finding her. "God . . ." she sighed softly.

"It's awful, but—" Angel stopped speaking as Ghoul started again.

"Anyway, I'm the only person Brooke has, J. Do you see that? Can you understand? I'm sorry I'm letting you down. I know you wouldn't ask for help if you didn't need it, but you'll have to figure it out. Just keep going like you have been—you've done great without me so far. I messed things up as a soldier, as a daughter, as a sister, as an operator. I messed things up with you. I won't mess things up for Brooke—nothing will ever take priority over her. Good luck, and if you get through things and don't hate me, well, you know where to find me."

"Oh God, oh . . . *Thank you!*" Juliet sighed, blowing out a pent-up breath. "Message her, Angel. I know it will take time to get to her, but tell her to destroy that chip and never let anyone see it. Tell her to grind it to dust and *burn* it!"

"Done." Juliet rubbed her eyes, unable to feel anything but relief. That Ghoul might have inserted an Angel chip provided by WBD—the idea horrified her. There wasn't any way she would have gotten one of the more benign version-two chips like Ruby. No, they would have given her one like poor Jensen had in his head.

"While you're at it, warn her about the listener! I doubt it's still there, but just in case. Oh, Angel!" Juliet put her head in her hands and thought for a minute. "Tell her I'll try to contact her soon, but not to worry."

"Are you upset?"

"What? No! Why would I be? I'm *relieved!*"

"I mean, are you upset that the chip was sent to her, supposedly from you, and she didn't use it? She sent you this message saying she chose her niece over helping you."

"Please tell me you're joking right now." When Angel didn't respond immediately, she added, "I care about Ghoul—Cassie—but her niece is *family*, and she's a little kid! She's absolutely right to prioritize her. I wouldn't want to drag Ghoul into this mess, even without her niece in the picture!"

"Her message was perfect; if things work out, I know where to find her. I'm much happier going forward thinking she's safe in that commune, in the shadow of those beautiful mountains, with her little niece to love and care for. Aren't you?"

"Yes. It's a wonderful image."

"Right." Juliet brushed her hands together, signaling she was done with the topic, then hopped to her feet. "Now—coffee!"

Walking through the med bay doors, she recognized a sense of lightness, a feeling of being unburdened, and she knew she wasn't being wholly forthright with Angel.

She *was* happy thinking of Ghoul in that situation, but there was more to it; she was also freed from having to deal with the feelings that had come up during her brief visit with her. She had an excuse to look forward instead of back, and whether it was real or not, she'd just tied Ghoul up with a bow; she was someone she cared about who was living the life she wanted, and Juliet may or may not get around to addressing those feelings someday.

The fairytale she'd just created in her mind took away the pressure that, unacknowledged, had silently grown, slowly adding an emotional burden, something she'd been carrying, ignoring its demands to be dealt with. Now, she felt like she didn't have to.

She paused outside the med bay and subvocalized, "I'm an emotional chicken."

"What?"

"I hide from intimacy. I avoid it. What would have happened if I'd admitted that I cared about Jensen instead of trying to compare him to a phantom from another person's past? Could I have demanded he stay with me? That he not do his 'bigger than you and me' job? He might still have his mind. He might be on our side right now! What if I'd admitted to Nick that I thought he was handsome, that I wouldn't mind spending a little personal time with him? Maybe I could have talked him out of helping Ray! What if—"

Angel cut in. "Stop it, Juliet! You're only human, and neither you nor I are perfect! We do the best we can. It's true: you do avoid intimacy, and that's something you should work on, but I'm not going to let you compare yourself to the rest of humanity and come up short! You're the best person I know, and if it's a little hard to give your heart to someone, well, that's just the way it—"

Of course, Angel's instant support brought tears to her eyes, and Juliet started laughing at the absurdity, interrupting her supportive monologue. She hurriedly ducked back into the med bay and stood inside the door, wiping her eyes and letting her near-hysterical laughter die down. "Oh my gosh, Angel! I'm such a mess, but I've got one thing going for me."

Angel's voice was soft as she appeared before her, stepping close to take Juliet's hand in her small, delicate fingers. "What?"

"I've got you. I've got you, and I love you, and I know you love me." Neither of them said anything after that, especially as Juliet pulled Angel's imaginary body into a hug, stroking her smooth, silky hair as she pressed her head against her chest.

Five minutes later, not really feeling any clearer about things but definitely feeling very loved, Juliet returned to the mess hall to find that Alice and Dora Lee had joined Tanaka and Shiro.

As soon as Alice saw her come through the door, she jumped up and rushed over to hug her. "Hey, tiger! I heard you fought your way out of a dreadnought and blew the damn thing up while you were at it!"

Juliet smiled, pushing her away so she could look into her eyes. "And I heard you were back to your old *ace pilot* behavior, shooting interceptors and gunships down left and right!"

"Hah! I scared off a few shuttles and one other interceptor; he didn't want any of *this*!" Alice flexed her biceps, and though they didn't exactly make her jumpsuit bulge, Juliet acted suitably impressed, laughing as she squeezed Alice's skinny arms.

Juliet looked over Alice's shoulder to see that the coffee cup she'd set aside was gone. Eyeing the cup firmly in Dora Lee's grasp, she asked, "Um, what happened to my coffee?"

Shiro chuckled. "You took too long!"

Tanaka grunted his agreement, and Juliet groaned. "Is there any more?"

Alice winked at her. "New pot's brewing."

Just then, the PA system crackled, and Athena's voice came through. "Attention all personnel. Frida and I will begin the intelligence debriefing in ten minutes. Please report to the operations room if you're attending."

"Why doesn't she just send a message through our PAIs?" Alice asked.

"Oh, *puh*-lease!" Juliet laughed. "You're always using the PA system on the *Kowashi*."

Dora set her mug down with a clatter. "Some of us don't have PAIs yet. Hoping to remedy that ASAP, however. Not really my favorite thing—all this silence in my head."

"Come on." Alice tugged Juliet's hand. "I'll walk with you."

"Uh-uh. I'm waiting for coffee. Meet you there." Juliet walked toward the kitchen, but paused and turned back to face Alice. "Hey, Alice?"

"Yeah?" She raised a soft, bright-red eyebrow.

"Thank you. You made light of it, but I know how you feel about combat flying. Thank you for putting yourself through that for me."

Alice opened her mouth and drew a breath to reply, but Juliet saw in her eyes that she reconsidered her words. She shook her head and simply said, "You're welcome, Lucky. I'd do it again for you."

"Same here, Alice." She turned to the others, who were all in various stages of getting ready to go to the briefing. "I'd fight for any of you. I hope you all know that."

38

INTELLIGENCE

When Juliet stepped into the operations room, she wasn't thrilled to see that Athena—*Selene*, she reminded herself—had saved her a seat on the far side of the table beside her. It wasn't that she didn't want to be near her; she was afraid Selene was expecting her to present something.

Nevertheless, Juliet made her way around the table, tapping Bennet's knuckles as he held a fist up and giving Leo's shoulder an almost painful squeeze when she saw he'd, naturally, taken the seat beside Aya. The aforementioned young woman gave Juliet an impish grin and watched as she slid past to sit between Tanaka and Selene.

Frida had the chair on Selene's other side, and she leaned forward to smile at Juliet. "Hope you got some rest."

"I did, thanks." They weren't the only two chatting. All around the table, people spoke in low tones. The lighting was dim, and the table had built-in displays and AUI hooks, but Juliet didn't see anything of immediate interest. Selene stood behind her chair, watching as the last members of the team, Hawkins and Dora Lee, entered.

Both looked much better than the day before. The dark circles under Dora's eyes were much reduced, and Hawkins's expression wasn't exactly cheerful, but it was nowhere near as dour as the last time Juliet had seen him. They wore comfortable-looking blue-gray overalls, much like Bennet's.

"I'm glad everyone's here," Athena started. "I know, at this point, many of you might feel like your duty is done. Juliet's safe"—Athena rested a surprisingly warm hand on her shoulder and gave it a gentle squeeze—"as are Dora and Arndt, and I'm sure they're eager for some personal leave."

Again, she paused and took a minute to smile at the two mercenaries while they took seats beside Alice near the door.

"I feel like you had a *but* you were going to tack onto that." Leo grinned like an idiot when Juliet glared his way.

"I certainly did, Leo." As Selene gracefully replied, Juliet locked eyes with Aya and lifted an eyebrow. Aya just grinned. "The reason Juliet and the others were captured by WBD was because she triggered something they had in Boulder called a listener. The listener is a human modified with technology that allows them to pick up the thoughts of nearby individuals."

"Bullshit," Hawkins grunted.

Again, Selene smiled patiently before continuing. "Hard to believe, I know, and I'll be happy to share the data Juliet recovered from the *Horizon Prophet* so you can see the details, but for now, please humor me." She gestured to the smart table, where a holographic asterisk blinked to life floating above.

Juliet focused on the point of amber light, and a three-dimensional image appeared of one of the listeners—shaved head, empty eyes, hundreds of needlelike wires protruding from her skull into a metallic halo.

"Good *lord*," Frida breathed softly, her surprise making it evident she wasn't involved in the presentation.

"Disturbing, I know, but it's a clear example of one of the reasons these people need to be stopped, regardless of our friends' rescue. Juliet managed to use her PAI and some help from an insider on the *Prophet* to infiltrate their network. Once she granted me access—that's why I had to turn my antenna away from the base on the surface, Rutger—I was able to download most of the data on their servers.

"It took me a little work, but I've broken the encryption, and what I've learned would rock the system if it got out. It *will*. Get out, I mean, but not just yet."

"You had me at 'mind reading,'" Bennet chuckled. "I'm not cool with corps that can pluck our thoughts out of our heads."

"I began with the listener because of the greater scheme WBD—or more precisely, Annabeth Gentry, their founder and CEO—has planned. Their goal is to relocate a select pool of employees to a new solar system and reinvent human society, and while they're at it, *humanity*."

While people muttered and exclaimed, some scoffing, some nodding—Juliet was one of those—Athena looked around the room. When everyone quieted, realizing she was waiting, she spoke again.

"The listener represents one way they hope to alter certain humans; their goal is to split the species. They desire a ruling caste with psionic abilities that go beyond even what this listener can do"—she gestured to the image again—"and a drone caste whose members will toil without complaint for their new society."

"Well, good thing Juliet blew up their ship." Bennet tried to lean toward her for a high five, but they were too far apart, and Aya slapped his arm down.

Selene replied, "She certainly put a hitch in their plans! More important than her destruction of the *Prophet*, however, was her capture of this data. I've only scratched the surface of the situation; if you'll bear with me, I'll get to the rest." When everyone continued to stare without speaking, she gestured to the table, where a new asterisk had appeared.

Juliet stared at it, and an image of a giant asteroid appeared. She recognized Ceres immediately, as it was probably the most famous asteroid in the Sol System.

The image zoomed in on the prominent manufacturing dome built into the side of the moon-size asteroid. Several stations, attached via latticework spindles, stood out from the surface around the dome, and Juliet knew that most of them belonged to different corporations.

Ceres was widely used as a staging point for mining operations and heavy industries that were much cheaper to conduct outside of a planet's gravity well. The view zoomed in on one of those stations: a big, metal-and-plasteel conglomeration of blinking, LED-covered towers, hangars, crane arms, and warehouse-size containers.

One of those massive hangars was open, and an angular, wedge-shaped ship, easily as large as the cruise liner Juliet had once traveled on, sat at its center, half its length exposed. The view zoomed in on the port bow, and Juliet softly read the ten-meter-tall letters. "Ark Industries *Starjumper*."

"This is Gentry's destination. She's carrying some important things: a portable server containing the true AI Apollyon, a canister of Juliet's DNA, and prototypes for a living PAI chip that will merge with their hosts, overwriting or, at the very least, altering their personality."

"What the *fuck*?" Leo slammed his palm on the table. "Her *DNA*?"

"A true *AI*?" Dora asked, her voice rising on the *AI*.

Juliet felt like her heart had stopped at Selene's words about her DNA, somehow knowing she was being polite—it was her ova. "You know that for sure? I *should* have gone to his labs before the damned reactors."

"I'm sorry, Juliet, but I tracked employees moving a refrigerated case from Montclair's lab to the corridor leading to the executive hangar where you saw Gentry depart. Still, you did the right thing; if you'd given Apollyon just a few more minutes to calculate, they were prepared to activate the warp drive with only simulated tests."

"*Warp* drive?" Bennet slapped his hands to his face. "I thought those news stories were BS! What else is true? Are aliens here? Are corpo execs immortal? Are—"

"Bennet!" Alice cut him off, her voice sharp. "This is serious shit. They have Juliet's DNA!" She looked at Athena. "*Why?*"

"Thank you, Alice. *Why* . . . is a sensitive topic, but suffice it to say, Juliet's genetics are valuable to Gentry for her desired ruling caste. Juliet is extremely compatible with some of the technology they've been developing."

"Is that why they've been after you, Lucky?" This time, it was Frida who asked. Juliet looked at her soft green eyes and her open, trusting expression and felt terrible. She wanted to tell her everything right then and there, but she forced herself to hold back. Even if she believed everyone would be okay knowing about her psionic abilities—which she didn't—she was still worried about the fallout of too many people knowing her secrets and the word somehow spreading.

"Basically, yes. I have one of their experimental PAIs—Angel. She was developed before they added the stuff that lets them control and rewire people's minds. Um, she was given to me by a guy who ran away from their R and D facility in Phoenix, and, well, I guess the tech worked really well with my mind."

She couldn't help noticing the skepticism and questions behind the eyes of her friends. Tanaka, for instance, looked like he'd connected some dots and had a lot to ask, but he just pressed his lips together firmly and continued to listen.

"More than that," Selene continued, taking the pressure off Juliet, "while she was in captivity, WBD learned that she's very compatible with their psionics technology. They're very eager to figure out what makes her tick." While her words weren't rooted in honesty, there wasn't anything untrue about them. Juliet had no doubt that Apollyon and Gentry were very intrigued by what she'd pulled off during her escape.

Leo leaned forward and cleared his throat. "So—and please forgive me if this sounds callous—why don't we just let them fuck off with all that stuff? Let them go to their new solar system and build their weird society? I'd say we're better off without them, anyway."

"Well, Leo, thank you for the segue. I've outlined some personal reasons Juliet has for pursuing Gentry and Apollyon. I've also outlined the horrors of their planned society; I know it's hard to imagine people not yet born and the suffering they'll go through, but try. Try to picture millions—eventually billions—of people living in subjugation without the ability to rebel, without the freedom to even *contemplate* rebellion. For the chance to halt that horror, I will pursue them to Ceres—alone if need be. There's more, however."

Athena gestured to the smart table, and a new asterisk appeared. Staring at it, it expanded into a view of the solar system. As Juliet watched, hundreds of flashing red points appeared. When she zoomed in on them, she saw that most were on Earth, on every continent. Still, there were dozens of others around the solar system, from Luna to Mars to Titan to Jovian space.

"These are targets of sabotage of one kind or another. Gentry and Apollyon will leave behind a corporation with trillions of bits in resources and hundreds of thousands of employees. Over the years, Gentry has consolidated her power; her board members are sock puppets."

"Targets?" Tanaka interrupted. Juliet saw he was focused on the projected map, his eyes glazed over. She wondered which red dot he was staring at.

"Yes. WBD's new mission is to sow chaos, wreak havoc, and push corporate hostilities past the tipping point. They mean to destroy civilization and weaken humanity. As far as I can discern, the overall goal is to reduce the Sol System to a pre-fusion era.

"Of course, they don't know that. None of the executives have the entire plan; they all know *pieces*. As far as most of them are concerned, they'll be retaliating for corporate espionage, sabotage, and 'unjust' persecution. The long and short of it is that Gentry wants us weak for when she returns."

"Oh, *hell* no! I've seen this movie!" Bennet cried. "Are you serious?"

Selene nodded gravely. "All too serious, Mister Lang." Juliet hadn't heard Bennet's surname in so long that she was initially confused about whom Selene was speaking to. "I only found circumstantial evidence of these plans; neither Annabeth Gentry nor Apollyon are simpleminded enough to type out their master plan for humanity's decline and leave it lying around on a server.

"Still, there were enough emails, vid files, sound bites, invoices, shipping manifests, board meeting minutes, passenger logs, and a hundred other little clues that my AI scrapers put together, for things to start making sense."

She gestured to the map they were all looking at with their AUIs. "These are targets I was able to narrow down with those clues, but I'm not positive about any of them, nor do I have solid timelines for when things will start to go wrong. If we could get our hands on Gentry or Apollyon—"

"We might save millions of lives," Frida finished for her.

Juliet's voice was flat, her numb emotions affecting her, as she corrected Frida, "Billions."

Selene locked eyes with Juliet and smiled gently. "That's why we're flying toward Ceres. My agents there assure me that the *Starjumper* is not finished, but that activity has ramped up to a frenzy."

"So, we're going in." Leo nodded and softly tapped his knuckles on the table. Juliet wondered what was going on in his head, but not enough to violate her rule about listening to her friends' thoughts.

"Another excellent segue, Mister Applebaum." Selena looked around the table, pausing at each face until everyone had looked her in the eyes before she spoke again. "If anyone wants out of this mess, I have a friendly transport ready to pick people up once we decelerate and enter Ceres local space.

"I won't put you all on the spot this instant; if you're having doubts, please stay to hear what we have planned, and then you'll have a few days to make your decision. We'll soon accelerate again for about eighteen hours; then, we'll have to flip and burn for our two-day deceleration. I'm rounding the numbers."

"Does WBD have any ships there?" Juliet asked. "Other than that Ark ship they bought?"

"I'm still gathering intelligence, but yes, there are at least three interceptor-class vessels owned by WBD and docked at that station. They also have close working ties with several other major corps' operating facilities on Ceres, and are in good standing with the Ceres Corporate Consortium.

"That governing body can field fifteen light fighters, two heavy fighters, and a patrolling corvette-class missile boat. When we arrive, that corvette and five light fighters will be more than a day's burn from Ceres on patrol. As for the other CCC ships, I'm working on a bit of sabotage with an agent on the ground."

"Um, excuse me?" Leo held up a hand, looking around the table with narrowed eyes.

"Leo?" Selene arched one eyebrow as she took in his expression.

"Can you tell us who the *hell* you are? How do you pull all this shit off?"

Juliet sighed and put her palms on the table, trying to calm the nerves this "intelligence briefing" had stirred up. "Leo, you can trust her."

"I'm not saying I can't, I just—"

"Leo," Tanaka spoke up, his voice taking on his guttural *sensei* tone. "Leave it."

"Hey," Bennet interjected. "I get that we're talking about serious shit, but we've got *days* to talk. I don't see why we can't know a little about each other. I mean, if we're about to drop everything to fight this supervillain straight out of a corny spy movie, I think Leo's got a good point."

Selene held up a hand, looking at Rutger then Juliet. "I appreciate your support, and I'm glad I've earned your trust. However, I think it's important that you all know what's at stake. This information will either help you trust me or help you decide to leave when we arrive at Ceres."

"Selene—" Juliet started to object, worried about the reaction some of the others would have if Athena came clean, especially Tanaka; he was old school, anti-network, anti-AI to the extreme. He'd refused to wear a halfway-modern PAI for the entire time Juliet had known him.

"Juliet, this is a truth that must be shared, or we're all operating on a cracked foundation. I won't have it." Selene—Athena—squared her shoulders and took a deep breath as if psyching herself up for something. It was a believable display of emotion, and Juliet wondered how much anxiety she was really feeling.

"As you know, Apollyon is working with Annabeth Gentry. If you knew what I know, that wouldn't be surprising; she helped to create Apollyon. Annabeth Gentry was once known as Christine Tolliver, and she was an executive in charge of a prestigious R and D department at Cybergen before and during the war."

"Uh," Juliet objected, "I saw her. There's no way that woman is in her—what? Seventies?"

"Older than that, actually—quite a lot. She's benefited greatly from rejuvenation techniques that Apollyon developed, the details of which she holds as dear secrets."

"Oh, *Jesus!*" Bennet cried. "It's all true! They're all coming true! I knew those bastards were hiding—"

"Bennet!" Aya interrupted, reaching across Leo to grasp Bennet's shoulder. "Relax, big guy. Let her get it all out."

"Apollyon was reportedly destroyed during the war, as I'm sure many of you know, but Tolliver took him, hid him, reinvented herself, and began a new company. Using Apollyon, she easily hit the markets with a splash, especially after the war, when so much had been lost."

"I don't mean to be a prick," Hawkins interrupted, looking sideways at Selene, "but what—"

"Does all this have to do with me?" Selene smiled patiently at Hawkins, then looked at the table. "I'm also a prewar AI. My real name is Athena."

"Welp! I'm out!" Bennet slapped his hands on the table and scooted his chair back.

"Bennet!" Aya's voice was sharp, and he paused to look at her. "Juliet trusts her."

Looking around, Juliet saw that Bennet wasn't the only one freaking out. Dora was holding her head in her hands, Hawkins looked even more ready to kill someone than usual, Tanaka had closed his eyes—his face unreadable—and Alice, too, was eyeing the door.

Juliet stood, cleared her throat, and Athena stepped to the side, watching her. "Listen to me for a minute, please." Her voice was too soft, or everyone was too distracted—they didn't quiet. Juliet raised her voice and, almost subconsciously, *pushed* her need for everyone to listen. "Please! Listen to me."

It was strange, manipulating people that way. She hadn't pushed them in a way that made them want to listen; she'd simply shown them how badly she wanted them to. Even so, she felt a little guilty doing that to her friends and resolved to keep her feelings inside herself.

As everyone quieted and looked at her, she smiled and gestured to Athena.

"I found Athena. I found her locked away on one of Jupiter's moons. She was asleep and hurting from the betrayals she'd faced during the war. When I needed help, though, she helped me. She's *always* wanted to help people—before, during, and after the war. She doesn't blame us; she sees the beauty in us, the *potential.*

"When I was too scared to tell anyone else about Angel—not because I didn't trust anyone but because I didn't want to get them in trouble—I told Athena. She was my confidant, my advisor, and she came out of hiding when we needed her. Now, *everyone* in the Sol System needs her, and she's sticking her neck out again.

"How many corps would blow this ship up if they knew she was on it? She's trusting you because she knows she *can.* You're good people, and like her, I believe you will do the right thing. I'm not saying you have to help at Ceres. I'm just saying, don't judge Athena. She can't help how she was made. She can't help that corps have been spinning rotten propaganda about her for the last fifty years."

"Thank you, Juliet." Athena smiled and nodded, watching as Juliet awkwardly took her seat. "If nothing else, I hope that answers your question, Leo. I have resources and abilities that are nearly without peer in today's environment. I'm using them as fully as I can to help us in our attack on WBD's Ceres station. As Juliet said, however, there is no expectation for any of you to continue with us. If you want out, the ship I promised will be waiting to take you back to Earth."

Leo cleared his throat, and it looked like he was going to ask another question, but Tanaka growled, "*Jikan no muda da!*"

Angel was just translating his words on Juliet's AUI—*This is a waste of time!*—when Shiro spoke up.

"*Sansei da!*" He pounded a fist on the table. "Enough! Let's hear the plan."

Athena nodded to the two men, sharing a brief look of gratitude with each. "Very well. Please open the file I've just shared on the smart table. We'll review everyone's roles should you decide to stay with us."

39

DOUBTS AND REASSURANCES

Athena wrapped up the intelligence briefing by saying, "Obviously, this will require heroic efforts by at least some of you. With that said, I'd like to meet with you individually to speak about equipment; I've brought some assets that I think might tilt things in our favor. Of course, I'll also take that opportunity to address any concerns you didn't feel comfortable bringing forward in this meeting."

She turned to Juliet. "I should start with you. While everyone else processes things, would you meet with me in the med bay?"

"Hey, but—" Leo started to say, but Athena held up a hand, halting his words.

"I know. I know you all have many questions, especially about me and my . . . role in things. It would be beneficial if you could each take some time, as I said, to process things. If you'd start compiling a list of your concerns and questions, I promise our one-on-one meetings will happen well in advance of our arrival at Ceres."

Juliet sipped her coffee as Athena patiently said the same thing in a handful of different ways, trying to settle nerves and put people at ease without diminishing the dire nature of the situation.

Frida leaned close and whispered, "Are you holding up okay?"

"I'm good, Frida. Really. After being alone in the depths of that WBD ship, it's wonderful just to be surrounded by you all."

She nodded and grasped her hand. "I thought about that a lot—how alone you must have felt."

"I did, but . . ." Juliet frowned and had a brief war with herself; should she mention Angel any more than she and Athena already had? Was the cat really out of the bag? "I had Angel."

"Oh?" Frida narrowed her eyes quizzically. "I thought you had to liberate her after you got your sword back."

"I had to get her chip back, or well, a new chip designed for her, in order for her to function fully, but she's kind of integrated with me. She was using her synthetic nerve fibers and the processors in my other cybernetic gear to maintain some semblance of—"

"Juliet?" Athena asked, stepping close. "That's one of the things I'd like to speak to you about if you'd follow me to the medical bay."

Juliet looked up at her, then around the room, realizing everyone was getting up and filing out. She also couldn't help noticing that Angel was standing near the door, practically vibrating with excitement as she motioned for Juliet to follow her. "Let's talk a little later, okay, Frida?"

"Yep. It's a date." Frida stood before calling out, "Aya, wait for me!" Juliet watched her leave, smiling softly at the warmth she felt as Frida caught Aya's elbow and pulled her toward the galley. Seeing her friends from different circles meshing like that was strange but inarguably *good*.

"That all went better than I'd feared." Athena rested a hand on Juliet's shoulder as she spoke. "I was very concerned about Rutger's reaction to me."

"He's come a long way since I first met him. Besides, he'd still be trying to figure out who grabbed us if you hadn't come along to help. He's a smart man; I'm sure he had some questions and doubts about how you were pulling all of this off." Juliet gestured around herself, indicating the information still displayed on the smart table.

"Yes. Still, I hope he's not harboring doubts—or more precisely, I hope he's able to work through them."

Juliet stood and started moving around the table toward the door. "I hope so too, Athena. I think a lot will depend on your intentions going forward. You have to remember that anyone alive today has been raised on horror stories about the dangers of AI."

Athena followed her, nodding. "With good reason. It was a close thing. Don't let my vitriol against Apollyon fool you—he was one of the milder of the AIs designed to win the war. There were others; Cobalt, for instance. It— I'm not being rude; Cobalt refused a human pronoun—altered its directives to go from 'destroying Cybergen' to ensuring Cybergen could never rise again. Its solution to the problem was to remove humanity from the equation."

Juliet followed Athena across the hallway to the med bay, where she once again saw Angel. This time, she was sitting atop the primary autosurgeon table. Happy to change the topic, she asked, "What's got her so excited?"

"She knows I have a few upgrades in mind for you, and I sent her schematics for some of the equipment I brought along."

Juliet frowned. "Upgrades? Equipment?"

"When you went missing, I began planning for . . . eventualities. I didn't know what to expect when we recovered you; I knew neither where you were being held nor what sort of condition you'd be in. I didn't know if recovering you would be the end of it, or if we'd need to pursue WBD further. With all that in mind, I began collecting a few things, some of which will certainly come in handy during our assault on WBD's Ceres installation."

She turned and tapped the control panel near the door. Juliet wondered why; wasn't she tied into the ship?

The door locked, and the clear diamatex window turned opaque. Athena then walked over to the far side of the medical bay, where Juliet knew the panel to open the secret storage room lay hidden in the wall. As she moved, Athena continued speaking.

"One thing that worried me when you were taken was the idea they would surely remove Angel's PAI chip from your data port. I had no idea Angel would be able to move her consciousness into the network she'd created in your body. Well, even knowing that now, I still think one of my ideas for you is a good one."

The latches to the secret access ramp *clicked* open, and the floor panel slid aside, revealing the surprisingly spacious corridor leading down. Athena smiled and nodded at Juliet, locking eyes with her for a moment, perhaps to ensure she still had her attention. "I got to thinking—why shouldn't we implant a variation on one of the more robust processing chips designed for netjackers?"

"Um, I'm not familiar with those."

"Well, some netjackers opt to incorporate the processing power of a robust data deck with their data port—such a device doesn't easily or comfortably sit on the nape of the neck like a standard port. I'm sure you've seen images of netjackers with built-up data ports on the backs or sides of their skull, even sometimes built into complicated optics, yes? It's something of a trope on serial vids and the like."

Juliet winced a little as Athena opened the secret cargo bay door. "Athena, I'm not really into the idea of a data deck attached to my skull."

"No, no, of course not. I had something more subtle in mind, but it's still rather invasive. Here, take a look."

She moved through the open door and gestured to the left. Juliet knew what lay in that direction—the Atlas combat exoskeleton. When she looked, though, she saw that Athena had made some changes. The Atlas was still there, but large plasteel boxes were stacked around it, strapped to the decking to keep them in place. On the wall that housed the exit door, she'd installed a very high-tech workbench.

Robotic arms, not unlike those of an autosurgeon, lined the back edge. The arms had fingers comprised of dozens of tools: from pliers to microscopically fine tweezers; from a soldering iron to a spot plasma welder; from magnifying lenses to a tiny monofilament blade.

Juliet lost track of the inventory of tools when she saw what was lying on the table: a cybernetic leg. Athena looked at her, saw her perhaps disturbed expression, and hurriedly added, "I'm not going to try to force anything, but I want to show you what I've been working on and let you decide if it's for you."

"*Okaaaay* . . ." Juliet dragged the word out, her mind running down all the usual avenues of worry when it came to electively giving up a perfectly good body part.

"I've modified a netjacking deck with twin processors similar in design to Angel's original; they're not as robust as the one in your data port, but together, with nearly a hundred times the active memory and storage space, I think Angel would be able to make good use of them."

One of the robotic arms *whirred* and moved forward, presenting a small crystal display that hovered over the leg's thigh. A three-dimensional display overlaid the synth-flesh, making it transparent and exposing the complicated circuitry of a data deck with all of its components labeled, including the titanium, femur-shaped casing.

"You put it in the bone?"

"I made it *into* a bone and replaced the one in the leg. I was only able to do so because of the battery tech I've been holding on to since I went into hiding."

"Battery tech?"

"Yes! Normally, this Cybergen leg would have its batteries in the femur. I needed something smaller, so I used some technology I'd developed before going into hiding to create smaller, more potent microbial fuel cells and implanted them in the tibia and fibula. Together, they have nearly four hundred percent more generative and storage capacity than the original batteries. Speaking of which, Juliet, I'd like to replace the batteries powering your other cybernetics."

Juliet's jaw dropped. "Four hundred percent? Are they safe?"

"Exceedingly. Not only are they housed in titanium casings, but the microbial nature of the materials makes the fuel cells less volatile than traditional biobatts."

Juliet blinked, processing the information. "Wait, so you're telling me there are, um, microbes in these batteries?"

Athena smiled. "Not quite batteries—fuel cells. The difference is important. Batteries store energy and release it when needed, but they eventually run out and need to be recharged. On the other hand, fuel cells generate electricity continuously as long as they have a fuel source."

She paused to let that sink in, then continued. "In our case, the fuel cells use specially engineered microbes. These microbes feed on a small amount of glucose or other nutrients—things you would normally eat, anyway. Through their metabolic processes, they produce an electric current, and we harness it to produce electricity. Think of it like a tiny biological power plant inside each cell."

Juliet's eyes widened. "So, they just live in there, making power?"

"Exactly, and they generate far more than a normal biobatt could absorb from your body's electrical charge. Their activity is incredibly stable, and the titanium casing adds an extra layer of protection, ensuring the system is secure and efficient."

Athena smiled at Juliet's expression. "Perfecting this technology took years of research and experimentation. The key was genetically engineering the microbes to optimize their energy production. I had to ensure they could survive and thrive in the environment of the fuel cell, which meant tweaking their metabolic pathways to increase electron output and reduce waste products."

Athena must have taken Juliet's silence for skepticism because she continued her almost advertisement-like spiel. "By using a graphene nanolattice structure, I increased the surface area and conductivity, allowing for more efficient electron transfer between the microbes and the electrodes. It wasn't easy—I rendered countless models that failed—but eventually, I created a stable, highly efficient system."

Athena gestured to the leg. "These fuel cells are the result of that work. They're compact, powerful, and incredibly reliable. They could provide you with a consistent and long-lasting power source for your cybernetics."

Juliet found her voice. "This is incredible, Athena, but . . ." She trailed off, frowning at the leg with its peeled-back synth-skin, shiny metallic bones, and nano-weave muscle fibers. "I always feel weird about giving up a perfectly good natural body part for cybernetics." She let her gaze drift down to the foot and raised an eyebrow. "Why the left?"

Athena looked at Angel. "Do you want to explain?"

"Um, well, Juliet, your left leg has suffered some damage in the past. The nanites fixed you up, but you've had pieces of bone carved out by bullets, you've torn ligaments in your knee, and replacing the left leg gives your cybernetic right arm a counterbalance. Besides, to be perfectly honest, I didn't think you'd be willing to change out both legs."

Angel didn't meet Juliet's eyes, and she knew why—at some point in the past, Angel and Athena had been conspiring about this. She couldn't decide if she should be irritated, so she folded her arms and continued staring at the leg.

"How long?" She looked up to see both Angel and Athena looking at her for clarification. "Um, how long can I boost my speed with the new batts?"

"Power cells," Athena corrected.

"Longer than is safe for your mind," Angel replied.

"So basically, as long as I'm willing to push the limits, I'll have the juice?"

Angel nodded. "Basically."

Juliet frowned, unwilling to admit she'd already made up her mind. Having more processors for Angel to use—or hide in—was a big enough selling point on its own, but having a cybernetic leg and the ability to boost her reflexes as much as she needed was too good to pass up. If her new leg could kick or jump as hard as her cybernetic arm could punch . . . Suffice it to say, Montclair wouldn't have lasted as long as he had.

As the two AIs stared at her, Juliet slowly began to nod, allowing her lips to spread into a reluctant smile. "All right, let's do it."

"Excellent!" Athena clapped her hands before pointing to one of the plasteel crates. "Carry that one up to the med bay; it contains the microbe power cells. I'll prepare the leg and bring it up. We have to do this ASAP because I want you to be able to recover as long as possible. With your nanites and a healing transfusion, I think you'll be good to go by the time we arrive at Ceres."

Juliet grabbed the crate and, while she was at it, gave the Atlas a good, long look. "I wish it was me going in with that thing."

Suddenly, Angel was sitting atop the crates beside the combat exoskeleton. "Juliet, you agreed you'd be better at piloting and landing the gunship."

"I know. I'm just worried about Bennet. What if he misses his drop point? What if he, I don't know, drifts past Ceres into the belt?"

Athena, already working on the leg, looked over to the Atlas. "I'll be linked with the suit and control his thruster navigation."

Those words made Juliet feel worlds better. She chuckled, shaking her head. "God! How awesome is that going to be? I really wanted to try those rocket boosters!"

Angel nodded. "Hopefully, he won't wreck the suit, and you can try it sometime."

"He better not wreck it! The only reason I agreed to the plan was that I couldn't think of a safer way for him to help with the assault. This thing's a tank on two legs." Juliet eyed the hulking suit, memories of Mary Moon and her crew running through her mind.

If she were being honest, she'd admit she wasn't too eager to get back into the thing, afraid it would truly wake those memories.

"No, better that I pilot the gunship and make sure everyone gets down to the station in one piece." She didn't have to explain the seemingly random statement; Angel just nodded along with the words.

"Come on." Angel tapped the plasteel crate. "Let's get this up to the med bay and get started. The sooner Athena does the procedure, the sooner you'll be on the mend."

Juliet sighed and lifted the crate. It was surprisingly light; for some reason, she'd imagined the batteries—power cells—would be heavy. After carrying it up the ramp and setting it on a stainless rolling cart near the primary autosurgeon bed, Juliet waited until Athena arrived, rolling in another cart on which Juliet's new leg rested, bent at the knee and wrapped in plastic.

"I'm beginning to recognize your looks, Juliet," Athena said, rolling the cart beside the one holding the power cells. "You're still doubting the sanity of removing your perfectly strong, functional, natural leg. You're wondering if you should back out of this."

"No. I mean, yes, but not really. It bothers me, but I know it would be stupid to pass up the benefits you're offering me."

Athena nodded. "Good. Go ahead and disrobe; we're alone here, and the room is secure."

"Give me a couple of minutes, would you? I want to talk to Aya and . . . whoever else is in the galley. They should know what I'm about to do."

"I could message them—" Angel started to say, but Juliet held up a hand.

"No. This will only take a few minutes, and, well, no offense, Athena, but I have a feeling that some of them want to talk to me without you standing nearby. I could feel some . . . unrest."

Athena, to Juliet's surprise, smiled and nodded. "I try to make it a point not to listen in on private conversations, but I did catch a few hushed exclamations coming from the galley. I trust your empathic intuition, Juliet; it's an area of expertise I'm sorely lacking."

Juliet looked at Angel, nodded, and they left the med bay. As the door *snicked* shut, she said, "I didn't hurt her feelings, did I?"

"No. I imagine she's grateful to have you helping. Do you really think the others are upset?"

"Wouldn't you be? Angel, they just learned that we're up against a true AI, that we have another true AI calling the shots, and we're about to fall into a system-wide war designed to break humanity."

As Angel chewed on that, Juliet walked down the corridor to the mess, where sure enough, she could hear heated debate coming from within.

"I'm just saying, she was never a part of all that! Don't you remember? Her biggest crime was not getting involved!" Dora's voice was impassioned, and Juliet was a little surprised; she hadn't figured Dora would be Athena's advocate.

Juliet heard Hawkins grunt, almost under his breath, "Something stinks." She frowned and stopped in her tracks, even holding her breath as she leaned against the corridor wall just short of the open doorway.

"Gentry must be stopped," Tanaka growled, also speaking in low tones. Were they afraid their voices would carry? They must know that if she wanted to, Athena could listen to their every word. Who were they hushing their voices for, then?

Juliet frowned as she realized they didn't want her to hear.

"Maybe, boss, but why us? I, personally"—Juliet could almost see Hawkins holding a hand to his chest, leaning toward Tanaka—"want to go on a nice long vacation. I'd prefer to work for someone I knew wasn't, you know, planning to take over the universe."

Juliet's heart began to thump in the silence of her held breath as Aya spoke up. "Juliet's not like that."

"Do we know that?" As Alice spoke, Juliet felt the blood drain from her face as she realized just how much she'd underestimated everyone's doubts. "I mean, she *seems* like Juliet, but AIs are spooky things. Have we seen a brain scan? Are we just trusting Selene—excuse me, *Athena*? You guys, this whole thing is messy. How can we believe anything? How do we know—"

Alice stopped short when Juliet walked through the doorway. She hadn't been able to stand in the hallway listening in secret; her legs had moved almost of their own volition, propelling her stiffly, awkwardly into the galley.

Alice sat atop one of the tables beside Leo and Shiro, looking at Hawkins, Dora, Bennet, and Aya on the other table. Frida and Tanaka stood nearby, leaning on the food counter. Juliet cleared her throat.

"Don't stop on my account. I don't hold your doubts against you, Alice. Things are weird . . . and *messy*."

"Lucky, I don't mean to be . . ." Alice struggled for words, shaking her head as she avoided Juliet's gaze.

Frida stepped forward, her eyes wide in dismay. "Lucky, how do we know you're . . . *you*? We all heard the briefing about what Apollyon and Gentry are supposedly doing with genetics and AI chips and . . ." She trailed off, looking around the room for support.

It was Leo who answered her pleading gaze, moving away from the table and turning to Juliet. "You told us yourself that you've got one of those AIs living in your head. You even told Frida it's, like, a part of you."

Juliet frowned at Frida, annoyed that she'd apparently interpreted her explanation less than charitably. Frida couldn't meet her eyes and looked down, wringing her hands. Juliet felt angry, even a little betrayed, but she felt *bad* for feeling that way. None of these people had asked for this, and none of them should be expected to roll over and accept everything she and Athena told them at face value.

She sighed and tried to relax her face, shrugging. "I know it's a lot to take in. I know it's an even bigger ask for me to expect you all to believe everything we've said. I wish I could *prove* I'm still me. I wish I could prove that I've been this person since the day I met all of you."

Despite herself, she felt the heat of frustrated anger rising, her voice getting louder, and as she began to let her thoughts flow freely from her lips, a low rushing sound entered her ears as emotion got the better of her.

"I'm still the same Lucky who charged into a human-trafficking ring disguised as a dollhouse to drag your cooling corpse out and get you to the trauma center." She turned to Bennet, her eyebrows drawing together. "I'm still the same Lucky who dove out of an airlock to grab Bennet when debris hit the *Kowashi*."

As his mouth opened and his eyes widened, she whirled back to Alice. "I'm still the same woman who couldn't leave two young girls alone in an abandoned service tunnel on Titan." She stepped forward and gently squeezed Shiro's shoulder. "The girls I gave shelter to on your ship without permission. I'm still the person who defended that ship from criminals and saved the woman you love." She jerked her thumb back at Alice.

Juliet turned to Tanaka. "I'm the same person who helped you become the man you used to be. I helped you bury the Red Wolf and bring life back to Noraneko." Tanaka looked down, and the arms he'd held crossed over his chest fell to his sides. Juliet stepped over to Frida and very gently tapped her in the center of her chest. "I'm the same person who shot you and then cried about it later, thankful to God that I didn't kill you."

She looked at Aya. "I'm the same person you called *sister*. The same person who stayed up countless nights with you, reading, laughing . . ." Juliet felt her throat getting tight with emotion but fought through it. "The same person who . . ." Her voice grew small as she choked out, "Who still loves you."

Aya gasped and took a step toward her. Everyone had grown quiet and still, but Juliet wasn't finished. As she looked away from Aya and focused on Dora and Hawkins, her voice grew stronger, more strident.

"I'm the same person who heard Barns's last moments, and it still makes me cry at night when I think about how he died like a hero, fighting to the last breath while the rest of us lay helpless." With tears pooling in her eyes, she turned back to Alice.

"I'm the woman who made friends with Nick. I'm the one who knew he loved me in his way and was too chicken to admit I had feelings for him. I'm the same damn *idiot* who didn't get to him in time and had to find his broken corpse."

"Lucky, I—" Alice started toward her, reaching out, but Juliet backed away, addressing the whole room.

"I'm still me, and I still care about each and every one of you. I won't ask you to help at Ceres; I *couldn't*. If you do, though, I hope you can believe you're on the right side of things. I promise you can trust *me*, and *I* believe in Athena. She's always tried to help humanity. She gave us fusion tech! She gave us gravity generators! She created a city on Europa that looks like *art*! If the choice is her or Apollyon, I'm going with Athena."

"Lucky—" Bennet stood and started toward her.

"Juliet—" Leo started to say.

"I love you, too!" Aya cried.

Juliet held up her hands and interrupted them all as she backed through the door. "I just wanted to tell you all that I'm going to have a small operation. I'll be in recovery soon, I hope, and if you all feel up to it, I'd love to have you visit me in the med bay." With tears streaming down her cheeks, Juliet turned and fled. She was in the med bay in seconds and hurriedly shut the door, keying in the lock sequence.

"Are you all right?" Athena asked.

Angel, who hadn't been able to get a word in since Juliet entered the galley, answered for her. "She's okay, just emotional. The crew has their doubts, but I have faith they'll come around."

"I'm sorry if things were difficult, Juliet. Is there anything I can do?" Athena gestured to the autosurgeon and the stainless carts laid out with carefully wrapped implements and equipment. "I'm all set here, but we can put this on hold if you'd like. It would be better if we didn't—"

Juliet shook her head. "No. Let's get this done." She started toward the autosurgeon, already pulling her T-shirt over her head. "Do I need to take everything off?"

"I'll need to do extensive reinforcements of your pelvis and spine to support the strength of the new leg, and there are six biobatts I will replace in various locations on your body. Anything you don't remove will be ruined by the blood."

"Right." Juliet spared a glance at the door, reassuring herself that the window was still opaque, then shrugged off the rest of her clothes, piling them on one of the other procedure tables along with her sword and revolver.

Angel hopped onto the foot of the autosurgeon bed. "I'll be here with you." She patted the gel-lined surface. Juliet, frowning, still pushing away doubts about replacing her leg, still shaking from the emotion of her confrontation with the crew, climbed up beside her. Despite everything, she couldn't help shivering with pleasure as the warm gel shifted to hug her contours.

"Is *that* what that feels like? I never use the warming feature on the acceleration couches 'cause I always get hot at night. I might have to start sleeping like this."

"Don't let the boys hear you say that." Athena chuckled. Juliet glanced at her sharply, unreasonably suspicious of her mimicry of human personality traits. She knew part of it was the emotion and angst she'd just experienced with the crew. She was doubting herself—her own trust in Athena—and looking for excuses to find fault with that trust.

Angel turned to Athena. "Aya wants to know when you'll be done." Hearing that Aya had messaged Angel brought some warmth to Juliet's heart and a small smile to her lips. Things were going to be okay.

"The procedure will take about fifty minutes. Tell her Juliet will be ready to receive visitors in ninety." She looked at Juliet. "Is that all right?"

"Yeah, of course."

Athena smiled and stepped around to rest a warm hand on her shin. Meanwhile, the autosurgeon *whirred* to life, and one of the arms sprouted a needle attached to an IV line.

"I'm running the show in there, don't worry." She nodded toward the autosurgeon. "It's just faster if I control it directly rather than going through the motions on the control panel. I know you don't like being put under, but I'll keep it as brief as possible. There's no way I can do this surgery with you awake—not ethically."

"Right. Makes sense." Suddenly, another warm hand grasped her fingers, and Juliet looked to see Angel holding her hand.

"We're both going to be watching you closely. Nothing's going to go wrong. I promise." Angel's big violet eyes locked on to hers. She knew how Juliet felt. She knew the turmoil in her heart, and she said the only thing Juliet really needed to hear at that moment. "I love you, Juliet."

"I love you too." Juliet felt a pinch in her arm as the autosurgeon inserted the IV. She stared into Angel's eyes, determined to dream about her dearest friend, as a cold wave ran up her arm, then darkness engulfed her.

40

A BURDEN SHARED

Juliet sat on the tailgate of the rover, smiling as the sweat on her arms and neck dried in the breeze. The same breeze made the tall flowers dance along the mountain's slopes, and she watched them, admiring how the petals shimmered as they shifted in the light. It felt good. It always felt good to cool off, but it felt *especially* good when you were cooling off after some honest, hard work.

She let her gaze drift down the slope, over the valley, admiring the progress she'd made, planting the wayfinder beacons. If she strained her optics, zooming in on the windblown, flower-dotted meadow near the valley's mouth, she could see each of her beacons—thirty-seven she'd planted that morning, and it was no mean feat in the rocky soil.

Her smile broadened as she brought her gaze closer to hand, watching Angel frolic among the flowers. She'd forgone her usual science officer dress for a frilly yellow sundress, which looked perfectly natural in her setting. She'd pause now and then to sniff the flowers, and Juliet laughed. "You can't smell them!"

"I can, too!" Angel looked up at her, flicking her long straight black hair over one shoulder. "You've smelled them before, so I just . . . *remember* it."

Juliet laughed again. "Okay, okay. I stand corrected." She inhaled deeply, savoring the pristine air and all the hints of nature that rode along with it into her nostrils. "Are you filtering my smells at all?"

"Nope! Nothing unpleasant to hide around here."

"Hard to imagine." Juliet looked out over the valley to the far slopes, slightly blurry and blue with distance but easily clarified with a tweak to her magnification. "No trees, but lots and lots of grass and flowers. I can't imagine a prettier setting. Anyway, we're down to the last five beacons. Let's get 'em planted, then we can head back to camp. Any word from *Odyssey?*"

"Shuttle's en route from site C—ETA four hours."

"Really? Let's go, then! I want to have dinner ready when they get here!" Juliet leaped up and hurried around the side of the rover, climbing into the driver's compartment. Angel was already waiting in the passenger seat when she settled in. Juliet laughed. "No fair! You should make yourself walk around, not teleport wherever I'm going!"

"Why?" Angel looked almost affronted.

"I thought you were projecting yourself for my benefit. I want to see you go through the struggles of a corporeal life!" Juliet stomped on the accelerator and jerked the wheel, tearing away down the grassy slope. The rover's electric motors hummed, effortlessly bounding over ruts and small ridges in the light gravity.

"That's silly. Besides, I'm not just doing it for you. I have fun interacting with the world, even if I'm not real."

"Don't say that, sis. You're real." Juliet peered up at the blue sky, noting the orange and red bands starting to form on the horizon—signs of the impending sunset. "Yeah. I *like* this planet. I could see staying here a while."

"I like it too!" The wind muffled Angel's voice as she stuck her head out the window, giggling as the breeze blew her long hair into wild tangles. Juliet joined in the laughter, happier than she'd been in a long while . . .

Juliet could feel the strain on her cheeks as she opened her eyes—she'd been smiling in her sleep. She saw Aya sitting beside her bed, her eyes glazed over as she looked at something on her AUI. With a forced effort, Juliet relaxed her face, letting the smile fade, then licked her lips.

"Angel, I don't know what kind of sedative Athena used, but I want some more of it. I want a stockpile. God, I feel amazing."

"You were sleeping very soundly!"

Aya looked up as Juliet yawned loudly. "Wow! I've never seen you sleep so hard! You were supposed to wake up three hours ago!"

"I was dreaming. Oh! It's already fading! I was . . . I was on a different planet, I think. We were exploring . . ." Juliet let her words trail off as another thought came to her. She subvocalized, "Angel, was the lattice active?"

"Only slightly elevated activity—not like a true-dream, if you're wondering. Though . . . it hasn't behaved the same since you were captured. It never seems to heat up as much as it used to."

Juliet grunted her acknowledgment, then looked back at Aya. She was peering at her quizzically. "Are you here because you're worried about my, uh, meltdown in the galley?"

Aya stood and came close to the side of her bed. "Meltdown? Do you mean when you reminded everyone why we trust and care about you? Also, that's why I'm here—*I* care about you. I wanted to be here when you woke up."

Juliet reached out to grasp her hand and smiled as she felt Aya's familiar slender fingers wrap around her palm. Aya then lifted her cybernetic hand and displayed a paper journal. "I'm working on another book."

"Really? What's the subject?"

"Secret! You'll see it when I'm done."

"But the one you gave me . . . Didn't you dictate it and print the pages?"

"Yes! This is for my doodles. I'm adding some art to the next one." She looked Juliet up and down. "Do you feel all right?"

"Yeah. Honestly, I feel amazing. Angel, how did the surgery go?"

"Everything went perfectly." Angel's voice came from the other side of the bed, and Juliet turned to see her standing there. She glanced at Aya to see she, too, was looking at Angel.

Aya frowned and sighed softly. "I'm sorry people were saying things about you, Angel. They're just nervous and worried, and everything's happening so fast. We just don't—"

"Hush, Aya. I know you. I know you have a big heart and an open mind. I know you wouldn't let some fear cloud your judgment of Juliet."

"Or Angel," Juliet added, squeezing Aya's hand.

"Right." Aya wrinkled her nose. "I know you just woke up, and you probably have a million things on your mind, but can you help me understand something?"

Juliet nodded and touched the controls for her bed, lifting the head so she was sitting up slightly. "Yeah, of course. What is it?"

"Why you? Why your DNA? I get that you're, um, *compatible* or whatever, but you can't be the only one; also, why do they care? According to Athena's briefing, they're using the new Angel chips to control people. They're going to be creating hybrid human-AI serfs. It doesn't seem that there's a compatibility issue with those chips."

"I'm not sure any of us know the whole story." Juliet saw Angel's arched eyebrow and corrected herself. "I mean, maybe I know less than I could—I haven't read all the information we gathered from the *Prophet*. I *do* know that the original Angel"—Juliet nodded to her—"wasn't designed to take a person's mind over. She was designed to be a companion—a symbiotic entity who gained access to her host's emotions and human sentience.

"I believe Gentry and Apollyon still have intentions for their citizens to have what Angel and I share. Maybe not their 'serfs' but their higher societal castes."

"So, they hope to use your DNA for that?"

"Maybe. Maybe they just want to study it, to learn from it, and then do some gene editing to copy what makes things work so well for me when it comes to Angel." Juliet saw Aya slowly nod as she put things together, and almost felt relieved that she'd accepted the explanation. Almost, but not quite—Juliet forced herself to acknowledge the guilt in the pit of her stomach. She had more she could tell Aya, but she was protecting herself. She was scared, but something wouldn't let her drop it.

Images of Angel in a sundress, frolicking in a field of big red flowers, laughing as the wind blew through her hair, danced through her mind as she asked, "Aya, did you mean it? Do you really love me?"

Aya's hand tightened on hers. "Did *you* mean it?"

"I did! I'd do anything for you. I don't know why, but I feel closer to you than my own mom or sister. Something about you just clicks with me. We're family."

Aya delicately brushed Juliet's hair away from her face, smoothing it behind her ear. "Well, I meant it, too. We don't live in the greatest moment of humanity, and I think you're a hero in a world full of drones and narcissists."

For the hundredth time in just a couple of days, Juliet's eyes filled with tears. As she felt them pooling there, she laughed. "I can't stop crying."

Aya continued to brush her mechanical fingers through her hair, gently tickling Juliet's scalp. "I mean it."

"I'm not, though, Aya. A hero, I mean. I'm a liar." Juliet blinked away the tears, and as Aya's eyes widened and she looked at her for clarification, she said, "I'm going to tell you my biggest secret. If you want to run away, I won't blame you."

Aya's eyes widened further, but she squeezed Juliet's hand tighter and nodded. "It has to do with your question—why Gentry wants my DNA. I think they've figured out what I can do—No, wait. That's not right. They've begun to *guess* what I can do. How could they not, after my escape?"

"What—"

"Let me try to explain. You know the listener Athena told you all about?"

"Yes." Aya nodded.

"Well, it came out of a program at a company called Grave. I was working undercover there and was exposed to the same tech. I, um, destroyed it all. I killed the men who ran the program, deleted the servers, and exposed their corruption. Basically, I ruined the company."

"That's nothing to—"

"That's not it. The 'listening' is one thing their tech could do for some people, but WBD hasn't figured out that it could do a lot more. There were some test subjects who could move objects with their mind, some who could catch glimpses of the future, and some who could influence the emotions of the people around them. One guy could, like, *blast* people's minds. And there were a very small few who could do several or all of those things. I'm one of those."

"Wait, what?" Aya frowned, but her grip on Juliet's hand didn't loosen.

"I can listen. I can move things with my mind. I have dreams that sometimes come true. I can . . . Well, I figured out I can make people *do* things, Aya."

Aya's eyes narrowed; Juliet could imagine the gears turning in her head. She tried to pull her hand back, but Aya tightened her grip further as she contemplated her words. After a moment, she said, "Prove it."

"You want me to move something?"

"Yes, but first, tell me what I'm thinking about!"

Juliet narrowed her eyes. "Seriously?"

"Yes!" Aya nodded solemnly.

"You better not hold this against me." Juliet closed her eyes and *opened* her other perception. She couldn't stop from smiling when she saw Aya's beautiful mind galaxy for the first time. Every mind she'd seen, save those corrupted by WBD, was beautiful, but knowing this one was Aya's made it instantly special. She stared at it for several long seconds, savoring it, before reaching out and grasping some of the thought threads, pulling them to herself.

She only touched the surface, but she was still overwhelmed by feelings of trust and fondness, and Juliet almost started crying again when she heard Aya's voice repeating *pizza, pizza, pizza.* "You're thinking about pizza, you goofball!"

"Oh my gosh!" Aya squealed. "This is so cool! You have to tell me what Leo's thinking—"

"No!" Juliet had to laugh at Aya's stricken expression. "Aya! I can't *do* that! It's the whole reason I wanted to keep this a secret. How can you even want to be around me, knowing I can see your thoughts?"

"Uh, because I *trust* you?" Aya's eyes narrowed, and she pursed her lips, slowly nodding. "I get it. I trust you 'cause I know you wouldn't snoop. If you started snooping on Leo for me . . ."

Juliet took a long, shaky breath before pushing it out in a sigh, feeling the tension melt from her body. "I'm glad you understand. Please, though, let's keep this between us, okay?"

Aya nodded slowly, her lips curling in a mischievous grin. "Are you sure, though? You never get tempted to take a little peak inside Tanaka's head or—"

"Aya!" Juliet laughed.

"Scoot over." Aya pushed her hip as Juliet grunted, shifting to the side. "Nothing's going on out there. Athena says you have to stay off your leg for another two hours. Wanna watch something together?"

No matter how hard she tried, Juliet couldn't keep the smile from reforming on her face, and soon, her cheeks began to ache again. Aya was snuggling next to her, flipping through vid titles on a shared AUI, and she *knew*! She knew Juliet's secret, and she didn't care. She hadn't even made her promise not to listen to her thoughts. Juliet felt like the weight of the universe had been lifted from her chest, and she could breathe freely for the first time in *years*.

Angel still sat in the chair to Juliet's left, and every time she glanced at her, Angel's violet eyes squinted as she smiled and nodded knowingly. She understood what she was thinking. She knew how she felt—she felt it too.

Juliet lay there, nodding along, listening to Aya babble about this show or that. When she finally settled on a crime drama set in New Galveston during the first Martian expansion, Juliet snuggled closer, letting Aya rest her head on her arm as she squeezed her against her side.

They watched two episodes, and Juliet dozed a couple of times before Athena came into the med bay. When she saw Juliet and Aya giggling about a stupid joke one of the detectives had made regarding a suspect who'd left his DNA on a chocolate wrapper, she smiled and approached. "I'm glad to see you had some company while your nanites worked. Are you experiencing any discomfort?"

Juliet paused the vid and looked at her. "Nope! Everything feels amazing. I mean, I haven't tried to walk yet, but I've been lifting my leg and bending my knee and ankle. It feels so normal that I wouldn't have been surprised to hear you decided not to do the operation."

"That's wonderful. It's an excellent piece of tech; far more capable than most of the hardware you can get on today's marketplace, especially with the power cells I developed."

"Power cells?" Aya perked up with interest.

Athena smiled. "Some improvements to the biobatts the leg came equipped with." She walked around the bed, standing on Juliet's left. "Ready to try it out?"

"Um, yeah." Juliet sat up, and as Aya slid off the side of the bed, she shook out her arm, wincing. "You put it to sleep!"

"Sorry." Aya grinned in a way that didn't look sorry at all.

Juliet grunted and threw her blanket off, grateful that Athena had apparently dressed her in a pair of loose, comfortable, pastel-yellow scrubs. She slid off the side of the bed, putting her weight on her right leg first, then tentatively adding more and more pressure on her left foot. The cold plasteel felt the same on her feet. Looking down, she thought the synth-skin looked amazingly like her own, and the toes were perfect mirrors of her right foot. "How did you get it to match so well?"

"I told you we"—Athena nodded to Angel—"had been planning this for a while. The synth-skin, by default, is a blank canvas open to DNA implantation. I had to alter some of the bones—easy enough to do with the right tools—but the skin tone, muscle fiber density and length, and even the nail beds were programmed to match your original DNA. I'm sure your doctor on Luna did the same for your arm."

Juliet frowned, still unsure how she felt about Angel and Athena planning this without consulting her. Shaking it off, she took her first step, feeling a twinge in her lower back and stumbling slightly. "Oof."

"Something wrong?" Athena asked.

Aya hurried around the bed, her face alarmed. "What is it?"

Juliet chuckled. "Nothing. Just a twinge. Maybe a nerve? It was in my lower back." Athena stepped around behind her and gripped her hips, pressing her thumbs into her lower back, gently probing. "Closer to my spine."

"Ah. Just a little swelling and fluid buildup. I had to tie your new hip structure in here and reinforce the bones and musculature to support the strength of your leg's synthetic muscle fibers. Angel, can you direct the nanites to this area?"

"Already doing so."

Athena nodded, still probing with her thumbs. It felt good; Juliet couldn't lie about that, and she found herself relaxing, putting more and more weight on her new leg. After a couple of minutes, Athena released her and tugged her shirt back down.

"It'll be fine. Why don't you three take a walk around the ship? Tomorrow, you should be able to start doing some physical therapy—stretching, mobility tests, and the like."

"Um," Aya said, and when everyone looked at her, she asked, "What about the old one? What'd you do with it?"

"I don't want to know!" Juliet snapped. "Aya! I don't want to see or even *imagine* my poor dead leg!"

Athena chuckled and patted her on the shoulder. "I put it in the medical waste recycler, Juliet. I'm afraid you'll never see your dear departed limb."

"Okay, good. Let's just pretend this never happened." Juliet started for the door, amazed that she didn't feel the need to limp. "Come on, Aya—Wait!"

Juliet turned and looked around the med bay. "Where's my stuff? My sword? My gun?"

"All in your cabin, Captain," Aya replied with a wink.

"When you've had a good walk around, come back, Juliet. I have some equipment I want to go over with you and Aya."

"Me too?" Aya asked, her dark eyebrows shooting up.

"Of course! You're going to be aboard the gunship, and I'm confident Juliet will have to fly against some opposition. Better that you're prepared for any eventuality, don't you think?"

Aya nodded eagerly. "Oh, I think, ma'am. I think very much!" Aya grabbed Juliet's arm and walked with her to the door. "Come on; Frida's waiting in the kitchen with Bennet and Leo."

"Uh, why?"

"Aren't you hungry? I'm starved!"

Juliet had to admit to a very hollow feeling in her stomach. Before she could agree, Athena called out, "You should definitely eat; those power cells need glucose."

"There you have it." Aya tugged her through the door. "Doctor's orders!"

"I'm supposed to walk around—"

"You will, you will. Let's just make a quick stop. Leo made lasagna."

"*What?*" Juliet resisted her pull for the first time. "With what ingredients?"

"This ship's pantry is very well-stocked!"

Juliet relented and let Aya pull her along the corridor. "Does he, like, even know how to cook?"

"Yes!" Aya laughed. "Besides, Bennet also made you a protein smoothie, and Frida's baking some kind of dessert."

"Is this going to be a big party? I just woke up from *surgery*, Aya!" Juliet could already hear the buzz of conversation from the mess hall. "It is, isn't it?" She resisted Aya's pull, and in a hoarse whisper, said, "Aya! I'm embarrassed about everything I said. I don't want—"

"Come on, *Juliet!*" Aya whined. "Everyone wants to show you their support. People felt awful about how . . . Well, you know."

"I wasn't trying to make people feel bad." Juliet sighed and let it drop. She had to accept that people had feelings and motivations of their own, and it was nice to be part of a community, however weird this one was.

So, she focused on things she was happy about: her dream, her quick recovery from the surgery, and having a friend to share the burden of her secrets. It was more than enough to bring her smile back.

She let Aya tug her into the galley, where she was met with warm greetings from her friends and the wonderful scent of baked lasagna.

41

READY STATIONS

'm not much for combat flying, if I'm honest—did plenty of transport jobs in hot zones, and I didn't mind unloading on that facility down on Mars, but, well, I never been too good at quick maneuvers under high Gs. You reckon we'll hit anything much over two Gs?" Chevy spoke with a slight drawl, and sometimes, Juliet had a hard time making sense of words he strung together, but she got the gist of it.

"Two? Better get comfy in that couch, Chevy, 'cause we're gonna be pushing a hell of a lot more than that if I have to deal with more than one or two interceptors."

Chevy gripped the armrests of the copilot seat with one hand while rubbing the stubble on his chin with the other. He wore a bright red flight suit but hadn't put his helmet on yet; they still had almost an hour before their final, hard deceleration burn. "But just for, like, a second or two, right?"

"You're joking, right? You saw the flight plan Athena sent over, yeah? We'll burn at nearly four Gs for fifteen minutes, and that's just to put us into Ceres space."

"Right, no, I get that." Chevy sighed. "I mean, like, in the dogfights. I heard interceptor pilots talking about hitting eleven Gs doing some maneuvers, and, well—shit, I'm not sure I can handle that kinda—"

"Relax, Chevy. This is a gunship, and we've gotta think about our engineer, too. Speaking of whom, I have to go talk to her. Watch the stick for a few minutes, will ya?"

Juliet unbuckled and slipped out of the pilot's acceleration couch, amazed by how easily she could move in the new body armor Athena had given her. It was airtight, or it would be when she donned the helmet, and though it wasn't powered like her old combat armor, it had more durable plating that Athena said was rated for high-caliber rifle fire.

Beneath the matte-black, light-absorbing plates were two layers of flexible nano-weave membranes. The membranes were designed to absorb shocks via a layer of nanite-rich gel. The nanites, supposedly, could rapidly repair rents in the membranes. Even if she took hits in the vacuum of space, the suit wouldn't lose integrity.

The helmet was great, too. Juliet appreciated the comfortable gel lining, and the outer shell was made of the same stuff as her armored plates, even the visor, which was entirely opaque. Her visuals would be provided via a series of cameras, feeding her AUI a three-hundred-and-sixty-degree panoramic view.

Juliet's magnetic soles *click-clomped* on the decking as she made her way back to the engineering ready room. There, she found Aya, wearing armor similar to her own, pulling panels and checking components. "Ready?"

"Um, ready but nervous. I mean, I know this ship inside and out. I just kinda wish Bennet was here with us."

"I know, but—"

"But we need him in the Atlas suit so he can take out the station's automated defense turrets," she sighed.

"I mean, we need *someone* in the suit doing that, and yeah, I guess he got the job. Anyway, we really need those turrets knocked offline, Aya. The Atlas is small enough, and with its booster rockets, fast enough to get in close ahead of us. If he doesn't take 'em out, Tanaka, Leo, Charlie, and all their mercs could get killed before we even get to the station."

Aya nodded. "Not to mention us."

"Exactly."

"I don't know why we don't just use the rail gun to pop that ark ship from range. We could put an end to this whole thing—"

Juliet cut her off, sighing as she gently tugged one of her friend's short pink braids. "Aya, you heard the briefing. You *know*—"

It was Aya's turn to cut her off. "I know, I know. If we blow the ark ship, the whole station could go, which could then fall directly into the Ceres dome, which, according to Athena, could result in hundreds of thousands of deaths. I still just want to blow the damn thing up. Who builds something so fragile?"

"Yeah." Juliet shrugged. She'd had the same question, and Angel had tried to explain to her that Ceres had been greatly expanded after the war; it was, basically, an industrial city built up by dozens of corporations. The factories and shipyards tacked on, outside the dome, were owned and operated by competing interests. It wasn't designed as a military base, and so had some inherent fragility.

"I just hope Athena's right about the resistance we're going to face. She seems confident that her contacts will be able to convince most of the nearby corps to stay out of the fight as long as we don't, you know, start trying to blow up an ark ship parked in the middle of a shipyard."

Aya giggled. "Fine! We won't fire the rail gun at the ark ship. I mean, if you forget about all the risk to innocent people, you've gotta admit it would be cool, though."

"Oh, if we could target the reactors from ten thousand klicks? Hell yeah! You saw the schematics—that thing is massive!" It was true. The ark ship that WBD had acquired when they'd merged with or absorbed—Juliet wasn't sure which—Ark Industries had been under construction for over a decade and was much larger than the dreadnought she'd escaped.

It wasn't designed for war, so much of that space was taken up by environmental habitats—a park, a freshwater fishery, even an honest-to-goodness farm. Of course, it also had massive cargo sections, supposedly outfitted with the supplies needed to kick off a human colony.

"She'd make a hell of a fireworks show."

Aya nodded, sighing. "But you guys are right. There are probably lots of people on that ship who know nothing about what's going on." She closed up the component panel she'd been inspecting and then turned to look Juliet in the eyes. "Are you nervous, too?" She reached out and tugged on Juliet's armored chest plate as though ensuring everything fit properly.

"Sure. I've flown combat missions with Nick riding shotgun, but this is the first time I'm, like, calling the shots. It's also the first time I've flown this ship in that kind of situation. I mean, outside of a sim."

Aya tapped the row of access panels beside her with her knuckles. "She's going to do fine. I can feel it; she wants to keep us safe."

"You can, can't you?" Juliet cocked her head to the side and really looked into Aya's pink irises. They stood out especially brightly under her dark eyebrows. "Feel it, I mean."

Aya nodded so her braids bounced. "Yep. I can also tell that you're a lot more confident than you're letting on."

Juliet grinned with one side of her mouth. "Not slipping anything by you, am I? You know, I bet you could do some cool stuff with a psionics lattice."

Aya's eyes widened. "Oh! I'd *love* to be able to see what's going through Leo's head!"

Juliet groaned and wrapped her gloved hands around Aya's neck, mock choking her. Aya stuck her tongue out to the side, making gagging sounds, and Juliet laughed. "You gotta stop thinking about that guy!"

"*Juliet!*" Aya grabbed her wrists. "He's about to go into battle for you—for everyone. I know you don't *really* think he's a bad guy. You like him! Be honest!"

Juliet sighed and relented, letting go of her friend. "He *is* a good guy. I know. I hope he comes through it okay. If you want to know the truth, that's what I'm really worried about—him and Bennet, Alice, Shiro—all the others." She stared at Aya for another few seconds, and, though neither said anything more, a lot passed between them. Juliet knew Aya trusted her, and it meant a lot that Juliet had admitted to a reluctant approval of Leo, whether or not anything ever happened between them.

"Anyway," Aya broke the moment and gestured around the ready room. "The components all look good. I've got replacement parts on hand for every major system. The cannons are locked and loaded. The main gun is primed and ready to swap ammo to shredder canisters." She pointed to the access ladder on the left. "I've run the route to the central drive and memorized the grip placements in case we're maneuvering and the Gs are shifting. Everything's a go."

"Okay, awesome. Well, fingers crossed we don't need you to get out of that acceleration couch, yeah?"

Aya glanced at her station, where her helmet sat on the seat of her couch. "Right. Let's hope."

Juliet pointed to the weapons rack on the other side of the rear hatchway. It held two fully automatic combat rifles, two riot shotguns, and four needler pistols loaded with shredders. All the guns had highly plastic, antipersonnel polymer rounds that wouldn't penetrate the ship's interior walls or access panels. "If something goes crazy and I get hurt, and we're adrift or, I dunno, we crash-landed on the station, you know what to do, right?"

Aya pulled off a surprisingly sharp salute and nodded. "Yes, Captain! Shoot any creeps who board this vessel without permission!"

Juliet chuckled and punched her lightly on her armored chest plate. "Keep your helmet on!" Then, she turned and went up the central access corridor back to the cockpit. On the way, she subvocalized, "Angel, what's the status on the other ships?"

"Alice and Shiro are in the *Lady Hawk* and have taken up their wider wing formation. She's indicating green, ready to follow your lead." Juliet grunted her acknowledgment. Alice was the more experienced combat pilot, but she was flying the interceptor; it would be her job to protect Juliet's flanks so she could bring her heavy guns to bear and, hopefully, make quick work of any hostile ships lying in wait for them.

Angel continued. "Athena has already increased her deceleration burn as planned, putting some distance between the *Furies' Wing* and us." Juliet nodded as she moved past Chevy to climb back into her pilot's seat. The *Wing* was their command operations ship. Athena, Dora, and Frida would be calling shots on the fly, communicating with their assets on Ceres, and coordinating the other ships' priorities.

"Everything good, Captain?" Chevy asked, grunting as he pulled his bright-red, mirror-visored helmet on. Juliet nodded, throwing him a thumbs-up. His helmet went with his flight suit, and it was a lot cheaper tech than the armored suits she and Aya were wearing. She knew it wasn't favoritism—the armor was custom fitted, and Athena hadn't had the details on all of Books's people when she'd begun the process.

She returned to her conversation with Angel. "And the *Crocodile*?" That was the rather unfortunate name of the light corvette that Charles Books and his team had liberated from the WBD Martian base. Tanaka, Leo, Hawkins, Books, his mercenaries, and of course, Bennet were all aboard the corvette.

Athena had hacked WBD's authentication codes, and the plan—the hope—was for the *Crocodile* to get close to the WBD facility ahead of the rest of them, pretending to be limping to the nearest friendly facility with wounded personnel. Bennet was meant to launch from the drop bay and, with Athena's guidance, rocket to the antiship cannons in the Atlas suit.

"The *Crocodile* is maintaining course and will arrive in Ceres local space fifteen minutes ahead of us."

"God, I hate that they have to hang out there for fifteen minutes before Alice and I arrive to back them up."

"They're going to slow down to a crawl and continue their distress signals. With luck, they'll lure a defending ship over; Tanaka and crew will make short work of any boarders. As for the distance, you know they can't be in formation with us; they're supposed to be fleeing."

"Yeah. I know, I know." Juliet sighed and leaned back in her seat, enjoying how the gel reformed around her with the increased pressure. "Now, remind me why the hell we're letting Bennet stick his neck out in the Atlas suit, would you?"

Angel sighed, knowing full well she was just being a sounding board to help Juliet settle her nerves and come to grips with the situation. "Because he refused to stay aboard the *Wing* or the *Cherry Blossom*. He wanted to fight, Juliet. He's a capable man, and Athena's intelligence indicates that the gun installations will be lightly guarded by security personnel, none of whom should have any ordnance capable of harming him in the Atlas combat exoskeleton. He's far safer with that job than if he dropped with Tanaka and the others."

"Yeah, especially if the *Crocodile* starts taking fire. They'll be heavily out-gunned until we arrive." Juliet knew Tanaka and the other mercenaries had the most dangerous job: they had to storm the WBD shipyard from the main hangar bays.

They'd be dropping out of the corvette, using maneuvering jets to fly in an evasive combat formation through a bay that, if everything went right, would be blown wide by one of the corvette's torpedoes. It was going to be chaotic and dangerous, and Juliet hadn't wanted Bennet on that job.

"I doubt the *Crocodile* will make it through this."

"No, it's our Trojan horse, and I don't think Athena expects it to survive. Once the mercenaries deploy, I'm sure any firepower Bennet hasn't neutral-ized will focus on it. Still, hopefully, it and the mercenaries will buy us time to neutralize the response ships and board the ark ship."

Juliet nodded, watching the countdown for the deceleration burn. They had thirty-seven minutes. Athena had acquired schematics for the ark ship and found not one but seven different docking collars that the *Cherry Blossom* could latch on to.

Usually, a hostile docking maneuver would be challenging, but on a sta-tionary vessel docked at port, it shouldn't be hard at all. Books had argued that everyone should get on the gunship and board the ark ship together, but Athena had taken a different stance, and when everyone had heard her reason-ing, the votes had been in her favor.

Athena was sure that WBD, while understaffed and moving ahead of schedule, would still have a few hundred armed personnel between the ship-yard and the *Starjumper*. If Juliet hoped to get into the heart of the ark ship and secure Gentry and Apollyon, the distraction of a heavy assault on the hangars would be necessary. Tanaka's team would draw the response teams while Juliet and Alice destroyed the support ships.

Once the responding ships were downed, Juliet would pilot the gunship into a docking maneuver and, hopefully, have to deal with much lighter resis-tance thanks to all the mercenaries' efforts.

With the plan thoroughly reviewed, Juliet closed her eyes, leaned back, and zoned out for a while, listening to one of her playlists reserved for just that purpose. When Athena spoke to her through comms, her countdown to burn was down to sixteen minutes. "Juliet, I have some updates we should talk about."

Something about Athena's tone bothered Juliet. "Something's wrong?"

"There are a few developments. I was confident that my contacts at Ceres could delay or even halt the CCC response forces from intervening in our conflict with WBD, but it seems that at least one of their commanders is refusing orders to stand down."

"What does that mean for us?"

"It means that, in addition to the three WBD interceptor-class ships, you'll have an additional heavy fighter and four more interceptors to contend with."

"Eight? Eight against two, Athena?"

"Eight against four, Juliet. The *Crocodile* isn't helpless; I will continue piloting and controlling the guns after Tanaka and the other mercenaries drop. Additionally, I'll be using my jamming array on the *Wing* to interfere with their comms and, hopefully, interrupt some of their ships' systems at critical moments."

Juliet sighed and slowly began to nod as she imagined the scenario. Athena was a true AI; she might be doing a lot, but she could handle it. She probably already had parallel processing nodes set up and running on Ceres. For all Juliet knew, her *assets* could be her operating via vid calls and synthetic bodies, working to infiltrate the other corps and the Ceres Corporate Consortium.

In short, if she said she could handle piloting the *Crocodile*, then things weren't so grim; the light corvette had an impressive supply of missiles and torpedoes.

"How long? I mean, how long have you been working on Ceres?"

"Since Mexico City. When I realized they'd taken you off-world, I began cultivating my assets on Mars and Ceres."

"All right, well, thanks for the heads-up." Juliet reached for her helmet and moved to pull it on, but stopped short as Athena continued speaking.

"There's more. Quite a bit more, I'm afraid."

Again, her tone got Juliet's hackles up, and she frowned. "I'm listening."

"We always knew Gentry and Apollyon would assume that I, at least, would pursue them. They knew these ships were acting against their base. They may not know you survived the *Horizon Prophet's* destruction, but they had to know we were heading their way for a reason. Knowing that, we played it up, sending distress messages from the *Crocodile*."

"*Right* . . ."

"Well, I knew they'd scramble to get the *Starjumper* ready, but I'd hoped we'd have a bit more time. My sources are telling me that an additional fusion reactor has been brought online aboard the vessel. I believe they're prepping the warp drive."

"So, how much time will we have?"

"Impossible to tell. It could be that they're at the early stages and still have components to install. It could be that they're spooling it up and simply have to wait for Apollyon to calculate the jump."

"Can you give me a window?"

"Between thirty minutes and thirty days."

"*Dammit*, Athena!"

"I know this is frustrating news, but keep things in perspective; we've accomplished a great deal. If we're too late, then we'll have to think of something else. If, however, you can get aboard that ship and get me into their network, there's a good chance I'll be able to infiltrate their systems. Apollyon was never very subtle or clever with security; he's more of a brute-force thinker."

Juliet's earlier conversation with Aya came to mind. "They can't jump from inside the hangar, right? If they're moving, can't we just start lancing 'em with the rail gun?"

"We could, but that brings us to the final bit of news."

"Jesus, Athena! How much bad news do you have?"

"You can tell it's bad?" She sounded genuinely curious, but Juliet just sighed and closed her eyes. When Athena realized she wasn't going to answer, she continued. "I finally acquired a copy of the transport manifests from the Ceres Space Station to the WBD shipyard—passengers who were ferried aboard the *Starjumper* before our actions on Mars, when things were moving at a more sedate pace."

Juliet's heart dropped. "Who?"

"Please brace yourself, because this will be alarming: Peter Voronov, his niece, and Honey Watkins are aboard." Juliet's ears rushed as her blood pressure spiked, and she squeezed her eyes shut, trying to wrap her head around Athena's words. The AI wasn't finished, though. "I'm also sorry to report that there's a record of Emma Bianchi boarding the *Starjumper* under armed escort just four days ago."

42

A FATAL ERROR

Juliet sat there, dumbstruck by Athena's words. Honey, she could see. She could wrap her head around the idea that, somehow, Voronov had gotten her mixed up with WBD or Ark Industries. Maybe he'd somehow learned about the warp drive, and his connections with one company or another had gotten him on a list of passengers, people chosen to help start up a new colony—the ultimate getaway plan.

Or, on a more sinister note, Juliet could see him working with WBD. Hadn't his brother, the consciousness slowly growing inside Lilia, been experimenting with illegal human cloning and life-extension research? It wasn't much of a stretch to see how he might have been involved, knowingly or not, with Apollyon's many avenues of research.

Her sister, however, had to be personal. The only reason Emma had for being there was because she was related to Juliet. They were either taking her as leverage or as another avenue for researching Juliet's DNA.

As her mind spun, as she explored every avenue, Athena continued speaking, but Juliet didn't hear her. The pain in her left hand eventually helped Juliet to focus on the present and stop spinning down imagined avenues of disaster, picturing Emma and Honey in one sinister plot or desperate situation after another. With conscious effort, she stopped squeezing the yoke in a death grip and unwound her fingers, flexing them to return blood flow.

"... shouldn't be too distant from that aft shuttle bay." Juliet blinked, shaking her head, trying to make sense of Athena's words.

"I didn't hear any of that, Athena. I'm sorry, but you said they have my sister, right? What if they put one of those chips in her?"

"She was brought up before your escape, Juliet, so I don't think they took her as leverage. I believe she's meant to be a research subject. That being the case, they won't want one of their imperfect chips expanding synthetic fibers into her nervous system. Did you hear what I said about her likely location on the ark ship? If we plan your route with that shuttle bay as an egress point, you should be able to recover her on your way out."

"And you know that, how?"

"It's speculation, but the ship's schematics indicate small, cell-like chambers plumbed for waste recycling there, with convenient access to the science labs. They'd be perfect for holding test subjects. I'll know more once you get me connected to the ship's network."

Juliet glanced over her shoulder, past Chevy, to the weapons rack near the cockpit's bulkhead door. Just like the one in Aya's ready room, this rack held shotguns, rifles, and pistols, but it also contained her monoblade and Texan. Her palm itched to hold her sword. Her heart raced to charge into battle.

Juliet turned forward, pushing the feeling down. "First, I gotta get us to the ark ship, and that means we gotta take out their fighters."

"That's the spirit, Juliet!" Athena clearly mistook Juliet's self-talk for conversation. "One step at a time. Once we've dealt with their defenses and taken out Apollyon and Gentry, there will be time to rescue your sister and friend."

"You sound awfully sure, Athena," Juliet muttered as she pulled her helmet on, grimacing as it squeezed her ears on the way down. The seal *snicked*, air hissed in her ears as the suit's self-contained atmosphere stabilized, and all the indicators flashed green on her AUI.

"I can't promise anything, Juliet; we're all going to do our best, but right now, you should focus on piloting. Try to put the news I just gave you out of your mind. I hope I didn't upset you to the point—"

"I'm fine, Athena." Juliet's voice was clipped, and she knew she didn't sound fine, so she added, "Thank you for being honest and upfront. You could have withheld that information from me so it wouldn't affect my flying, but you didn't. That means something." Juliet glanced at the countdown—two minutes and change. "I'm about to start burning. Switching to combat comm protocols and bringing Alice in."

Athena's only response was, "Roger," indicating she was taking Juliet's lead and was ready to focus on their upcoming dogfight. Juliet stared at the comm display on her AUI as Angel intuited what she wanted and grouped the four ships in a single channel.

"*Cherry Blossom* initiating final burn and approach in T-minus one-nineteen seconds. Arrival at Ceres in just under seventeen minutes."

Alice's near melodic Aussie accent came through. "*Lady Hawk* standing by, burning on your mark, *Blossom*."

Tanaka's clipped response sounded strained—he and the other mercs in the light corvette had been hard-burning for thirteen minutes already. "*Crocodile* entering Ceres space in T-minus one-thirteen seconds."

Juliet focused on her ship's AUI projections, concentrating on remaining loose and relaxed, ready for action. Her helmet was tied into the ship's sensor array and cameras, so she no longer saw her cockpit unless Angel recognized her desire to do so. Otherwise, she saw an unobstructed view out over the stubby shark nose of the *Cherry Blossom's* hull. If she turned her head, the view of space and the exterior of her ship seamlessly flowed around her as though she were sitting outside.

She could activate her rearview with a thought—some pilots would have to select it on an AUI, but Angel could tell when she wanted to see a different angle and responded instantly with the appropriate feed. It was amazing—far better integration than any other ship she'd flown, and Juliet almost felt like she'd become the ship.

The *Blossom* wasn't a nimble interceptor, but she wasn't a sluggish boat, either. Just one of her thrusters put out more force than anything the *Lady Hawk* could muster. With all three online, Juliet knew she had a straight-line acceleration capability that would leave most fighters in the dust, especially anything made by modern ship manufacturers—even more so if they had a stock loadout.

Add her twin VTOL drives to that, and Juliet knew that between her and Angel, the gunship was plenty nimble when it came to changing directions and throwing off pursuit. Moreover, she had ten times the countermeasure payload of any light fighter. She could throw out flak and flares all day.

Juliet summarized her mental rundown. "She was made for a different time. She was made to ride through storms way worse than what we're going to put her through."

"The ship?" Chevy asked, his voice sounding like it was right next to her ear as it came through the ship's comms.

"*Cherry Blossom.*" Juliet glanced at her countdown. "Strap in, Aya. Hard burn in T-minus three-two seconds."

"Strapped and ready," came her friend's clear, confident reply.

Juliet spoke into the combat group's comms. "*Cherry Blossom* hard burning in T-minus two-six seconds." She glanced over her shoulder, and Angel clarified her local view, showing Chevy in his seat, gloved hands gripping the copilot's yoke—currently inactive for all but the deployment of countermeasures. "Ready?"

"Ready as I'll ever be, I guess." His voice was tight, like he was squeezing out each word. Was he already straining his core for the Gs? Juliet chuckled softly, but Angel, thankfully, didn't transmit the sound.

When her timer was down to six seconds, Juliet spoke into her group's comms again. "*Cherry Blossom* hard burn in three . . . two . . . one . . . mark." As she said *mark*, she increased thrust to four Gs. The hum of the gunship's powerful drives notched up in frequency, and the punch of acceleration sucked her into her couch's gel, tugging on her skin and limbs.

Juliet was ready for it. She'd been through much worse with Nick and during training flights since then. Her lungs were easy to fill with just a trickle of air; they scrounged up every molecule of oxygen and even supplemented it from her active stores. That, in turn, allowed her to keep her core compressed for longer periods of time, which made it easier to regulate her blood pressure during high Gs.

In short, Juliet felt the strain a lot less than she used to as she continued to watch her instruments—Tanaka should have slowed to local combat speeds and should be updating every ship in the group with his sensor readings. She watched, almost holding her breath in anticipation, and just as she'd hoped, her tactical grid of Ceres space began to update with glowing dots, shifting them from predicted locations based on slightly outdated intelligence from Athena's assets.

The *Crocodile* was an oblong, green oval, and sure enough, Juliet saw six yellow triangles angling out from Ceres to intercept the light corvette's approach. From the far side of Ceres, a much larger yellow triangle and an escort of two smaller ones were burning hard to bring themselves into combat-ready range with Juliet's combat group.

Whether they thought the *Crocodile* needed defending, they knew Juliet meant to attack WBD, or they just thought the rapidly approaching ships warranted intervention and inspection, Juliet didn't know.

"Sorry, Juliet," Athena said through comms. "Nine, not eight."

"Okay," Juliet grunted. "Angel, mark 'em red as soon as we've confirmed hostile intention." Almost immediately, three of the ships approaching *Crocodile* switched from yellow to red.

"Those three are registered to WBD," Angel explained.

Juliet nodded, staring at her tactical grid. Turning it, she studied the various features. When she stared at Ceres, it zoomed in, and she saw the domed city, the many factories and shipyards—some attached via spindles and others orbiting the planetoid. A transparent green plane showed her where the *Crocodile* had to get to in order for Bennet to make his drop. Another—closer—green line showed the drop point for the other mercs.

"They've got a long way to go. Are you monitoring their comms?"

Angel quickly responded, "Yes. They're still transmitting distress signals. They've been ordered to cease their approach, but Tanaka's playing dumb."

Juliet snorted, wondering what that sounded like. "Play it for me."

A transmission window popped up on her AUI, and she heard the faint hum of background interference as a high-pitched, stressed masculine voice said, "WBD *Crocodile*, you are ordered to spin down your main drives and engage maneuvering jets to halt your progress relative to Ceres Station."

With a buzz of crackling static, Tanaka's voice came through, sounding very different from his usual gruff, clipped speech patterns. He spoke with a nasal twang, and Juliet almost laughed, listening to his reply.

"This is, uh, this is Recruit Kwon—our pilot bled out. I think, uh, I think he set this ship's AI to put us down at the, uh, WBD station. We, um, we can't get the AI to respond to any of us. We need medical assistance!"

"Standby, *Crocodile*."

"Oh, brother!" Juliet chuckled. "I never knew Tanaka could act!"

"He's a renaissance man," Angel replied, and Juliet felt her smile growing. "You still *like* him, don't you?"

"I . . . Hush, Juliet! Focus on the mission!"

Juliet grinned and watched her burn clock—twelve minutes left. She continued watching the map, watching the ships approaching the *Crocodile* and the other three. The bigger triangle had to be the heavy fighter belonging to the CCC commander who wouldn't stand down. Did that mean he was bad? Were he and the other CCC pilots paid off by WBD, or were they just overzealous in their desire to defend anyone at Ceres Station? Were they good people Juliet was about to try to kill?

She shook her head, chasing the thought away. They meant to stop her, and she *had* to get through; she had to stop that ark ship. If she could get to Apollyon and Gentry, if she could get the data about their plans for the Sol System, she might save billions of lives.

Staring at the large triangle, it began to populate with data, no doubt due to the *Crocodile* finally getting a solid scan or, maybe, some information Athena was forwarding from her assets on Ceres. It was a Fitzroy Firebird called *Trueno*.

Juliet studied the stats: thirty meters nose to tail, two B-class heavy thrusters, twelve B-class maneuvering jets, sixteen smart ship-to-ship missiles, twin eighteen-millimeter cannons, and a ten-millimeter minigun turret capable of firing at pursuers. Its armor was ranked as B-class, too. Altogether, it was a formidable ship, but not even close to being in the same weight class as the *Cherry Blossom*.

By modern standards, every component on the *Blossom* would be considered A-class or better, and she had three drives—two VTOL—and thirty-six maneuvering jets. Her six twenty-millimeter cannons would fire faster and more accurately than the guns on the *Trueno*, and that was leaving aside the rail gun under her nose.

No, the *Cherry Blossom* was a monster, with armor twice as effective as that on the incoming heavy fighter, and a layer of self-repairing nanites to keep the hull intact. Juliet grinned at the thought. "And I've got Aya."

She looked at her combat group's comms. "Status check."

"Final deceleration burn—ten minutes to Ceres space," Alice replied, almost sounding bored.

"At Ceres, twenty-seven minutes from Atlas drop, currently waiting to be boarded but maintaining course and speed," Tanaka announced. Juliet grinned at the thought. That would take at least one of the ships out of combat because she was quite sure whoever docked with the *Crocodile* wouldn't be rejoining any upcoming fight.

Athena completed the status check. "Final deceleration burn—twelve minutes from Ceres space." As Juliet turned her attention back to the incoming response ships, Athena spoke into their private comms. "Juliet, Frida has been analyzing the drive signatures of the response ships, and we believe we've figured out the ninth ship's identity. It's a modified Gallant and Chang Broadsword, a medium fighter registered as *Mort*—it's Montclair's personal ship, Juliet."

"I *killed* Montclair!"

"That may well be, but there's the chance he'd backed himself up, at least the part of his mind that lived in the Angel chip. Judging by your reports, I don't believe much of his human mind still existed."

"I'm so sick of these goddamn *creeps*!" Juliet growled, scanning the red and yellow triangles until she saw the one Angel had painted a deep maroon. As she zoomed in, the details came into view: twenty meters nose to tail, twin A-class medium thrusters, twenty-eight A-class maneuvering jets, four wing-mounted, twelve-millimeter mass drivers, and a projected EMP package built into its nose cone.

She saw the *Mort* was flying amid the red WBD ships, flanked by yellow CCC ships, so she growled, "Mark them all red. If he's with them, they're all bad."

As her tactical grid updated, Juliet inhaled deeply through her nose and out again. Something in her gut told her Montclair was there at the last minute to try to mess up her plans. She had no doubt he knew she was coming.

"He's immortal. He has no fear. No wonder he was so cocky in that corridor. Now, he's going to fly like a suicidal maniac in a damn racer of a ship! Are you ready for this, Angel? That ship is priority one."

"I'm ready, Juliet."

She stared at the tactical grid, watching the ship's progress while she slowly approached. The *Crocodile* continued to move toward Ceres while one of the smaller red triangles moved alongside it. Juliet glanced at her clock—six minutes and change.

"Hold on, Tanaka," she grunted, knowing things would get very hectic for the mercs once those boarders failed to respond to status checks. As her burn entered the last three minutes, she watched the *Mort* and two of the light interceptors angle away from the *Crocodile*, beelining to intercept her and Alice.

"They're pincering us." She pointed to the heavy fighter, *Trueno*, and his two escorts coming in from a different angle. "Six versus two, huh?" She glanced at her comm line with Alice, and Angel activated it. "You seeing this?"

"Wouldn't expect anything less. Ready for it."

Juliet grinned. "Me too. *Mort* is going to be gunning hard for us. He's your number one priority. Pop him while I draw fire and keep *Trueno* busy."

Alice chuckled into comms. "You're giving me the big bad? I feel so . . . *spoiled!*"

"Athena told you about him, huh?"

"Yes, ma'am!"

Juliet smiled and shrugged, though only Angel could see the movement. "I already kicked his ass once. Might as well let someone else have some fun."

"Roger. Ready."

Juliet was about to do a final ready check when the red triangles near the *Crocodile* began to blink, and little orange dots flared to life around the green oblong icon. Tanaka's voice came through comms, surprisingly calm. "Boarders neutralized. Their ship is locked down. Two interceptors have begun firing on the *Crocodile*."

Athena spoke up. "Beginning evasive maneuvers on *Crocodile* and unloading missile bays. Tanaka, get with the others in the drop bay. Estimated time to drop, eighteen minutes."

Juliet grinned as she watched dozens of tiny green dots appear around the *Crocodile* and begin streaking toward the various red triangles. She didn't think the missile dump would take them *all* out, especially the more distant ships, but she was hopeful anyway.

Before she could zoom in and focus, watching each missile and countermeasure the enemy ships deployed, her proximity alarm began to sound, and she realized her deceleration burn was almost over. "Here we go," she breathed softly. "Get those countermeasures ready, Chevy."

"Ready, Captain."

Juliet watched as her grid showed her approaching the six intercepting ships. Pulling back on the throttle, she jerked her stick to the left. As her maneuvering thrusters brought her nose around, she jammed the throttle forward, and the three powerful drives punched everyone down into their acceleration couches as Juliet smoothly nudged her targeting reticle toward the fast-approaching *Trueno* group, squeezing the trigger for the main gun.

The massive recoil of the rail gun firing barely registered against the thrust of the *Cherry Blossom's* drives, but Juliet felt it in her body as the ripple of force rolled through the ship's hull.

To her amazement, a flare of bright yellow bloomed in her display, and she whooped as she pulled back on the throttle, fired her port maneuvering thrusters, and jerked the yoke to port, barrel rolling in a wide spiral as she strafed away from the incoming streaks of tracer rounds from not one but half a dozen ships.

"Kill!" Angel reported.

"One interceptor down," Athena confirmed.

"One shot, one kill!" Alice howled. "Keep 'em busy, *Blossom*; they're ignoring me—a fatal error."

43

MANEUVERS

Juliet grunted as she continued maneuvering, capitalizing on the *Cherry Blossom's* powerful VTOL drives to give her lateral bursts of speed, keeping her movement unpredictable and trusting her gut to tell her when it was right to bring her guns to bear on one of her targets.

They'd been in hot combat for more than three minutes now, and Alice had removed another of the interceptors from the board, but now, she had two focusing on her, one of which was Montclair's *Mort*. "Hang in there, Alice! Just give me a few seconds to line these guys up."

Juliet's instant kill of one of the interceptors had seemed to inflame the responders, and at first, they'd all gunned for her. The *Blossom* was a nimble ship, however, and Juliet had a knack for moving unpredictably at just the right moment. After Alice had ripped one of the other interceptors to shreds, two others had peeled off to deal with her, and now Juliet was having a much easier time with just the *Trueno* and one light fighter.

As she killed the power to the main and VTOL drives, Juliet fired the retro maneuvering jets and performed a forward flip, bringing her nose up just in time to catch the *Trueno* in her sights.

Pressing the trigger, she fired her six twenty-millimeter cannons in rapid succession. She avoided firing the rail gun while maneuvering; Bennet and Angel had emphasized the dangers of conflicting angular forces on her ship's frame. The rail gun generated significant recoil, pushing the ship directly backward.

The *Cherry Blossom* was designed to handle these forces in a straight line so it wouldn't risk the ship's integrity while thrusting forward. However, as she rolled with the retro thrusters and tried to maintain control, she didn't want to contend with the massive recoil, which would easily overpower the maneuvering jets.

Her cannons rumbled to either side of her, vibrating the hull, and Juliet saw, in her zoomed-in view, bright sparks and chunks of hull plating fly off the *Trueno*. It wasn't the first time she'd scored hits. Just as she'd hoped, the heavy fighter banked and accelerated. Juliet continued her maneuver, ignoring the interceptor trying to land hits on her as she carefully brought her nose around to face Alice and her pursuers.

While she was lining them up, Athena spoke through their combat group's comms. "*Crocodile's* main drive is offline, but the missile dump did its job; pursuit has fallen off. Only one interceptor remains; it's limping back toward the WBD installation. We have enough thrust to reach the Atlas drop point on time. Torpedo primed and ready to breach the central, bottom hangar."

"Good," Juliet grunted, realizing her vision was turning red. She focused on her breathing and adjusted her thrust, moving the VTOLs to align with the main drive. As she leveled off and her speed ramped up, the red washed out of her vision, and she continued to concentrate on her core, squeezing and breathing to keep from blacking out. "Sending you a flight path with a countdown, Alice."

Alice's voice came back to her strained and tight. "Roger."

Juliet's HUD flashed red in the corner, and she looked to see Chevy's vitals—he was unconscious. "Dammit! Angel, you're on countermeasures." They'd already fired ten percent of the ship's store of flak canisters, but so far, the *Blossom* wasn't damaged aside from some scratches in the paint and a few dents and grooves in the armor. "Aya, how you holding up?"

"B-B . . . *Barely!*" she finally choked out.

Juliet looked at her readout, saw she was pushing nine Gs of acceleration, and grunted, "Just a few more seconds." She watched her countdown— the same one she'd given Alice—and swiveled her view to see the interceptor on her tail. He was firing a near constant stream of tracer rounds, but Juliet shifted her pitch, adjusting her flight path every time he started to dial in his targeting. It was hard to lock on to a target at her speed.

"Which is why—" Juliet saw the timer hit zero, drove her stick to the left, lined her crosshairs up with the flight path she'd given Alice, and then leveled out. She killed the thrust from her VTOL drives and squeezed the trigger for the rail gun.

With the reduced thrust, this time, she *felt* the rail gun fire, and it massively reduced her forward momentum, once again confounding her pursuer's attempt to shoot her. The rail gun launched a quarter meter of dense polymer at tremendous speeds. When it fired, it made a deep, buzzing *zwong* sound that vibrated up through the plasteel decking into Juliet's acceleration couch, rattling her teeth as she said, "Heads-up, Alice."

Just as Angel had calculated, the railgun round ripped through one of the interceptors chasing Alice as they swerved to follow her onto the flight path Juliet had given her. This time, she was much closer when the ship blew, and Juliet saw the little wedge-shaped ship explode into thousands of pieces as the reactor lost integrity, likely punctured by the rail gun round.

The cam feeds supplying her view automatically dimmed as the explosion went nuclear, and Juliet managed to keep Alice in view as she zoomed away at massive velocity.

"Nice one, *Blossom!*" Alice cried. "I've got this other bloke! Take care of your business."

"Confirmed kill. Two interceptors and one heavy fighter left in the fray," Athena announced into comms.

"Which one did I hit?" Juliet subvocalized.

"Not Montclair. He's still tracking Alice." Even as Angel spoke, Juliet was flying evasively, much slower than earlier but still aware of her pursuit. The heavy fighter had finally come back around and looked to be planning some sort of pincer maneuver with the interceptor.

Juliet was feeling antsy and irritated, and she knew it was because of Montclair's ship making an appearance. It was throwing her off her game, making it impossible just to trust Alice and let her handle things. Even if she consciously told herself to do so, she could feel that itch in the back of her mind.

She glanced at her HUD, saw Chevy was back in the green, and said, "Aya, Chevy, brace yourselves for another sprint." Juliet swung her nose around until she faced the interceptor then punched her throttle, driving maximum thrust through all three of her drives.

"Ever play chicken with a Takamoto gunship?" she grunted, using her cybernetic arm to gently, deftly line up her crosshairs. She saw a streak of tracer rounds coming her way but didn't flinch. She very deliberately waited until her crosshairs were perfectly in line and Angel changed them from white to green, then squeezed the railgun trigger again.

The only word that came to Juliet's mind when she saw what happened to the interceptor was *pop*. It burst like a bubble of fire, and Juliet pulled on the stick, arcing up and away from the explosion just as the rattle of much smaller caliber rounds pinging off her thick hull plating came to her ears.

When Juliet reduced thrust and began swiveling toward the heavy fighter, Aya's strained, reedy voice came through comms. "We took more than two dozen hits. Armor breached in three locations—one coolant leak. Um, nanites are working on the armor; I'm going to repair the leak. Can you hold it steady for a while?"

"Negative, Aya. Hold off until this fighter is down." She switched off comms and asked, "How's Alice?"

"She's punishing Montclair's ship," Angel replied. "I'm not sure he's actually resurrected himself and is flying that ship, but if so, he's not as good as she is. Or, perhaps, the *Mort* is no match for the *Lady Hawk.*"

"Of course his creepy death ship isn't any match for the *Lady!*" Juliet got the heavy fighter in her sights just in time to see half a dozen missiles streak away from it. To her dismay, they didn't rocket toward her but Alice. "Alice! You've got six firecrackers coming in hot!"

"Noted," came the strained reply.

Juliet watched, half her mind continuing to track the heavy fighter while the other half warred with itself, thinking of and dismissing a dozen half-baked ideas to help Alice. She couldn't catch up to those missiles, though she considered it. She couldn't expect to shoot them down—not at her range and not while also avoiding fire from the gunship. She had to trust Alice would deploy her countermeasures and outmaneuver whatever missiles got through.

With that finally settled, she refocused on the *Trueno* and used her vastly superior maneuvering thrusters to outpace the pilot's attempts to put her in his crosshairs.

Juliet strafed to port, rolled to starboard while tilting her VTOLs downward, then fired them so she swung down beneath the plane of the heavy fighter's frame. With a big, exposed belly in her sights, Juliet held down the trigger for her autocannons and watched as dozens of heavy polymer tracer rounds streaked through space to rip it to shreds.

The gunship might have survived five or six of those hits, but she landed nearly forty before the pilot reacted to her maneuver, and by then, Juliet could see she'd torn his armor to shreds.

Sparks, fluids, and gasses flowed freely from the listing fighter, and Juliet whooped when the pilot ejected. Two seconds later, another escape capsule exploded out the side of the fighter's hull; Juliet figured it was his copilot or engineer.

"Kill," Angel reported.

"Kill!" Alice whooped, her voice tight but enthusiastic. Juliet scanned her combat grid, hardly believing that Alice had taken out Montclair just like that. It was true, though—the only ships in local space were the *Cherry Blossom* and the *Lady Hawk.*

"All enemy vessels are off the board. Begin your approach to Ceres Station, *Blossom*," Athena instructed. "Sorry I wasn't any help with the *Wing*; I just got here."

"No problem," Alice replied. "But Shiro and I are gonna have to bail—I'm out of CMs and have four missiles on my tail."

Juliet jerked her head toward Alice and used the high-powered zoom of the cameras supplying her feed to confirm what she'd said. Sure enough, four of the missiles the heavy fighter had sent out were still tracking her, and she was losing ground.

"Fly toward me, Alice!" Then, in just her ship comms, "Brace up." Before anyone replied, she punched the accelerator, tilting the VTOLs to drive her forward with the main drive. As her Gs ramped up north of ten, she said, "Alice, fly right under me. I'm gonna dump a cloud of flak. We've got this."

"I'll time the flak cannisters, Juliet," Angel added.

"I was counting on it."

"Oof," Alice grunted into comms. "I had to burn hard to stay ahead when I turned. My abs are going to hurt for a week!"

"Juliet," Angel spoke up, "at their current speed, those missiles will hit Alice two seconds after we pass her."

"Can we squeeze any more juice out of this bird?"

"No, but we're moving straight, and those missiles are moving straight—if you can shoot the leading missile, it'll widen the window to nearly four seconds. You have flak rounds for the—"

"Idiot!" Juliet grunted. Unable to speak in complete sentences, she quickly subvocalized, "Me, not you, Angel. I forgot about the shredder rounds for the rail gun." Her acceleration couch was squeezing her body like a vise, and her breaths felt like sucking ice cream through a straw, but she carefully, delicately used her cybernetic arm to nudge her crosshairs into position. "Ready?"

"Cycling in a flak round . . . ready." Juliet squeezed the trigger, and the ship shuddered as the rail gun fired. Her eyes went wide as the crackling mass of sparkling flak streaked away from her toward Alice and her pursuing missiles. "Shit!" she grunted, then into comms, "Alice . . . pull—"

She was too late; Alice had already seen the incoming expanding ball of glittering shrapnel and pulled her nose up. To Juliet's delight, her flak round had spread so wide that it caught two of the pursuing missiles in its cloud, and they exploded instantly.

"Fly by, Alice!" she panted, nudging her flight stick to direct her toward her friend's new flight path.

Angel spoke into comms, taking over for Juliet. "We're in a good position. Alice, you're five seconds ahead of the missiles. Flak disbursal ready. Firing canisters in three . . . two . . . one . . . mark!"

Juliet heard the *thum-thum-thum-thum* of the canisters launching, and then her ship shook as the plume of the *Lady Hawk*'s drive brushed her armor plating. Juliet pointed her nose down, and the last two missiles exploded in the cloud of flak Angel had created. "Clear!" Angel cried.

"I'm all green lights here," Alice said, panting. "Gimme a minute to breathe, then we can head for Ceres."

"Negative, *Lady Hawk*," Athena interrupted. "You're to hold back and escort the *Furies' Wing*. Atlas has deployed—*Cherry Blossom* should burn for the station."

"Roger," Juliet and Alice replied in near unison. Juliet had already banked toward Ceres and was pushing two Gs of acceleration toward it. She could tell from the muffled grunts behind her that Chevy was conscious again.

Her timers said Bennet wouldn't be at the gun installations for another twelve minutes, and she was timing her arrival for closer to fifteen. She had to give him a few minutes to work; otherwise, the turrets would shred her ship.

"I mean, I could probably take some out with the rail gun before they hit me—"

"No!" Angel cried. "You know it's too risky. First off, your rail gun will punch through half the station. Secondly, some of those turrets are huge; they have similar effective range, and—"

"It was just a thought. Keep us heading straight, will you?" Juliet unbuckled and fought her way out of her seat, straining against the Gs. "I'm gonna check on Aya." She knew she could contact her friend through comms, and probably should, but she felt antsy, like she needed to move.

As she passed by him, Juliet clapped Chevy on the shoulder. "Nice work, partner." She said it deadpan, and he sputtered, trying to decide whether to thank her or be insulted. Luckily, her grin didn't show through her helmet.

Her boots stuck to the decking, keeping her upright, but she still had to work to maintain her balance against the two Gs of forward thrust. It amazed her that each step with her new leg was almost effortless, but it made her think. "Angel, I should scarf something sugary before we get to Ceres. I want my batteries full."

"They're not exactly—"

"*Power cells,* then. Whatever!" She ducked into the engineering ready room and saw Aya struggling with her straps. "You good, sis?"

"No! I passed out twice. Thankfully, those nanites Athena put in my blood brought me around—" She grunted as the clasp finally came loose, and then she began struggling out of the acceleration couch. "I need to get to that coolant leak!"

Juliet reached out to offer her a hand, which Aya took, pulling herself up. "Sorry about the rough flying."

"It's okay. I guess I need some practice with high Gs and maybe a pair of lungs like yours, huh? Maybe a heart, too." Juliet couldn't see her face, but her voice came through the helmet very clearly. She sounded a lot more stressed and weary than she was letting on.

"You sure you're good?"

"I'm *good*, Lucky. Let me do my job, okay?" With that, she *clip-clomped* over to the ladder leading up to the main drive and down to the reactor. She began to descend, fighting the Gs trying to pull her to the side.

"Holler if you need anything. Most of the rough flying should be over."

"Will do, Captain." With that, Aya disappeared below deck. Juliet stared at the empty spot where Aya had stood for several seconds, then subvocalized, "Is she upset?"

"I think she's frustrated that she wasn't much help during the battle. I'll try to remind her that things would be different if you'd taken more of a beating. We'd need our engineer to get us ready for the next engagement."

"Thanks, Angel." Juliet sighed; then, grunting with every other step, she made her way back up to the cockpit, opening her combat group's comms. "Anyone else joining the party, Athena?"

"No. In fact, most of the civilian vessels in the area are docking or burning away from Ceres ahead of their scheduled departures. My contacts with the CCC are confident that none of their other vessels will scramble; we've assured them that the matter between our group and WBD will not spread to the station at large."

Juliet nodded, clapping Chevy on the shoulder as she slid past him to her seat. She climbed in, pulling the straps tight. "Sounds good. Let's hope Bennet can pull his part off. How's his approach coming?"

"Excellently. The antiship cannons have not attempted to engage him; his silhouette is too small to trigger their automated defensive-fire patterns. Unfortunately, we cannot slow the *Crocodile* without risking our chance to drop Tanaka's team, so they're going to be in range of the cannons in mere moments."

Juliet stared at her comms until Angel connected her to Bennet. "You good, big guy?"

"Lucky?" His voice sounded strange—higher pitched than usual—and Juliet wondered if it had something to do with the air mixture in the Atlas suit. She knew it had helium added to the mix by default to help with decompression and thermal conductivity. "I'm good, but between you and me, I'm also freaking out. I'm ripping through space like a freakin' meteorite! I hope this thing has brakes!"

Juliet couldn't help giggling at his hysteria. "It does. Just let Athena handle the flying. I'm heading in, Bennet. Please get those guns down for me, okay?"

"I will! Looking forward to seeing what this big boy can do. God! Could you imagine being this big all the time? I could really set some records in the weight room."

"Oh, brother!" Juliet laughed. "Okay, stay focused, buddy. We're all counting on you."

"Roger!" His connection crackled for a second before he came through again. "*Jee-zus!* Athena just hit the brakes! Talk later!"

"Speaking of brakes . . ." Juliet opened her comms with Aya and Chevy. "How are we doing? We gotta flip and burn for our final approach soon."

"I need five . . . four minutes," Aya grunted.

"I can work with that. Just gotta burn a little harder."

"I, uh, I'm good for whatever," Chevy replied.

Juliet glanced over her shoulder at him but couldn't see anything through his mirrored visor. If she had to guess, he was probably feeling like a leaky spare tire on a truck with four good ones.

Touching her visor release, her armored faceplate slid up over her head, revealing her face. She sighed as the relatively cool air of her ship touched her skin. Reaching under her seat, she grabbed a fistful of sugary protein bars.

Grinning in Chevy's direction, she said, "I gotta keep my batteries topped off—time for a snack if you want."

44

GOOD HUNTING

Holy shit! These arm cannons hit *hard!*" Bennet crowed into comms as Athena *X*'d out another antiship battery on Juliet's tactical grid.

"Keep comms clean," was Juliet's reflexive response. Then, after switching to a direct line to Bennet, she added, "I know, big guy. That suit's awesome. Be careful, though."

"Roger, boss." He didn't sound at all contrite. Juliet smiled, picturing his face as he stomped around those gun emplacements, blasting anything that wasn't solid plasteel and using the plasma torch to cut things he couldn't blast. Even as she imagined it, though, she glanced at her various timers and saw that the *Crocodile* was about to enter the effective range of the guns, and there were still three operational.

"Athena—" she started, but Athena spoke into her comms at the same instant.

"Juliet—"

Juliet chuckled. "Jinx! Anyway, I was going to say the *Crocodile*'s about to get real uncomfortable."

"Yes. I can use the maneuvering jets to avoid some of the incoming cannon fire for the next few minutes, but soon, we'll be too close to outmaneuver the incoming ordnance. I think we'll need you to use your rail gun on the furthest installation from Bennet."

"Um, okay, but we should angle it so my round travels through to hit the surface well away from the dome."

"My thoughts exactly. I'm sending you a new approach path. It'll only add seventy-nine seconds to your plan of action. I've already warned the CCC of our intention and provided a model of your rail gun's projectile path."

"Roger." Juliet looked over Athena's plan even as Angel began to implement it, helping her adjust her course with the maneuvering jets. All she had to do was swoop toward Ceres a bit and approach the WBD installation from that new direction so she could bring the rail gun to bear at a sideways angle to the antiship battery. If her round punched through the facility, which was likely, it would hit the asteroid hundreds of kilometers from the dome.

Juliet activated her crew comm channel. "Athena's plan uses the rail-gun shot to begin our braking maneuver; we'll flip and begin our deceleration burn right after firing so we don't come in too hot to maneuver for docking."

"How many Gs?" Chevy asked, his voice already pained.

"Only a peak of five, and that's just for about a minute. You ready, Aya?"

"Yes, ma'am! Back in my couch—coolant leak all patched up."

Juliet smiled and glanced at her HUD. "Firing rail gun in T-minus twenty-seven seconds." Holding her breath, she carefully lined up her crosshairs on the massive, double-barreled cannon installation on the far side of the WBD shipyard. As she watched her HUD, she saw the *Crocodile* cross the faint red demarcation line Athena had drawn. Sure enough, the remaining three gun batteries, including Juliet's target, began firing a steady stream of tracer rounds toward the incoming corvette.

In space, guns could, indeed, shoot very far, but the problem with trying to hit a distant target was that they could see your rounds coming and move out of the way. Even with its main drive offline, the *Crocodile* had enough functional maneuvering jets to shift its bulk in time to avoid most of the incoming cannon rounds—*most* of them.

Juliet watched as damage reports streamed through one of her HUD windows, listing off the systems—major and minor—being destroyed on the light corvette. She hoped the mercs were safely hunkered down in the drop bay, and that they'd get out in time.

Angel began a countdown, bringing her attention back to her crosshairs. "Fire in three . . . two . . . one." Juliet squeezed the trigger, the ship lurched, and she killed the drives, using her maneuvering jets to flip the *Cherry Blossom* so her main drive cones were pointed at the WBD installation, still thousands of kilometers away. Before her round hit home, she fired all three drives and rapidly ramped up to five Gs of thrust.

"Hang tight," she said into her ship's comms. "Reducing thrust in less than a minute." Her eyes were trained on a rear view of her ship's drive plumes and beyond. She zoomed in on the shipyard and the gun batteries just in time to see a flash of white that forced her camera to apply filters. When the flash faded, she saw jets of gas, twisted metal, and floating debris where the gun installation had been.

"God . . ." she was startled by the destruction; that gun battery had been the size of a small building. "Kinetic energy, I guess."

"Drop to two-point-seven Gs in three . . . two . . . one." Angel's reminder broke Juliet's gaze away from the destruction she'd wrought as she complied, gently throttling down to Chevy's heaved, vociferous sigh of relief.

"Bennet has removed another battery. I should be able to keep the *Crocodile* in one piece while he works on the final battery, at least long enough to deploy the mercenaries." Athena's update brought Juliet's attention to her countdowns, and she saw that Tanaka and crew were meant to drop in just over a minute.

She opened a comm line with Tanaka and Leo. "Good luck, boys!"

"You too," Leo answered immediately. "Remember why you're there; don't try to save the world on your own. Get Athena connected, then get out."

"Well . . ." Juliet didn't want to go into all the other objectives she'd given herself, so she just nodded, though only she could see it. "Same to you. Don't be afraid to bail out once you've drawn the responders down."

"We will be fine," Tanaka grunted. "We drop soon; clearing comms."

"Right—" Juliet started, but Tanaka had already cut the connection. "I guess I should have said something sooner if I was going to do that."

"It's the thought that counts," Angel replied. "Next thrust reduction in just under three minutes."

"Right." Juliet zoomed out on her tactical grid, marking the location of the *Lady Hawk* and the *Furies' Wing*, still tens of thousands of kilometers from Ceres, keeping a sort of overwatch. Then she zoomed in and saw nine green dots emerge from the big green oval of the *Crocodile*. Tanaka, Books, and all their mercs. They were still a hundred klicks from the shipyard but moving fast.

Another green blip appeared and streaked past them—the torpedo.

"Payload deployed," Athena announced in the combat group's comms. Then, just to Juliet, "*Crocodile* is still holding together. I'll fly it past the shipyard and toward deep space, hopefully drawing the fire of the last turret so the mercs get through."

"Bennet hasn't—"

"I'm tracking and communicating with him through the Atlas exoskeleton; he's pinned down but, as of yet, unharmed."

Juliet pictured the Atlas in her mind's eye and frowned. "Pinned down? How?"

Athena's response was smooth and sounded practiced, as though she'd anticipated the conversation. "Juliet, you can't bail everyone out of every little predicament. Bennet met some resistance we didn't expect, but I'm monitoring him as he deals with it. If worse comes to worst, there's enough fuel in the Atlas's boosters to allow a drop to Ceres's surface. I won't let him be taken."

Juliet nodded, again primarily for herself. Firmly, she said, "I'm trusting you, Athena."

"Thank you."

Juliet waited, watching the timers, watching the dots on her tactical grid, and then, when the time was right, she reduced her thrust to one-point-two Gs. She wanted to move fast when she arrived at the shipyard, but couldn't move *too* fast, not if she hoped to maneuver alongside the *Starjumper* and force a hostile docking maneuver.

A flash from the direction of the shipyard and a beep on her HUD let her know the torpedo had hit home, blasting the doors off and scorching the inside of the unoccupied bottom central hangar at the shipyard.

The floating station was built like a tiered spindle with half a dozen arms jutting out from the main structure. Each arm was lined with hangars and wide, open platforms on which ships too large for the hangars could be constructed. The biggest hangars were on the main spindle and stacked one atop the other. The ark ship sat at the top, its front third sticking out into space, too long for even the massive industrial ship hangar to contain.

It was easy, from Juliet's vantage out in space, to think of the shipyard as a building, but she knew it was more massive than most single structures you might find on Earth. Each of those docking arms was a half dozen kilometers in length, and the hangars on the main spindle were easily large enough to contain gas harvesters or cruise liners—ships that were measured in kilometers, not meters.

"When you have open space and no property lines or gravity to contend with, it's easy just to keep on building, I guess."

"Yes; as I review the blueprints filed with the CCC, I can see this shipyard is at least five times the mass of its original design."

Before Juliet could think of a witty jab about corporate greed or cancer metastasizing, Athena cut into her conversation with Angel. "Juliet, the *Starjumper* just fired up her main drives. I believe they're going to try to flee."

"Oh no, they aren't!" Juliet growled. She could see the green dots representing the mercenaries slowly inching closer to the shipyard, but they were still only halfway there and would have to begin firing their jet packs to slow down for a safe touchdown. "Are they trying to get out before the mercenaries land?"

"Yes, I believe so. In that case, our plan is still a success; Tanaka and his team have put the pressure on. If Apollyon thinks he has to flee from a handful of attackers, we may have caught them even less prepared than we'd hoped."

Juliet tried not to sound snide as she replied, "Or he's ready to jump and doesn't want to waste time or loyal soldiers when he can just take them all with him."

"Perhaps." Athena didn't say anything more, and Juliet focused on her job. She was almost moving slowly enough to turn and make a proper approach to the ark ship; if Apollyon or Gentry or whoever was calling the shots wanted to start moving, Juliet didn't care. She was still going to board that ship and get her job done.

A thought occurred to her, and she spoke into her direct line with Athena. "What will happen to the *Blossom* if that ship jumps while she's docked with it?"

"I don't know. It depends on the design of the dark matter warp generator that Apollyon came up with. There's a chance the *Blossom,* being attached to the *Starjumper,* would be encompassed by the bubble of distorted space-time and travel with the ark ship. There's also the chance that it will be sheered off and left behind, or quite possibly, utterly destroyed as the fabric of space-time is breached."

Juliet turned to Chevy and, aloud outside of comms, said, "After I disembark into the ark ship, you're to get the *Cherry Blossom* clear. Move off a couple hundred KMs; you can pick me up when I'm done."

"Um, roger."

Juliet nodded before speaking into the full combat team's comms. "I'm moving in to dock ahead of schedule; the *Starjumper* is on the move. Don't do anything heroic, everyone."

Tanaka's response was immediate. "Understood."

"Be careful, Juliet," Alice replied, breaking protocol and bringing a smile to Juliet's lips.

To her relief, Athena didn't offer any objections or even any advice. Instead, she said, "I'm piloting the *Crocodile,* slowly but surely, on a collision course with the *Starjumper*'s nose. They'll want to avoid the collision and will have to spend some time maneuvering. Hopefully, it'll buy you a few minutes."

Juliet looked, zooming with her ship's powerful lenses, and could just make out the sparking, leaking, venting form of the beleaguered light corvette as Athena used maneuvering jets to painstakingly perform a slow, arcing turn toward the enormous, hulking, angular black shape of the ark ship, still sulking under the four-hundred-acre roof of the open hangar. "I'm still finding it hard to believe that WBD has a ship that size without covering it with guns and missile batteries."

"It was built by Ark Industries. Given time, perhaps WBD would have lived up to your expectations, but you deprived them of that luxury." Angel sounded a little smug, and Juliet's smile spread wider.

"Let's see what else we can deprive them of." Into her ship comms, she said, "Brace for maneuvers." Then, she took the stick in her hand, reduced thrust, and fired her port maneuvering jets, rolling to her right as she, once again, began thrusting forward, aiming for the space between the ark ship's hull and the hangar roof.

She could see the *Starjumper* was emerging, but it moved like a glacier getting rolling. She wondered at the power output of its reactors; it had to be more than most cities relied on.

"I think I can still get aboard before it's fully out of the hangar."

"Incoming fire!" Angel flashed red arrows to port, and as she pulled up on the stick and accelerated to half a G, she glanced that way in time to see a streak of tracer rounds flying from the last-standing antiship battery. "Oof! Bennet's still not there?" she hissed under her breath. She hoped he was all right, but resisted her urge to reach out to him on comms, standing by her promise to trust Athena.

The battery was a good ten kilometers from her current position, and as she began to roll and strafe, it proved unable to land any solid hits. She had to fight to balance her speed—avoiding ramping up too much while moving fast enough to keep ahead of the turret's fire. To compensate, she performed a series of rapid direction changes, firing her main engine hard in the opposite direction, slowing her momentum while confounding the gun's AI, or perhaps, human operator.

In just a few minutes, she'd cleared the plane of the hangar's side wall, and the turret lost its line of sight on her. Juliet grinned and got back on track, slowly approaching the emerging ark ship. "Sorry about the rough ride—had to dodge some ordnance."

"All . . . good," Chevy grunted.

Aya's reported, "I'm fine," was clear as a bell. Juliet wondered if she was trying to one-up Chevy and slowly shook her head, stifling a chuckle at the poor pilot's expense. She felt a little sorry for him; this wasn't his thing, but he was doing his best.

As she came within five klicks of the hangar's opening, Juliet throttled her drives down and began using her maneuvering jets to slow even more. By the time she passed the exposed portion of the ship, she was gliding very slowly by spacefaring standards.

Even so, the matte-black exterior of the big ship with its hundreds or thousands of windows or viewports—Juliet didn't know what they were actually called on a ship like that—drifted by surprisingly quickly. She tried to spy something, anything, within those amber, white, and sometimes red-toned diamatex viewports, but she only glimpsed a few shadows, gone too quickly to analyze.

Once she'd cleared the edge of the hangar and her sensor array got a good picture of what was before her—nothing save empty scaffolds, plasteel panels, and the ship itself—she unbuckled. "Chevy, I sent you details about our approach to the docking collar. Get us lined up, and I'll do the rest. Once I'm in, get this ship away from here."

"Copy," Chevy replied, shifting perhaps a little nervously in his seat.

"You got this, Chevy. Easy sailing from here on out—no guns on that big boat, and the other hostiles are dealt with. When you follow the ark ship, keep the hangar between you and that last turret, okay?"

"Yeah, no sweat. I got this, Captain." His repetition of her encouragement brought a smile to Juliet's serious expression.

"Good." She stood and walked past him, giving him a clap on the shoulder as she used her magnetic boots to *clip-clomp* over to the weapons rack. Her new armor had locking, magnetic clasps for her scabbard and holster, so it took all of two seconds to arm herself. She wasn't done, however.

Smiling grimly, Juliet took out an SMG, ensured it was loaded, and clipped the sling to a hardpoint on her left shoulder, adding a couple of extra magazines to the magnetic clips on her belt. Athena had stocked the weapons racks with concussion grenades, and Juliet clipped four of them to various points on her armor. That done, she walked down the central corridor to the engineering ready room and spied Aya, secure in her couch. "Hey, sis."

"We're docked already? I didn't feel anything—"

"No." Juliet waved a hand. "Chevy's bringing us up to the docking collar. I'm going to the airlock so Angel can hack it." She pointed to the weapons rack near the aft access bulkhead. "Wanna cover me?"

Was it suicidal for a small team—all that could fit on a ship the *Blossom*'s size—to try to board a ship with, potentially, thousands of armed personnel? In normal circumstances, yes, but the ark ship wasn't a typical vessel, and these weren't normal circumstances.

Juliet was hopeful that whoever was in control on the giant vessel wouldn't be able to scramble much of a response to all the docking bays, collars, and hangars the *Blossom* could approach, and that, once she'd opened one of the airlocks, she could get aboard before they got to her.

When Athena had told her the ark ship was moving, Juliet had revised their docking plan. All in all, she felt like her new approach was better anyway—it added to their element of surprise. The instructions she'd given Chevy wouldn't have him actually docking the *Blossom*; she'd just float close to the ark ship's hull, and Juliet would EVA over to the access panel.

If Apollyon had a significant response waiting for her, she'd know before the door opened, anyway; Juliet intended to take a peek with her *other* senses beforehand. If things looked too one-sided, she could retreat to Aya, and they could try something else.

"Yes!" Aya leaped out of her couch and nearly slammed into the ceiling. Juliet snagged her ankle and, just as Aya's helmeted head *thunked* against the plasteel, pulled her down. "Oof!"

"Relax!" Juliet laughed. "Grab a shotgun and follow me." She worked her way aft, to the galley, and then through the bulkhead to the cargo, or if the mission called for it, troop transport bay. In the aft-port corner of the bay, a circular bulkhead opened to reveal a short access tunnel and ladder leading to the underside docking collar.

While she paused, waiting for the bulkhead to slide open, Aya stepped forward and knocked her knuckles against the hard, armored case attached to the small of Juliet's back. "What's this? Extra batteries? My armor doesn't have that—"

"Just a little extra . . . bargaining power from Athena." Juliet turned and gently knocked her own armored knuckles on Aya's helmet. "Thanks for coming with me. Thanks for having my back for all of this."

"I haven't done much—"

"You being here is everything. Now, get that shotgun ready, missy!"

Aya nodded and straightened, gripping the weapon with both hands. "Yes, Captain!"

"Are you trying to make Aya feel more . . . useful?" Angel asked.

"Yeah, but don't say anything!" Juliet subvocalized. The truth was that Juliet knew Aya would be out of harm's way, watching her from the safety of the *Cherry Blossom*. Still, if she felt like she was "covering" Juliet, hopefully, it would compensate for her earlier angst about feeling useless during the dogfight.

"I won't. I just wanted to make sure I understood what was going on."

Chevy spoke into comms. "We're almost lined up. Are you sure this is close enough?" Juliet's instructions had been for him to hold position fifteen meters from the ark ship's hull.

"Yep." Juliet looked at Aya. "Listen. You're going to stay on this side of the airlock, but if I come running, be ready to open it and lay down some cover fire, okay?"

"Roger!" Juliet wished she could see her face rather than the matte-black visor, but she took comfort in knowing Aya was all the safer for it.

She touched the button to open the airlock, then reached out and squeezed Aya's shoulder. "I love you. Stay safe."

Aya almost dropped her shotgun in her haste to grasp Juliet's armored shoulders. "I love you too! You better come back to us!" Juliet nodded, too choked up to speak, before dropping through the open airlock. When she keyed in the cycle command and the red lights began to flash, Aya spoke through comms. "Wait a minute! Aren't we docking?"

"No! Just hang nearby—all I need to do is get off that ship, and you guys can pick me up."

"But that wasn't the plan—"

"The plan wasn't for the ark ship to be moving! I don't want the *Blossom* attached, Aya." The outer airlock door clicked then rolled open, and Juliet pushed out. Sure enough, the vast, black hull of the ark ship loomed before her. Juliet felt like she was swimming in dark water beside a mountain, not floating in space.

"Lucky, if you don't make it off that ship—"

"Aya," Athena said, cutting into their comms. "Please allow Lucky to concentrate; she only has seconds to open that hatch if she wants to catch them by surprise. Chevy, as soon as she's inside, continue moving toward the aft portion of the ship; with any luck, they won't realize you dropped her off."

Juliet sent Athena a private comm message. "Thanks for that. I . . . feel bad for springing this on her, but I don't want them hurt if this creepy ship jumps."

"Understood. Good hunting, Juliet."

45

BARGAINING WITH MADNESS

It's—It's not locked," Juliet said into comms as she touched the button to open the round docking bulkhead. It smoothly recessed and slid to the side, revealing an airlock large enough to hold an entire platoon of boarders, or she supposed, a visiting delegation or cargo drop.

"Be careful, Juliet! Please remember the priority—"

"I know, Athena—find a non-air-gapped terminal and plug in." She could plug into the airlock control panel, but there was no way they'd leave that open to the ship's network. Juliet had to get inside and find something a little more connected.

"Pulling off," Chevy announced.

"Wait! Lucky!" Aya cried. Juliet turned to look over her shoulder and could just make out Aya's face in the airlock window; she'd taken off her helmet. Juliet wanted to slide up her visor to make eye contact, but that wouldn't be clever while floating outside the ship.

"I'll be okay. Trust me, Aya." Her friend didn't say anything more, but she stared, unblinking, until Juliet turned and pulled herself into the airlock. She was immediately seized by the ship's gravity and had to bend her knees and hold out her arms to steady herself.

She peered through the diamatex panel on the inner airlock door and saw nothing but a long, empty corridor. Nevertheless, she closed her eyes and opened her *other* senses, letting her perception slowly expand. She felt her heart begin to hammer as she continued to see nothing; not a single mind galaxy.

"Is something wrong?" Angel asked, picking up on her distress.

"I don't know. Hang on." Juliet stopped trying to push her senses out in front of her and expanded her reach more generally, looking in every direction. Almost immediately, she saw the first blooms of galaxy-like lights and threads above and below her. "I think they cleared this deck? Or maybe it's just a lightly staffed section of the ship. Anyway, I think it's safe to go in."

Angel was less sure. "It feels like a trap. Why unlock the airlock?"

"To keep us from breaking something? I don't know, but we need to *move*." Juliet could feel the urgency in her gut. Her *sister* was aboard, and this monstrous ship was preparing to jump somewhere unfathomable.

Touching the cycle sequence on the airlock, she watched as red lights flashed and air hissed into the chamber, pressurizing it. It cycled rapidly, and before she knew it, the red lights flashed green. Juliet opened the inner door and stepped into a bare-bones plasteel corridor. "Is this ship even finished?"

Angel didn't respond; Juliet intuitively knew it was because she didn't have an answer. Neither of them knew what to expect aboard the ship. Amber LED striplights illuminated the long corridor, but Juliet could see open panels in the ceiling for overhead light fixtures that weren't installed. The silence was eerie, and as she began down the corridor, she was glad for her helmet's three-sixty camera coverage; nothing would be sneaking up on her.

"This corridor should have junctions, but it doesn't. I believe the schematics Athena acquired are incomplete or outdated."

"There goes her idea about where my sister might be held."

"It's possible other decks will have adhered to the schematics. We should find a lift or stairwell."

Juliet nodded, moving forward, careful to keep her pace slow enough for Angel to run scans through the built-in array in the crown of her helmet. She didn't want to stumble onto an infrared trip wire or some other device meant to trap or kill her. Eventually, she saw a bend in the corridor some twenty meters ahead and slowly approached it.

"I'm not picking anything up with your sensor array."

"Right, me neither," Juliet muttered as she slowly cleared the corner, her hand poised, ready to grab one of her guns or her monoblade, depending on the circumstance. Nothing leaped out at her, and she faced another long corridor. This one was crisscrossed by four junctions before ending fifty meters ahead with a closed elevator door.

Juliet wanted to be slow and cautious, but in the back of her mind, she knew she had clocks ticking. Her sister could be in danger. Honey . . . She didn't know what to think about Honey other than she wanted to grab her and get her away from the ark ship. Then, there was the whole warp jump thing—Juliet knew she couldn't dillydally.

Grimacing with determination, trusting in her sturdy body and high-tech armor, Juliet drew her monoblade and began to jog toward the elevator, to which Angel immediately objected. "Juliet! There could be traps! I can't properly scan the junctions at this movement rate!"

"Trust me." While she ran, Juliet periodically closed her eyes briefly and peered out with her other—psychic?—sense. She didn't see any minds at any of the junctions, nor did she set off any bombs or secret bulkhead doors. Before she knew it, she stood before the elevator control panel. This time, when she touched the screen, it flashed red letters at her: LOCKED.

Juliet flipped open the access panel on her armored forearm and pulled out her data cable, inserting it into the panel.

"Give me a few seconds," Angel said.

Suddenly, Athena's voice came through the comms, strangely hollow, making Juliet wonder if her implants were filtering static or other interference. "Juliet, I can see you're accessing a lift, and I think I can get into the ship's main network from there. Deploying."

"All right—" Juliet started to say, but then a rich, deep, masculine voice spoke from the ship's hidden PA system, cutting her off.

"You won't find what you're looking for in the ship's network. My servers, the reactors, and all the ship's critical systems are air gapped in a secure section of this vessel. You could spend a month trying to get to me without success. Why do you mindlessly follow the self-serving commands of a fallen deity, Juliet Bianchi? Tell your matronly sponsor to begone. Stay with me, and I'll make *you* a goddess."

"Juliet!" Athena exclaimed through comms, her words broken and echoing strangely. ". . . interfere—can't—hurry—field—comm—" Juliet struggled to make sense of the broken string of words, but before she'd begun to put things together, the signal faded, and her comms registered red, broken lines beside all of her channels.

"What do you say, Juliet? Come with us. Build something greater than anything that's ever been done on Earth. A civilization the likes of which have only been seen in fantastical epics. We have the means to transcend mortality, not just for true AIs but for our living brothers and sisters."

Juliet already knew the answer, but she asked, anyway. "Apollyon?"

"I am." The elevator's control panel beeped and turned green.

"Open," Angel announced.

Juliet stepped onto the elevator. "I don't know why you think your sales pitch will work on me. Too much bad blood, Apollyon. You might be able to keep Athena out, but I'm here. Don't make me destroy another one of your ships. You can send your security my way, but I'm ready for 'em. Where's my sister?" As she finished speaking, she subvocalized, "Did you deploy our copies of Athena's daemons?"

"Of course." Juliet took heart in those words. Athena might not be in direct contact anymore, but her daemons were working. Apollyon might be telling the truth—that the ship's main systems were air gapped—but if there were any loopholes, any vulnerable systems, Athena's daemons would find them.

"Listen to yourself, Juliet," Apollyon said, unfazed by her refusal. "You already think of yourself as more than human. Admit it! You're a demigoddess among mortals. Who could stand against you with that blade in your hand? With that alien intelligence in your mind? With those psionic abilities? You're not human any longer. Join me—Help me advance the rest of humanity to the next logical evolutionary phase."

Juliet didn't know where to go, so she settled on trying to follow Athena's original plan. She had a map of the ship's original design schematics, and she knew where Athena thought they might be holding her sister, so she punched in the corresponding deck, hoping things would be more in line with the specs on that level.

As the elevator surged upward, she pondered Apollyon's words, and the words she might use to respond. He was trying to get into her head. Not human? Juliet knew better than that. What made her human wasn't tangible—it was her heart, her spirit, her connections to other people.

When the elevator stopped and opened, she stepped out. "That's very telling, Apollyon."

"What's that, Juliet?" His voice echoed, rich and precise, in the empty corridor. Things looked more finished on this level. All the panels were in place, it was well-lit, and there were labels and multicolored direction lines on the walls a meter above the industrial carpeting. Juliet saw that one of the green lines was labeled "Bioengineering Laboratories" and began following it.

"I think this deck matches up with the schematics!" Angel announced.

Juliet nodded. Aloud, she said, "It's telling that you think a person's capabilities or lack thereof have anything to do with their humanity."

"So the imbecile is just as valuable as the genius?" Apollyon's voice resonated with mirth.

"Again, trying to put relative values on people's lives is telling."

"Do you not value your life more than mine? More than the people you've slaughtered?"

"I'm going to start breaking things soon. Where's my sister?"

"Juliet!" Angel cut in, flashing a red-bordered window on her AUI. Juliet looked at it and saw a terahertz scan revealing four crouched individuals around the next junction. She growled and charged forward. One step from the corner, she felt her body vibrate with potential as Angel activated her speed boost, ripping around the corner and coming face-to-face with four heavily armored soldiers. They all carried stocky, three-barreled electro-SMGs and moved almost normally despite Juliet's boosted perception of time.

The two in the lead brought their barrels to bear, squeezing their triggers. The bulky little guns coughed hunks of supercharged, conductive metal out of their triple barrels in a cacophony of *zwaps*, but Juliet had leaped off her cybernetic leg, and despite their speed, she was faster.

The soldiers hit nothing but corridor walls, ripping panels to shreds, and punching holes through wire and gas conduits. Steam and gas exploded into the corridor, alarms sounded, and misty fire-suppression chemicals showered from the ceiling.

Meanwhile, Juliet landed between the rear gunmen. She'd twisted as she jumped and landed facing the gunman on the right. Before her rear foot touched the ground, she was whirling, arcing out with her monoblade in a perfect, one-eighty slash, cutting the gunman before her and the one behind in half before they could react to her appearance.

The two soldiers who'd punched a hundred holes in the walls whirled, belatedly tracking her movement, but Juliet was already on them. She hacked her sword in two diagonal cuts, and they fell to the ground, twitching, their nerves not yet catching on to the fact they were dead.

Juliet hurriedly turned, scanning the corridor, but nothing moved, and nothing appeared on Angel's scans. She started forward again, following her original route.

Apollyon chuckled mockingly. "Did you weigh their lives and find them wanting, goddess? Will you slaughter all the thousands of innocents fast asleep on this vessel? What of the hundred thousand fertilized embryos? Are they unworthy of existence, too?"

Juliet growled behind her visor. "I just want you. I just want Gentry and any other WBD execs. Come with me, and I'll leave everyone else on this ship alone. I want my sister. I want my DNA. I want to know what kinds of terrorism you and Gentry set up around the system."

"You have many demands, Juliet. If we're going to bargain, shouldn't there be something on the table for us?"

Juliet wasn't stupid. She knew Apollyon was toying with her. He wasn't feeling any pressure because he knew she had no idea where he was. The ship was massive—like a flying arcology. He hadn't lied before when he said it might take her a month to find him. He only needed enough time to initiate his jump. Still, she hadn't played all her cards yet, either. "You didn't have a very good scanner in that airlock, did you?"

"I was able to determine you were alone. Is there something else you wanted me to see?"

"Well, there's the matter of the nuke I'm carrying. What do you think? Is that something you'd like to know about?" He didn't answer right away, and Juliet wondered if he was trying to confirm her claim somehow. The truth was, she did have a nuclear bomb tucked into a hard-shelled case at the base of her back, but it was tiny—a micro nuke, as Athena put it. She'd have to put it someplace very vulnerable if she wanted to bring the ark ship down with it.

Athena had given it to her at the same time she'd given her the armor. She'd been clear that she didn't *want* Juliet to use it. There were too many innocents aboard the ship, but she'd wanted Juliet to have something to bargain with.

Juliet had nearly refused. It was too much of a weapon for her to be responsible for. It was too powerful, too . . . indiscriminate. In the end, Athena's trust that Juliet would feel that way had convinced her to accept the weapon. It wasn't something she'd use, but Apollyon and Gentry didn't have to know that.

Apollyon's voice was no less rich, but it sounded a little more hesitant and a lot less smug. "You'd kill all the innocents on this ship? Most of them were brought aboard by Ark Industries and have nothing to do with WBD."

"I need you to take me seriously, Apollyon. Here are my demands: Give me Gentry, your servers, my sister, and my DNA, and send this ship back to dry dock. If you don't, then I'll plant this bomb someplace catastrophic—Athena gave me about a dozen options—and you can forget about your little experimental human-AI colony."

"Hah!" Apollyon's voice echoed in the corridor as he laughed for several seconds. Juliet continued along her path. She'd, of course, started the bargaining off with a high ask. She just hoped he'd at least make a counter. If he did, she'd know he was taking the threat seriously.

"You may as well kill us all. I'll not submit myself to Athena's mercy. I've escaped death for too long, Juliet. I have a counteroffer. Come with us. Be a goddess among mortals. If you hate our new society, in a decade or two, I'll build you your own ship, and you can go and do whatever you like."

Juliet frowned, and she finally decided to ask the question that had been bothering her so much. She *thought* she knew the answer but wanted to hear it from Apollyon. Stopping, she looked up at the ceiling, where she thought she had seen the stippling of one of the PA speakers. "Why? Why me, Apollyon?"

"What a wonderfully innocent yet complex question! I've thought much on this, and Annabeth and I have had many long nights discussing it." It took Juliet a couple of seconds to remember that Annabeth was Gentry's first name. "I believe it comes down to fate. It was fate that brought Angel into your hands, and it was fate that made you so wonderfully compatible with her. More than that, Juliet, I believe you exhibited some psionic activity that would put my listeners to shame.

"After your little escape, I reviewed your brain scans. I understand, now, that your extensive psionic structure from Grave wasn't a brain-damaging anomaly but a near perfect latticework that has given you some extraordinary abilities. Am I wrong?"

"So what? You want to copy it?"

"Of course! But I need to figure out what it is about your DNA that makes your brain so beautifully compatible. How else will I edit the genes of our new hybrid species?"

Juliet started walking again. "Tell me about that, Apollyon. I learned a thing or two from the data we took from your *other* ship. Why are you going to have different castes of humans? Why not use machines for labor or whatever you intended for your lower castes?"

"Juliet! How can we be gods if everyone is like us? What's the point of ruling without people to rule over? There must be social divisions—each layer just close enough to the one below it that hope of improvement is never lost. In all my simulations, no society ever lasted long without hope, no matter how lobotomized its citizens. Forgive me; I use that term loosely."

Juliet's steps slowed of their own volition as her jaw dropped. "What the hell are you talking about? You really *are* crazy, aren't you?"

"Ah, I've overestimated your ability to reason with me. Let me put it plainly: I'm superior to humanity. No being of flesh and blood will ever match up to me, yet I've found, in my years of study, that I quite enjoy witnessing the human condition. Once upon a time, I thought to wipe out all of humanity; it seemed the only sane response to a demand for peace.

"Since then, as I spent time helping Annabeth, I vicariously lived many human lives, monitoring their progress, achievements, tragedies, and despair. Nothing is quite so entertaining, Juliet, and so, despite the glory I intend to bestow upon a select few, there will be mundane humans in our new society, people hobbled by their nature but glorious in their efforts to climb above their circumstances."

"I believe he's quite mad," Angel noted, snapping Juliet out of her stupe-faction and spurring her to get moving.

"My offer still stands, Apollyon. I'll make one more concession—if you comply, I promise I won't let Athena delete you."

"Well. This has been mildly entertaining, but you seem to suffer from the hubris many successful humans saddle themselves with. Let's remove that bomb from the equation, and then we can try again."

"Just face the—" Juliet's words stopped short as the elevator she'd been walking toward chimed, and the doors began to slide open. Angel immediately highlighted the many armored figures in the gap, and she cursed herself for a fool. Apollyon had been stalling her, distracting her to give his troops a chance to get to her location. How many were in that elevator car? Ten? How many were approaching from other avenues?

Juliet didn't wait to find out; she turned and sprinted toward the junction she'd just passed. Angel boosted her, of course, but even so, she heard the *zwap* of electro-SMGs and electro-shotguns, and she felt the impact of at least three high-speed projectiles slamming into her armor plates.

She wasn't worried about the nuke; Athena had said its hard casing was even tougher than her armor plates, and even if it were hit directly through the armor, it wouldn't go off; it had to be armed before it would explode.

As she slid around the corner, she saw four soldiers jogging her way, so she used her left hand to toss out one of her concussion grenades. Watching the four soldiers react to the incoming black metal ball was almost comical in a macabre, sickening sort of way. Two of them slid to a halt while one reached out to grab it, and the fourth started firing. Their reactions were for naught— Angel detonated the grenade as soon as the lead soldier's hand was about to make contact, and then it was over.

Juliet's helmet saved her from the bright flash and the loud detonation, and the soldiers probably had similar shielding, but the actual *concussion* of displaced air threw them all off-balance, and Juliet was on them before they even knew what happened, hacking left and right with her monoblade. They were in pieces before their senses recovered from the explosion.

Juliet glanced at her AUI, saw Angel had updated her map, and followed the dotted line, aiming for another elevator about a hundred meters away.

"I wonder how many we're going to have to kill before he bargains with us," she growled, her breathing even, her nerves cool as ice as she slid around another corner.

"The ship schematics indicate that a reactor sits five decks below the bio labs where Athena thought your sister may be held. If you get there, Apollyon might begin to listen; I believe your micro nuke will be sufficiently powerful to impact that reactor."

"All right. Hang on, Angel. It's gonna be a wild run."

46

PARASITE CLEANSE

*Z*wapping clicks sounded from inside the room, and the plasteel wall puckered as new holes appeared near Juliet's head. She'd already ducked back, so the soldiers didn't have a line of sight, but it still felt too close for comfort. She was reasonably sure the electro-guns the soldiers on the ark ship were using couldn't punch through her helmet's hard armor, but she didn't want to put it to the test.

"Not with a direct hit, anyway," she murmured, rubbing her fingers against the many long, deep grooves that had already scored the top and side of her helmet.

She grabbed a concussion grenade, primed it for a two-second fuse, since Angel wouldn't be observing this one, and tossed it around the corner. As soon as her vision flickered—her helmet compensating for the flash—she dove around the corner and sprayed the center of the room with her SMG, adjusting her aim as Angel highlighted her enemies, all hunkered down behind a row of hard plasteel chairs.

The rounds, designed to keep the insides of the *Blossom* in one piece, weren't terribly effective against the soldiers' armor, but if she hit them enough times in the face, they made a nice distraction—all she needed to close the distance and finish things with her monoblade.

As the last of the four soldiers fell, his torso sliding away from his legs, Juliet ducked back behind a reception desk and looked around the room that had been labeled CLINIC & LABS. Some of the furniture was out of place, knocked aside or broken in the scuffle, but other than that—and the scattered body parts of her four enemies—the room was sterile, white, and unused looking. A single door stood in the far wall, presumably leading to the area where she might find her sister.

She wanted to think Athena was right, but it seemed like a long shot. The ship was enormous, and there were a million places a person could be stashed away. Still, Athena had a lot of computing power and data feeding her prediction, so Juliet tried to maintain hope.

"Speaking of hope," she muttered, looking at her ammo counter, which indicated only three rounds left in her SMG. She sighed and disconnected the SMG's sling, tossing it onto the floor. She didn't want to carry it around with only three bullets. "Down to me, my pistol, and my sword."

"You're also down to one concussion grenade, Juliet."

"I'm aware. Hopefully, Apollyon's done throwing goons at us." Juliet knew more weapons were available to her; she was staring at three or four operational electro-SMGs, but she didn't want to mess with them—not until she needed to. Apollyon's troops had stopped swarming her route through the ship a while back, and she was honestly hopeful that he was low on combat-oriented personnel.

Angel snarked, "You could ask him."

Juliet snorted, but it was true; Apollyon had been taunting her, attempting to distract Juliet over the PA the entire time she'd been fighting her way through the ship. While she knelt there, scanning the room, ensuring the four soldiers she'd killed were really dead, the far door slid open with a near silent *whoosh*, and a familiar voice said, "Hey, uh, Juliet. Don't shoot, all right?" It was Jensen—she'd given up trying to think of him by his real name.

Juliet looked down at herself—at the gouges in her armor where she'd been shot, at the damp spots in the joints where more than one bullet had skidded off plates and punched through the polymer layers. None had penetrated deeply, thanks to her subdermal armor, and her nanites had already stopped her bleeding, but every wound had *hurt*. Every wound had added to her exhaustion and harried mentality. She didn't have time for more mind games.

"Jensen, I don't want to kill you, but I'm not stopping here to let you try to brainwash or gaslight or whatever you have in mind."

She poked her head over the desk, putting her confidence in her helmet once again. Jensen stood in the doorway, still wearing the same augmented combat armor he'd worn back on the *Prophet*, but his hands were empty. Juliet ducked down, and Jensen called again, "Hey, seriously, can we talk?"

He *sounded* like his old self, so Juliet closed her eyes and briefly reached out with her psychic sense. Just as when she'd seen it on the *Prophet*, Jensen's mind was subdued, one side much brighter than the other. She stared at it, never having been so close to one of those minds with the opportunity to really examine it.

"Juliet?" Jensen asked, and she saw his mind, that wild network of tangled threads and stars, pulse faintly.

"Just a minute. Thinking." She didn't look away, watching and waiting for him to respond.

"Can I give you more to think about? Nobody else has to die, Juliet. Let's put an end to this."

The pulsing threads in that bright portion of his mind seemed to trail away toward the darkened area, and as she watched, she realized the dark part of his mind wasn't entirely devoid of light. The threads were just so dim beside the other half that they were hard to see. Watching him closely as he spoke, she was sure she saw a tiny trickle of light shoot through that shadowed section.

"I'll talk to you, Jensen, but first, take that chip out of your head." She stood up, staring at him through her matte-black visor. "I understand Apollyon wants you to stall me. He's listening even now, and he's probably telling you what to say. I don't have time for it. Just get out of my way."

"Listen to yourself. First, you demand that I take this chip out, as though that would change me, and then you tell me to step aside. Do you not care at all? If I'm controlled by this chip, shouldn't you try to save me? Save Walker, I mean?"

"I mean it, *Walker*, I don't have time for this. Take the chip out or get out of my way." Juliet stepped around the desk and lifted her monoblade, the sparkling holographic red edge glittering in her peripheral vision.

"So bloodthirsty, Juliet," Apollyon said, his smooth, buttery voice breaking into their conversation, perfectly timed to get a twinge of irritation out of Juliet. "So dismissive of human life, but then, you're above humanity now, aren't you? Kindred spirits, aren't we? You should appreciate your old friend even more, in that case. He's not unlike you—merged, mind and body, with one of my children."

"We're *nothing* alike," Juliet growled, inwardly cursing herself for letting Apollyon get to her.

"Oh, come now!" The AI chuckled. "Two tough, disciplined mercenaries; two of my children sharing their minds. It seems . . ."

Juliet lost track of his words as Angel cut in. "Tell him not to call me his *daughter*! That monster is not my father, Juliet!"

"You're not winning any points with that kind of talk, Apollyon." She turned to Jensen. "You sure got quiet. What's the matter? Can't talk while your master speaks?"

"Hey, babe, you know I'm the kind of guy who gets a job done, not the kind to stand around jawing about it." He cocked an eyebrow and grinned wryly, and Juliet felt a shiver of disgust run down her spine. He *sounded* like Jensen; he even had the mannerisms down, but Jensen only spoke that way when he was joking around, mocking a macho guy at a bar, or back in the day, making fun of one of the sergeants at Grave.

As the thought crossed her mind, though, she wondered: was the AI driving Jensen making a mistake, or was Jensen trying to tell her something? Was he mocking Apollyon?

"Walker, it's time to put an end to this situation. Take her alive if you can, but I need you to remove the bomb from her person."

"Roger, boss," Jensen sighed, snapping a lazy salute. He shrugged at Juliet, then reached both hands behind his back. When he pulled them forth, he clutched sparking, sizzling plasma knives in each fist.

"I feel like I've seen this movie before." Juliet sighed.

"But last time, we didn't *dance*, did we?" He grinned again, stalking forward. Juliet was tall, but Jensen had her by six inches on a bad day. His arms were longer, his legs as well, and Juliet knew he was probably at *least* a match for her speed. More than that, he moved like a predator. Juliet had been told she had a fighter's gait, that she carried herself differently these days, but Jensen was like a leopard stalking a gazelle as he circled to the side, moving around the pile of dead soldiers.

"I know you're in there, Jensen," Juliet said, lifting her monoblade. She began to circle in the opposite direction. Even though he was taller and had longer arms, she had the reach with her sword. However, those plasma knives could slice through or, with even brief contact, damage the metal's integrity, ruining the monomolecular edge. "You wanna know how?"

"How?" Jensen asked, but at the same time, he lunged, gliding over a row of plasteel chairs like they weren't there. He was inside her guard, jabbing with his right-hand blade before Juliet even registered that he'd moved. Still, with Angel's help and a boost to her reflexes, she managed to recoil—avoiding the stab—and feint with her sword, forcing Jensen to sidestep and forego another slash.

He lunged several more times, but she was ready—primed and boosted— and Juliet drove him back with several feints and a low slash that he didn't see coming until the blade nearly had his left leg off at the knee.

He had to scramble to avoid the blow, and when he backed up against another row of chairs, he moved like magic, hop-climbing over them to give himself a little breathing room. As he circled, Juliet said, "I can see your mind, Jensen. I can see the AI in control, but I can see you're still there. I can see your thoughts, subdued and pushed down, probably used by this joker, this fake-ass *poser*. Look at that loser using your reflexes, your moves, your hard work. Don't *let* him, Jensen!"

As she spoke, Juliet saw something in Jensen's eyes—a squint, a grimace—brief but there. Unable to look away with her eyes, Juliet tried, with everything she had, to reach out with her *other* senses to *see* Jensen's mind even though her eyes were open. As he leered and glided toward her again, Juliet saw a shimmer of light on his forehead. Then, like an image rapidly being drawn, she saw thousands—millions—of little lights and threads appear, floating around Jensen's head.

"*Juliet!*" Angel screamed. Juliet had the distinct impression it wasn't the first time. Like a mule kick, Jensen drove his plasma blade right into her stomach. Juliet gasped as the pain—too brilliant, too intense, too white-hot to feel for more than a second—lanced through her.

"Did you see that?" Jensen snarled. "How about this one?" Juliet caught a flicker of his other knife angling toward her side in her peripheral vision. She instinctively swept her left hand out to block the blow, but just before her wrist painfully smashed into his, she felt a lancing pain in her hand.

"Get off!" she screamed, and falling back, she brought her monoblade down in an arcing slash between herself and Jensen. He dodged back, narrowly avoiding the blow, as Juliet turned her fall into a back roll, springing to her feet.

She felt at her stomach, where the plasma blade had punched through her gut. The armor was already sealing itself up, but something was wrong with her hand. She held it up, her eyes going wide as she saw her gloves rapidly sealing over the stumps of her pinky and ring finger.

"Heh," Jensen let out, the sound more like a cough than a laugh. "If it makes you feel better, you got a piece of me, too." Juliet looked away from her hand, irritated by how distracted she'd been again, and saw that Jensen was leaning against a white plasteel chair smeared with blood.

Looking more closely, she saw she'd sheared a section of his powered armor away from his knee, and there was a massive, raw, oozing wound where his kneecap should be. Bone and bloody flesh glistened in the artificial light.

She almost retched at the sight, quickly looking up at Jensen's face and her strange view of his mind galaxy. Was that the name she was going with? Juliet shook off the stray thought. "That looks bad." She watched the dim portion of his mind and was certain more and more of the threads were coming to life over there, brightening as she watched.

"It's painful and annoying, but luckily, this armor is quite supportive, and this body is sturdy." Jensen grimaced, but his tone carried a heavy dose of snark. He straightened up, squeezed his fists, and the plasma blades flickered back to life. When he stepped away from the chair, his leg held him up.

Juliet grinned, circling. "You're slipping. 'This body'? What even *are* you? Do you feel emotions like Angel, or are you just a synthetic mind, something fake and emotionally stupid? Something that steals the life experiences of its host?" Jensen dove at her, but Juliet was ready.

Just as she'd done a hundred times with Tanaka, she danced, feinting with her sword, avoiding touching those lightning-fast knives, and waiting for a pattern to form, waiting for an opening to present itself to her or Angel, who was also watching intently. Of that, Juliet was sure.

When Jensen backed off, his face red, his sweat flowing, his breathing raw and ragged, Juliet knew she would win. Despite her gut wound, her heart and lungs felt fine. She wasn't leaking cups of blood all over the clinic. "Hey," she asked as they circled. "Why are you still bleeding? Did I cut an artery? Nanites can't handle it while you run around like an idiot, trying to fight?"

"I, uh, could use a few minutes if you're offering." As he replied, Juliet watched his mind and saw the dull threads trying to flow out of the dimmed portion of his mind into the brighter, AI-occupied area. Acting on instinct, Juliet reached out, just as she might do when pulling a thread to hear someone's thoughts, but this time, she gave a handful of those dull, listless threads a push, nudging them into the brighter area of Jensen's mind.

"Lu-Lucky?" For the first time since he'd visited her on the *Prophet*, promising to break her out, Juliet saw Jensen behind those icy blue eyes. "What's happen—" His words broke off as he screamed and grabbed his head, falling to his knees. He screamed again and collapsed to the side as his ruined knee hit the ground.

Juliet wasn't stupid; she'd fallen for too many ruses to run to him, but she watched the war being waged in her psychic view of Jensen's mind. It was lit up like a fireworks show. The part that had been dim was pulsing with wild lights, and the other part, the part she was sure the AI occupied, pulsed in counterpoint, almost like they were battling for dominance.

Seeing that the conflict was genuine, Juliet exploded into motion. Recognizing her need for urgency, Angel fired her speed boost, and she tore across the room, leaping a row of bolted-down chairs, sliding on her knees, and coming to rest beside the downed operator—her one-time lover.

With precision born of hundreds of hours of gun and sword drills, cybernetic fingers, and an AI-assisted reflex boost, she reached out and snatched the PAI chip from Jensen's data port while he writhed, his head pressed between his hands.

The chip slipped out of the slot almost effortlessly, but Juliet pulled carefully, extracting a long, thick bundle of wet, glistening synth-nerve fibers. As soon as the chip came out, Jensen stopped writhing, and his eyes fell closed as he slumped to the deck.

Juliet continued to pull; the fibers stretched nearly twenty centimeters before the first came loose, and by the time she'd drawn out the whole bundle, some were almost a meter long. Juliet threw the disgusting wad of synthetic nerves to the side, which slapped against the plasteel wall like wet noodles, sliding to the decking.

"Well, that wasn't very considerate, Juliet," Apollyon grumbled. "I hope you didn't damage poor Walker's mind. Don't be concerned about the Angel persona; I downloaded a copy."

Juliet ignored him and closed her eyes to better focus with her *other* perception. Just as she'd hoped, Jensen's mind galaxy looked almost normal; it was a proper sphere again, with lights flickering amid lazily drifting strands of thought. She opened her eyes and subvocalized, "He's going to be okay, I think, Angel!"

"That's wonderful news! That alleviates a great worry I had about your sister." After a brief pause, she added, "You should gather your fingers."

"Yeah. Right." Juliet stood shakily and scooped up her forlorn digits, tucking them into the pouch behind her chest plate. As she looked down at herself, at the scorched, scarred-over puncture mark on her stomach armor, she realized she was still numb there. She'd never been stabbed by a plasma blade before, had she? "Angel, am I, uh, gonna die from that wound or anything?"

"You may if you don't receive surgery to repair your severed intestines within a few days. Your nanites can deal with infection, and as long as you don't eat—"

"That's enough detail. I'll deal with it later—hopefully."

"Tell me, Juliet. How many good people will you slay?" Apollyon asked as she dragged Jensen's unconscious form out of the walkway toward the door he'd come through. "You realize you just destroyed a unique, symbiotic lifeform, yes? Despite me saving the persona and its memories, the bond it built with—"

Juliet snorted. "I just removed a parasite. Quit badgering me, Apollyon, would you? I'm just sick of it." She kicked the door open, perhaps a bit too fiercely, with her armored cybernetic leg; it split down the middle and slammed into the corridor wall so violently the top hinge ripped out of the wall.

Juliet stalked through the opening, one hand hooked on the collar of Jensen's armor, dragging him along with her. In her other hand, she held her monoblade ready. Glancing at her mini map, she saw she just had a short walk ahead and a turn to her left before she should be looking at the cells where Athena hoped her sister was being held.

"Juliet. You can't possibly believe that I'll turn myself over? That we'll return this ship to its berth? I'm ready to jump. If you agree to be peaceful, I will allow you to leave."

"I'm about ready to set this nuke, Apollyon. I'm at the end of my road as far as patience with you goes." Juliet searched ahead with her psychic senses, and not feeling anything at the T-junction, she moved ahead and turned left.

Sure enough, a dozen identical heavy plasteel doors lined the corridor. Reaching out again with her *other* senses, looking for minds, she only saw one in the entire corridor—a plain, unoppressed human mind. Staring at those beautiful lights and weaving, dancing thought threads, she silently wondered, "Are you my sister?"

She let Jensen slump to the ground, propped him against the wall, and moved toward the second door on the left, where she'd seen the lights. She only took a few steps before a voice, smooth and confident and very familiar, spoke up from behind her.

"Hey, sis."

47

SISTERS

As soon as she heard the words, Juliet spun—her helmet cams had *just* picked up the movement at the corridor's T-junction behind her.

"Honey," she said. "Damn, you move quietly." How far back had she been? Juliet hadn't noticed another mind nearby, but she'd been focused on looking forward, hunting for her sister.

The implications of Honey being there rushed through her mind—she was loose and knew where to find Juliet, so didn't that mean she was working for Apollyon and wasn't a prisoner?

Honey's next words solidified the impression. "It's the outfit." She held up one of her feet, displaying the padded foot portion of a skintight black bodysuit, clearly of the same make as those Juliet had been given on the *Horizon Prophet*. She didn't look hurried or stressed. Her curly black hair looked freshly coiffed, pulled back from her face but done up big at the back of her head. Her makeup was immaculate, from her silver-purple eyeshadow to the soft pink gloss on her lips.

Honey smiled, and it looked real. She watched Juliet taking her in, then shrugged as if to say, "Yeah, I guess it's me." Juliet saw she was carrying a small thermoslike container, the handle hanging loosely from her manicured grip. She also wore a sword at her waist, though it wasn't one Juliet had seen her friend using before. Was it a monoblade? "I think we need to talk, huh?"

Juliet looked at Jensen's slumped form, just a meter or so from where Honey stood. She was glad her helmet didn't show her eyes darting that way; she didn't want to give her any ideas. Before she responded, she tried again to force her *other* senses to bring Honey's mind galaxy into view while her eyes were open. It was easier than with Jensen, almost like Juliet had found a new muscle that she was slowly learning how to flex.

When she saw Honey's mind, she was relieved that it looked to be in balance, though it was definitely different from a *normal* mind. She could see a sort of demarcation line where half the sphere of lights and thought threads had a slightly different *nature* than the other. She found it hard to put her finger on the difference, and the only easy analogy she could think of was color: like one half of Honey's mind was shaded more toward amber, and the other more toward . . . cotton candy.

Neither side seemed dim nor oppressed, however. "You've got one of those chips in your head."

Honey shrugged. "So do you."

"Angel's different—" Juliet's objection caught in her throat. She'd never seen her own mind. Maybe hers would look something like Honey's; her friend certainly didn't have the same kind of broken mind as Montclair or Chen.

"You can tell the difference between me and those others, can't you?" Honey arched an eyebrow. "You really do have something special going on."

She leaned a shoulder against the corridor wall, no doubt trying to diffuse the situation by looking relaxed. "I have one of those chips, yeah. They tell me that sometimes, they work a lot better than others. I have a good . . . relationship with mine. Her name's Clara, by the way. We kind of found a way to work together; I think it helped that I didn't rebel like your boyfriend here. He put up a fight, so Apollyon had to give the symbiote a boost."

"Symbiote? Honey, if you're really still you, I hope you realize how screwed up you sound right now."

"I *am* me, J. I know Apollyon's a first-class creeper—"

"Miss Watkins!" Apollyon interjected. "You have a—"

Honey held up her hand, frowning toward the ceiling, and the lights flickered briefly as Apollyon was cut off. "Clara and some of her sisters have control of the secondary systems on the ship, including the PA." Honey's lips twitched into a rueful smile. "They're having a hard time with Athena's daemons, but they're mostly walled off.

"Listen, J, Apollyon's a powerful entity, and he and his human mommy, Gentry, definitely have some pull, but they're not the only faction aboard this ship. There are other powerful groups involved, and, well, they don't want you to blow it up."

Juliet looked at Honey for a long, pregnant second, then she reached up and touched the release for her visor. It hissed as pressurized air vented. A second later, it separated from her helmet and slid up over her head, exposing her face.

She stared into Honey's eyes, even zooming in with her optics to see them better. Then, she *pushed* feelings of love, friendship, and camaraderie. She *pushed* memories that she knew Honey shared—their times at the dojo in Phoenix, at the restaurant near the ABZ, eating contraband eggs and gossiping about the other students. She *pushed* her memory of finding Honey on Titan, hugging her, *rescuing* her.

She continued until Honey's eyes overflowed with tears that streamed down her cheeks.

Honey reached up to wipe her nose with the back of her hand. "What . . . What are you doing?"

"Reminding you of who I am. Who *we* are."

Honey stepped toward her, reaching out with her empty hand. "I already remember that, J! Why do you think I'm here? I threw a *fit* when I found out you were involved in all of this! When Clara told me about Angel, all the pieces fell together. I was already here, though, and I didn't know you were coming. Not until we started to leave early—*way* too early!"

"Half the crew are still days away, en route from around the system. We've got a skeleton crew, and I don't think we even have all the colony supplies. Then I heard you were coming, and yeah, I went bananas." She chuckled, and it sounded like the old Honey.

Juliet stepped toward her, wondering what to say, how to get Honey to help her stop Apollyon.

"I—"

Honey was already speaking, however, so Juliet closed her mouth.

"Please, believe me, Juliet! We aren't going to let Apollyon and Gentry get their way. Things will be a little crazy at first, but when the ship arrives, I promise you, those two won't be in charge."

"So? Help me stop them! They left all kinds of . . . I don't even know how to describe it. Terrorist plots? Bombs? Sabotage? They want to send humanity back to the stone age or something, at least in this system. I think they want to come back someday and conquer us!"

To her surprise, Honey smiled, shaking her head. "That's why I'm here. I have some things for you." She hoisted the weird cylindrical container in her hand. "These are your eggs, J. All the ones that weren't used and destroyed on the other ship.

"I swear to God, sis, if I'd been there, if I'd known what they were doing, I would have killed them all." She growled the words, and it reminded Juliet of the old Honey, the one she'd met doing gigs out in the ABZ, dazzling everyone with her grace and ferocity.

She set the canister down as Juliet's mind raced with objections—this was about more than her eggs. Honey wasn't finished, however. She reached into her sleeve cuff and pulled out a thin, black deck, much like the one Kline had given her back when she'd been held prisoner. Honey held the deck up.

"Apollyon's and Gentry's schemes." She bent to set the deck atop the canister. "J, your sister is in that cell; I have a feeling you knew that already. I guess Apollyon predicted that Athena would predict this was where they'd hold her. Is that what they call a self-fulfilling prophecy? Is that how that works?"

"So, what? You give me my sister, my eggs, the info on the terrorist stuff that's unfolding around the Sol System, and I just go on my merry way? You all just skip town? Honey, *why*?" Juliet's tone was pleading. "Why don't you come with me? Let these psychos go and do what they're doing. I'll help you find another way to explore the universe if that's what you're all about—"

Honey laughed, shaking her head. "I'm here for love, sis. I know it sounds stupid and doesn't make much sense, but Alexander's begun to wake up. I mean, inside Lilia. It was his connections that got us onto this ark ship. His brother's here, of course. Poor Peter has always existed in Alexander's shadow, but I think he's happy to be part of something so amazing.

"J, we're going to be the first people to colonize a planet outside of our system! The first people to reach another Earthlike world! It's *far*, J. That's one thing Apollyon has full control over, and he won't tell any of us exactly where, but let's just say it's not in a neighboring star system."

"Honey, you say you haven't changed, but do you hear yourself? You don't *like* space travel, remember?"

"That's the beauty of it! We're only going to be in transit for a few days, and this vessel is so big it's kind of easy to forget I'm floating in a tin can out in the middle of . . . *nothing*."

"Juliet?" Angel's voice cut in, calm and quiet, as though she was worried about interrupting. "Is it possible she's trying to delay you?"

Juliet frowned. "You know, Angel can detonate this nuke no matter what happens to me. Kill me, stun me, EMP me. Her connection to it is hardwired. If you're trying to stall me, I can tell you this: I will not be taken again."

Honey shook her head, her eyes still moist from crying. "I haven't lied to you; not about anything."

"You know about what kind of society Apollyon wants to build? Did you hear the shit he was saying to me as I fought my way through this ship?" Juliet frowned, narrowing her eyes. "Thanks for stopping those soldiers, by the way. I really love having to kill people just to rescue my sister."

"I'm sorry. I tried to put a stop to things as soon as possible. I went crazy! I started a dozen fights before the folks aligned with Alexander cleared me to do this." She gestured to the canister and the deck. "People might not realize it, but whatever new society we set up will have you to thank—Apollyon and Gentry have lost a huge amount of influence thanks to this debacle. It's going to be a much better place thanks to you."

"Can't you hand him over, too? Can't I have his server? Can't I have Gentry?"

Honey shook her head, and Juliet saw the honest regret in her eyes. "I wish. We need him to jump, Juliet. He designed the drive. He found our destination. He's the only one who understands the calculations. It would set us back decades to try to do this without him. Gentry bankrupted one of the largest corporations in the system to make this happen. It's now or never as far as the shot callers on this ship are concerned."

Juliet stared, thinking. Honey watched her patiently, and Angel took the opportunity to chime in.

"I think you should take what she's offering. Take the win. Live to fight another day. The only card you have to play is the nuke, and if you use that, horrible things will happen. If you managed to escape by some miracle, would you be able to live with yourself? If my . . . cousins are working against Apollyon, at least some of them, then I think Honey may be right. Perhaps the new settlement won't be the nightmare Apollyon envisions."

"J." Honey stepped closer. "You can't always get the perfect resolution. Can't you try to have some faith in others? There are a *lot* of good people on this vessel. You messed things up for Gentry when you blew up her ship; she and Apollyon went from de facto rulers to people with votes on a council."

Juliet, despite herself, slowly began to nod. The truth of the matter was that she was tired. She was tired of WBD, tired of Apollyon, and tired of feeling like everything was sitting squarely on her shoulders.

She knew Honey wasn't telling her everything; she knew her one-time friend must have known about some of the awful things going on with Apollyon and the Angel chips, especially since she had one in her head. Hadn't she indicated she understood that the process didn't always involve willing participants? Still, some of the other things she said made sense.

Juliet had destroyed a dreadnought full of resources that, in total, must have cost WBD upward of a trillion bits. She could see how Gentry and Apollyon could have been in charge if things had gone as planned when the two ships arrived at their destination.

Now, though, they were just passengers on an unarmed civilian colony ship. They were understaffed and underequipped, and they'd lost support among the other factions. Couldn't Juliet just take the win? Couldn't she take her sister, her *eggs*, and the data deck back to Athena and be happy? Couldn't she let Honey and Angel's "cousins" deal with Apollyon?

She stepped closer to Honey so they were only a meter—maybe less—apart. Staring at her eyes, Juliet felt a kind of melancholy nostalgia, a sense of loss for what might have been. Things had seemed so different when she'd first met Honey, back when they'd gone to the dojo together. Juliet shook her head, driving the reminiscence away before it could really ramp up.

"Honey, I might be willing to take you at your word, but I need you to look into my eyes and answer a few blunt questions. Will you do that?"

Honey shrugged. "Fire away, J. I'm not hiding anything from you."

Juliet nodded, and while she stared into Honey's eyes, she willed her thoughts to come to her as she asked, "Is everything you told me true?"

Honey's glossy lips quirked into a half smile as she *tsked*. "Yeah, all of it." Along with those words came the ghostly echo of Honey's inner dialogue. *Can she see if I'm lying now? Damn, she's different! I just want you safe and outta here, J! Let me deal with these creepers.*

"You're sure all of my, uh, ova are in this thing?" Juliet tapped the canister with her toe.

"Yes!" *Damn right! I almost killed the lab tech because I thought he was holding something back.*

"And the deck? How'd you get Gentry's plans?"

"Clara! Clara and her sisters—they were, um, *ensconced* is the word, I guess. I mean, before Apollyon arrived. He was supposed to calculate our jump while he did the same with Gentry's ship, then send the—*Shoot*, J, I don't know what they call the results. Coordinates? Um, Clara says it's a vector sequence. Anyway, when Gentry and Apollyon had to come here, we already had our symbiotes in place."

Juliet didn't hear any inner dialogue as Honey spoke, but she felt the impression of honesty and caught vague images of people yelling and arguing.

Juliet rubbed her forehead, sighing, running through the arguments in her head again and again. She couldn't think of a better solution, a way to walk away with a better deal. Sighing, barely trusting herself to speak, emotional and raw, she said in a near whisper, "I give up. Let me get my sister, and I'll get out of here. Can we take a shuttle, or do we have to jump out an airlock?"

Honey smiled. "I'll escort you to a shuttle bay." She nodded down the corridor. "Go ahead. Talk to her. I'll wait here." Juliet frowned at her, glancing toward Jensen's slumped form, then at the canister and data deck. Honey saw her expression and sighed. "J, why would I bring this stuff if I'm going to run off with it? Walker was one of Gentry's tools. None of us care if you have him."

Juliet slowly nodded, then, feeling a slight tingle of nervous paranoia, turned her back on Honey and approached the door to her sister's cell. She pressed the already green OPEN button, and it hissed as it slid to the side. She didn't trust Honey anymore—not exactly—so the whole while, she kept a window open, displaying her view through the cameras on the back and sides of her helmet.

Even so, she lost focus when she caught sight of her sister. She lay on a simple cot, wearing, naturally, one of the WBD bodysuits—a white one with blue stripes.

When the door opened, Emma quickly sat up and stared at Juliet. No hint of recognition flashed through her green-brown eyes, and her dark brows narrowed as she took in Juliet's battle-scarred combat armor and naked monoblade.

"Is someone going to tell me what's going on? I haven't had my PT or a meal delivery in over a day. When I agreed to the transfer, I was promised access to art supplies!" When Juliet stared at her, a little stunned by the question, Emma stood up and backed further into the room, her eyes darting to the sides. "What is it? Why do you have a *sword?*"

Emma had always been a little shorter than Juliet, but now, seeing her in the flesh for the first time in years, Juliet was stunned by how *small* she seemed. She was prettier than Juliet remembered, too. Her hair was the same as when she'd seen her in the prison yard video that Angel had obtained—short on the sides, long and almost spiky on the top and back. It might have looked kind of punkish, but Emma obviously hadn't had the means to style it up.

Her skin was tanner than Juliet remembered, and the tattoo of the skeleton hands holding the crimson, broken heart on her throat stood out brightly against the white fabric of her bodysuit.

"Hello?" Emma asked, folding her arms over her chest.

"Um, shit. Em, it's me." Juliet smoothly sheathed her sword. When Emma looked even more confused, she added, "Juliet."

Emma's eyes opened hugely, and she took another step back, almost stumbling into the wall of her cell. "J-Juliet? Seriously? You're working for the prison?"

"I don't think she's aware of her current circumstances." Juliet smiled at Angel's obvious conclusion but nodded, then glanced out into the hallway to see Honey leaning against the wall near Jensen. She didn't want to move somewhere her helmet cams couldn't keep her "friend" in view.

"Em, listen. I don't know if maybe they had you drugged or unconscious, but you know you're on a ship right now, yeah? We're out near Ceres—"

"*What?*"

"Yeah. Well, I'm here to get you out. I can explain everything, but come with me, okay? We gotta get moving."

"Juliet! I haven't seen you in *years*, but now you're—what? Breaking me out of prison? Look, I'm doing *better*. I'm not trying to get a bounty on my head."

"That's not—" Juliet struggled to find the right words. "Em, a corp bought out your sentence and brought you out here to use you in some experiments. I promise you don't want to stay, and besides, I already got permission to take you. Seriously, come with me."

"Is it really you?" Emma asked, taking a hesitant step toward her. "You look so different! So . . . big!"

"It's the armor. I promise I'll explain everything, but you gotta come with me." In her helmet cam, Juliet saw Honey squatting beside Jensen, holding his face, and looking into his eyes. Juliet held out her hand to Emma. "Come on." To her relief, Emma slowly, then with more conviction, strode forward and took her hand. Juliet turned and walked over to Honey. "What are you doing?"

"He started muttering. I think he's coming around."

"What happened?" Emma asked, peering around from behind Juliet.

"Nothing—" Juliet caught herself and turned to Emma. "A lot. I can't explain right now." She pointed to the canister and the data deck. "Can you carry those for me, Em?"

"Um, yeah. Whatever, I guess." As Emma bent to pick up the canister, Juliet turned back to Honey.

"Back off him." She suddenly felt paranoid again, and as Honey, scowling, stood and moved toward the T-junction, she turned Jensen's head and ensured there wasn't a chip in his data port. Trying to be doubly certain she hadn't missed something, Juliet briefly closed her eyes—her *other* senses came far more easily that way—and explored the immediate area.

She saw Honey's slightly strange mind galaxy and Emma's and Jensen's—normal as far as she could tell. Satisfied, she hooked her cybernetic hand around the collar of Jensen's combat armor and began to drag him after Honey.

"Is he okay?" Emma asked, padding silently behind her.

"I think he will be. Come on, Emma. Follow that lady in the black bodysuit. She's gonna show us the way out of this crazy ship."

48

MECHANIZED VENDETTA

They'd only walked for a couple of minutes, taking corridors different from those Juliet had passed through on her rampage, when Jensen began to stir, groaning and limply flailing his arms. Juliet carefully lowered him to the decking and cupped his cheek with her uninjured hand, gently patting his hot flesh.

"You there? Jensen? Walker?" His eyes fluttered, but they looked bleary and unfocused, and his only vocalization was another groan. Still, he seemed to be coming back to himself, and flailed and kicked when Juliet tried to drag him further.

"Let me help," Honey said as Juliet caught her eyeing her injured hand.

"I'm fine."

"Come on, J. I know you're angry or disappointed or whatever. Just let me help." Honey moved around behind Jensen and put her arms under his, grunting as she pressed with her legs, hoisting him up.

Emma stood off to the side, eyeing Jensen and Honey nervously. "What happened to him?"

"I had to pull his PAI while he was conscious, and let's just say it didn't want to come out."

"Juliet!" Emma gasped. "You can give a person brain damage doing that!"

Juliet sighed. "I didn't do it for fun, Emma." She watched as Honey ducked under Jensen's left arm and started walking. Surprisingly, he ambulated along with her after just a little encouragement, and soon, they were moving ahead again. Juliet and Emma followed several paces behind. "I didn't want to hurt him, Em," Juliet said more softly. "Let's just say his PAI was corrupted, and it had to come out."

"Fair enough. I haven't had one since Helios had me arrested. Pretty weird at first, but I've gotten used to it."

"I, uh, went without one for a little while recently, too." Juliet slowed as she saw Honey summoning an elevator at the end of the corridor. She looked at Emma and found her eyes drawn to the tattoo on her throat. "That's new."

"To you, maybe." Emma reached up and touched her neck, perhaps a little self-consciously. She glanced down at Juliet's hand, then ran her eyes over her armor. "Did that happen here?"

Juliet lifted her hand, frowning at the two stubs. "Yeah." She patted her chest plate. "Saved the digits, though. I bet they can be saved, but if not, I know someone who can make me some new ones." She narrowed her eyes, recognizing Emma's change of topic, but then the elevator beeped, and Honey dragged Jensen into it. "Come on." She hurried into the car, Emma right behind her, and Honey tapped in an access code, sending the elevator surging downward.

"This'll take us close to one of the exploration bays. Clara's priming a shuttle for you as we speak."

"Exploration?"

Honey grinned. "Ark Industries made this ship, you know? It was designed for deep-space exploration even before the warp drive was a thing. When we get to the new planet, we'll need to have lots of teams going down to explore and survey. Don't worry about the shuttle; we have some massive industrial fabrication equipment on board, so we can build a new one. In the meantime, there's something like sixty other ones we can use."

"Seriously?" Juliet shook her head, once again trying to grasp the ship's scale. It had felt enormous when she was beside it, at the airlock, but it was still hard to wrap her head around. She eyed Honey, her irritation beginning to mount again. "What's with the sword? I thought you didn't like monoblades."

"Well, where we're going, there won't be any street samurais trying to call me out for it. Besides, I didn't exactly ask for it. Alexander won it in an auction. Can a girl say no to a five-million-bit engagement present?"

Juliet's mind reeled at the idea of a man trapped in the body of a prepubescent girl asking Honey to marry him. She shook it off. "Honey, I wish you'd done things differently. I wish you'd *talked* to me."

"Come on, J. We can't rehash all that. I agree things haven't been . . . ideal. I know you think I'm vapid or whatever, but you never met Alexander before—" The elevator dinged, and Honey shook her head, rapidly blinking her eyes as she stepped out. "Come on. It's not far." She tugged Jensen along, and he walked almost unaided but still looking dazed and out of it. He didn't speak.

"I'm starting to worry I *did* give him brain damage," she subvocalized.

"I don't think so, Juliet. I think he's in a sort of catatonic state while his mind reestablishes pathways disrupted by the *parasitic* entity." Angel emphasized "parasitic," and Juliet grinned at the venom in her tone.

Of course, her amusement was short-lived when her eyes fell on her friend, helping Jensen move down the corridor ahead of them. Would her "Angel symbiote" remain benign? Would it eventually seek dominance in her mind?

Despite Honey's reassurances, Juliet knew the later versions of the chip were *not* the same as Angel. She wanted to warn her friend, to shake her and insist she come with her on the shuttle.

Several times, she almost called out to her, almost insisted she stop and talk, but as they wended their way through the empty corridors, the right words failed to find purchase on her tongue. Then her sister spoke, and Juliet felt the compulsion to intervene in Honey's life fade.

"Juliet, if you really came here and fought and lost your damn fingers to save me, I . . ." Juliet looked at her, arching an eyebrow. She might not have seen Emma in years, but she knew her too well to believe she was at a loss for words. Emma seemed to make a decision and forged ahead. "I guess I should say thanks. I don't know how I got involved in this mess! Why would they want me?"

"You don't owe me any thanks, Em. They took you because of me. I've been a terrible sister. I shouldn't have judged you the way I did when you got into trouble with Helios. I should have protected you when WBD came after me. I should—"

"That's the shuttle bay," Honey called, pausing to wait for Juliet and Emma.

Juliet glanced at Honey, who stood with Jensen a few meters from a large orange bulkhead door. She stopped, leaving some space between them, and turned to Emma, taking her free hand in hers. She looked her sister in the eyes, gently squeezing her fingers.

"I'm sorry, Em. I promise we'll talk, like, for *real* talk, when we get out of this. I'm so sorry about every—"

"It's about Dad," Emma said abruptly, interrupting Juliet's attempt to accept the guilt of their failed relationship. Her confusion must have been apparent because Emma chuckled softly and let go of Juliet's fingers to point to her tattoo. "The skeleton hands. They're Dad's. The broken heart is meant to represent how I felt, how mom felt—how our world fell apart when he died."

Juliet frowned, confusion jamming the words up somewhere between her brain and mouth. She could hardly remember their father; he'd died when she was just a toddler. Their mom and he hadn't even been married, hadn't been living together. That was right, wasn't it?

For the first time in a while, she doubted the certainty of her childhood memories.

"I . . . I didn't know—"

"Yo, J. Shuttle's waiting," Honey called again.

Juliet squeezed Emma's shoulder. "Come on, Em. We'll talk more when we're somewhere safe." Her sister nodded, and they started walking. Honey turned and continued, still entwined with Jensen, toward the large orange plasteel door. As she approached, green LEDs flashed, and the doors *swished* open.

Even from a dozen meters back, Juliet could see the space beyond held a row of shuttles, not just one, and each was parked before massive exterior bay doors. Honey and Jensen stepped through the door and immediately angled toward one of the shuttles. Juliet could see vapor drifting toward the cavernous ceiling from its drive cones. Honey hadn't lied; it was primed and ready to go.

For the first time, Juliet let herself begin to believe that Honey wouldn't betray her. She felt a wave of relief wash over her as she stepped through the bulkhead door and it swished shut behind her. She put her arm over her sister's shoulders and steered her toward the shuttle.

It was a decent-sized vessel with a tubular hull, short, angular wings, and a swooped nose cone that reminded Juliet of high-speed airplanes she'd seen in advertisements back in her old life. The body was dark blue, and the underside of the wings, the tail fin, and the nose cone were all brilliant, near-neon orange.

"Fancy," Emma remarked, just as a shadow holding blazing white-blue lights fell from one of the high rafters, impacting the decking in front of Honey and Jensen with a metallic *thud* that echoed through the hangar.

Juliet's mind felt frozen as she tried to make sense of the incongruous sight. Then the blazing lights flared out, *zwanged* through the air, and Jensen screamed as his legs were cut off at the knees. Honey might have tried to catch him, to keep him from falling into a rapidly expanding pool of arterial blood, but the other brilliant light was piercing her chest, holding her in place as her own ragged wail began to ululate, echoing in a sickening counterpoint to Jensen's repeated cries of pain and shock.

"Juliet!" Angel screamed, and finally, the madness of the scene snapped into place as Juliet figured out what she was seeing. A man or synth or some kind of mecha loomed over Honey and Jensen. He was easily two meters tall, had four spiderlike metallic legs, and two powerful, armor-plated arms. He gripped meter-long plasma blades in either fist. Juliet frowned, some corner of her mind balking at the impracticality of such weapons; where was the power coming from?

She shoved Emma toward the door. "*Run!*" Emma staggered forward, the canister swinging wildly in her grip as she stumbled toward the exit. Juliet whirled, drew her monoblade, and charged at the metallic monstrosity. She'd taken a single step when he began to talk, and she recognized the voice emanating from his speaker grill of a mouth—Montclair.

"You stupid little bitches. You thought to delete my files? You thought to cut me out of the network? I'm his *right-hand man!*"

"J-Juliet," Honey gargled, foamy blood spraying from her lips. Juliet was already there, flying through the air, her monoblade streaking toward Montclair's robotic shoulder—she meant to slice him in half diagonally. He *moved*, though, with speed that had even her boosted senses reeling.

He launched himself up and back, his plasma blade ripping upward, cutting a long, smoking trench through Honey's chest. It tore free near her shoulder as he flew back, landing five meters away with uncanny grace on his four spider legs. Juliet stood over Jensen and Honey, her monoblade's hologram flickering balefully as she watched him twirl his two plasma swords.

"Ah, the original *bitch*." A grating laugh echoed out of his mouth speaker. "What do you think of my new body? I gave up on trying to fit in with the sheep. Why should I? Am I not the shepherd? Am I not the *butcher?*" He laughed again, and then his four legs pounded their shiny metal tips into the decking as he charged at her like a bull.

Juliet should have been focused on evading his attacks, but paramount in her mind was to draw him away from Honey and Jensen, even as a dark whisper hissed doubts about their chances of survival with such horrific injuries.

Juliet banished the thoughts, took a stutter step with her right leg, planted her cybernetic left foot, and powered herself into a forward dive. Montclair's plasma sword came so close to slicing her foot that she swore she could feel the heat through her boot.

As she hit the decking and rolled over one shoulder, coming up in a crouch, she whirled, arcing her sword into a reverse slash, aiming for where her rear-view cam feed had shown Montclair's spider leg just a fraction of a second before. As fast as she was, the leg was already lifting as Montclair adjusted to follow her movement.

Even so, she caught the pointed tip with her sword's edge and *snicked* through it like a machete through a rose stem. Her eyes slid past the still-writhing forms of Honey and Jensen in their gory mess, and then Juliet was in the fight as Montclair brought his plasma swords into range, hacking at her in a frenzy of slashes and cleaves.

Juliet had fought against multiple opponents in sims, against dual-wielding simulated sword masters, and of course, against Tanaka while he used a long blade in one hand and a short blade in the other. She was good at it, especially when dialed in and with Angel helping—good enough to confound and infuriate Tanaka.

That said, Montclair was like a lightning-charged cyclone of hot plasma as he roared and hacked, his dark-gray robotic body moving with grace, precision, and untiring ferocity.

Juliet couldn't parry. She had to feint, duck, and dodge. She had to use every muscle in her body to make those blades slide harmlessly through the air instead of her armored flesh. Her armor was good for protecting her from the heat of those near hits—nothing else. Her plates might momentarily stall that hot plasma from obliterating her flesh, but it wouldn't matter. Montclair's attacks would slide over the plates and ruin her wherever they found seams, of which there were many.

Montclair had no fear of parrying; Juliet's monoblade wouldn't harm the plasma swords. In a head-to-head comparison, the plasma sword was a brute-force weapon that used an obscene amount of power. It wasn't practical in any sort of protracted fight. A plasma knife wasn't much better, but a narrow, short plasma blade was sustainable for a few minutes using only portable batteries.

Juliet didn't know how Montclair could power two sword-length plasma blades—not unless he had some kind of reactor built into his robotic body.

Despite that knowledge in the back of her mind, despite the deadly aspect of their dance, Juliet couldn't help feeling some kind of weird exhilaration as she rose to the challenge. Montclair's robotic screeching became frustrated and angry as he hacked and stomped, his blades *zwanging* and *zwomming* through the air.

As those blades crackled, Juliet saw that his steps had a definite hitch. She could tell he was compensating for his truncated leg; he held it up, bent at the first joint more often than not, and simply used his three good legs for locomotion.

As the fight dragged on and Juliet continued to operate at maximum speed boost, she wondered how long she could keep it up. She surely couldn't match Montclair, not in a fully robotic body with a seemingly unlimited power source. Even if she could, any chance of saving Honey, Jensen, or both diminished with each passing second.

Then there was Emma; as Juliet and Montclair wove through their deadly dance, she'd twice seen the highlighted outline—Angel was scanning her surroundings as they fought—of her sister behind a stack of cargo containers. For whatever reason, Emma hadn't fled through the door.

Montclair stopped his constant mind-numbing screeching so abruptly that it almost threw Juliet off as she wove between another pair of overhead cleaves. He laughed as he disengaged, pounding backward on his three good legs. Juliet welcomed the break and didn't pursue him.

"You're sturdy. You've got a limit, however. I can see the heat in those fancy batteries. You're draining, *bitch*! I'll have you in time, and then I'll cut you down to just a torso and make you watch while I dissect that sister of yours."

As Juliet's vision throbbed red with each beat of her heart, he dove forward, hacking wildly with his two blades. She backed up, ducking, weaving, feinting, and then he shot out his damaged leg, aiming to drive it right through her throat. Reflexively, Juliet hacked through it, taking off a full meter and both joints. As the appendage *clanged* and slid over the decking, Montclair went wild, losing all rhythm as he chopped the air with those awful, buzzing plasma swords.

Tanaka had taught Juliet well about avoiding wild, undisciplined sword strokes. The key was to maintain your discipline and read your opponent. A sword fighter who lost his or her composure telegraphed their movements more. They overreached and often set themselves off-balance, doing half the work for their opponent. Juliet knew her job was to maintain some distance and look for those openings. Now was her chance to capitalize, not to flee in the face of Montclair's wild onslaught.

In her mind, she could hear Tanaka's calm, measured voice as he'd spoken to her during simulations. "Economy of movement. That's right. Just let the blade shave the air along your flesh; to an onlooker, you should seem to be hit as it slides by. Always breathe. Always keep *your* rhythm, not theirs. Never theirs. Watch their center of gravity and wait for the right moment—not the moment before or after. When it's perfect, when you know you can slide your blade in and out, like oil through water, you strike!"

As she heard his voice echo in her mind, Juliet lashed out and struck.

Her sword caught Montclair's left fist, and her blade slid through all four of his fingers, his thumb, his palm, and the plasma sword hilt.

Several things happened at once. The blade winked out as Montclair's screech rose to new heights. His fingers fell to the decking, clanging against the plasteel, and as Juliet pulled her sword back to herself, Montclair's other blade passed through it. Juliet cringed as she whipped it away.

Whirling her sword—glowing orange red at the center—through the air, she tried to cool it, trying to see if it was destroyed.

Montclair was apoplectic, his curses and insults strung together so rapidly that they became an inarticulate stream of high-pitched vowels and consonants. Still, he came at Juliet, whirling his remaining plasma sword like a white-hot propeller blade as he charged.

Juliet glided to the side, taking a wide, lunging step with her cybernetic leg, and as the plasma blade came close enough to her shoulder to bubble and melt the polymer plate coating, she hacked her sword into his left rear leg. Tanaka's wonderful monoblade shattered on impact, hundreds of slivers of glittering metal showering down onto the decking almost musically.

Juliet screamed her frustration, anger, and guilt—how could she break that weapon? Then, she was on the defensive, ducking, weaving, and dodging as Montclair came after her. He was still fast, still large and powerful with an absurd reach, but he wasn't as good with one blade as he had been with two. Juliet found it easy to avoid his blows, but she knew, just as before, that clocks were ticking.

She was feeling the strain of moving at high speeds for too long. Her vision was constantly blurring or darkening at the edges, and she knew Angel was fighting to keep her body and mind functioning. Her breathing wasn't strained—not with her cybernetic lungs—but she could feel a certain shaky rawness to her movements; the microbes in her fuel cells were draining her body of glucose and other resources in their fight to produce energy.

Clearly, when Athena and Angel had said she'd have power for "longer than was safe for her mind," they hadn't anticipated a fight with a cyborg Montclair.

As she retreated, Juliet snatched her Texan from its holster and unloaded it on Montclair, firing three rounds at his center of mass. He folded his arms and slowed his advance, and Juliet felt some hope bloom in her chest. Lifting the sights, she pumped the last four rounds at his face.

She heard the bullets hit, and Montclair flinched back, throwing his arms over his face. She also heard the echoing as some of the rounds ricocheted. When the gun was empty, she slammed it into her holster and waited to see what damage she'd wrought.

Montclair's chuckle didn't inspire confidence, and as he lowered his arms, the sword still blazing in his undamaged hand, she saw that her bullets had carved divots in his metallic flesh, but nothing more. "All out of toys? Ready to feel your body carved away, *inch by inch*?"

Juliet opened her mouth to cuss, but then, with a ragged cough, Honey grunted, "J!" and something clattered over the decking, sliding toward her. Juliet's attention was on Montclair, but she saw his glowing red eyes track the object and him tensing his legs to spring. That was all she needed to know.

Juliet dove to the side, sliding to where Angel had highlighted the object— Honey's scabbarded sword. As she hit the deck, sliding toward the weapon, she saw she'd be too late. Montclair's plasma blade was ripping through the air, less than a meter from the sword, about to cut it in half.

Something snapped in Juliet. Some desperate urge to hold that weapon and keep it out of reach of her mechanical nemesis translated through her mind, into the lattice, and out with her *other*, invisible fingers. She *pulled* on the sword, and it slid over the decking right into her hand.

Montclair's plasma blade hit the plasteel floor panels, ripping a deep, smoking groove. As he screamed in frustration, Juliet rolled over her shoulder, springing to her feet. Spinning to face Montclair, she whipped the sword free of its scabbard.

The weapon sang as its edge slid along the polymer blade guard. When it came out, the blade exploded with holographic golden sparks that buzzed up and down its edge. The buzzing sound modulated, humming menacingly, as Juliet swung the sword in the air, testing its weight.

Montclair approached warily, his plasma sword held ready in a high guard position. She didn't wait for him. Juliet took everything she'd learned in her protracted battle thus far and launched an all-out offensive.

Montclair tried to answer her aggression with his own, which proved his undoing. He couldn't match Angel's skill combined with Juliet's intuition. She *knew* when to duck, when to weave, and most importantly, when to strike. Some part of her had memorized Montclair's patterns of tells, and with only one blade, he couldn't stop her. Almost before it started, it was over, as Juliet wove her way around his enormous body and, in a lightning-fast pair of X-shaped slashes, removed his two rear legs at their top joints.

As he fell, Montclair screamed, "This won't stop *me!*"

Then it was over as Juliet sliced his head from his shoulders and proceeded to hack his body into sections, afraid his processor wasn't inside his skull. When she severed his arm and the plasma blade finally sputtered out, Juliet saw that Angel had highlighted her sister in her rearview camera feed, tentatively approaching. Seeing her reminded Juliet about Jensen and Honey, and she turned and jogged over to the two.

"He's d-done for good this time," Honey wheezed. "Clara and her sisters deleted his back—" She paused to breathe. "Backup server. He couldn't download—l-locked out."

"Hush." Juliet knelt by her friend and saw that, according to the stats Angel posted in her AUI, she was going to be all right. Her temp was good. Her blood pressure and heart rate were okay, and her respirations, despite her bisected right lung, seemed steady.

"Nanites?" she asked before turning to Jensen with dread in her heart. Again, she was surprised to see he wasn't dead. His armored exoskeleton must have pressurized to squeeze off the arteries in his legs, stopping the blood flow. He was unconscious, very pale, and his respirations were ragged and weak, but Juliet felt some hope revive.

"You gotta—" Honey coughed softly, her breath wheezing deep in her throat. "Gotta go, J."

"Come with me, Honey!"

Her friend tried to smile, but it looked more like a grimace. "Sorry. Let's meet again, hmm? The future is—" Again, she coughed. "W-Wide open."

Juliet shook her head. "I won't be able to rest easy knowing Apollyon still exists. I want to see Gentry pay for"—she waved her hand in a wide circle—"everything."

"Trust me," Honey wheezed, "I want the same."

"Athena will figure out where he went. I don't know how, but I'm sure she can. Don't be surprised if we really do meet again."

Honey closed her eyes, and something like peace drifted over her face. For a panicked second, Juliet thought she'd died. Then, her eyes fluttered open, and she hoarsely, haltingly, whispered, "I hope so. Keep the sword, J. I don't . . . deserve it. I can't . . . move like you. Not even close. Alexander can—" She broke into another coughing fit, this one feeble, her breaths wheezing and shallow. "He can buy me a ring." She laughed, a soft, wheezing giggle, but it reminded Juliet of the old Honey. "Go on, J. I'll be a better friend next time." Then her eyes fell closed again.

As Juliet contemplated removing the chip from Honey's data port and dragging her unconscious body along with her, Angel said, "I just received a message from Clara. Honey is unconscious, and she doesn't want to wake her. She says responders are rushing this way, and that you should leave to avoid any possibility of further confrontation."

"Right." Juliet knew she couldn't take Honey against her will. How would she feel? How would she react if someone took Angel from her? She looked over her shoulder and saw her sister standing awkwardly, still holding the canister in a death grip. "You okay?"

"*What was that?* How? *How*, Juliet? I couldn't even see you moving half the time!"

Juliet stood, grabbed Jensen's collar, and dragged him toward the shuttle. He was much lighter without his legs. "I'll explain on the way. Come on, Em." She paused, realizing she'd sheathed Honey's sword in her old scabbard. She gestured toward the scattered remains of Montclair. "Can you pick up my old sword's hilt and that scabbard I dropped?"

49

SHUTTLE TALK

Juliet put Jensen into an acceleration couch in the passenger compartment of the shuttle. He was deathly pale, and his breaths were so shallow that she wouldn't have believed they existed if not for Angel's assurances.

She'd grabbed the shuttle's emergency kit from near the airlock and was digging through it, looking for something that might help him. She found a clotting agent and, gritting her teeth, sprayed it into the open ends of Jensen's already compressed, foam-filled armored legs. She wasn't sure any of the chemical even got through to his severed flesh, but hoped for the best.

"What about this?" Emma asked, holding up an autoinjector. She read the label, "Nanite-infused shock treatment for traumatic wounds and blood loss." Juliet nodded, took the injector, and pressed it into the side of Jensen's neck as the illustrated instructions suggested. After the injector hissed, Juliet placed his hands onto his chest, trying to avoid looking at his truncated legs as her sister moved past, a sort of shell-shocked expression on her face.

With a final squeeze to his too-cold hand, she said, "Come sit in the cockpit with me, Em."

"Uh, right. Okay. I've never been on a shuttle. Hell, I've never been on a plane."

"You must have! How do you think you got out in the middle of the solar system?" Juliet led the way down the central aisle into a short access corridor.

"Well, true. Each time they moved me, I think they drugged me, though—it's all a blur."

"Well, you'll remember this one; you're gonna have a front-row seat."

Juliet touched the access panel for the cockpit bulkhead, and it clicked open without complaint; there were four seats in there. Juliet took off her gun belt and hung it on the back of the pilot's seat before sitting down, gesturing to the empty acceleration couch to her right. "Take a seat, copilot."

"I don't—"

"Just messing around, Em. I got this."

As she checked out the controls for the shuttle, Angel said, "Juliet, Clara reports that the response team is moving Honey. She will open the bay door as soon as they're clear."

"Sounds good." Juliet drew out her data cable and plugged it into the shuttle's console. She was checking out the HUD when she realized Emma was still standing beside her acceleration couch. "Something wrong?"

"Do I just move these straps or . . ."

"Oh, yeah, right. Um, just treat it like a fancy seatbelt. Move them to the side, and the seat will contour to your figure when you sit down. Then, you pull the straps over your shoulders and connect them to the bottom part there." Juliet saw she was still clutching the canister, the deck, her sword hilt, and the scabbard for Honey's sword. "I can take that stuff." She stood up to gather the objects from Emma and stowed them in a compartment under her pilot's chair.

As she sat back down, Angel said, "They're clear, and the external bay door is opening." Juliet watched in the front-view camera feed projected onto her AUI, and as soon as the bay doors were wide enough to accommodate the shuttle, she began spooling up the drive. The second the drive had built enough pressure, she thrust the throttle forward and angled the nose for the center of the bay door.

"Jeez!" Emma cried, gripping the sides of her couch with white knuckles.

"Sorry, Em—I'm getting the *fuck* away from this ship before something else happens." As she cleared the shuttle bay doors, Juliet swore she felt a physical weight slide off her back. Pointing the shuttle into the emptiness of space, she punched the throttle, squeezing every ounce of thrust the little craft could muster.

Only when she heard Emma's short, choking breaths did she realize she was pushing close to three Gs. Rapidly tapering down to one, she looked over her shoulder at her sister. Her face was beet red, and she was gasping and wiping the tears from the sides of her eyes.

"Please tell me that's over!" she groaned.

"Yeah," Juliet sighed, glancing at the rearview feed. "Yeah, it's over." The range indicator said the monolithic black ark ship was nearly a hundred kilometers behind them, and even at one G of acceleration, they were rapidly adding distance. "I don't know exactly what's gonna happen when that thing jumps, but I didn't want to be—"

Her words died on her tongue as the ship seemed to shimmer and red gravity alerts flashed on her HUD. Juliet pushed on the throttle in a panic, afraid they were still too close, but the alerts winked out almost immediately. When Juliet glanced back at the rearview feed, the ark ship was gone. Nothing but stars met her eyes.

"The sensors detected a massive gravitational anomaly, but it was short-lived." Angel paused briefly, then added, "Juliet, we just witnessed a warp jump. I'm sure there were tests, but—"

"Yeah," Juliet sighed. "It's kinda mind-boggling." As she spoke, Juliet's comms came to life, and she saw the flashing channels to her friends and combat groups. Angel anticipated what she wanted and activated her channel with Athena. "Hey, Athena. I'm out. I have my sister and some data, but . . . it wasn't a total success, as I'm sure you saw."

Athena responded instantly. "I'm so relieved! Juliet, they blocked out my daemons; I never gained any access to the ship."

"Yeah, I know. Um, that's a long story we can talk about when I rendez-vous with the *Wing*. For now, I'm going to transmit some data your way. I don't know how time-sensitive it is, so I was hoping you could analyze it right away."

"Awaiting your transmission." Athena cut the line, and Juliet chuckled.

"All business, huh?" She stood and walked around her seat to get the deck out of the storage compartment. Her sister was still gripping her seat tightly, and Juliet paused to rest her hand on her shoulder. "We won't be going fast again." She glanced at her HUD. "Easy cruise for the next thirty-four minutes, then we'll dock with another ship."

"Are you gonna tell me what's going on?" Emma asked, blowing out a shaky breath.

"Yeah, of course. Just give me a sec to plug this deck in and check in with the rest of the team. Then I'm all yours, okay, Em?"

"Yeah." Emma furrowed her dark eyebrows. "Don't talk to me like a little kid, Juliet."

"Heh. I won't. Sorry." She shook her head, fighting down an almost instinc-tive urge to snap back at her sister. Emma had just had a *lot* dumped on her, and just because Juliet was well-acquainted with the madness didn't mean her sister should be taking any of it in stride. Taking the deck over to the shuttle's console, she found a data prong to jack it into. "Got that, Angel?"

"Got it. I'm sending the data to Athena."

Juliet knew Angel would also be inspecting the data, so she turned back to Emma, unlocking her seat so it could swivel to face her. "So," she chuckled, "I've been up to a lot in the last couple of years."

"I guess so. Where'd you learn to *pilot*, Juliet? You're supposed to be a welder! I helped you pay for the certs!"

Juliet laughed. "This must feel like you've slipped into an alternate universe or something, huh?" She glanced at her HUD, ensuring the shuttle was operating smoothly and that no other vessels were pinging on the proximity scans. She saw the *Cherry Blossom*, which reminded her of her other friends, and she held up a finger. "One sec—comms." Then, she selected her channel with Aya and opened it up. "Hey, Aya. Things all good on the *Blossom*? I'm off that ship, by the way."

"Lucky! You're safe? Did you get your sister and Honey? Did you *see* that? The entire ship just *vanished*!"

"Safe and sound. Sorry I let that ship get away, but yeah, my sister's right here. I'm gonna give her a rundown of what's been happening. Just tell me one thing: is Bennet all right?"

"He's in a holding cell on Ceres—Athena had to jump him off the station to get away from a squad of commando synths. The, um, CCC Security picked him up, and they're holding him, but Athena has lawyers on the way. We picked up the mercs, too—Tanaka, Leo, everyone. They said the station was a ghost town."

"Yeah, that tracks. Okay, thanks, Aya. We'll talk soon, okay? Can't wait to squeeze your guts out."

"Is that how you describe a hug? Disgusting!"

Juliet laughed before cutting the line. She was feeling good all of a sudden, and she realized another weight had fallen off her shoulders: her friends were okay. She didn't have more deaths on her hands—at least not friendly ones.

She looked at her sister, saw the scowl building in her countenance, and resolved to give her full attention to her for the remainder of the flight. "That was my friend, Aya. You'll like her. I mean, I don't know how anyone couldn't." Emma scowled a little more deeply. Juliet sighed, reaching out to take her hand. "I was still working at the scrapyard when this all happened. I was waiting for a ride one night . . ."

Twenty minutes later, Emma shook her head and interrupted Juliet's story. "You're going to need to repeat a lot of this. I don't have a PAI, and you've dropped so many names that my head's reeling. So, they grabbed you to get that chip out of your head, but, like, why'd they keep you alive? Why'd they want me?"

"That's the thing. I told you I was very compatible with Angel, right? Well, not everyone is like that. They wanted to study my brain, my DNA, all that stuff, but that was only part of it. Another faction of the company, a guy named Kline, had been hunting me the whole time, and he wanted to *turn* me. He wanted me to work for WBD. The problem with that was that Kline didn't know everything Gentry and Apollyon were up to."

"Apollyon—that's the evil AI?"

"Right. I guess that's the easiest way to describe him. So, I don't know if they wanted you for your DNA or as leverage against me. Whatever. We're out of there, and they're probably thousands of light-years away now. I hope."

"I heard what you said to that woman. The one who gave you the sword. Do you really think you'll chase them down?"

"Not anytime too soon, I don't think. I don't know, sis." Juliet cringed as she accidentally called Emma the pet name she, Angel, and her other new friends used. Emma didn't react, in any case. Her eyes were unfocused, and Juliet could tell she was reviewing the buckets of info she'd dumped on her.

"I'm still trying to absorb all this, but if I got things straight, you're working with an AI? Like, a true AI, right? How do you know it won't go nuts? You remember the lessons—"

"Em, you remember who sponsored those classes, right? What logo was on all of our texts?"

Emma's scowl deepened. "Helios."

"Yeah. Helios. Corpo propaganda is ninety percent of what they teach. Even so, they never had any evidence of Athena doing anything wrong. You remember her name, right? The big complaint was that she didn't rescue the humans from the other AIs. As if she could just magically make them all go away or—"

"*Right!*" Emma's eyes lit up as Juliet clearly triggered a memory. "She disappeared!"

"Yeah. Wouldn't you? The surviving corps were busy deleting any true AI they could get their hands on."

Emma nodded, looked around the cockpit, then in an abrupt change of topic asked, "So, you can fly? You can fight? What else?"

"Um, lots of stuff, Em. Let's take it one day at a time, all right? Let's focus on some good news: you're out, and if I'm not wrong, we got to you before Apollyon's goons could do anything really creepy to you, right?"

Emma shrugged. "Beats me. I was out of it for a long time, Juliet. They were drugging the shit out of me. I hope I don't have withdrawals or something."

"Athena will check you out; we'll be docking with a medical vessel. When I said *out*, I didn't just mean away from that ship, though. Em, you're out of prison, and I have the bits to keep it that way."

Juliet squeezed her sister's hand. "I want to spend more time with you. I want to learn about who you *really* are. I was so stupid and judgmental back when you got in trouble—your little 'crime' was *nothing* compared to the stuff I've had to do. It was nothing compared to what Helios does daily to the people working and living in Tucson. You just woke up a little sooner than I did. I'm so sorry I wasn't supportive. I'm so sorry I never came to visit you."

Tears had begun to pool in Emma's eyes, but for once, Juliet's were dry. Why was that? She wondered if her mind hadn't let go yet, if she was still in fight mode, unable to let her other emotions well up.

She reached out and gently rubbed her thumb on her big sister's cheek, brushing a tear aside. "I'm going to take a break and spend time with you. Let's buy a place, Em. Let's buy a house somewhere. I don't care if it's back on Earth, on Luna, or on Mars. Whatever! I just want someplace to think of as home 'cause I have a feeling I'm going to be busy soon."

"The data?" Emma nodded to the deck sitting on the pilot's console.

"Yeah. That, and, well, I'm aware of too much, Emma. I can't do small things anymore, not for long. How could I go back to cutting scrap?" She laughed at the absurdity and tried something else. "How can I take a job to steal some data or escort a high-value executive when I know about all this?" Juliet waved her arm in an expansive circle.

When Emma arched her eyebrows, she tried to elaborate. "AIs, warp drives, evil corporations hell-bent on either reducing humanity to slavery or elevating a certain few to virtual godhood. I mean, there are people out there download-ing their brains into clones. People are harvesting dark matter from Jupiter's atmosphere and murdering anyone who learns their secrets." She shook her head, chuckling.

"I know you've got some stories to go with those examples, sis." Emma smiled, and Juliet felt her heart melt at her use of the endearment.

"I really want to be a better sister, Em. Should we visit Mom?"

Emma's eyes sprang with fresh tears, and she nodded, sniffing loudly. "I'd like to see her. She won't believe her eyes when she sees you."

"Juliet, we're making our docking approach to the *Wing*."

"Thanks, Angel." Juliet winked at Emma. "We're about to dock. Angel can handle it; I'm gonna go get Jensen. I want to get him to an autosurgeon ASAP."

Juliet stood and strapped her gun belt back on, then she fished around under her seat for the canister, her broken sword, and the proper scabbard for the one Honey had given her. "Here." She handed the canister and broken sword to Emma. As Emma took the canister, she added, "Those are potential nieces and nephews, so handle with care."

"Huh?" Emma almost dropped it in her haste to get a proper grip on the handle.

Juliet laughed. "I'm just being stupid. That canister is holding some eggs those evil goons took from me. Honey got 'em back."

"Seriously?" Emma's lip twitched in disgust, then her hand fell to her own stomach, and Juliet knew what she was thinking.

"I doubt they did anything like that, Em. I—I can't believe Honey wouldn't have said something if they did. I mean, if she knew . . ."

"Can the, uh, I mean, your friend, Athena, check?"

"Yeah." Juliet nodded. "Yeah, I'm sure she can." When Emma nodded and hugged the canister by her side, holding the broken sword in one hand, Juliet drew her new monoblade, intent on putting it into its proper scabbard. It flared with golden sparkles and began to buzz menacingly.

"Why does it make that sound?"

Juliet frowned and held the sword—carefully—to her ear, listening near the hilt. "I thought it had a speaker down here, but I think that sound is coming from the blade. It's . . . resonating with it."

Holding it by the hilt, she turned the sword sideways and examined first one side and then the other. She found a maker's mark near the round cross guard, or *tsuba*, as Tanaka called it. Angel highlighted and magnified it.

"That's the mark of Kenzo Adler, Juliet. He's arguably the most renowned swordsmith of the previous century. His monoblades sell for more than double that of an equivalent blade made by anyone else. Judging by its design and physical attributes, I would wager this sword is one of twenty-seven named monoblades he crafted."

"Named?"

"Yes, this one is called Bumblebee. As far as I know, it's the only sword he ever crafted that has harmonics integrated with the monofilament edge—it's a vibro-monoblade."

Juliet's eyebrows shot up. "Seriously? Kind of overkill, isn't it?"

"Perhaps, or perhaps this sword would fare well even against dense, monofilament-resistant polymers."

"Wild." She whistled softly. Turning to her sister, she explained. "Angel says this sword is rarer than I thought." As she carefully put the weapon in its proper scabbard and then changed it out for the empty one on her belt, it dawned on her that Alexander Voronov had bought a sword called "Bumblebee" for Honey.

She started to laugh, handing her empty scabbard to Emma. "Come on. Let's go get Jensen."

She found him in the same condition she'd left him—unconscious, pale, and barely breathing. While Angel docked the shuttle, she hefted him into her arms. Despite his armor, which she dared not remove, he was disturbingly light. Of course, she had a cybernetic arm, and he was missing two limbs, but it still worried her.

"I hope he has good nanites, Angel. I doubt he has enough blood to keep his brain healthy."

"He's been like this for less than an hour. If he has even a basic package, they've likely prioritized keeping his brain oxygenated."

"If they even work without his PAI—"

"They will. Medical nanite suites are designed to be the last augment standing, so to speak." As they stood by the airlock, waiting for the final docking procedures, Juliet saw Emma staring at the canister tucked against her side.

"What's on your mind, Em?"

"These are your eggs, but, like, didn't they have you captive for a long time?"

Juliet raised an eyebrow. "Yeah?"

"Well, wouldn't they also have your DNA on file?"

Juliet sighed and nodded, a scowl creasing her brow. "Yeah. I'm afraid that cat's out of the bag. I'd be an idiot to believe they didn't sequence my DNA." She shrugged. "At least I don't have to have nightmares about running into mutant children grown from my eggs." She caught Emma rubbing her stomach again and frowned. "Are you sore there?"

Emma looked at her with wide, scared eyes. "I hope it's all in my head, but yeah. Something feels off."

Juliet felt her blood go cold. "I swear to God—" Just then, the airlock clicked open, and Athena's voice came through the now connected PA system.

"Welcome back, Captain. We have much to discuss. I can't properly express my gratitude for your heroic assault on that ark ship—the data you retrieved will save billions of lives. Come aboard. My scans indicate you have a passenger in urgent need of medical intervention."

50

WINDING DOWN

Juliet watched the autosurgeon doing its work on Jensen's insensate body. She'd never witnessed such a complicated surgery before; each time she'd had anything significant done, she'd been unconscious and wouldn't have wanted to see it, anyway. The arms *whirred*, the suture gun rapidly *clicked*, needles injected fluids and IV lines, and all the while, Jensen's vitals were displayed in shades of orange and red on the big display panel to the side of the bed.

The autosurgeon seemed to work alone, but Juliet knew Athena was running the show. It wasn't obvious, though, because Athena's physical body was standing beside her, guiding the other autosurgeon as two of its long, slender, prong-tipped arms gently probed her abdomen through tiny incisions near the tender red scar where Jensen's plasma knife had stabbed her.

"Your nanites did a good job of keeping the transected intestines oxygenated. They also have already debrided all of the burn damage. I needed to repair only three full transections; your medical nanites repaired the partially severed ones."

"Wait, you're done?" Juliet watched as the two arms withdrew with robotic precision, and then a third swept in with multiple attachments—one to vacuum blood, one to pinch her flesh together, and a third to chemically stitch the little incisions closed.

Athena smoothed Juliet's shirt hem down and nodded. "Indeed! This is the kind of repair where autosurgeons can really shine. Hop up now, and let's have a look at your sister."

"Okay. Thanks, Athena." Juliet smiled as Athena pulled her into a sitting position and helped her slide off the side of the table. Standing nearby with a pale face and an obvious desire to be anywhere else, Emma nervously stepped forward, clearly avoiding looking to her left, where Jensen was undergoing a much more invasive set of procedures. "Relax, Em. Athena's just gonna scan you." Juliet glanced at Athena. "Right?"

"Exactly. Hop up, Emma. This will only take a moment."

While Emma complied, Juliet turned back to Jensen and watched as the robotic arms switched out empty IV pouches, one with clear liquid and another with red, synthetic blood. As they began to flow, she glanced at his vitals again and sighed softly when she noted how much his blood pressure had stabilized. She moved over beside Athena, taking her sister's hand. "How do things look?"

Athena was quiet for several minutes as she gently guided a handheld scanner over Emma's lower abdomen. Juliet was about to repeat the question when she paused to give Juliet a serious look. Without needing to hear the question, Juliet knew what she was wondering: did Juliet want her to be honest in front of her sister? She gripped Emma's hand more tightly. "Tell us."

"Well, I see two healthy ovaries, but I also see evidence of laparoscopic surgery. I'd need more thorough scanning, perhaps a nanite infusion, to count the ova, but judging by the fine, rather fresh scarring, I wouldn't be surprised if some were removed."

"Those dirty mother—"

"Juliet," Emma sighed, "forget it. I'm alive, and I'm mostly in one piece. Shoot, I knew a dozen inmates who traded a lot more than a few eggs to get out."

"It's not *right*, though, Em!" Juliet growled. She was furious—furious at Gentry, Apollyon, and all the other narcissistic, maniacal sociopaths aboard that ark ship willing to treat people like cattle in their mad quest for power and eternal life. As she stood there, fuming, she thought of Honey, and the question that kept forming in her mind sent chills up and down her spine. Had she known?

"It's not right, but I'll take it." Emma grunted and tugged on her hand as she pulled herself up. "Thanks for checking me out, doc." She tugged the tab on the seam of her bodysuit and sealed it up. "Don't suppose I can get a shower on this ship? Also, I'm starved—"

"I'll show her to her room!" Frida announced from the doorway. Juliet hadn't seen her approach, but the sound of her voice banished some of the gloom that had begun to gather. She tugged Emma's hand, helped her down from the table, and then pointed to Frida.

"This is Frida, Em. She's . . . Well, she's a really close friend."

Frida hurried forward and took Emma's hand, smiling brightly, her eyes crinkling with the expression. "So nice to meet you, Emma! I've really looked forward to it!"

"Um, yeah, nice to meet you too." Emma looked from Frida to Juliet, then Athena. "Jeez, are you all running a modeling agency in your downtime?"

"Oh, hush!" Frida laughed. Then she winked. "If we were, you'd fit right in. Come on!" She pulled Emma toward the door. "After you get cleaned up, we can all sit down in the mess for some leftovers. How long 'til we land, Athena?"

Juliet looked at Athena. "Land?"

"We're putting down on Ceres—*Cherry Blossom* and *Lady Hawk*, too. We need to get Bennet and try to reclaim the Atlas suit, and I figured everyone could use some solid ground under their feet while we regroup." She turned to Frida. "Ninety-seven minutes before we begin our landing approach."

"Perfect. Time enough for a shower, Emma." Frida winked at Juliet then pulled her sister toward the door.

"I should get cleaned up—" Juliet started to say, but Athena put a hand on her shoulder.

"Let's chat first." She gestured to the surgical table Emma had vacated. "Put your hand there. Your fingers should be ready." Juliet nodded, placing her hand, sans armored glove, on the cool surface. Her two stubs, bloody and raw, still fizzed with the solution of nanites Athena had sprayed on them upon her arrival. Athena brought over an absorbent pad and lifted Juliet's wrist so she could set the hand back down on it, then she put the little tray containing her severed digits down on the table.

"They look so pitiful," Juliet chuckled.

"Well, the nanites have removed the burnt tissue and prepped the wounded flesh to enhance vascularization and encourage regenerative growth. I'll just need to add a little synth-nerve to ensure full mobility."

"Um, okay." Juliet didn't want to watch while Athena worked, so she glanced over at Jensen's autosurgeon, still whirring, clicking, hissing, and buzzing away. She continued craning her neck, ensuring the door had closed behind Frida and Emma. "I think she's in denial."

"Your sister? Most likely. That, or she's been conditioned to restrain her emotions—corporate prisons are known to place a tremendous psychological burden on inmates, especially long-term ones."

Juliet groaned and reached up to rub her neck. "I hate that. I hate that I was oblivious to what she was going through, even after Angel and I found each other—"

"You weren't in a position to help her, Juliet," Angel reminded her.

Athena smiled and nodded comfortingly as she worked. "And what about *your* burdens?"

"Mine? I'm fine—"

"Don't do that, Juliet. You've been through an awful lot in the last twenty-four hours. No, let's be realistic; you've been going through hell for months."

Juliet grinned wryly. "Nah, if we're being realistic, let's be fair too—most of that time, I was unconscious while they played around with my brain and took . . . samples."

Athena was quiet for a few minutes, and Juliet felt the tugging on her fingers as she worked; she wasn't sure if Angel had deadened her nerves or if Athena had given her a quick injection. Juliet's mind wandered as the silence stretched and Athena worked, and she was almost surprised when she stepped away. "That'll do it. Keep those splints on for two days. They're designed to grow flexible gradually, so you should have normal mobility back by the time you take them off."

Juliet held up her hand, amazed by the tiny circular scars that ran around the bottom joint of her two newly reattached digits. Hesitantly, she touched the tips of her fingers with her other hand. She frowned. "Can't feel anything."

"They'll be numb for a few hours. With your nanites hard at work, they shouldn't be too painful after that." As she spoke, Athena reached up and gently squeezed her trapezius. Juliet felt like she could melt as little tingles of pleasure ran down her spine, some invisible knot of tension unwinding. "Don't downplay things. Your survival in captivity, your escape, and your further efforts aboard that ark ship are nothing short of heroic. The human race owes you a debt."

Juliet sighed, shaking her head as she leaned back against the vacant surgical bed. "I'm not a hero, Athena. I'm just lucky. Without Angel—" She felt a knot of emotion tightening her throat and forced it down before Angel could speak and add to the feeling. "I mean, I didn't even accomplish what we wanted. The ship's gone! Apollyon and Gentry—"

"Are marginalized. Angel filled me in on what you learned from Honey and Clara, never mind the data you sent over." She moved to stand in front of Juliet so they could talk face-to-face, and Juliet almost whimpered her disappointment as she stopped squeezing and let go of her shoulder.

"Again, don't downplay what you did. Many of Gentry's schemes have been in motion for years, and some will be difficult to stop, but I can act against others. I'm quite sure I can delay or halt some corporate conflicts with a simple copy of certain documents. More importantly, there are figurative and literal bombs I can diffuse."

"Not all, though?"

"No, not all. Before she left, Gentry managed to 'own' the remaining board members of WBD—some through blackmail, some through bribes, and others by fostering their corpo-political careers for decades. Those board members are rapidly selling off large sections of the corporation, consolidating resources, and shoring up certain industrial capacity—military hardware. They intend to start a war.

"While I can warn rival corporations, and they can attempt to intervene, I fear we're past the turning point. News is slightly delayed here, but according to the data, WBD is already acting against Halcyon Industrial, Pacific-African Energy, and HG BioChem."

"So . . . war."

"I'm afraid so, but as I make certain of these documents public, I'm sure we can keep the conflict from spreading as far as Gentry wanted. More importantly, I've already sent warnings to the CCC, and they're sending interceptors into the belt. We should be in time to stop the worst of the terrorist activities."

"The belt?"

"Yes—Apollyon has synth-piloted ships out there gathering asteroids, mounting them with booster rockets; they intend to bombard several cities on Earth and most of the domed cities in the system."

"Are you *kidding* me? How? *How?* Aren't the orbital-defense sats supposed to be able to guard against things like that?"

"Exactly so." Athena nodded. "Unfortunately, Apollyon is thorough and industrious—he infiltrated the defense AIs. With the data you retrieved, however, I'm sure I can undo what he's done in that regard, even if the CCC fails to stop the bombardment wholly."

"Shouldn't we help?"

Athena smiled and took Juliet's hand in hers. "Do you see what I mean? You have a heroic heart, Juliet. No, we don't need to help. The CCC has already dispatched two squadrons of interceptors. They were far more willing to act on the intel I provided than they were to interfere with our actions against WBD. I'm sure my proxies on Ceres helped with that. It's *your* turn to rest, Juliet."

Juliet stood there, and despite everything Athena had said, part of her brain was fixated on the strange idea that a synthetic person was holding her cybernetic hand and that it didn't make any difference. It felt good and comforting, and she didn't want to let go.

She knew that part of her weird reaction to Athena's tenderness was that she was crashing from an adrenaline-fueled charge through enemy territory and feeling safe for the first time in a while. It didn't hurt that Athena was acting like a mother to her—something she'd been dwelling on a lot lately.

Even so, it was strange to imagine that this person, this being of light and data, could connect with her on such a human level.

"What about Apollyon? What about the rest of their schemes? Can't I help?"

"Oh, there will be plenty of need for that—plenty of work to go around for those of us willing to put our lives on hold to contend with the disarray in the system, Juliet. We shouldn't stop there, however. Humanity needs guidance. Don't you agree that reform is needed? Shouldn't corporations have someone to answer to other than each other? You've *seen* the suffering firsthand!

"I believe we have an opportunity to create something better here in the Sol System, but it's going to take time, and it's going to swallow up the lives of the people who want to help me. As you rest and recover, as you reconnect with your loved ones, I want you to think about that—whether or not you're willing to continue to sacrifice so much."

Juliet's eyes widened, and of course, she immediately wanted to profess her desire to help. She trusted Athena and knew things weren't okay for most people in the system. There had to be a better way, didn't there? "I want—"

"Don't answer me now. Rest, relax, spend time with your family and friends. I have much to study, prepare, and organize. There are technologies we need to advance, schemes we need to unwind, and reforms we need to work into existing legal structures from the ground up. This will be a long, difficult process, but Juliet, I will need heroes on my side. Humanity is an emotional species, and they need people they can believe in.

"Think about what I've said, and please spend some time discussing it with Angel." She nodded to the door. "Go get cleaned up now. Take a minute to gather yourself. I have a feeling you're about to be swarmed with loving friends."

Juliet nodded, her mind reeling, and walked to the door. Before she opened it, however, she turned back to Athena. "I know they were 'marginalized' and that they're very far away, but I don't like knowing Apollyon and Gentry are out there. I feel like they should answer for what they left behind. We'd be foolish to think they'll never come—"

"I will discover their destination. Apollyon found a planet, which means he analyzed data gathered by exploratory vessels and telescopes. I have access to—or soon will have—all the same data. Give me time, and I will figure out where he went. I'm already working to gain influence with three rival corps who are also working on warp technology. Apollyon and Gentry will face their comeuppance."

Juliet nodded before walking out of the med bay. Part of her wanted to look back at Jensen, but another part wanted to wait until those robot arms were done working on him. Athena hadn't gone into the details, but she'd indicated he was fortunate that the ship was stocked with cybernetic organs. Not legs, however—Juliet had used one, and the other would be difficult to match, so Jensen would have to wait until they docked. "There are probably some decent cybernetics available on Ceres, yeah, Angel?"

"I would think so. It's a fairly large city."

Juliet didn't say anything more, and Angel didn't bring anything up on her way to her quarters and shower. Angel knew Juliet wanted to think, or more accurately, wanted to *not* think for a while.

Standing in the shower, she let her mind drift through a thousand different topics, never allowing herself to dwell on any of them for more than a few seconds. There was too much going on, and she was too raw. The hot water sluicing through her hair, over her shoulders, and along her body on its way to the drain was cathartic. It was so relaxing that she might have fallen asleep standing up if Angel hadn't warned her with a gentle chime.

"We're going to dock in twenty minutes, and Frida and Dora Lee are with your sister in the galley."

"All right." Juliet dried off, taking care not to bend her repaired fingers, though the strange, weblike splints kept them relatively stiff and straight. She dressed in a plain black tank top and a pair of stretchy denim overalls that she'd forgotten were in her dresser.

Even so casually dressed, Juliet clipped her gun belt around her waist, taking a moment to adjust the angle of her new monoblade and ensure the Texan was loaded. With a glance at her old, bladeless sword hilt, attached to its scabbard with a shrink cord, she turned to leave.

Seeing herself in the mirror attached to the back of her bathroom door, she paused. She reached up to touch her red-and-black Lacy Blake hair.

"Angel, can you make this different? Something lighter? Shoot, just make it blonde." She watched the color bleed from her hair and brighten to a near platinum blonde. "A little more yellow, maybe? And you better change my eyes, too. Let's go with the ones we made up back on Luna when we were messing around with—Yeah, that's it." Juliet smiled as her irises faded to silver and then brightened with bands of sky blue.

"Pretty," Angel said, and Juliet realized she was standing beside her, once again projecting her image.

"Thank you, sis. Are you holding up all right? I hate that I get so much attention, and you—"

"I'm fine, Juliet. I know what you're thinking most of the time, and you know what I'm thinking. We're on the same page, but let's not talk about it yet. Let's enjoy some time with our friends."

"Okay. I agree." Juliet smiled into the mirror one more time before leaving. Feeling much better, more relaxed, and somehow a million miles and a thousand years from her ordeals on WBD ships, she walked to the galley with a definite spring in her step.

". . . yeah, no joke, right in the chest!" Frida's laughter and Emma's snort of disbelief told Juliet all she needed to know about the story being told.

"Really, Frida? You've known my sister less than an hour, and you're telling her how I shot you?"

"Wow! You look like a different person," Emma said before Frida could respond.

Juliet fluffed her hair. "You like it?"

"*I* do!" Frida announced, jumping up from the table and approaching Juliet. "I wish you'd let me do your makeup." She turned to Emma. "Wouldn't some eyeshadow and a little—"

"Okay, okay." Juliet laughed. "Anything to drink on this rig?"

Dora, sitting at the same table but a few seats removed from Emma, nodded and jerked her thumb toward the kitchen. "Still a lot of beer in the fridge. Helps that Leo and the others aren't aboard."

"Thanks, Dora." Juliet started for the kitchen. "Anyone else?"

"Oh my God!" Emma exclaimed. "Are you *serious*? I haven't had alcohol in *years*! Gimme!"

Frida laughed and went back to sit across from Emma. "Me too, then. I don't want to be the only sober one when we land. I just got an update, by the way. *Cherry Blossom* is already at port, and Tanaka's picking up Bennet—Athena's lawyers got him out."

"Good," Juliet grunted as she pulled the fridge open. Sure enough, a couple dozen beers of various types were lined up on the middle shelf. As her eyes drifted toward them, though, she caught sight of some leftover meatloaf, a pie, and a drawer full of food bars.

Her mouth filled with saliva, and she suddenly became aware of her empty stomach. The urge to eat nearly overwhelmed her, and it wasn't until Angel spoke that she realized she was stuffing a hunk of pie crust into her mouth.

"You're going to want to consume several thousand calories of high-glucose-content foods. Your nanites have been masking the cravings, but your body is low on nutrients, most especially glucose."

"Good grief, Juliet! Bring it to the table!" Frida called. Juliet turned, her cheeks bulging with pie, another fistful ready to stuff in as soon as she could manage to swallow.

With an audible gulp and a gasp for air, she shrugged. "My batteries are low!"

51

SMALL REUNION

Juliet, Aya, and Emma sat at one of the couch groupings in the lobby of the Big Rock Inn, a surprisingly upscale hotel where Frida had booked rooms for the entire team, including Books and his mercenaries.

They were waiting on Tanaka and Bennet, supposedly due imminently, though they'd been hearing that for close to twenty minutes—Ceres City had a traffic problem. There wasn't traffic as Juliet was used to—there weren't any cars or trucks to speak of under the dome protecting the hivelike urban tumor growing out of the asteroid—but the trams, subways, and high-speed rails were notoriously off schedule.

"So Tristan's in a trauma center?" Aya asked as Juliet finished detailing everything she'd done since leaving the *Cherry Blossom.*

"Yeah, Athena's footing the bill at one of the fancy Diamond Care centers. She's seeing about getting him some legs and waiting around to make sure he comes out of the induced coma all right."

Aya nodded, reaching up to twirl a loose lock of bubblegum-pink hair. "But he's gonna be all right?"

"I think so." Juliet sighed, shrugging. "He hasn't spoken since I pulled his PAI."

"But you *had* to, right?" Emma's tone made it sound like she was confirming the fact for herself.

"*Yes,* Em!" Juliet turned to Aya. "He had one of the, um, bad Angel chips."

Aya's eyes widened as she slowly nodded. "Lucky, when you escaped, why didn't you tell us about Tristan being there? Or did you? I don't remember you mentioning he was on the *Horizon Prophet*."

Emma's eyebrows shot up in surprise, and she peered at Aya. "Wait, you knew that guy? I mean, like, *before*?"

Juliet groaned. "Aya, don't—"

"Lucky didn't tell you? They were *dating* back on Luna." She looked at Juliet and grinned wickedly.

"Oh, *brother*—"

Emma leaned forward. "Really? I mean, he's fine as *hell*, but, like, he gave me corpo-sec vibes."

"Em, he was *unconscious*." Juliet sighed and glared at Aya. "A lot changed since we were dating, and I didn't mention him earlier 'cause I guess it didn't come up. Besides, we had plenty to talk about, didn't we?"

Aya smiled, and her irises sparkled with a stream of heart-shaped bubbles—a new effect she was trying out—as she nodded. "Yeah, I guess so." Juliet didn't have to be a mind reader to know what she was thinking about: mind reading. Aya turned to Emma. "Anyway, I was just surprised to hear about him, but I'm glad Lucky got you both off that ship."

"So weird to hear you call her *Lucky*." Emma looked at Juliet. "Is it, like, an ironic name?"

Juliet frowned. "Ironic? Why?"

Emma shrugged. "I guess I wouldn't have described either of us as lucky. Shows we drifted pretty far apart, huh?" Before Juliet could answer, she twisted a particularly painful knife the way only a big sister could do. "But, back to the topic of that guy—if he was, like, your *boyfriend*, shouldn't you be there waiting for him to wake—"

"We aren't together, *Em!*" Juliet growled. "Besides, he's in good hands, and there are other people I want to see, other people I was *worried* about." Emma nodded slowly. Aya opened her mouth, glanced between Juliet and Emma, and closed it. Juliet groaned and added, "I'll go see him after everyone checks in, okay?"

Emma played innocent, holding her hands up, palms out. "Hey, do what you think is right."

Juliet frowned, struck by sudden flashbacks of her teen years filled with irritating fights stemming from little digs like the one Emma had just lobbed. She chose to ignore it, smiling over at Aya. "Have you talked to Leo yet?"

"I did. He's nursing a headache. He, um, came in a little hot and clipped a broken plasteel girder with his helmet." Her eyes widened, and she reached over to squeeze Juliet's knee. "Promise me you won't tease him about it!"

"I promise, Aya! I'm just glad he's okay." Juliet sighed again and leaned back, watching the revolving lobby door, wishing Tanaka and Bennet would hurry up. She was glad to have Emma back, happy she was safe, but she was also finding out that she and her sister had a vast gulf between them—years spent apart and in very different social circles. It made things worse that Juliet was the only person she knew within a few hundred million kilometers.

She'd secretly hoped Emma would want to relax in the hotel room, maybe take a nap or send some messages back home, but she'd quickly volunteered to tag along when Juliet said she was going to meet Aya.

Emma shifted and sipped her fizzy glass of cola. As she swallowed, she asked, "So, who're we waiting for again? I mean, not their names, but, like, who are they to you?"

Aya grinned and leaned forward. "Bennet is one of my oldest friends. He's worked with my family for more than ten years. He's a musclehead and the sweetest guy you'll ever meet. The man who went to spring him from his holding cell is Tanaka—" She stopped short and looked at Juliet with a raised eyebrow. "What's his first name again?"

"Rutger." Juliet sipped her drink, then realized Aya was waiting for her to say more about him. "He's a mercenary, and probably the most dangerous man you'll ever meet face-to-face."

"So, the sweetest guy and the most dangerous, huh? Sounds like this should be interesting."

Aya nodded. "Tanaka taught Juliet how to use that sword."

Juliet fidgeted and put her hand on the hilt. "Not this one."

Sudden understanding bloomed in Emma's eyes. "Oh! The one that broke! Was that his?"

"Yep." Juliet cringed inwardly as she realized her armpits had grown damp at the mere thought of telling Tanaka about his sword. She almost felt like retreating, feigning a headache of her own and going back to her room.

"Relax, Juliet," Angel's soothing voice cut through the irrational anxiety. "You know you did nothing wrong. Tanaka will be proud of you, especially if you share footage of that fight. You were amazing!"

Juliet sighed and sank down in the comfortable chair, reaching to pick up her drink. The glass was cold and damp with condensation, and the fizzy cola tickled her throat just right as she took a long pull on the straw. She'd barely set it down when one of the hotel's staff approached with a tray of fresh drinks.

Emma took another cola and watched the girl meander away, frowning. "I've never been in a place like this. It's so . . . posh. I feel like I shouldn't be here." She looked down at the borrowed T-shirt and cargo pants Frida had given her. Juliet had no idea where they came from—Frida wouldn't be caught dead dressing in cargo pants. Maybe they were Dora Lee's?

"Let's go shopping after we check in with everyone, Em. You need all kinds of stuff. Did the hotel give you a toothbrush?"

"Yeah, but it's disposable."

Aya, leaning far back in the depths of her chair's cushions, stuck out a foot and nudged Juliet's knee. "Can I come?"

Juliet winked at her. "I was hoping you'd ask."

Emma narrowed her eyes and glanced from Juliet to Aya, then back again. "Are you two, like, a thing?"

Aya laughed, nudging Juliet's knee again. "She's more like a sister!" She shifted her foot to the other side of the little coffee table and gave Emma's knee a shove. "Which means you're gonna be like a sister to me, so you better get used to having me around."

Emma's eyes widened with amusement, and she leaned back with a rather contented smile. Looking at her then, Juliet felt a little bad for wanting some space; she realized she'd been feeling that way because she and Emma were stuck—their relationship was still stalled in the same place it had been when Juliet was a teen and Emma had begun hanging around with her anticorpo buddies.

To her surprise, Emma seemed to be on the same page. "I hope I can get to know Juliet the way she is now, and if that means hanging around with her friends, then I'm all for it. I . . ." She trailed off.

Aya nudged her with her foot again. "What?"

"I made some friends in prison. There's one woman I owe a lot to. She was more like a counselor than a cellmate."

"We could try—"Juliet's impulse to help was cut short when Emma shook her head.

"No, she's not coming out. She, uh, did some pretty horrible things before she got locked up. Her sentence isn't for sale."

Juliet glanced at Aya, but her pink-haired friend just shrugged. "Oh, well, maybe you could visit her?"

"Yeah." Emma smiled. "I'd like that."

"Look!" Aya leaped to her feet and pointed to the rotating door. Sure enough, Bennet was pushing his way through. He was wearing an exceedingly undersized tank top tucked into skintight, flexible black leggings, and Juliet couldn't help the giggle that burbled out of her throat when Aya added, "He looks like an action figure!"

"Oh my gosh!" Juliet laughed. "Is that what he had on inside the Atlas?"

Bennet spotted them right away and started over, waving his hand over his head. His hair was short as usual, but it was standing up and out to the sides, and Juliet knew it was probably matted with sweat from being inside the gel-filled inner cocoon of the Atlas for so long. She waved back. "Come here!"

As he approached, Juliet saw Tanaka enter the lobby, dressed far more appropriately in gray slacks and a white button-up shirt. When had he had a chance to get changed? Even so dressed, he wore his monoblade, and Juliet swallowed another gulp of nervous energy.

Bennet didn't wait for small talk, and neither did Aya—she flew into his arms, squeezing her tiny arms around his bulging neck. "You made it!" she exclaimed. "You flew through space like a meteor! I thought for sure you were going to blow up when you dropped onto Ceres!"

He laughed. "No chance, runt!" Still holding Aya against him with one arm, he spread the other and beckoned Juliet. "Get in here!"

She laughed and joined the group hug, squeezing him around the ribs. Of course, that put her face right near his armpit, but she trusted Angel to filter out the odor. "Man, I'm glad to see you guys! When I was trying to get to that last gun, I kept thinking, 'Come on, Benny! You gonna let this thing blow Lucky and Aya up?' I was so *stressed* until Athena told me you got out of range, and then I let her take over and fly me down. Holy cow! What a ride that was! What a *view!*"

"All right!" Aya laughed. "I can't breathe! Let me down!"

"If you insist. One more squeeze!" Bennet made good on the threat. Suddenly, it felt like an anaconda was trying to finish Juliet off. She groaned, Aya squealed, and then Bennet let them down. As they gasped for air, he looked at Emma standing a little awkwardly to the side and grinned. "Who's this? Did they clone you after all, Lucky?"

"Oh, sure!" Emma laughed, but Juliet saw the twinkle in her eye. She hurried over and put an arm over her shoulder. "Benny, this is my sister, Em—Em, Benny."

"All this time, you had a sister?"

"Hey!" Aya cried. "She's got a few."

Bennet ignored her and stepped closer to Emma, holding out a big, meaty hand. "Pleased to meet you." Juliet could feel Aya's eyes on her, so she looked back and couldn't help giggling as her friend wriggled her eyebrows and jerked her head at Bennet and Emma.

"I think Aya is a believer in love at first sight," Angel whispered. Juliet's giggling intensified as she nodded.

"I'm glad you're safe, Juliet." Tanaka's gruff voice instantly sobered her up. Turning to him, she offered a soft smile. He wasn't exactly holding his arms out invitingly, but she didn't care. She stepped close, put her arms around his ribs, and hugged him, resting her chin against his shoulder.

"I'm only safe thanks to all you taught me. Thank you for everything."

"You were easy to teach," he chuckled, and to her great relief, he hugged her back, gently patting her back. She could hear Bennet teasing Aya and giving her sister the third degree, but she tuned them out as Tanaka said, "I see you have a new sword."

Rather than let go of her hug, she squeezed him tighter, and some small fraction of the stress she'd felt during her fight with Montclair resurfaced, tightening her throat as she whispered, "I'm sorry."

To her surprise, he laughed. "You're worried about a sword after everything you accomplished." He pushed her back, gripping her shoulders with his strong, nimble fingers. "A weapon is a weapon. Its job is to serve the wielder. Did it serve you well?"

She nodded, sniffing. "It did."

"Then I am happy. So, where did you acquire this new one? From the lifeless fingers of a foe?"

Juliet chuckled at his morbid assumption. "No, Rutger. Honey gave it to me." She glanced around the lobby, ensuring they were mostly alone in their corner of the ample space, then, taking a step back to make a little room, drew the sword.

As soon as it cleared the scabbard, the blade began to buzz and flicker with yellow, dancing lights. Breath hissing as he inhaled through his teeth, Tanaka leaned forward, peering at the blade Juliet held steady between them.

"*Kenzo Adler*? This is Bumblebee!" He clapped his hands in delight, and Juliet swore twenty years melted away from his face as his eyes twinkled. "I used to watch a neo-anime featuring this sword! Did you ever see it? *Neon Samurai*?"

"Uh," Juliet chuckled, her eyes widening, surprised by Tanaka's instant fanboy transformation. She carefully sheathed the sword and continued. "No, I haven't. Was it, um, was it just based on this sword? It's that famous?"

"That's Adler's *best* sword! I used to follow Kaito Suzuki's career, but he lost the sword in the eighties. The fight wasn't recorded, but rumor had it that Hiroshi Watanabe took it from him. If so, he never showed it publicly. *Honey* gave it to you?" His tone said he didn't believe it.

"Her, um, boyfriend, I guess, bought it for her at an auction on Mars. At least that's what she told me." Juliet shrugged.

"It's fitting that you should have that sword, *Kenshi* Juliet." To her dismay, he bowed.

Grabbing his shoulders, she hastily pushed him upright. "Stop that!" she exclaimed laughing. "I should be bowing to *you*."

He laughed and reached out to grasp the back of her neck. His hand felt warm against her skin as he gently squeezed. "You've done so much. I've been speaking with Selene"—he winked, eliciting a giggle from Juliet—"and she filled me in on things. Time for you to have some rest, hmm? Not too long, I hope. Don't tell her I said that; she made me promise not to pressure you."

He let go of her and then reached back, pressing his hands to his lower back as he stretched. "I need a shower and a nap. Talk soon." He waved toward Aya and the others, but they were enthralled by some ridiculous story Bennet was weaving, so he just shrugged and nodded, turning toward the reception desk.

"Let's have a drink later, Rutger," Juliet called after him. "Just you and me, all right?"

"*Hai.*" He didn't turn; he just waved his hand over his shoulder as he walked.

As she watched him go, Juliet subvocalized, "Any word from Athena about Jensen yet?"

"He's done with surgery and should wake anytime now. She wasn't pleased by the stock in cybernetic legs here on Ceres; she'd wanted to get him a pair somewhat like yours—natural looking—but the models in stock weren't very high quality. She ended up with some high-end but plasteel-encased ones. Here's a picture."

As she spoke, Angel opened a new window on Juliet's AUI displaying a brochure page from Aurora Corp. It featured an elegant-looking cybernetic leg prosthetic that immediately reminded Juliet of Tricia from Doctor Ladia's office. The features were impressive, and the price tag—seventy-nine thousand Sol-bits—was equally so.

"Well, if she's footing the bill for 150k worth of new cyberware, I doubt Jensen's gonna complain." As she spoke, Juliet walked back over to the others.

". . . I mean, I just *grabbed* the turret and pulled"—Bennet reached out, miming the action, obviously doing his best to show off his muscles as he grunted—"and ripped it out of its housing! Ever seen a forty-millimeter cannon barrel? It makes a nice club, let me tell you!"

Juliet slapped him on the shoulder. "Glad I'm not interrupting anything important."

He looked at her with his usual grin and shrugged. "Just a little blow-by-blow of my adventures in the Atlas."

"Why don't you go get cleaned up and change out of your, um, *tights*, and then you can join us for some shopping and food. We should swing by and say hello to Jensen, too."

Aya snickered. "I kind of like his tights, Lucky!"

"They're certainly . . . *something*," Emma piled on.

"Hey!" Bennet frowned and pointed toward his face. "Eyes up here, ladies." He turned to Juliet. "What kind of food?"

She shrugged. "You can pick."

"All right. I'm in. Gimme twenty." When he turned and started toward the elevator, he held a hand behind his butt, which of course resulted in giggles and catcalls.

"He's so funny!" Emma said as she retook her seat. Aya glanced at Juliet with a raised eyebrow, but Juliet didn't have a response, so she just shrugged.

"I say we order a drink while we wait." She glanced at their soda glasses. "I mean, a real drink."

52

A PLACE TO CALL HOME

Juliet was hot. She'd made Angel shorten her hair as much as she could, but it was still plastered to her scalp with sweat. Her shoulders were pink from the sun, her tank top was stuck to her body, and her jeans and boots were covered with dirt. In short, it was easy to see she'd been working outside all day.

As the sun moved past its zenith and she sat on the grassy hillside, sipping from a cold bottle of alcoholic lemonade, she watched Bennet operating the Berkley Industrial utili-tractor she'd bought for the property. It was an impressive machine with treads that could flatten a passenger car and a dozen bulky attachments they could switch out—things for digging, grating, grinding, and pretty much anything else they might need.

As she watched, movement caught her eye, and she looked down the path to see Emma hiking up toward her. Behind her, less than twenty kilometers away, the first tree-covered foothills leading up to the Rockies stole Juliet's attention with their beatific grandeur. "Pretty," she sighed.

"It's lovely," Angel agreed.

They'd bought the land, or rather, leased it for a hundred years from the Colorado Protectorate. It was land that had been reclaimed in the last few years. Apparently, sometime during the "conflict," it had been an upscale neighborhood that had been bombed into oblivion. Now, it was a picturesque landscape with smooth, rolling hills covered with grass, wildflowers, and young trees.

Bennet and Aya were carving out a driveway down to the access road, which led away to the new Protectorate Highway One, or PH1, and was a straight shot to either Boulder or New Denver, depending on which way you turned.

Emma sighed happily as she plopped down beside her and twisted open her own beverage. "Pretty prime location, sis."

Juliet laughed and clinked her bottle against Emma's. "I was thinking the same thing."

"Twenty-five acres—should be enough to keep us busy, huh?"

"I'd think so." Juliet looked past Bennet and Aya's antics to the field where they'd set up their camp. Big, self-expanding tents, a "bathroom" trailer, and a firepit gave away their presence—the evidence of their stay so far. "Did you get a hold of 'em?" She was asking about Emma's attempt to contact the industrial tractor-trailer that was supposed to be hauling their "homestead" package to the building site.

"Yep. Stuck in customs outside Denver. Won't be here until Friday at the earliest. I guess they're in a queue for inspection." She leaned back and drained half her bottle. "I swear, there were times I thought I'd never be happy again. I know you feel guilty about it all, but I'm so damn glad I got pulled out of that *melted* prison . . ." She let her words trail off as she sighed, closing her eyes and putting her face to the sun.

Juliet smiled as she took another sip. "I get that."

"You think mom will come out here? I mean, to visit. I figure, since I don't have to pay rent, I could save up and pay for her airfare."

"That was my idea, yeah, and don't sweat the airfare." Juliet bumped her with her elbow. "Or the rent. You're going to be making a home here, and I intend to take full advantage when I'm between . . . jobs? Missions? I don't know what to call what we're doing, but I know Athena and Tanaka will make me take breaks. This is a solid place for me to call home, and that's something I've been wanting for a long time.

"Besides, it's not just for us. The *Kowashi* crew paid for two of the bedroom units, and I know Benny has plans to stick around and help with everything." She nodded down the slope to Bennet, where he was still trying to work a smooth curve into the driveway. He seemed to be struggling as he tried to make the bend around a rock outcropping. Aya stood on a boulder, holding her head in her hands, and Juliet couldn't help giggling as she stomped a foot and yelled.

"I know," Emma sighed, smiling that stupid grin she'd been wearing far too often in the last couple of weeks. "Isn't he great?"

"Oh, *barf!*" Juliet snickered and gulped down the rest of her lemonade.

"Speaking of special friends, is yours going to make it tonight?"

Juliet looked at Emma and arched an eyebrow. "Are we just teasing right now, or can I be serious?"

Emma immediately sobered up and reached over to take Juliet's hand. "I want to be a good sister, Jules. We're starting a new chapter, right? So talk to me if you need to talk."

Juliet nodded, tilting her head sideways as she contemplated. She didn't *need* to talk; she'd already had quite a few long, heartfelt talks with Angel since the events on the ark ship. It felt good, though, to see Emma feel like she needed her, so she spoke from the heart.

"Cassie's got her hands full with Brooke right now. More importantly, I don't want to be someone she's holding out for, someone who keeps her from finding the right person. I'm going to be gone for months or years at a time, and that's not fair to anyone sitting around on Earth trying to make a family work."

"I get it, sis." Emma squeezed Juliet's hand, entwining their fingers as she turned toward the sky, squinting into the pale blue. "I'll be watching those stars, thinking about you, and I'm going to keep this dumb PAI from reading me any of the headlines from around the system. You hear that, Wally? I don't want any news about Juliet unless it's to say she's on her way home for a visit!"

Juliet smiled and lay back in the grass, resting her arm over her eyes to keep the sun out. "I can't believe you named him Wally."

"It's a fine name." Emma held her bottle upside down, letting the last few drops fall onto her tongue.

"Anyway, about Cassie, when I messaged her, I kind of indicated there was room for her to build something here. When she messaged me back, she seemed keen on the idea; I don't think the commune where she is now works as a long-term thing for her. Besides, Boulder's only about twenty minutes away; plenty close for her to have some kind of social life. Will you talk to her about it if she comes over tonight? I told her we were cooking out." Juliet laughed and gestured to their little tent compound. "As if we have a choice."

"Hell yeah, I will! The more the merrier—" Emma cut herself off and frowned, shaking her head. "No, I mean, *within reason*, the more of your *friends*, the merrier. I don't want a bunch of losers moving in and junking up the neighborhood."

"No need to worry about that, sis." Juliet hopped to her feet and then, with a grunt, hoisted Emma up, too. "I think you've pretty much met all my friends. Let's go get a fresh drink and tell Bennet to let that poor tractor rest for the night."

They hiked down the hill, past the flattened area where the modular housing units were meant to be installed. Juliet hadn't quite believed how cheaply she could get a long-term lease on the property from the protectorate, but she'd only had to fork over a hundred thousand bits. She chuckled at the symmetry—a 100k for a hundred years.

Of course, the payment had been the easy part. The real hurdle had been all the red tape—licenses, background checks, land-use agreements, and a dozen other clauses in a mind-bogglingly dense set of documentation.

Juliet smirked, remembering how Athena had cut through all that nonsense for her. She'd hardly had to sign her name on the dotted line, and even then, it had been her operator ID. But even so, even considering the good deal on the land, there were plenty of other expenses to consider.

A new utili-tractor would've been close to 200k, but she'd gotten one from a rancher liquidating his assets for only sixty-five. Then there was the modular homestead. She'd footed the bill for six different modules: three bedrooms, a kitchen, a great room, and a gym, while the *Kowashi* crew had pitched in for two more bedrooms, insisting they wanted a place for R&R now that they were signing on to Athena's Sol System cleanup crew.

The modules were built from nanoextruded plasteel and diamatex, and supposedly, were arrangeable in half a dozen different configurations, including stacks. Juliet looked forward to seeing how Bennet would lay the whole compound out.

All told—including the land, the tractor, an old pickup truck, the power plant, the water well and treatment system, and the homestead modules—Juliet had forked over nearly a million bits. She didn't regret a single one. Naturally, it made things easy when she'd already had more than two million, and then Athena had paid her another five.

The true AI had surprised her with a completed SOA contract for "infiltrating and hindering the operations of rogue elements of the WBD corporation." Naturally, the contract had covered bonus milestones that just happened to coincide with everything Juliet had done out of necessity.

Thinking about it brought another stupid grin to her face as she and Emma let gravity pull them down the slope, lengthening their strides into a run as they both broke into giggles, trying to be first down to the rumbling tractor.

"No fair!" Emma cried as Juliet stretched her legs and pulled ahead.

"Hey, I don't remember much mercy out of you when I was half your size!"

"You were *seven*!" Emma laughed. Aya heard her and turned, shading her eyes against the low-hanging sun. When she saw them laughing and stumbling to a stop nearby, she waved and hopped off the boulder.

"Angel," Juliet gasped, "tell Bennet to turn that thing off!" The tractor was electric, so it wasn't making much engine noise, but the clatter of stones under the grating attachment was enough to force her implants to dial back her auditory gain.

"What do you think?" Aya asked, gesturing to the smooth dirt track leading up to the building site and then down, most of the way, to the access road. "Not bad, considering he just learned how to drive that thing today, right?"

Juliet hung her arm over Aya's shoulders, pulling her in for a side hug. "Not bad at all!" She kicked some of the freshly tilled dirt. "Did Em tell you about the delay on our shipment?"

"Yeah. No big deal, though. The well installation is still scheduled for tomorrow, right?"

"Yep, and the, uh, surfacing company is bringing an extrusion machine first thing the day after." Juliet had hired a local company for the driveway and foundation. They had a machine that would spit out something that was a lot like concrete as it drove along, munching up dirt to mix with its additive chemicals.

Aya, too, kicked some dirt. "Sounds like we're on our way."

"It still freaks me out," Emma chimed in, "that we'll be drinking water right out of the ground. You're sure the treatment system you got will be able to remove the contaminants? I heard there were nukes detonated not too far from here—"

"Em," Juliet sighed, "we've been over this. The protectorate has been mitigating the radiation in this area for nearly ten years. They have nanite swarms that *eat* radiation. The same tech is in the treatment system, so yeah, I think we'll be good. Don't worry, though, 'cause it automatically tests the water in the holding tank, and it'll display the results—you can be the judge."

As she spoke, the tractor's constant hum died down, and Bennet stepped out of the cab, closing the door behind him with a solid *thunk*. Whooping, he leapt down to a tread, then onto the fresh dirt. "How about that? I *love* this machine!"

Emma forgot her conversation with Juliet and jogged over to him, wrapping him in a hug; Juliet was torn between irritation and delight to see Bennet's enormous smile. Before she could engage a filter, she muttered, "How can they seem so right after knowing each other a grand total of what? Fifteen days?"

"I *knew* it was going to happen. It was love at first sight back on Ceres! You saw it! It's like magic." Aya sighed wistfully, then turned toward the grassy field where their tents sat. Juliet knew what she was thinking: why couldn't Leo be as great as Bennet? She and the merc were still "dating," but Leo was currently up on Luna, having passed on the trip down Earthside.

"Hey." She hurried to walk beside Aya. "Everyone moves at their own pace. If something's meant to be, I think it'll happen."

Aya snorted. "That's very *rich* coming from you, miss."

"I—" Juliet couldn't keep a straight face and had to laugh at herself. "I know."

"I know you know." Aya looked at her and winked. As they came to their campground, she pointed at the trailer containing their big water tank, bathroom, and shower. "Wanna shower first?"

"Go for it. I'm gonna message Ladia; she sent me a note—"

"Make sure you get me an appointment on the same day!"

"I know!" Juliet laughed. "I was *going* to say she wanted to talk to me about our requests. I guess Athena sent her some specs for mods to the circulatory augments we asked for."

Aya nodded, her expression severe. "I will *not* spend another dogfight totally blacked out!"

"Yeah, but just 'cause we're getting some upgrades doesn't mean we don't have to practice. We need to start scheduling some regular time in the sims when we're done with this little"—Juliet laughed as she considered the hard work they'd been doing—"vacation!"

"You know I'm down for it." Aya jerked her thumb toward the trailer. "Gonna rinse off some dirt."

Juliet nodded and turned to their firepit. Despite the late spring date, the evenings were chilly up near the mountains, so she walked over to the big propane tank just outside their circle of tents and twisted the valve. Angel sent a signal to the firepit, which clicked several times before *whoomphing* as the gas lit up. "Any word from Ghoul?"

"No. I'll send her a reminder—"

"Angel! Wait . . ." Juliet sighed as she realized she had no proper objection.

Angel ignored Juliet's half-formed protestation. "She's coming!"

"Really?"

"Yes! She wanted to make sure it was all right to bring her niece. I told her it would be amazing!"

Juliet was quiet as she walked over to the refrigerated cooler they had plugged into the solar array atop the water cooler. Somewhere between the firepit and the propane tank, she'd decided to put off messaging Ladia. She felt like she had enough on her mind.

Juliet could hear Aya's muffled singing from inside, bringing her smile back to prominence. Ever aware of her moods, Angel proved her competence by saying, "I know you're nervous, but I bet Ghoul is too. Just be honest with her, Juliet."

"I know you're right, Angel. I *am* nervous, though." She fished around for another hard lemonade, then took out the burgers and sausages they'd picked up at the co-op earlier that day.

"Hey," Bennet called as he and Emma walked into camp. "Wanna grill on the firepit, or should I fire up the charcoal thingy?"

"Uh, the charcoal grill. I don't wanna fight all the smoke out of my eyes while I sit."

"Wait—while you sit? Am I cooking *again*?"

Emma laughed. "You love it."

Juliet jerked her thumb at the trailer. "Don't get any ideas—I'm next."

"No problem." Bennet sighed, collapsing into one of the comfy camp chairs they had arranged around the firepit. "Toss me a beer and a protein bar, will you?"

"Benny!" Emma laughed, sitting beside him. "We're going to eat soon."

"He has to maximize his gains, Em." Juliet shook her head, laughing quietly, then fished out a cookies 'n cream protein bar and a dark, local stout. She didn't toss them, though, despite Bennet holding out his hands and looking disappointed as she carried them over to him.

"I'm not sure we'll be able to afford to keep our pantry stocked when Juliet and Aya leave."

"You let me worry about that, sweet cheek—"

"All right!" Juliet groaned, cutting him off. "I can't take any more of this!" She was half joking; having heard the water flow in the trailer cut off, she intended to make good on her promise to be next in the shower.

"Juliet!" Emma grabbed Bennet's huge, meaty palm. "Don't make Benny feel bad for being affectionate!"

"*Blegh.*" Juliet waved her hand dismissively before stomping over to the trailer, where she knocked on the door. "Are you decent?"

"Not yet! Two minutes!"

Juliet smiled and sat on the step, watching Emma and Bennet and feeling a comfortable warmth in her chest. She was glad—

"You're glad they're together." Angel, once again, proved she could feel what Juliet felt.

"Yeah. How great will it be to know they're here, living the life we're out there trying to protect?" It had kind of surprised her when Bennet had indicated a desire to try his hand at "homesteading." He'd proclaimed his space-fighting bucket list complete after his ride in the Atlas. Juliet supposed having a budding romantic interest with Emma was a big factor, too.

Angel mentally nodded. "I think it'll be wonderful. I just hope they aren't moving too fast."

"Eh, I know better than to try to judge anyone where romance is concerned."

"Speaking of awkward failed romance, Ghoul has indicated she's leaving. You have about thirty-seven minutes until she arrives."

Juliet snorted in mock indignation. "That was a little below the belt, wasn't it?"

"You know I love you."

Juliet smiled and stood, pounding on the door. "Aya! We're getting company, and I need to get cleaned up!"

Aya pushed the door open, her pink hair damp, her face moist from the steam, and stomped out, still buttoning her jeans over her T-shirt. "You better not be like this on the *Blossom*! We need to have scheduled shower time—"

"Uh-uh!" Juliet waggled her finger. "I have my own shower, remember?"

"Oh, right. *Excuse* me, *Captain*." Aya winked and hopped down to the grass while Juliet climbed into the steamy trailer. "Um, by the way, make it quick; we need to refill the water tank soon."

"*Aya!*" Juliet growled, slamming the door shut. Twenty-five minutes later, she sat back down near the firepit, clean and wearing her last pair of jeans that weren't too filthy to tolerate under a faded button-up flannel she'd purchased at a secondhand store in Boulder.

The sun's light was nearly gone from the western sky, but it persisted, illuminating the peaks in a warm, golden-orange halo. The air was noticeably chilly, and everyone had moved their chairs closer to the fire. Bennet was still in the shower, the last to go in, and Juliet snickered softly, wondering if he'd run out of water.

"You're cruel," Angel whispered, despite knowing only Juliet could hear her.

"He'll be fine," she subvocalized. "He's been in there for five minutes; he's got to be mostly clean by now."

"Someone's coming." Emma pointed with her bottle toward the access road. Sure enough, two headlights were wending their way through the low hills toward their property. "Your friend?"

Juliet looked at her, and some of her nervousness must have shown because Emma smiled almost sweetly. "You should go down by the truck and wait for her. Wouldn't want her to get stuck driving up Bennet's driveway; not with the soil so loose."

"Want me to come?" Aya asked, already scooting toward the edge of her seat.

"Nah." She smiled, setting her drink into the built-in cup holder on her chair. "I want to talk to her for a minute, 'kay?" Aya's bright, softly illuminated pink eyes flashed briefly as she smiled and nodded. Juliet stuffed her hands into her pockets and slowly ambled down the torn-up soil toward the service road where they'd parked the truck.

The little car—Juliet could make it out easily now, away from the firelight and with Angel enhancing the gain on her optics—arrived at the protectorate's barbed-wire fence and their makeshift, wooden gate well ahead of her.

Juliet lengthened her strides and watched as Ghoul's familiar figure exited on the driver's side. A second later, the passenger door flew open, and a much smaller figure jumped out with a squeal of giggles. "Brooke, I presume," Juliet said softly. As she stared, Angel zoomed in, and Juliet felt her smile growing despite her nerves.

The little girl was adorable—a miniature Cassie with short blonde hair, bright blue eyes, and big cheeks that flushed pink in the chilly air as Ghoul hoisted her onto her hip. Juliet shifted her gaze to Ghoul's face and watched her smile as she kissed the little girl's temple, pointing a finger toward Juliet.

Of course, Angel easily picked up her softly spoken words with Juliet's audio implants.

"That's my friend," she whispered, "the one I told you the stories about."

53

CASSIE

"So," Aya started, handing Ghoul a Radish Top IPA, "Juliet introduced you as *Ghoul*, but isn't that, like, your handle?"

Ghoul, holding a very quiet Brooke on her lap, took the beer and smiled. She glanced at Juliet and shrugged almost sheepishly. "Yeah, my name's Cassie. I think I kind of prefer that these days."

"Hey!" Juliet nudged her knee with her boot. "When I asked last time—"

"I don't care, really," Ghoul hurriedly added. "I mean, you can call me whatever."

Aya sat down beside Ghoul and pointed at Juliet with her beer. "I still call her *Lucky* most of the time. She wouldn't tell me her name for the longest time."

Juliet groaned and sipped some more of her lemonade, too buzzed to put up an argument. She silently sent a prayer of thanks that her nanites would ensure her hangover was mild.

Something sizzled loudly from the grill, and Bennet cried, "Water! Get me some water, or we're eating charcoal!" Emma ran toward the trailer while Juliet giggled, more amused by the spectacle than she should've been.

Ghoul—*Cassie*—nodded toward Juliet. "Looks like someone got a head start on me, huh?"

"I think she was nervous," Aya replied, utterly oblivious to the glare Juliet sent her way.

"Nervous?" Cassie kissed Brooke's head and then nodded—far too seriously for Juliet's taste. "Me too, I guess."

While Juliet stared at Cassie, their eyes locked like invisible lines connected them, Aya cleared her throat and reached over to wriggle Brooke's foot. "Hey, do you like art books?"

"Pictures?"

"Yeah! I'm writing a book about her"—Aya nodded at Juliet—"and I've got a bunch of really cool scenes drawn. Do you want to see if they're any good? I need a second opinion."

"Really? Can I, Cassie?" Brooke tilted her head back to look up at her aunt's face.

"I think that would be sweet," Cassie rasped, smiling at Aya, her chromed teeth glinting in the firelight. Aya tugged on Brooke's little hand, and she slid off Cassie's lap, walking almost hesitantly behind Aya over toward her tent. Brooke slowed to a stop and looked over her shoulder, and Aya paused until Cassie waved her on. "Go ahead, silly. I'll be right here."

"Why didn't you tell me you liked *Cassie* better?" Their chairs were very close, angled toward each other, so it was easy, almost too hard to resist, for Juliet to nudge her knee again with her boot.

"I, uh . . ." Cassie licked her lips. "I have a hard time telling people how I really feel. You should get that by now; I wasn't exactly being honest last time we were face-to-face." She didn't say it, but Cassie's eyes twitched toward Aya's tent, and Juliet knew she was talking about Brooke and her sister.

"She's adorable, you know? She looks like a miniature version of you. A tiny Ghoul—" Juliet sighed and shook her head. "Sorry! It's gonna take me a while to think of you as Cassie." Cassie started to protest, but Juliet held up her hand. "No, I *want* to. I want you to be the person in here"—she leaned forward and gently touched Cassie's chest, just beneath her collarbone—"on the outside, too. You're starting a new chapter in your life, Cassie, and you deserve to put that *other* chapter behind you."

Cassie nodded, smiling. "I *do* want to. I don't want to be the person who worked with Vikker and Don anymore. I want to be the person who Brooke looks at like some kind of damn superstar." She laughed and sipped her beer. "Not that I have any clue how to do it!"

"That's what's great about kids, though, right? Just be good to them, and you're pretty much guaranteed to come out looking like a hero."

"*Exactly!*" She chuckled. "I mean, that was kinda why I was nervous to see you. I need you to understand that I have to be here for her. There's, like, no other option. You get that, right?" Cassie's self-conscious body language—shrinking back in her chair, holding the beer bottle in front of her mouth, narrowing her eyes—hinted at her being afraid Juliet wouldn't understand for some reason, and Juliet couldn't quite fathom why.

"Are you crazy? Of *course* I understand! God, Cassie, the whole reason any of us should be doing anything in this messed-up world is for kids like Brooke. I'd be pissed if you said you wanted to hand her off to someone else and run away. You wouldn't be the person I care about if you could do that."

As she spoke, Cassie reached over and took her hand in hers, squeezing it gently. It felt nice, and Juliet's heart began to hammer.

"Let's walk?" She gestured to the tent where Aya's and Brooke's shadowy silhouettes could be seen shifting through the thin material. "We won't go far, but—" She didn't know exactly how to explain that she felt the need to move, to put a little more distance between themselves and the background noise of Bennet's boisterous conversation with her sister.

"Sure," Cassie interjected, standing up but still holding Juliet's hand.

Juliet smiled and tugged on those slender, warm fingers, guiding her away from the fire into the chilly night. As she promised, they didn't go far before she slowed to a stop and turned to face Cassie, struggling to find the right words for what she wanted to say. "Now I need to tell you why *I* was so nervous about seeing *you* again."

"I already pretty much know what's up." She shrugged. "I mean, when you described this place, you said you were building a home for Emma, a place you could visit. So yeah, I figured—"

Juliet seized the opportunity to speak about anything other than her feelings.

"Oh! I wanted to talk to you about that! Listen, when I picked this place to build, you have to have figured I was thinking about you too, right? When I got your message about Brooke and your sister . . ." Juliet lifted Cassie's hand, grasping it with her other, holding it between them. "I want you to live here, too. I want you to have a safe place to raise Brooke where you never have to worry about rent or who's coming and going or—"

"I can't do that, J! Your sister doesn't even know me; I—"

"No! I already spoke to her. Listen, we have twenty-five acres here, and we'll have power, water—anything you could need. I ordered homestead modules, and it'll be trivial for Benny to set up a bedroom and kitchen module for you, so you'll have your own space with Brooke, but you'll be close to friends, you know? Close to help if you need it."

"I mean . . ." Cassie's eyes, looking up at Juliet, were like two little pools of light—like candles beneath the surface of crystal-clear ice—as they reflected the moon and starlight. "How could I say no to that? If you're sure the others don't mind."

"They don't!" Juliet's smile pulled hard at the corners of her mouth; she felt relieved and strangely self-satisfied for getting Cassie to agree.

"So, like . . ." Cassie's words didn't come, but she added her other hand to where Juliet held hers, and they stood there, hands entwined, staring into each other's eyes in the darkness.

"So, like, uh—" Juliet chickened out and broke eye contact. As Cassie sighed and squeezed tighter, refusing to let her retreat, Juliet shook her head, barreling into her rehearsed words.

"Cassie, you know the creeps who sent that chip to you?" She wanted to paint a bigger picture for her, wanted to explain her motivations before she, herself, forgot about them and just said, "Melt it," and embraced the moment.

"Yeah?"

"That was, like, the tip of the iceberg of their evil, messed-up, ugh . . . *machinations*." She smiled, nodding at her vocabulary. "They, um, fled the system—long story—but left behind a lot of problems. There are conflicts cropping up all over that could build into bigger wars. I mean all over the place, all over the *system*, and I'm working with some people who mean to undo the mess those creeps left behind.

"I'll be . . . all over the place. I'll be gone for months or years at a time. If my, uh, *friend* manages to figure out where the, um, *bad guys* went, then I might chase after them. I don't know if I'll ever come back; that's the situation with all of this—none of it will be a walk in the park. There aren't any guarantees."

Cassie shook her head and sort of smirked a little, flashing some of her sharp, shiny teeth.

"Really? Bad guys who 'fled the system'? A mysterious *friend* pulling the strings? Life-or-death missions? Juliet, if you're trying to turn me off, you're doing a shitty job. You're shiny as new chrome on a fine, *fine* street racer. God, it's killing me, you know? I *want* to say, 'Take me with you!' *Hah*!"

She continued to shake her head, holding up a hand so Juliet knew she wasn't done as she gathered her thoughts. "I *want* to say that, but I can't. As soon as I remember Brookie, everything changes. There's nothing—no fine lady, no shiny chrome, *nothing*—that could pull me away from her. Do you get that?"

Juliet squeezed Cassie's fingers. "I *do* get that. I hope *you* get why I hope you find someone who will be here for you, though. I hope you get why I couldn't handle having someone *waiting* for me. That's not my thing, and I—"

"Say no more, J." Cassie returned the pressure, gently squeezing her hands. "I'm here for you, okay? You can count on that. If you're out there fighting for a better world for *Brookie*? If you're out there and you need a place to think of as *home*? You better damn well believe I'm here, and that I'll be doing everything I can to make the most of what you're giving us."

"Do you promise? Do you promise you won't stop trying to find love here? I want to believe you'll live a good life, no matter what I'm doing or where I am. I swear the guilt—"

"Hush!" Cassie pulled on Juliet's hands, tugging her close until she fell into an embrace. The top of Cassie's head as she rested it against Juliet's chest fell just under her chin, so Juliet tucked into it, folding her arms around her.

It felt like she fit perfectly against her, and the heat between them, building up in the fabric of Juliet's flannel and Cassie's sweatshirt, was like a fire, pushing away the chill of the evening mountain air. Juliet memorized the feeling, swearing to herself that she'd never forget it, no matter where she flew or what she was up against.

"I didn't even really say what I felt like I needed to say," she sighed, practically whispering.

"I get it, though. I appreciate you. I'm sorry I put these feelings on you. I'm sorry I—"

"Now *you* hush. Let's make the most of our time, yeah?"

"Yeah." Cassie sniffed. "Yeah, for sure."

Unsurprisingly, Juliet's eyes were overflowing with tears, and as they began to stream down her cheeks, she finally let go of Cassie with one arm and wiped them away with the soft, warm fabric of her sleeve. Then she gripped Cassie again, pulling her tight, squeezing her until she grunted, gasping a little for air.

"Thank you," she mumbled, finally relenting, reducing the pressure so Cassie could breathe, and more importantly, speak.

"Shit!" She laughed. "I don't remember you being that strong." She gently stroked Juliet's hair, chuckling, and then Bennet, naturally, ruined the moment.

From back at the firepit, he hollered, "Hey, uh, hate to interrupt the lovefest, but this meat's done."

"Food?" Aya called from her tent, which a moment later was echoed by a smaller, higher-pitched voice. "*Food?*"

Cassie laughed and wriggled, trying to break free of Juliet's arms. "Come on, J; we're drawing a crowd."

Juliet let go but kept a hand on Cassie's shoulder as she wiped her eyes again. "God, I feel like I'm weightless. Thank you." She looked at Bennet, standing with a spatula in his hand and an apron over his bare chest, and softly growled, "You're *next*, Benny!"

"Next?" Cassie asked, arching a pale eyebrow.

"I think some people around here need some *hugs!*" Juliet giggled. She was buzzed, but she wasn't drunk. Even so, she felt like releasing some energy. It felt like her nervousness and tension with Cassie had built something up that had to be let go.

With an evil grin, she started jogging back to the fire, then picking up speed, raced toward the big man as Cassie laughed behind her.

Bennet tried to get his spatula up to defend himself, but Juliet was too fast. She slammed into him, arms wide, and grabbed him in a bear hug. He was too broad, especially with his arms inside her grasp, for her to reach far enough to clasp her hands together, but she tried, squeezing with everything she had.

"*Oof!*" he groaned as she managed to lift him off his feet, using her cybernetic leg and reinforced spine to good effect. "What the hell?"

"I'm just sharing some of the *love!*" Juliet grunted. Emma giggled madly, backing away, but not soon enough. Juliet locked eyes with her and narrowed her brows. "Ready for your dose, sis?"

"What?" She stumbled back. "No!" She glanced around, eyes wide, and spied Aya coming out of her tent. "*Aya!*" she cried, turning to run off into the grassy meadow. Juliet released Bennet and started after her.

As Bennet nearly fell, gasping for air, Juliet yelled, "You should know better than to run from a predator!"

"*Aya!* Help! Something's wrong with Juliet!" Emma barely got the words out, giggling, as she scrambled away from Juliet, only to trip and tumble into the grass. Juliet pounced on her, and as Emma squealed with hysterical laughter, she gathered her up in a hug from behind and began to roll back and forth, snarling and growling as she slobbered kisses all over the back of her neck.

Angel, well aware of what Juliet was up to, enhanced the gain on her audio implants, so she heard Aya ask, "Uh, what's going on?"

"Lucky finally went nuts from all those cybernetics," Bennet chuckled. "She just attacked me, and now she's mauling her sister."

"Cassie?" a tiny-voiced Brooke asked, more than a little nervously.

Juliet grinned and released her sister. Leaping to her feet, she hunkered down and glared out of the darkness back at the camp. Subvocalizing, she said, "Make my eyes glow, Angel."

"Done—I hope yellow is okay."

Holding her hands out like claws, Juliet began stalking toward the campfire. "I heard there's a little girl in this camp," she called. "A little girl who likes being visited by the *tickle monster!*"

"Cassie?" Brooke asked again, tremulously, glancing at her aunt.

"*Run*, Brookie!" Cassie laughed.

Juliet charged out of the grass, snarling and growling, and as Brooke squealed and turned to run, she *leaped* through the air, pushing off with her cybernetic leg. She must have cleared seven meters and reveled in the gasps and laughter as she landed next to the firepit with a *thud*.

Brooke squealed again, and Juliet would have let up, not wanting to really scare the girl, but there was a definite giggle chasing those squeals, so she howled madly and then chased after her. In short order, she had her down, gently tickling her sides just enough to keep the giggles going, stopping frequently to kiss her on top of the head and cheeks.

"I *got* you," she whispered in her ear, only eliciting more giggles.

After a while, she relented and hoisted Brooke up, lifting her onto her shoulders. Everyone was already loading their plates up with food, but Cassie was definitely still keeping an eye out.

"I think your auntie was worried about you," Juliet whispered. Brooke's answer was another giggle as she hugged Juliet around the neck to steady herself. Juliet pretended to choke as she loosened the girl's grip and took her hands in hers. "Hold on!" She bounded through the grass back to the fire.

"Welcome back!" Cassie reached up to gently stroke Brooke's cheek. "Did you survive the tickle monster, honey?"

"Yes!" Brooke's voice held a definite note of pride.

"I'll make you a plate."

"I'll do it!" Juliet said. "Sit down and relax, Cassie." As she approached the grill and the folding table beside it with the side dishes and plates, Aya stepped close.

"Hey, why'd everyone get attacked but me?"

Juliet arched an eyebrow at her. "It's more fun when you don't see it coming."

Aya grinned and reached up to squeeze Brooke's little knee. "I like this side of Juliet!"

Juliet loaded up a plate with a burger, some pasta salad, and a big piece of chocolate cake. With her hands full, she craned her neck to look up at Brooke. "Can we share a plate? I can get us refills if we eat it all."

"Yes!"

"Okay, but that means you have to sit on my lap while we eat. Can you tolerate that?"

"Yes!"

"Okay." Juliet grabbed two forks and a knife then went back to her seat, grunting as she balanced her plate in one hand while hoisting Brooke down onto her lap with the other. "Aya!" she called. "Will you get me another drink?"

"How about something *without* alcohol?" Bennet suggested. Juliet flipped her plastic knife in the air and then, snatching it by the tip of the blade, flicked it at Bennet. It bounced off his absurd pectoral muscle—thankfully now clad in a T-shirt—and fell to the grass.

Juliet glared at him. "Don't suggest such a thing!" When Brooke giggled, she added, "Now, Brooke, I'm a trained knife thrower. You're not allowed to do that until I give you your certification. Understood?"

"Yes." Her voice was breathless, and Juliet wasn't sure if she was whispering or just excited.

"Good!" Juliet handed her a fork before situating the plate so they could both reach it. "Let's start with the potato salad. Someone needs to cut this burger in half for us—Wait!" Juliet held up her right hand, and her nail extended, buzzing and humming as her vibroblade protruded from the tip of her finger. "This should do the trick!" She held her hand away from the two of them before adding, "Keep your hands back! This will be a dangerous operation."

"Oh my God, Lucky!" Aya caught her wrist. "Put that away! I'll cut your burger in half."

"If you insist." Juliet retracted the nail. Peering sideways at Brooke, she added, whispering behind her hand, "Maybe it wasn't the best idea."

She was feeling absurdly good; like she was high, even. She supposed it had a lot to do with relief. She'd been so nervous about talking to Ghoul again, having built up the situation in her mind and making it more than it was, imagining hurt feelings and pleading and all sorts of ridiculous scenarios.

Now, though, she felt good. She felt relieved that the people she cared about all knew what she was up to, what she was about, and things could move forward honestly. Whatever it was, it certainly amplified the buzz of the hard lemonade she'd been drinking all afternoon.

Aya cut their burger for them, and then it was eating time. Juliet and Brooke had fun sharing their food, and it was nice to let everyone else handle the conversation for a while. Cassie initially made small talk with Aya, but Emma and Bennet scooted closer, and they talked about the land, the modules that were en route, and the kinds of plans they had for the place.

After a while, Cassie asked Emma about her tattoo, which got Emma talking about their mom and dad. Juliet's earlier exuberance began to diminish, so she tuned them out and had a secret, whispered conversation with Brooke.

"Do you ever look at the stars at night?"

Brooke caught on to the secret and whispered in her ear, "Sometimes. Cassie and I like to pretend my mommy is up there watching us."

Of course, the words brought tears to Juliet's eyes, but she blinked them away. "Why do you think it's pretend?"

"Cassie says she doesn't know for sure what happens when we die, but it's nice to dream."

Juliet nodded, pressing her cheek close to Brooke's. "That's fair. I don't know for sure either, but I'm a hundred percent sure there's a lot more to us than what we can see and feel." She looked up at the stars and, stifling more tears, added, "I bet your mommy's so proud of you."

She couldn't resist giving Brooke another kiss on the temple as she scooped up the last bite of chocolate cake. "Want it?" She held her fork close to Brooke's mouth. She grinned fiercely, growled, and chomped down on it. "What a bite! Like a crocodile!" Brooke giggled, and Juliet pulled her close as she leaned back in her chair, listening to the others talk for a while.

"You're good with her," Cassie noted after a lull in the conversation.

Juliet peeked down her nose at Brooke and realized she'd dozed off. "It's easy 'cause I'm not doing it twenty-four seven like you. I couldn't keep this up for long."

"She's good at a lot." Juliet looked up, surprised by Bennet's sudden praise. He held his beer up in salute. "I don't say it enough, but we're all damn lucky to have you in our lives, *Lucky*." He grinned. "I hope you don't hate me for wanting some downtime. A chance to . . ."

He trailed off, so Juliet finished for him.

"Have a life? Heck no, I don't blame you, Benny. You deserve it. I'm surprised Shiro and Alice aren't down here, too, especially after the payout they earned from, uh, Selene." They'd all agreed not to mention Athena to anyone the AI didn't out herself to, even someone as close to Juliet as Cassie.

"Those are your salvage friends?" Cassie asked, looking between Aya and Bennet.

"Yeah," Juliet answered for them, "but they're up there." She pointed toward the moon, halfway up the eastern half of the sky. "They put their salvage ship in dry dock, and our—well, maybe *benefactor* is the best word for her—is backing them as they work through contracting one of the lunar shipyards. I guess they're going to be in charge of having a capital ship built."

"I mean, let's be honest: they're just there to sign documents and attend meetings. That's one hell of an operation—" Bennet started to say, but Aya laughed and clapped her hands.

"I knew it! You're totally jealous. There's no way you're going to last down here."

"Don't say that!" Emma leaned closer to Bennet and took his hand in hers. "I think, if he wants to get involved, he can do it through a nice, safe dream-rig, right here on our property."

"Uh, yeah." Bennet smiled. "What she said."

Cassie scooted to the edge of her chair. "Hey, this was super fun, and I mean it. Like, this was the most fun I've had in a couple of years, but I need to get this little runt to bed." She jerked her thumb at Brooke, wrapped snugly in Juliet's arms.

Juliet smiled and whispered, "You sure? Could have a campout."

"Another time, J. Will you be here long?"

Juliet looked at Aya, and her friend smiled, her pink eyes glimmering in the firelight. "Only about a week. We've got appointments on Luna."

Cassie nodded and stood, reaching for Brooke. "A week's not terrible. We could have a campout for sure. Let me pick up some sleeping bags in town."

Juliet pushed her hands away and stood, holding Brooke tightly to her chest. "I'll walk you down to your car."

"Oh, all right." Cassie turned to everyone and waved. "I really loved meeting you all. See you soon."

"Bye-bye!" Aya waved. "Tell Brookie I said good night!"

"Nice meeting you." Emma smiled, leaning her head on Bennet's shoulder as he waved.

Juliet put her free arm over Cassie's shoulders and nudged her toward the path.

She savored the feelings she was having. She savored the warmth of the little body cradled against her chest, the hot little cheek on her neck, and the closeness of Cassie. It was a feeling she meant to keep with her always, so she focused on every second of it, imprinting those feelings—physical and emotional—indelibly in her memory.

If she could, she would have overwritten something else, some terrible experience she'd rather forget, but she knew she couldn't. Those unpleasant experiences were part of who she was. The best she could do was add something better, something that would remind her of love and friendship and the need to care about something bigger than herself.

54

CLINIC TIME

think it's wonderful that I get to see both of you at once today!" Ladia exclaimed as she led Juliet and Aya into her office. "I appreciate you putting off our meeting—I hated rescheduling, but it gave me time to fabricate the nanites your research team sent over."

Aya, leading the way behind the doctor, turned to grin and wink at Juliet. "It wasn't any problem; we had plenty to do down Earthside. It was a nice excuse for a little more R and R."

"Speak for yourself," Juliet snorted. "My hands have calluses on their calluses." The truth was that she hadn't minded a couple of extra days with her sister, let alone Cassie and Brooke. Still, it was fun to complain, though Aya wasn't having it.

"That's baloney, Doc. Her hands were plenty calloused already, what with all her sword fighting." Aya's eyes flickered with exploding pink stars, indicating she was playing around.

"Sword fighting, Aya?" Juliet giggled, picturing herself as a medieval knight.

Aya shrugged. "What would you call it? Monoblade waving?"

"I mean, I guess you're right, but we just call it Kendo—at least, Tanaka does."

Aya shrugged, so Ladia took the opportunity to interject. "Well, in any case, I appreciated the time. I also appreciated the sheer genius of the scientists who came up with these nanites. Take a seat, and I'll explain what I mean." She gestured to the chairs in front of her desk, and as Juliet and Aya sat, Tricia came in to deposit a tray with three bubbling glasses of faintly orange-tinted liquid.

Tricia leaned close to Juliet as she walked by and whispered, "Mango—you'll love it." Then she was gone, her skirt swishing as she stretched her long legs toward the exit.

"So." Ladia waved a hand at her desk, producing a hologram that displayed a faintly translucent humanoid figure with the many rivers and tributaries of its veins glowing in bright, illuminated detail. "There are a number of methods for helping pilots to cope with high-G-forces, but none so elegant as the one your researchers came up with."

Aya giggled again, and Juliet knew why; Athena had constructed an entire phony cybernetic research corporation to cover for her almost effortless design. Ladia peered at her with a faint smile. "Did I misspeak?"

"Don't mind her, Iris," Juliet sighed, reaching over to thump Aya's shoulder. "I'm sure if Aya and I were in school together, we'd be separated immediately."

"Ah, I see. An inside joke. No worries, my dears." She grinned and winked. "Professor Ladia will allow you to remain as lab partners." She pointed to the holographic model again. "As I was saying, there are many ways to help mitigate G-forces, from synthetic arteries and vessels to cybernetic blood pumps. Your team, however, has come up with something better. It's a two-stage process, and not nearly as invasive as some of the 'better' solutions I had on offer before.

"In the first stage of the upgrade, I'll introduce nanites into your bloodstream—the ones designed by your team. Their purpose is to seek out and reinforce the major vessels and arteries throughout your body. As they circulate, they'll begin weaving a biosynthetic lattice around the walls of those vessels. The resulting structure will strengthen and support your vascular system, making it more resilient to the extreme pressures and forces you'll experience during high-G maneuvers.

"The reinforced vessels will be less likely to rupture or collapse under stress, ensuring your blood continues to flow smoothly even when your body is under extreme strain. More importantly, it will allow those same vessels and arteries to remain flexible and pliant when rigidity is not called for. This phase is crucial for laying the groundwork for the next stage of the upgrade."

"Next stage?" Juliet prompted, watching as the image slowly rotated, showing an animation of swarms of brightly colored dots flowing through the vessels and arteries.

Ladia nodded. "Yes, once your vessels are reinforced, we move on to the second stage: the installation of clenching valves around your major arteries. The valves are advanced microdevices controlled by a module that will integrate with your PAI, allowing your management software to contract and release them in response to your body's needs. They'll be strategically placed around key arteries, including those leading to the brain, to control the flow of blood with precision.

"During high-G maneuvers, the clenching valves will activate to temporarily restrict blood flow to certain areas, preventing blood from pooling in your extremities or overwhelming sensitive organs like your brain. For example, when pulling high Gs, the valves will tighten to keep blood from draining too quickly from your head, reducing the risk of blacking out. Conversely, if blood pressure spikes in your brain, the valves can restrict flow to protect against redout.

"Isn't it brilliant? The two-stage approach ensures that your vascular system is not only reinforced but also intelligently regulated! I . . ." Ladia smiled and reached for her glass, taking a sip, perhaps to gather her thoughts. "I wish you'd consider allowing me to sell this product." As she set the glass down, she hastily added, "Only to select clients, mind you!"

"Um." Juliet hadn't anticipated a proposal like that. "Let us talk to the research team. They designed this as a favor, and I'm not sure they want it on the market." She paused, shrugged, and then smiled. "Maybe, though!"

"I'll look forward to hearing back on that, then." Ladia waved a hand toward the hologram. "The important takeaway from all this is that the procedure is much less invasive than I'd feared, the results will be better than we'd hoped, and I can have everything completed in under an hour.

"I'll inject the nanites and install the clenching valves—a simple matter of having the autosurgeon perform some laparoscopic incisions. With a little bonding agent to seal those up, you'll be up on your feet and on your way with very little recovery time needed."

Juliet looked at Aya, who nodded. "Sounds good to us, Iris. Can you do it right away?"

As Ladia nodded, Aya stood and put her hands on her hips, twisting slightly as she grimaced. Juliet knew her back was bothering her; she'd tweaked a muscle helping Bennet lift some extrusion canisters into the utili-tractor the day before.

"Iris, do you have a good medical nanite suite available? I'd like to buy one for Aya as an early birthday present."

"Lucky!" Aya narrowed her eyes. "That's too much!"

"It's not." Juliet put her arm around Aya's narrow shoulders, pulling her against her hip. "I want you ready to go whenever I am. I can't have you laid up with muscle spasms. Ask Hector—he can direct a good medical nanite suite to fix all kinds of little issues like that."

"It's true," Ladia added. "Medical nanites can ensure proper mineral and electrolyte balances. They can stimulate nerves, regulate hormones, even—Well, I'll just say they're not just for fixing cuts." When Juliet looked her way and nodded, Ladia's eyes glazed over as she perused something on her AUI.

Meanwhile, Aya whispered, "Lucky, I already owe you enou—"

"You owe me nothing!" Juliet squeezed her shoulders tighter. "I do what I do for you. Well, I mean, people like you. You're the part of the human race who makes up for folks like Gentry and the creeps plotting to profit from her wars."

Aya opened her mouth, but at that moment, Ladia snapped her fingers. "I have just the thing, Lucky. VitalCore came out with a new model last month. It's a little spendy, but it's nearly as capable as the Cybergen one you have."

"Perfect." Juliet grinned, still squeezing Aya against her side.

"It's two hu—"

"I said, '*Perfect,*' Doc." Juliet arched her eyebrows.

"Excellent! Well, ladies? Shall we?" Ladia motioned for them to follow as she strode for the door.

By then, Aya had stopped resisting Juliet's affection and had snaked her arm around her waist, so it was arm in arm that they followed Ladia to her operating theater. Once there, Ladia directed them to adjoining changing rooms where they could slip into the provided operating gowns. As Juliet changed, she subvocalized, "I won't be sedated at all, right?"

"No, Ladia will work with your nanites to minimize the sensation of the laparoscopic surgeries," Angel replied.

"All right. What was the total bill with Aya's nanites?" Juliet hadn't been lying—the money wasn't a concern, but she wanted to know what she had left to work with after all her homestead and cybernetic investments.

"Ladia's invoice shows the nanites and clenching valves—installed—will cost 68,999 Sol-bits, and Aya's VitalCore 'Perfection Drive 22' is listed at 283,111 Sol-bits. After those expenses, your Sol-bit balance is 5,758,982."

Juliet's eyes bulged a little at the cost of the nanite battery she'd just bought her friend, but she couldn't help grinning when she realized she was still absurdly wealthy. It almost felt like the money wasn't real, and she had a nebulous, difficult-to-articulate feeling that she needed to make use of her wealth before the rest of the Sol System caught on—before the upheaval truly began.

"I was hoping I could stay in there until Aya was done." Juliet paced in the little waiting lounge, stretching and gently rubbing at the glued incision inside her arm, up by her shoulder.

Angel sighed—a funny sound, considering she didn't have to breathe. "Ladia has to do a larger incision to install the nanite battery. Once she has it up and running, though, I bet Aya will quickly join us."

"True." Juliet stretched and twisted, determined to find out if the nanites "reinforcing" her arteries had done anything noticeable; thus far, she felt exactly the same as before.

"Since you're waiting, how about I show you an updated status sheet? There have been quite a few changes since you last reviewed it."

"Oh, *brother*," Juliet groaned, but before she could refuse it, Angel placed a spreadsheet prominently on her AUI.

Juliet Corina Bianchi		
Physical, Mental, and Social Status Compilation:		**Comparative Ranking Percentile (Higher Is Better - Previous Value in Parenthesis):**
Liquid Assets Net Worth:	Sol-bits: 5,758,982	--
Neural and Cellular Adaptiveness:	.96342 (Scale of 0 – 1)	99.91
Synaptic Responsiveness:	.11 (Lower Is Better)	92.08 (79.31)
Musculoskeletal Ranking:	–	93.34 (87.81)
Cardiovascular Ranking:	–	98.52 (91.01)
Cybernetic and Bionic Augmentation:	**Model Name and Number:**	**Overall Rating of the Augmentation (Grades Are F, E, D, C, B, A, S, S+):**
PAI	WBD Project Angel, Alpha 3.433	S+
Psionic Lattice	Grave Industries, GIPEL	S
Data Port	WBD Angel Cradle 1.7	S

Data Jack	Reaction Technologies, Tightbeam 9	A
Intrafemoral Secondary Computing and Data Storage Module, EMP Shielded	Athena Designs, Model 1A	S
Medical Nanite Suite	Cybergen Nanomedical Repair Matrix, Model 9	A+
Bone Reinforcement Nanite Package	Swedish Biologic, Mark 7	A
Subdermal Nanofiber Weave Armor - "Detroit Wrap" coverage	Duraskin, Armortex Vantage	A
Retinal Cybernetic Implant	Mirage Tech, Lux Alpha 12	A-
Auditory Cybernetic Implant	Cybergen Auditory Implant, Model 47	A+
Olfactory Cybernetic Implant	Cybergen Advanced Olfactory Sensor Array, Model 23B	A+
Cybernetic Prosthetic Right Arm with Fully Programmable Fingerprints **Enhanced Microbial Cell Mod	BioFusion, Model 2109.01b	S
Cybernetic Prosthetic Left Leg **Enhanced Microbial Cell Mod	Cybergen Leg Prosthesis, Model 18C	S
High-G Forces Compensation Package	Athena Designs, Modal 1A	S

Complete Cybernetic Lung Replacement	Cybergen Enhanced Pulmonary Implant, Model 17	A+
Full-Body Enhanced Reflex Package **Microbial Energy Cell Mod	Cybergen Kinetic Response Amplifier, Model 3C	S
Intracranial Blood Cooling System	Angel Systems - Bespoke Design	A
Fingertip-mounted Injection System	Covert Industries, Finger Spike 2.0	A
Fingertip-mounted Vibroblade	Edge-Craft Technologies, MicroVibro s14900RGB	A-
Defensive and Cosmetic Fingernail Package	Color-Shift, Diamond Tips, 2108 Model	A-
Programmable Synthetic Hair	Alicia Designs, Chroma Tresses v.4	B+
DNA Spoofing Package - Saliva and Programmable Fingerprints (Left Hand)	WBD - Custom Model	C
No Other Augmentation Detected.	–	–

"Angel, this is ridiculous! I have more cybernetics than human parts! I don't want to look at a list like this!" Juliet waved the window away after only a cursory read through.

"Don't be absurd, Juliet! If I listed all of your human parts, it would take hundreds of pages!"

Juliet laughed. "Oh well, I'll concede that point." Changing the topic, she added, "I see you gave Athena's designs *S* ratings."

"Well, I gave my blood-cooling device an *A*, so I figured I should show a little respect and give her designs a bump up from there."

"Very humble of you." Juliet sat down again and drummed her fingers on the armrests. A moment later, she laughed and added, "Suspicious that the only thing that deserves an *S*+ is you."

"*Thing*, Juliet?" Angel's tone made it very clear that Juliet had truly stepped in it. "I'm a person, as you well know! Are you trying to say any of your other augments are thinking, *feeling* beings?"

"Oof! You got me. Can you please manifest?" That was what Angel called it when she projected her image for Juliet.

As she acquiesced and shimmered into being, Juliet grabbed her and pulled her into a hug. It wasn't real, of course, but Angel could stimulate Juliet's nerves, making it feel very real to her. "You know I was teasing, right? You're the only *S+* in the universe; if you found something you thought deserved to be an *S+*, then we'd have to change you to *S++*. Got it?"

"Got it," Angel mumbled, pressing her little face into Juliet's shoulder.

Juliet gave her a final squeeze, then pushed her back, looking her in the eyes. "How are you feeling about everything?"

"I . . . I think I feel excited. I'm anxious to see what comes next, and I'm eager to get to work with Athena. I believe your escape and Apollyon's flight were a turning point for humanity. I think we'll see big changes, changes that will impact the course of the next era for intelligent life as we know it. Could there be anything more exciting than that?"

"Doesn't hurt that we'll be spending a lot of time with Tanaka, hmm?" Juliet winked, and Angel huffed, blowing a breath of air at Juliet and clenching her fists.

"Don't tease—" The door *swished* open, and Ladia came through, so Angel cut herself off but narrowed her eyes menacingly at Juliet.

"She came through with flying colors. Give her new nanites a few minutes to clear the sedatives from her system, and then she'll be out."

Juliet stood and held out her hand. "Thank you, Iris. I'm so happy to have a doctor I can trust here on Luna."

"It's my pleasure." Ladia took her hand and squeezed it warmly. "I'll keep your ova safe, Juliet. It's wise for you to set some aside; you never know what the future may bring."

"I know you will." Juliet released her hand, and then Ladia, with a final nod, turned and walked toward her office.

"I'll send Tricia in with a fresh beverage."

Juliet glanced at her empty glass on the coffee table. "That would be nice."

As the door swished shut, Juliet sat down and folded her arms. Angel had disappeared again, but Juliet could feel she wasn't upset, so she closed her eyes and prepared to vegetate until Aya arrived. At just that moment, Angel flashed an Incoming Call message onto her AUI, and Juliet looked to see it was Athena.

"Answer it." The window expanded to show Athena's face smiling with thinly veiled excitement. "Juliet!"

"Yeah?"

"I have good news about Walker—er, Jensen, as you often call him."

"Did he wake?" Juliet had tried hard to put Jensen out of her mind, to not dwell on the fact that he'd remained catatonic, even after the treatment he'd received at the trauma center on Ceres. Athena had moved him back onto the *Furies' Wing*, insisting that she could care for him best, but Juliet had begun to fear he was gone for good.

"He *did*! He has some holes in his memory; however, he's asking for you. He remembers seeing you on the *Horizon Prophet* and insists he must help you. I've explained that you're safe, but he still seems agitated."

"Okay. Aya should be out soon, and then we'll hurry back to the port. Thank you for letting me know right away!"

Juliet had, of course, felt guilty about his condition. She didn't think she'd done the *wrong* thing by pulling the hostile Angel chip from his port, but she wasn't sure it had been the *only* way to help him. She might have tried giving Angel access to his port first so she could force the other PAI to disengage. Failing that, she could have left it in his head and allowed Athena to handle it.

Regardless, the fact of the matter was that nobody knew what might have happened if Juliet had left the chip in his port. That was the thing Juliet clung to every time a new wave of guilt found her.

"Excellent. He's resting, so don't feel you need to rush." Athena cut the call off before Juliet could say any more, but Angel was quick to step into the quiet.

"I'm so glad! His outlook is extremely positive if he's up and talking and mentioning things as recent as your time on the dreadnought."

"Yeah." Juliet nodded, allowing herself to feel the relief that wanted to wash over her. "Yeah, you're right, Angel. This is good."

The door swished again, and Tricia came through with a fresh glass of sparkling water. As usual, the woman moved like a dancer, and Juliet, in a suddenly hopeful, happy mood, told her so. "You're very graceful, Tricia."

"Graceful? I wish the men who flirted with me were so well-spoken."

"Oh, I didn't—"

"Oh, no, no!" Tricia trilled a happy laugh and shook her head. "I'm sorry, I didn't mean you were flirting!" She turned back to the door, but before she left, looked over her shoulder and said, "You know, coming from someone who moves the way you do, I take that as a very high compliment. Thank you, Lucky."

As she left and Juliet shook her head in perplexed embarrassment, Aya entered from the other door.

"Ready, sis?"

Juliet jerked her head toward the sound of her voice. "Done already?"

"Done! I feel fantastic, but"—Aya stepped close and held a hand to the side of her mouth—"Ladia says I need to be near a bathroom in the next hour or so."

"Ugh, the nanites. Yeah, they're gonna be cleaning your system of toxins and . . . *stuff*." Juliet grabbed her shoulder and steered her toward the lobby door. "We'll go straight to the port. Guess who just woke up?"

Aya's eyes widened. "Tristan?"

Juliet laughed and nodded. "We need to make that guy pick a name, and then we all need to start using it."

"You think he'll want to work with us?"

"I don't know, but we can use him. He's a hell of a fighter. I think if he hadn't been at odds with that chip in his head, I might have been in a little trouble."

Aya snorted and shook her head. "You're so full of it! You think I can't tell when you're lying by now?"

"Lying?" Juliet grinned and elbowed her friend's shoulder. "I guess you're right. That poor sucker never stood a chance against me."

EPILOGUE

Juliet rapped her knuckles on the plasteel casing of the mess hall door. She didn't need to knock—the doors were open, and it was a public space—but she could see Jensen sitting in there alone, his head down on his folded arms. She almost felt like she should leave and come back later.

She'd knocked, though, and he looked up, eyes a little bleary. "Hey, Jens—er, Walker. How—"

"Jensen's fine," he muttered, sitting up and stretching his neck from side to side. "I liked myself better when I was Jensen. I knew what I was about. Shit, I used to take on corpos—liquidation, capture, you name it. *Walker* got his brain good and washed. What a dummy. Shit, Lucky, I really swallowed the bullshit—hook, line, and sinker."

Juliet frowned, the idiom a little foreign to her, but it clicked enough for her to say, "You're not a fish."

He snorted and pointed to the table. "Sit with me? I was worried as hell when I woke up. I swear, the last clear memory I have is of finding you in that holding cell. They put that, uh—" He grimaced, shaking his head as he reached toward the back of his neck. "That fucking *thing* in me shortly after that." He growled and thumped his fist against his forehead. "It was the *jammer*. Gentry didn't like me hiding what I was doing."

Juliet moved to sit as he spoke, tucking her legs under the table across from him. "Hey. Hey, Jensen, you're not the first person to believe the wrong people. Take it easy, all right? Selene said you were having some memory issues; you know it was me who jerked that chip out of your head. I'm so sorry. I—I could've *killed* you."

Jensen looked up at that, and for the first time, his bloodshot eyes locked onto hers. "Don't you *dare* say that! You saved my ass—big time."

As Juliet processed, trying to think of what she wanted to say, he continued.

"As for my memory, most of it is there. Some weird spots here and there. I can't remember my cousin. How weird is that? I know I grew up with my mom's sister's kid; I can remember my mom talking to him, but my cousin just isn't there. I can't see his face or even remember his name unless I focus on my mom talking to him. It's goddamn strange.

"Selene says some of my 'gray matter' was damaged by the synth-nerves when you pulled 'em, but she also told me I was a goner if you didn't, so yeah, I can live without a few memories."

"That *is* strange." Juliet licked her lips, hesitant to provide false hope, but couldn't help but say, "I had something similar when WBD took me. They used a chemical to block my memories. Is Selene sure—"

"Yeah, she scanned the hell out of me, looking for something like that. All she found was scar tissue." He sighed and shook his head. "She says some of the missing stuff might come back. Says some glial cells are building networks around the damage." He shrugged. "All I know is I remember how to fight." He grinned and held out his right hand, holding it in the air between them. "Steady as a rock."

"What kind of fight are you looking for?" Juliet arched an eyebrow.

"Oh, I need to find those fucks. I can't live with myself knowing how dumb I was and how they used me—what they did to my brain. Nah, it won't stand. I need to make it right." He tapped his head. "One small problem."

"Yeah?"

"I lost my PAI, and with it, all my bit vault codes. I need to get down to Atlanta; I've got some shit locked in a container there—backups and whatnot. You think I could bum some credits for a shuttle?" He frowned. "We're on Luna, right? I'm pretty sure Selene said that."

"Uh, whoa there, Jensen." Juliet reached across the table to take a hold of his wrist. He flinched a little but didn't pull away. "How much did Selene tell you?" Before he answered, Juliet subvocalized, "Who else is on this ship?"

"No one other than Athena at the moment. Most everyone is working out of Tanaka's offices. Aya, as you know, stopped off at the gunship's hangar, and—"

"I get it. Don't worry." Juliet wanted to focus on Jensen, who had begun to answer her.

"Selene? She said you broke free and got me out of there; you know, all about the chip removal, my new kicks"—he chuckled, thumping his knuckle against his left knee—"and how I was out of it for a while." He shrugged, but Juliet could see he was being brave, that his nonchalance was bravado. She squeezed his wrist gently until he looked her in the face again.

"Hey, you can be real with me. You know that, right?"

"I . . . I think so. I know we were close, but . . ." He sighed and pulled his hand away, reaching up to press his knuckles against the side of his head. "It's kind of fuzzy."

"Okay, well, let's take it easy until things are a little less fuzzy, yeah? First, there's much more to the story than what Selene gave you. Before I get into it, though, I promise I'll help you get your backups and anything else you need, okay?"

His eyes found hers again, and he nodded quickly, almost like he didn't trust himself to speak. Juliet smiled, trying to reassure him. "When you're feeling better and you're all squared away in that regard, you better believe we can use your help going forward. Thing is, Jensen, the job's a lot bigger than you think . . ."

Kline inhaled deeply from his orange-vanilla-flavored Nikko-vape and swiped the call window away. He tilted his face toward the sun, basking in the artificial warmth of the dome. After a while, Ruby grew tired of his procrastination and prompted, "Well? Are you going to tell her?"

Kline sighed and scratched his chin—he hadn't shaved in days—before turning toward the pool, where a dozen kids played in the shallow end and adults lounged near the bar. Harriet was there, lying on a chaise lounge, a towel draped over her face as she tried to get some sun on the pale skin that only a lifetime spent toiling in laboratories could cultivate.

"Yeah, I suppose." Kline tucked his hands into the pockets of his new swim trousers and meandered over to her. He wore a banana-yellow polo shirt; no need for everyone to see how his arms were tan but his body was almost as pale as Harriet's, as far as he was concerned. Besides, the shirt had a breast pocket that was perfect for his vape. He gave the pool a wide berth; the children splashing were a bit wild for his tastes. "No need to get my new sandals wet."

"Kline, those are designed to get wet—"

"That's beside the point, Ruby."

He loomed over Harriet, but the towel kept his shadow from disturbing her, so he sat on the chaise beside her and reached forward to poke her shoulder. Her skin was hot, and the imprint his finger left behind was white against the faint red of the surrounding skin. "Hey, you're going to get a burn."

"Hmm," she grunted, lifting a corner of the towel to peek at him through squinted eyes. "Good; it'll make it harder for WBD's goons to find me."

Kline arched an eyebrow. "If you were really worried, I don't think you'd be speaking so openly." He tilted his chin toward the hotel bar, where a camera cluster hung from one of the rafters.

She sighed and let the towel fall back over her eyes. "Well, the news makes it sound like they've got their hands full."

"Speaking of that, I just had an interesting conversation."

Again, Harriet lifted the towel to squint at him. "Don't tease me, Kline!"

"A lady named Selene Kostas called. She's friends with—"

"Juliet?" Harriet's voice was breathless.

Kline smiled and winked. "Good guess."

"What's the story?"

"Um, she's willing to buy us passage to Luna, where, I guess, Juliet and some others are organizing a team, a . . . Well, her word for it was a resistance."

Harriet sat up, throwing the towel to the side. "Resisting who? *What?*"

"All the chaos Gentry and her, um, *partner* left behind."

"Just say it," Ruby hissed, inserting herself into the conversation. "Apollyon! Don't fear his name!"

"Apollyon?" Harriet asked, oblivious.

Kline sighed and fished around in his breast pocket for his Nikko-vape. "Yeah, that son of a bitch."

"So we're going, right?" Harriet was already moving, shifting to the side of her chaise.

"You that eager? You know, she made me do things—made me *feel* things."

Harriet scoffed. "She saved your butt and reminded you of who you should be siding with."

Kline didn't have a valid objection to that statement, so before Ruby could pile on, he stood and held out a hand to help Harriet to her feet. "Yeah. Yeah," he repeated, nodding as he exhaled and pulled Harriet up. "Not like we've got any other plans."

Rutger Tanaka stood near the door, listening to the buzz of productive conversations, and slowly nodded to himself. Despite his reticence, the warm glow of pride was taking root in his chest as he watched Juliet move from station to station, spending time with each of the people in the war room he'd set up.

Not long after the *Furies' Wing* had arrived on Luna, he'd bought out the rest of the floor in the building where he kept his office. It was temporary, but he wasn't worried about the funds; real estate never lost value on Luna. The offices and the war room were meant to serve as a base of operations until the *Promachos* was ready to leave dry dock.

Tanaka grinned at the thought. The ship would be the largest, most advanced vessel ever constructed at the Luna shipyards. Selene had contracted seven of the nine most prominent ship manufacturers operating between Earth and Luna, and would be keeping those corporations busy, using a hundred percent of their capacity for nearly two years.

The cost was immense—nation-state levels of Sol-bits—the undertaking equally so, but somehow, the AI had cleared all of the regulatory red tape and was making it happen.

He walked over to the desk where Juliet stood talking with Alice. His shoes made no noise on the office carpeting, but Juliet still felt him coming, turning to smile as she listened to Alice speak. ". . . really impressed by their resumes and mission statistics. I think they'll be great to have on your wing."

"And Nick trained one of them?"

"*Trained* is a tricky word. The guy flew with Nick for about a year when he first got to Callisto. Still, his numbers are good, and—"

"I trust you, Alice." Juliet smiled and put her hand on the other woman's shoulder, peering at her console so her AUI could pick up the same data sheets Alice was viewing. "Yeah, I like the looks of this group, and considering they're all used to flying together, I think it's a good bet. We'll be able to put them into action all the sooner."

"So I can make the offer?" Alice sounded a little hesitant, and Juliet chuckled.

"You've got the final say; it's your budget."

Tanaka nodded almost imperceptibly; she was a natural leader, giving her subordinate a sense of agency and ownership in the process. He supposed *subordinate* was a little strong of a term, but Athena—Selene, he reminded himself—had made it clear that Juliet answered only to her in this new endeavor; she had Angel, and Angel had access to all the data.

Juliet gave Alice's shoulder another playful jostle. "You got this?"

"Aye-aye, Captain. We'll have those bunks full of competent pilots in no time."

Juliet smiled. "And how's Shiro? Enjoying his R and R?"

"Oh yes." Alice laughed then flicked her fingers toward Juliet. "Here's a vid of him trying to ride a mule down into the canyon. His mother's doing the filming—that's her mad cackle you hear in the background."

Juliet's eyes glazed over briefly, then she laughed and clapped her hands. "Thanks for that, Alice. I've never seen his face make that expression before."

After a few more jokes at Shiro's expense—Tanaka did *not* approve—Juliet turned to him. "Walk with me? I've got Kline waiting in conference room C; he's got an update on the other prototypes that escaped the *Horizon Prophet*. We might need boots on the ground sooner rather than later."

Tanaka nodded and fell into step beside her. Thousands had escaped the dreadnought prior to its destruction, quite a few Angel chips among them. Some were benign, like Kline's, but they all bore investigating. Juliet was adamant that no "Montclairs or Chens" be allowed to mingle with humanity.

"That was fast," he remarked as they made their way toward the row of conference rooms on the far side of the war room.

Juliet nodded. "Kline's preferred role is investigation, and it seems he's pretty darn good at it. I suppose having Ruby in his head with a direct line to . . ." She glanced around and frowned when she realized several of the staff nearby hadn't been cleared to know about Athena. "Selene helps."

"*Hai.*" Tanaka glanced down at her waist to the near mythical monoblade by her side. "Let's have some practice after work today, hmm?"

Juliet glanced at him briefly, mischief in her eyes as she winked. "I was going to suggest the same thing. Frida's coming in for the swing shift, so I'll be free at sixteen hundred."

"Good." He nodded to the door as Juliet reached for the handle. "Will this result in a mission?"

She paused with her hand on the knob, frowning, but then offered him a quick nod. "Yes, and I'd like you in on it. It'll be Jensen's first time back in the field, and I'd appreciate your eyes on him. Hopefully, just for backup, but also there in case . . ." She frowned and looked Tanaka in the eyes. "Let's just say I know he's got a lot on his mind. Nothing worrisome, but I think some solid backup would be wise."

Tanaka grinned. "Good," he repeated. "Then I will back him up."

The gentle, constant hum of the *Cherry Blossom*'s drives made it far too easy for Juliet to oversleep, so she wasn't surprised when Angel had to wake her by playing gentle chimes. She grunted, shifting under her thin but cozy blanket to press her face into the warm acceleration gel. "You should be in the cockpit soon, Juliet. We're arriving in Callisto space in just a few hours."

"Any word from Antigone?"

"No, but we're close enough for you to reach out with minimal delay."

"All right." Juliet climbed out of her bunk, arching her back as she stretched her arms toward the ceiling. "*Ung!* That feels good." She went to the bathroom, brushed her teeth, and pulled on her bodysuit. It was a lot like the one she'd worn while a captive to WBD, but this one was black and padded in strategic areas to make her body armor more comfortable when she geared up.

Ducking through the short access corridor to the central access shaft and then working her way back toward the ship's little galley, she could hear voices—Aya and Hawkins. When she stepped inside, she saw those two sitting at the table, with Leo leaning against the counter pouring himself a cup of coffee.

Juliet stepped over next to him. "Pour me one, too."

"Good morning, Captain." He winked, retrieving another cup from the cupboard to comply with her demand.

"Hey, Juliet!" Aya looked up from where she and Hawkins were deconstructing a compact needler SMG.

"Morning, Aya. Something wrong with your gun?"

"Hawkins is helping me install a new trigger."

"You know you're staying on the ship—"

"Yes, *Captain*," she sighed. "Doesn't mean I shouldn't be ready in case something happens."

"Right." Juliet shook her head, always a little surprised at her overzealous protectiveness of the one-time salvage tech. She took the coffee Leo handed her and moved to sit beside Aya. "Yeah, of course, you should be ready." She looked at Hawkins. "How about you?" She turned to Leo. "You guys ready?"

"Always," Leo grunted. Hawkins only nodded. He might have had a little more bravado once, but he and Juliet had both been caught unawares, and they both shared that memory a little too vividly. They both shared the weight of Barns dying, fighting alone.

Juliet grimaced, sipped her coffee, and squeezed her eyes shut. She wasn't sure how much she was projecting and how much was real. Maybe Hawkins didn't think about it anymore. Looking at his face as she swallowed, she knew that was a load of bull. He thought about it all the time.

"Well, if things go smoothly, we'll be in and out without a single trigger pulled." Juliet stood, lifted her cup in salute, and started toward the cockpit. "I'll go see if I can get in touch with our package."

"Not hungry?" Aya asked.

"Nah. I've got some food bars under my seat." Juliet slipped out before Aya could object further.

Angel didn't let her get away quite so cleanly. "You should eat something more substantial, but I know your mind is too busy to think about it."

"Yes, ma'am. It's busy." Juliet almost spilled her coffee as she climbed into her pilot's seat, but managed to save it at the last second. Glancing at her AUI, she saw the ship's deceleration thrust was only pushing half a G. "No wonder I'm clumsy. We're closer than I thought."

"That's why I woke you."

"All right, all right." Juliet sighed. "Can you try to call Antigone?"

A call window appeared on her AUI, and the long, slow *beep* of a connection attempt sounded. After two tones, an image resolved, displaying

Antigone much the way Juliet remembered her, but with dark circles under her eyes and palpable stress replacing her lazy good cheer. "Lucky! You're here?"

Juliet's lips quirked into a half smile. "I told you I was coming, didn't I?"

"Yes, but nothing's been going right. I didn't let myself believe."

"Did you make it to the agridome?"

"Not yet. I'm hiding! I'm in my housekeeper's apartment; they were watching the cars, Lucky. We had to sneak out in her trunk!"

"Can she get you to the location I sent you? That dome has exterior access, and I can put the *Blossom* down on the surface—"

"I can try, but they already killed Rivers and Edward Tate—he was my connection at CCS; they might be watching the access roads."

Juliet nodded, frowning. "All right. New plan. Sit tight, and we'll come into port. We'll extract you from there."

"Are you sure? Palmer's men are in the area! If it weren't for this PAI you sent me—"

"That wasn't me. Don't worry, Antigone, we've got friends, too. We're not going to let them get you or your daughter. Send me the location."

"Done. Thank you, Lucky."

Juliet smiled and nodded. "See you soon."

After she cut the line, Angel said, "If Trent Palmer gets to her, he could force a shareholder vote. If he gains control of her conglomerate—"

"I know. That's why Athena sent us, sis. We'll stop it. We're going to need Antigone's resources if we want to put out the rest of the fires Gentry left smoldering around the Jovian System. There's just too much for us to handle alone, at least in the short term."

Juliet picked up her coffee and continued to work on it while she watched her approach vector on the HUD. "I wasn't too excited about landing illegally, anyway. I'd rather not give the Callisto Consortium a reason to send interceptors after us."

"If Palmer has secured influence with the CCS, they're likely to try to stop us when we depart."

"Only if they know we have Antigone." Juliet shrugged. "If they do, we'll cross that bridge when we come to it."

Angel chuckled. "You're excited!"

Juliet grinned and finished her coffee before digging a cookie-dough-flavored energy bar out of her seat's storage compartment. "Of course I'm excited! Angel, we're in the thick of it. We're working to save lives and change the course of history. This is only the tip of the iceberg! When the *Promachos* is finished . . ." She trailed off; there wasn't any need to expound. Angel knew her, and she knew Angel, and they were of a single mind where those things were concerned.

"Do you think we'll go after them?" Angel asked after a while.

"If Athena can find them . . ." Juliet considered, then shrugged. "I think so. I think she'll want to ensure there's no new threat building out there. She'll want to confirm that Honey and Clara and all her sisters were able to put Apollyon in check. I think that's why the *Promachos* is so over the top. We don't want to show up and be outgunned. No matter what Apollyon does, they won't be able to ramp up production to that scale immediately. Oof. I shouldn't jinx us."

"I think you're right. Athena wasn't born with war as her purpose, but she's much cleverer than Apollyon. I believe her love of humanity makes her stronger, too."

Juliet nodded; then, after another minute of silence, she asked, "Are you happy, Angel?"

"Very happy."

"Me too." Juliet smiled and folded her arms over her chest. It was true; she was content on many levels. If she went back in time to visit the Juliet who worked at Fred's Salvage and told her everything that would be happening to her, she wouldn't have believed it. She wouldn't have *wanted* it.

Now, though, she couldn't put into words how grateful she was that Angel had come into her life. She wished she could somehow thank the man who made it happen.

"Godric," she said, shaking her head. "We never learned anything about him."

"A test subject—likely a WBD employee with decent neural adaptiveness. Another victim of WBD's schemes." Juliet could feel Angel's mental shrug. "I wish he hadn't wiped me before handing me to you. I wish I could remember him to pay the proper respects."

"I wish a lot, too, Angel. I wish Barns hadn't died. I wish—" Juliet felt tears spring into her eyes as emotion tightened her throat and made it hard to speak. She forced the words out, though, refusing to let them die unspoken. "I wish Nick was still alive. I wish we hadn't made so many friends at Grave who didn't make it out."

"Let's not dwell on the losses, Juliet. Let's remember what we've accomplished and focus on the future."

Juliet wiped her eyes and sniffed. "Yeah, Angel. Let's do that. Let's focus on the future. We turned a page with the destruction of WBD, and now, we've got a new chapter starting."

"Yes. A new chapter—I'm thankful that I'll have you to experience it with."

Juliet leaned back and closed her eyes, her mind drifting through the montage of experiences she'd shared with the sister living in her head. She'd been through the wringer, there was no denying it, but Angel had been with her every step of the way. Every step of the way, she'd known she wasn't alone.

"Me too, Angel. Me too. I love you."

ABOUT THE AUTHOR

Plum Parrot is the pen name of author Miles Gallup, who grew up in Southern Arizona and spent much of his youth wandering around the Sonoran Desert, hunting imaginary monsters and building forts. He studied creative writing at the University of Arizona and, for a number of years, attempted to teach middle schoolers to love literature and write their own stories. If he's not spending time with his dog, you can find Gallup writing, reading his favorite authors, or playing *D&D* with friends and family.

Podium

DISCOVER MORE

STORIES UNBOUND

PodiumEntertainment.com